VENTUS

For Janice

VENTUS

Karl Schroeder

A TOM DOHERTY ASSOCIATES BOOK
NEW YORK

VENTUS

Copyright © 2000 by Karl Schroeder

Edited by David G. Hartwell

A Tor Book
Published by Tom Doherty Associates, LLC
175 Fifth Avenue
New York, NY 10010

Tor® is a registered trademark of Tom Doherty Associates, LLC.

Design by Jane Adele Regina

ISBN 0-312-87197-X

Printed in the United States of America

Acknowledgments

Many people helped make this book happen. Thanks go to my editor, David Hartwell, and to Jim Minz at Tor for wise editorial decisions. Particular thanks go to the Cecil Street Irregulars, for the reams of constructive criticism and support they've provided over the years. And, as always, I am grateful to my family and friends for encouraging me to keep working at my writing even in those times when I had nothing to show for it.

. . . Frankenstein's monster speaks: the computer. But where are its words coming from? Is the wisdom on those cold lips our own, merely repeated at our request? Or is something else speaking? —A voice we have always dreamed of hearing?

—from *The Successor to Science*, Marjorie Cadille, March 2076

PART ONE

The Heaven Hooks

1

THE MANOR HOUSE of Salt Inspector Castor lay across the top of the hill like a sleeping cat. Its ivied walls had never been attacked; the towers that rose behind them had softened their edges over the centuries and become home to lichen and birds' nests. Next to his parents, this place was the greatest constant in Jordan Mason's life, and his second-earliest memory was of sitting under its walls, watching his father work.

On a limpid morning in early autumn, he found himself eight meters above a reflecting pool, balanced precariously on the edge of a scaffold and staring through a hole in the curtain wall that hadn't been there last week. Jordan traced a seam of mortar with his finger; it was dark and grainy, the same consistency as that used by an ancestor of his to repair the rectory after a lightning storm, two hundred years ago. If Tyler Mason was the last to have patched here, that meant this part of the wall was overdue for some work.

"It looks bad!" he shouted down to his men. Their faces were an arc of sunburned ovals from this perspective. "But I think we've got enough for the job."

Jordan began to climb down to them. His heart was pounding, but not because of the height. Until a week ago, he had been the most junior member of the work gang. Any of the laborers could order him around, and they all did, often with curses and threats. That had all changed upon his seventeenth birthday. Jordan's father was the hereditary master mason of the estate, his title extending even to the family name. Jordan had spent his youth helping his father work, and now he was in charge.

For the first four days, Father had hung about, watching his son critically, but not interfering. Today, for the first time, he had stayed home. Jordan was on his own. He wasn't altogether happy about that, because he hadn't slept well. Nightmares had prowled his mind.

"The stones around the breach are loose. We'll need to widen the hole before we can patch it. Ryman, Chester, move the scaffold over two meters and then haul a bag of tools up there. We'll start removing the stones around the hole."

"Yes sir, oh of course, mighty sir," exclaimed Ryman sarcastically. A week ago the bald and sunburned laborer had been happy to order Jordan around. Now the tables were turned, but Ryman kept making it clear that he didn't approve. Jordan wasn't quite sure what he'd do if Ryman balked at something. One more thing to worry about.

The other men variously grinned, grunted, or spat. They didn't care who gave them their orders. Jordan clambered back up the scaffold and started hammering at the mortar around the hole. It was flaky, as he'd suspected—but not flaky enough to account for the sudden outward collapse of stones on both sides of the wall. It was almost as if something had dug its way through here.

That raised dire possibilities. He flipped black hair back from his eyes and looked through the hole at the vista of treetops beyond. The mansion perched on the highest ground for miles around and butted right up against the forest. Jordan didn't like to spend too much time on the forest-side of the walls, preferring jobs as far as possible inside the yards. The forest was the home of monsters, morphs, and other lesser Winds.

The inspector who built this place had been hoping his proximity to the wilderness would win him favor with the Winds. He used to stand on the forestward wall, sipping coffee and staring out at the treetops, waiting for a sign. Jordan had stood in the same spot and imagined he was the inspector, but he was never able to imagine how you would have to think to not be scared by those green shadowed mazeways. That old man must not have had bad dreams.

Bad dreams . . . Jordan was reminded of the strange nightmare he'd had last night. It had begun with something creeping in through his window, dark and shapeless. Then, as morning drifted in, he had seemed to awake on a far distant hilltop, at dawn, to witness the beginning of a battle between two armies, which was cut short by a horror that had fallen from the sky, and leaped from the ground itself. It had been so vivid. . . .

He shook himself and returned his attention to the moment. The others arrived and now began setting up. Jordan had scraped away the top layer of mortar around the stones he wanted cleared. Now he swung back along the edge of the scaffold, to let the brawnier men do their work. Below him the reflecting pool imaged puffy clouds and the white crescent of a distant vagabond moon. Ten minutes ago the moon had been on the eastern horizon; now it was in the south and quickly receding.

He looked out over the courtyard. Behind him, dark forest strangled the landscape all the way to the horizon. Before him, past the courtyard, a line of trees ran along the three hilltops that lay between his village and the manor. To the right, the countryside had been cultivated in squares and rectangles. He could see the trapezoid shape of the Teoves's homestead, the long strip of Shandler's, and many more, and if he squinted he could imagine the dividing line that separated these farms from those of the Neighbor.

All of this was familiar, and ultimately uninteresting. What he really wanted to look at—up close—was sitting right in the center of the courtyard, with a half circle of nervous horses staring at it. It was a steam car.

The carriage sat in front, separated by a card-shaped wooden wall from the onion-shaped copper boiler. A smokestack angled off behind the boiler. The tall, thin-spoked wheels made it necessary to board the carriage from the front, and the gilded doors there had been painted with miniatures showing maids and plowmen frolicking in some idealized pastoral setting.

When the thing ran, it belched smoke and hissed like some fantastical beast. Its owner, Controller General of Books Turcaret, referred to it as a machine, which seemed pretty strange. It didn't look like any machine Jordan had ever heard about or seen. After all, if you weren't putting logs under the boiler it just sat there. And last year, on Turcaret's first visit, Jordan had watched the boiler being heated up. It had seemed to work just like any ordinary stove. Nothing mechal there; only when the driver began pulling levers was there any change.

"Uh-oh, there he goes again," grunted Ryman. The other men laughed.

Jordan turned to find them all grinning at him. Willam, a scarred redhead in his thirties, laughed and reached to pull Jordan back from the edge of the platform. "Trying to figure out Master Turcaret's steam car again, are we?"

"Winds save us from inventors," said Ryman darkly. "We should destroy that abomination, for safety's sake. . . . And anyone who looks at it too much."

They all laughed. Jordan fumed, trying to think of a retort. Willam glanced at him and shook his head. Jordan might have enjoyed a little verbal sparring before, when he was just one of the work gang. Now that he was leader, Willam was saying, he should no longer do that.

He took one more glance at the steam car. All the village kids had found excuses to be in the courtyard today; he could see boys he'd played with two weeks ago. He couldn't even acknowledge them now. He was an adult, they were children. It was an unbreachable gulf.

Behind him Chester swore colorfully, as he always did when things went well. The men began heaving stones onto the rickety scaffold. Jordan grabbed an upright; for a moment he felt dizzy, and remembered last night's dream—something about swirling leaves and dust kicking into the air under the wing beats of ten thousand screaming birds.

A group of brightly dressed women swirled across the courtyard, giving the steam car a wide berth. His older sister was among them; she looked in Jordan's direction, shading her eyes, then waved.

Emmy seemed in better spirits than earlier this morning. When Jordan arrived at the manor she was already there, having been in the kitchens since before dawn. "There you are!" she'd said as he entered the courtyard. Jordan had debated whether to tell her about his nightmare, but before he could decide, she bent close. "Jordan," she said in a whisper. "Help me out, okay?"

"What do you want?"

She looked around herself in a melodramatic way. "*He's* here."

"He?"

"You know . . . the controller general. See?" She stepped aside, revealing a view of the fountain, pool, and Turcaret's steam car.

Jordan remembered Emmy crying at some point during Turcaret's visit last summer. She had refused to say what made her cry, only that it had to do with the visiting controller general. "I'll be all right," she'd said. "He'll go away soon, and I'll be fine."

Jordan still wasn't sure what that had been about. Turcaret was from a great family and also a government-appointed official, and as father said constantly, the great families were better than common folk. He had assumed Emmy had done something to anger or upset Turcaret. Only recently had other possibilities occurred to him.

"Surely he won't remember you after all this time," he said now.

"How can you be so stupid!" she snapped. "It's just going to be worse!"

"Well, what are we going to do?" Turcaret was a powerful man. He could do what he liked.

"Why don't you find some excuse to get me out of the kitchens? He comes by there, ogling all the girls."

Jordan looked up past the scaffold at the angle of the sun. He wiped a bead of sweat from his forehead. It was going to be a hot day; that gave him an idea.

He put his hand on Willam's shoulder. "I'm going to fetch us some water and bread," he said.

"Good idea." Willam grunted as he levered another stone out of the wall. "But don't dawdle."

Jordan swung out and down, smiling. He would get Emmy out here for the morning and keep his men happy with a bucket or two of well water in the face. It was a good solution.

He was halfway down when a scream ripped the air overhead. Jordan let go reflexively and fell the last several meters, landing in a puff of dust next to the reflecting pool.

Surprisingly, Willam was lying next to him. "How did you . . . ?" Jordan started to say; but Willam was grimacing and clutching his calf. There was a huge and swelling bruise there, and the angle of the leg looked wrong.

Everybody was shouting. Flipping on his back, Jordan found the rest of his men plummeting to the ground all around him.

". . . Thing in the wall," somebody yelled. And someone else said, "It took Ryman!"

Jordan stood up. The scaffold was shaking. The men were scattering to the four corners of the courtyard now. "What is it?" Jordan shouted in panic.

Then he saw, where the men had been working, a bright silver hand reach out to grab one of the scaffold's uprights. Another hand appeared, flailing blindly. Bright highlights of sunlight flashed off it.

"A stone mother," gasped Willam. "There's a stone mother in the wall. That's what made the hole."

Jordan swore. Stone mothers were rare, but he knew they weren't supernatural, like the Winds. They were mechal life, like stove beetles.

"Ryman reached into a hole and the silver stuff covered him," said Willam. "He'll smother."

The second hand found the upright and clutched it. Jordan caught a glimpse of Ryman's head, a perfect mirrored sphere.

Jordan knew what was happening. "It's trying to protect itself!" he shouted to the scattered men. "Ryman was sweating—it's trying to seal off the water!"

They stood there dumbly.

Ryman would be dead in seconds if somebody didn't do something. Jordan turned to look at the open doors of the manor, twenty meters away. Clouds floated passively in the rectangle of the reflecting pool.

Jordan decided. He reached down, splashed water from the pool over his head and shoulders, then started up the scaffold. He could hear shouting behind him; people were running out of the manor.

He pulled himself onto the planks next to Ryman. Jordan's heart was hammering. Ryman's head, arms, and upper torso were encased in a shimmering white liquid, like quicksilver. He was on his knees now, but his grip on the upright remained strong.

Ryman was stubborn and strong; Jordan knew he would never be able to break the man's grip. So he reached out a dripping hand and laid it on the oval brightness of the man's covered head.

With a hiss the liquid poured over Jordan's fingers and up his arm. He yelled and tried to pull back, but now the rest of the white stuff beaded up and leaped at him.

He had time to see Ryman's blue face emerge from beneath the cold liquid before it had swarmed up and over his own mouth, nose, and eyes.

Jordan nearly lost his head; he flailed about blindly for a moment, feeling the coiling liquid metal trying to penetrate his ears and nostrils. Then his foot felt the edge of the platform.

He jumped. For a second there was nothing but darkness, free-falling giddiness and the shudder of quicksilver against his eyelids. Then he hit a greater coldness and soft clay.

Suddenly his mouth was full of water and his vision cleared, then clouded with muddy water. Jordan thrashed and sat up. He'd landed where he intended: in the reflecting pool. The silver stuff was fleeing off his body now. It formed a big flat oval on the water's surface and skittered back and forth between the edges of the pool. When it caromed back in his direction, Jordan jumped without thinking straight out of the pool.

He heard laughter, then applause. Turning, Jordan found the whole manor, apparently, standing in the courtyard, shouting and pointing at him. Among them was a woman he had not seen before. She must be traveling with Turcaret. She was slim and striking, with a wreath of black hair framing an oval face and piercing eyes.

When he looked at her, she nodded slowly and gravely and turned to go back inside.

Weird. He glanced up at the scaffold; Ryman was sitting up, a hand at his throat, still breathing heavily. He caught Jordan's eye, and raised a hand, nodding.

Then Chester and the others were around him, hoisting Jordan in the air. "Three cheers for the hero of the hour!" shouted Chester.

"Put me down, you oafs! Willam's broke his leg."

They lowered him, and all rushed over to Willam, who grinned weakly up at Jordan. "Get him to the surgeon," said Jordan. "Then we'll figure out what to do about the stone mother."

Emmy ran up and hugged him. "That was very foolish! What was that thing?"

He shrugged sheepishly. "Stone mother. They live inside boulders and hills and such like. They're mecha, not monsters. That one was just trying to protect itself."

"What was that silver stuff? It looked alive!"

"Dad told me about that one time. The mothers protect themselves with it. He said the stuff goes toward whatever's wettest. He said he saw somebody get covered with it once; he died, but the stuff was still on him, so they got it off by dropping the body in a horse trough."

Emmy shuddered. "That was an awful chance. Don't do anything like that again, hear?"

The excitement was over, and the rest of the crowd began to disperse. "Come, let's get you cleaned up," she said, towing him in the direction of the kitchens.

As they were rounding the reflecting pool, Jordan heard the sudden thunder of hooves, saw the dust fountaining up from them. They were headed straight for him.

"Look out!" He whirled, pushing Emmy out of the way. She shrieked and fell in the pool.

The sound vanished; the dust blinked out of existence.

There were no horses. The courtyard was empty and still under the morning sun.

Several people had looked over at Jordan's cry and were laughing again. "What—?"

"How could you!" A hot smack on his cheek turned him around again. Emmy's dress was soaked, and now clung tightly to her hips and legs.

"I—I didn't mean to—"

"Oh, sure. What am I going to do now?" she wailed.

"Really—I heard horses. I thought—"

"Come on." She grabbed his arm ran for the nearby stables. Inside she crossly wrung out her skirt in a stall, cursing Jordan all the while.

He shook his head, terribly confused. "I really am sorry, Emmy. I didn't mean to do it. I really did hear horses. I swear."

"Your brain's addled, that's all."

"Well, maybe, I just . . ." He kicked the stall angrily. "Nothing's going right today."

"Did you hit your head when you landed?" The idea seemed to still her anger. She stepped out of the stall, still wet but not scowling at him any more.

"No, I don't think so, I just—" A bright flash of light in his eyes startled him. He caught a confused glimpse of sunlit grass and white clouds, where straw and wooden slats should be.

"Jordan?" His elbow hurt. Somehow, he was on the floor.

"Hey . . ." She knelt beside him, looking concerned. "Are you okay? You fell over."

"I did? It was that flash of light. I saw . . ." Now he wasn't sure what he'd seen.

Emmy gently felt his skull for bruises. "Nothing hurts here, does it?"

"I didn't hit myself, really." He brushed himself off and stood up.

"You looked really weird there for a second."

"I don't know. It's not anything." He felt scared suddenly, so to cover it, he said, "No, I was just joking. Come on, let's check on Willam. Then we'd better get back to work."

"Okay," she said uncertainly.

Willam and Ryman were still with the surgeon, and nobody knew what to do about the stone mother, so Jordan told the rest of the men to take an early lunch. He went to the kitchens and found a stool near Emmy. They wiled away some time near the warmness of the hearth.

Jordan had just decided to round up his men and get back to work when he suddenly felt a horse under him and saw grasslands sweeping by. A thunderous sound, as of many mounted men, filled his ears. This time, he was lost for what seemed a long time.

His hand gripped the reins tightly, only it was not his hand, but the sunburned hand of a mature man.

In an eye blink the vision was gone, and he stood again in the kitchen. He hadn't fallen, and no one was looking at him. Jordan's heart began to pound as if he'd run a kilometer.

He waved at Emmy urgently. She was talking to one of the bakers and ignored him until he started to walk over. Then she quickly intercepted him and whispered, "What?" in that particular tone of voice she used lately when he interrupted her talking to young men.

"It happened again."

"What happened?"

"Like in the stables. And outside. I saw something." Her skeptical look told him to be careful what he said. "I—I do think I'm sick," he said.

Her look softened. "You look awful, actually. What's wrong?"

"I keep seeing things. And hearing things."

"Voices? Like Uncle Wilson?"

"No. Horses. Like in the dream I had last night."

"Dream? What are you talking about?"

"The dream I had last night. I'm still having it."

"Tell me."

"Horses, and grasslands. There was a battle, and the Winds came. All last night, it was just like I was there. And it keeps happening today, too. I'm still seeing it."

Emmy shook her head. "You are sick. Come on, we'll go see the surgeon."

"No, I don't want to."

"Don't be a baby."

"Okay, okay. But I can go on my own. You don't have to come with me."

"All right," she said reluctantly. He felt her concerned gaze on him as he left.

The surgeon was busy with Willam's broken leg. Jordan stood around for a few minutes outside his door, but the sound of screaming coming from inside made him feel worse and worse, until finally he had to leave. He sat in the courtyard, unsure whether to go back to work or go home. Something was wrong, and he had no idea what to do about it.

He couldn't stay idle, though. If he went home, his father would treat him with contempt at dinner; Jordan always felt terribly guilty when he was sick, as if he was doing something bad.

He thought of the walk home, and that made him think of the forest. There was someone there who could help him—and maybe solve the problem of the stone mother, too. It was a long walk, and he didn't like to be in the forest alone, but just now he didn't know what else to do. He stood up and left the manor, taking the path that led to the church, and the house of the priests.

THE CHURCH LAY several kilometers within the forest. Jordan relaxed as he walked, frightening as the forest was. Father Allegri would help him.

The path opened onto the church lands abruptly: Jordan came around a sharp bend where towering silver maple and oak trees closed in overhead, and there was the clearing, broad and level, skirted at its edges with low stone buildings where the ministers lived. In front of the church itself, a broad flagstone courtyard, unwalled, was kept bare and clean.

The priests' house stood off to one side, under overhanging oaks. It was a stout stone building, two stories high, with its own stable. Jordan had been inside many times, since his father helped in its upkeep.

With relief he saw that Allegri was outside, seated on the porch with his feet up, a news sheet in his hands. It must be something important he was reading. The priests received regular news about the Winds from all over the country.

Allegri looked up at Jordan's shout and quickly walked to meet him. Now that he was here, Jordan ran the last part, and appeared on the porch huffing and puffing.

"Jordan!" Allegri laughed in surprise. "What brings you here?"

Jordan grimaced; he didn't know where to start.

"Is something wrong? Shouldn't you be at work?"

"N-no, nothing's wrong," said Jordan. "We're taking a break."

Allegri frowned. Jordan shrugged, suddenly unsure of himself. He pointed to the paper Allegri held. "What's that?"

"Copy of a semaphore report. Just arrived." Allegri sent Jordan another piercing look, then sat, gesturing for Jordan to do the same. Jordan dropped on a bench nearby, feeling uncomfortable.

"It's fascinating stuff," said Allegri. He waved the paper. "It's about a battle that took place yesterday, between two very large forces, Ravenon and Seneschal."

Jordan looked up with interest. "Who won?"

"Well, there hangs the tale," said the minister. "It seems each side lined up, on the edges of a great field east of here, on the Ravenon border. They camped, and waited all night, and then in the morning they donned their armor, took up their weapons, and marched against each other. Very deliberate. Very confident, both sides."

Jordan could picture it clearly; this sounded so similar to the nightmare he'd had last night. In his dream, the mounted horsemen had clashed in clouds of dust on the ends of the lines. Bracketed by the horror of dying men and screaming horses, stolid infantry marched up the center. In his dream, Jordan could tell from the angle of the sun that it was nine o'clock in the morning. He had stood on a hill above the battle, surrounded by flying pennants and impatient horses.

"What colors?" he asked.

Allegri raised an eyebrow. "Colors?"

"What were the colors of the pennants they were flying?"

"Well, if I recall correctly, Ravenon flies yellow pennants. Those are the royal colors, anyway. The enemy were the Seneschals, so they'd be red," said Allegri. "Why?"

Jordan hesitated before speaking. To say this to Allegri would be to make it real. "Your semaphore ... does it say that the Seneschals had these steam cannons hidden behind their infantry? Like fountains in a way, gray streams of gravel flying up and into the back ranks of the Ravenon foot soldiers."

"Yes." Allegri frowned. "How did you know? I just got this. We're relaying it on to Castor's place right now." He gestured to the farside of the clearing, where one of the brothers was yanking the pulleys on a tall semaphore tower.

"I dreamed this battle." There, he'd said it. Jordan looked down at his feet.

"Is this why you came to see me?" Allegri asked. "To tell me you'd dreamed today's news?"

Jordan nodded.

The priest opened his mouth, closed it, and said, "Where were you in this . . . dream?"

"On a hillside. Surrounded by important people. I think I was an important person, too. People kept looking at me, and I said things."

"What things?" Allegri prompted.

It wasn't like remembering a dream. The more Jordan thought about it, the more like memory it became. "Orders," he said. "I was giving orders."

He closed his eyes and recalled the scene. His own lines were wavering, and the infantry fell back even as his cavalry outflanked the Seneschals on the right. A group of his cavalry rode hard at the steam cannon, and cut down their operators, but some were lost in the last moments as the cannons were laboriously turned against them. Ravenon now had the Seneschal forces bent back like a bow, but their own lines were stretched thin. Jordan described this to Allegri.

Allegri shook his head, either in surprise or disbelief. "What happened then?" he asked. "The news just reached us—but it's unclear. Unbelievable. What do you know about it?"

Jordan squinted. He didn't want to remember this part; he could see bodies strewn across the grass below, some writhing, and in places where the line of battle had passed, women walked to and fro, cutting throats or administering first aid depending on the color of a helpless man's uniform. Jordan saw one man play dead and then leap up and run down a woman who had approached him with her knife drawn. Three others converged on him and cut him down in turn.

In the dream Jordan had looked away then, and spoke. "We deployed a new weapon," said Jordan now.

"Describe it." Allegri's hands twisted in the cloth of his robe. He sat hunched forward, eyes fixed on Jordan.

"We had the breeze to our advantage. My men set fire to some sort of long tubes filled with . . . sulfur, I think. They made a horrible reddish-yellow smoke." Jordan didn't want to talk about it any more, but once he had started it was hard to stop. And Allegri was staring at him as if he could force the story out of him by willpower alone. "The smoke went over the Seneschals. They started to fall down, they choked on it. The lines broke. We had time to regroup, we got ready to charge."

"And then?"

Jordan swallowed. "And then the Winds came."

From the hillsides all around the battle scene, a cloud rose as the birds, the bugs, the burrowing animals, and the snakes all rose and marched into the valley. The grass itself began to twist and come to life, and the earth trembled as great silvery boulders wrenched themselves out and sprouted legs. The men and horses around Jordan milled in panic. He could see they were screaming, but their voices were drowned by a tumbling, roaring, and shrieking mass of life descending on the battle lines.

"It was the sulfur," he said quietly. "They smelled the sulfur and became angry at us. It was okay as long as we were cutting each other up. Beating each other to death. But the smoke . . ." Jordan relived a feeling of terrible helplessness, as he watched both armies dissolve under a tumult of fur, feather, and scale. Only a few stragglers and quick horsemen escaped. The steam cannons exploded with ringing bangs, and mist and sulfur clouds hung low for many minutes until, drifting away, they revealed an encampment of the dead. The animals slunk away into the hills, shaking the bloody fur of their backs as they passed the stunned witnesses.

"It's okay, you're safe," Allegri was saying. Jordan came to himself to find the priest at his side, arm around his shoulder. He realized he was shaking. "It wasn't your fault."

"But I was the one on the hill. The one who gave the order!"

Allegri shook him gently. "What are you saying? That you got up in the middle of the night, grew some centimeters and an army, and commanded the battle yourself? It's more likely that you've been using that fantastic imagination of yours." The priest laughed. "Maybe you heard something last night, from Castor or his men. After all, he might have the news from some other source. Did you maybe sit near some conversation last night, that you maybe didn't realize you were listening in on? Some word or phrase you caught that came back to you as you were going to sleep?"

Jordan shook his head. "I went straight home." He wiped at his eyes.

Allegri stood up and started to pace. "The semaphore said there was a battle yesterday, near a town called Andorson. Everyone died, it said. We looked at that and didn't understand it. Everyone died? But who won? What you've just said clears it up. It could be this was a true vision you had."

"A vision?"

The priest chewed on a fingernail, ignoring Jordan. "A vision, for the son of a mason. Won't this upset the applecart. Do we tell Turcaret and Castor? No . . . no, that wouldn't do at all."

Jordan stood up and grabbed Allegri's arm. "What's going on? What's this about visions?"

Allegri scowled. He was more animated than Jordan had ever seen him. "You know some people can talk to the Winds. Turcaret claims the power; it runs in his family." Jordan nodded. The whole foundation of sensible government was men like Turcaret, who had a proven connection to the Winds, hence the authority to guide the hands of economics and bureaucracy. "The Winds often speak in visions," said Allegri. "Or dreams. But they rarely speak to someone of your class."

"What does that mean? Am I like Castor?" The thought was absurd; Castor was hereditary salt inspector for this province. His pedigree was ancient.

"I admit it's unusual, but most of the great families got their start with somebody like yourself, you know." Allegri pointed toward the church. "Let's talk in there."

"Why?" asked Jordan as he followed the rapidly walking priest.

Allegri shook his head, mumbling something. "It's a shame," he said as Jordan caught up with him.

"What do you mean, a shame? This means our family could get a government post, doesn't it?" Was that really the voice of some spirit that had entered his dreams last night? The idea was both exhilarating and terrifying. Jordan found himself laughing, a bit hysterically.

"Am I going to get my own manor house?" As he said it, he realized something: "But I don't want that!"

As they entered the church, Allegri frowned at Jordan. "Good," he said. "I had higher hopes for you—you've always been inquisitive. A lot of the ideas you've spoken to me about are like ones from the very books Turcaret bans. I'd hoped you would show an interest in the priesthood. After all, it's the one thing you could legally do besides being a mason."

They stood now in the pillared space of the church. Allegri gestured at the cross that hung between the tall windows at its far end.

"If Turcaret and his like had their way, this place would not exist," Allegri said, gesturing around.

"What do you mean?"

"Turcaret and his kind have power because they claim—*claim*, mind you, that's all—to know the will of the Winds who rule this world. All they know, really, is merely how far the Winds can be pushed before they push back. The inspectors and controllers use that knowledge to control the affairs of men. They claim to serve Man; really, they serve either the Winds or themselves. And those who serve the Winds do not serve God.

"Jordan, I hope you don't become such a one. Whatever the Winds tell you, you can choose how to use the knowledge. But beware of becoming their tool, like the controller and his men."

Jordan looked around at the quiet space, remembering many evenings he had spent here with Mother. Father did not attend church; he was not a believer. Only about half the people at Castor's manor were. The rest adhered to one or another of the Wind cults.

"What should I do?" asked Jordan.

"I'll consult by semaphore with the church fathers. Meanwhile, tell no one. If these visions disrupt your day, claim sickness. I'll back you up. Hopefully we'll get some guidance in a day or so."

Jordan brought up the subject of the stone mother. Allegri called one of the brothers over and they consulted, returning after a few minutes with some suggestions for handling the mechal beast. Jordan thanked Allegri, and they made their farewells.

He felt as if a great weight had been lifted off him as he walked back to the manor. Whatever was happening to him, he had put it in Allegri's hands. The priests would know what to do.

THE USUAL BUSTLE of the hallways was muted today, out of deference to Turcaret, whom they needed to impress, if for no other reason than that Castor wanted not to seem too provincial to his rich visitor. The silent summer air weighed heavily in here, as outside, and when he had stopped puffing Jordan headed straight for the back stairs to the kitchen.

"She's quite a filly, eh?" That was Castor's voice, coming from behind the wood-inlaid door to the library. "Turn around for Turcaret, Emmy."

Jordan stopped walking. Emmy. He looked around, then put his ear against the door.

"A fine girl." Turcaret's dry, sardonic voice. "But hard to appreciate in all that getup."

"Emmy, you hide your beauty too much," said Castor. Jordan heard a faint whisper of motion as someone walked across the room. "Turn around."

An appreciative noise from Turcaret. "Clasp your hands behind your neck, girl."

"Sir?"

"It's all right, Emmy," said Castor. "Do as the controller general says. Stand up straight."

Something about the tone of the voices made Jordan uncomfortable. He put his hand on the doorknob, hesitated, took it away. He had no excuse to be entering the library.

"Emmy, whatever happened to that dress you had last summer? The off-the-shoulder one? That was quite pretty."

"I-I outgrew it, sir."

"Do you still have it? Hmm. Why don't you wear it tomorrow, then?"

Emmy said something Jordan didn't catch. Dry laughter from the men. Then she gave a little shriek: "Oh!"

"Here comes the lady," said Turcaret suddenly.

"All right, Emmy. That will be all," said Castor in a distracted tone. "Remember what I told you about tomorrow."

Jordan heard the door on the far side of the library open. Castor started to speak, but he was cut off by a strong female voice Jordan had never heard before. "All right, gentlemen, what about our agreement?"

Another door, this one around the corner of the same hallway Jordan was in, opened and closed. He left off eavesdropping and ran around to find his sister leaning against the wall underneath a watchful portrait of one of Castor's ancestors.

"Emmy!" She looked up, then away. To his surprise, she turned and started to walk away without even acknowledging him.

"Hey! What are you doing?" He caught up to her. He felt a fluttering uneasiness in the pit of his stomach. "I talked to Allegri—everything's all right. There's nothing wrong with me."

Emmy rounded on him, grabbed him by the shoulders, and pushed him against the wall. "Where were you when I needed you?" she shouted. "Everything is *not* all right. It's not!" She thrust herself away and ran off down the hallway. Jordan stayed leaning on the wall for a long moment. Then, still feeling the prints of her hands on his shoulders, he slouched back the way he had come. What had happened? It was as if last night some veil had been withdrawn from reality, showing behind it an ugly mechanism.

For just a second, he saw blue sky, clouds, heard the snorting of a horse. "Oh, stop," he murmured, squashing the palms of his hands against his eyes. "Just stop."

2

JORDAN'S MOTHER LADLED out a thick soup and revealed a spread of cheese, salad, and fresh bread. She smiled around the supper table with proprietary kindness, while Jordan's father talked on about the stone mother and Jordan's bravery.

"Ryman can't say a bad word about the boy now. Ha! What a change. But the fact is, when it came to the moment, he panicked, and you didn't."

"Thanks." Jordan found himself squirming. All this sudden fame was strange, and tiring on top of everything else that had happened today. Despite his exhaustion, he was afraid of going to sleep tonight. The nightmare might return.

He wanted to tell his family about Allegri's idea that he'd been blessed by the Winds. He opened his mouth to speak, but a cold feeling deep in his stomach stopped him. Father kept printed broadsheets detailing the escapades of the inspectors and controllers; Jordan could see several tacked up by the door if he turned his head. That was all Mother would allow as decoration, the rest being relegated to a chest on the porch. Father would be thrilled and proud beyond description if he thought Jordan might be able to gain a government position. But it wasn't what Jordan himself wanted.

He had always assumed he would follow in his father's footsteps and was content with that. Jordan's highest ambition was to have a comfortable home, a family, and to be considered a solid member of the community. What more could a man ask for?

So he said nothing. It was desperately necessary that the peace of the supper table not be disturbed. His mother's careful preparations, her cleanliness, and little touches such as the chrysanthemums in the center of the spread were talismans, protective as was his father's way of hovering about all problems without alighting his attention on any, and smoothing all troubled waters with belittling wit.

His father had said something more. "Hmm? What?" He blinked around the table.

"Where's your head?" His father's smile was puzzled, traced with a little sadness as it often was. "Have more potatoes, they're good for you," he said, but he looked like he wanted to say something else.

What he did add was, "I met a man today, a courier for the Ravenon forces named Chan. You know about the war they're having with the Seneschals?" Emmy nodded dutifully. Jordan sat up straight, his food forgotten.

"This fellow said there was a battle yesterday. On the border."

"Is the war coming here?" Emmy asked.

"No. I don't know if the war is going to continue. It seems the Winds intervened in the battle. Stopped it."

"The Winds are mighty," said their father. "That's the lesson; though truth to tell, this fellow Chan seemed more amused by the tale than anything." He shook his head. "Some people . . ."

He turned his attention to Emmy. "Your brother did well today, didn't he?" he asked.

"He did okay," she said in a monotone.

"Okay? Well, aren't you proud?" She said nothing. "Well, how about you?" he asked. "Did you get to see our master's guests? Did you meet Turcaret?"

Emmy glanced up; her eyes met Jordan's. He looked down, squirmed in his chair. "Yes," said Emmy.

"He's pretty grand, isn't he? I hear his house is twice the size of Castor's. Mind, that would be twice the work, I expect."

"I—I don't like Turcaret," blurted Emmy.

Their father reared back, raising his eyebrows. "What? That's a pretty definite opinion to have for somebody you've barely met, especially one of your superiors. What brought that on?"

Emmy didn't answer immediately, hunkering down over her meal. Finally she said, "He got Castor to make me wear my old dress tomorrow."

"What dress?" asked their mother.

"The canary one."

"But you've outgrown that dress, dear."

"I told them that."

There was a brief silence. Jordan felt a familiar tension and the clamoring need to defuse it. He cast about for something funny to say, but his father was faster. "You still have it? I thought you gave it to Jordan as a hand-me-down!"

Everybody laughed except Emmy. She looked a bit sick, actually, and Jordan's own laugh died in embarrassed silence.

"Well, after dinner we can try to let it out a bit," said Mother.

Emmy looked at her aghast. Then she pushed away from the table and ran for the stairs.

"Emmy!" thundered their father, then more weakly added, "come back."

They sat in silence for a few moments, then Mother got up. "I'll talk to her," she said quietly, and padded up the stairs after Emmy.

Jordan and his father completed their meal in silence.

AFTER DINNER JORDAN took a walk to the spot where he planned to build his own house. He was heartsick. He strolled the rutted red tracks that joined the houses of the village, but it took only a few minutes to cover them all. He stopped to talk to a few people, family and friends who sat in the lazing sun and talked while their hands busied with spinning and mending. He was distracted, however, and soon resumed walking again. The Penners were fixing their roof, along with a mob of relatives. Jordan avoided them; they would just want his advice.

This village was his home, always and forever. Jordan enjoyed hearing tales of the outside world and often dreamed of a life as an traveler. But outside the village waited the forest.

The forest appeared in the fading daylight as a ragged swath of green-black across the eastern horizon, exhaling its hostility across the reach of fields and air to Jordan. The forest was a domain of the Winds and of the morphs that served them. Unlike the morphs, the true Winds had no form, but only a monstrous passion sufficient to animate dead moss and clay. They drove the wall of trees forward like a tidal wave, slowed to imperceptibility by some low cunning, but just as unstoppable. The previous summer, Jacob Walker had gone to the back of his fields to cull some of the young birch trees that had invaded his fields. His son had seen the morphs take him, and the way Jordan heard it, the trees themselves had moved at the morphs' command. Walker's farm was abandoned now, saplings spiking up here and there in the field, the crops turned to wood sage and fireweed, poison ivy and thistle. The Walker family now lived in another village and did odd jobs.

Some things could not be avoided, or confronted. There must have been a time, Jordan felt, when he was unaware of the pressure of the sky on him, of the eyes of conscious nature watching from the underbrush. He vaguely remembered running carelessly through the woods when he was very young. But he was swiftly educated out of that. Once, too, he had run and laughed in the corridors of the manor, but he knew now that however familiar Castor might be, he was something different than Jordan and his people, hence in his own way a force of nature like the Winds. To be obeyed, his anger sidestepped if possible, else accommodated. Jordan could not become that.

Better not to think about it. His pace had increased as his thoughts drifted back to the manor, and the visiting Lord. Jordan slowed his pace, consciously unclenched his fists. From here, at the edge of the village, he could see the roof of his parents' house over those of the neighbors. Everything looked peaceful in the goldening glow of evening. He had come to a fence, past which a row of haystacks squatted, surfaces alive with attendant grasshoppers, wise blinking birds sitting on their peaks. He sat down on the stile and propped his chin on his hands.

Across the road was an expanse of unruly brush, interspersed with trees. It was far from the forest. Jordan had decided when he was ten years old that he would build his house here. Although he had yet to buy the land, only just having begun to earn a wage, he felt the place was already his. Lately he had begun drawing up plans for the building. Father had laughed when he saw them. "That's a bit optimistic, isn't it?" he'd said. "Better start small."

Jordan had kept the plans as they were. His house would have a big workshop where he could do stonework. Why limit himself to repair work? People would need detailing for new buildings. He could do that. So he needed that extra space, regardless of what Father said.

Evening canted slowly over the village, lighting and deepening the roofs as planes and parallelograms of russet and amber. There came a time when there were shadows, and Jordan knew this was when he should go back. The hammering from the Penners' had stopped, and now only a few lazy laughs drifted in, mixed with the barking of dogs called on to herd the goats back home.

Jordan heard a sound behind him. It was only a blackbird taking off, but he realized it too late to stop a cold flush of adrenaline. He stood up, brushing dust off the backs of his pants, and glanced at the dark line of the forest. Yes, go back.

He did feel better now, his mind calmed of any bad thoughts. His father was sitting in the doorway of the cottage, whittling, as he did sometimes. Yawning, Jordan bade him good night; his father barely glanced up, only grunting acknowledgment. Jordan saw no sign of his mother or sister inside. He padded up to the attic and threw himself on his narrow bed.

As he drifted off, he saw and heard flashes reminiscent of his nightmare last night. Every one would jolt him awake again, a little pulse of fear setting him to roll over or hug the blankets tighter about himself. He imagined something creeping in through the little window and whispering in his ear. He was sure someone had touched his face while he slept last night, and that this had set the nightmares off. What if it had been a morph?

Jordan sat up, blinking in the total darkness. It had not been a Wind. It was a person, someone unfamiliar whom he had seen, sometime today. Turcaret? He couldn't remember.

He had been so absorbed in battling memory that he hadn't noticed the sounds coming from downstairs. Now Jordan could plainly hear his father and his sister arguing. It sounded as if it was coming from the back room.

"I won't go back there," she said.

"What are you saying?" said their father. "What will you do instead? There is nothing else, nowhere else to go. Don't be silly."

"I won't."

"Emmy."

"He's an evil man, and he makes Castor evil whenever he comes. They were . . . they were looking at me. I won't wear this."

"Castor commanded it. He's our employer, Emmy. We owe everything we have to him. How can you be so ungrateful? If it weren't for him, where would we be? Huddling in the forest with the windlorn."

"You'd let him . . . you would . . ." She was in tears.

Father's voice became softer, placating. "Emmy, nothing is going to happen. We have to trust Castor. We have no choice."

"It is! It is going to happen! And you won't see! None of you!"

"Emmy . . ." Jordan heard the door slam open, and quick footsteps recede into the night. He leaped out of bed and went to the window. A slim form raced away from the house, in the direction of the black forest. Jordan's scalp prickled as Emmy vanished in the shadow of the great oaks.

His father had heard the boards above his head creak. "Go back to bed, Jordan!"

He remained standing. Downstairs, his father and mother spoke together quietly; he couldn't hear what they were saying.

Jordan fell back on the bed, his heart pounding. The murmured conversation continued. Why weren't they following her? He listened, a tightness building in his chest as his parents' inaction continued. After a few minutes he realized they were praying.

There were morphs in the forest, and maybe worse things. Jordan felt a sudden certainty that Emmy was going to stumble into its arms. She must be trying to get to the church, but the path was difficult even in daylight. At night, the forest was so dark you couldn't see a tree trunk centimeters from your face, and, he knew, every sound was magnified so the approach of a field mouse sounded like a bear was coming.

Emmy had never feared the woods. He should have told her what had happened to him today. Jordan put his hands to his eyes and squinted back tears. At that moment, he felt terribly, awfully helpless and abandoned, because she was abandoned. Their parents were doing nothing!

And neither was he. He went to the window again.

"Jordan." His father's voice filled him with sudden loathing. His father was afraid of the forest. He wouldn't follow Emmy because he was scared of the dark, and he was sure inaction would cure whatever was wrong.

Jordan sat on the bed, seething with hatred for his parents. The tightness in his chest was growing, though. *Do something*, he commanded them silently. Sitting in the dark with his fists clenched, he tried to move his parents with sheer willpower.

The tightness had him gasping. Finally, he admitted to himself that they would do nothing—not tonight, not tomorrow, or ever. Their desperate fear of any disturbance in their carefully ordered lives paralyzed them utterly—and it always had.

He hurriedly dressed, not caring how much noise he made, and thudded down the steps. Candles lit the kitchen, where his parents knelt on the gritty wooden floor. Both looked up as Jordan appeared.

His father opened his mouth to speak, then closed it. He met Jordan's eye for only a moment, then looked down. His mother nervously fiddled with the bow of her night dress.

Some spell had lifted, and Jordan walked past them with no feeling of compulsion to stop, obey, or even heed what they might say. He stepped into the cool August night and turned toward the forest.

He took the lantern that always hung outside the door, fumbled for the matches that were stuffed in a crack nearby. Frowning, he lit the lantern as he walked. Behind him he heard a shout, but he ignored it. Somehow, the action of lighting the lantern, of picking the likely path his sister had taken, absorbed his attention and he felt no emotion as he walked. No emotion at all.

Once he was under the trees, the lantern seemed to create a miniature world for him. This little universe was made of leaf outlines, upstanding lines of grass, and gray slabs of trunk, all stuck in the pitch of night. Without the light, he would be stuck here, too. It was inconceivable that Emmy could go any distance in here; but he had to admit she knew the paths. He had once asked Allegri what he would do if he lost his light in here, and the priest had said, "It happens now and then. But the trees are cleared near the path, so if you look straight up, rather than ahead, and sweep your feet ahead of you as you walk, you can do it." It was like walking backward using a mirror. Emmy knew this.

But she could have fallen, could be lying two meters away, and he would never see her.

He opened his mouth to call her, heard a croak come out, and his own voice, circling around to his ears, somehow broke the dam of numbness that he had preserved as he left home.

"Emmy!" His shout was louder than he'd expected, and his voice cracked on it.

A few meters into the blackness he saw a small footprint in the mud; she had come this way. Emmy must be making for the church. She wouldn't go to the neighbors; they would just bring her back home. And she wouldn't go to the manor. The church was the only other refuge.

"Emmy!" He started to say, *come back*, but what came out was "Wait for me!"

He walked for a long time, calling out now and again. There was no answer, though once he heard a distant crashing in the brush, which froze him silent for a long moment.

She couldn't possibly have gone this far! Had he missed her in the dark? Maybe she hadn't come this way at all, but just skirted the forest, and was even now back home, waiting for him with the others. That thought made Jordan's scalp prickle, as if he were the runaway . . . but that was silly.

The lamp was starting to gutter. "Shit." He was going to wind up huddling the night under some bush; in the pit of his stomach he knew he'd lost Emmy. And now he was alone in the forest.

He bent down, placing the butt of the lantern on his knee, and opened the glass to check the wick. There was probably enough oil to get a kilometer or so. It was more than that back to the village. The church was probably closer.

So he had to go on. Somehow he felt reassured by this. He stood up to continue.

A little star bobbed within the blackness ahead of him. He stared at it, biting his lip and remembering stories of spirit lights that led travelers off cliffs. But such lights were supposed to be green, or white, and to flicker and dodge about in swampy country. This light was amber and swayed just as a lantern would if someone were walking with it.

He raised his own light and shouted, "Hallo!" The sound echoed flatly away.

The little light paused, then bobbed up and down. He started toward it, along the path. Maybe someone had found Emmy, and was returning with her. The thought sped him up; his heart was in his throat.

It was a lantern, and it was an ordinary person carrying it. But . . . Jordan had expected a man, a woodsman or even Allegri, but this was a woman stepping delicately over mossed logs and bent reeds. Not Emmy. And alone.

She raised her light again, and he recognized her. He had seen her at the doorway of the manor kitchen, asking for water. She must have accompanied Turcaret here in his steam wagon. When he'd seen her this morning she had been dressed in a long gown, but now she wore buckskin pants like a man, a dark shirt, and a cape thrown over her shoulders. She stood in stout muddied boots, too, and had some kind of belt around her hips, from which several leather pouches hung. Her glossy black hair was drawn tightly back, only one or two careless strands falling past her dark, arched brows. Her eyes gleamed in the lamplight.

"What a happy meeting," she said. Her voice was melodic and strong; she seemed to taste each syllable as she spoke it, weighing how it might best be pitched. "What are you doing so far from town?"

"Looking for my sister. She . . . she came this way." He felt suspicious suddenly, wary of admitting Emmy's vulnerability. "Have you seen her?"

"No . . ." She tasted the word as if it had some special savor. "But then I have only just ventured onto this trail. Perhaps she went by earlier?"

"Not long ago." He heard himself groan faintly, knowing he must have missed Emmy somewhere in the dark. "Please," he said, "can you help me? I'm scared for her. I can't find her. She should have been . . . back there." He looked around at the curtains of black. "Maybe I missed her."

"All right." She came up to him, and her fingers lightly touched his shoulder as she walked past. He found himself turning as if she held him tightly. They began to pick their way back along the trail.

"I've seen you up at the mansion," she said. "You're the lad who outwitted the stone mother, aren't you?"

"Yes, ma'am. Jordan Mason."

"Yes." She was smiling now, as if delighted. "It's fortunate I met you just now, Jordan. It saves me a lot of time."

"Why?"

"I wanted to talk to some of Castor's people. On my own, you know?"

Jordan thought about it. She didn't trust Castor? "Is that why you were out at the church?"

"Yes." She shot him a dazzling smile. She was, he noticed, notably taller than he.

His lantern guttered and finally went out. "Shit," he said, shaking it. "Excuse me."

"You're not afraid of the dark, are you?" she asked, chiding.

"No, ma'am. I'm afraid of what's in it."

"I see." He heard, rather than saw, her smile in the sound of the words.

The lady appeared to be thinking. She glanced about herself, then said firmly, "I heard voices a ways back. Was your sister going to meet someone?"

"No . . ." But what if she had met Allegri or someone else coming from the priest's house? "Where did you hear the voices?"

"This way." She held the lantern high and walked back the way she'd come. He followed, hopeful that they would meet Emmy coming back from the priest's house.

The lady paused at a fork in the path. The way to the priest's was on the right, Jordan knew. The left way led deeper into the forest. She stepped onto the leftward way.

"Wait!" He hurried forward. "She wouldn't have gone this way. It doesn't lead anywhere."

"But one of the voices I heard was that of a girl," said the lady, frowning. "And they came from down this way." She stood hipshot, radiating impatience. "You are keeping me from my own errands, young man. I need not help you at all, you know."

"Of course. I'm sorry." He followed her onto the lesser of the two paths.

This way was half overgrown; the lady seemed to have no trouble seeing the path ahead of them but to Jordan every way quickly came to look the same. He glanced behind them and saw only a thatchwork of tree trunks and ferns, framed in black.

"Are you sure this is where you heard the voices coming from?" he asked after a few minutes.

"Of course. Look, there's a footprint." She lowered the lamp for him to see. Jordan peered at the ground where she pointed, but he couldn't see anything.

"I don't see—"

"Are you questioning me?" said the lady. "You are keeping me from my duties. What will Castor and Turcaret say about my lateness?"

"You mustn't tell them!"

"Well, then, stop dawdling."

Jordan was silent for a while, but his heart was sinking. Could Emmy have run afoul of a bandit, or worse, a morph? Who else would be out in this blackness?

"What were you doing out here alone, ma'am?" he asked boldly. "Were you visiting the priests?"

"Yes, of course," she replied promptly. They continued on over the uneven ground, until the thickets and trunks surrounded them tightly, and there was no longer any indication of a path underfoot.

The lady had one foot on a fallen log, about to step over it, when Jordan said, "Stop."

"What?" She stepped up and balanced precariously on the mossy log.

"This is crazy. She can't have come this way. Sound plays tricks in the forest. Maybe the sound came from somewhere else."

"Maybe." She sounded doubtful.

"We need to go back and get help," he said. "I'll roust my work gang. There's no need for you to worry yourself, ma'am. You have your own business to attend to."

"True." She started to step down from the log, but slipped. Jordan saw the lantern fly in an arc, then complete darkness fell around them.

"Damn!" He heard the lady groping about for the lantern.

Jordan put his hands out and hesitantly edged in the direction of the sounds. The darkness was total. "Are you all right, ma'am?"

"I'm fine. But I can't find the lantern."

Now that he was completely drowned in darkness, Jordan realized Emmy could never have come this far. It was impossible to take two steps in any direction without encountering a wall of uncertainty more solid than any tree trunk.

"Hmmf. Well, that's that," said the lady. "It's broken. Give me your hand." He reached out tentatively, felt her warm fingers entwine his own.

"Come. This way."

"What are you doing?"

"We were headed uphill. I'm just going to go down. I'm sure we'll find the path again."

"Begging your pardon, but we should stay right here. You're not supposed to keep walking if you're lost in the—"

"We're not lost!" Her voice expressed outraged anger. "And I am not going to miss my appointments tonight!"

"But—"

"Come." She tugged, and though his every instinct was to remain still, Jordan followed so as not to lose contact. Slowly, they walked hand in hand over the uneven path.

Jordan was completely blind and was sure he would blunder into a tree at any moment, but the lady's pull was steady. Jordan fought within himself and craned his neck up, looking for small swaths of starlight overhead instead of straining to make out the logs and stones underfoot. He tried to feel his way. And she did seem to know where she was going, for she did not stumble at all.

It seemed so strange, placing his feet by faith, seeing only the occasional star, and feeling acutely the touch of this stranger's hand. It was at once intimate and solitary. He cleared his throat and said, "What's your name?"

"I am the lady Calandria May. Turcaret was my traveling companion, but I am not in his employ."

"Oh." So she might be Castor's equal; Jordan felt uncomfortable to be holding her hand. She was his superior, so she could take his, but he could never have touched her so first.

"Careful." She stepped him over another fallen log. He hadn't felt or heard her hit it, but then he was concentrating on staring up. He didn't remember this log from a few minutes ago, and his footing was much rougher now. Round stones rolled under his shoes, and long drooling fronds of grass wet his thighs. He smelled the metallic tang of moist earth, mixed with many green and fetid odors.

The strip of starlight was disappearing. He kicked himself for not looking up when he'd first come this way, to judge now where they were. They were not on the path. "We're not on the path," he said.

"Yes we are," she said in the same calm, even tone with which she had pronounced her name. Jordan stumbled over a root; her hand pulled him leftward, then back, and he felt tall brambles tug by. By instinct he had looked forward, and his free hand was out to ward him. When he looked up again, the stars were gone.

He craned his neck to try to see behind him—futile, naturally. His mouth was open to protest that they really were off the path, but her grip tightened, and she pulled him ahead with renewed speed. His warding hand brushed something slick—a tree trunk, he realized even as he snatched his hand back with a gasp.

"Steadily now, Jordan," she said.

"But—"

"Come now," she said. He heard gentle humor in her tone. "We are on the path. After all, we haven't hit any trees, have we?"

It really wasn't his place to question a lady. Her hand was his only life-line, she his only recourse here. But how could she see in the dark? Was she a Wind? The thought nearly made him break his contact. She sensed something and gave a reassuring squeeze.

"How can you see in the dark?" he blurted.

"I am as human as you," she said.

How was he going to find Emmy now? "We should stop and wait here for morning," he said, insistently.

She let go of his hand.

Jordan shouted in surprise.

The lady's voice issued from very nearby. "You may wait here, if you'd like," she said crossly. "I am going on back to the manor, and a warm fire and good companionship. You can sit here in the damp and stew in your own fears, or you can come with me. Which is it to be?"

Then silence. He couldn't hear her moving away, couldn't hear her breathing or moving at all. The silence stretched uncomfortably; Jordan could hear his own breath rasping, and the sounds of crickets, wind in the treetops. Nothing else. Had she left him?

"Please," he said.

Her fingers twined in those of his outstretched hand. Her touch, in the dark, made him remember last night, when a dark-haired woman had come to stand over him in his half sleep and laid her hand on his brow.

"Come," she said.

3

DAWN FOUND THEM walking. Jordan was cold and almost deliriously tired. For hours now, he had let the wet leaves slide over his face without raising his hand to fend them off. The lady's hand remained clamped on his, and a strange passivity made him follow her. For the first part of the walk, she had spoken constantly and unhurriedly to him, her voice and the feel of her hand the only realities, until he seemed to lose touch with his body entirely. It seemed they were a pair of spirits, drifting through the underworld.

Morning in Memnonis, Jordan's country, began with the gradual realization of shapes in the dark of the forest. Jordan began to see outlines of tree branches if he looked up, although they seemed etched onto a medium as dark as themselves. And as more became visible, the cold of the night settled to its absolute bottom. In the distance, he heard first one, then another bird begin to sing. The sound made him realize that, for hours, all he had heard was the dumb crashing of his feet in the underbrush and the slight breaths of the woman ahead of him. Now he could see her, caped back swaying slightly as she trod over the matted leaves and fern beds. She was very close to him, the hand that held his fallen to her side, his own held stiffly in front of him. His own fingers felt numb; hers were warm.

His self-awareness returned with the light. No sharp line divided his passivity from memory and decision, any more than day came like the lighting of a lamp. He simply became more aware of his situation as he became able to see around himself. He was far from home; his sister remained lost and in some peril he may well have not been able to save her from. It was partly to salve his own conscience that he had run after her, and he did feel better for having tried; but as he walked he was troubled by the inadequacy of his parents' response—and his own, for what had he planned to do when he found her?

Now, as color returned to leaf and branch around him, he considered what Emmy had done, and the decision it had forced on him. Whether she and he returned to their home again, they could never again be the daughter and son he had always imagined they were. He and Emmy stood apart from their parents now, and that meant they would have to stand together.

But they could only do that if he could find her. He and the lady Calandria May were now profoundly lost in the woods. Was Emmy going to creep back home after a cold night in the woods, finding him gone and no one to stand with against mother and father—and Castor and Turcaret? Jordan knew the consequences if a search party was called out, and if she was found alive and in good health: she would find the anger of the whole village aimed at her.

The first fingers of sunlight slanting through the treetops overhead told Jordan exactly which direction he and the lady were walking. They were going northeast.

"This is the wrong way," he said. "I knew walking was a bad idea. Who knows how far we've gone?"

"This is the right way," said the lady quietly. Her steps did not falter.

Jordan opened his mouth to object, then stopped himself. She knew they were going the wrong way. It had never been her intention to return to the manor. And somehow, she had mesmerized him into following her. The last few hours were a blur; and even as he realized this, he continued to follow her, step by step.

He stopped walking. "What did you do to me?"

She turned, her face serious. "I need your service, Jordan Mason. Last night, you were too wrapped up in your search to listen to what I had to say. Now, in the light of morning, perhaps we can talk like adults."

Morning light provided Jordan his first good look at the lady. Her oval face was beautiful and strong: her dark brows and the lines around her mouth spoke authority, while her soft skin and the delicate bones of her jaw opposed them with an impression of fragility.

He decided to tell her the truth. "I must return," he said. "My sister . . . she's not just lost. Tucaret . . . he is after her."

She frowned.

"I'll make a deal with you," she said. He stood still, glaring at her. May crossed her arms and sighed. "Look, I can save your sister from Turcaret. All I have to do is send a message to one of my people. She'll be safe."

Cautiously, Jordan stepped closer. "Why would you do that?"

"In return for your coming with me. And if you don't, then I don't send the message, my man doesn't find her, and Turcaret does; and you'll still come with me!" She turned abruptly, brushing leaves from her cloak. She glowered over her shoulder at him. "Consider her my hostage." She walked away.

Jordan was sore and stiff and emotionally battered. "Why are you doing this?" he mumbled as he followed her.

"Because you have information I need," she said. "Very important information."

"I don't," he protested weakly.

"Come come," she said, her voice no longer smooth but peremptory. "If I promise to protect your sister, will you promise to come with me?"

"How do I know you can protect her?"

"Astute." She pointed through the trees to a brighter area. "Clearing there. We'll camp and catch up on our sleep." She waved him ahead of her. "You know about the war between Ravenon and the Seneschals?"

He nodded. "I work for Ravenon," she said. "Right now I do, anyhow. I'm searching for a renegade from the Ravenon forces."

"But the battle," he protested. "They were all killed by the Winds."

"Not all of them. I'm not alone on this journey, Jordan, and Turcaret is in debt to my people. He'll do as I say, at least for such a small matter as your sister."

She was probably lying, but it might do him good to let her think he was gullible. Meanwhile, he stumbled through the brush to an area where young, white birch trees thrust up through the ruined stumps of a very old fire.

May looked up at the open sky. "Six o'clock," she said matter-of-factly. "Well, do we have a deal?"

"Yes," he said. He resolved to escape later, as she slept. She was not of Castor's family. She had no real hold over Jordan unless he decreed it.

"Good." She kicked at an old log, judging how decayed it was, and sat in the single ray of amber sunlight that made its way almost horizontally through their clearing. Little wisps of her black hair floated up, gleaming in the light. "You weren't well prepared when you left the house last night," she said. Jordan had nothing other than his clothes and the lantern that had banged against his hip for the last few hours. He looked down at himself emotionlessly, then around at the soft moss and wildflowers that had taken over the ground. The need to sleep was overpowering.

"Go ahead," she said. Reaching up, she unclipped her cloak and held it out to him. "It's still cold, cover yourself with that. I'm going to go send word about your sister."

He took the cloak. "What's to stop me running away while you're away doing that? Are you going to tie me up?"

"I'll send the message from here." Uncomprehending, Jordan knelt down, then let himself topple sideways onto a mat of vivid green moss and tiny, finely etched ferns. He started to draw the cloak over himself, but was asleep before he finished the motion.

CALANDRIA ADMINISTERED A sedative shot to the youth. Probably not necessary, judging by his condition, but she didn't want to take any chances.

She sat back and let the exhaustion she'd walled off these last few hours wash through her. Finding Mason last night had been unbelievable luck. His disappearance, which she had been trying to arrange for days, would now be seen as misadventure, a family tragedy to be sure, but unlikely to be caused by foul play. Because search parties would be out in force by noon, however, she'd had to get him as far away from the village as possible, and chose the deepest uninhabited forest to hide them.

She would program herself for three hours' sleep. But first, she had to adhere to her part of the bargain. She had no idea if such a bargain would help with the boy, but it was worth trying; and he needn't know that, as soon as she learned the trouble his sister was in, Calandria had resolved to do what she could about it.

Closing her eyes, she activated her link. "Axel," she subvocalized. Spots of color floated in front of her eyes, then coalesced into the word *calling*.

"Cal?" His voice sounded pure and strong in her head, as it had on the several occasions they'd talked last night. She had been in touch with Axel Chan from the moment she found Mason on the trail. If the youth had gotten away from her, Axel would have scooped him up.

"What's your status, Cal? I read you as ten kilometers northeast. Still have Mason?"

"Yes. But I have a job for you, to help cover our tracks."

"Go ahead."

She told him about her arrangement with Jordan. Axel grunted once or twice as she spoke, but made no other comment. "Think you can take care of her, Axel? Keeping her safe from yourself too, I might add."

"Cal!" He sounded hurt. "I like 'em experienced, you should know that. Yeah, she's safe, as soon as I find her. What about you?"

"I'm taking Mason east and then north. There's a manse located about twenty-five kilometers from here, we'll make for that first. Then west again. What say we rendezvous at the Boros manor in one week?"

"Unless you get Armiger's location first, right?"

"Exactly."

"Will do. I'll call you as soon as I get the girl."

"Good. Bye."

The connection went dead, but Calandria did not open her eyes. She accessed her skull computer and told it to initiate a scan of the area. "Check for morphs," she told it.

Gradually, from left to right, a ghost landscape appeared behind her closed eyelids. The scan was registering all the evidence of the Winds in this vicinity; mostly, it showed lines like the ghosts of trees, and the pale undulating sheet of the ground. But here and there, bright oblongs and snake shapes indicated the third of Ventus's divisions of life—the mecha, distinct from the ordinary flora and fauna.

The scan showed evidence of a morph about three kilometers south of her, but it was moving away. Still, that was a bit close for comfort. She hoped it hadn't heard her transmission to Axel.

She opened her eyes. The scan had shown a very small mechal life form nearly at her feet. She squatted and shuffled leaves aside until she spotted it, a nondescript bug form.

Watching it crawl brought a strange sense of betrayal to mind, as though the world around her were somehow fake. It wasn't—but of all the planets she had been to, Ventus was somehow the oddest. Maida had been a world of glaciers and frozen forests; Birghila was enwrapped in lava seas, with skies of flame; and Hsing's people lived on a strip of artificial land hovering in tidal stress thousands of kilometers above the planet itself. But Ventus seemed so like Earth; it lulled the visitor, so that when you ran into a morph or a desal or witnessed the serene passage of a vagabond moon or the buzz and smoke of mecha-life forms devouring the bedrock, a kind of supernatural unease was awakened. She'd felt it when she first arrived, and watching that little bug, knowing the earth and air were full of nanotechnology as thickly as with life, made the prospect of lying down to sleep here unpleasant. The sooner she accomplished her purpose and left Ventus behind, the better she'd feel.

There was no indication that any of the nano around her was aware of her. It should have been; this was the greatest puzzle of Ventus, why the Winds did not acknowledge the presence of the humans who had created them. It seemed to have become a small hobby of Axel's to discover why, but Calandria was merely grateful she could pass unseen.

She checked once more to make sure the morph was really heading the other way. Then she lay down on the damp earth next to Jordan and compelled herself to sleep.

JORDAN AWOKE IN another place, and his hands were on fire.

He was screaming. For a moment he thought he was in the battle again, because he was surrounded by flame—orange leaping sheets of it to all sides, a smouldering carpet underfoot, and blue licking tongues above his head. But he stumbled against a post, and the fires around him shook and long tears ripped through them. The flaming walls of the tent he was in began to collapse.

For some reason Jordan didn't feel the pain, though he saw flame licking up from his hands, the backs of which were black and bubbling. And he could hear himself scream, only it wasn't his voice. It was the worst sound he had ever heard.

The tent pole snapped, and the broken bottom half scraped up his side. He stumbled, flailing his arms wildly as, in a strange spiral fall, the heavy burning fabric of the tent came down on him. The impact, as if he were enfolded in an elemental's arms, brought him to his knees. He breathed smoke and could no longer scream. His throat spasmed.

From somewhere he heard voices shouting. Men. He was pulled to and fro violently, and he heard the ring of swords being unsheathed. Blows all about. And the arms and chest of the elemental branded him, burned away his hair, stripped his skin, pressed against his raw muscles in a hideous, intimate massage.

The cloth over his face was torn free. He tried to blink; could see with one eye; watched bright blades held by desperate men tear at the burning canvas. But although his mouth was open, he could not breathe.

Then he was free. He staggered to his feet, straining, arms lifted to grasp at the sky itself, as if he were trying to climb the air. Jordan heard a deep clicking breath escape from inside himself. He caught a glimpse of men standing in a semicircle, expressions of horror or grim calculation on their faces. They wore military jackets and turbaned metal caps; one or two held muskets. Behind them was a green field crowded with tents.

He heard a deep voice say, "He is dead."

He mouthed the words. Then he died.

Jordan struggled to awake. He reached blindly, hoping to find the headboard of his bed; he felt cloth. That jolted his eyes open. Was he enshrouded in canvas? But no, it was a leaf-green cloak he pulled away from his face.

He arched his back with the effort to breathe. Rolling back, he blinked up at a ceiling of pale leaves, blue sky, and white cloud beyond them. He heard himself gasping.

He tried to sit up, but it was as if someone very heavy were sitting on his chest; he struggled halfway up and collapsed back, his arms out at his sides, hands up to grab the air. For a few seconds, he struggled to just breathe.

This wasn't the nightmare of fire and death, but it was no better. He wanted to be in his bed, awaking to an ordinary day. The curtain wall wasn't patched yet, and what was the work gang going to think if he didn't turn up for work? He desperately longed to be there, digging at the mortar.

When his breathing settled down, he concentrated on raising his right arm. It moved like a leaden object, hand flopping. He brought it across his chest and vainly tried to roll over. What was wrong with him? His body had never betrayed him like this before.

His head fell to the side. A meter away, a woman slept on her side, hands folded in front of her as though in prayer. Seeing her, Jordan knew what was wrong—or at least why. The witch had paralyzed him so he wouldn't run away. She intended some evil for him, that was certain.

He moaned, and her eyelids twitched. Suddenly more afraid of being helpless with her awake, he held his breath. His vision began to gray after a few moments, and he started gasping again. She took no notice.

He was trapped, his choice either to be awake in a nightmare reality where his family was lost—or to be asleep and open his eyes in an inferno. He whimpered, then shut his eyes, and the very act of doing so propelled him into a dizzying spin that ended in unconsciousness.

CALANDRIA AWOKE REFRESHED. She was on her side facing the youth, who was sprawled awkwardly as though he'd been fighting with her cloak. The sun was higher overhead and the morning was warming up nicely. She sat up, brushing leaves and bits of bark from her cheek, and smiled. The air was fresh and the sounds of the forest relaxing. Her job was going very well. Feeling lighthearted, she cleaned herself up, rolled the boy into a more comfortable position, and set about making a small fire. When that was going to her satisfaction, she rooted through her pouches, considering the rations situation. They would need more than the concentrated foods she had on her. Best reserve those for an emergency.

The Mason lad would be asleep for a while. Meantime, she would get them dinner.

First, she sat in full lotus, closed her eyes and scanned the vicinity. There were rabbits on the other side of the clearing. They were keeping an eye on her, and she would never be able to run them down. Luckily she wouldn't need to.

Fluidly, she moved from the lotus position into a crouch. From her belt she drew the pieces of a compound bow. She put it together quietly, strung it, and reaching in another pocket, drew out one of a number of coiled threads. These had an arrowhead on one end and feathers on the other, but were limp as a string. She unrolled the one she'd selected and gave it a whipping yank. Immediately it snapped straight and stiff.

Armed now, Calandria crept very slowly over the log next to Mason, under the canopy of a young pine, and into a nest of rushes by a stagnant puddle where midges hovered. She could see the dome of ferns under which the rabbits were eating. They were invisible to normal sight, but by closing her eyes and scanning she could pick them up easily.

Eyes closed, she straightened slowly and drew the bow. A moment to aim, battling the urge to open her eyes, and then she let fly. A thin squeal sounded from across the clearing.

She walked over the uneven ground and flipped back the canopy of ferns. Her rabbit lay twitching, well impaled. She smiled and broke down the bow while she waited for it to stop kicking.

"Transmission," said a voice in her head.

Calandria smiled. "Go ahead, Axel."

"Got her. She was hiding near a brook a few hundred meters inside the forest. Seems to have been one of those old kids' forts. Scan picked her up just in time—there's a morph hanging around here, and it had located her, too. Now that I have her, what do I do?"

"Hire her."

"What?"

"Axel, she's compromised where she is. She may be in a position to embarrass Castor or Turcaret, which makes her vulnerable. She'll get no help from her family. Best to make her independent of them for a while. Designate her Ravenon's postmistress for this area. She can handle dispatches between the Ravenon couriers. She's of age, and we see women handling positions like that all the time. It's a good chance for her, because it's a light job and won't last more than a year or two. Once the war's over, she'll be able to move right back into her community, because she'll have been there all along. Meanwhile, she's independent of her family, and Castor won't touch her because she's one of ours."

"Yeah. I see it. So you want I should brazenly walk into Castor's place and install her?"

"Why not? See if there's a house you can buy for her. And send a dispatch to Ravenon to open up a route here."

"They might not do that."

"Doesn't matter. It's appearances that count right now. We've got the cash and the seals of authority, we might as well use them." She watched the rabbit kick one last time and go still. She reached down and picked it up by the arrow through its belly.

"Sounds pretty complicated, Cal."

She smiled. "Just curb your tongue and your appetites, Axel, and pretend you really do work for Ravenon. The indignant knight, discovering a cowering maiden in the dawn light. Make yourself legendary. Isn't that why you came on this expedition?"

He hmmphed. "You make it sound like a bad thing." She laughed. "What about your man?" he added.

"Asleep. I'll see what I can get out of him today. Maybe knowing his sister's safe will make him more reasonable."

"Reasonable—" Axel bit back on whatever he was going to say. "Treat him gently, Cal." He broke the connection.

She dropped the rabbit by Jordan's feet and sat down on the log to contemplate him. He looked strong enough. Whatever did Axel mean?

Gently. She frowned down at the smooth skin of her hand, matched it against the mossy bark of the log. She was as gentle as water, she knew. It was only that today, and with regard to this youth, she was as purposeful as a river in flood.

She went to work skinning the rabbit.

JORDAN AWOKE TO the smell of cooking. The lady had prepared a stout meal for him. He avoided her eyes as he ate. She watched him expressionlessly for a while, then said, "You sister is safe."

He sat up, eyeing her suspiciously. "Tell me."

She explained that she had gone to a nearby road and intercepted a courier she knew was scheduled to pass. She'd told him of the girl's plight, and he went in search of her. Later, he'd sent another runner back with news she'd been found.

"How could all that happen in just a few hours?" he wondered sullenly.

"You needn't believe me. Axel said he found her in some kind of kids' fort, a hundred or so meters in the forest. Does that sound familiar?"

Jordan looked down. It did. He hadn't thought of the place in his own rush; the other kids had used it more than he, because of his fear of the forest. Emmy probably had more memories of it than he.

That meant he'd passed her almost immediately last night.

He ate silently for a while, his mind paralyzed in a catalog of if-onlys. Finally he said, "I want to see her."

"When we've finished with our job," she said.

"What job?" He felt a faint spark of hope; she hadn't suggested before that she was going to let him go at all.

"You have to help me find the man I'm after," she said. "Armiger. Do you know him?"

"No. Why would I?"

"He knows you." She leaned forward, squinting a bit as she appeared to examine him over the small campfire. "He visited you years ago and left something of his behind. In there." She pointed at his forehead.

Jordan reared back, eyes wide. Was there some kind of thing in his head? He pictured a worm in an apple and touched his temple with suddenly trembling fingers.

This had to have some connection with the visions. Was that thing their source? But if it had been there for years, he would have had visions for years, wouldn't he?

"You're crazy," Jordan said. "There's nothing in my head but me. Plus the headache you gave me!" he added.

She scowled. She stood up, stretching her slim arms over her head. "We'll figure this out later," she said. "Put out the fire, will you? We have some walking to do."

He sat obstinately for a few seconds, until she fell out of her stretch and snapped, "I can carry you if I have to. You'll be safe, and you'll see your sister again, but not until I'm done with you."

Reluctantly, he moved to obey—for now.

JORDAN CRASHED THROUGH the trees, his heart pounding. There was no way he could run quietly in this brush. It didn't matter anyway; he knew she was right behind him.

The first time he'd tried to escape, he had slipped away while Lady May was engaged in her toilet behind a bush. She had caught up with him half a kilometer away. That time, she had simply stood in front of him and frowned fiercely, her hands on her hips. He had tried to laugh it off, and followed her for a while. It was obvious she was faster than he was, though, and he no longer believed there would be a moment when she slept while he did not.

So, when he spotted a stout but dead branch right in his way, Jordan had reached up with his free hand and snapped it off. May did not look around.

He had tried to transcend his exhaustion, summoning what strength he could behind the blow that he landed on the back of her head. She fell, and he was free.

His legs were like jelly from walking all night over uneven ground, and now, only minutes after he struck her, he was only able to stagger from tree to tree, following no path but only trying to get away.

Suddenly his legs went out from under him and he was facedown in the leaves. "Huff!" Lady May squatted on his back, and twisted his right arm painfully behind him.

She spat some word in a language he didn't recognize, then said "Nice try," in her slow measured way. Her voice was full of menace.

"Let me go, you witch!" he shouted into the dirt. "Either kill me or let me up, because I'm not going with you! Let me find Emmy! You took me away from her!"

He heard her muttering angrily in that strange language. She said, "You damn near broke my head, boy."

"Too bad I didn't!" He tried to struggle, but she had him completely pinned.

She sighed. "Okay, I guess I had it coming." Without loosing her hold, she left his back in a crouch and rolled him over. Her free hand rubbed the grit away from his face; his wrist was still pinned at an awkward angle. If he moved too much, he was sure it would break.

She let go of Jordan's wrist. A trickle of blood down the center of her forehead lent her a fearsome aspect, as it seemed to point at her eyes, which were narrowed accusingly at Jordan.

"I have done you a great disservice, Jordan. I know that. But you must understand, it is a matter of life and death, for everyone we know, your family included. Your friends will call you a hero when we're through. And I should only need you for a few days. Please trust me about your sister. Will you please wait a day or so, until I can give you proof that she is safe? All this running is doing neither of us any good."

He thought about it. "I will wait for a day."

She nodded wearily, rubbing her forehead, and winced. "Then get up. We only need to walk a little more today, I'm tired, too. A rest will do us both good."

. . .

SOON SHE WAS smiling in her enigmatic way, asking him to name the various trees and birds they passed and letting him pause for breath when he wanted. Her anger was swift and volatile, and though he had hurt her, she fell out of anger quickly. He expected the unforgiving smolder he had always seen in his parents and had feared because he'd always felt each bad thing he did diminished their love for him permanently; this woman had flashed into fury, dragged him back to her invisible path, and then forgot her anger. He hated her for what she had done to him, but she seemed incapable of hating him, and this confused him. He decided to be insulted by it.

The countryside they passed through was deeply forested by black oaks that trailed moss, muffling the birdsong. The forest floor was bathed in a secretive green twilight, broken by dust motes sparkling in infrequent shafts of sunlight. The air was warm, but held the expectant fullness of late summer, as if Life were resting. They were far from the habitations of men.

When darkness fell Lady May decided to camp again. Jordan was worn out and grateful for the respite. She made a quick fire and roasted some more rabbit, and he ate his and fell asleep immediately. His mind had been going all day, running up against walls of fact and memory, and it was mental exhaustion more than physical that put him under.

The last thing he was aware of was Lady May watching him with something like sympathy in her eyes as she languidly fed the fire.

THEY SLIT OPEN his belly and dumped out his organs. He did not protest. His eyes remained fixed on the ceiling of the tent. Muttered voices all around; the sharp tang of incense; and outside, professional mourners wailed hypocritically.

The two men who were preparing his body were elderly, their long gray hair tied back with strands of hair from the corpses they'd worked on. They wore black velvet robes sewn with many pockets, and from these they produced a variety of vials filled with noisome chemicals. These they dripped on and into his body and painted over his skin with brushes.

The ceiling was aplay with shadows of underworld spirits, from statues placed around the perimeter of the tent. The shadows elongated and bent, shortened and faded, as if the spirits were waging a war with some unseen enemy across the amber heaven of the canvas.

A metal handle clanked; the bucket containing his blood was taken out of the tent, to be burned. One of the attendants bent over him, holding a mallet and a long spike with a T-shaped head. Placing the spike under his chin, the man hammered it up, nailing his tongue against his palate, piercing the palate and the nasal palate and imbedding the iron deep into his brain. The T held his slack jaw shut.

"Speak no more," said the attendant, and putting down the hammer he nodded to someone at the door of the tent.

Six men entered, looking solemn. Some stared at him; some looked everywhere else. They lifted the pallet he lay on and he passed from under the sky of canvas, to the sky of night.

Diadem, the only moon of Ventus, was up and glittering like a tear. The rest of the sky was clear and splashed with stars, rank on rank, gauze on gauze of finest points of white. The river of the galaxy ran across the zenith. The human mourners fell silent, leaving only cricket sounds that seemed to come from the stars themselves.

The night air lessened the smell of burned meat that had pervaded the tent.

Torches to the left, right, ahead, and behind. Spirals of gray moved up to dissolve among the stars. Murmuring voices and the sound of shuffling footsteps, as he was carried out across the plain toward a dark hill.

The hillside rose steeply, blocking the stars. The torches lit a deep cut in its side, where a bare rock face had been smoothed, maybe centuries ago. Deep letters were carved over a slotted doorway uncovered by a huge stone slab. The slab had been tilted to the side and now leaned heavily on a scaffold made from catapult parts. Rough soldiers sat on the scaffold, passing bottles back and forth. They watched impassively as he passed under them.

Another sky drew overhead, this one of yellow stone. The ceiling was centimeters away. The deeply pitted sandstone was painted in abstract clouds of gray and black by the passage of many torches. The smoke from those burning now swirled up and around him, settling into a layer of trembling heat.

Around a corner, and now he was being carried down a steep flight of steps. His bearers spoke back and forth as they lowered him carefully. Ten meters down, then twenty, into a region of dead air and penetrating cold where squat pillared halls led away to either side. His bearers moved more quickly now, and the torchlight flickered off an uneven ceiling and dark niches in the walls where objects, long or round, were piled.

He was lowered to the floor in front of a black opening and unceremoniously slid in. The ceiling here was just above his nose. Bricks thudded down just behind his head. What little light there was disappeared, and of sound, only that of stones being mortared into position. After a few minutes, even that ceased.

There had been no name carved above the niche. So, after a while, he raised one hand, slid it across his opened chest, knuckles scraping the stone, and felt behind his head. There, in a band of moist mortar, he wrote the word:

Armiger.

JORDAN SAT UP screaming. Calandria was at his side instantly, holding his shoulders while he shuddered.

"What is it? A dream?"

"Him, him again—I saw him . . ." He seemed not to know where he was.

"Saw who?"

"Armiger!"

Calandria lowered him back onto his bedroll, and when he closed his eyes and drifted off again, she smiled.

4

IN THE MORNING he awoke feeling sore and frustrated. He expected Lady May to raise the subject of his dream last night, but she didn't, as if daylight were not the proper time for such things. She did seem even more cheerful than she had yesterday, though. When Jordan awoke she had already hunted, for there were two pheasants near his head, which she indicated he should tie to his belt. She had also gathered several handfuls of mushrooms and some other roots he recognized as edible. At least they wouldn't starve any time soon.

"Come," was all she said, and they set out again.

He was content not to talk for most of the morning, but the warm sunlight and the shared exertion of the walk was bound to loosen his tongue eventually. She might have been counting on this. Even so, he cast about for a long time for a subject other than the dark vision he'd had last night, finally asking, "Why are we going this way?"

Lady May looked back, arching an eyebrow in apparent amusement. "It speaks," she said. "That was a question you should have asked yesterday, Mason."

He glared at the ground.

"We're avoiding the people who are searching for you. I had my man say he'd seen you going south, but even so they may search north. But not this far into the forest."

"Did Emmy hear that?" he asked sharply. "She thinks I ran away?"

"I don't know what he told her," she said. "He's a compassionate enough man, if a bit of a libertine. I'm sure he wouldn't hurt her by telling her that, if he thought he could trust her with the truth."

Jordan chewed on that. Just how much could Emmy be trusted with something like that? He had to admit he didn't know; she kept secrets pretty well, he thought, but what about the secret abduction of her brother? It made more sense to let her believe the lie everybody else had heard.

In which case she would believe he had abandoned her.

After a while he asked, "How can you know where we are? You say you aren't a morph, but you're not using a compass or anything. And you can see in the dark." *And you're pretty strong*, but he didn't say that.

They were walking through an area of new growth now. Slender willows and white birch stood in startled lines all around, and the sun had full access to the ground. Very high in the sky, mountainous white clouds were piling up over one another.

Lady May squinted up at them. "Storm coming," she said.

"What are we going to do when it rains? We'll get soaked."

"Yes." She shrugged. "We should be under shelter in time."

"How do you know that?"

Lady May sighed. "It's rather difficult to explain," she said. "And I really didn't want to get into it yet. But you and I are going to have to make an agreement to work together, I mean really work together, and I'm going to tell you some things and you're going to tell me some. Understand?"

He nodded. He didn't want to talk about Armiger; even in daylight, he vividly remembered the embalming tent and the slot in the hillside and the disturbing implication that he had been looking through the eyes of a corpse.

CALANDRIA DEBATED HOW much to tell the youth. There was no law as such against revealing galactic news to the isolated and backward people of this world. At worst, the various anthropological groups that studied Ventus would be furious at her for muddying their data.

There was little, however, that Jordan Mason could do with anything she might tell him about the wider world. He was a prisoner of this place, like all his countrymen. There was no prospect of rescue or escape for the people of Ventus; compassion dictated that she not even hint that Mason's life could be other than it was.

She was going to have to tell him something, though. It might as well be the truth, as far as he was able to understand it.

They skirted the edge of an escarpment for a while. This path gave a great view of the endless, rolling forest and of the towering thunderheads that were bearing down on them. Calandria sniffed at the air, feeling it change from dry and still to charged, anticipatory. There was no way they were going to get to the manse in time.

It was ironic, she thought. In idle time before landing she had stood at the window of her ship, the *Desert Voice*, and contemplated this world.

Gazing down at Ventus, the human eye lost itself in jewel-fine detail. Her eye had followed the sweep of the terminator from pole to pole, gaining a hint of the varieties of dusk of which this world was capable. Somber polar grays melted into speckled brown-green forests, along a knee of coastline reddened by local weather, and in a quick leap past equatorial waters her gaze could touch on this or that island, each drawn in impossibly fine detail and aglow with amber, green, and blue. Each, if she watched long enough, summoned into night.

She had wondered then if the original colonists had felt the way she did now. When they first beheld Ventus and knew that a chapter of their life was ending, and a new one beginning, had they felt the same unease? And the anticipation?

She had tried to picture what their imaginations brought to the pretty little islands that had caught her eye. Standing above this canvas, each must have painted it with his or her own colors, drawing the boundaries of new states and provinces. It would be irresistible, at a new world, to wonder what the forest looked like from underneath; how the rain smelled; what it would be like to sleep under the stars here.

At that time the skies weren't as empty as they now appeared. The Winds were still visible, like gossamer-winged creatures dancing above the atmosphere. All frequencies were alive with their singing and recitative. They were almost as beautiful as the planet itself—as intended—and they took human shapes to communicate with the colony ships. This was expected; they had been designed that way.

The Winds sang and danced in slow orbits in time to their singing. In those last moments before the nightmare began, the colonists' eyes must have beheld a perfect world, an exact embodiment of their dreams.

Thunder grumbled. It was so different when you were down here, she knew now. The invulnerability of space was a dream. Calandria found her steps quickening, not so much because of the coming rain, but because once again she was reminded that Ventus was not the natural environment it appeared to be.

They rounded another arc of escarpment, and there it was, right where the *Desert Voice* had said it would be: a manse. Jordan hadn't spotted the long rooftop yet, obscured as it was by trees. Calandria smiled at the prospect of warmth and comfort the manse promised.

Jordan was ignoring the view. In fact, he seemed to be sniffing at something. She raised an eyebrow, and cleared her throat. "What are you doing?"

"Death," he said. "Something's dead. Can't you smell it?"

Damn if he wasn't right. She should have been more alert. Jordan had walked several steps off the deer path and now gingerly parted a spray of branches. "Lady May, look at this."

She looked over his shoulder. In a dark, branch-shaded hollow of loam and pine needles lay a giant bloated object. It looked like nothing so much as a big bag of mangy fur. At the top was a kind of flower of flesh, which, she realized uneasily, had teeth in it. As if . . .

"What is that?"

"Looks like it used to be a bear," whispered Jordan. Its mouth had folded back to become a kind of red-lipped flower atop the bag of flesh, and its eyes had receded into the skin. She looked in vain for signs of its four limbs; save for the vestigial head, it was little more than a sack of fur now.

A sack in which something was moving.

She stepped back. For once, Mason seemed unfazed. In fact, he looked back, caught her obvious distress, and grinned.

"A morph's been here, maybe two, three days ago," said Jordan. "It found this bear, and it's changed it. I don't know what's going to hatch out of it, but . . . looks like several things. Badgers maybe, or skunks? Whatever the morph thought there was a lack of in this part of the woods."

Of course. She'd been briefed on morphs, she knew what they were capable of. It was a very different thing to witness the result.

"They'll come out full grown," said Jordan as he backed away from the clearing.

Thunder crashed directly overhead. Calandria looked out over the escarpment in time to see a solid-looking wall of rain coming at them.

"Come on!" she shouted. "It's only a little farther."

Jordan looked at the rain and laughed. "Why hurry?" he asked. "We'll be wet in two seconds."

He was right—in moments, her hair was plastered down on her head, and cold trickles ran down her back. Still, Calandria hurried them away from the disturbing thing that had once been a bear. They continued to skirt the top of the escarpment for a hundred meters, then came out near what might normally have been a good deer path down the slope; it was a torrent of muddy water.

"What's that?" Jordan pointed. Perhaps two kilometers away, warm lights shone through the shifting gray of the rain.

"Our destination. Come," she said, and stepped onto the downward path. Her feet went out from under her, and Calandria found herself plummeting down the hillside in a flood.

Jordan watched Calandria May get to her feet at the bottom of the hill. "I'm soaked!" she shrieked, laughing. It was the first time he'd heard her laugh in any genuine way.

She was a hundred meters below him, with no obvious way back up. He debated turning and running—but he had no idea where to go.

Doubtless she'd be able to track him down, even if he got a half hour's head start. He sighed, and started picking his way down the hill.

About halfway down he took a long look at the lights burning in the distance, and he felt a chill greater than the rain settle on him. He ran the last few meters a bit recklessly, but arrived next to May still on his feet.

"Don't you know that's a Wind manse?" he said, pointing at the distant lights. "If we go in there, we'll be killed!"

She had that serene, unconcerned look about her again. "No we won't. I have protection," she said. Ahead of them, tall stately red maples stood in even ranks. The underbrush was sparse, as if someone regularly cut it back.

Jordan shook his head. They jogged through tall wet grass and into the shelter of the trees. Calandria pointed to a brighter area ahead. "Clearing. I guess there's extensive grounds around this one."

She led him on. After a minute he said, "So you've been in other manses?"

"Yes. I have a way of getting in." She stopped and rooted around in one of her belt pouches. "This." She brought out a thick packet of some gauzy material, which she shook out into a square about two meters on a side. "We wear this over us, like we're playing Ghost."

She held it out to him and he touched it. The material was rather rough, and it glittered like metal. It crackled a bit when it folded.

"Stand close." Reluctantly, Jordan did so. She pulled the sheet over both their heads. It was easy to see through, but a little awkward to walk with, as it tended to bell stiffly out. They had to take handfuls of the stuff and hold it close. "Put your arm around my waist," she directed him when it became apparent they were not walking in rhythm. Jordan did so with the reluctance of someone touching a snake.

He forgot his wariness when they came out from under the trees. His hand tightened around her and he gasped. Calandria stopped as well, and smiled.

The forest was cleared here in a perfect rectangle almost a kilometer long. They stood at one end of a green, clipped lawn dotted here and there with artfully twisted trees. Square pools of water trembled now under the onslaught of the rain; under clear skies they would be perfect mirrors. Softened by the haze of rain, made shadowless by the cloud, a great mansion rose up at the far end of the lawn. Its pillars and walls were pure white, the roofs of gray slate. The windows were tall and paned in glass, which lit up every few moments with reflected lightning. Behind some of the windows, warm amber light shone.

Jordan indicated the lit windows with his chin. "They're home. How can we get in when the Winds are home?"

"They're not home." She nodded sagely. "That's part of the secret. The Winds never visit these places. You have a lot to learn, Jordan."

"Everybody knows the Winds live here," he said sullenly.

"I know they don't. You may have a lot to learn, but you are going to learn it, never fear. Let's call this a good first lesson for you. This way." She stepped onto the lawn and led him along the edge. "Wouldn't want to be hit by lightning on the way in," she said.

There were no horses tethered at the front of the huge building. Though light glowed from its windows, Jordan could see no movement within. The marble steps leading up to the tall doors were well swept, but there were no servants visible. He hung back as May trotted up the steps; she took his arm and pulled him gently but inexorably after her.

He held his breath as she reached out to the door handle and turned it. She pushed the door open, letting a fan of golden light out into the blue-gray afternoon. "Come," she said, and stepped in.

He hesitated. Nothing happened; there was no sound from within. Reluctantly, he put his head around the doorjamb.

"I'm soaked!" Lady May yanked the water-gemmed sheet off and tossed it down. "Look at this." Her legs and backside were covered in mud.

Jordan stared past her uneasily. It was warm here, and dry. Light came from a great crystalline chandelier overhead. That meant there must be servants to tend the lights. They were bound to show up at any moment.

"Close the door please, Jordan." He eased in, closed the portal but kept his back to it.

This place was bigger than Castor's mansion. They stood in a bow-fronted vestibule at least two stories tall. Two wide marble staircases curved up to either side. Ahead was an arch leading to darkness. There were tall wooden doors at the foot of both staircases. Everything looked clean and straight, but the style was ancient, as if he'd stepped into one of the etchings in his father's book of architectural mannerism.

He looked up past the chandelier. Gold arabesques over the windows. The ceiling was painted with some torrid mythological scene, framed at the edges by ornate gold guilloches.

Lady May followed his gaze. "Derivative," she said. "Venus restraining Mars."

Jordan had heard of neither of them. He looked down. They were both dripping on the polished marble floor. Suddenly horrified at how wet, muddy, and disreputable he must look, he said, "We have to get out of here."

"Find the lavatory," she said.

"No, what are you saying? They'll catch us!" He fought a rising tide of hysteria, which clicked in his throat.

"Jordan," she said sharply. "There is no one here. No one to take notice of us, anyway, as long as we keep this with us." She held up the silvery gauze square. "It disrupts their sensors."

He shook his head. "The chandelier—"

"—needs no tending," she said. "And is tended by nobody. There are things here, and I suppose they're servants of the Winds, but they're just mechal beings. You know mecha?"

He nodded guardedly. "Flora, fauna, and mecha. Like the stone mother. But those are just beasts."

"And this is like a hive for some of them. It looks like a human house for reasons it would take hours to explain. It's not a Wind place; just a mecha house."

"Then why are people killed who try to enter?"

She sighed. "The same reason people are killed when they enter a bear's den. They protect their territory."

"Oh."

"Come on. Let's find the lavatory." She picked up the gauze, half wrapped it around herself, and walked dripping up the stairs. Jordan hurried after.

The halls upstairs were carpeted luxuriantly. Lady May indifferently trailed mud through the red pile. Jordan walked in her footsteps so as not to soil it even further. His heart was pounding.

Lady May found a huge marble-sheathed room full of fixtures and appliances somewhat familiar to Jordan, but more ornate and absurdly clean. As she entered, light sprang up from hidden lamps near the ceiling. Jordan started and stepped back, but she ignored the indication that their presence was known and went to a large black tub. "Aaah," she sighed, letting her cloak slide off her shoulders. "I need this." She began to let water into the tub from somewhere.

"You've been here before," he said accusingly.

"No. This is just a very familiar building plan." She began to unlace her shirt. "I am about to bathe," she said in her slow drawl. "We must both remain close to the sensor sheet, so do not leave the room; but I would appreciate it if you turned your back while I disrobe."

Embarrassed, Jordan turned around. "What you might do," she said, "is clean my clothes for me. I'll do the same for you while you bathe." A sodden bundle of cloth and leather hit the marble next to Jordan with a splat. "Just dump the cloth in that hopper there, and put the leather in the one beside it for dry cleaning. The boots can go in there, too. The mecha will clean them for us."

"Why would they do that?" he asked as he went to comply.

"The mecha keep this house for inhabitants just like us. They have ever since the beginning of the world. The manses were to be the estates of the first settlers here, as well as libraries and power centers. Their tenants never arrived—or at any rate, they didn't recognize them when they did arrive. So they wait. But they're more than happy to fulfill their household functions as long as they don't think we're intruders."

"And this cloth somehow fools them?"

"Yes. It's a machine." He heard her stepping into the water. "Aaah. Do you know machines?"

"Yes. Machines are a kind of mecha."

"Other way around, actually. Mecha is a kind of machine."

He puzzled over that, as he sat down cross-legged facing the still-open door. The hallway was dark; he heard the sound of rain tumbling against distant windows.

"When we've bathed and eaten, Jordan, I will explain to you why I had to take you away from your family, and just what your dreams about Armiger mean."

"You know why I'm having them?"

"I do. And I can end them. If you cooperate. That's why I came to you."

"But—," he started to say for the tenth time that he knew nothing that could help her, but a sound from the hallway stopped him. He scrabbled backward on hands and knees. "What was that?" he whispered.

Lady May was sitting up in the tub, one arm across her breasts. Steam wreathed her. "Probably some mechal thing. Cleaning the carpet, I'll bet. Here, come close and get under the sheet." She drew it up from the floor and draped an end over herself.

Jordan hurried to comply. They could hear a delicate clinking sound now, like wine glasses tapping one another, and then a long slow sliding sound, like a rough cloth being drawn across the ground. Jordan was terrified and huddled next to the tub. Lady May sank back under the water, just her face showing. The gauze fell into the water and made a flat floor across it.

Something moved in the doorway; Jordan held his breath, eyes wide. He thought he caught a glimpse of golden rods rising and falling, of glass spheres cradling reflected lightning, and then the thing was past, tinkling on down the hall.

He let his breath out in a whoosh. Lady May sighed, and her wet hand rose to clutch his shoulder. "You're safe, Jordan, much safer than you realize. Safer than you were in that village, after you started dreaming."

"I don't believe you," he said.

"Your worst enemy is yourself," she said, and her hand sank back again.

THEY ATE WELL in a dining hall of royal proportions. Jordan had spent the most luxurious half hour he could ever recall bathing in the marble tub. His clothes were now clean and dry, and Lady May had lit a fire here in the hall, in a large hearth with stone gargoyles on the mantelpiece. It looked as though no one had ever lit a fire there before. Warmth against their backs, they contemplated the rain-streaked darkness of the windows, and Lady May told him the names of some of the people on the painted ceiling.

"The stories those paintings tell are traditional stories, older than Ventus itself."

"How can a tradition be older than the world?" he asked.

"Mankind is older than this world," she said in her measured, confident voice. "The Winds made Ventus for us to use, but then they rejected us. Have you never heard that story?"

"Yeah," he said, looking down at his plate. "We made the Winds, the Winds betrayed us and trapped us. They teach us that at chapel lessons." His fingers traced the perfect circle of the china; he was here, and alive, in a place of the Winds. "It always seemed very remote from real life."

"You're very lucky to be able to say that," she said. "Listen, when did you start to dream about Armiger?"

"A couple of days . . . a day before Emmy ran away, I think. Was it you who did that to me?"

Now it was her turn to pretend to examine her food. "Yes, but I had no idea it would be so traumatic for you. And it wasn't originally our plan to kidnap you this way. But let's go back a step or two. How do you think I was able to get you to dream about Armiger?"

"You said he put something in my head," he said. "But why should I believe that? I never felt it before. I think you put it there, that night."

"You believe what you want," she said with a smile. "Meanwhile, I'll tell you my version anyway. Armiger did put it there, probably six years ago, when he first arrived on this world." He looked over quickly. "Yes," she said, "Armiger is not from this world."

"What other world could there be?"

"We'll get to that," she said. "Armiger came from another world. And when he came to Ventus, he made you and a number of other people into his spyglasses. He could see through your eyes, hear through your ears, all these years."

Jordan suddenly lost his appetite. He put a hand to his forehead, thinking of all the minor shames and crimes of his youth.

Lady May went on indifferently. "He didn't care about you or what you did, of course. He was looking for something."

"What?"

She sat back, her mobile face squinched into a speculative look. "Not sure. But we think he came here to conquer the Winds."

Jordan shot her the kind of look he reserved for Willam's less-successful jokes.

"Hmm. I guess it would sound crazy to you. Tell me, what specifically did you dream about Armiger?"

Any former reluctance he'd had about revealing his dreams was gone;

Jordan now hoped May would be able to remove them, the faster the better he satisfied her. He began with the first dream, and she listened
patiently as he described Armiger's death and burial.

"You remember him writing his name in the mortar? That was real,
not an actual dream?" Jordan nodded; he felt he could tell these visions
from dreams.

"Strange. He's faked his own death. I wonder why."

"Tell me what they mean!"

"Okay." Lady May turned her heavy wooden chair around to face the
fire and stuck out her boots. Something clittered by in the outside hall,
and her hand hovered near the protective gauze until it was gone. "In
the first dream, you say you saw a great battle, which the Winds interrupted.

"If that was a true vision, he has been defeated here, just as he has in
space. Maybe Armiger only just received a transmission telling him about
the greater defeat off-world. You see, a little while ago a battle was
fought among the stars. I was there. And I helped destroy a creature
rather like the Winds. A thing that went by no name, only a number:
3340." Firelight caressed her features as she spoke. "This creature had
enslaved an entire world, a place called Hsing. There are other worlds,
Jordan. Other places than Ventus where men walk." He shook his head.
"Well, anyway, 3340 has been destroyed. But some of his servants survive. One of these servants is Armiger.

"Armiger was sent here six years ago by 3340, who hoped to find a
way to enslave the Winds and thus take all of Ventus as its own. And
Armiger sent out his machines to try to find the Achilles' heel—the secret
vulnerability—of the Winds.

"I'm sure you know the Winds destroy all machines that are not of
their own devising. They did this to Armiger's first probes. He tried hiding some probes in animals, but the morphs discovered them and took
the probes out. But he had learned that the Winds do not change humans
the way they do other life here. The morphs can kill, but they do not
change people, do they? Only animals. So he realized he could hide his
probes in people. And he did so. One of those people was you."

"I would remember," he protested.

"No, it was done in your sleep, using very small mecha. That's all the
probe is, a mechal infection on your brain. *Nanotech*, we call it. And for
six years he roamed Ventus, casting a wide net to learn as much as he
could about this world. In order to learn how to conquer the Winds."

"You can't conquer the Winds," he said. "The idea is absurd. Armiger
must not be very bright."

"Maybe, maybe not." She shrugged. "His master had enough power to
spare to send him on a mission that had no guarantee of success. But what
if he did find a way?"

She left the question hanging. Jordan stared at the fire and tried to imagine the sovereign Winds bowing to another power, to the thing that had scratched its own name on the inside of its tomb.

"Armiger," Lady May said, "wanted to become god of this world. But he had a master, from whom all his power came. Armiger is only a spy, possibly an assassin. And he has learned that his master is now dead." She steepled her hands and glared into the fire. "So now what? Is he free to pursue the plan on his own? Your story suggests he's gone mad, but he may just be going to ground, dropping from sight, which would make sense if he suspected we were going to come after him."

Jordan blinked at her. This was too strange to question; he could not fit any of it into his understanding of the world.

Lady May seemed to sense his confusion. "The rest is simple," she said. "All 3340's agents are being hunted down and killed. Axel Chan and I have come to find Armiger and destroy him. Destroy *it*; Armiger's not a human being like you and me."

"But he died."

"And you went on receiving from him after he died? He's not dead, although he might not realize it himself yet, if he has gone insane. When we came here, Axel and I could not discover Armiger, but we found you. And we found there was maybe a way to use you to find him. Our intention was to hire you away from your father, as an apprentice. I traveled with Turcaret for credibility's sake, to negotiate that with Castor. Castor would have none of it, though; maybe it was Turcaret poisoning his mind about your sister, he realized he couldn't shatter the whole family and chose Emmy. We were stuck until your sister ran into the woods. You see," she shot him a conspiratorial smile, "it was the perfect opportunity, and I really had no time to explain."

"So you made me dream."

"I'm not sure why that's happening. He seems to be broadcasting a signal to his remotes. Trying to summon them home, maybe. A good happenstance, since we still can't track Armiger directly through your implants. But you can tell us where he is. Better and better."

"For you, maybe." He stood up and walked away from the fire to peer out the rain-runneled window. Instead of telling him something he could make sense of, she'd prattled a tale of insanity. "You're telling me you're from the stars, too."

"I am." She laughed. "Oh, Jordan, I'm sorry we had to meet this way. Our intention was to hire you, and you were to receive all the benefits of our knowledge and skills. We were going to pay you better than in coin for your service, and you would return home equal to Castor or any of the monks in your wisdom. You see, we did plan to tell you something about the world you live in—the truth, not the myths you were raised on."

He heard her stand and approach. Close behind him, she said, "And I will still honor that intention. We have more to make up for now, but I promise you we will make it up. Money is the easiest thing; I can pay you in knowledge and wisdom."

Jordan had lost the safety of his village and family. Calandria May had told him a tale that, in the normal course of things, would have sparked his imagination; it made a good tale, people up there in the sky, fighting nameless gods and stalking a demonic assassin across the plains and mountains of the world. Now, though, he could only shake his head dumbly and try not to think at all.

For a while they stood looking out at the storm; when he glanced at Lady May again, her eyes were hooded, her carven features masklike. But she caught his eye and smiled, not with her usual harsh amusement, but with sympathy. In that moment she was beautiful.

"Let me show you something," she said.

SHE LED HIM from the dining hall to another giant room. Though there was no fire, it was just as warm in here, almost too warm. Jordan had seen lights coming on as they entered other rooms, so he was ready when those strangely steady spots of illumination pinioned scattered armchairs and tables. He wasn't ready for the vista of the walls around them.

"Books!" Castor had a library, but it must amount to a twentieth of this bounty. The ornately decorated wooden shelves rose to three times his height, and they covered all the wall surface. "There must be thousands!"

"Yes," she said. "A tiny portion of the knowledge of the human race as of one thousand years ago—when Ventus was settled." She strolled along the shelves, trailing one hand along the spines. "Ah. Try this one." She pulled a thick volume out. "You can read, can't you?"

"A little." The book she handed him was well made, leather bound, and solid. It had a title written in letters he knew, but the words made no sense: *Baedeker's Callisto*, it said. He flipped the book open to a random page.

"What language is that?" she asked.

"Not sure. . . ." He puzzled over the text, which was perfectly inscribed. Actually, he recognized a lot of the words, and with a bit of puzzling, he could make out what it said. "It's a description . . . of some place where you can eat?"

She looked over his shoulder. "Ah, yes, the Korolev restaurant strip. I don't think that exists any more, but the city of Korolev does." She flipped the page for him; Jordan found himself looking at a colorful map of roads and towns, all on a surface strewn with circular formations.

"This is a tourist guide," said Calandria. "For another world. It's written in an archaic version of your language. Now, why would the Winds have books? Aren't they omnipotent and all-knowing?"

"I . . . don't know."

"Books are for human readers," she said. "As are armchairs and lamps. This manse was made for you, Jordan. But the makers and maintainers no longer know that."

He flipped to another page. This one held a photograph, of much better quality than those hanging in Castor's great hall. It showed a white landscape under a black sky. There was a moon in the sky, but it looked all wrong: orange, banded, and huge.

"There is much to the world," said Calandria May. "And there are many worlds. Come, it's time we slept."

JORDAN REMAINED AWAKE long after they bedded down in a room opposite the marble washroom. He lay staring at the canopy of the great bed that had swallowed them both. He was afraid to sleep lest he open his eyes in a cold tomb, but also he was aware of a deep current within himself, bringing a change he was not ready to face. The lady had told him a fabulous story, and he wanted none of it. He wanted his home, his work—even Ryman would be good company right now.

He had been stripped of that—and stripped of the only other thing he knew, which was the certain safety of his own mind. And yet he still breathed, and walked and ate. Then who was he? He no longer knew.

In the mythology known to Jordan, there were demonic Winds who gave and took away. In one story he knew, such a creature granted immortality to the generalissimo who craved it—but only after removing his sight and hearing. These Winds often gave and took away, but sometimes they only gave, and the torment of the recipient of the gift took the form of doubt: why should the demon give me this if demons only harm? In some stories, the gift's recipient came to hate and fear the gift because no harm had come from it, where everything they had heard told them some should. Suspicion ate these people from within.

It was easy to see Calandria May as such a gift-giving Wind. It was clear what she had taken away; at the same time, her words placed Jordan in the middle of a tale so wild and fabulous he could not believe it. But when he closed his eyes they opened in Armiger's face, and she was the only one who made that experience sensible to him.

He tossed and turned, and also lay at times looking at her. She seemed to sleep like a stone—the sleep of the just? Her ability to sleep soundly was another sign of her arrogance, he felt. But in sleep her features softened, and he told himself that maybe her true character was revealed now, maybe she was gentle at bottom, maybe he could trust her.

At length, still wide awake and needing to relieve himself, he rolled to the edge of the bed and groped underneath for a chamber pot. There wasn't one. Maybe it was on her side. He crawled out into surprisingly warm air and rooted around past her boots. There was no pot under the bed. What did these people do if they had a need, he wondered, then remembered that no actual people lived here.

He had almost grown used to this place. There was nothing threatening in this room, and the gauze draped over their covers guaranteed their safety. Still, he wasn't about to venture out of the room without it. The washroom was right across the hall. No harm would come to Lady May if he walked across and back carrying the gauze; he would be able to watch the doorway from the washroom. Gently, he drew the gauze off the bed and folded it once around himself. Then he padded to the doorway and peeked out.

Nothing. Quickly he hurried across to the marble room and felt about in the dark for the toilet. He pissed hurriedly, feeling exposed the way one does in the woods.

He heard a faint gasp. He frowned and turned to look to the doorway, and as he did Calandria May screamed.

"No no no!" He ran out into the hall, but stopped in the doorway to the bedroom. A thing was on the bed, and its great golden limbs bounced from the canopy and down again as it tried to stab Lady May. She was holding onto the yellow blades at the end of the thing's arms and was raised and flung down repeatedly as it tried to get past her hands to stab her. Blood ran black down her wrists and from her throat. She was still screaming.

Jordan stood frozen in horror. It could not have crept past him as he stood in the lavatory, he would have seen or heard it. That meant it had been in the room all along, either on top of the canopy or . . . under the bed.

He backed away. He had the gauze—he could make a break for it now, and nothing in this place could touch him. If Lady May wasn't dead she would be in moments. He could escape.

And run until he had to sleep? And then to awake with Armiger in his tomb? What, now, could he escape to?

One of the golden thing's legs was right at the edge of the bed. Jordan tried to shout—it came out as a choking sound—and running forward, he kicked at that leg. The thing lost balance and toppled past him onto the floor.

It rose in a flurry of hissing, whirring limbs. He expected it to attack him but it didn't, instead moving around him to remount the bed.

"No!" He dove onto the bed, raising the gauze above himself. Terrified, staring into glass curves and white metal, he still heard Lady May moving behind him. "The sheet," she croaked.

The mechal thing's arm struck past him. It lifted Calandria May and tossed her across the room in one motion as though she weighed nothing. She broke an ornate side-table in her fall and skidded on into the wall. The thing went after her.

Before it reached her she was on her feet, eyes and teeth glinting in the faint light from the window. "Bastard!" she hissed, and Jordan didn't know whether she meant it or him for abandoning her to it.

It struck at her but she ducked out of the way and came up with a piece of the table, which she swung like a club. She hit it and the bit of table shattered. The mechal killer fell back.

"The sheet!" she screamed. Jordan leaped off the bed and ran to her. They hunkered down under the thin stuff. It seemed a suicidal maneuver to Jordan. But the golden thing paused, glass globes whirling this way and that. And then it reached down and picked up part of the ruined table—and another part, and more, piling wooden flinders in its arms. It was cleaning up.

Lady May groaned and slumped against the wall. Jordan took her hands and opened them, expecting to see her cut to the bone and her tendons severed. She had numerous long thin gashes on her palms and up her wrists, but nothing very deep. And the wound in her throat was also shallow; it had nearly stopped bleeding, though the thin shirt she had worn to bed was soaked.

"How . . . ?" Jordan snatched his hand back from the examination. She opened her eyes and smiled faintly at him.

"No bruises, no deep cuts. I know. I wear armor, Jordan, but under my skin, not over it. I can't be cut deeply. And in my blood is a substance that goes rigid for an instant if it is shocked. Getting thrown across the room is . . . nothing." She coughed. "Almost nothing."

"Let's get out of here," he said.

She stared at the golden creature, which was tidying up the bed now in a fussy manner. "Actually, yes, let's."

They gathered their shoes and clothes from under the bed. As they staggered out of the room she said, "Next time you have to go, use the chamber pot."

He started to protest that there hadn't been one, then thought of the golden thing hiding under the bed. Incongruously, the image of it putting the chamber pot into his groping fingers came to mind. To his own horror, Jordan chuckled, and wonder of wonders so did she, and then they were both laughing out loud, and it felt good.

5

ARMIGER TRIED TO open his eyes. Something had changed. Deep within him, all his voices still mourned. But something had pulled him back into this body, where he had never expected to return.

His eyes wouldn't open completely. The lids were drying to stiff leather, and the orbs beneath had shriveled. All he saw was ruined blackness. He was still in his niche, closed in on all sides with stone, as was proper. His neighbors were the dead, and he should feel kinship with them now. He was also dead.

Life to him had been so much more than this one body that its own survival meant nothing. He was a god, composed of living atoms and enfolding within himself the power of a sun. His had not been a single consciousness, but the coordinated symphony of a million minds. Each thing he touched he felt in all ways that were possible; and each thing he saw, he saw completely and was reminded of all things. All was in all for him, and he had acted decisively across centuries.

He had been brought low by an army of creatures as thoughtless compared to him as bacteria. They were led by a woman to whom he was incidental, merely an obstacle to be removed. And when she killed him, she had no idea that something whose experience exceeded that of her entire species had died. All the questions she could ever have asked, he had answered long ago. She was ignorant, and so all of his wisdom was lost.

This body had no purpose without that greater Self. The fact that it still moved and breathed was irrelevant; the motivating soul was gone.

But lying here, senses blocked, embalmed and shriveling as was proper, Armiger had continued to think. He was locked in the paralytic cycle of grief; all his thoughts had turned on the higher Self, predicated by its existence, and with it gone, every thought hit an impasse and locked hard. He could have no notion, no memory, that did not run up against that barrier, so Armiger's mind was now a chaos where no thought finished forming, no purpose completely crystallized. Jagged nightmare images, half memories, and monotonous fragments of impulse echoed on and on. The flesh of this body would turn to dust, but Armiger's real body was a filamentary net of nanotech, and that would last for centuries. So would the echoes of grief.

And nothing should matter, or disturb his rest. But his eyes had opened.

A faint vibration sounded—footsteps. The sound of someone walking in the catacombs had woke him. Whatever walked was bipedal, with the same period to its step as a man—but it could still be anything. Maybe one of Ventus's mechal guardians, come to dissect him.

It didn't matter. He tried to shut his eyes, but they would no longer obey him at all.

He couldn't stop listening, either, as the footsteps approached, paused nearby, and came even closer. A second set of steps approached, then a third. Now he heard voices. The men were standing just outside his niche.

Anger emerged from the chaos in Armiger's heart. He should be left in peace. Humans had no idea of his pain; they had killed him, and were they now here to desecrate the remains, play with his corpse? His throat caught in a gesture that would have formed a growl, if he still had lungs to breathe with. His fists rose at his sides, struck the stone overhead, and fell again, trembling.

The anger possessed him. It stilled the mourning voices. Armiger's attention turned to the wall behind his head as the first blow of the hammer fell outside.

"HE'S A GENERAL, he's not going to have jewelry," muttered Choltas. He looked around uneasily.

The oldest of the grave robbers, Enneas, watched him good-humoredly. Choltas had been into a couple of mounds near Barendts city; the operations had consisted of surveying and tunneling, based on the assumption that the burial chamber was at the center of each mound. They'd been right once, but the chamber had collapsed long ago. They had sifted through clay and stones in a suffocating tunnel by the light of fireflies tethered with horses' hairs. The operation had taken weeks, but was worth it when they turned up some sintered metal, a little gold, and a jade pendant in the shape of a machine.

Choltas had been scared then; how much more so was he now in his first catacomb. This hall was low and wide, so that Choltas's lantern lit a spot of floor and ceiling and only hinted at the rest of the space. He kept starting and looking around, because every now and then the lantern light would gleam off a slick surface of one of the pillars that lined the place. Enneas knew they could play tricks on the eye; he had been here before. If you let your imagination run away with you, the pillars looked like men, standing still and silent all around.

"He could have anything," Enneas said. "You never know what a man will choose to be buried with. If nothing else, if he's highborn, there's the gold in his teeth."

Choltas grunted. Corres, the third member of the party, waved impatiently from a ways down the gallery. His impatience, Choltas knew, was not due to fear, but a simple desire to get an unpleasant job done. Corres had no imagination, no apparent feelings, and seldom spoke. Enneas had no idea what he did with the money he made in these tombs.

They joined him near one wall of the passage. "It's somewhere along here," said Corres. He swung his lantern, making shadows lean up and down the hall. Corres was merely trying to get a good view, but Choltas watched the moving darkness with growing alarm.

"It's okay," Enneas said, patting him on the shoulder. He pitched his voice at a conversational volume. "This is our place of employ. We belong here." Choltas stared at him wide-eyed. Enneas chuckled.

Well, it was almost true. Fear battled anger in Enneas's stomach every time he entered a tomb like this. The fear was natural; he'd never reconciled himself to death. The anger was more powerful, though, and it had to do with Enneas's legacy: his family had fallen from one of the highest positions in the republic. The deciding moment in his life had been the day his mother took him to visit burial mounds of some ancient warlords. "Your ancestors are buried here," she had said, gesturing at the earthen hills, each surmounted by a fane of pillars. He'd imagined men and women with his family's faces standing at attention under those hills, watching him. Their eyes had accused: you are poor, they had said. You are no longer one of us.

Enneas had naively believed that fortunes lost could be regained. His youth had been a comedy of failure; he could enter no guilds, influenced no inspectors with his painstakingly written political letters. Business ventures begun with pride and faith in his fellow man had ended in betrayal by his customers and friends. One day he had found himself wandering penniless near the field of mounds. He was damned if he would beg. And his ancestors' eyes followed him as he walked among them. He decided to shut their eyes once and for all and had started digging.

And now he was wealthy. Choltas, too, was from a fallen house, though he was too young to be bitter. Enneas had taken it upon himself to spare the youth the detours that had brought him to this point. Even now Choltas wasn't sure he wanted to live this way, but Enneas kept at him. Tonight was an important test for the boy.

The wall was full of niches. They were not shallow and broad, as in most catacombs, but were deep holes into which a body could be inserted feetfirst. The builders of this place had planned it to be used for many centuries, but their nation had been overrun sometime in the dim past. The city this tomb had served no longer existed, so it was seldom visited. The general's army had been camped nearby, otherwise he would have been buried elsewhere. Good luck for the robbers, for although the heavy stone that covered the main entrance could not be moved by less than thirty men, there was another way in which Enneas knew about. It had been easy to convince Corres to come here—nearly impossible to convince Choltas.

"I don't like this," said Choltas. His round face bobbed palely in the lantern light. He stared in frank terror at the bricked-up niches Corres was passing his hands over.

"Quiet," said Corres. "Look for new mortar."

"The sooner we find him the quicker we can be out of here," Enneas sensibly reminded the boy. He joined Corres at the wall. The floor around this whole area was scuffed. The burial party had come straight to this section of wall. No set of footsteps ventured into any of the other halls, unsurprisingly. The superstitious soldiers who'd put the general in here had wanted to get the job done as quickly as they could and get out again. Enneas imagined they'd looked around themselves fearfully just as Choltas did now.

And his own pulse was racing. He wanted to leave—but each time he thought that, he remembered poverty and disappointment, and his feet remained planted right here.

"It's none of these, they're all old," Corres complained. "And the letters make up other names, I think."

"Yes." The general had not been buried in any of the top or middle niches. Enneas lowered his own lantern and examined the row of low openings at floor level. Several were bricked over, and two of these fell in the center of the scuffed area. "It's one of these."

Choltas backed away. "We shouldn't be doing this," he said.

They both looked at him. Corres was unslinging the smith's hammer he carried for this kind of work. "Getting traditional on us?" he asked.

"It's—it's wrong," said Choltas. "There must be a better way to—"

"To live?" Enneas was annoyed. Choltas was shaking; this would not do. "You can be a beggar, Choltas, you can do that. Go on—leave us and take up your position on some rainy street. And every time a copper piece clinks into your cup, remember that for every one of those, a hundred gold sovereigns hang in the purse of a dead man, vaulted away underground where they'll never buy any child a year of meals, least of all yours. And when they spit on you and call you useless, think how useless those sovereigns are. Now don't be foolish. We have a job to do." This was a rehearsed speech, but his delivery had real passion behind it, and it seemed to work. Choltas's shoulders slumped.

Corres tapped against each niche. "The right one seems newer," he said. "It's hard to tell."

"We'll open it first, then try the other one," said Enneas. Corres swung the hammer back, then glanced at Choltas. He stood and handed the hammer to the youth. "Go."

Breathing raggedly, Choltas leaned over and swung the hammer with both hands. The hollow thuds it made didn't echo, though all the stone around them should have promoted that effect. Enneas imagined the corpses in their bricked niches absorbing the sound, shifting a bit and settling with every blow. He glanced around uneasily.

One of the bricks dented inward, and on Choltas's next blow it disappeared, leaving a black window. "Shit," said Choltas as if he'd wanted the wall to stand firm.

"Good." Corres knelt and, putting his hands in the aperture, pulled. The bricks around the opening twisted out, then fell with a clatter. Choltas dropped the hammer.

Enneas's own fear reached its peak. This was always the hardest part for him—facing the body. He knew what to do from long experience, however: use his anger to deride the fear, make fun of it, and thus extinguish it completely.

"Allow me," he said. Corres grunted and stood up, dusting his hands fastidiously. Deliberately, Enneas didn't shine his lamp into the opened niche. He knelt and stuck his arm into it.

There was no real odor coming from this niche. It couldn't be the general's, then. Oh well, it might still have some valuables in it. Enneas kept a casual smile fixed on his face as he groped around. His heart nearly stopped as his hand fell on a rounded surface covered with lank hair.

Might as well have some fun. "Here he is," he said. He got a good grip on the hair and pulled. The skull came away with a brittle pop. He stood up and thrust the skull at Choltas, not looking at it himself. "Meet General Armiger," he said.

The other floor-level niche exploded outward.

Corres was standing right in front of it. For a moment he looked down in bewilderment at the brick dust covering his boots. Then his eyes widened impossibly, and his head ratcheted over a bit, down a bit, until he stared at the black opening that had appeared by his feet.

A black hand snapped out into the lamplight. It grabbed the edge of a brick and shoved it into the corridor.

Choltas began to scream. Enneas stepped back, raising the skull to his chest as a feeble shield. He wasn't really thinking, and later he couldn't remember fear. But he remembered Choltas screaming. And he would always remember Corres standing helplessly, watching coal-black, half-dried arms widen the opening they had made and then clasp its sides to drag a foul-smelling, lolling thing onto the floor at his feet.

One of the black hands touched Corres's boot, and he finally moved, stepping away quickly. "Hammer," he said, but Enneas barely heard him over Choltas's screams.

The general stood up. His dress jacket was open, and showed his split torso; there were no organs inside, only darkness. His eyes had dried half open. He swayed unsteadily, like a puppet held aloft without the use of its legs. His right arm swung out widely, then came back to paw at his throat. The fingers closed around a metal bar there, and pulled.

Corres had found the hammer. He stepped forward, shouting the name of a Wind Enneas had never heard him espouse, and swung. The hammer caved in Armiger's split chest, banging him against the stone wall. The general's head rolled around helplessly.

He made no sound as he stepped forward. His hand moved down, drawing a long T-handled spike out of his jaw. Now his mouth gaped open, but still he made no sound.

In the lamplight Enneas saw the black burns that covered his head and arms, and pale white flesh like ivory elsewhere. The image was burned into his memory in the instant Armiger stood with the spike in his hand, then the general moved, almost too quickly to follow.

He stepped up to Corres, and his arm came up and drove the spike into the hollow at the base of Corres's throat. Corres's eyes bulged, and his lips writhed back. No sound came, only blood.

Armiger took another step, his arm rigid before him, and the force carried him and Corres outside of the circle of lantern light.

Choltas stopped screaming and ran. The wrong way. And that was too much for Enneas, who also ran. He banged into the stone jamb of the door to the hall and swung himself around it to stagger in total darkness toward their entrance shaft. Anything could be waiting ahead, but he knew what was waiting behind. He heard Choltas start screaming again.

He tripped over a loose stone and fell, banging his chin and twisting his arm. Pain lanced up his neck. He stood anyway and lurched into the opening he knew was there. He expected fingers to encircle his ankle as he grabbed for each hand-hold in the rough stone shaft.

Enneas pulled himself out of a pit into starlight on the top of the hill. He ignored his sacks and supplies and ran until he tripped and rolled over and over down the slope. He came to rest at the bottom, not badly hurt but bruised and shaken. When he stood up, he continued on at a limp, eyes fixed on the horizon where dawn was hours away.

And though the fear didn't go away, as the hours passed, Enneas began to feel again all the anger of injustice and betrayal he thought he'd overcome years ago. When he wept it was from frustration, at the end of the only chapter of his life that had been in any way successful.

ARMIGER'S EYES HAD dried out, but he could see. His ears had withered in his skull, but he could hear the sough of wind across the top of the shaft as he neared it. Stars glowed above the lip of the pit.

He had already forgotten the humans. A deep passion they would not have understood moved him now. He climbed swiftly, as if chasing something, but what he pursued was his own meaning.

CHOLTAS HAD HEARD the footsteps of the devil fade away. He knew it would be back unless he stayed very still. This was the thing's home; it would never venture out into the world above. So though he couldn't hear it, he knew it was there. If he stayed completely still, wrapped around himself in this corner in total darkness, it might not find him. But if he so much as sneezed, he knew it would be on him instantly.

Even now it might be creeping up on him silently. He wrapped more tightly around himself, and tried not to breathe.

Time passed, but Choltas did not move. When thirst began to torture him, he stayed still. He wet himself and shat in his pants quietly. And eventually, delirium overcame him; he heard his mother's voice, saw drifting pictures of his home.

He kept his arms around his knees, and his face buried there against his own flesh. And he breathed weaker and weaker, aware at last only of the murmur of his own heart and the torment of cold and thirst, overridden by a fear he could no longer identify.

Stay still, stay still.
Its hand hangs above me.

6

JORDAN BECAME AWARE that the jolting of the cart they rode had stopped. He blinked and looked up. He didn't remember much of the past day; all he could see was the startled face of that man in the tomb, as an arm that seemed to be Jordan's own pushed the spike through his throat. And then the ticking footsteps to the stone shaft, and up and out into bright starlight.

Armiger was walking in the world again. Jordan could hear the creaking of his dry joints, as if the dreams had begun to infect his waking life. If he closed his eyes, he could even see the afterimage of some other place, a field or clearing. Armiger's steps fell like the beat of a metronome, far past human confidence. Steady and fast, day and night, he was going somewhere.

He hadn't told Lady May much. She knew Armiger was out and moving, and that he still seemed to be dead. In the dream Jordan had looked down at himself and awkwardly buttoned up his jacket to cover the hole in his chest. The skin of his fingers was taut and black, but in the last day it had turned an awful yellow and become more flexible.

A horrible thought had come to Jordan this morning. Surely Armiger could see what Jordan saw; wouldn't he know that Calandria May was after him by now? He had asked Calandria, and she had said, "The changes I made to your implants are supposed to prevent him from receiving you." All Jordan heard of that was the phrase *supposed to.*

He was sure Armiger was coming after them. If Armiger had power over life and death, how was Lady May going to destroy him? She seemed gay and unhurried. The only reassurance he had was the memory of her apparent invulnerability during the fight with the mechal butler at the manse.

He was numb by now from fear and horror, so he said nothing. He'd only spoken once or twice, when Lady May pressed him for details of the countryside Armiger moved through, and when he had asked her, "Are you like him?"

"No," she had answered vehemently. "I am flesh and blood like you." She took his palm and put it to her cheek. "I've sold nothing of myself to gain the powers I have. Remember that." She smiled in her quietly confident way.

Now she was smiling in that same way, looking at the stone posts of a large gate they had come to. The road ran on, but the track through those gates was well rutted, as if from much recent traffic. This belied the impression given by the dead ivy thronging over the posts and the verdigrised metal gates, which seemed frozen open.

"Where are we?" he asked weakly.

Her arm encircled to hug him quickly. "Refuge," she said. "We'll meet Axel here. Then we'll decide how to eliminate Armiger."

She flicked the reins, and the horse obediently turned through the gates. They'd bought this cart and the horse in a village yesterday. Lady May had paid the startled ostler well for it, forgoing the usual haggle over price and quality. Although she treated the horse well, Jordan had the feeling she took her ownership of it lightly and would cheerfully abandon it and the cart the moment she ceased to need it. Jordan would have to work two years at Castor's to afford such a beast.

They passed down an avenue of trees. Gaps to the right showed well-tended grounds, much more extensive than Castor's. At first no one was visible, then Jordan spotted three children in bright clothing running across a lawn. The path wound down, and Jordan revived a little at the sight of warm shafts of sunlight piercing the green canopies, one lighting a stone trough by the road carved with well-worn images of the Diadem swans.

Two giant oaks signaled the end of the grove. In the bright sunlight beyond, Jordan could see green grass and the beige stone of some vast mansion in the far background. But nearer, a few yards past the oaks, a table had been planted on the lawn. A clean white cloth draped it, held down by bowls of fruit and meat, plates and cups and tankards. Three people dressed in white livery stood by, gathering up platefuls of food. Now he could hear a continuous murmur of voices, laughter, and the thud of hooves, coming through the remaining screen of trees.

As they passed beneath the twin oaks, two attendants appeared from behind them. They bowed, and one took the bridle of the horse.

Jordan barely noticed them. He was staring at the beautiful lawns, where a party was taking place.

Tall beribboned poles had been planted in the ground at wide intervals. At least six tables were scattered around the field, each piled high with food. Servants ran back and forth between knots of people—and the people, when Jordan turned his gaze on them, were amazing. They were brown skinned, white skinned, dressed in bright colors or somber black, or barely dressed at all. Sunlight flashed off jewels at the throat of a laughing woman. Nearby, a man with iron-gray hair patted his hands on his velvet trousers and tried again to mount a pair of stilts held for him by two long-faced jugglers. A small knot of red-skinned men were having an archery competition, their target a melon on top of one of the poles.

Calandria May looked puzzled. "What's the occasion?" she asked the servant leading their horse.

He looked back, arched his eyebrow, and said, "Aren't you family?"

She hesitated almost imperceptibly. "Guests," she said. "Of Inspector Boros. Our arrangement was made some weeks ago, but we were delayed, I fear. It seems we've arrived at an unfortunate moment."

The servant smiled arrogantly. "We have plenty of room." He gestured to the manor.

This place put Castor's to shame. Massive fluted pillars framed the entranceway, iron lamps perched upon their capitals. They did not hold up a roof, but were open to the sky. The building's facade was of tan stone, filled with windows, each framed by pillars. Statues posed on the rooftop corners, and more stood in niches in the walls. Three stories were indicated by the windows, and by the width of the place it must sprawl around a central courtyard large enough to hold Castor's mansion.

Behind the profusion of chimneys on the roof, a bleak gray fortress tower rose incongruously. Its sides did not curve smoothly, but in juts and acute angles; it seemed to have been built of stone triangles. Black stains like tear tracks wove down its sides.

As the cart passed near a group of revelers, a tall woman in severe black and scarlet excused herself and walked over. The servant stopped them as she approached, and Lady May hopped down from the cart and curtsied to her.

"Good grief, are you a boy or a woman?" The lady laughed in a deep voice; Calandria was still dressed in buckskins. The lady made a fluttering gesture with her hand near her breast. Silver chain in her hair glinted as she cocked her head. "And which side of the family are you from?"

Lady May curtsied again. "Neither side, I fear, Madam. I am Lady Calandria May, and this is my charge, Jordan Mason." Jordan started at the sound of his own name. He stood awkwardly and bowed. "I wrote asking for the hospitality of the house some weeks ago and received it." Lady May went on. "If we have come at the wrong time, please let us know."

"Nonsense," said the lady. "Make yourselves at home. I am lady Marice Boros. My husband is, alas . . ."—she smiled for the first time as she looked around—"missing. You see, we are having the first family reunion in a full generation, and the clan has grown to unmanageable proportions. These are all my kin." She swept her hand to indicate the throng, then turned and frowned at the vista. "Oh dear, they are, aren't they? Well, no matter, we will accommodate you. Alex," she said to the man holding their horse, "put them in the tower." She nodded sharply to Lady May. "I trust you will join us for dinner? I'm afraid we shan't be able to give you too much attention today; I've not spoken to some of our family members yet and will be doing that at dinner."

"We understand. Though I hope we will be able to converse at some point, your obligations are clear," Lady May said. "Oh—we were to rendezvous here with an acquaintance. Sir Axel Chan. Has he by any chance arrived?"

"Chan. Ah, of course." Lady Marice's eyes narrowed. "I think you can find him right over there."

Jordan and Lady May followed Marice's pointing finger. In a clear area of grass, two men circled each other. One wore a sky-blue silk uniform with winglike feather epaulets. The other, shorter man wore black leather. They were surrounded by a small crowd of young men, who either sipped delicate glasses of wine or negotiated bets among themselves. Abruptly the man in black stepped forward, took the wrist of his opponent, and without appearing to move, flipped him over to land with a thud audible all the way to the cart. Scattered laughter and jeers drifted over.

Lady May sighed. "I was afraid of that. I will take him off your hands, Lady Marice."

"Thank you." Marice curtsied, and walked away. Lady May started in the direction of the fight, and Jordan stepped down to follow.

The youth who'd been flipped stood up angrily. ". . . Slipped!" he shouted. Two of his friends shook their heads as they paid the ones with whom they'd bet.

The man in black grinned like a gargoyle. He was not tall, slighter than his black jacket and leggings tried to suggest, but broad chested. His features were strange—flat, with a broad triangular nose and dark hooded eyes. His hair was a black tangle kept tied back in an unruly ponytail. But when he smiled, his teeth were perfect, and he smiled very broadly when he saw Calandria.

"My lady," he shouted, spreading his arms and stepping forward to embrace her.

Lady May shifted her weight slightly and shrugged. Axel Chan flew over her cocked knee and onto his face.

The crowd erupted in laughter. The young man whom Axel had humiliated smiled and bowed to Lady May as Axel picked himself up.

Jordan's attention wavered between Axel and Calandria May. As she had before, now she changed before his eyes, her mobile face taking on a rakish smirk as she played up to the young men. "Dear sir," she said, "Our friend is not well known to you; he is to me. Hence, you can be forgiven for not being prepared for him. I, however, am surely ready for any meeting with Axel Chan." She put a hand on Axel's shoulder and shook him lightly. Axel grinned stupidly.

"Axel, you will show your worthy opponent what you did to him—later. For now, I need your ear. Get yourself cleaned up, and I will meet you in your quarters."

Axel winked at the youths. "In your dreams, Axel," added Lady May, as she turned to go.

Jordan stayed where he was. After a moment, Axel noticed him, and his expression became serious. He waved away the questions from the other men and came to stand before Jordan, hands on his hips. He smelled of wine and sweat.

"Well. Mason, isn't it?" He stuck out a grimy hand. "Axel. I met your sister."

Jordan wasn't sure he liked the idea of this rogue coming anywhere near Emmy. "How is she?"

"Fine." Axel glanced after Lady May, who was remounting the cart. "Don't tell her ladyship there, but I told Emmy what's up. I have a letter she wrote you." He grinned at the way Jordan's face lit up. "Don't do that! She'll figure it out. This is between you and me. I'll let you have it later, whenever we can escape from her clutches for a minute or two."

Jordan opened his mouth, countless questions crowding for expression. Axel gave him a friendly shove. "Be on your way, boy. She wants you. We'll talk later."

Jordan nodded, and practically ran back to the cart. He remounted it next to a scowling Calandria. ". . . About as inconspicuous as a tart at Communion," she was muttering. "He'll be the death of us all."

They were led to the main doors of the manor, where they dismounted. Another servant preceded them into the giant rotunda of the place and through a wide greeting hall to a glass-walled chamber that let out onto the central courtyard.

The manor wrapped almost all the way around the courtyard, which was packed with statues like a forest of stone. The neat procession of pillared windows and beige wall was broken at the far end by the strange angles of the old tower. The manor seemed to have grown out of one of its corners.

Jordan marveled at the workmanship of the statues. They depicted men and women, mechals and desals, and other fabulous creatures, and one or two were attempts at modeling the Winds themselves. He paused before one of these, which was a human form made of tortured folds of cloth carved in marble. It looked realistically windblown. The servant noticed him looking and said, "Lady Hannah Boros, six generations ago now. This was her workplace. She made all our statues," he added proudly.

One statue near the dark entrance to the tower was missing its head. The blond stone in the wound was fresh; Jordan could see a few chips half covered by grass at its feet. "What happened to that one?" he asked.

"Hush," said Lady May. "Be discreet." The servant pretended not to have heard them.

Jordan was still puzzling over that exchange when they were shown their chamber. It was squarish and about six meters on a side, but the ceiling was a spiderweb of buttresses. One narrow window looked out over the courtyard. There was only one bed, but the servant told them another would be brought up. Other than that, the place held only a dresser and wardrobe and a small writing desk. Sheepskins were scattered about the stone floor; it smelled of camphor and wood smoke here.

Lady May thanked their guide. "I need clothes," she said to him on his way out. "Can you send me a tailor?"

"We have the best here, Lady. Dinner is at six."

"Thank you." He left, and she collapsed backward onto the bed. "Whew."

"Why are we here?" Jordan asked. He was admiring the stonework. This place was very solid, much more so than the manor house itself. It might even be strong enough to keep Armiger out.

Lady May had stripped off her left boot and was massaging her toes. She peered at him through the window her legs made. "We will be staying here until we know exactly where Armiger is. You have to get hold of yourself now, Jordan. We need you to tell us exactly where he is and where he's going. When we locate him, we'll strike."

"Why should I help you any further?" he asked. "When I tell the Boroses what you did to me—"

"Do you want the nightmares to stop?" she asked quickly. "When Armiger is no more, they will cease," she continued. "But only Axel and I of all the people on Ventus can destroy him. You can surely escape us, Jordan, but by doing that you guarantee you will never escape Armiger."

"Well?" she asked after they had glared at one another for a long moment.

"He's coming here," Jordan said sullenly.

She dropped her foot and sat up. "Are you sure?"

"Yes, he's after me!"

"How do you know that?"

"I . . . I just know."

She grimaced. "I don't think so. At least, we've seen no evidence that he's aware that his connection with you is still open. As I told you, we've taken steps to disable it so he can no longer see through your eyes. But we'll determine all of that soon. This is our headquarters now, Jordan. We are also guests here, and I expect you to behave accordingly."

"What do you mean?" he asked suspiciously.

She patted the bed next to her. He sat on the linen; it was softer than any bed he'd known, except maybe the one in the manse. Lady May leaned over and massaged his shoulders delicately. "I'm going to go talk to Axel. When the tailor comes, I want you to ask him to dress you. Not in servants' clothing—you are no one's servant now, you are the equal of anyone in this building. So waistcoat, evening dress, the lot. Do you understand?" He nodded. "And do not wander too far, but please do not enter any of the servants' areas—when you walk, you will walk in the main halls like the owners. I think this might be hard for you, but it is necessary."

He frowned. He hadn't thought about it, but it definitely would be hard. Never in his life had Jordan walked the halls of a manor as if it were his home. He was used to ducking from stairwell to stairwell, never straying beyond areas where he could justify his presence. She was right: his instinct would be to find the back halls, eat in the kitchens, and leave the building when night came. He shook his head. "I'll try."

"Good." She rolled off the bed. "I'm off to tackle Axel. Wish me luck."

He watched her go and bolted the door when she'd left. Then he went to examine the mortaring around the window and tried to gauge its strength.

AXEL HAD WEASELED his way into the main building, naturally. Calandria had no difficulty getting directions to his room; all the servants knew him. He'd only been here two days.

She took the steps up to the third floor two at a time. Despite herself, she smiled as she thought of Axel tossing that fop on his ear. Outside his door she paused, looking down at herself. She still wore ragged outdoors gear. It would have been so much better if they'd arrived first, then she could have met him in a proper gown, with pearls at her ears. She sighed, then rapped on the door.

"Enter." She stepped into a lavish bedroom. It was huge—and had a perfect view of the grounds. Velvet draperies hung everywhere, over the windows and framing the bed. The bedposts were carved with leaf motifs and painted gold. Or maybe they were gold. A woman's slipper lay half concealed under the bed. Yes, this was Axel's room all right.

He rose from a writing desk. He had discarded his jacket and wore a billowing blue silk shirt. "Ho!" He opened his arms as he came to her. "And don't hit me this time!"

She returned the embrace warmly. He still smelled of wine, but she knew him; he'd have taken a restorative before meeting with her. He held her for a second longer than she'd have liked, but that too was normal. As he broke away he gestured at the room. "Quite a place, no?"

"I expected no less of you," she said, eyeing the slipper.

It constantly amazed her how well Axel did in situations like this. After all, he wasn't a professional, like her; Calandria had been trained in espionage and intelligence gathering by people who made a religion of such things. They had plucked her out of the crude reformatory she had ended up in after her mother's arrest and death and erased all links with her past and home world. Then they had given her not a new identity, but a repertoire of identities. Calandria had spent every waking moment since then acting. Only after she had turned rogue on her employers could she behave like something approaching her true Self—and then only with close friends like Axel.

She had met Axel in deep space, on a remote, frozen planet without a mother star. He was a smuggler. They dealt to their mutual satisfaction several times, and each time she was a different person. It took him quite a while to wise up to her act, and by the time he did she had taken a liking to him. When he confronted her, she took the opportunity to chastise him for his inattention. "If I'd been hired to trap you, you'd be undergoing decriminalization now," she told him. "Count yourself lucky." He had laughed at that.

Calandria needed her disguises to move through the different societies and subcultures demanded by her work. Axel just seemed to make friends whereever he went, without changing one iota of his appearance or style.

"Here, look at these pictures," he was saying now, as he dragged her to one wall. The walls were hung with large, faded photographs, apparently of ancient members of the Boros clan. "Printed on porcelain," he said. "So they don't deteriorate. Good idea, no?"

She arched an eyebrow. "I suppose." Photography was permitted by the Winds, along with other gentle forms of chemistry; Axel knew that, so why should he care about these examples? They were nothing compared with even the most primitive hologram.

Axel had picked up a decanter of wine. "Oh, do stop," she said. "It's not even dinnertime yet."

"I think these pictures are fascinating," he said. "Especially this one—it's printed on vellum." He put the decanter down on an ornate dresser under one and stretched to grab both sides of the frame. He lifted it off the wall.

An irregular hole was revealed. Set into the plaster was the verdigrised mouth of a large horn. Calandria blinked at it. Axel cupped his hand at his ear. He adopted an exaggerated listening stance. Then he made a talking gesture at her with the other hand.

She cleared her throat. "I wonder how they did that?"

"The porcelain, or the velum?" Axel picked up the decanter and gestured at the horn. She shook her head.

He shrugged, then upended the decanter into the horn. Red wine gurgled as it drained down into some pipe in the wall and, she imagined, straight into the ear of whoever might be listening at the other end.

Axel cackled with glee, and grabbing up the silk doily on the table, stuffed it down the horn after the wine. Then he replaced the picture and dusted his hands. "That was the only one," he said. "Now we can talk."

"Oh, come now," she said. "Why would they be bugging us? We're just visiting."

"Timing," he said. He flipped a white plush-cushioned chair backward and sat in it, leaning his arms on the back. "The whole Boros clan is here, and that's bad. Old Yuri may think we're spies."

"Why? They seem like a friendly enough bunch. Not that I've had the time to talk to any of them. . . ."

"Ah, you will. You're better at this than I am, I suggest we attend dinner and you can tell me who intends to kill whom. They are a murderous lot—did you see a certain statue in the courtyard?" She nodded. "Yesterday night. A duel. I didn't see who, or who lost, mostly because it wasn't preannounced. Ambush, maybe? Who knows."

"Really." She sat at the writing desk, and looked out over the grounds. "I've never been anywhere quite like this."

"It's positively medieval," said Axel with a nod. "But then, look at their history. Six hundred years ago these people were still scrabbling in the muck, living in mud huts. Only a few warlords had any kind of power. It's actually pretty amazing how far they've come as a society, considering the ancestors of people like the Boros."

He waved at the grounds. "All this is very European in style. I'm pretty sure people must have raided manse libraries here and there over the centuries. How much would it take, do you think, to build a nation? One book of economics? Another about gardening? They saved very little from the initial disaster, so they must have supplemented it from the manses, but it was obviously hard-won knowledge, or there'd be more of it."

Calandria pictured a group of soldiers armed with pikes trying to face down several of the golden creatures she and Jordan had seen—battling their way to a manse library, grabbing a few books at random, then bolting with crystalline things at their heels.

That was interesting, but not what she had come here to talk about. "What's the occasion for this reunion?" she asked.

"Yuri called it—the patriarch, you met his wife. Marice. Good name. There's some kind of power struggle within the clan, and he wants to resolve it. The Boros are old money in three nations: Memnonis, Ravenon, and Iapysia. The revolt of the parliament in Iapysia has tipped the balance of power somehow, and Yuri wants to make sure it trickles through the family correctly. The Iapysians don't mind—they get to call in favors to consolidate their position back home. Problem is, there's two factions represented there—the parliamentarians and the royalists. If you look you can probably make them out—at opposite ends of the grounds."

"Hmm." Calandria did look out. "Dinner will be fun."

"It gets better. There's some dispute over Yuri's position as patriarch. Which side will he support in the Iapysian thing? That's a touchy question, because the loser might decide to open the old wound of his legitimacy. That's all happening down there even as we speak."

"My." She smiled at him. "We do pick the most interesting hotels."

"Yeah. Well, we'll have to be careful not to get involved. Now, how's Mason?"

"You saw him. What do you think?"

Axel shrugged. "He looks tough. Does he know where Armiger is?"

"If he did we'd be able to send him home," she said. "No, he doesn't. That's our job for the next day or two—locating Armiger. Jordan's a bit wrapped up in his own misery right now, so we'll have to show him the advantages of his position. He's afraid Armiger is coming here."

Axel frowned. "Is he?"

"I don't know. That would surprise the Boros, wouldn't it? I guess Armiger is a walking corpse at the moment, though he may be recovering. We have to know how powerful he is before we face him. I'm wondering how we can get Jordan to find out for us."

"Yeah, yeah . . ." Axel chewed on one knuckle absentmindedly. "We need more power."

"Political?"

"No, guns, damn it. I don't like this planet, Cal. The damn Winds are always watching. If you bring anything higher-tech than a wristwatch in here they'll pounce on you and rip it off. We can't face Armiger without real weapons—a plasma cannon would do."

She laughed shortly. "We stick to the plan. When we've got him in our sights, the *Desert Voice* will hit him from orbit."

"And then the Winds will blow your starship out of the sky!"

She glowered at the tabletop. "My reading of the Winds is that they have an abysmal reaction time. They let us bring the cutter down, and it got back to the *Voice* okay. Nothing technological stayed on the surface, as far as they know."

"Yeah, but they'll object to Armiger getting nuked. I have another idea."

She didn't really like the current plan, either, so she said, "Go ahead."

"We contact the Winds ourselves. Tell them about Armiger. They're like the immune system for the entire planet; any foreign body gets eliminated eventually. Like we will be, if we stay here too long. I don't know how Armiger's lasted this long; superior technology, I guess—"

"Well, precisely," she pointed out. "He's more sophisticated than the Winds. Even if we knew how to carry on a rational conversation with the Winds, do you think they'd believe us? I'm sure Armiger's totally invisible to them. And I doubt it's going to change."

"Ventus is a lot more complicated than we thought," he said. "Some people do talk to the Winds; I've heard more stories in the past couple of days—"

"Stories? Axel, this planet breeds myths like fungus! None of the locals has a clue what the Winds are, and if they did they can't affect them at all."

"They can—there are ways. Do you seriously believe humans would cohabit this world with them for so long without working out ways to deal with them?"

Calandria looked out over the grounds again. This manor was centuries old, and the civilization that had built it was older still. And the Winds were as constant as their namesake in these people's lives. Axel could be right. "So how do they do it?"

"It's actually pretty simple. A couple of their main religions are ecologically based, right? The inner doctrine seems to be emulation of the Winds. If you act like the Winds, they treat you like one of them. And then they'll talk to you."

"Sounds too easy," she said. "And suspiciously mystical."

He threw up his hands and stood. "Believe whatever the hell you want! But it makes sense, Cal: the Winds are confused about humans to begin with. They don't know whether we're vermin or part of their grand design. How do you think agriculture gets done on this world? People placate them. It works. I think we should look into it."

"All right," she said. "You look into it. Meanwhile, I'm going to work on Jordan and find out where Armiger is going."

Axel frowned. "He really is on the move?"

"Maybe. The *Desert Voice* located the site of the battle he talked about, but the forces that survived it are dispersed across hundreds of kilometers of territory. I'm going to try to get some more lucid descriptions from Jordan."

"And what if Armiger is headed this way?"

Calandria looked out at the forest woods beyond the manor grounds. "Then Jordan had better be able to warn us when he's due."

7

JORDAN SMOOTHED THE lapels of his vest nervously. He had never worn clothes like this. Their strange fit and discomfort in the oddest places was a constant reminder of his role tonight as apprentice to Calandria May. The stiffness of the fabric and the cut of the shirt and pants drew his shoulders up and made him constantly arch his back. All the other men stood and walked the same, in an almost exaggerated, prideful posture. He had always assumed that went with their station. The idea that their clothes were made to hold their noses up amazed him. He couldn't look at them with quite the same awe as he used to.

He stood just outside the dining hall in a swirl of young men, who mostly spoke among themselves. He knew the language, but had no idea what they were talking about—rights, obligations, and fine points of the pecking order, it seemed. As far as possible Jordan tried to stay out of any dialogue, only nodding and smiling when it was needed. He knew his accent was guild class, and although Calandria claimed to be able to fix that, she hadn't yet. He gave his name when it was required of him, but nothing more.

"Ah, there you are!" boomed a familiar voice. Axel Chan's hand descended on his shoulder like a vice. "Where's the lady?"

"Changing," Jordan said tersely. Axel had spoken so loudly that heads turned all over the chamber. Jordan wanted to shrink into the floor to avoid all those high-class gazes.

"Good. If she's not about, I'll borrow you for a moment." Axel steered him away from the men, past the ladies, who were preening and talking behind their feather fans, and out of the antechamber. He led Jordan halfway down the lower, stone-floored corridor that ran between the antechamber and the stairways, then stopped under a high window. Evening light suffused the corridor, gilding the stones that Axel leaned against. He grinned, slouching, and put his hands in his pockets.

"How are you doing, lad?" he asked.

"I don't like this," said Jordan, pulling at his jacket.

"It's a fine uniform. Red and gold—your choice?" Jordan nodded guardedly. "Very nice. Tasteful. We'll make an inspector out of you yet."

"Calandria says she can teach me to talk like them."

"It's no trick. You just speak slowly and flap your lips a bit, as if," he switched into an overdone upper-crust accent, "you could barely care to speak at all." Despite himself, Jordan grinned at the imitation.

Axel leaned close. "Don't worry. We're all pretending; that's what events like this are all about."

"Why are we doing it at all?"

"To fit in. Better that we be there to be spoken to than absent to be spoken about." Axel stood away from the wall and smiled archly as two ladies walked past. They ignored him. He slouched back again and said, "Now, I promised to show you the letter from your sister. Can you read?"

"A bit. I can do figures and architectural terms, and a little more."

"I'll read it to you. Your sister dictated it to me." Axel pulled a sheet of paper out of his pocket. He flipped it open and began to read.

"Oh, Jordan, I miss you so much. I wish you were here right now, but Sir Chan says you have to finish a job for him first. Then you'll be back and bring lots of money.

"I'm sorry I ran away. Mom and Dad are really mad at us, though they won't say it. They just don't talk about that night. And they pray for you to come back all the time. I can't talk to them! I wish you were here so I would have somebody to talk to.

"Sir Chan told me to write something so you would know it was me. Remember that turn on the stairs in the manor, where we found the crack? Remember the note we hid there before Dad mortared it up? I know what the note says—only me and you know. The first word is 'Boo!' Remember that?"

Jordan let his tension out with a big breath, then leaned heavily against the wall next to Axel. He smiled at Axel.

"So, it's really her, is it?" asked Axel.

Jordan nodded.

Axel continued: "After Sir Chan found me, he gave me letters of appointment to the king of Ravenon. I can't believe it—neither could anybody else, but Castor did. And Turcaret—you should have seen his face when Sir Chan showed him the letters. He wanted to kill Chan, I could tell, but he was afraid to. But Castor—he almost smiled, I think. Anyway, he told Turcaret not to argue, and he signed the letters, and Sir Chan lent me money to move in with the Sanglers, which is where I am now. Waiting for dispatches from Ravenon, who will come to me before they come to Castor. I'm so proud, and scared at the same time. And lonely. I hope you come home soon. Sir Chan says you are okay and having an adventure. Please write me and tell me all about it."

"Can I?" Jordan asked.

Axel nodded. "But you can't talk about what we're doing or say anything about Armiger." He looked over Jordan's shoulder at something and smiled. "And speaking of ladies, here she is! You're a vision, my dear."

"Thank you, Axel," Calandria said, smiling. She wore a long emerald-green skirt, a bodice worked with beads of gold, and a white loose-sleeved blouse. Her hair was piled up and held in place with pearl-tipped pins. A gold necklace completed the ensemble. Her face glowed with an inhuman perfection that Jordan had guessed at but which had hitherto been hidden under a layer of grime and disarrayed hair. Surely she wore makeup, but he could see no sign of it. Despite all that she'd done to him, in that moment Jordan thought she was the most beautiful woman he had ever seen.

He stammered something and blushed. Calandria lowered long lashes and made a near smile. "You look the proper gentleman, Jordan. Shall we join the dinner party?" She cocked her elbows; Axel immediately stepped out to take one of her arms, and Jordan hurried to place himself on the other. He felt a burst of pride as they entered the antechamber and conversations died left and right. Calandria's smile grew even more subtle, and Axel's face had hardened into an imperious mask. Jordan had no idea what he himself looked like, but strongly suspected he was ruining the effect. He tried to draw himself up as Axel had done and don a suitable air of contempt.

The hall was brightly lit by gas lamps. Jordan could see all the way to the blond stone groin vaults of the ceiling a good fifteen meters overhead.

The hall was as wide as it was high, and twice as long. Tapestries hung between the narrow buttresses, depicting scenes from the long, industrious history of the Boros inspector generals: collection and taxation figured prominently, but instead of glorious victories, as true nobility would boast, the few battle scenes showed Boros's militia sweeping away mobs of rioting citizens. A huge fireplace roared at one end of the hall, silhouetting the raised chairs and table of Yuri Boros and his family and filling the room with the smell of wood smoke. Long tables had been laid out down the sides of the hall, each length overhung by wrought-iron arches holding a lamp and trailing flowers. People were seating themselves now with the aid of black-coated servants, who paced up and down in the clear runway that stretched from the main doors at the foot of the room to the raised table and fireplace at the head. A low murmur of voices lofted up and echoed down from the arches.

When Jordan was very young, he had once watched a gathering like this through a crack in the kitchen doors at Castor's hall. He remembered none of the logic of the occasion, only the brightness and laughter and the amazing variety of food that was carried past him. All adults had been like gods to him, the controllers and inspectors more so. He longed to find some door to hide behind, some safe vantage from which to watch the tables. At the same time, he wanted to be here, seated with his betters as if he had the right. For at least tonight, Calandria's aura protected him. So, as they took their seats at an obscure table at the back of the room, Jordan sat at his place in wonder and delight and wished fervently he could also be peering through the crack in the kitchen door, his self there pulling the strings of his self here.

He glanced at Calandria's perfect face and had a flash of insight: were she and Axel standing somewhere aloof from themselves at moments like this, pulling the strings of their public faces?

His contemplative spell was broken by the bray of a horn. Everyone was seated now; Axel and Calandria had put themselves to either side of Jordan, effectively isolating him from conversation, which was fine with him. It came to him just where he was, and he had one of those moments that is later permanently impressed on memory; his finger traced the edge of a blue-china plate such as he had seen but never touched back home, and the sleeve of his arm was red and beautiful in the white light that flashed off the knife and forks by the plate. He looked up, and as he did the main doors to his right opened, and a procession entered.

They had done this at Castor's, too, he remembered, and the familiarity mixed with strangeness sent a shiver down his back. Servants dressed as highborn men and women entered the hall, walking sedately in pairs. Each wore a finely crafted mask—the death masks of the Boros ancestors. These masks probably resided in a room of their own, somewhere near the front of the manor. The ones at Castor's manor were racked on the wall in pairs, with lines painted on the wall between the hooks, plainly showing the family tree.

At festival occasions they were taken out and worn, as now. The Boros ancestors had come to visit their descendants.

The horn sounded again. Everyone stood. The masked procession proceeded up the hall within the space between the tables, and each figure bowed or curtsied politely to the head table before it turned to walk back. Polite guests were expected to have already learned the names and histories behind these masks; Jordan had never thought to do so, but then, he had never been any highborn person's guest before. He resolved to visit the mask room and learn the Boros pedigree as soon as he could.

Lady Marice stood. "On behalf of my husband, I welcome you. We have much that is serious to discuss amongst ourselves, but I pray you first enjoy this fine meal we've brought you, and forget your cares for a space."

"What does she mean about serious stuff?" Jordan whispered to Calandria.

"Something's up," Axel responded cryptically. Almost imperceptibly, he gestured at the table opposite. Jordan looked, but didn't see anything odd or unusual—just two family groups seated near one another, each attentive to Marice. Now and then glances were exchanged within each group, but not between them.

Axel nodded to the patriarch of the family closer to the head table. "That's Linden," he whispered. "Direct heir to Boros." Linden was a thin, whippish man with pale hair drawn back in a ponytail. His eyes were fixed on Marice as she spoke. "And that," Axel indicated the square-faced head of the other family, "is Brendan Sheia, bastard son of Yuri and a lady from Iapysia. By the laws of Iapysia, he is the heir."

"Isn't there a civil war in Iapysia?" Jordan whispered back. Axel nodded.

Calandria touched his arm. "Can you tell me who here is a royalist and who is a parliamentarian?"

Jordan looked from one family to the other, then down the rows of the tables, where many more sat. Marice had finished her short speech, and as she sat down, the buzz of conversation started again. Now Jordan was eager to see who spoke with whom, but there was no easy dividing line.

"Bright lad," Axel said behind his head. "He's looking for the battle lines already." Calandria nodded.

Waiters swirled up carrying trays of food. A very complicated service began; Jordan knew vaguely that there was a protocol to which dishes one took and in what order, but had no idea what that was. In a fit of inspiration, he decided to watch the apprentices of two households opposite and choose what they chose. Once a plate came to him before either of them, and he felt a moment's panic. He appealed silently to the waiter, who smiled and gave a slight nod. Relieved, he took the dish.

And so it proceeded, through a grueling two hours of careful eating, followed by a grueling hour of ambiguous speeches and circumlocutions. Jordan alternated between relaxed enjoyment and extreme discomfort. Despite himself he began to fight back yawns, and to keep himself awake he let his thoughts drift to his sister. He didn't want to think about his parents beyond acknowledging to himself that he was still angry with them. But as postmistress, would Emmy attend banquets like this one? He would have to tell her about the evening and reassure her that she could do the same at Castor's.

He shut his eyes, weary and worried again about Emmy. Her official position was a thin shield, he knew. Somehow he must accomplish what Calandria demanded of him and return to her. Tonight or tomorrow; soon.

Suddenly dizzy, he opened his eyes. To sunlight.

Jordan blinked, and again he saw the tables and the guests, under lamplight. He craned his neck back. Shafts of evening light still shone through the oculi high overhead, but it hadn't been those he'd seen. For a mere instant, he'd seen forest light, leaves, and sky.

He shook his head and sat up a little straighter. *Must be the wine*, he thought hopefully. With an effort, he returned his attention to the banquet.

Linden and Sheia still ate stone-faced, though their wives seemed animated enough. At the head table, Yuri seemed most relaxed, his slack-jawed pale face shining in the gaslight. But, Jordan noticed, his hair was plastered to his forehead with sweat, and it wasn't hot in here. Of course, Yuri was right next to the fire.

In more ways than one, Jordan thought, and smiled. "You wouldn't wish to have the troubles of the highborn," Jordan's father had told him more than once. Just now he agreed.

Jordan leaned back and closed his eyes.

HIS RUINED HAND brushed aside twigs, revealing a forest path. With a sigh he stepped down to it. For a moment he swayed, and put one hand out to steady himself against a tree. Then he sat down.

Armiger looked up at the sky. Night was coming. He had been walking for two days now without pause; night merely slowed him down. At first it had been mechanical, aimless activity. Gradually as he walked, though, the bright air and thrum of life all around him awakened something in him—a kind of recognition, an identification with the things that grew and struggled all around. If he squinted at the sky, his healing eyes could perceive the faint threads of the Diadem swans wavering in their high seats. The Winds still did not know he was here. But while the sight of them filled him with a deep pang of loss—for they were his own kind, if distantly related—it was the buzzing insects and the gaudy flowers that he drew strength from. The swans, like his greater self, were inaccessible.

As he walked, Armiger for the first time contemplated what it meant to be mortal.

Now as he paused on this tenuous path, he forced himself to take stock of his body. Hitherto the body had been just a vessel, rugged but ultimately disposable. Today as he walked he had begun to come to grips with the idea that this was his only body now—that his resources were finite and concentrated in this ruined husk.

His wounds were healing. If he tried he could articulate words with his split tongue, and his fingers could grip again. The terrible wound in his chest had closed, and great sloughs of skin had fallen away to reveal flesh new and pink. As he walked he had stuffed leaves into his mouth to make up the mass he'd lost, dimly aware as he did so that the human biology of his body protested. He overrode it to command digestion and assimilation. After all he was not human; he was Armiger, agent of a god.

Or he had been. What he examined now in the failing daylight was a badly wounded man, dehydrated and staggering on blistered feet. In his experience in the field, he had seen men like this weeping as they collapsed by the side of his marching columns. They tended not to rise again.

When he closed his eyes and listened to this human body, Armiger knew why. Yesterday as he walked he had wondered how the small lives around him experienced existence, unaware that he need only pay attention to his own body to know.

As long as he thought of himself as Armiger the demigod, this body's problems seemed trivial, as he had treated those dying men's tears as trivial. After all, they were so stupidly unaware of themselves as parts of the systems of army, ecology, and planetary action, which Armiger felt in his deepest being. What was a body or even a mind? Get rid of it, there was more, the important thing was the system. Armiger had been the systems' awareness; they had been it also, but never knew.

While he had his tie to the omniscient power that had created him, Armiger had rarely used the brain of this human body he was in, except when he needed to understand the irrational actions of his soldiers. This body thought, and felt, like any human's, but he didn't need to use that mind, for he had access to the far greater mind of his master, whose own thoughts could themselves be conscious entities.

Previously Armiger had existed as god and mind, with the body merely a tool. Now he was only mind and body. He ran his hands over this body, finding the strains and infections. He stank, he realized. The human instincts he had ignored so long quailed at the damage, the humiliation of his state. For the first time, Armiger opened himself to those instincts.

This was what his men had felt, fighting and dying. This was the essential experience of the deer and foxes he had sighted as he walked: pain and loneliness.

Armiger no longer had the god to center him, make him complete. Humans and the animals of this world had existed without such a god. How? Who are you? he asked his human side.

In wonder, Armiger realized he had sunk to his knees, was clutching himself, and crying in wrenching gusts. And now he knew the feeling of the human misery he had heard so much on this world.

"CALANDRIA!" JORDAN CLUTCHED at her shoulder.

"Shh!" She put a hand on his lips angrily.

He started to protest—he needed help, the visions were back—then noticed the silence.

Jordan turned his head. A few people were staring at him. The rest had their eyes on the head table, and only one voice in the whole hall was speaking. It was Yuri, who had risen and now stood with his arms crossed, staring at nothing while he spoke. Jordan had not heard him speak before; his voice was a high tenor, very mannered and hard to hear, even in this attentive silence.

". . . Are aware of the Iapysian tragedy. The Boros clan has an obligation, as nobility in that state, to not stand aside and allow it to continue. We also have an obligation, as nobility in other states, to avoid any action that might seem to be foreign interference. That is the reason I have not acted before now. It is the reason you were called here. All three nations know the Boroses are meeting, and that we are meeting at our ancestral home because it is our home, and for no other political reason.

"Now, there are many stories circulating about the nature of the catastrophe in Iapysia. It is popularly held to be a punishment by the Winds, who are popularly held to have installed Queen Galas to begin with. First, though, she was the legal heir, so she would have inherited without their help. And second, she has been committing all manner of atrocities in the name of 'reform,' many of which have struck at the very heart of our social order."

Brendan Sheia glared at Yuri. "Is reform a bad word around here?" he boomed.

Yuri held up a hand, cocked his head, and said, "Not at all. But we have to face the prospect of a nation ruled only by the rabble, in the form of the Iapysian Parliament. Regardless of Queen Galas's crimes, no right-minded man or woman would want to see the state headless. We would all have to deal with the consequences, and I believe, the Winds would not look favorably upon Iapysia. And we, the Boroses, are part of Iapysia."

Calandria put her hand on Jordan's sleeve. "Are you all right?" she asked in a whisper.

He wanted to tell her about the visions, but that would end the evening for sure. It wasn't that Jordan was enjoying this assembly, but it was a very big thing to be here at all. He wanted to stay until the end.

He shook his head. "I'm fine." But he was beginning to sweat.

Yuri continued: "The queen earned the wrath of Parliament, and much of the nobility, by creating a number of 'experimental villages' in which the laws of the land were replaced by mock laws of her own devising. In one such, every citizen was entitled to both a husband and a wife—male and female." Yuri nodded sagely at the shocked expressions of his audience. "In another she repealed law entirely, replacing it with crass public opinion. And in yet another, she inverted all the laws of the land, so that no one was punishable for any act—instead of being punished for acting unjustly, people were rewarded for acting justly. In short, she flung a challenge into the face of decency in all its forms. All in the name of some nebulous 'reform.'" Yuri looked down his nose at Brendan Sheia. "We are all ashamed of the actions of this queen, and no amount of condemnation would be sufficient.

"But she is queen, and if she is to be dealt with, it should be by the landowners, not the rabble. So, my dear family, we find ourselves on the horns of a dilemma, for the army raised and ruled by Parliament is winning the war against the queen."

STRANGE, HOW REASSURING tears were. They were right for this body, a healing action. Armiger had never known that about tears before, had always taken them to be some reflex reaction of his men to pain. But they freed up sorrow, and this body of his, now his only one, thanked him for allowing them.

Now he stood, wiped his eyes, and gazed up and down the path. What else did this body need? It seemed he should take it into account now that his greater self was gone. He required proper food, yes, and shelter, warmth, and rest. Rest . . .

He had not known that his body was so weary. All the energy he had poured into it over the past day had poured right out again as he walked. He was healing despite his great expenditure of energy, not because of it. If he wasn't careful, the body would give out again, this time permanently. He would have to find another or exist only as the ghostly net of threads that had first come to this world. While he could survive that way, Armiger feared the loss of his human body—it was his anchor. Without it he would drift into the madness of his own sense of loss.

His body wanted the comfort of its own kind to heal it. He would see where this path led to.

JORDAN COULDN'T MOVE. His perceptions seemed doubled: he knew he was sitting at the table in the banquet hall, but at the same time, he was far away, watching through another set of eyes. His other hand brushed leaves aside; he stumbled, and Jordan tried to put his right hand out to steady himself. It worked!—he grabbed a branch. But then the hand let go again, before he willed it. No, he was not controlling this body, only reacting in synchrony with it.

"SO IT IS with reluctance and in full awareness that this decision will please no one, that I have to tell you the official position of the house of Boros." Yuri frowned around at the assembled family members. "In the interest of eventually returning a true monarchy to Iapysia, we must support Parliament at this time."

THE PATH WOUND down a hillside, and there on a shoulder of the hill, under tall trees, sat a cabin. Extensive gardens were carved out of the brambles at the bottom of the hill, where a small stream wound through this wooded ravine.

Armiger paused, breath heaving. He felt conflicting impulses—to avoid this place, since he was not strong and his body might not survive a hostile encounter—or to seek help for it now. He was desperately ill, tired, and wounded.

He stood shifting from foot to foot, aware of jabs of pain every time he moved. Where else could he go? Would he walk to the edge of the world? Or until the Winds found him and wrapped him in their own unwanted embrace? That prospect was daunting.

A gasp from behind him caught Armiger by surprise, and he tried to turn, only to lose his footing. With a raw shout he tumbled down the slope, quite helpless. At the bottom he lay wondering at his weakness. Never, even in the tomb, had he felt this way. His energies were failing from the effort it took to restore his body to life. Coughing, he blinked at the pale leaves high above.

"Goddess!" The voice was a woman's. "Are you all right?"

A shadow bent over him. He heard another intake of breath. "Goddess, you are not!"

Armiger tried to lift his hand. "Please," he croaked. "Help me." His black fingers closed in fine hair.

. . .

"No!" JORDAN WAS barely aware that his plate was skittering across the table, and off to shatter on the floor. He had fallen forward, fighting to hold back Armiger's distant body. "Run! Get away from him!"

No one was paying any attention to him. Brendan Sheia was on his feet, shaking his finger at Yuri. "This is a calumny!" he shouted. "We all know the real reason you're supporting Parliament, Father. It's to cut me out of my birthright!"

A gasp went around the room. Then everyone was shouting at once.

No one could hear Jordan—not those in the banquet hall, transfixed as they were by the drama unfolding here, nor the distant woman, too close to Armiger. Jordan felt her hands on him—or were they Calandria's?

A torrent of outraged voices enveloped him: "Your anger does you no credit, Brendan!" "Quiet, Linden, you traitor." Chairs toppled; ladies scurried for cover as the two Boros heirs confronted one another below the head table.

None of this mattered to Jordan. He tried with all his will to take control of Armiger's body, but it was futile. That hand in her hair . . . He dimly knew that Axel had him in an armlock and, together with Calandria, was marching him from the banquet hall.

He fought the wrong bodies, and even as they resisted, in that distant place the one who should resist, should flee, did not. Instead, her gentle arms gathered him up.

8

CALANDRIA POURED SOME wine and handed Jordan the cup. He accepted it gratefully and hunched farther under the blanket next to the fire Axel had lit in the fireplace. Axel now paced angrily at the doorway to their tower room. He had barred the door. Several times people had knocked, but he'd shouted that things were under control, Jordan was fine.

It seemed he'd disgraced them at the banquet. Jordan could still taste vomit faintly; he gulped at the wine to mask it. His hands shook, and he stared at them dumbly.

"What's wrong with him?" Axel demanded.

"He seems to be becoming more attuned to the implant. He was only able to receive when he was asleep before. Jordan, can you hear me?"

He drew himself closer to the fire. Reluctantly, he said, "Yeah."

Her fingers alighted on his shoulder. "Are you all right?"

"Yeah." He drained the wine, facing into the fire.

"This is too much for him," Axel said. "We should stop."

"We don't know where he is yet!" she retorted. "The avatar is a threat until we find him and neutralize him. You know how the gods are. We have no way of knowing whether 3340 hid a resurrection seed in Armiger. If it did, and the seed sprouts . . . then, everything we've done is threatened."

"There are other ways to find him."

"No!" They both turned their heads. Jordan glared at them. At that moment the two of them reminded him of his parents, ineffectually mouthing words instead of acting. "We have to do something now! He's hurting people."

Calandria came to sit next to him. "What do you mean?"

"We have to find out where he is right now," Jordan insisted. "You promised you would take the visions away when I'd told you where Armiger is. Well, let's do it. I thought after the manse that things would get easier, since you said you knew what was happening, and I thought you could do something about it. But you didn't expect what happened tonight, and it's getting worse!" He hunkered himself down, trying to pin her with the reproach of his gaze.

Calandria and Axel exchanged looks. Axel shrugged, appearing almost amused. "There are three of us in on this venture now, Cal. He's got a point."

"Where's the wisdom you were going to trade me for telling you where Armiger is?" Jordan pointed out. "I haven't got anything out of this. You kidnapped me and put visions in my head till I'm almost crazy!" He was mildly astonished at his own outburst. Of course, he'd had a few cups of wine tonight, but really enough was enough. An echo of the force that had driven him into the night after Emmy drove him to speak now.

"You seem like the Winds sometimes," he said, "but you haven't done anything for me. You said you would."

Calandria stood. "I'm sorry," she said. "I promise to make it up to you. And I realize I made a mistake in bringing you to the banquet. I didn't think you would find it so stressful."

"Wait a second," said Axel. "So he was under extreme stress tonight. And started having visions. Is stress the trigger?"

She nodded, and sighed. "Sorry, Axel. I wasn't sure of it before, so I didn't mention it. But the banquet proves it. There's a correlation between stress and his receptivity."

"Maybe if he can control his stress reactions, he can control the visions," said Axel. Jordan looked up again at this.

Calandria looked pained. "Yes, but we don't want to eliminate them entirely. On the other hand, he won't be able to learn to control himself fast enough to prevent us learning what we need to know."

"We can at least teach him how to avoid the sort of thing that just happened." Axel nodded, his arms crossed and his eyes on Jordan. "Teach him some of your tricks. Relaxation games. Mind control. We owe him that much, and you'd said we'd pay him in wisdom. So let's start paying."

Calandria looked from Axel to Jordan and nodded wearily. "All right." She sat down again. "Jordan, we will start your education right now, if you want."

"Yes!" He turned to face her. *Finally.*

"This will take time, and a lot of practice. It might not even work for the first while, but with practice you'll start to get it. Okay? Good. The first thing you must learn is that you cannot do anything if you cannot control your own mind—your emotions and your reactions. So, that is the first thing you will learn. Beginning with how to relax."

Jordan forgot the heat at his back and the wine in his cup and listened.

Two ANXIOUS DAYS passed. Armiger wasn't moving, so Jordan had nothing new to report to Calandria. He knew she was frustrated by the delay; they went over his previous visions time and again, but he could provide nothing new for her. He often saw her meditating with her eyes closed, and often after these sessions she had new questions for him about the landscapes he had glimpsed: "Was there a tall rounded hill in the distance? Did the forest extend in three tongues near the horizon?" He had no answers.

On the third day, on one of his infrequent breaks, Jordan went to the roof to stretch. The Boros estate sprawled out below. People went to and fro about duties that were all familiar to him. He could tell what was happening by watching the servants, though the purposes of the Boroses themselves were impossible to read.

Though politics as such was beyond him, Jordan could read the story of the Boros family home from its very stones—could tell what was added when, and in what style. If you went by the boasts of the visiting family members, the clan had always been prominent. But this tower was ancient, and the manor house new, and in between were traces of buildings and walls in styles from various periods. Jordan could imagine each in turn, and he saw large gaps between the apparent razing of one set of buildings and the growth of the manor. If this were the Boroses ancestral home, it had lain unoccupied for up to a century at a time.

This exercise was a good way to take his mind off things. And, he had to admit, he was starting to relax despite himself. Over the past days he had constantly practiced the skills Calandria May had taught him. He'd never known he should breathe from the belly, not the chest—or that his body carried tension in tight muscles even when his mind was relaxed. He scanned his body every minute or two, and every time he did, he found some part of it had tightened up, usually his shoulders. He would concentrate for a second, relax them, and go back to what he was doing. The feeling of being pursued that had plagued him was receding.

Best of all, the visitations by Armiger were no longer arbitrary and uncontrollable. He still dreamed about the demigod, but in daylight he could tell when a vision fit was creeping up on him. Using the relaxation exercises Calandria had taught him, he could usually stop it dead. Calandria encouraged him to think of the visions as a talent he could master and not as some alien intrusion.

He knew this worked to her ends, but was prepared to go along because, at last, her ends paralleled his own. He was able to think about the visions with some objectivity, and report what he saw and heard in detail to her.

Most important, what he saw and heard had changed. Armiger lay in bed in a cabin somewhere to the south. He was being nursed by a solitary woman, a widow who lived alone in the woods. In his convalescence Armiger seemed like an ordinary man. His terrible wounds were healing, and the small snatches of dialogue between him and his benefactor that Jordan caught were mundane, awkward, almost shy. Armiger had not eaten her, nor did he order her about. He accepted her help and thanked her graciously for it. His voice was no longer a choked rasp, but a mellow tenor.

Jordan didn't doubt Armiger's capacity for evil. He was not human. But what Jordan saw was no longer nightmarish, and that, too, was a relief.

"Hey, there you are!" Axel Chan's head poked up from the open trapdoor of the tower's roof. He emerged, dusted himself off, and came to join Jordan at the battlement. "What are you doing up here? The gardens are fine today. Soaking up the sun?"

Jordan nodded. "I like it up here. I can see all the buildings." Gardens didn't interest him; they were the provenance of gardeners, not stoneworkers like him.

He hesitated, then asked something that had been on his mind. "We're not staying here, are we?"

"We'll be leaving as soon as we have a fix on Armiger." Axel leaned out carefully, and spat. "Hmm. Twenty meters down." He looked slyly at Jordan. "You wouldn't be hiding from Calandria up here, would you?"

"No." It was the truth, though Jordan did know what Axel meant. "She works me pretty hard." If she had her way, Jordan would spent sixteen hours a day on his exercises.

Axel shrugged. "She's trying to pack as much information into you as she can in a short time."

"But she won't answer all my questions."

"Really? Like what?"

"I asked her what the Winds are. She said I probably wouldn't understand."

"Ah. No, you probably won't. But that doesn't mean we shouldn't tell you," added Axel with a grin. "You want to know? The unabridged version?"

"Yes!"

"Okay." Axel steepled his hands, looking out over the estate. "Has she told you what gods are?"

"Primal spirits," Jordan said. "Superior to the Winds."

Axel scowled. "You see, here's one of those places where the questions will go on forever. Okay, first of all, the gods aren't spirits, they're mortal. Second, humans existed before the gods. Third, we made the first gods, centuries ago. They were experiments in creating consciousness in mechanisms. Nobody knows where 3340 came from, but He was the same kind of thing as the Winds, and just as out of control."

"How could a god be a mechanism?"

"Hmmf. Look at it this way. Once long ago, two kinds of work converged. We'd figured out how to make machines that could make more machines. And we'd figured out how to get machines to . . . not exactly think, but do something very much like it. So one day some people built a machine that knew how to build a machine smarter than itself. That built another, and that another, and soon they were building stuff the men who made the first machine didn't even recognize. Some of these things became known as mecha, which is the third order of life here on Ventus. Mecha's as subtle as biological life, but constructed totally differently.

"And, some of the mechal things kept developing, with tremendous speed, and became more subtle than life. Smarter than humans. Conscious of more. And, sometimes, more ambitious. We had little choice but to label them gods after we saw what they could do—namely, anything.

"Most of the time gods go on about their own concerns. 3340 decided its concern was us. Luckily we—humans—know how to create things of equal power that serve us. The Winds were intended to be your slaves, not your masters. Apparently there's stories here to that effect."

Jordan nodded.

The Winds were created by humans and given the task of turning Ventus from a lifeless wasteland into a paradise where people could live. They did so—except that when the colonists arrived, the Winds didn't recognize you. Something had gone wrong. And the original design of the Winds had been lost during a period of civil unrest on Earth.

"It seems there was no way to communicate with them. One of the things we don't know to this day is what the chain of command within the Winds was supposed to be. There seems to be no central 'brain' that rules the planet. And communications between the Winds seems spotty and confused. It's as if they've all gone their own ways.

"A lot of people think this is what happened. The Winds all concern themselves with the ecology of the planet, but at different levels. The vagabond moons worry about the overall distribution of minerals and soil nutrients, so they scoop here and dump there; they want to do in centuries what evolution and tectonics would take billions of years to accomplish. The mecha embedded in the grass are advocates of the grass, and they may object to the moons' dumping crap on them, say. There's no central brain telling both it's a good idea. But maybe there was originally supposed to be a central plan, that they would all have access to. Knowing this plan, the grass would acquiesce to its death by salting or by drowning in a new lake made by the desals. So, though none of the Winds were to be answerable to any of the others, they would all be answerable to the plan, because that was the only way to guarantee the proper terraforming of Ventus.

"Humans don't seem to be mentioned in the programming of the Winds. We were supposed to be the apex of the plan, represented as its ultimate purpose. That's what went wrong—no plan, no accommodation for the arrival of the colonists.

"So a strange double world has developed on your planet. Each object seems to have its resident spirit—the microscopic mecha, or what we call 'nano,' that coordinate that object's place in the ecology. Originally these resident spirits were supposed to have a common goal over and above the survival of their hosts. They were to put themselves at our disposal—be our tools. But now, it's anarchy. War in the spirit world. The only ones aloof from this war are the greatest Winds, the Diadem swans, the Heaven hooks, and the like."

Jordan had only understood a little of this speech. "But some people do speak to the Winds," he said. "That's how the inspectors and controllers know what crop yields should be or where they can build a waterwheel. The Winds tell them what's allowed."

"Hmm . . ." Axel raised an eyebrow. "I'd heard that from other people here, too. Up there," he jerked a thumb at the clouds, "people don't believe it. They say your inspectors are a bunch of charlatans, holding onto power by pretending they can talk to the Winds."

Jordan crossed his arms. "I don't know. I just know how we do things."

"Right. That's fair."

"So what is Calandria May?" asked Jordan. "Is she a Wind or a thing like Armiger? Or just a person?"

"She's . . . just a person. But a person with special skills and with enhancements to her body, such as the armor under her skin. I've got that, too," he said, rubbing his wrist. "And I'm still human, aren't I?" He grinned.

"So how did you get here? I know you followed Armiger, but . . ." Jordan had too many questions; he didn't know where to start.

Axel frowned down at the distant gardens. "We were at war against 3340—all humanity was. It wanted us all as slaves. It had all its godly powers; we had our supermecha. And a few agents who were more than human, but less than gods, like Calandria May. Last year she infiltrated a world called Hsing, which 3340 had enslaved, to try to find a way to turn the population against their unchosen god. She found 3340 had been changing ordinary people into demigods—Diadem swans or morphs, if you will—by infecting them with mecha that ate them from within, replacing all their biology with mechalogy. Then 3340 enslaved these demigods much more brutally than even the humans. Cal found a way to turn them against 3340, and she did that during our attack six months ago."

"How?"

"She had to briefly become one of them herself. You or I couldn't have done it, but Calandria was able to leave her humanity behind. She became a goddess, only for a day or so. And she killed 3340."

"If she became a goddess, why didn't she stay that way?"

Axel shook his head. "Don't know. She could have kept fabulous powers; she would have lived for thousands of years if she wanted. She didn't want to. I think she was crazy to give that up. Don't understand. I really don't."

Jordan was thinking. "So after 3340 died, you came here. To kill his servant, Armiger."

"Exactly." Axel leaned against the battlement, and squinted at the sun. "What does all of this imply about the Winds, now?"

Jordan hesitated. What came to mind was impossible.

Axel nodded smugly. "You're smart. Isn't it clear? The Winds are made of the same stuff as the mecha. They are alive. And they, too, are mortal."

Jordan turned away. "Crazy talk. If the Winds are mortal, then every-thing could be—the sky or the sun or the earth itself."

"You're beginning to understand," Axel said. "Now understand this: what is mortal can be murdered."

THE DOOR TO their tower room was bolted; the fire was lit and candles sat on the table. Jordan, Calandria, and Axel sat in imitation of some domestic scene, each bent over an evening task. Except that Calandria was not darning, but poring over a map on the tabletop; and Axel was not repairing tools or his boots, but polishing the steel of a wicked sword; and Jordan was not playing games or cleaning, but sat cross-legged in the center of the floor, hands on his knees, eyelids fluttering. He was trying to count to three, one digit per breath, without allowing any stray thoughts to intrude on the way. Tonight he felt he was finally starting to get the hang of it.

At two and a half breaths, he caught himself thinking *Hey, I can do this!* Stop. Back to one.

"Shit." He slapped himself on the forehead. Calandria laughed.

"You're doing well," she said. "You can rest now."

"But I had it once or twice!"

"Good. Don't push it, or you'll get worse rather than better."

He unwove his legs and stood. Two deep breaths, just as she had taught. Jordan felt great, relaxed and able to deal with things. He'd never really felt like this before . . . oh, maybe when he was very young and didn't know what the world was like. All his cares and worries seemed distant, and he was able to pay attention to the here and now. He smiled and plunked himself down on the edge of the bed.

"Axel tells me you have quite a mind," Calandria said. "He told me you figured out your own history of the Boros clan by reading their architecture."

"Yeah," he said suspiciously. He and Axel had moved on to talk about that this afternoon, after their conversation about the Winds and 3340 had ended in an impasse. Axel had been quite unaware of the contradiction between the Boroses' official history and what the stones suggested.

"Do you want to move on to a new study? You must continue to practice what I've taught you, of course."

"Sure!" He felt ready for anything. "What do we do?"

Calandria folded her map and put it aside. "We can build on what you've already learned. If you can relax, you can concentrate. If you can concentrate, you can do marvels."

"Like what?"

"Perfect memory, for instance. Or perfect control of your body, even your heartbeat. Tonight, I'll show you something to help you control your visions."

"I thought that was what I was learning."

"You've been learning how to stop them. Now you'll learn how to make them happen."

Axel looked up, surprise written on his mobile face. "Do we know that?"

"Everything's consistent," she said. "I'd be very surprised if this doesn't work." She motioned for Jordan to sit on the floor and seated herself in front of him. "Now, close your eyes."

Jordan wasn't sure he wanted to be able to make the visions happen—he was happy that they were going away. But he obeyed. Armiger was not so frightening any more, and if he could stop a vision once it started, the prospect was less daunting.

"Now," Calandria said, "without actually doing it, imagine you are raising your hand in front of your face." He did so. "Examine your imaginary hand. Turn it back and forth. Make a fist." He obeyed. "Look closely at your hand. Picture it as clearly as you can."

Jordan did his best. "Do you keep losing the image?" she asked. He nodded. "Do you get little flashes of other images?"

Puzzled, he sat for a while. Then he realized what she meant: the hand was replaced for a split second here and there by pictures of inconsequential things, like the washbasin in the corner or a vista of trees he couldn't identify. "I see it," he said.

"This is what goes on behind everybody's eyes," she said. "A constant flicker of visions. As you practice the counting exercise and your concentration improves, you'll be able to damp them down and see what you want to see for longer and longer.

"Now, as you've imagined your hand, imagine you can see your entire body. Keep your eyes closed and look down at yourself." He moved his head, imagining his bent knees and bare feet against the flagstones. "Good. Now, keep your eyes closed and don't move. Imagine this second body of yours is your own, and stand up in it."

He did. "Look around." Jordan pretended he was standing and looking around the room. It was hard to maintain the images; they kept sliding away. He said so.

"That's okay. Now pretend to turn around. Do you see the bench where Axel's sitting?"

He concentrated. "Yes. . . ." He kept seeing it as a memory, from the position of the bed where he'd sat earlier. He tried to imagine seeing it as if he were standing in the center of the room.

"See his pack on the floor next to it?"

"Yes."

"Go over to the pack. Open it up. Look inside. What do you see?"

He pretended to do as she said. "There's . . . a knife, a book, a glass liquor bottle."

"How full is the bottle?"

Jordan pretended to hold it up. It seemed to be a quarter full. "A quarter." That was just a fancy, of course; he had no idea what was in Axel's pack.

Calandria said, "Axel, open your pack. Is there a bottle in it?"

"Yeah."

"How full is it?"

"A quarter full, but hey this is just a memory trick. I was drinking from it earlier, you both saw me."

"Jordan, do you remember seeing Axel drink from the bottle earlier?"

"I . . . I don't know. Maybe."

"Maybe. But you're not sure. And yet you see the bottle, and you know how full it is, and where it is. How strange, hmm?"

A strong exultation gripped Jordan. He had seen it! What he saw with his imagination was somehow real.

"Parlor trick," muttered Axel.

"Be silent!" she commanded. "Now try this. Sit your body down again where your real body sits. Close your imaginary eyes." He did so. "Imagine blackness. Now . . ."

Her hand touched his shoulder. Jordan struggled to keep his eyes closed. "Practice your deep breathing. Calm yourself, and see deeper and deeper black." He felt the center of his consciousness dropping through his body, to rest finally in his belly, where great strength drove slow breaths in and out.

Calandria's voice had taken on its most hypnotic lilt. "You will open your inner eyes again, but this time, the hand you see before you will not be yours, but rather Armiger's. Do you understand?"

He nodded.

"Open those eyes."

He did so.

THE CEILING WAS low and beamed. He could see the cross-pattern of thatch crooks flickering above that in the firelight.

Armiger sat up. The effort was easier this time. He looked around, fingers opening and closing on the soft cloth that was draped over his naked body.

The woman sat near the fire. Megan, she had called herself. She held a cloth sack draped across her knees and was just positioning the second of two buckets at her feet. It was probably the scraping sound of the buckets that had woken him.

All Megan's possessions were visible within the one room of this cabin. She had three chairs, a full set of pots, cooking and fire implements, two hatchets by the door, and a spinning wheel. Chests were wedged into the corners. Dried herbs and kindling hung from the rafters. Everything was rough-hewn, except three items of furniture: the posted bed Armiger now sat in, a fine oaken dining table, and at the wall behind Megan, a wooden cupboard with inlaid patterns of leaves. Yesterday he had lain for a while, too exhausted to move, and examined the pattern on that cupboard from his position here.

Megan was in her thirties. Her hair was gray, her face lined and wind-burned. She was very strong, though, and still slim under the red peasant dress she wore. Now she plunged her hand into one of the buckets, and brought out a fistful of brown-and-white feathers. She began riffling through the mass with her other hand.

"What are you doing?" he asked. His voice sounded stronger.

Megan looked up quickly, and smiled. "How are you?"

"Better." He rolled his head, surprising himself when his neck cracked. It never used to do that. He fingered the underside of his jaw. The scar was almost gone. "I'd like to try to walk today."

"Tomorrow. It's evening."

"Oh." She began stuffing feathers into the open end of the sack, and he realized she was making a pillow. "I've been using your bed. I . . ." He wasn't sure what he was going to say. Thank her for that? But he had been ailing. It was a human thing for her to do, he knew; not that any of his men would have willingly done the same. "Where have you been sleeping?"

"Oh, I slept there with you the first night," she said, looking down at her work. Her hair hid her face. "You were so cold, I thought you might not survive till morning. The last few times, I've used the table. With some quilts on it, it's quite fine. The bed's mattress is only straw, anyway."

Armiger imagined her lying on the table, like a body in state. He pushed the image deliberately out of his mind.

"I'm sorry to be a burden to you," he said stiffly.

Megan frowned. "Don't talk like that. It's no trouble; all else I have to take care of is me. And I am fine. Anyway . . . what else could I do?"

"I was dying," he said, wondering at the thought. "You saved me."

"I've tended the dying before," she said. "Last time, with no hope he'd recover. I had not that hope this time, either. So I am happy, you see, if I could save someone." Her face fell as she thought of something. "At least this time . . ."

"You lost someone close to you?" He looked around, noticing the fine wooden table and bed frame. "Your husband."

Megan nodded as she reached for more down. "You see I know about losing things. And about trying to keep them." She looked at him, almost fiercely. "You always lose it in the end—what you want to keep. The harder you try to keep it, the more it goes. So now I know how to keep things right."

"How is that?"

"You can never keep a whole thing. But you can keep a part of anything." She looked sadly at the wooden cupboard. "Be it only a piece of furniture. And if you can learn to be content with that, then you can let anything go." Megan stood and walked to the cupboard. She smoothed her hand over the fine wood grain. "I would sit and watch him as he made this. He spent so much time on it. We were in love. When you lose your husband, you think you've lost everything—nothing has any value any more. Funny, how long it took to know that this was still here, and other little things. The parts of him I could keep."

She shrugged, then turned to Armiger. "And what have you lost?"

He felt a surge of rage at the mindless presumption of the question.

As if she could comprehend what he'd lost! Well, maybe to her, losing her husband was the equivalent of his own disaster. "I lost my army," he said.

Megan laughed. "And nearly your life. But soldiers don't worry about that sort of thing, do they? I admire that."

He scratched absently at the back of his arm. "Good lady, soldiers worry about nothing else."

She came and sat down on the edge of the bed. He smelled pungent chicken feathers. "Now," she said seriously, "maybe I do believe that. Because you've lost something. More than your way."

Armiger stared at her. There was no way he could talk about this— words could not encompass it, they were too small. The part of him he had communed with had been beyond words, or any of a human's five senses; it had invented senses, and sense, to suit its intimacies.

He wanted to speak to her in thunder, in torn ground and shocked air. Would have, had he only the strength.

Reminded that she had given him what strength he did have, he looked down.

"I think . . . I did die," he said. It was the only human analogue he could think of. "I died when . . . she died." "She" was completely wrong to describe his higher self; but Megan's people thought their souls were feminine. He struggled to find words, wrapping his arms around himself, glaring past her. "More than a wife. More than a queen. My god died, who gave meaning to more than just my life, who infused everything, the stones, the air, with it."

Megan nodded. "I knew. From things you said in your sleep. From the look of you." She sighed. "Yes, you see, we are together in that."

"No. Not like you." He sat up angrily, feeling sharp stabs of pain in his side. Megan stared at him, patient and undaunted.

He wanted to pierce her calmness, her certainty that her own pain was as great as his. "She wasn't a human being," he said. She was . . . a Wind."

Megan blinked. Her brow wrinkled, then cleared. "Much is made clear," she said. It was his turn to look surprised. Megan reached out, slowly, and touched the healing scar under his chin. "I know the rites of death," she said. "I have had to perform them myself."

Armiger sat back. His anger was deflated. For some reason, he felt unfulfilled, as if he had lied to her, and not merely told her what she would understand.

Everything was graying out. "Sleep," she said. "My morph."

He lay back, listening to her move about the cabin. Just before he drifted off again, he heard her say, maybe to herself, "And what part of this are you going to keep?"

9

"THIS MAY BE our last warm night of the year," said Megan the next evening. "It pleases me to see you enjoying it."

Armiger smiled at her. He stood in the center of the clearing next her cottage. The sun had just set, leaving a rose band across the western horizon. The moon Diadem was rising. The moon received its name from the scattering of brilliant white craters on its surface, which made it a dim oval studded with diamond-bright pinpricks of light. On other nights Armiger had praised or cursed those gleaming points, depending on whether night visibility was to his army's advantage or not. Tonight, possibly for the first time, he was able to admire the sight for its own sake.

He felt content. He knew it was because he was free from all responsibilities during this convalescence.

"Strange," he murmured.

Megan looked up at the moon, then back at him. "What?"

"I should be dead," he said.

She touched his shoulder. "Your wounds were terrible. But they're healing quickly. Isn't that normal for a morph?"

"I'm not exactly a morph," he said wryly. "Just something like one. But yes, you're right." The lie came easily to his lips. Then he thought about it. Could he explain this to a mortal? He would never have thought he had an obligation to try.

Armiger lowered his eyes from the moon and studied Megan in the pale light. She was a creature he didn't understand. His plans had rarely included women. But she stood next to him now, easy in the cricket song and darkness, and played none of the dominance games males played. She took her own obligation to him, the wounded soldier, for granted.

"My link to my higher self," he began, then stopped. "It was more than love. We shared an identity. When . . . she died, I should have died, too. Because there was only one of us. Or at least that's what I believed."

Megan nodded. "We all think that of our life's love. But one carries on."

At first Armiger thought she had simply not understood him. Then he thought of another possibility: Megan knew his experiences were not like hers, but she was making an effort to translate them into terms she could understand.

It surprised him to think that she might be spending her time with him doing such an odd kind of work. For it would be work, finding commonality with a stranger's experience. Armiger himself did so only as a way of anticipating the next move of an opponent.

If she'd kept her conclusions to herself, he might have believed she was doing that, too. But she shared them.

"Was she killed in the war?" Megan asked.

He started to say no, since this local brushfire he had been involved in had nothing to do with the interstellar conflict that had resulted in his greater self's demise. But he could play the same game as she: what would make sense to her, on an emotional level? "Yes," he said.

"You won't go back to being a soldier, will you?"

He barely heard her. *Why am I alive?* When his Self died, he should have been extinguished, or at least turned back into an aimless machine.

"I thought I knew what I was," he said. Armiger had pretended to be human since arriving on Ventus. Before that, he recalled bright light and deep vacuum, vision encompassing 360 degrees, radio song in his head, and others' thoughts as well. In that existence, there had been no distinguishing his own mind from those of his companions, the other servants of 3340. And the god's will was the same as their own. The part of that vast identity that was Armiger thought of himself as an extension of the greater whole. He had assumed that when he thought, it was 3340 who was thinking, and when he acted, it was the god acting. It had always been that way.

No, not always. . . .

Suddenly the presence of this woman at his side felt threatening. Something ancient, a memory perhaps, made him turn away from her. "I need to be alone now," he said. The harsh tone of his own voice surprised him.

"But . . ." she began. Then she seemed to think better and turned and walked away quickly.

Armiger glanced back. Humans were biological creatures—mortal animals. For a second there, though, he had touched on some deep-buried feeling within himself. Megan had loomed in the darkness as real as 3340 itself. For an instant, he had . . . remembered? Remembered standing with someone, a human being, who was every bit his own equal. A creature like himself.

A woman.

And there and then a memory unfolded within Armiger like a long-dormant flower: of himself walking and laughing, a young man with a young woman on his arm, on a world with two moons. On a night like this.

That memory was a thousand years old.

Had he once been human himself? That could explain why 3340 had chosen him for this job. On the other hand, the god could have crafted his personality from the remnants of captured human minds. After all, a memory was nothing more than a synaptic hologram. He was sure 3340 could manufacture any sort of memory for its agents.

Armiger stalked through the long wet grass, swiping at it absently with his hands. The moon and the warmth of the night were forgotten now. He came to the edge of the woods, and turned to pace back the way he'd come, scowling.

If that had been a manufactured memory, why should it remain submerged for so long? He would have expected the god to make only useful memories and provide them all to his agent's consciousness.

This memory . . . her hand in his . . . was an alien thing. He couldn't fit it into his purpose or identity as 3340 had given them to him.

He realized he had been kicking the grass out of his way as he walked, tearing it up by the roots. Armiger stopped, then glanced back at the cottage. Megan stood silhouetted in the doorway.

He ran his hand through his hair. Well. Evidently there was some fragment of human mentality in him, and 3340 would not have sent him on this mission were that not the case. It could explain why he was still alive: for some reason 3340 had given him the same instincts for autonomous self-preservation as biological creatures had.

He told himself not to jump to conclusions. He had yet to really take stock of himself. Hitherto the overwhelming fact of his bereavement had kept him from exploring what was left to him. Maybe it was time.

He walked back to the cottage. Megan still stood in the doorway, a frown on her face. "I can't say I haven't done that myself," she said. "I'm sorry if I reminded you of things you didn't want to think about."

Armiger felt tired, in body and mind. "I need to thank you, actually," he said. "You've provided me such a safe haven here that I can finally face some of these things."

Megan beamed. She seemed to struggle for something to say. "Oh," she managed at last. Then, slyly, "then I can take your ripping up the garden as a good sign?"

"Garden?" He glanced back at the darkened field.

"You tromped right through one of them a minute ago."

"Oh." What to say? "I'll repair the damage in the morning."

She laughed. "Just do your best. I can't picture you as a gardener, whatever else you may be."

Awkwardly, he tried a grin in reply. Megan combed her fingers through her hair and bumped her shoulder against the doorjamb a couple of times.

"I'll heat up some stew if you'd like," she said at last.

"Thanks. I'm going to sit out here and meditate a while."

"Okay." She ducked back in, leaving the door open to the fragrances of night.

Armiger sat down stiffly on the uneven boards of the cottage's small porch. There was just enough space next to Megan's rocking chair for him to sit in full lotus. He gazed out over the breeze-runneled grass. Diadem's light cast shadows like nodding figures under the trees. He closed his eyes.

Armiger decided to avoid a full neurophysiological exam for now. He just wasn't psychologically strong enough to take an objective look at how much intelligence, memory, and will he had lost with 3340. He could treat his body dispassionately, however, so he started with that.

His resources were painfully low. The gossamer nanotech that made up his real body had unfurled from its usual position at the spine and spread throughout this human form, right to its extremities. Nearly all his energy was devoted to shoring up the body's ravaged immune system. He had manufactured nano to move in and repair the dead cells of his own corpse, and until a day or so ago he had been warm and breathing only because the nano had replaced normal cell processes with their own harsh metabolism. Now the nano were easing out of revived cells and were being reabsorbed into his filamentary body. His strength was growing, but very slowly. At this rate it would be many months before he recovered fully.

He regretted having been so profligate with his power when he arrived. To think he had detached parts of his own gossamer and implanted them in humans, just to use them as remote eyes and ears. . . .

Armiger opened his eyes. He had completely forgotten about the remotes. It wasn't surprising, with everything that had happened; they had always been a minor part of his plans, the mental equivalent of posting picket sentries around a camp. They did contain valuable nano, however. He could considerably speed up his recovery if he recovered some of that.

If it hadn't been too badly damaged by the catastrophe, he should still have links to each remote. They operated on superluminal resonances, undetectable on the electromagnetic spectrum; he had set up the links this way to prevent the Winds from homing in on his position. It was still possible to trace the signal back from one of the remotes, but that would require an understanding of human physiology and psychology that he knew the Winds didn't possess. Superluminal links were always two-way—what affected one station affected the other. Armiger knew of no Wind capable of exploiting the fact to turn one of his remotes into a receiver, so he had felt safe in making them.

Shutting his eyes, he called up their perspectives. The system was weak from damage and disuse, but after a few seconds the remotes began to respond.

There should have been twelve. By the time the system was fully up, Armiger could see through only six pairs of eyes.

Even that was nearly overwhelming. Somewhere in the catastrophe he had lost the ability to process multiple sensory inputs. What came to him now was a chaos of sensations: blue cloth waving near a fire, water down a horse's flank, the feel of stone on his bare back, a warm hand on his belly—

—Pounding heart and ragged breaths gulped into a tight and painful chest.

He recoiled in pain. It was too much to take all at once. After opening his eyes and breathing quietly for a minute, he resumed, this time singling out one remote's perspective.

This other's hands smoothed the chestnut flank of his horse one last time, then turned away. Armiger saw he stood in a small stable, the sort attached to country inns all across Ravenon. This perspective belonged to an engineer who traveled the country repairing and updating the heliographs in royal signal towers. He saw a lot of the country in his travels, and more than once Armiger had used his perspective to gather intelligence.

Tonight he was idle, walking slowly out of the stable, through a light drizzle to the door of a thatch-roofed inn. Armiger stayed with him only long enough to see him slide aside the curtain to a private closet; a candle already burned next to the small cot there.

Armiger turned his attention to the next perspective. This man was in bed already, but not alone. Several people sat on hard wooden chairs next to the bed in his small plaster-walled bedroom. Armiger's remote was talking to them.

". . . Came at me like that out of nowhere. Why? What did I do to deserve this?" He gestured at his leg, which lay exposed above the bedding. It was thickly wrapped in bloody bandages.

"How many did you say there were?" asked a man wearing the crimson ribbons of a priest.

"Five, six. I don't know! It all happened so fast."

"Well, you must have done something to offend them."

"Not necessarily," said another man. "Maybe someone else did. Matthew was passing by. He was a handy target."

"I don't understand," whined the man in the bed. "How am I going to work now?"

"Don't worry. We'll help you."

Armiger left this perspective for the next.

Still on her back. Cold stone and pebbles ground against her hips. Her legs were wrapped around the broad torso of the man who moved against her. Past his shoulder, Armiger could see bright stars.

He moved to the next remote.

Stumbling in the blackness, he went down on all fours. His own breath was a rasping rattle in his ears. This man stood, staggering now from a broad scrape down his leg, and ran.

Through leaves and dancing branches he ran—down a hillside, recklessly, barely keeping to his feet above prancing stones—and into an orchard. The limbs of the well-tended trees stretched skyward like supplicants' arms to heaven. He barely glanced up at them. After weaving his way down an alley between the trees, he allowed himself to slow, then to pause, and look behind him.

Nothing pursued him in the darkness. He looked up.

The night here was overcast, making the darkness near total. But past the crest of the hill he had just come down, above the clouds, light shone as though men with lanterns rode some causeway there. The lights were coming closer, with apparent slowness.

He gave a cry that was more a painful gasp, then turned to run again. A cottage was visible now at the end of the rows of trees. Low, stone, with a goat pen attached, it glowed with internal firelight, warm and inviting. He renewed his run, breathing harshly.

Armiger felt the boards under him dip as Megan came out onto the porch. She said something. He raised one hand to still her.

The runner had reached the cottage. "Lena!" he cried, then flung himself to hang on the fence around the goat pen. He shuddered.

"Perce?" A young woman appeared in the cottage's doorway—uncannily silhouetted as Megan had been earlier. "Perce! What's wrong?"

"They're coming! Just like the old man said they were."

"No. That can't be. He's crazy, we all know it—"

"Look!" He reeled around, and pointed at the glowing sky.

She screamed.

"What's going on here?" An older man and woman appeared behind the girl.

"Perce!" She ran to him. Perce reached over the fence as she threw her arms around him. "What's going to happen?"

"The old man said they wanted to take me away." Perce laughed giddily. "We never believed he really spoke to them, remember? All those years . . . He said they'll take me. And I'll never see you again."

She buried her face in his neck, crying. He could see her parents standing in awkward confusion nearby. They were staring at the sky.

"I came to say good-bye."

"No," she said, muffled. "You can hide here. We'll take care of you. They'll go away."

"I tried hiding," he said. "They found me—started to pull the stables down around me! I ran to the river—dove in and let the rapids take me awhile. That's the only way I got as far ahead as I did. If I stay they'll kill you to get at me. But I couldn't go without saying good-bye."

She shook her head.

"There's so much I want to say," he mumbled. "Something—I wanted to say something to let you know how much you mean to me."

He pulled away, leaving her reaching for him over the fence. "All I could think of was when we were twelve. Remember when we played hide-and-seek in the orchard? That day? I dream about it all the time. Have, ever since."

Turning away to face the darkness, he said, "That's all—I remember that day. Good-bye, Lena."

She screamed after him, but he ran with renewed energy. Armiger deduced he wanted to get as far from the cottage as he could before whatever was coming found him.

Perce ran around the goat pen and down a laneway that led between more orchards. Low fieldstone walls lined the laneway, and in the darkness they closed in claustrophobically. Perce's eyes stayed down though; he seemed to know what in the dark he was afraid of, and it was nothing that might lurk behind those walls.

He had gone perhaps half a kilometer, and was beginning to stagger desperately, when he heard a ripping sound overhead. It was a sound almost like a flag in the wind, almost like the blurred noise of a sword on the downstroke, but it went on and on, rising to a deafening crescendo. Dust leaped from the laneway around Perce, and he coughed, and stopped helplessly.

Giant claws crushed him. He shouted blood as they spun him around and pulled him into the sky.

Perce saw his hands reaching down to the receding lines of the laneway, then he saw the jewel-box perfection of Lena's cottage glowing below him. It was intact. Drops of blood trailed off his fingertips and fell toward it.

Darkness fell over him like a cloak.

Armiger cursed and opened his eyes. Megan stood above him, her expression quizzical.

Something had severed his link to the remote.

"What is going on here?" he asked himself.

Megan laughed lightly. "I was about to ask you that myself. What are you doing?"

He shook his head, scowling into the night. Suddenly the shadows Diadem cast across the clearing didn't look so benign.

I have to leave, he thought. But, looking up at Megan, he found he didn't want to say that to her. In its own way, that was as disturbing as the vision he had just had.

He pushed the heel of one hand against his forehead, a gesture one of his lieutenants had favored.

"You're a mess," Megan said sympathetically.

Armiger thought about it. Then he squinted up at her. "Dear lady," he said, "I believe you are right."

RETURNING FROM EXPLORING the local town, Axel found the road to the Boros estate blocked by a number of wagons. They sat listlessly in the hot sun, waiting for some obstruction ahead to clear.

His horse snorted and turned to look at him. Axel stretched and grinned. "You hate to wait, don't you?" he said to her. She swung her head away again.

He had gone into town to look for a good pair of horses for Calandria and Jordan. He'd found only one suitable horse. It was a start.

He cantered over to the wagons. "Making camp?" he inquired of the driver of the wagon that sat square in the middle of the gateway. The man looked at him wearily.

"Everybody's a comedian. Sir," he added, noting the way Axel was dressed.

"Seriously, what's the holdup?" One very large wagon blocked the wrought-iron gates to the estate. Axel supposed he could ride around through the underbrush. He didn't, but leaned forward as the other man pointed down the road.

"Breakdown up ahead."

Axel laughed. "Some things never change. Any chance you can move that cart a meter or two and let me by?"

"Yes, sir." The driver urged his horses forward a bit. Axel's own steed balked at the narrow opening between the stone gate post and the side of the wagon, so he dismounted and led it through.

Six or seven wagons waited on the roadway ahead. He didn't bother to mount again as he passed them.

Funny, he thought, but these wagons looked awfully familiar. Then he looked past them, and understood why.

Turcaret's steam car sat wreathed by smoke and mist a little down the road. The controller himself stood next to it talking to a potbellied man in greasy velvet robes. Axel passed the lead wagon and walked up the center of the road to meet Turcaret.

When he spotted Axel, Turcaret turned and casually waved. He was a tall man who appeared forever to be posing for his own portrait. He wore a red velvet riding jacket, and spotless black boots. He stood ramrod straight and held his chin high so that he could look down his long, pointed nose at Axel.

"Ah, the wandering agent of Ravenon," he said. "I see you made use of my suggestion to visit the Boros. How is the lady May?"

"Never better, sir." Axel peered into the pall of smoke around the steam car. He hated Turcaret. "Having a little mechanical problem?"

"Nothing we can't fix. I've sent a man ahead to tell Yuri we're arriving. I trust you've found the Boroses accommodating?"

"That we have." What was Turcaret doing here? He had outlined his travel itinerary at length in several tiresome dinner conversations prior to their arrival at Castor's. Cal had decided to take up the hospitality of the

Boros family precisely because Turcaret was not expected to come here. The fewer people to compare notes about them the better.

Might as well admit surprise, he thought. "And what brings you here? I thought you were heading straight for the capital after Castor's?"

"Oh, I was." Turcaret smiled one of his strangely infuriating, smug smiles. "But then I was given some information that I thought Yuri simply must know about. So I thought it best to come here directly."

Axel felt his smile grow a bit wooden. "Information? What information?"

"Oh, that would be telling," said Turcaret.

"Yes, well . . . I hope to see you at dinner, then?" Axel remounted his horse.

"Oh, you'll be seeing me, Mr. Chan, count on it." Turcaret smiled again and turned back to inspecting his steam car.

This can't be good, Axel thought as he spurred his horse to a trot. He'd had a very good time here at the Boros estate, but the worm was in the apple now. What would happen if Turcaret and Yuri compared notes? Maybe nothing . . .

But he would start packing anyway, he decided, just as soon as he'd told Calandria the news.

10

ON THE NIGHT of Turcaret's arrival, Jordan awoke somewhere around 3:00 A.M. For a moment he thought he must be back in Armiger's mind, because the sound that had awakened him was the sound of metal striking metal: clashing swords. He sat up and looked around. This was definitely the tower room, with its odd triangular stonework. The sound had come from the window. Outside it was the courtyard of statues.

The sound was faint and intermittent. For a few seconds he thought he might be imagining things. Then it came again.

And again, silence. Jordan pictured two figures circling one another, in unspoken agreement that no alarm should be given. Unless one was already dead?

He rose and padded quietly to the window. The smell of the rain, which had cascaded down all evening, came to him. Calandria slept in her usual comatose way, limbs flung akimbo, body entangled in the sheets. Jordan stood on his tiptoes and peered down at the darkened well of the courtyard.

His scalp prickled. He had never seen the courtyard after lights-out. Not even the glow of a lantern filtered down from the tall windows of the manor. Lady Hannah Boros's statues posed like dancers at some subterranean ball, who needed no light, whose music was the grumble of bedrock settling, and whose dance steps took centuries to complete. Jordan had no doubt, after seeing the manse, that such places existed.

One of the statues leaped out of place and dodged behind another. Jordan heard labored breathing and the slide of metal on stone. Shadowed darkness near one wall roiled, showing another figure in motion. Jordan's breath caught, and he pulled himself up farther to look straight down.

These two seemed to be alone. If there were seconds to this duel, they must be invisible in some darkened doorway. Jordan doubted there was an attending physician present; there was the grimness of vendetta about the silence and darting motion of these men.

Holding onto the edge of the window was hard. The opening was little more than an arrow slit, meant to provide light and a good firing point if one pulled up a chair to stand on. The chairs in the Boros manor were huge, heavy, and old, and he was bound to wake Calandria if he tried to drag one over. He clung as long as he could, catching frustrating glimpses of movement below. Then he fell back, flexing his arms in frustration.

If he awoke Calandria, she would order him to stay here while she investigated. No way he was going to let that happen.

The whole thing was probably none of his business, but Turcaret's steam car had puffed into the estate this afternoon. Where Turcaret went, bad news followed, Jordan had decided. And Jordan knew that Axel and Calandria had decieved Turcaret; they were both worried about his arrival. It was always possible, he told himself as he headed for the door, that one of the embattled shadows downstairs was Axel Chan.

He raced down the steps, slowing to a loud skip as he reached the first floor, and poked his head around the corner of the archway. Directly ahead was the door to the courtyard; to either side long halls led off in dark, punctuated by coffin-shaped opals of light from the windows. These halls connected the tower to the main manor house at ground level.

A black figure reared into sight in one of these lighted spaces. It crossed the beam of crooked light, then disappeared again in shadow. He watched for almost a minute, until it appeared again in a lozenge of lunar gray farther down the hall.

Though the night watchman must be a thirty meters away by now and facing the other way, Jordan still held his breath and tiptoed very quietly across to the door. He eased it open, letting in a breath of cold, misty night air.

Jordan felt exposed just peering around the doorjamb. The statues seemed to be staring at him. Aside from them, there was no sound at all now.

The two men might still be circling in the dark, only meters away for all he knew. Now that he was here Jordan had no idea what he was going to do. Sound the alarm? That would be the sensible thing to do—but this was doubtless some political feud, and Calandria's dress-up games aside, he was still only a mason's son, and it was not his place to interfere. He had already drawn the attention and wrath of the household for fainting at dinner. He was not about to compound that by waking the place, especially since the courtyard seemed empty now. Maybe the duelists had lost their nerve and fled, or one had capitulated.

The silence drew out, and the outside chill began to penetrate Jordan's bones so that he shivered as he clung to the door. Then he heard a cough, followed by a faint groan.

The duel was over then, but the outcome had not been peaceful. Now what? Wake the household? Run back for Calandria, tell her a man was bleeding to death in the courtyard?

"So what," she would say. She was too ruthless and seemed to think it best if Jordan unlearned empathy as she sometime had. But he couldn't do that.

He eased out into the night air and paused, half-expecting a dark figure to rush him from the forest of statues. Nothing moved.

He heard the groan again, and this time he was able to locate its source. Huddled near one wall of the manor was a man. He held his stomach with both hands, and his mouth was open wide as he struggled to breathe. His épée lay neglected on the grass nearby.

Jordan ran to him and knelt down. The man flinched away from him. "It's all right," Jordan said. "I'm going to help you."

"Too . . . too late for that," the man gasped. He was tall and rangy, with a hatchet-shaped face. Lank black hair lay plastered across his forehead. He was dressed in the livery of Linden Boros's household. "I . . . I lost. Let it be."

"What are you talking about? You need help, or you'll die."

"I know." Black liquid welled up between his tightened fingers. "Got me . . . a good one." He gritted his teeth and raised his head to look at his belly.

"Yes, you lost fair and square. But he didn't kill you, did he? You've got another chance."

The man shook his head. "Can't . . . face them. Now. Too humil—, humili—." He didn't have the breath for the word.

"What?" Jordan was desperate that the man would die in front of him. He sat back on his haunches, suddenly angry. "You can't face them? Is that supposed to be brave or something?"

The man glared at him.

"I've always admired soldiers for their bravery," Jordan went on in a rush. "Being willing to die for your pride seemed honorable. But I guess some men are willing to die because they're brave enough to face defeat, and some because they're afraid of facing their friends after being defeated." He crossed his arms and tried to stare the man down. "Sounds like you're the second kind."

The man fell back with a groan, closing his eyes tightly. "I'd . . . I'd kill you," he gasped. "If I could stand."

"Yeah, that way you wouldn't have to listen to me. Cowardice again. Are you going to let me help you?"

"Go to hell."

"What's the problem?" Jordan nearly shouted in exasperation. "Where is everybody? Where are your friends? What's so awful about getting yourself sewed up? Who's that going to kill?"

"House . . . house rules." The man opened his eyes again, to stare at the stars and wind-torn clouds. "Boros rules. No dueling . . . allowed. I call f-for help . . . Linden loses. Loses face. Maybe more."

"We'll take you to Linden's doctor. He can cover up for you, surely?"

"Ordered . . . not to treat . . . duelists." The man began to shiver violently.

"Oh." Jordan looked back at the tower, which stood in black silhouette against the troubled sky. "So your surgeon won't treat you because he's ordered not to, and Yuri's won't for the same reason. I suppose it was one of Brendan Sheia's men who stabbed you, so his surgeon certainly won't help." The man nodded fatalistically.

"Lucky for you I'm not a member of this household, nor one of yours, or Sheia's," Jordan went on. "I've been given no orders against helping you."

"Are you . . . surgeon?"

"No, but," he guessed, "my lady is."

The man tried to sit up. Jordan slipped an arm under his shoulders and helped him. "How can . . . lady be . . ." A violent shiver took hold of the man. "C-c-cold."

"Come. We'll stand up. Then we'll see." Slowly and gingerly, he drew the man to his feet.

CALANDRIA CURSED IN a language Jordan had never heard before. He needed no translation.

"Look at the trail of blood!" she snapped. "How are we going to hide him as you're suggesting? And what if he dies? We'll have a corpse in our room!"

"Not . . . my . . . idea," whispered the bleeding man.

"Lie back," she said to him. She knelt, whipping her nightdress around herself crossly, and poked at the embers of the fire. "You're going into shock. I'm going to get the fire well up, then we'll see to your wound." Jordan sat with his hands pressed hard on the man's stomach. Blood flowed everywhere, but no more than at the butcher's; Jordan was more worried by the amazing paleness of the man and the coldness of his skin.

"Don't mind her," he said to keep his mind off these things. "What's your name?"

"A-August. Ostler." By Ostler he might have meant his family name or profession; Jordan didn't pursue the issue.

"I'm Jordan Mason. This is Lady Calandria May."

"Jordan, stop it! You're wasting his strength." Calandria thumped two logs onto the churned embers. Sparks flew up, and she poked the wood into position so it caught. Jordan had noticed before that she wasn't very good at tending fires, a strange lack in someone so otherwise talented. Luckily these logs needed no encouragement to catch.

"Get Axel," she said. "I'll take over here." She pulled her pack from under her bed, spilled its contents on the floor, and came up with two white metal tubes. Without glancing up, she added, "Then clean the blood off the steps, and yourself, too."

Jordan ran.

He was glad now that they had taken the tower room. The place was set apart from the main manor, so comings and goings like this would be much less noticeable than in the house. Still, Jordan slowed to a cautious walk when he reached the downstairs gallery and paused every few steps to listen for the night watch.

Infrequent lamps dimly lit the halls of the manor. Jordan's bare feet made no noise on the cold stone floor. He took servant's ways; the idea of walking the main halls still bothered him, especially now when no one should be afoot. This also allowed him to pause at the cistern outside the kitchen. Low voices came from inside. He cautiously ladled water into a bucket and washed himself. He took the bucket with him up the tall narrow stairs to the top floor. If anyone stopped him, he could come up with any number of plausible servant's explanations for carting water about at two in the morning.

Even with this prop in hand his heart was pounding. As he reached the top of the stairs, he heard voices again. He plunked the bucket in a corner and quickly cast about for a place to hide. Finally he stood behind the door to the hall. Stupid, but what choice was there?

The voices became louder: a man and a woman in quiet conversation somewhere nearby. Very nearby. He held his breath and waited for them to open the door.

Nothing happened. They must be standing just on the other side. Jordan waited for several minutes, but they did not move. But he had to get to Axel. Time to brazen it through. He took a deep breath, picked up his bucket, and opened the door quickly.

There was no one on the other side.

The voices continued. Jordan put the bucket down and placed his palms over his ears. The dialogue continued, within his own head.

"Shit! Not now!" He staggered back, nearly tipping the bucket. All the excitement tonight had made him vulnerable, and Armiger had stepped into his mind again. Now that he knew what it was, the voices were obviously those of Armiger and Megan.

He stood for a minute in silent panic, waiting for the vision to wash over him completely. He would lose himself here, just when Calandria and Axel needed him. Maybe someone would find him wandering like an idiot, bloodstained. If August died, he would be taken for the murderer.

As he thought this, the top-floor landing did begin to fade. He thought he saw the inside of Megan's house, lit by a single candle. She and Armiger sat close together, talking earnestly. The vision became sharper with each passing second.

Jordan reached out blindly and felt the bannister at the head of the stairwell. He held it tightly in both hands to anchor himself. It was the panic he had to fight. There was no other way to stop the vision.

He put his awareness into the tip of his nose and breathed slowly, in and out, counting his breaths as he did so. Over the next few minutes he used every trick Calandria had shown him to engender calmness, and gradually the voices faded. When he was confident he had them at bay, he let go of the bannister. He could see again.

Jordan wasted no more time, but grabbed up the bucket and went straight to Axel's room. He debated whether to knock or walk in, knowing Axel might be with someone. He stooped to peer through the keyhole, just in case.

A candle burned on the table by the window. Axel sat there in a loose robe, his hands steepled. He was speaking in a low voice to someone out of sight. Jordan craned his neck to see who he was speaking to.

". . . The local humans don't seem to be in great awe of the Winds they deal with every day," Axel was saying. "They know the morphs and desals moderate animal populations. People treat morphs like they do bears or moose, with caution but not fear. But they mythologize the Winds they know the least—you can see it in their names for the geophysical Winds—like 'Heaven hooks' and 'Diadem swans.' They can't connect the activities of these greater Winds with their day-to-day lives."

He still couldn't see who else was in there. Well, there was nothing to be done about it. Jordan knocked lightly on the door. Axel stopped speaking immediately. Jordan heard him approach, and then the door opened a crack.

"What the hell do you want? Do you know what time it is?"

"Come quickly," Jordan said. "We need your help."

Axel opened his mouth, thought better of it, and went to dress. He left the door wide open, and Jordan was able to satisfy himself that indeed, there was no one else in the room.

.   .   .

HE WAS NOT surprised to find August asleep and breathing easily when he and Axel arrived. Calandria had removed the man's bloodstained jacket and shirt and was examining a harsh gash under his sternum. Amazingly, the gash was not bleeding.

"I had to use nano on him, or he'd have died," she said without preamble.

August had been bundled under several blankets. The fire was roaring nicely.

"Bad move to save him," Axel said. Calandria said nothing.

"What was I supposed to do, let him die?"

"What were you doing out there in the first place?" Axel shot back.

"What does that have to do with it? I was there. He was in trouble." Jordan stuck out his chin. "What was I supposed to do?"

"The question is," Calandria said drily, "what are we supposed to do, now that we have him? I let the nano work just long enough to suture the wound. I think I got it all out, but he may wake up in the morning without a wound at all. That's going to be hard to explain. Our discretion in this place seems to be evaporating. Once again you are the cause of the problem, Jordan."

"It's hard to think ahead when somebody's dying in front of you," Jordan said quietly.

Axel and Calandria glanced at each other. "All right," said Axel, "we're going to have to handle this carefully. He can't be moved right now, obviously. But he must be moved tomorrow night. You," he pointed at Jordan, "will be his nursemaid tomorrow. Then you will help me sneak him out and into town tomorrow night. Understand?" Jordan nodded. "We're lucky he's feeling personally humiliated. The fact that he wasn't supposed to be fighting will work in our favor; he won't come back here for a while—if, as you say Cal, he's not totally healed by morning."

"How could he be?" Jordan asked.

"Science," Axel said blandly. "Not the kind we're teaching you, though."

"Nano, right?"

Calandria swore in that other language again, and Axel laughed. "Yeah, nano. Shit, Cal, it was your idea to snatch Jordan in the first place. Live with it." She glowered at him for a second, then composed herself: the anger seemed to drain away totally, and she was once again her usual poised, calm self. This sudden calm was in its way more unsettling than the anger.

"How are we going to explain August's miraculous recovery to him?" she asked.

"He wasn't exactly in a position to judge how bad it was," Axel said.

"All he knew was he had a hole in him. If it turns out to be less of a hole than he thought, well, he'll just thank the Winds, I suppose. We'll bandage him thoroughly, and if there's no hole there at all tomorrow, I'll put one in—cosmetic, of course, don't look at me like that."

Calandria shook her head. Axel smiled. "You're good at planning," he said. "I'm good at improvising. That's why we get along."

"When we get along," she said with a sphinxlike smile.

Jordan sat down on his bed, suddenly very tired. In the back of his head, he heard Armiger and Megan still talking. It didn't matter. At that moment, he had to wonder which was the more real, the quiet, ordinary dialogue taking place in his head, a thousand kilometers away, or the mad conversation Calandria May and Axel Chan were holding, barely a meter away from him.

"Jordan!" He looked up. "Did you clean the blood off the steps?" Calandria asked.

He shook his head, then rose to do so. He'd left the bucket outside, ready for this.

"I'll help," said Axel unexpectedly. After they got outside and shut the door, he said, "Are you all right?"

"Yeah."

"You did the right thing," said Axel as they both knelt to dip rags in the bucket.

"She doesn't seem to think so."

"Oh, she does. She just gets angry when something happens she can't control."

Jordan sighed and began swabbing at August's blood. "Why?" was all he could think of to ask.

"Cal has her own problems," said Axel quietly. "She's never been a happy person. Why should she be? She never had a real childhood."

"What do you mean?"

"Cal was inducted into a military organization at a young age, after her mother was sent to prison. Over the years, they made her into a tool, an assassin who could serve the causes they were paid to support. She can change her face, her height, her voice . . . I don't know what she can't do. She can read a book and memorize every word the first time or learn a language in days. She's probably the best fighter on this planet. She has amazing powers, but she's never really had her own life. She ran away from her masters, the ones who made her, and for years she used her talents to support herself. Then she got tangled up in the war against 3340.

"People had tried to destroy 3340 from without," Axel continued. "Cal found the way that worked—she killed him from within."

"You told me."

Axel shook his head. "I gave you the sanitized version. You know

3340 was in the habit of 'promoting' humans—turning them into demigods pretty much at random by making them immortal, replacing their biological cells with nano, that sort of thing. He'd subverted the whole human civilization on Hsing to this perverse lottery. Once you became a demigod, though, he took control of your mind using some sort of sophisticated virus program. One of his 'conscious thoughts,' I guess. The place really was hell, there was no morality there, everyone just scrambled to try to become immortal and didn't care what they had to do to get it.

"Thirty-three forty looked unbeatable. But we kept hearing rumors that one demigod—and only one—had beaten the virus thought and thrown off 3340's enslavement. Calandria tracked him down and got the secret. Then she arranged to be 'promoted' by 3340."

"How did she do that?" Jordan had been dabbing at the blood spots one at a time; now Axel upended the bucket and poured the contents down the steps. "It'll be dry by morning," he said.

Axel looked at his now-wet feet. "You needed to really impress 3340 to get promoted. So Calandria betrayed us." He glanced up and, apparently satisfied by Jordan's shocked look, nodded. "The whole underground that Choronzon and the Archipelago had built up on the planet. Had us arrested, thrown in jail . . . sentenced to be eaten by 3340's data gatherers.

"It worked." His voice had become uncharacteristically flat. "The god took notice of her. He promoted her to demigod status on the spot. She became sur-biological, able to shape-shift, split her thoughts off into autonomous units, invent new senses for herself. They tell me it's the ultimate experience, short of real deification, but you're not even remotely human anymore. And of course, he slipped his virus thought into her, and it took her over."

Jordan had forgotten the wet steps. "Her plan didn't work?"

Axel half grinned. "Our ally god Choronzon had arrived in force, but his navy was being cut to pieces. Calandria went straight into the heart of the battle. But once she got there . . . she fought off the virus and flew through 3340's ranks, showing all the other demigods how to get free.

"So suddenly 3340's whole navy turned on him. Both navies chased him down to a mountain on Hsing, and Calandria and Choronzon con-fronted him there and killed him."

Jordan shook her head. It sounded like myth, but Axel was telling it in a bald matter-of-fact way.

"It must have been overwhelming for her." Jordan shifted uneasily, trying to imagine what it would take to deliberately choose to become like Armiger. "But you say she's human now?"

"She rid herself of all her powers—had her nanotech commit suicide by building itself back into normal human cells. She did it publicly to show the people of Hsing that being human was better than being a god."

He shook his head. "Me, I'd have stayed immortal. Think of the fun you could have."

"Why did she do it?"

He shrugged. "Like I said, she has her own demons—metaphorically, I mean. I think they pursued her even into godhood. She found some way of coming to terms with them by becoming human again. I don't know the details, she won't talk about it. She's also the most fanatically moral person I ever met," he added. "She thought it was the right thing to do.

"The thing is," he added gently, "you impressed her tonight by saving August. She wouldn't have left him to die, either, no matter what she might say. She just doesn't understand that at heart she's no different from any of us.

"And that, my friend, is a scar I don't know how to heal."

11

WHEN JORDAN AWOKE again, it was to the sound of a flock of geese honking their way south. He climbed stiffly out of bed and went to the window to watch them. Calandria was already up—or she had never returned to bed at all.

Winter was coming. The smell of wood smoke pervaded the estate, and the dawn chill reminded him of waking at home to find snow on his blankets. He would drag his clothes into bed—icy and stiff, they would start him shivering immediately. Better to warm them under the covers than to step into the cold air of the loft and put them on there. Quickly he would stomp downstairs, carrying his chamber pot like a lamp to set near the fire if its contents had frozen, otherwise by the door. And then to the chores and breakfast.

Sleepy winter. He felt a sorrowful ache, remembering and knowing things would never be the same. Resting his head on his hands, he stared out at the brooding sky.

He heard movement near the fire, where they had lain August. He was awake, staring at the ceiling with a puzzled expression on his narrow face.

When Jordan walked over to him, August said in a thin voice, "It doesn't hurt."

"It will if you move," Jordan warned. Axel had coaxed him on that point. August was almost completely healed. They would have to trick him into thinking he was still hurt.

"I'm thirsty." Jordan nodded and went to get some water from the table. He tilted a cup to August's lips, and the man drank awkwardly.

"Where are we?"

"The tower. We're going to move you to town tonight. You can recover there, out of sight of the Boros."

"Ah." August appeared to consider this. "Will I have a commission to come back to? Dueling is frowned on."

"What about self-defense? You can claim you were attacked while you were out taking a piss." Jordan shrugged. "We'll think of something."

August's eyes squinched shut for a second. "Thank you," he said. "I'm beholden."

"I don't think so." Jordan sat back on the wood floor. "Why were you fighting?"

August sighed. "I saw Sheia's man Andre acting suspiciously. I think he was stealing. Anyway, I followed him and challenged him, and he took me on. Maybe I should have raised the alarm, but . . . Linden has a curfew, and I was breaking it. I'd have had to explain myself, too. And what about you? What were you doing out of your room?"

Jordan pointed to the window. "You woke me up."

"Oh. Sorry." August grinned ironically. "We thought we were being so quiet."

Jordan scowled. "Dueling is stupid."

"I know." August looked very serious now. "My older brother was killed in a duel."

"So why did you do it?"

August stared at the ceiling pensively. "It gets easier to risk your life as you get older. I think women understand that when they have children. Suddenly they know they would give their life for their child, and it doesn't bother them. With men it's different, but we . . . trade our allegiance in the same way. At some point, if you've grown up at all, you have to decide that something outside yourself is more important than you are. Otherwise you'll be a miserable bastard, and you'll die screaming." He closed one eye and peered at Jordan. "That make sense?"

"I don't know," Jordan said uncomfortably.

"You get perspective. You can stand outside your own death, a little. Not while you're dying, though." He frowned. "Shit, I was scared. Scared . . ." He closed his eyes.

"You should sleep more," Jordan prompted.

"No. I like being awake. Alive, you know?" His face wrinkled; for a moment he looked as though he would cry. Jordan sat back on the wooden floor, blinking in surprise.

August swore. "Stupid, stupid, stupid! Things are coming to a head between my master and Sheia. He needs me right now, and I've let him down."

"Yuri decided in favor of your master," said Jordan.

"Yeah, but we know Sheia won't stand for it. He's going to lose everything, because his queen is going to lose her war. His only hope was to shelter under the Boros title. Now he can't do that. We don't know what he's going to do, but he's going to have to do it soon. Yuri's living in his garden if he thinks Sheia will just accept his decision."

Jordan shook his head, puzzled. "But what can Sheia do about it?"

"Don't know." August scowled. "He's devilishly clever, the bastard. He's probably celebrating my death right now; one less man to defend Linden."

"Linden should leave."

"And leave Sheia alone with Yuri's family? No. We stay."

A key rattled in the door. It opened, and Axel poked his head in. "She here?" he asked.

"No."

"Okay." The door slammed again.

Jordan sighed. "You'd better rest," he said to August. "I have to go study."

AXEL FOUND CALANDRIA on the manor's roof. He'd thought she might be here; this was a good spot from which to signal her ship. The *Desert Voice* maintained a high orbit, waiting for its order to obliterate Armiger, and Calandria came up here to listen for its pulsed radio beacon every day. She seemed to need the reassurance of its presence, which was one of those unlikely character traits that people who didn't know her well would find hard to credit.

"How are you doing?" he asked as he settled onto one of the crenels beside her. She was staring moodily out over the estate.

"Fine." She shrugged. "Things are getting more and more complicated, that's all. I was hoping we could get out without impacting the local culture at all. That seems unlikely now."

"These people are used to miracles," he said. "They're part of the natural order here. Look." He pointed east, where a pale crescent hung high in the sky: a vagabond moon. Another made a tiny dot above the southern horizon. "We aren't doing anything supernatural, as far as these people are concerned."

"I don't like it," she said. "Especially after last night. August's wound is almost totally healed. That's one miracle already. The *Desert Voice* is going to nuke Armiger, which is two."

"Well, I'm afraid I have to add to the complications," he said dolefully.

"Why? What's happened now?"

Axel puffed his cheeks out. "This time I really was minding my own business. I went for a walk in the gardens. You know me, I think better on my feet, always have. Anyway, there's the usual conspirators, sitting in shady bowers here and there in pairs. Very silly. As I'm walking, who should I see coming down the path, but the bastard himself."

"Turcaret?"

"The very same." Axel rolled his eyes. "Anyway, he calls me over like I'm some sort of lapdog, you know"—he gestured with one hand, as if to bring something to heel—"and says, 'I need to have a talk with you. Meet me in my quarters at eight o'clock tonight.'"

"Talk?" She frowned.

"Yeah." Axel shrugged uneasily. Their cover story here might be blown. "So I said yes," he finished unhappily.

"He's forcing our hand," she said.

"So what do we do? I told him I'd be there."

"Wise, but obviously we can't just react at this point. I wanted just a day or two more to pinpoint Armiger, but . . ." She nodded decisively. "I think we have enough."

"You know where he is?"

"About a hundred kilometers from the Iapysian border," she said. "Almost due south. More important, I think we've figured out where he's going."

"The queen?"

She nodded. "He seems to be interested in war. If he can use his powers to save Queen Galas, he might take over Iapysia. I thought before that the battle where the Winds intervened was a test. He may have wanted to find out what it would take to attract their attention. But it could be that he really does want to conquer a kingdom. Maybe he needs a large number of men to help him search for the Winds' Achilles' heel, or some other resource he's after." She shrugged. "It's all speculation."

He grinned loosely. "So let me get this straight: we cut and run now, Turcaret sends the king's guards after us, and where are we running, but straight into a war zone."

She half smiled. "Essentially, yes. The problem is what to do about Jordan."

"We can't very well leave him," he said.

"We can't very well take him with us, either. Not only because he'll slow us down. You and I are prepared for the danger, but he is not."

"That's where August comes in," he said brightly.

"Absolutely not. We've already involved too many people."

Axel threw up his hands. "Will you stop whining about that! It's their world—you can't treat these people like children. So a few of them find out what's going on—what kind of crime is that?"

"That's not the point. We keep adding extra concerns that just muddy the main issue, which is how to deal with Armiger as quickly as we can and get out."

"Is the job all you care about?" He hopped down from the crenel. "These people aren't going to cease to exist just because we go away. We kidnapped Jordan. What's he going to do when we cut him loose?

Haven't you considered that, or were you just planning to get him away from Turcaret and then cut him loose?"

She glowered at him. Obviously, she had been thinking just that.

"You're not playing the whole game, Cal, you never do. We're not just here to eliminate Armiger, we're here to act like decent human beings. What's wrong with getting to know people and helping them live their lives? And letting them help us live ours? I like Jordan. He did the right thing last night; he'll be a man of solid character once he's able to support himself."

"Well," she said coldly, "you've decided the right and wrong of it all, I see. So my opinion now isn't going to matter."

Axel clutched his black hair. "Your opinion matters! So does Jordan's. So does August's! We're not just assassins, that's all! Why don't you get to know these people? Maybe you'll like them. Maybe," he laughed, "you and August will hit it off! What's so bad about that?"

She stalked away. "We'll leave tonight—with Jordan," was all she said as she yanked up the lead-sheathed trapdoor.

Axel watched the door slam, then cursed. She hadn't understood a word he was saying.

ARMIGER STOOD AND wiped the sweat from his brow. He had been trying all afternoon to repair the damage he'd caused to Megan's garden last night. Short of using some of his own nano, there was nothing more he could do.

"Very good," she said. He turned. Megan leaned on the tall stump that marked the end of the garden. She smiled. "But seldom have I seen a man so grimy."

"I told you I would fix it."

She laughed. "One does not 'fix' growing things, Armiger. But . . . with practice, you could become a good gardener. I may leave the task to you for a while."

He brushed back his hair. She seemed happy at the thought, and he did not want to disappoint her. Still . . . "I can't stay," he said.

Her face fell. "Why not? You're not going back to your damnable army?"

"This is another army, and another war." He shrugged uncomfortably. "I want to talk to Queen Galas. She's the only one on this off-chart world who seems to know what the Winds are. The only human on Ventus with vision. Naturally, she's going to be killed for it. So I have to reach her immediately."

Megan folded her arms under her breasts. "You know this queen?"

"No. Never met her."

Megan watched him pick his way carefully out of the garden. He hadn't said he was in love with the queen. Still, he was willing to leave Megan to see her.

He paused next to her, waiting for her to fall into step as he headed for the cottage. His recovery had been unnaturally swift, so that by now he showed no sign of having been at death's door. Quite the contrary; his face glowed with health, and he moved with a catlike grace he had sometimes caught her admiring. None of this surprised Megan; he was a morph, or some spirit very like that, so such powers were to be expected. But he was still a wounded man, she knew, regardless of his bodily strength. He walked and ate like one in shock, and their conversations had continued to be brief and awkward. Some men trod heavily on their own hurt; the worse it was, the harder they would push it down, but it showed—in premature age, in lines of exhaustion and anger in the face. And she well knew that a man who will not salve his own pain will often put all his energy into healing that of others. To Megan, such brutality against oneself combined the most noble and foolish that men were capable of, and men of this sort drew her like magnets. Her own Matt had been like that. She believed only a woman could ease the intolerable pressure these men put on themselves.

So, Armiger was leaving. But she would be going with him, though he did not know it yet—and she had only this moment decided.

"I have money," she said. "Enough for a horse, maybe two. Riding palfreys."

"I only need one horse," he said. Men were so obtuse sometimes; she half smiled.

He strode easily through the thick grass, muscles moving in that fascinating synchrony she saw only in horses and men. "I'm not letting you in the house until you're clean," she said mischievously.

"You might have a long wait, then." He grinned back at her. "Your little well only draws a cupful at a time. Do you propose to wash me a palm's width at a time?"

"That might be delightful," she said. "But wait and see."

When they reached the cottage, he laughed in surprise. "How long did this take you?" She had filled an entire washtub while he was in the garden.

"Well . . ." She put her hands behind her back and kicked the dirt. "I rather thought you would need it. So I started just after you left."

"I do need it." Unself-consciously he stripped off his shirt. Her eyes widened as she saw he meant to do the same with his pants.

Armiger had only bathed in the presence of other men—officers and enlisted men, at river's edge or encampment. It took him a moment to notice her sudden silence, then he realized he might be shocking her. By then he was naked and had already stepped into the water.

He turned and their eyes met. Even as she stepped toward him, he felt his sex stirring. Since becoming embodied, he had not made love; it wasn't necessary. Still, he had seen others do it many times, although the rapes performed by his men were distasteful, nothing like the lovemaking in which he had seen his remotes indulge.

Megan took a washcloth and wordlessly ran it up his leg. She did not look at him as she laved his calves and thighs; but his excitement was visible, and she raised her eyes to his as she brought the cloth there.

He reached to touch the nape of her neck. She sighed heavily, and ran her wet fingertips along his member. She kissed the flat of his stomach, then stood into his embrace.

Part of him wondered why he was doing this—an old, inhuman side whose voice had been losing strength and confidence over the past days. Another part of him, young and ancient at the same time, almost wept with desire and relief as he drew her dress down to bare her shoulders, and buried his face in her hair.

Megan dropped the dress completely and stepped into the basin with him. "It's been so long," she whispered.

"Yes." He lifted her onto him. The feeling awoke a torrent of memory—false or real, it no longer mattered. He encircled her with his arms. "Too long," he murmured. Their mouths met, and neither spoke again.

JORDAN CAME TO himself suddenly. Calandria was standing in front of him, bathed in slanting evening light. Her face was framed by a wreath of fine black hair, tendrils of which caressed her forehead and the nape of her neck. She smiled at him. Jordan cleared his throat.

"How is our patient?" she asked, nodding to August. "Well enough to travel?"

"I feel fine," said August. "The wound doesn't seem so bad. I think I could even manage to hide it from Linden."

"Really?" Calandria brushed a hand through her hair absently. "That might not be such a bad idea, after all."

Jordan was surprised by this. Last night she had been adamant about getting August out of the way so that he would not call further attention to them. The state of his wound was bound to be cause for comment, after all. Of course, if he himself hid it from his masters . . .

"Jordan, can I speak to you alone for a moment?" she asked. He nodded, smiled at August, who shrugged, and followed her into the hall.

She closed the heavy door and said, "Our plans have changed." Jordan felt a quickening sense of excitement, but said nothing. "We are leaving tonight," she continued. As she spoke she watched his face closely. "I want you to pack our belongings and wait for me to return. Be prepared to move quickly," she said.

"What about Armiger? I thought we were staying because we hadn't figured out where he was."

"Well. We have enough to make a start, don't we?" she said brightly. Then she walked away, apparently confident.

Jordan reentered the room and closed the door. "What's up?" August asked him. The man was stretched out, seemingly at leisure, on his bedroll next to the fire.

Jordan shook his head. "I have no idea," he said.

AXEL RAISED HIS fist, then carefully loosened his knotted muscles and knocked politely on the tower door. It was a hard climb up here, past Turcaret's guards then up a narrow windowless spiral stairway. He could barely make out gleams of light coming through cracks in the door. After a moment he heard shuffling footsteps, and the door opened inward.

"Come in, come in." Controller Turcaret waved him inside.

Axel was surprised to find the controller was alone. The tower room he had been given was lovely. Tall leaded windows in all four walls admitted long shafts of afternoon light to gleam on the leaves of hundreds of plants festooning every surface. The chamber was tall, maybe six meters, and stone floored. Whoever normally lived here had trusted to the sturdiness of the place and had potted several young trees of respectable size. One, a willow, curled its long branches down over an iron-framed bed. Another overshadowed a writing desk. A wardrobe, several cabinets, and a table sat half hidden behind the foliage. There was a fireplace by the bed; the place might be quite cozy in the wintertime.

Axel crossed his arms, trying to manage a diplomatic smile. "Well. How are you?" he asked. It really should be Calandria at this meeting; but Turcaret had asked for Axel in particular, so Cal was off getting the horses ready, and he had to pretend to like this man for a few minutes. He manufactured a smile.

Turcaret brushed some leaves and a beetle off the table and motioned for Axel to sit. "Come in, Chan," he said as he rummaged in a cabinet. "Make yourself comfortable." He produced a bottle of wine and two glasses.

Axel eyed the bottle. "Are we celebrating something?"

Turcaret laughed darkly and uncorked the bottle. "We might be. That depends on how cooperative you are."

"Does it have to do with your reasons for visiting the Boros?" asked Axel. What he really wanted to ask was, *Did you follow us here?*

"All in good time, man." Turcaret made a shooing motion toward the wine glass. "Try it. I think you'll appreciate it."

Axel scowled, but picked up the glass. He took a sip. Instantly his diagnostic nano went to work. They detected no common poisons, although the liquid was full of substances foreign to them. That in itself was normal for Ventusian wine, Axel had discovered.

"Hmm." He dismissed the paranoid thought that Turcaret might try to poison him and took another sip. It was delightful stuff, so strong it seemed to dissolve into his soft palate before reaching the back of his throat.

He smiled at Turcaret and raised his glass. "All right," he said. "Now what did you want to talk about?"

"Ah, that." Turcaret steepled his hands and smiled. "It has to do with the little matter of your being an imposter."

DAYLIGHT WAS SEEPING away outside. Jordan was fairly sure Calandria would wait for darkness before making any moves, but knowing that didn't make the time pass any easier.

The time dragged. Jordan had packed everything in the ten minutes after Calandria left, and after that all he could do was wait. August had eyed him while he worked, but said nothing. He seemed content to let Jordan speak if he wished, but Jordan was distracted, and too upset to give the man much notice.

What confused Jordan even more was that Armiger and Megan were making love next to her fireplace. If he closed his eyes for even a second, he was there, seemingly touching her himself, and the vision was so mesmerizing he didn't want to look away. It was powerfully arousing, and he couldn't afford that—not tonight, and not with August in the room.

August kept twisting his body, flexing his arms, and touching his wounded side. He looked puzzled. Obviously he was trying to find some motion that would hurt enough to locate his wound. Jordan seized on the distraction.

"I told you, we've put something on it to kill the pain. You'll just open it up if you move about."

"No," said August. "I can feel everywhere around there. It seems . . ." He threw the blankets off.

"Stop!"

August stood up. "I'll be damned," he said. He pressed his hand to his side. "It feels . . ." He looked up suddenly.

Jordan heard something. "Quiet!" he hissed. August looked up in surprise.

"What—?" Jordan waved him silent. He sidled over to the door and put his ear against it.

August hitched his pants up and came over as well. "What is it?" he whispered.

"I heard footsteps. They stopped just outside the door," Jordan whispered back.

August planted his ear against the door. "I hear voices. Snuff out the candle, will you?"

Jordan ran to obey. August flattened himself against the wall next to the door, and Jordan barely had time to duck down behind the bed before someone pushed the door open, and three men stepped into the room.

12

TURCARET GLANCED OUT the window to check the angle of the light. It was almost dark. Almost time.

"I sent a semaphore message to the king of Ravenon," he said to Chan. "Shortly after you left Castor's manor. The king had never heard of you, or the damsel who calls herself Calandria May. You are not couriers for Ravenon. We don't know what you are, but I did receive permission to have you arrested and sent back to the capital in irons if I chanced upon you again."

Chan took another sip of his wine, his expression bland. "We're alone in this room," he pointed out. "If you wanted to arrest me, you would have already done it."

"True." At least Chan wasn't the idiot he looked. "I had a better idea," Turcaret admitted.

"I'm all ears," said Chan. Turcaret had never heard that expression before; the image was so bizarre he laughed.

"I originally intended to turn you in," he said. "After all, you rendered me a tremendous insult."

Chan sat up straight. "In what way? I'm sure we intended none."

"You intended none?" Turcaret couldn't believe his ears. "Well, to start with, you stole my property away on a pretext."

"What property?" The fool looked puzzled now.

"The Mason girl."

A look of disgust slowly spread across Chan's face. He tilted the glass, pouring the wine out on the floor. That was all right, Turcaret decided; he'd probably drunk enough by now.

"People are not property," said Chan quietly. "They have rights, even in this godforsaken country."

"Rights? Yes, let's talk about rights, now," said Turcaret. "That girl was just a thing, of no consequence, and no one would protest her fate, because no one can do anything about it. She was my right, she was the payment of a debt, and that was the beginning and end of it. But you! You have the gall to be indignant about that little trollop when you are nothing but a thief yourself—the thief of a title of Ravenon! You are the one befouling propriety here, and I'd be within my rights to have you summarily executed right here and now."

"You and what army?" asked Chan. He shook his head stupidly; the plant extract the priests had prepared for Turcaret must be starting to work.

"You're referring to the fact that we're alone. Perhaps you think you could take me in a fair fight. Maybe. But you wouldn't get far, even if you avoided my men and escaped the grounds."

" 'Zat so?" Chan seemed to suddenly realize what had happened to him. He tried to stand, unsuccessfully.

"Oh, yes, you've been drugged," said Turcaret. "But that's not why you'll never get out of here. The Winds have chosen you to play a part in the events that are about to unfold. The Winds are on our side. We know they favor us. By the time this evening is out, everyone will know it."

"Go to hell," muttered Chan. He didn't seem afraid at all. Angry, maybe. Turcaret supposed he was stupider than he looked, after all.

The controller smiled, not trying to hide his smugness. "You have been sent to us, sir. You might think you were the author of your own actions, but you are not. A higher power has sent you to us."

Chan shook his head sloppily. "Yer delusional." He tried again to stand, unsuccessfully.

"Feeling a bit weak?" Turcaret asked. "Good. Stay there, I want to show you something."

He reached behind the orange tree and brought out the wrapped packages his man had delivered just prior to Chan's arrival. He leaned the long cloth bundle on his own chair and put the smaller package on the table. He unwound the cloth that wrapped it. Chan blinked at him owlishly as he did so.

Turcaret spared a glance outside. The sun was down. It was time.

"Recognize any of these?" Turcaret unrolled the smaller bundle to reveal a dagger, a cloak pin, and a wide ornate belt.

"Hey!" Chan fell forward over the tabletop. "Those're mine! You stole 'em?"

Well, that was finally a satisfying reaction. Turcaret casually unwound the cloth from the longer bundle. He held up the sword and let the last drapes of cloth fall from its tip. "And how about this?"

Chan stared at the blade. He said nothing. He had obviously expected to see his own sword revealed under the wrap, correctly assuming that it had also been stolen from his room. This was not his sword, but rather a much more ornate, finely made épée. "Yuri's favorite sword," Turcaret said. "He keeps it in his bed chamber. I've only borrowed it, don't worry. It's going to be back there in an hour or two."

Shaking his head, Chan tried to rise. "Hey, wait. Just wait a—" He fell back, head lolling.

"You should see yourself," Turcaret said. "You look pathetic. That's no way to die, Chan. I would have expected more of an 'agent of Ravenon.'"

He raised the sword, aiming it straight at Chan's heart. "I've been told to kill you neatly and quickly," he said. "And I will. But not before you tell me something."

"Huh?" Chan levered himself up with his arms; his legs seemed unresponsive. Turcaret stepped forward and kicked him behind the knees. The man went sprawling off his chair.

Turcaret raised the sword, turning it so that it gleamed in the lamplight. Chan's eyes were fixed on it.

"Tell me this, or I'll make it a slow death rather than a quick one," Turcaret said. "Why are the Heaven hooks coming to take Jordan Mason?"

AUGUST'S ÉPÉE FLASHED in the dimness. One of the men who had entered the room screamed and fell, clutching his leg. The other dove forward, reaching for his own blade. This brought him up against the bed.

Jordan looked up into the startled eyes of a man wearing Turcaret's livery.

"Run, Jordan!" August's thrust clove the air where the man had been an instant ago. Jordan rolled sideways and ended up in the middle of the room. He could see the other two struggling, hands locked to wrists. The man August had stabbed was crawling toward the door; his left calf streamed blood. August had hamstrung him.

"Run!"

Jordan staggered to his feet and ran. He was in shock from the unexpected violence, and he didn't even bother to check whether there were more men in the hall. He stumbled down the steps, mindless, until stopped by a heavy thump above him. A dark silhouette with a sword appeared at the top of the stairway.

"Jordan!" He stopped, and let August catch up to him. The man was clutching his side, where he had been wounded last night.

August grabbed Jordan by the shoulder and shook him. "What's going on?"

"What do you mean?"

"Don't you try that with me," said August in a deadly tone. "My sword wound!"

"What about it?"

"There's a shallow cut there that looks fresh, but I can't feel anything deeper. It's healed!"

"Uh . . ."

"And why were two of Controller General Turcaret's men invading your chamber?"

"I don't know!"

"You! Stop!" Several men with swords had appeared at the top of the stairs.

"Later, then. Go!" August shoved Jordan down the last few steps. This time Jordan didn't hesitate, but ran. The ring of steel echoed after him as he shouldered open the door to the courtyard, and then he was dodging between statues, as the sounds of the fight faded behind him.

AXEL TRIED FOR the fifth time to stand. "Go to hell!" he muttered. *Concentrate*, he told himself. *Think of a way out of this.*

The damned controller kicked him in the ribs. It didn't hurt much, but there went his equilibrium again. Whatever it was they'd spiked his drink with, it had gotten past his usual immunities, and so far the diagnostic nano hadn't caught it. *Cheap hardware. Never should have bought it from Choronzon.*

He had left his sword and dagger in his room, where all his gear was packed for their flight from this place later tonight. Etiquette had prevented him from wearing them to what he'd been told was a simple meeting with Turcaret; they'd known that he'd leave them behind, so it must have been simple for someone to slip in and take them.

He tried to use his radio link to call Calandria. It needed some pretty specific mental commands to operate, and he couldn't focus well enough to give them. "Damn!"

"Tell me!" insisted the controller. "Why are the Heaven hooks coming for Mason?"

"I don't know what you're talking about," said Axel.

"The Heaven hooks will take the Mason boy tonight," said the controller. "I know all about him, though you tried to hide him from me. The Winds have not told me why they want him, though. All they will say is that he threatens 'thalience.' What does that mean? What is thalience?"

Axel had never heard the word before. He said so. "Who's really pulling your strings, eh? Tell me that, I'll tell you what the Winds want with Jordan."

Turcaret raised the sword, face white. Then he thought better. "If you paid attention to something more than the scullery maids and the location of the better wines, you'd know what's going on," said Turcaret. "We're putting Yuri's mask in the parade room. He backed the wrong man."

"You're in bed with Brendan Sheia?" Axel had to laugh. "You're an idiot! He's going down in flames! The queen is going to lose her war and then he'll be stateless. He hasn't a prayer of convincing the family he's the rightful heir. You know that."

The controller had calmed down. In fact, he looked much too calm now. "Well, Mister Chan, maybe I know something you don't. Unlike Yuri, we have the backing of the Winds. We know the Truth about them, you see." Axel was sure Turcaret had put a capital *T* on Truth. "That the Winds are ultimately destined to be our servants."

He swung the sword in a bright arc over his head, and brought it down on Axel's neck.

JORDAN WAS HALFWAY to Axel's room when the new vision began.

He could sense Armiger, somewhere in the back of his mind. He knew the man was still in bed with Megan, but had stoically managed to stay away from them. Armiger's senses were seductive, dangerously so.

This new thing was something else, another voice or voices. Despite himself, he stopped, bewildered.

He stood in one of the main halls of the manor. He could distinctly hear voices coming from one of the salons. Layered on top of that was a confused jumble of whispers, whose origin he could not place. They seemed to be coming from all around him.

Many of the whispers were in languages he didn't know; some were in his own. He also caught fragmentary, strange glimpses of things: black sky; the side of a building at night; something that looked like a tiny model of the Boros estate, viewed from above.

He shook his head, trying to remain calm. As he had the last time, he would have to pause now and damp the visions down, or else he would be unable to get to the safety of Axel's room. If he was to do that, he would have to find a secluded spot, or Turcaret's men would find him.

He moved as quietly as he could to the door to the mask room. No one would be here at this hour. As he pushed the door open, he leaned against the stone lintel, and the touch sent an electric sense of awareness into him.

"What . . . ?" He snatched his hand back. The murmuring voices hushed again. They might have been coming from the ranked masks on the wall, but somehow he sensed it was more than that. Still, the vacant eyes of the masks sent a shiver down his spine. He turned his back on them.

Tentatively, Jordan reached out and touched the stone wall with his fingertips. Again he felt a sense of connection, as though he had stepped from a silent corridor into a bright hall full of people.

"What is this?" he whispered.

The voice was strong this time. *I am stone*, said the stone wall.

CALANDRIA HAD VISITED the kitchens and filled a pair of saddlebags with food. Then she'd gone to the stables and overseen the provisioning of Axel's and August's horses. Leaving at night was bound to cause talk but she hoped not until morning, when they would be many kilometers away.

When everything was to her liking she went back to her chamber to tell August Ostler he should make ready to travel.

She could tell something was wrong from the bottom of the stairs. The door to their room hung open. Calandria moved silently up the steps, watching for any movement. The room seemed empty, but she saw fresh blood on the floor.

She cursed under her breath and stepped inside. There was no one here. Had Ostler attacked Jordan? The blood was smeared inside the room, but she could see drops of it receding down the hall. Whoever it was that had been hurt, they had left under their own steam or had been carried.

None of this made any sense, and not knowing the situation alarmed her more than any certainty would have.

She opened her radio link to Axel. *"Axel? Where are you?"*

There was no answer. Now fully alarmed, she stalked past the discarded blankets by the fireplace and began stuffing her few possessions into a bag. She scowled down at the beautiful gown she wore; it would be very difficult to ride wearing this confection. Although her instincts told her to run from the room, she paused long enough to shuck the gown and pull on her tough traveling clothes. Then she hefted her bags and turned to go. These few things would have to do.

Where next? *"Axel?"* Still nothing. He had not activated his transponder, so she couldn't locate him that way, either.

Jordan's few things lay on his bed, and she eyed them. He had not taken anything with him, a sign that he had not gone willingly.

Axel was supposed to be visiting Turcaret right now. She could go that way, or she could follow the bloodstains to where Jordan might be in danger.

Axel could take care of himself, but Jordan was only here because she had kidnapped and coerced him to be.

Cursing foully, Calandria wrestled her cape into position, threw her bags over her shoulder, and went to follow the blood trail.

As she left the room, a voice emerged from the darkness ahead of her.

"You're in quite a hurry for an innocent traveler, Lady May."

TURCARET STARED AT the place on Yuri's sword where it had broken cleanly in half.

Axel Chan's hands were at his throat. He gurgled. Then he rolled to one side, spat, and gasped.

"The sword broke," whispered Turcaret. "On your neck . . ."

Axel put his hands under himself and carefully rose to a kneeling position. Then he grabbed the edge of his overturned chair and used it to brace himself as he stood up. He tried to speak, but only a cough came out.

His throat was red and lacerated where Turcaret had hit it with the sword. Little blood flowed; the wound seemed superficial.

Obviously, he had struck the stone floor with the tip of the sword before the rest of the blade had touched Chan's throat. That must have been what happened.

No time to worry about that, Chan was on his feet. Turcaret grabbed the man's own dagger off the table. Chan made a clumsy grab for him but Turcaret stepped inside his reach and stabbed up, right under his heart.

The dagger tore through Chan's shirt and grated across his ribs. He staggered back, coughing. Blood flowed freely from the wound. Turcaret could plainly see he'd raised a flap of skin the size of his palm—but the blade had not penetrated.

Surprised, but not worried, Turcaret jumped after Chan, who was trying to get to the door. "Die, damn you!" He reversed the dagger, grabbed Chan's shoulder, and stabbed him again and again. It was like stabbing a table. Each blow cut Chan's shirt as the blade scored across his skin, and plainly he wore no armor. But the blade would not penetrate more than a few millimeters. Finally it, too, broke against the man's shoulder.

Turcaret backed away. "How have you done this?"

Chan huddled against the closed door, gasping. His whole upper body was covered in blood. This was not going to be the clean kill Brendan Sheia had demanded. There was no way Chan would appear to have been killed by Yuri's dying blow. Maybe it could be made to look like more of a fight had taken place, but they had wanted to avoid that because the question would be raised why no one had heard anything. But the man would not die!

Chan turned now and uncovered his eyes. He might have been vulnerable there, but Turcaret had not thought of it in time. Chan's face was transformed. The skin around his mouth was pure white, and his eyes were wide. He was shaking, but not, it seemed, from fear.

"Help," Turcaret said under his breath. Then he screamed it. "Get in here and help me!"

JORDAN WAS NO longer sure where he was. When the wall spoke to him he'd bolted, then came to himself briefly to find himself here outside on the front lawn of the estate. He tried to keep going, to somehow escape the noise in his head, but made it only fifty steps before he went blind again. He could see—with a clarity that was itself frightening—but no longer through his own eyes.

The spirits surrounding him were handing vision back and forth, like a ball. All the parts of the Boros estate had their spirits, it seemed, and each kind of thing perceived the world in a different way. They were all speaking at once, looking about themselves, as though awoken from an ages-long sleep to find themselves startled by the world.

Something had awoken them. Something was coming.

The trees told of a gargantuan weight descending through the air and of a shadow between them and the twilight sky. The stones could feel an electricity spreading in a kind of wave, coming from the east. Jordan understood these things because the stones, and trees and water, were speaking in common terms of reference, some of which were actual words and phrases he could understand, some images, some physical sensations.

He staggered to a stop, swaying, unsure whether he was even still on his feet. No, he seemed to be above the ground now, very high up. He could see the rooftops of the manor, and he saw the windowed facades (last rays of sunlight touching them gold) and felt the draft of the passage of human bodies through the halls within. The attentiveness of the estate seemed to draw a tighter focus, bearing him images of people. He seemed to touch the faint trails of heat left by the cooks in the kitchen, as reported by an archway there. The flagstones in the courtyard felt the pressure of walking feet, and measured the passage of four people. The sound of voices echoed weirdly, as if from a long distance.

The spirits were searching for someone, he realized—a man or woman who was somewhere on the estate.

He knew he wasn't really in the air; this was just a vision. Jordan began to move again, perversely wishing they would notice him because then he could see where he was, if only through their eyes. He put his hands before him like a blind man and walked.

The heavens . . . something was coming down from the sky. The estate knew it, and increasingly the snatches of vision Jordan caught were images from a vast height, far above the highest trees.

If he wasn't able to fight back these visions, he was as good as dead. Was he just going to stand here and let whatever it was that was coming take him?

Angry at his own helplessness, Jordan stopped walking, dropped his arms to his sides, and breathed in deeply. Once. Twice. He called on all the things Calandria had taught him and tried to subdue the panic. All so he could have his own eyes back, for just a moment.

He felt the kaleidoscope of visions clearing and tilted his head back. He saw the cloudless sky, scattered with the first stars of evening like the finest jewels on blue silk.

And he saw the Heaven hooks.

LINDEN BOROS DISPLAYED the family smile to Calandria. It was no more charming coming from him than it had been from Yuri or Marice. He was dressed in dark riding breeches and a red embroidered jacket, as if he had just arrived from the stables. He had ten men with him, all armed. August Ostler stood near him, looking uncomfortable.

"August told me there was a fight," said Linden. "Were you a witness to it, Lady?" His bodyguards had their swords out.

Calandria looked at the swords, wide-eyed. "What is this about?"

"It would seem my bastard brother has overstepped his boundaries," Linden said dryly. "Through his friend Turcaret." He gestured for her to come up the steps. She walked up to stand before him.

"Where is my apprentice?" she asked. "He should be with your man here." She indicated Ostler.

Linden's brows furrowed slightly. He glanced at Ostler, who shrugged. "Not my concern," he said. "But I think you owe us an explanation."

Calandria cocked her head to one side. "Explanation? Regarding what? That we saved your man here from death requires no explanation—unless you are one of those who would not save a life unless it profit you. That we hid him? It was at his own request. He was a bit ashamed of himself after breaking the rules of the house."

"And why are you dressed for riding at this late hour, Lady?"

"Considering the kindness I've done your man, Mister Boros, I think I'm entitled to keep that to myself."

He scowled. "May I remind you that you are a guest in this house?"

"Not for much longer," she said. "And I am not the guest who transgressed the rules," she added, nodding significantly at August, who shrank back.

Linden folded his arms. In this light he appeared quite menacing, slim and poised, with his sword loose at his side. The blond hair cascading down one shoulder was bound with black ribbon. Standing this close to him, Calandria caught a scent of leather, horses, and sweat. "Speaking of transgressing rules," he said with some irony, "the Winds might be upset to know just how much science you carry around with you, Lady May."

She didn't reply. "Our poor August, here, was done for, by his own admission," Linden continued. "Someone tried to disguise a freshly healed sword wound with a new and shallower cut, but it's a clumsy job. Especially since there's a corresponding scar on his back. I've never seen such a pair of scars like that before . . . most people with that sort of wound don't last a day. Now August assures me his blood is actually rather thin, making it difficult for him to clot a cut finger. He says you did something to him . . . something scientific, which brought him back from the brink of death. The last person to try that was general Armiger, whose entire army was destroyed by the Winds."

"But—" she started.

"But," Linden interrupted, "you happen to be right. You did save my servant's life, by his own admission. I'm not sure what it is you are doing, but those who attacked August the first time just returned to finish the job. That tells me you are not one of them yourself. I don't know who you are, but—"

He was stopped mid-sentence by screams and shouts breaking out below them. A man ran up the stairs recklessly, shouting, "Sir! Sir! He's dead!"

Calandria had bent to pick up her packs. She hesitated, as the man stumbled on the top step, skidded to his knees, and shouted, "They've killed Yuri!"

Linden's eyes widened. "Brendan! I knew it!" He rounded on Calandria. "If you have some involvement in this, Lady, then you won't live to see trial. But you saved August, so if you love our house then come with me!" He raced down the stairs.

Calandria reached for her packs, but August already had them. "Where is Jordan?" he asked her, as men raced around them like a river in flood.

"Don't you know?"

He shook his head. Then they turned as one and ran after the mob.

AXEL REACHED FOR the first thing at hand. It was a potted spider plant.

"B-bastard," he managed to croak. His throat burned like he'd been branded. Every time he moved, his arms and shoulders screamed pain. The subcutaneous armor worked just as Calandria had advertised, or else he would be dead by now. It wasn't enough to prevent loss of blood and deep bruising. He had to hope Turcaret didn't realize just how close to collapse he really was.

He threw the pot. Turcaret dodged it easily. Axel's reflexes were still pathetic, but the dizziness was passing.

"I'll kill you," Axel told the controller, trying to sound confident. He stepped into the center of the room. Turcaret backed to the window. Axel stared at his stolen possessions, laid out on a piece of cloth on the tabletop as if they were for sale. They were going to plant them wherever they killed Yuri, in case they didn't get Axel himself. Good plan.

Turcaret stepped to the window and shouted, "Men! Get up here!" loudly.

"Oh, right—" Axel began, but just then the door behind him burst open. Four large men with swords spilled into the room. They stopped their onrush when they saw Axel, bloody by the table, and Turcaret backed against the window.

The leader's eyebrows hopped up and he sneered at Turcaret. "Shall we finish him, sir? It's well past time for—"

He had laid himself wide open, so Axel put a side kick into him. The man sailed across the room and shattered a fine lacquer cabinet. Axel staggered and nearly fell over.

A sharp blow to the shoulder drove him to his knees. This time he had the sense to roll forward, and came to his feet on the far side of the table. The man who had tried to chop his head off was looking at his sword in surprise.

Two of them came around opposite sides of the table. Axel hopped onto it and let one stab him in the chest. He reached out and took the man's wrist; Axel twisted it and took the sword out of his hand while the other bodyguard watched in confusion.

He couldn't let these men catch him. He turned to see a good view of Turcaret's rear end, as the controller struggled to get out the window.

Axel put the pommel of the sword into its owner's face and got off the table. He kicked a chair between himself and the other bodyguard and ran for the window. Turcaret had made it outside and was clinging to the casement, some three meters above the roof of the manor.

No more time to look—they were converging on him. He grabbed the window frame and pulled himself through it as they howled after him.

The fall would have broken something had he been unarmored. As it was, he was stunned for a second. When he pulled himself to his knees on the rooftop, he could not at first spot Turcaret.

But there he was, struggling with the metal door set into the rooftop. Behind him the moon was rising, huge and white. Axel barked a laugh and painfully pulled himself to his feet.

Turcaret looked up in fear—and it took a moment for Axel to realize the controller was not looking at him, but past, at the sky.

Ventus had only one moon, and Diadem was small. The thing Turcaret was silhouetted against was huge—larger than Earth's moon—and growing by the second. It glowed from within.

Turcaret was staring at something behind Axel. He turned around, and looked up . . . and up.

"Oh, thank you," Turcaret said.

THE BOROS FAMILY feud really wasn't any of Calandria's affair, but right now she was surrounded by shouting men for whom nothing could be more important. She let herself be swept along with them, thinking that by doing so she might find Jordan. Linden raised a hand. "Silence!" he thundered. "Where?" he said to the man who had told them of Yuri's death.

"In his bedchamber!"

"Oh, pray he was not butchered in his sleep." They hurried out into the courtyard, which was ablaze with torches. The sky was lit by the crepuscular glow of a vagabond moon, huge and lowering over the estate. Servants crowded everywhere, gawking. Linden's men were rallying under the main doors to the manor. "Where is Sheia?" roared Linden.

"We've got his men barricaded in their rooms!" crowed a lieutenant. "Don't know where he is—doubtless he's run, like the cur he is."

"Where is Marice?"

"With Yuri."

"Come then." Linden hurried into the manor. They followed. August stayed close to Calandria, but said nothing.

Yuri's bedchamber was on the third floor, at the front of the house. It had a commanding view through many floor-to-ceiling leaded-glass windows. Two fireplaces faced one another across the room; Yuri's giant canopied bed hulked near the one to the right. Linden's men crowded in after a whole mob of people, who were babbling and wailing incoherently.

Everything had been knocked about in the course of Yuri's final battle. Tables were overturned, chairs smashed. It was astonishing no one had heard the fight—but then, the walls were thick stone, and the door was four-centimeters-thick oak.

Yuri lay on his back on the bed. His belly was slit, and intestines bulged blue out of the wound. His eyes were still open, glaring at the ceiling.

Lady Marice stood next to the bed. There was no expression at all on her face; it was as if she were carved from stone. She watched as people ran back and forth shouting.

"The assassin fled," someone said to Linden. He stepped up to Marice and took her hand. She snatched it back, and turned away from him.

"But he left his sword." The man pointed to the floor by the bed.

"Did he now?" Linden knelt and prodded the blade that lay there. "And whose is this, I wonder?"

Calandria gasped. It was Axel's sword.

13

THE BOWL OF the sky was being filled. Jordan could see stars only near the horizon; the rest of the firmament was taken up by the dark mass of a vagabond moon. He had never seen one so low to the ground before—had never realized how big it was, like a thunderhead. It seemed ready to drop on him at any moment.

From a distance the moons seemed featureless, but up close he could make out tiny patterns in its dark skin, like the veins of a leaf. And directly above him, in the center of the bowled-in sky the moon made, he saw a deeply black star-shaped opening appear, and motes of light drifted silently down from it.

The Heaven hooks. He could see them among the lights now: black filaments, like spider's thread, with the lights strung along them like paper lanterns at a fair. Everyone knew the hooks rode on vagabond moons, reaching down through clouds like the hands of a god to scoop up entire fields. He had never seen them before—no one he knew had. But he knew the stories.

The entrance to the manor was only a hundred meters away. Jordan put his head down, and ran for the doors.

. . .

LINDEN BOROS PICKED up Axel Chan's sword. The blade was covered in blood. The lord turned it over in his hands thoughtfully. "Foreign make," he said. "Could be Iapysian?" A fresh commotion was breaking out in the hallway outside Yuri's bedchamber. The whole estate, it seemed, was erupting with noise.

"What does it matter," said the lieutenant at his side. "We know Brendan Sheia is behind this."

"*Is that so?*"

Silence fell like a cloak across the room. Calandria stood on her tiptoes to see what had happened.

Brendan Sheia stood in the doorway. He had one hand on the pommel of his sword, otherwise he appeared calm. "Is it wise to jump to such conclusions, brother?"

"I'm not your brother!" Linden paced up to him. "It was very stupid of you to come here, Brendan. I suppose, though, it saves you the humiliation of being run to ground."

"You're too quick to jump to conclusions," Brendan said. He went to Marice, and gravely bowed. "My lady, I don't know what to say. This is terrible." Again, Marice turned away.

Brendan Sheia wheeled about like an actor on stage. He knew he had the attention of every person in the room. He was a hulking man with a square face, black hair, and beetle brows. He wore a housecoat, embroidered with the family crest, and simple gray breeches, a doubtless calculated attempt to look like he had come from his own bedchamber, which the sword spoiled.

He would have had to be insane to enter this room without the weapon, judging from the way people were looking at him.

"What is that?" He nodded at the sword Linden held. "The murder weapon?"

"Yes," said Linden, "and as soon we find which of your men it belongs to, we'll pin him to the south wall with it—just ahead of you."

"One of my men?" Sheia frowned. "Not likely. That belongs to one of our other guests . . . the tawny fellow, you know, the irritating one."

"Sir Chan," said Linden's lieutenant.

"Yes, that's the one. Where is he during all this commotion?"

Linden looked at Calandria. She had nothing to say, but simply shook her head.

"Perhaps you do need to tell us the reason for your traveling clothes," Linden said to her.

"Well then." Sheia crossed his arms and glowered at Calandria. "It seems straightforward."

"Not necessarily," said Linden. "They have no motive. Quite the contrary."

"Maybe they were hired by Sheia," said the lieutenant.

Sheia guffawed. "They're agents of Ravenon, by their own admission. By this one stroke they've sown disorder in both Memnonis and Iapysia. Considering the troubles Ravenon's having, they'd love us to squabble within ourselves. If you don't see that, Linden, you're an idiot."

Linden stepped toward him, white-faced. Sheia ignored him, turning instead to Calandria. "So Lady May was taking the servants' stairs, was she?"

"If the assassin got away," Calandria said, pitching her voice clear and steady, "why did he leave his sword? That seems like a rather large oversight."

"Perhaps he was overwhelmed by what he had done. Or, maybe he was hurt?" Sheia appeared to consider that idea. "It looks like quite a fight happened here. That being the case, *brother*," said Sheia, "wouldn't you agree we should be hunting for Chan?"

Linden appeared to have regained his poise. He snapped his fingers at two sergeants, who came to attention and hurried from the room. "There," he said. "Now let us get back to the question at hand: namely their connection to you." He nodded to two more men. They moved forward to flank Brendan Sheia.

"Before you make an ugly mistake," Sheia said, "consider your options. Who are you going to put to the question here? I did not kill Yuri. With him gone, the family needs us united—it is imperative to our survival. If my men hear you've imprisoned me, there'll be a bloodbath, and nobody wants that. You can find out for sure who killed Yuri. Ask her."

Linden laughed humorlessly. "We will. But you're not going anywhere until we're done. Bring her." He turned to leave.

"Wait!" August jumped between Calandria and the Boroses. "She is no assassin. I can vouch for her."

"And bring him, too!" Linden cried. He flipped his cloak about himself angrily as he stepped from the room. Sheia laughed richly as he followed.

"Wait!" August shouted. A soldier clouted him on the side of the head, and he went down on his knees. Another man took Calandria's arm and pushed her roughly toward the doors.

She had just turned to snap something rude at the man when the ceiling caved in.

Turcaret laughed spitefully. "You are too late. The Heaven hooks have come, to take your young apprentice. Doubtless they will take you, too."

Axel stared at the sky. "Oh, shit," he whispered.

The biggest aerostat he had ever seen was hovering over the manor house. They were a common enough sight in the skies of Ventus and very similar to the aerostat cities he had seen on gas giants and dense-atmosphere planets. The thing was just a hollow geodesic sphere about two kilometers in diameter. It didn't much matter what you built one with; at that size it would remain airborne despite its mass because, due to its high surface-to-volume ratio, sunlight would trap enough heat inside to create buoyancy. On other worlds entire cities lived in the bases of the things; here on Ventus, Axel had been told, they served as bulk transport for minerals and other terraforming supplies. No human had ever entered one and come out again, of course—they were purely tools of the Winds.

The belly of this aerostat had opened out like the petals of a flower—or more ominously, like the beaked mouth of an octopus. Hundreds of cables woven round with gantries and buttresses tumbled into the high air from this opening. He could see them spiraling down at him in glimpses highlighted by Diadem, the world's one true moon.

"They will take you, Chan!" Turcaret shouted. "It was going to happen, if you lived. Somehow you and yours have offended the Winds. They have taken notice of you! My killing you was an act of kindness, don't you see? I would have spared you this!"

"Shut up," Axel said distractedly. What the hell was the thing doing here? This couldn't be some random event; his briefings on Ventus had never mentioned an attack like this. But the Winds treated any technology not of their own creation as a pathology to be removed. Axel had thought he and Calandria had succeeded in hiding their nano and implants from the rulers of Ventus. Maybe it hadn't worked.

Axel had to get to Calandria, and Turcaret happened to be standing on the only door. "Out of the way, you bastard," Axel said. Turcaret's face was lost in darkness, but Axel could see he was shaking his head.

"I will deliver you to them," said the controller. "It will be my pleasure." He shouted something into the sky in some old language. Past his dark outline, Axel saw a thing like a caged claw, big as a house, fall straight at them. Just before it hit, great lamps like eyes blazed into life from its cross beams.

The roof disappeared with a great *slap* Axel felt in his bones. Dust and scraps of shingle and wooden beams shot into the air, and he was airborne, too, before he knew it. He landed on his side on the roof, which swayed and pitched like the deck of a ship. Something bright as the sun, and howling like a million saws, planted itself in the roof next to him and twisted this way and that. He smelled hot iron and ozone.

Axel rolled onto his stomach. Turcaret was crouched two meters away, also looking up. Axel willed himself to stand up, but his strength momentarily failed him. As he was struggling onto his elbows, Turcaret sent him a silent, contemptuous glare and hopped down through the hole in the roof.

A metal tower reaching all the way to the heavens was heaving its base back and forth through the ruins of the manor. Only part of one wing had collapsed, so far, but the thing had hundreds of arms, and these pounced out and down into corridor and chamber, and through the dust he could see some of these arms passing struggling human forms inward to the thing's central cage. Horrified, he rolled away from the sight.

He came up against the door, which had popped open. The stairs leading down appeared quite unscathed. A last glance back showed Axel that other giant arms had landed on the grounds and by the stables, in a rough circle around the main building. They were eating the trees.

Axel wailed and fell through the open door.

CALANDRIA SORTED HERSELF out of the tangle of lead triangles and glass flinders on which she had landed. She had never read of, seen, or VR'd someone jumping through a *leaded* glass window before; it had turned out to be a lot more difficult than she had expected.

It had taken two tries, but she was on the ground now. Poor August was still upstairs, but there was only so much she could do. She rolled to her feet, rubbing blood out of her eyes.

Madness had fallen from the sky. She had a perfect view of the grounds from here in the bushes by the front steps of the manor. People were running back and forth, trying in equal numbers to get into and out of the house. An aerostat hovered over the estate, visible in the light of fires that were springing up all over. Calandria stared at it for a moment, then shook her head to clear the muddle of half thoughts that filled it. Bits of glass flew from her hair.

A deep crash sounded from inside the manor; the front doors flew open, and a waft of dust blew out. There was no going back in there—but she had to find Axel. She bounced on the balls of her feet for a moment, debating whether to use radio to contact him.

A huge metal arm plowed into the earth a hundred meters away. Its end flopped there for a second or two, then split into a hundred bright threads, which coiled outward. Each thread—which must be a motile cable as thick as her body—bent and probed the ground ahead of itself as it moved. She realized suddenly that this thing might be able to smell her out from the radio waves, and her scalp crawled with sudden fear. She had been about to contact Axel. Its cables continued to unravel and lengthen, and some were heading toward her.

With a terrible rending crash, one wall of the manor fell outward. Calandria screamed as the air around her was filled with flying stone. At least ten people had been hurrying across the patch of ground the wall had hit.

She stood back and cupped her hands around her mouth. *"Axel!"*

Twenty meters away, a gleaming metal snake reared into the air, its mandibled tip quivering. It slid deliberately in her direction.

A hand fell on her shoulder. It was Axel, coughing and covered head to foot in blood and gray dust.

"You're hurt!" She gingerly peeled his sticky shirt aside.

"It's superficial. You look a bit rough yourself. You okay?" he said.

"So far. Look at that!" She pointed at the questing snake.

He glanced at it briefly. "Yeah. Let's get out of here."

"Which way?"

"We need our supplies. Where's your stuff?"

"August's got it. He's . . . well, we got separated. How about yours?"

Axel pointed wordlessly at the heap of rubble even now being picked through by metal scavengers.

"Inside!" She went to grab his arm, then thought better of it; she didn't know where all his wounds were. "Oh, Axel, what happened?" She gestured for him to follow her up the pillared steps. The snakelike thing was only a few meters away now.

"Can't we just run for it?" He stood swaying slightly, staring at it.

"Come on!" Abandoning care, she hauled him inside. The foyer of the manor was a chaos of screaming people. One staircase had collapsed; a weeping woman dug frantically at the wreckage, screaming, "Hold on! I'm coming!" Some soldiers with their swords in their hands stood in a knot, staring hectically at the shadowed ceiling. Men were hauling injured people and corpses in from one of the side corridors.

"There's nowhere else to go," said Axel.

"What's happening?" She pulled Axel to face her; his expression was lost in darkness, since the only light came from a couple of oil lamps, and from fires burning outside.

"Turcaret says they're after Jordan," said Axel. "I guess his implants set them off somehow. The bastard did this to me," he said, raising his arms then wincing. "Tried to set me up for the murder of Yuri."

She shrugged angrily. "Yes, I saw the result. Where's Jordan?"

"No idea." One of the front doors fell off its hinges. With everything else that was happening, this didn't seem momentous. But harsh cones of electric light pierced the dust from outside. Calandria heard a loud whirring sound, accompanied by undulating movements in the doorway.

"What do we do now?" she said.

"Nothing," he said, staring into the light.

"Not nothing!" She let her breath out in a rush, coughed on dust, and said, "We shoot down the aerostat."

Axel's eyes widened. "With what?"

"Call the *Desert Voice*. Land her here. Have her take out the aerostat on the way."

"But Jordan—"

"Axel, we're done here! We need to get Armiger and get out of here. Axel"—she couldn't prevent her voice from rising as she spoke—"they're killing everyone here! Because of Armiger!"

Axel's lips were drawn in a tight grimace. He clenched his fists and glared at her while around them people screamed. "All right!" he said finally. "Do it!"

Calandria closed her eyes and opened the link.

TURCARET DUCKED INVOLUNTARILY as something nearby fell with a crash. The manor was coming down around him, but he couldn't leave it until he had taken care of his people.

He fought his way past running servants to his people's quarters. The maids and footmen were clustered at the windows, staring outside in disbelief. "Run!" he barked at them. "Quickly now. Get outside before the rest comes down."

"What's happening?" wailed one. "Is it the war?"

He shook his head. "Just go."

They made for the door.

He sighed. Duty was satisfied; now to find Jordan Mason.

He had no idea whether the assassination of Yuri had gone off successfully, but that seemed unimportant now. The Heaven hooks were in a rage. He could hear them, a deep sussurating chorus in his mind.

Never in his life had Turcaret been in the presence of such powerful Winds. He had heard voices as a child and, long before he met anyone who could explain them, had decided they were Winds. Little things spoke to him, trees and stones, and sometimes he could reply. They generally rambled about subjects he didn't understand, but every now and then they brought news of the hooks or the Diadem swans, and once or twice they had told him of the activities of the desals. He clearly remembered the day he learned that the desals had chosen to put the lady Galas on the throne of Iapysia. She was blessed by the Winds; it was this fact that finally made him throw in with Brendan Sheia.

Now the voices discussed their search for a man. The Winds were acting to eliminate a threat—but how could that be? In all his years, Turcaret had never heard the Winds speak of any sort of danger to themselves or the world. They were all-powerful.

Sometimes when the Winds were very near, Turcaret could see secrets within things. That was happening now, but on a scale he could never have imagined. Everywhere he looked, ghostly words and images seemed to hover in front of objects—the chairs, walls, casements, and jittering chandeliers each had its orbiting retinue of tiny visions. He knew if he had time to stop and examine them, each would reveal some secret about

144 ∞ Karl Schroeder

the object behind it. You could learn all the crafts, from masonry to bookbinding, this way.

He had always felt exalted by such gifts. They were proof that he was special, destined in some way to be a great leader and master over both man and nature. When he heard whispers of the coming of the Heaven hooks last night, Turcaret had assumed they knew of his plot with Brendan Sheia and were preparing to marshal the forces of heaven itself behind their attempt to wrest control of the Boros family. Sheia didn't believe him when Turcaret told him, so they had continued with the conservative approach: framing the visiting imposters for the assassination. But Turcaret had suspected such detail work would prove unnecessary in the face of what was to come.

Now the Winds had arrived, and they were destroying the estate! He would have thought they disapproved of Yuri's assassination, were it not that he could hear plainly they wanted only one thing: Jordan Mason.

At the foot of the stairs, people were spilling into the courtyard. He could see Linden Boros trying to organize his men among tilting statues. The terrifying arms of the Hooks reared overhead.

Turcaret ignored them; they were no threat to him. He scanned the faces in the courtyard. He had seen Mason once, being hoisted aloft in Castor's courtyard for some minor victory. And indeed, there he was coming out of the front hall. He looked more boy than man, his dark hair tousled, eyes wide.

"Give me your sword," Turcaret demanded of a passing soldier. Dazed though he was, the man hurried to comply. Turcaret hefted the blade and walked through the mob, eyes fixed on Mason.

What was this boy to the Winds? He was nothing but a loutish tradesman, and yet the Heaven hooks were willing to kill everyone on the estate to get at him. "You!" Turcaret leveled his sword at Mason. "What did you do to anger them?"

"I don't know!" shouted the boy. He shook himself and glared at Turcaret. "And who are you to accuse me?"

Anger always calmed Turcaret; it gave him focus. He smiled now at the boy. "You've spent too long with Chan. Answer me! What have you done to offend the Winds?"

Uncertainty crept into Mason's eyes again. He was lit in intermittent flashes of lightning, making him seem to shift in place. If he tried to run, Turcaret was prepared to kill him.

"I don't know why they're doing it," Mason said simply. He seemed guileless; whatever he had done, he was probably too stupid to remember or connect it to tonight's events.

The Heaven hooks would keep tearing the estate apart until they found Mason. He was the cancer at the heart of the night, and only his removal would restore the correct order to things.

Killing him would also surely make the Winds notice Turcaret at last.

"Stand still," he instructed the youth. He stepped forward and raised the sword.

Lightning flashed again, and Turcaret caught a glimpse of Mason's eyes. In them Turcaret saw something he had never believed he would see.

Words and images flickered like heat lightning in those eyes. Somehow, this youth was both man and Wind. The whispering voices of nature spoke from within him. All the people on this estate—all people everywhere—appeared to Turcaret as absences, silhouettes against the glow of the Winds. All except Mason, who shone like nature itself.

Mason glanced up at the sky. Suddenly everyone in the courtyard was screaming.

Mason jumped back. People were running for the walls, so finally Turcaret tore his gaze away from the youth.

He just had time to count the claws on the giant hand before it fell on him, took him, and crushed out his life.

JORDAN MET AUGUST Ostler in a cellar hallway choked with dust and swarming with terrified people. The soldier looked stunned, and Jordan had to take him by the shoulders and shout in his face to get his attention.

August blinked at him. Despite the warm red light of the torches, August's face was deadly pale. "The Heaven hooks have come," he said.

"I know," Jordan said impatiently. "Where's my lady?"

A series of scraping thuds sounded overhead, like the footsteps of a bewildered giant. The crowd grew suddenly silent; their gleaming eyes rolled and glanced to and fro.

Jordan felt curiously detached. He knew he would be in the same state as these people, if he didn't know who the Heaven hooks wanted. But they wanted him; knowing that made his mind wonderfully clear. He was sure he was as afraid as anyone here, but his fear was focused and sharp. He knew the thudding steps above were the gropings of a god that was determined to take the manor apart stone by stone until it found him.

August stammered. "Last I saw, she was being held by Linden's men. They suspect her of killing Yuri!"

"Killing Yuri? That makes no sense!"

A giant roaring collapse took place somewhere above. It shook dust from the ceiling. People had begun to talk again, and this silenced them.

Jordan strove to compose himself. It seemed everything that went wrong in his life did so when he lost control. He folded his arms across his chest, closed his eyes, and tried his breathing exercises. With an effort he began mentally reciting one of the nonsense mantras Calandria had taught him.

He would have to leave the building. The Heaven hooks would get him for sure, but it sounded like it was just a matter of minutes anyway before they dug down to where he was now.

Once he came to this decision, he felt calmer. He opened his eyes.

August stood near him, eyes downcast. Only now did Jordan notice the bags he was carrying.

"These are Calandria's!" He fingered the strap of one.

"Yes, I was carrying them because . . . well, never mind."

"Give them to me!"

August did so without complaint. He seemed relieved, in fact, to be free of the responsibility.

Jordan sat down on the cold flagstones and began rooting through the bags. His mind was racing, spinning between the terrible feeling that he was somehow responsible for this disaster and a hope that he might be able to set it right.

"August, what do the Heaven hooks look like to you?"

August shook his head dumbly.

"Come on! What do they look like? Animals?"

"No."

"Trees?"

"Almost . . . no. They are what they are, Jordan."

"Do they look like mechanisms?"

August frowned, then nodded.

Jordan had found what he was looking for. "Listen, August, when Calandria and I were on our way here, we stopped one night in a manse of the Winds. We slept there, unmolested."

"Impossible."

"I thought so, too. I didn't want to go in." Jordan half rose and poked August in the spot where the man had been run through. "Remember this? The wound that nearly killed you *last night*? That's now gone? Calandria May has more tricks than that. One of them is this." He held up the gauze they had used to avoid the mecha in the manse, and he told August how they had used it.

He had the man's attention now. "I swear to you," Jordan said, "the Heaven hooks are after me! I'm not Calandria's servant or Axel's apprentice. I'm just a workman. But I've been cursed, and the Winds are after me. They're tearing the manor house apart because I'm down here! If I leave, they'll stop."

"If that's true . . ." August didn't finish, but Jordan knew what he was thinking. August believed him. It was best for Jordan to go out there, and if he wouldn't go voluntarily, he should be forced. And yet, from the look on August's face, he had no love for the idea.

Could it be that August felt some sort of loyalty to Jordan because he had saved the man's life? Ridiculous. Other people were worthy of such admiration, but Jordan knew he was not.

He had no time to think about that now. Renewed crashings sounded above them, as did deep thuds that seemed to be coming nearer. "Listen," he shouted over the din, "Lady May says mecha are a kind of machine. If the Heaven hooks are like the mecha, maybe this will hide me from them."

"Then they will go berserk for sure," said August. "But anyway, the Winds are different from live things, and different from machines."

Jordan shook his head. "Maybe, maybe not. Anyway, I've got no intention of just disappearing." He told August his plan.

THOUSANDS OF KILOMETERS above Ventus, a thing like a bird sculpted in liquid metal heard Calandria's call. The *Desert Voice* was named for the voice of conscience that had driven Calandria from the employ of the men who had trained her. The *Voice* knew the origin of her name and was proud of it and of her mistress. When she heard Calandria's call she was nearly over the horizon, following her orbit; she instantly reversed thrust. A bright star appeared in the skies over Ventus.

The *Voice* had been sailing a very quiet sky. There was no radio traffic from the surface of Ventus except for localized tight beams between the vagabond moons and the Diadem swans. The swans themselves were invisible, wrapped in radar-proof cloaks. They knew the *Voice* was there, but the starship had been discreet after dropping Calandria and Axel off.

They were about to become very interested in the *Desert Voice*.

She broke orbit entirely and dropped to hover directly over the Boros estate at an altitude of two hundred kilometers. The fire from her exhaust pierced the ionosphere and created an auroral spike visible over the horizon. To the survivors huddled in the ruins of the Boros estate, the vagabond moon that eclipsed the sky glowed faintly for a moment.

"She's here," said Calandria.

The *Voice* assessed the situation. The aerostat between her and her mistress was a big one: two kilometers in diameter, composed of a thin carbon-filament skeleton covered with quasi-biological skin. It was surrounded by a haze of ionized air, which it created and directed around itself to control its movement. It was completely empty except for a ring of storage tanks and gantries in its belly, which was of insignificant mass compared to the lift the sun-warmed air inside it gave.

It stood five hundred meters above Calandria's position. The *Voice* could see it straining to maintain its place: lightning shot from its waist, and a vast electrical potential roved its skin, pulling the air about. It was creating its own weather, and it would have to lift soon or the instabilities would drag it into the ground.

The *Voice* reviewed her options. Eliminating the aerostat without having it fall on Calandria was going to be tricky. She could send a nuke into the center of the thing and blow it to smithereens, but a lot of the debris would fall on the mistress. Better to blow a hole in its side—but a quick calculation told her that the aerostat could stay on station for many minutes despite huge structural damage, simply because it would take a while for the warm air inside to be replaced by outside air.

She could nuke a spot some miles *above* the aerostat. The updraft would loft it into the stratosphere . . . but might also tear it in half.

Her thoughts were interrupted as, all across the sky, the Diadem swans threw aside their cloaks and came for her.

"GOOD-BYE, AUGUST," SAID Jordan. They shook hands. August looked grim.

"I think I'll see you again, Jordan," he said. "You're a mad fool, and such people have a way of surviving."

Jordan laughed. His heart was hammering. "I hope you're right!" He turned and stepped out the servants' door.

The grounds of the estate were lit by fires and the savage beams of lantern light cast by the hooks. Jordan ran with Calandria's magic gauze wrapped about himself, and though he passed close to several of the vast armatures, none moved in his direction. They continued pounding at the ruins of the manor. He could see very few people. Only here and there survivors huddled under the shelter of trees, or in archways. They watched the approach of the metal arms of the hooks with increasing apathy.

Jordan tripped through deep gouges and ran around uprooted trees and fallen blocks until he reached the middle of the field, where he had first stopped to look up at the hooks. There was rubble all the way out here, a hundred meters from the house.

He didn't give himself time to think, just threw aside the gauze and screamed at the sky, "Here I am, you bastards!"

For a moment nothing happened. Then he saw the great arms that had buried themselves in the manor were lifting up and out. And above him, a pinpoint of light began to grow into a beacon, as something new fell toward him.

"Oh, shit," he whispered. He had been hoping he was wrong, that the hooks were here to avenge someone else's transgression.

A wind blew up suddenly, carrying with it a strong smell like air after a thunderstorm. Dust and smoke swirled up and began to wrap around the base of the vagabond moon.

Certain he had their attention, Jordan wrapped himself in the gauze again and ran for the trees.

A big metal crane slammed into the spot where he had been standing. The impact threw Jordan off his feet, but he was up and running again in a second. He heard the thing thrashing and digging behind him, but though his shoulders itched with expectation, nothing grabbed him. He made it to the edge of the forest, then paused to look back.

Several arms now hunted over the grass. None were coming after him. Better yet, those limbs that had been demolishing the manor were gone, lifted back up into the belly of the moon. The thunderstorm smell was stronger, though, and fierce, and conflicting gusts of wind blew across the treetops. The moon seemed to be hanging lower and lower in the sky.

Jordan had run for the screen of trees that separated the road from the grounds. He stood at the entrance to a pathway that he knew led to the stone trough at the side of the road.

He unwound the gauze. "Hey!" he shouted, waving his arms over his head. "Over here!"

The questing arms rose into the air and silently swung in his direction.

He covered up and stepped into the shelter of the trees.

"It's moving away," Axel observed. He and Calandria stood with some others watching the departure of the arms that had harried the manor. In the sudden silence he could hear the shouts and screams of trapped and injured people. Blocks of stone still fell from the sky at intervals, so everyone's attention was directed upward; few people were moving to help the injured.

It did seem like the aerostat was moving away, and the strong winds were probably the reason. Along with the smoke Axel smelled ozone. Electrostatic propulsion? Probably.

"Think the *Voice* scared it?"

Calandria shook her head. "I doubt it. Anyway, we've seen no sign. Maybe it decapitated the aerostat, though; we might not know until it hit the ground. As soon as it's far enough away I'll call the *Voice* and check."

Axel nodded. He returned his attention to ground level. A shame. A real shame. "Our first priority is to help these people," he said. "There's still some trapped in the rubble."

"I'll dig," she said. "You'd better sit down."

He looked down at himself. He was covered in blood, with open cuts up and down his torso. He hurt all over, too.

"Yes," he said as he lowered himself onto a stone. "I think I'd better."

Jordan made it to the highway. He was out of breath and covered in sweat, but the hooks hadn't caught him yet. From here on the countryside was open, which could pose a problem; but he remembered the golden monster in the manse reaching around him to pick up shattered wood after he had merely raised the gauze. It had not seen him even though he was right in front of it. By now he was fairly sure the hooks would not spot him even in open country, as long as he had this protection.

He would make for the forest. It was a day or two's travel away, but he wouldn't feel he could rest until he was under the trees, gauze or no gauze. And then, if he survived, he would try to find his way home.

Or would he? He had started walking, but paused now. He might lose the Heaven hooks for a while, but something else would come after him in time. The Winds were everywhere. He had only delayed the inevitable— unless he were to wear this accursed cloth for the rest of his life and shun any community that the Hooks might dismantle to reach him.

Jordan realized that if he survived, it was going to be as an outcast unless he was willing to risk everyone around him. Was that how he was going to end his days? Hiding from god and man alike in the forest?

He lowered his head and wept as he ran.

A FEW MINUTES later there was a brilliant flash of light in the sky, like sheet lightning but as bright as the sun. A few seconds later, a violent *bang* and grumble of thunder sounded.

The vagabond moon had lit up like a lantern in the flash. In the aftermath of the thunder, Calandria and Axel stood from their digging to watch as the moon dipped lower, until its base disappeared behind the trees. Then it seemed to crumple like the finest tissue, even as it continued to move east. Over the next few minutes it spent itself across the fields, in a trail of girders and torn skin many miles long. There were no fires, no explosions, and only faint distant rumblings as it fell.

It came down closer to Jordan, and he saw the bottom ring with its mouth full of hooks touch the earth and shatter, spilling stone blocks, trees, and human figures. Many of those figures lived and struggled free of the wreckage; the moon had not fallen straight down, but glided slowly into the earth at an angle. Most of those alive when it hit were still alive afterward.

Jordan saw this, but he could not stop, because he could not be sure some new horror would not follow. He continued walking, nursing a stitch in his side. If he could not go home because of the voices in his head; and if Calandria May was wrong about Armiger, as he had begun to suspect; and if even she could not prevent the Heaven hooks from coming after him; then he would have to find help elsewhere.

He was no longer walking east. His goal now lay to the southwest.

WHEN THE AEROSTAT had finished falling, Calandria May knelt down, closed her eyes, and signaled her ship. Axel watched as her brows knit, and she frowned. She remained kneeling for longer than he thought should be necessary. When she opened her eyes, she looked at him with an expression of tired acceptance.

"The *Desert Voice* doesn't answer," she said. "I'm afraid, Axel, that we may be stranded."

PART TWO

The Wife of the World

14

... WE SHALL WIN *new feelings, superior to love and loyalty, from the field of the human heart.*

General Lavin put down the book, and rubbed his eyes. It was late. He should be sleeping, but instead he kept returning to these damnable pages, to stare at words written both by a familiar hand and an alien mind.

Distant sounds of crackling fires, canvas flapping, and quiet grumbled conversation reassured him. His army sprawled around him, thousands of men asleep or, like him, uneasy in darkness. Lavin felt a tension in the air; the men knew they were close to battle, and while no one was happy, they were at least satisfied that waiting would soon be over.

He had closed the book four times this evening, and every time began pacing the narrow confines of his tent until, drawn equally by loathing and hope, he returned to it. The things Queen Galas said in this, a collection of private letters liberated from one of her experimental towns, were worse than heresies—they attacked basic human decency. Yet, Lavin's memories of her from court were so strong, and so at odds with the picture these writings suggested, that he was half convinced they were someone else's, attributed to her.

This was the hope that kept him returning to the book—that he would discover some proof in the writing that these were not the writings of the queen of Iapysia. He wanted to believe she was isolated, perhaps even imprisoned in her palace, and that some other, evil cabal was running the country.

But the turns of phrase, the uncanny self-assurance of the voice that spoke in this pages; they were undeniably hers.

He sighed, then sat down in a folding camp-chair. He was having more nights like this, as the siege lengthened and Galas continued to refuse to surrender. The strain was showing in his face. In the lamplit mirror his eyes were hollows, and lines stood out around his mouth. Those lines had not been there last summer.

Some kind of discussion broke out in front of his tent. Lavin frowned at the tent flap. They'd wake the dead with those voices. He cared for his men, but sometimes they behaved like barbarians.

"Sir? Sorry to disturb you, sir."

"Enter." The flap flipped aside, and Colonel Hesty entered. The colonel wore riding gear, and his collar was open to the autumn air. He looked haggard. Lavin tried to take some satisfaction in that: he was not the only one who found it hard to sleep tonight.

"What is it?" Lavin did not make to rise, nor did he offer Hesty a seat. He realized he had spoken in a certain upper-class drawl he was usually at pains to disguise from his men. They seemed to think it was effete. With a grimace, he sat up straighter.

"They've found something. Over in the quarry." Something in the way he said it caught Lavin's full attention.

"What do you mean, 'found something'? A spy?"

Hesty shook his head. "No. Not . . . a man. Well, sort of a man."

Lavin rolled his head slowly and was rewarded as his neck cracked. "I know it's late, Hesty, and one's vocabulary becomes strained at such times. But could you expand on that a little?" He reached for his coat, which he had carelessly slung across the back of a chair.

Hesty raised one eyebrow. "It's hard to explain, sir. I'd rather show you." He was almost smiling.

Lavin joined him outside. The air was cool, but not yet cold. Autumn came late and gently on the edge of the desert; south, in the heart of the land, it never came at all.

South and west lay the experimental towns, now mostly razed. Flashes of memory came unbidden to Lavin, and he suppressed them with a shudder. "It's hard to sleep, now that we're so close," he said.

Hesty nodded. "Myself as well. That's why I think a little mystery might do you some good. I mean, a different kind of mystery."

"Does this have to do with the queen?"

"No. At least, only very indirectly. Come." Hesty grinned and gestured at two horses who waited patiently nearby.

Lavin shook his head, but mounted up. He could see the palace over the peak of the tent. Looking away from that, he tried to find the path to the quarry. The valley was a sea of tents, some lit by the faint glow of fires. Columns of gray smoke rose from the sea and disappeared among the stars.

Hesty led. Lavin watched his back swaying atop the horse, and mused about sleep. Some nights he struggled with exhaustion like an enemy, and got nowhere. Maybe Hesty did the same thing, a surprising thought; Lavin respected the man, would even be a bit afraid of him were their positions not so firmly established, he the leader, Hesty the executor. After one battle, he remembered, Hesty's sword arm had been drenched in blood. Lavin had killed a man himself and felt proud and ashamed, as one does, until he saw Hesty. Hesty had been grim, his mind bent to the task of securing the town—unconcerned with himself. There was a lesson in that.

It was possible the man was acting that way now—simply doing his duty to try to ensure a night's distraction for his commanding officer. Lavin smiled. It might work, too. Sometimes the only way to win the struggle with insomnia was to let it carry you for a while—ride it like he rode this horse.

As they left the camp, he found his thoughts drifting. The movement of the horse lulled him, though it was a hard rocking from side to side, never subtle, not swaying the body like a dancer swayed. Which made him think of dancers; how long had it been since he had attended a dance? Months. Years? Couldn't be. No one seemed to host them anymore. None like the one where he had first seen Princess Galas, anyway. It wasn't hard to believe that was twenty years ago—easier to believe it was a hundred.

Swaying was how he had first seen her. She was finishing a dance. At that time she could have been no more than seventeen, a year or two younger than himself. He had stood in a corner with some friends, plucking at his collar. They had all craned their necks to try to locate this storied mad princess in the moving maze of dancing couples. When she did appear it was very nearby, as the song broke up—she curtsied, laughing to her older partner. He bowed, and she spoke to him briefly. They drifted apart as the next dance began.

She stood nearby, miraculously alone. This baron's hall held easily a thousand people, and all had to meet her, or be seen to try for etiquette's sake. Her father's spies would know who did and did not pay her compliments. She, like any princess, was a vessel for his favor. Lavin saw her sigh now, then close her eyes briefly. *She wants to recover her poise,* he thought.

His friends huddled together. "Let's meet her!" "Lavin, shall we?"

"We shall not!" He said it a bit too loudly, and she looked up, her eyes widening just a bit. For the first time Lavin had realized she might have come to rest here because his was the only group of people at the ball near her own age. Everyone else was middle-aged or older, a fact that had been making Lavin's group squirm.

So he smiled and bowed to her, then said, "*We* shall not meet the princess. If she wishes, the princess will meet *us.*"

She smiled. Galas was willowy, with large dark eyes and a determined thrust to her chin. She held herself well in her formal ball dress; Lavin envied her such poise. But she was of royal blood, after all. He was merely noble.

His companions had frozen like rabbits caught in a garden. Lavin was about to step forward, say something else ingenuous (although he seemed to have exhausted his cleverness with that one statement) when suddenly Galas was surrounded by courtiers. They had rushed, without seeming to rush, around the edge of the dance floor, and homed in on her like falcons.

Galas became caught in a tangle of clever opening lines. They led her, without seeming to lead her, away to the lunch tables. Lavin stared after her, not heeding decorum.

When they had almost reached the tables, she turned and glanced back. At him.

He would always remember that moment, how happy he had been. Something had begun.

Harsh shouts ahead. Lavin opened his eyes. Hesty had led them to a deep gash in one of the hills near the city. Here, under the lurid light of bonfires, gangs of prisoners labored through the night to create missiles for their steam cannons.

Lavin and Hesty dismounted, and the colonel led him into the pit, where captured royalists cursed and wept on the stones they were chiseling, while Lavin's men whipped them.

Over the years workers had taken a large bite out of the hillside. The layers below proved to be made of salt. Lavin had not been here before, and he marveled at the cleanness of the carved walls. In daylight they would probably glow white. The whole place stank of oceanside. The scent made him smile.

The salt was precious, and the entire site was under guard because his men wanted to walk off with the stuff. They had tried quarrying for proper stone but it was a good distance underground. Lavin wanted a heap of rock the size of a house near his cannons when it came time to fire on the city. The salt was available; precious or not, he would use it. His men could collect the shards off the street later and buy their own rewards with it. Lavin couldn't buy what he wanted, so he was indifferent to its lure.

"It's over here!" One of the overseers waved at them from across the pit. A large crowd had gathered there, numbering both soldiers and prisoners. The prisoners showed no fear, but glanced up at Lavin with frank eyes as he strode past. Their attitude made him uncomfortable—they were her creations, and he didn't understand them.

"Sir!" The overseer saluted hastily. His broad belly gleamed with sweat in the torchlight. He stood over a large slab of white salt, perhaps twice the length and width of a man, and at least half a meter thick. Two brawny soldiers were brushing delicately at its surface with paint brushes.

Lavin cocked his head skeptically and looked at Hesty and then the overseer. "You got me up in the middle of the night for this?"

"Sir. Look!" The overseer pointed. Lavin stepped up to the slab.

There was a man buried in it. The outline of a man, anyway, blurred and distorted, visible through the pale milky crystals. Lavin stepped back in shock, then moved in again, repelled but fascinated.

"Where . . ."

"The whole slab came off the face over there," the overseer pointed, "about two hours ago. Killed the man it fell on. When they went to get him they thought he'd climbed out and died on top of the thing—they saw the outline, see? But his leg was sticking out from underneath." He laughed richly. "Three legs was a bit unlikely, eh. So they looked closer.

Then they called me. And . . ." He seemed to run out of steam. "I called the colonel."

Hesty traced the outline of the figure with his fingertip. "We have the quarry foreman. He thinks the layers we're working in were laid down eight hundred years ago, by the desals."

Lavin lifted whitened fingers to his face. The sea. "So at that time, this area was a salt flat? How then did it become hilly?"

"Mostly runoff, but this is more of an underground salt mountain than a flat. Otherwise the whole area for kilometers would be mined. But sir: look at this."

Below, and a little to the right of the body, a dark line transected the crystal block. "What is it?"

The soldier, Lavin saw, wore some kind of uniform. He could make out the bandoliers. And poking over his shoulder was, unmistakably, the barrel of a musket.

Lavin caught his breath. Muskets were the property of the royal guard. Always had been, as far as he knew . . . and he was right. Even so many generations ago, Iapysia had been exactly as it was when Lavin was a boy. And then came Galas, to break all the ancient traditions and bring her people to ruin.

Something else glinted in the torchlight. He bent closer to examine what might be the soldier's hand. "More light. Bring some hurricane lanterns here. I want to see it." People hurried to obey. Lavin heard Hesty chuckle behind him.

Yes, your distraction worked, Hesty, he thought. *Be smug about it if you want.*

When they had brought the lanterns Lavin took another good look. He was right: preserved in the salt, wrapped around the withered finger of the soldier, was a silver ring.

He stood back, knuckled his eyes and was rewarded by a salty sting. "I want that."

"Sir? . . ."

"The ring. Get it off the corpse. Bring it to me." He blinked around at the men. They looked uniformly uncomfortable.

"I'm not grave robbing. We'll return it to him after the siege, and accord him full honors as a member of the king's guard when we inter him. But this ring is a powerful symbol of the continuity of the dynasty. Think about it. I want it on my hand when I ride into battle."

With that he turned away to remount his horse.

Back in his tent he prepared for bed. Something told him he would sleep this time. His lamp still burned above the camp table, and as he bundled his shirt to use as a pillow, his eye was drawn to Galas's book, which still sat open to the passage he had read earlier.

Lavin marveled that he had been so mesmerized by the words. Now, the book beckoned again, and he wondered if Hesty's distraction had been enough to break the spell it had cast over him. He hesitated; then, when he realized he was acting like he was afraid of the thing, he stalked over quickly and bent to read:

An ancient sage held that in different ages, humans held the senses in different ratios, according to the media by which they communicated and expressed themselves. Hence, before writing, the ear was the royal sense. After writing, the eye.

We say that similar ratios pertain between emotions. Each civilization has its royal affect and its ignored or forgotten feelings. Or rather—there are no distinct emotions. You have learned that in the human heart, love resides within such and such a circle, hate there in another, and between are pride, jealousy, all the royal and plebeian emotions. We say instead emotion is one unbounded field. Our way of life causes us to cross this field, now in one direction, now another, again and again on our way to the goals to which our world has constrained us. The paths crisscross, and eventually the field has well-traveled intersections and blank areas where we have never walked.

We name the intersections just as we do towns but not the empty fields between them. We name these oft-crossed places love, hate, jealousy, pride. But our destinations were made by the conditions of our lives, they are not eternal or inevitable.

We know that the answer to human suffering lies in changing the ratio of emotions so grief and sorrow lie neglected, even nameless, in an untraveled wild.

The task of a queen is to rule a people truly. The task of the Queen of Queens is to rule truth itself. We know that the highest act of creation is to create new emotions, superior to those that, unguided, have fallen to us from Nature. And this We shall do.

As We have won new fields and towns from Nature, We shall win new feelings, superior to love and loyalty, from the field of the human heart.

Lavin closed the book.

Hesty had done him more of a favor than he might know. Despite all he knew about the queen's excesses, and even after all the atrocity and hatred he had seen during the war, Lavin still had his doubts. She had been his queen . . . and more.

The night stars and the rounded hills reminded him now of permanence. Thinking of the ancient soldier they had found, he remembered that those same stars had gazed down upon his ancestors, and they would smile on his descendents, who because of him would speak the same tongue and live their lives as he would prefer to live his. Things would again be as they once had been. He had to believe that.

A messenger coughed politely at the flap of the tent. Lavin took a small cloth bundle from him, and unfolded it to reveal the soldier's ring. It was shaped like a carven wreath, the tiny flowers still embedded with salt crystals like dull jewels. He sat on his cot for a long while, turning it over and over in his hands.

Then he put it on and blew out the light. He felt calm for the first time in days. As he drifted off to sleep, Lavin felt his confidence return, flowing from the immeasurable weight of the ages lying heavy in his hand.

BELOW AND BEHIND them, a horse nickered in the dark. Armiger glanced back—though Megan could not fathom how he could see anything in that shadowed hollow. Their horses were no doubt safe, but Armiger had to assure himself of everything.

They crouched on a hilltop overlooking the besieged summer palace of the queen of Iapysia. The palace was dark, a blot of towers against the sky, sinuous walls hugging the earth. The pinprick sparks of campfires surrounded the city on all sides. Thousands of men waited in the darkness below this hill, and Armiger had earlier pointed out pickets on the surrounding hills as well. This hill's sentry watched the palace a hundred meters below the spot where Armiger and Megan hid.

"I count ten thousand," Armiger said. He squirmed forward through the sand, obviously enjoying himself. Megan sat back, brushing moist grit from the cloak she sat on.

"It's sandy here," she said.

"We're right on the edge of the desert," Armiger said absently. He cocked his head to look at the hills to either side.

"Who would build a city in a desert?"

"The desals flood the desert every spring," he said. "The Iapysians seed it in anticipation of the event, and harvest what comes out. The desals are using the desert as a salt trap and don't really mind if the humans introduce life there. It probably saves them some trouble, in fact. A good arrangement, so Iapysia has thrived for centuries."

"Then why's it all coming apart?" She tried again to count the fires, but they flickered so much she quickly lost track.

"Galas."

There was that name again. It seemed a name to conjure by. If she breathed it too loudly, would those ten thousand men stand as one? Ten thousand hostile gazes turn on her? The queen was bottled up in that palace down there, and in days or hours they were going to storm its walls and kill her. Megan mouthed the name, but nothing seemed to happen.

"Is it rescue you are planning?" she asked. "What will you do, ride in and ask for her? 'Pardon me, coming through, would you hand me the queen, please.'" She smiled.

"Rescue? No, I'm sure she'll die when they take the place."

"Then why are we here?"

"Not so loud."

"Excuse me." She placed a finger over her mouth, and whispered past it, "Why are we here?"

Armiger sighed. "I just want to speak to her."

"Before or after they kill her?"

"They have the palace well surrounded," he said. "Withal, I'm sure I could reach the walls; after all, they're watching for the approach of a large armed force or for sallies from inside. The trouble is, how to get inside."

"Once *you're* there?"

He rolled over to look at her. It was too dark to see, but she pictured a puzzled expression on his face. "Why do *you* want to get into the palace?"

"You are an inconsiderate lout."

"What?"

"You're going to leave me here where the soldiers can find me?"

"Ah." He stared into the sky for a moment. "Perhaps you had better come with me, then."

Megan growled her frustration and stood. She grabbed up her cloak and stalked down the hill. After a moment she heard him following.

Armiger was without a doubt the most insensitive man she had ever known. She tried to forgive him, because he wasn't an ordinary person— but she had always assumed the Winds were better than people. Armiger, strange morph that he was, was worse much of the time.

Men, after all, were usually wrapped up in their own schemes and thought about the things that mattered rarely if at all. She was used to having to prod them into remembering the basic duties of life. Armiger, though! On the day she took him in, Megan had taken on a responsibility and burden greater than any woman should have to bear. For it quickly became evident that Armiger was not really a man. He was a spirit, perhaps a Wind, one of the creators of the world.

Many times during the week-long ride here, he had gone from seeming abstracted to being totally oblivious to the world. He had leaned in the saddle, eyes blank, slack jawed. This sort of thing terrified her. He forgot to eat, forgot to let the horses rest. She had to do his thinking for him.

Megan had come to understand that Armiger needed his body as an anchor. Without it, his soul would drift away into some abstraction of rage. She had to remind him of it constantly, be his nurse, cook, mother, and concubine. When he rediscovered himself—literally coming to his senses—he displayed tremendous passion and knowledge, uncanny perception and even, yes, sensitivity. He was a wonderful lover, the act never became routine for him. And he was grateful to her for her devotion.

But, oh, the work she had to do to get to that point! It was almost too much to bear.

She had thrown her lot in with him, and this was still infinitely better than the loneliness of rural widowhood she had left. Fuming about him was an improvement over brooding about herself or the past. He was coming to appreciate her, and the vast walls of his self-possession were starting to crumble. She was proud that she was making the difference to him.

Surprisingly, she felt jealous of this queen, as if the great lady might steal her mysterious soldier. Well; anyone could be stolen, and as likely by a peasant as a princess. She found herself frowning, and resolutely pushed the thought away.

She reached the horses and murmured reassurances to them. They had lit no fire tonight, and the darkness was unsettling. Megan was used to the presence of trees, but they had seen the last of the forest days ago. She felt naked amongst all this yellow damp grass.

She heard him coming up behind her, and she smiled as she turned. Armiger was black moving on black, his head an absence of stars.

"We need help from inside. We have to get a message to the queen," he said.

Megan crossed her arms skeptically. She knew he could see her. She just looked at him, saying nothing.

"There is a way," he said. "It will weaken me."

"What do you mean?" She reached quickly to touch his arm.

"I can send a messenger," he said. "It will take some of my ... life force, if you will, with it. With luck, we can recover that later. If not, I will take some time to heal."

"So my careful nursing is being thrown out with the dishwater? I don't understand! Why is this so important? What can she give you that matters? She's doomed, and her kingdom, too."

He stepped into her embrace and smoothed his hands down her back awkwardly. Armiger was still not very good at reassurance.

"She is the only human being on Ventus who has some inkling of what the Winds really are," he said. "She has spent her reign defying them, and I believe she has asked questions, and received answers, that no one else has thought of. She may have the key to what I am seeking."

"Which is?"

He didn't answer, which was no less than she had expected. Armiger had some purpose beyond any he had told her about. For some reason he didn't trust her with it, which hurt. If it were something that would take him away from her, she should worry, but Megan was sure that as long as he could hold her, his other purposes mattered little. She closed her eyes and clung to him tightly for a while.

"What do you have to do?" she asked when she finally let go.

"Will you keep watch for me? This will take all my concentration."

"All right."

He sat down and vanished in the shadow.

"I can't see. How can I keep watch?"

He didn't answer.

For a while Megan moved about, fighting her own exhaustion and worrying about what he was up to. She stood and stared up at the stars for a long time, remembering how she had done that as a child. The constellations had names, she knew, and everyone knew the obvious ones: the plowman, the spear. Others she was not so sure of. Her brother would know, but she had not seen him in years; he had never left their parents' village and lived there still with his unfriendly wife and four demanding, incurious children.

How strange to be here. She repressed an urge to skip and laugh at the strange turns life took. The day when she found Armiger half dead on the path near her cottage had started just like any other. Before she knew it, she was nurse to a wounded, emaciated soldier, listening to him rave in the night about the Winds and gods . . . and three days later she awoke in awe to the fact that he was so much more than a soldier, more than a man.

And he had let her come with him. They were, at least for now, a couple. It was as though she were suddenly living someone else's life. She shook her head in wonder.

A gleam of red in one of the horse's eyes brought her attention back to ground level. At first she thought Armiger had lit a fire, but the glow was too small and faint for that. She went over to him and crouched down.

Armiger sat cross-legged, his eyes closed. His hands were cupped together in front of him, and the glow came from between his fingers.

Seeing this, Megan stood and backed away. "Don't," she whispered. "Please. You're still too weak."

He made no move. The glow intensified, then slowly faded away. When it was completely gone, he stood up, hands still cupped. Then in a quick motion he flung his arms up and wide and brought them down again loosely. His shoulders slumped.

"There," he said. "Now we wait."

"What have you done?" She took one of his hands. The skin felt hot, and there were long bloodless cuts in his palms.

"I have called the queen," said Armiger. "Now we will see if she answers."

15

GALAS WAITED IN her garden. It was a cool night, the air laden with water after evening thunderstorms. Their clouds still mounted up one horizon, giant wings lit by occasional flickers of lightning. The rest of the sky was clear, and stars were thrown across it in random swatches. The moon had not yet risen, but the night flowers were opening all around her, giant purple and blue mouths appearing from dense hedges that ringed deep pools. The garden was made around its pools, each one isolated by some artifice of growth so that it seemed a world unto itself, and a thousand years of tradition had dictated as many rules for its seeming disarray as the queen had for her court.

She had decided to pause beside a long rectangular pool. Diadem, the moon, would rise directly above this pool tonight; that was what this pool was for, to catch the rays of its light on this and the following two nights of the year, to prove that harvest time was over. Throughout the rest of the year it was tended carefully by men and women whose lives were dedicated to the garden, but who would never see this nocturnal vision. All the night flowers would bow to Diadem, all transformed at the critical moment into a magical court, the queen herself its centerpiece. She loved this pool, and this garden, as few other places in her land.

She pulled her shift around her and delicately sat on the stone bench that was hers and hers alone to sit upon. Her maids had woven diamonds into her pale hair, in anticipation of the lunar light; her shift was purest white, belted with onyx squares, and she carried in her right hand her short staff of office, carved of green jade.

Queen Galas smiled at the placid water. Total silence blanketed the garden. She knew quite well that Lavin was encamped within sight of the garden walls, but he was forbidden to attack on this and the next two nights by ancient custom more strict than law. It was the Autumn Affirmation and war was forbidden for its duration. It was a fine irony, she thought, that she should have this time to prepare for his coming. She smiled at the pool's beauty. Aware as she was that death and ruin lay in wait outside her gates, she marveled that such peace should maintain itself within.

"Flowers will grow on your grave, too," she said to herself. "The moon also smiles on slaves and cripples."

The smile broke, and she lowered her eyes.

For a long time she sat like that. When she looked up again, Diadem was fully visible, like a brilliant jewel held aloft by the arms of carefully tended trees. Its reflection came slowly down the water toward her, lighting up the curves of bole and stem and creating that lovely illusion of animation that happened only once every year. She had missed the beginning of the event. She frowned a chastisement to herself and sat up straighter.

But a flaw had appeared in the full whiteness of the moon. She stood up quickly, as it resolved into a giant black night moth, two hand spans across, of the sort that inhabited the mountains many days east of the palace. It dropped from the moon and fluttered across the surface of the pool, directly to Queen Galas. It paused in the air before her.

She sat down. "What do you want, little one?"

It dipped down, then up, and then appearing to gather its courage, landed on her knee. She had never feared insects and sat admiring it, trying to pretend it was some sort of omen. That was no good, though—she was well past the stage where omens could tell her anything she didn't know. Lavin was coming; nothing would change that.

The moth beat its wings, but didn't rise. Suddenly it seemed to sprout another pair of wings, and then it gave one flap and . . . unfolded.

She blinked at the single sheet of paper that now lay on her lap.

Galas's fingers trembled as she reached to touch it. The sheet was square, smooth and dry, and slightly warm. Writing was faintly visible on it.

The skin of her neck crawled. She had never seen anything like this, never heard of such an occurrence. The morphs could change animals, she knew, but they didn't understand writing. Could this be a message from some new Wind, whom she had never met? Or had the desals, the Winds who had helped her take the throne, decided to intervene again in her life?

She picked up the letter by one corner, and turned it to the moonlight. She read.

May I humbly beseech Queen Galas, wife of this world, to grant an audience to a traveler? For I have not rested on green earth since before the ancient stones of your palace were laid, nor have I spoken to a kindred soul since before your language, O Queen, was born.

I came as a falling star down your sky and now feel again what it is to breathe. I would speak to one such as myself, whose eyes encompass this whole world, for I am lonely and own a question even the heavens cannot answer.

Signed: Maut.

Below this was another line of text. She read it and shook her head in wonder. Here were clear instructions as to how she could meet this being who had written her. Meet him or her tonight.

Galas looked up, wondering if she would catch sight of a trail of light across the skies. She looked at the paper in her hand. *Of course I will speak with you.*

She restrained an urge to leap from the bench and race inside. Whom could she tell? Her heart was thudding and she was suddenly light-headed. She buried her face in her hands for a moment. She breathed faint rain-scent from the paper she still held.

Galas commanded herself to become calm. She turned her attention back to the pool. All along its edge now waited handsome and graceful courtiers, fair and clothed in dewdrops and ivy. The garden's plants were cultivated just so they would appear this way for a few moments on this night. Ever since she was a girl, she had marveled at the human ingenuity that could create such art, and in the past the sight had served to strengthen her resolve to cultivate her land as though it, too, were a garden.

The shadowy figures all faced toward the rising moon, and the pool appeared like a flow of glass between them, a mirrored way down which Diadem's reflection moved to meet her.

This contemplation was uplifting, but sad this time. She imagined the faces of her real courtiers on these ephemeral shapes and fancied herself the reflection of the moon. All brief, a mere shadow play soon to be ended by the blades and guns of the insolent general waiting outside. One shadow overtaking another.

Fear surged in her, and she closed her eyes. *Stop,* she told herself. *I am not the reflection.* "I am Diadem herself. All things take their light from me." *Even the general who comes to kill me.*

She looked down at the paper and laughed a little giddily.

Then she stood to go inside.

THE ROOM WHERE she chose to wait was really an old air shaft con-structed to cool the Hart Manor, which was the center of the palace. Originally several other floors had openings onto the shaft, but some paranoid ancestor had walled them off. Galas had discovered the place as a girl, but it had gained new, symbolic significance for her after the desals placed her on the throne.

She came here sometimes to pace the three-by-three-meter square floor, or scrawl insults on the walls, or scream at the clouds framed by tan brickwork far overhead. She had torn her clothes here, and wept, and done all manner of unmentionable things. Now she lay on her back and stared at the stars.

Her visitor should be approaching the walls now. Its instructions had been simple: let down a rope at the centerpoint of the southern battle-ment, and be ready to pull. She had wanted to meet it there herself, and even now her hands pressed against the cool stone underneath her, eager to push her to her feet. But whatever happened she must not blunder out like a gauche ingenue. If this was a Wind coming to see her, she must meet it as an equal. She would wait.

But she wasn't dressed for this! With a groan she stood and left the shaft. One of her maids curtsied outside. Galas waved at her. "Our black gown. The velvet one. Be prompt!" The girl curtsied again and raced away.

Galas entered the shaft again and closed the stout door she had made for it. "Why now?" she said.

She kicked the door with her heel. "I'm almost dead! A day, two days." Crossing her arms, she walked around the room. "Bastards! You strung me up, after putting me here in the first place!"

Well, it's not like I haven't done everything in my power to disobey the Winds, she reminded herself.

She'd been wracked with tension for weeks now; so had everyone here. Her courtiers and servants were true Iapysians and had no idea how to discharge such emotions. Galas showed them by example: she laughed, she cried, she paced and shouted, and whenever it came time to make a decision, she was cool and acted correctly.

But it was all too late. Lavin had come to kill her—of all people, why him? She had loved him! They might have been married, had not an entire maze of watchful courtiers and ancient protocols stood between them. She wondered, not for the first time, if this was his way of finally possessing her. She grimaced at the irony.

"Come on, come on." She hurried back to the door. Ah, here came the maids, bearing gown and jewel box.

"Come in here." They hesitated; no one but her ever entered this place. She was sure all manner of legends had grown up about it. "Come! There's nothing will bite you here."

The three women crowded in with her. "Dress me!" She held her arms out. They fell to their task, but their eyes kept moving, trying to make sense of what they saw. Galas sometimes spent whole nights in this place. She often emerged with new ideas or solid decisions in hand. The queen knew, from faint scratches around the hinges of the door, that at least one person had given in to curiosity and broken in. She imagined they had reacted much as these women to discover there was nothing here—no secret stairway, no magic books, not even a chair or a candle. Only a little dirt in the corners and the sky for a ceiling.

They had wondered about Galas her whole life. Let them wonder a little more.

"Has the guest suite been prepared?" she asked.

"Yes, Your Majesty."

"How are the supplies holding out?"

"Well enough, they say."

"Reward the soldiers who bring Our guest over the walls. Give them each a double ration. Also convey Our thanks."

"Yes, Your Majesty. . . . Ma'am?"

"Yes, what is it? Bring me a mirror."

"Who is this person? A spy of some sort?"

"A messenger," she said brusquely. Satisfied with her appearance, she gathered her skirts and swept from the chamber. They followed, casting final glances about the shaft.

Out of a sense of devilment, Galas decided to leave the door open— the first time ever. She hid a smile as she paced toward the audience hall.

As a girl she had made up stories about the figures painted on the audience hall's ceiling. Later she learned the struggling, extravagantly posed men and women were all allegories for historical events. By then it was too late; she knew the woman directly above the throne as the Smitten Dancer, not as an idealized Queen Delina. The two men wrestling on the clouds near the west window were the Secret Lovers to her, not King Andalus overthrowing the False Regent. Every time she entered this room she glanced up and smiled at her pantheon, and she knew that those observing her assumed she was drawing strength from her family's history, and knowing that made her smile again.

She composed herself on the throne and waited. When had she had a visitor who had not closely studied the history of Iapysia? If this stranger was truly from the heavens, would he know whom the frescoes represented? Or would he be in the same state of innocence as she when she wrote her own mythology on them?

Or would he know all histories, the way that the desals had? She scowled and sat up straighter.

The doorman straightened. He looked tired and confused, having been rousted out of bed for this one moment. "Your Majesty . . ." He read the card he had been given with obvious puzzlement. "The Lord Maut, and Lady Megan."

MAUT? MEGAN STOPPED in her tracks. "What name is this?" she hissed at him.

"My name," Armiger said simply. "One of them, anyway." He smiled and strode into the vast, lamp-lit chamber as if he owned it.

GALAS RESTRAINED AN urge to stand. Now that he stood before her, she had no idea what she'd been expecting. This was no monster, nor by appearances a god.

He seemed mature, perhaps in his early forties, his hair long and braided down his right shoulder, his face finely carved with a high brow and straight nose and a strong mouth. He was a little taller than she and was dressed in dusty traveling clothes, with soft riding boots on his feet, an empty scabbard belted at his waist. As he paused four meters below the throne, she saw the light traceries of character around his eyes and mouth, indications of both humor and weariness.

Behind him, like a shadow, stood a peasant woman. Her face shone with a mixture of timidity and defiance. As Maut bowed, she curtsied deeply, but when she raised her eyes she looked Galas in the eye. There was no hostility there, or respect; only, it seemed, unself-conscious curiosity. Galas liked her immediately.

Galas held up the folded letter. "Do you know what this says?" she asked the man.

He bowed again. "I do," he said. His voice was rich and deep, quite compelling. He gave a quick smile. "May I humbly beseech Queen Galas, wife of this world, to grant an audience to a traveler? For I have not rested on green earth since before the ancient stones of your palace were laid, nor have I spoken to a kindred soul since before your language, O Queen, was born."

Galas saw the woman Megan start and stare at Maut as he spoke. Interesting.

"What are you?" she asked. "And—maybe more germaine—why do you speak of me as a kindred soul?"

Maut shrugged. "As to what I am—you have no words for it. I am not a man, despite appearances—"

"What proof do you have of that?"

For a moment he looked angry at her interruption. Then he appeared to consider what she had said. "My moth was unconvincing?"

"There are people who make a life's work of tricking others, Maut. Your moth was highly convincing—but just because something is convincing, that does not make it true. It is merely convincing."

He waved a hand dismissively. "It cost me energy to perform that minor miracle. I have very little to spare, and no time to recover any I lose now."

Galas leaned back. She felt betrayed and suddenly cynical. "So you have no more tricks? Is that what you're saying?"

"I am not a trick pony!"

"And I am not a fool!"

They glared at one another. Then Galas noticed that the woman Megan was covering a smile with her hand.

Galas forced a grim smile of her own. "You know our situation. This is not the time for frippery or lies. Is it so strange that I demand proof?"

Grudgingly, he shook his head. "Forgive me, Queen Galas. I am much reduced from my former station, and that makes me tactless and short-tempered."

"But unafraid," she said. "You are not afraid of me."

"He is not afraid of anything," said Maut's companion. Her tone was not boasting—in fact it was perhaps a little apologetic. Or resigned.

Maut shrugged again. "It seems we've gotten off to a bad start. I am very weary—too weary for miracles. But I am what I say I am."

"But, you have not said what that is!"

He frowned. "There is an ancient word in your language. It is not much used today. The word is *god*. I am—or was—a god. I wish to be so again, and so I have come to you because, of all the humans on Ventus, you are the only one who has caught a glimpse of the inner workings of the world. You may have the knowledge I need to become what I once was."

"Intriguing," said Galas. It was still unbelievable, on the face of it. But . . . her fingers caressed the letter in her lap. She had seen what she had seen.

As to his flattery—well, she knew, as an absolute certainty, that no one in the world had the knowledge she held. It was perhaps slightly charming that he recognized it.

"And why should I tell you what you wish to know—even assuming that I have the knowledge you need?"

Maut put his hands behind his back. He seemed to be restraining an urge to pace. "You have looked up at the sky," he said. "All humans have done that, at one time or another. And you have asked questions.

"You want to interrogate the sky. And you of all people, Queen Galas, would interrogate nature itself, everything that is *other*, in your human search for understanding. Everything you have ever done proves this. You are human, Galas, and your madness is very human: you wish to hear human speech issue from the inhuman, from the rocks and trees. Could a stone speak, what would it say? Your kind has ever invented gods, and governments, and categories and even the sexes themselves as means of interrogating that otherness.

"That the world should speak, as you speak! What a desire that is. It informs every aspect of your life. Deny it if you can.

"Allow me my ironic bow. I am here, madam, to perform this deed for you. I am everything you are not. I was blazing atoms in an artificial star, have been resonances of electromagnetic fire, and cold iron and gridwork machines in vast webs cast between the nebulae.

"I am stone and organism, alive and dead, whole and sundered. I am the voiceless given a tongue to speak.

"I will speak."

AND YET, THE irony was not lost on Armiger that on this world, stones *did* speak; that the very air sighed its voices in his ear. It was the humans who were deaf to the language of the Winds. Armiger, though he heard that language, did not understand it. The sound of his own words was quickly absorbed into the stone of the walls, the ancient tapestries, the lacquered wood cabinets. And in all these things the Winds resided.

Armiger knew they could listen if they chose; he suspected they did not care what he said. The masters of Ventus went on about their incomprehensible tasks, whispering and muttering all around him.

He had spoken half for their benefit, but they ignored him, as they had since he had arrived on Ventus. So, he thought, his words dissolved into the stone, into the carpets, into the wood. Save for the two women who stood with him, none heard his brave boast.

Yet, though none in the palace heard, still his voice went out. It penetrated the chambers and halls of the ancient building and passed through the sand and stone of the earth as if they were an inch of air. In the high clouds from which the raindrop-dwelling Precip Winds gazed down, Armiger's voice flickered as unread heat lightning on a frequency they did not attend. Even the Diadem swans, swirling in a millennial dance within the Van Allen belt, could have heard had they known to listen.

No swan heard, nor did any stone-devouring mountain Wind or any of the elemental and immortal spirits of the world. But a solitary youth, lonely and sad by a campfire, mouthed Armiger's words and sat up straight to listen.

16

Tamsin Germaix spotted the man by the road first. Her uncle was busy talking about some grand ball he'd been to in the capital. Her eyes and hands had been busy all morning on a new piece of embroidery, much more difficult than the last one Uncle had her do. But every now and then (and she hid this from him) she had to stop because her hands began to shake. Now was such a time: she frowned at them, betraying as they were, and looked up to see the man.

The figure was sitting on a rock by the road, hunched over. It would take them a few minutes to pass him, since Uncle was more interested in his story than in speed, and anyway every jolt of the cart sent spikes of pain up Tamsin's sprained ankle. She had the splinted shin encased in pillows and wore a blanket over her lap against the chill morning air; still, she was far from comfortable.

Certainly they had passed farmers and other lowborn persons walking by the road. This track was what passed for a main road in this forsaken part of backward Memnonis. Why, in the past day alone, they'd met three cows and a whole flock of sheep!

"... Hold your knife properly, not the way you did at dinner last night," her uncle was saying. "Are you listening to me?"

"Yes, Uncle."

"There'll be feasts like that again, once we're back home. It'll only be a few days now." He scratched at the stubble on his chin uncertainly. "Things can't have changed that much."

She watched the seated figure over the rounded rump of one of their horses. He looked odd. Not like a farmer at all. First of all, he seemed to be dressed in red, a rare color for the lowborn. Secondly, she could see a fluff of gold around his collar, and at his waist.

"Uncle, there's a strange man on the road ahead."

"Huh?" He came instantly alert. "Only one? Is he waving to us? Ah, I see him."

Uncle Suneil had told her about bandits and how to identify them. This apparition certainly didn't fit that mold.

As they drew closer Tamsin levered herself to her feet and looked down at the man. He seemed young, with black hair and dressed nattily. His clothes, though, were mud spattered and torn, and he had a large leather knapsack over one shoulder. He held a knife in one hand and a piece of half-carved stick in the other. He was whittling.

He stood up suddenly as if in alarm, but he wasn't looking in their direction. He had dropped his knife, and now he picked it up again and started walking away up the road. He seemed to be talking to himself.

"I still think he's a bandit. Or crazy! He must have taken those clothes off of a victim."

Her uncle shook his head. "A proper young lady knows fine tailoring. Look, you'll see his clothes have been made to fit him nicely. Now sit down, before you fall off the wagon."

She sat down. He certainly looked mysterious, but after all, they didn't know who he was. She knew the mature thing to do would be to pass him by; she knit her hands in her lap and waited for her uncle to prod the horses into a faster walk.

Uncle Suneil raised a hand. "Ho, traveler! Well met on the road to Iapysia!"

ALL HE HAD done for two days was walk. Jordan was exhausted now and was beginning to think his journey to meet with Armiger might be impossible. Calandria had bundled food for several people into her saddlebags, but it weighed a lot. He rested when he needed, and he carefully lit a fire before bedding down each night. Despite that, his feet hurt and his shoulders were strained from carrying the heavy bags. So, as midmorning burned away the cold of last night, he sat down on a stone by the side of the road to rest.

He would have given up walking, were it not that whenever he paused to rest, he saw visions of far-off places and knew they were real. Knowing that fed his determination to keep going.

He needed an activity to keep the visions at bay. He had taken to whittling, and now he pulled out a stick he'd begun this morning and began carving away at it, lips pursed.

Last night Jordan had sat rapt at his meager fire as Armiger spoke to Queen Galas. "You wish to hear human speech issue from the inhuman, from the rocks and trees," the general had said. "Could a stone speak, what would it say?" It was almost as though the general knew he was listening.

Armiger had not gone on to tell his story. It was late, and the queen had deferred the audience until some time today. Jordan was not disappointed; he had lain awake for hours, thinking about Armiger's words. He had pushed aside his self-pity and exhaustion and made himself come to a decision. It was time to take the step he had been avoiding.

Despite his private miseries and loneliness, Jordan had not forgotten for a moment that Armiger's was not the only voice he could hear. On the evening when the Heaven hooks descended, Jordan had learned he could hear the voices of the Winds, too. Until this morning he had deliberately tuned them out, because he'd been afraid that at any moment the Heaven hooks would rear out of the empty sky and grab him up.

He had bundled Calandria May's golden gauze into a kind of poncho, then awkwardly buttoned his jacket over that. The gold stuff stuck out behind him like a bird's tail, and up around his neck like a dandy's ruff. But he was pretty sure it was still doing its duty. The Winds did not know where he was.

As the Heaven hooks descended on the Boros estate, Jordan had learned that he could hear the little voices of inanimate and animate things. Each object within his sight had a voice, he now knew. Each thing proclaimed its identity, over and over, the way a bird calls its name all day for no reason but the joy in its own voice. Now that he knew they were there, Jordan could attune himself to the sound of that endless murmur. Last night and this morning, he had worked at tuning into and out of that listening stance as he walked.

If he closed his eyes, he could see a ghostly landscape, mostly made up of words hovering over indistinct objects. He could make little sense of that, so he left that avenue alone.

It seemed that he could focus his inner hearing on individual objects, if he concentrated hard enough.

He held up the knife he had been whittling with and concentrated on it. After a few minutes he began to hear its voice. *Steel*, it said. *A steel blade. Carbon steel, a knife.*

At the Boros estate, Jordan had spoken to a little soul like this, and it had answered. *I am stone*, a doorway arch had said to him. This ability to speak to things didn't surprise him as much as it might have, considering everything that had happened. According to the priest Allegri, some people had visions of the Winds, and the Winds didn't punish them for this.

Allegri had told Jordan that he might be one of those with such a talent. He had been wrong at the time; what Jordan had been experiencing then was visions of Armiger—and those, the Winds surely disliked.

But this? This communion with a simple object seemed to have nothing to do with Armiger. Maybe it had been enabled by whatever Calandria May had done to Jordan's head. But was it forbidden by the Winds?

Well, he had Calandria's protective gauze. Jordan was confident he could hear the approach of the greater Winds in time to don it and escape.

It came down, then, to a matter of courage.

"What are you?" he asked the knife.

"*I am knife*," said the knife.

Even though he was expecting it, Jordan was so startled he dropped the thing.

He picked it up and began nervously walking. "Knife, what are you made of?"

The voice in his head was clear, neutral, neither male nor female: *I am a combination of iron and carbon. The carbon is a hardening agent.*

He nodded, wondering what else to ask it. The obvious question was, "How is it that you can speak?"

I am broadcasting a combined fractal signal on visible frequencies of radiation.

The answer had made no sense. "Why can't other people hear you?"

They are not equipped to receive.

That was kind of a restatement of the question, he thought. *How will I get anywhere if I don't know what to ask?*

He thought for a moment, shrugged, and said, "Who made you?"

"Ho, traveler! Well met on the road to Iapysia!"

For just a split second he thought the knife had said that. Then Jordan looked behind him. A large covered wagon drawn by two horses was coming up the road. Two people sat at the front. The driver was waving to him.

Suddenly very self-conscious, he slipped the knife into his belt. He knew the gold gauze was sticking out at his collar and waist, but there was no time to do anything about that.

"Uh, hello." The man's accent had been foreign. He was middle aged, almost elderly, with a fringe of white hair around his sunburned skull. He was dressed in new-looking townsman's clothes.

The other passenger was a woman. She looked to be about Jordan's age. She was dressed in frills and wore a sun hat, but her face under it was tanned, the one whisp of stray hair sunbleached. She held an embroidery ring in strong, calloused hands. She was scowling at Jordan.

"Where are you bound, son?" asked the man.

Jordan gestured. "South. Iapysia."

"Ah. So are we. Returning home?"

"Uh, yeah."

"But your accent is Memnonian," said the old man.

"Um, uh. We have houses in both countries," he said, mindful of the Boros example. He was itching to listen in to the voices again; he had to know if his dialogue with the knife had alerted the Winds. At the Boros manor, the whole landscape had come alert, almost overwhelming his senses. That wasn't happening now. But he couldn't be sure without checking.

"My name's Milo Suneil," said the man. "And this is—"

"Excuse me," gritted the young woman. She stood abruptly and climbed into the covered back of the wagon.

". . . My niece, Tamsin," finished Suneil. "Who is not herself today. And you are?"

"Jordan Mason." He affected the half bow that the highborn Boros had used on one another. It was harder to perform while walking, though.

"Pleased to meet you." There was a momentary silence. The cart was moving at just the pace Jordan was walking, so he remained abreast of Suneil. From the back of the wagon came the sound of things being tossed about.

"Calm weather, for autumn," said Suneil. Jordan agreed that it was. "Clouds moving in, though. Not good—clouds could hide things in the sky, don't you think?"

"What do you mean?"

"News travels slowly, I see!" Suneil laughed. "You're dressed like a highborn lad, surely you've heard the news about the destruction of the Boros household!"

"Ah, that. Yes. I did hear about it," he said uncomfortably.

"I'm itching to find out what really happened," said Suneil. "We've had ten versions of the story from ten different people. When I saw you walking by the road; coming from the direction of the estate, I thought, could it be? A refugee from our little disaster?"

Jordan, unsure of himself in this situation, merely shrugged.

Suneil was silent for a while, staring ahead. "The fact is," he said at last, "that my curiosity has gotten the best of me. If we were to run into someone who actually knew what had happened at the estate—or Winds forbid, someone who was actually there!—then I might be inclined to give that person a ride with us, provided they told their story."

"I see," said Jordan neutrally.

"My niece has sprained her leg," added Suneil. "And I'm not as young as I used to be. We'll need someone to gather firewood, the next day or so."

Jordan was very surprised. People didn't trust strangers on the open road. Then again, one never traveled alone, either.

Do I look that harmless? he wondered.

"It's all right," said Suneil reasonably. "I'm not a Heaven hook, nor am I in league with them. I just deduced that you were at the Boros place, because you're walking from that direction, and you're dressed well, except for the mud stains and wild hair. Actually, you look like you fled somewhere in a hurry. We've passed a couple of people who looked like that—only none would talk to us."

Jordan eyed the cart greedily. He was very tired. A few days ride in return for some carefully edited storytelling couldn't hurt anything. In fact, it might be the only way he'd get to Iapysia.

"All right," he said. "I'm your man."

TAMSIN COWERED BACK into the wagon. Uncle must be insane! He was picking up strange men on the highway—they were sure to be robbed and raped by this crazy person who talked to himself and had gold cloth stuffed in his shirt.

She felt the wagon dip deeply as the man stepped up onto the front seat. Then it commenced rolling forward. She sat down on a bale of cloth, disconsolately picking at her embroidery. Finally she threw it on the floor.

Some days were fine. Today had started out that way. Some days, she could wake up in the morning, and clouds would be just clouds, water just water. She could actually smell breakfast as she cooked it and feel hungry. Some days she could listen to Uncle's plans and tease into life a small spark of enthusiasm that he seemed to know she had. She could look forward to being an ingenue at Rhiene or one of the other great cities of Iapysia. So there were days when she practiced her curtsies, her embroidery, and recited the epic poems Uncle had coached her in.

And then there were days . . . Her hands trembled again as she reached down to massage her leg. She couldn't remember why she had been running—all she remembered was the overwhelming bleakness of the landscape. Bare trees, yellow grass. Cold air. Her own thoughts and feelings were inaccessible to her. One thing was sure, she was certainly not looking where she was going that morning. No wonder she'd sprained her leg.

Sometimes the tiniest little annoyance would set her off in a fit of temper that made her Uncle's eyes widen in disbelief. Once it was because she had dropped a stitch! He did nothing to calm her down, but let her play it out. Afterward, she was always listless and ashamed.

I will not explode, she told herself. *Even if Uncle is trying to get us killed.*

They were talking up there—chatting like old friends. Of course, he did that with strangers all the time, but it was normally when they stopped at roadside markets or near towns. Uncle was an insatiable vessel for news, and these last two days he had been stopping everyone for information about the horrible incident at the Boros estate. It just wasn't like him to pick people up off the road to talk.

Tamsin gritted her teeth and glared at the canvas flap. It was true an extra set of hands would be good right now. Rationally, she understood it. It didn't stop her seething.

She sat in the dimness for a while, arms crossed, trying not to think. Thinking was bad. It led to things worse than anger.

This will all end soon, she told herself. *When we get to Rhiene everything will be different.* Meanwhile, she would have to make adjustments and test her patience. So, after a little while, she adjusted her hair, planted a smile on her face, and opened the front flap of the cart's canopy.

"Hello," she said brightly to the startled young man who was in her seat. She held out her hand. "My name's Tamsin. What's yours?"

CALANDRIA MAY SLUNG the bag of potatoes over her shoulder and made her way out of the market. The place was still buzzing with talk of the Boros catastrophe; the consensus was that the Winds had finally gotten around to punishing the family for unspecified past excesses. Attendance at church here in the town of Geldon was decidedly up.

There was some confused discussion of Yuri's assassination. It was laid at the feet of Brendan Sheia, and two spies from Ravenon were named as accomplices. That explained why Calandria was currently disguised as a boy. She had cropped her hair and changed her voice and mannerisms. Right now she used the bag of potatoes to add swing to her shoulders as she walked, since otherwise her lower center of balance was harder to disguise.

People were also talking about Jordan Mason. No one knew his name, but some people had witnessed a confrontation between Turcaret and a young man. The controller had accused the youth of bringing the Heaven hooks down on the household.

Her shoulders itched as she walked—a familiar feeling that she was being watched or followed. It had nothing to do with any townspeople who might glance at her on the way by. This was an older, and more fundamental, fear.

If she closed her eyes, Calandria could invoke her inscape senses: infrared sight and the galvanic radar that told of the presence of mecha or Winds. She couldn't help herself—every few minutes, she paused, closed her eyes, and looked around using these senses.

Ever since the night that the Heaven hooks came down, Calandria had refused to let herself be lulled back into thinking that Ventus was a natural place. She was trapped in the gears of a giant, globe-spanning machine—a nanotech terraforming system that barely tolerated her kind. This appeared to be ordinary dirt she walked on, but it had been manu-

factured; it took more than the thousand years that Ventus had been habitable for soil like this to form naturally. The air seemed fresh and clean,
but that, too, was moderated by unseen forces.

Those unseen forces were a threat. They might yet kill her. So she
remained vigilant.

Calandria turned into a narrow alley and went through a rough-hewn
door that had a latch but no lock. Up a flight of stairs, through another
door, and she was home.

This was the safe room where they had intended to hide August
Ostler. The room was about four by six meters. It had one window,
which let out on the street—not an advantage, because mostly it just let in
the smell of the open sewer that ran down the center of the lane. The
place was built of plaster and lath. Calandria could hear the landlady
snoring in the room next door. But it was out of the elements and warm
at night. That was all that mattered.

Currently everything she had was in this room or on her person. Their
horses had been killed in the destruction of the Boros stables, and she had
never recovered her pack with its supplies of off-world technology. That
had complicated matters over the past couple of days.

Axel Chan grunted something and shifted in his sleep. His face was
still flushed from the fever that had gripped him since Turcaret's attack.
His diagnostic nano were supposed to be able to handle routine infections. They didn't seem to be working. Without the proper equipment,
Calandria couldn't determine why, though she suspected the local mecha
were suppressing the off-world technology.

Would the same mecha contact the Winds and warn them of the presence of aliens here? Each night as she lay down, Calandria found herself
imagining the harsh armatures of the Heaven hooks reaching down to
pluck this small room apart.

It wasn't like her to be afraid. But then, she was never afraid of merely
physical threats. This was something else.

She put the potatoes down on the room's one table. Axel coughed and
sat up.

"How are you feeling?" Calandria ladled some cold soup out and put
it next to Axel. He drank it eagerly.

"As the good people of Memnonis like to say, I feel like a toad in a piss
pot. Is this brackish swill the best you could do?"

She sighed. "Axel, have you ever been truly ill in your life?"

"No."

She nodded. "Why?" asked Axel after a moment.

"Because your nurses would surely have strangled you in your bed,
the way you carry on."

"Oh, ho," he said. "Leave then. I'll be fine on my own." He coughed weakly. "I'll manage somehow . . . I'll feed on the rats and bugs, and be sure to die somewhere out of the way, where no one will trip over my shriveling corpse."

She laughed. "You do sound much better."

"Well . . ." He raised his arms and examined them. "I no longer feel like I'll leak all over if I just stand up. I should be able to ride in a day or two."

She shook her head. "It's going to take longer than that. We need you in top form when we go after Armiger."

He nodded, then sank back on the straw bed. "Any word on Jordan?"

"No one knows what happened to him, and I have no way to track him now. We used the *Desert Voice*'s sensors to locate Armiger's remotes the first time. With the *Voice* missing, we don't have that option. Anyway, Jordan's probably on his way home. No reason he shouldn't be."

Axel shifted uncomfortably. "I don't like it. I still feel responsible."

"I know," she said. "But our first responsibility is to find Armiger and destroy him. If we don't do that, then Jordan won't be safe, no matter where he is."

Axel appeared to accept this logic. "I assume," he said, "that we're not going to take Armiger on ourselves at this point. Just track him down."

She nodded, coming to sit next to him. With the loss of the *Desert Voice*, they no longer had the firepower to destroy Armiger themselves. They would need help. At the same time, having the firepower wasn't enough: they had to find Armiger, run him to ground. Calandria wanted to be sure of where he was before they left Ventus for reinforcements.

Axel looked better, but was still pale. He'd lost weight. "As soon as we get a ping from a passing ship we'll try to get off-world," she promised. "Meanwhile, we can't afford to lose track of him."

"We may have already." He closed his eyes, wincing as he tried to turn on his side. "We don't know for sure that he's going after the queen."

"Yes. Well, it's all we've got." Axel didn't reply, and after a moment she stood and went to the window. His breathing deepened with sleep behind her, as Calandria looked out and up at a blue sky full of rolling white clouds. She fought the urge to look behind that facade at the alien machinery that maintained it.

Losing the *Desert Voice* was a catastrophe. She loved her ship, but more than that, they would have needed its power in order to destroy Armiger. Somewhere out there, beyond the rooftops and the clear air, he was hatching his schemes. She should be able to see him, like a stain on the landscape, she thought. It was horrifying that he should be invisible to the people he was setting out to enslave.

Calandria hugged herself, remembering what it had been like on the one world of 3340's she had visited. The people of Hsing had been traumatized to the point of madness; their only goal in life—more an obsession—was to win the attention and favor of 3340 by any means possible so as to avoid destruction and win immortality as one of its demigod slaves. People would do anything, up to and including mass murder, to gain its attention. And once enslaved, they became embodiments of their most base instincts, in turn enslaving hundreds or thousands of innocents; or simply slaughtering them as unwanted potential competition.

And all the while, 3340 had eaten away at the skies and earth, rendering the planet progressively more toxic for the few unchanged humans who struggled to survive in the ruins.

Armiger might find the key he was looking for at any moment. Irrevocable change would come sweeping from over the horizon like a tsunami, and this time Calandria would not be able to stop it.

She sat down by the window and forced her hands to stay still in her lap. There was nothing to do but wait. Wait—and watch the skies for a sign that the world was ending.

17

MEGAN HAD NEVER seen so many books. They crowded on high shelves around all the walls of a large room on the third floor of the palace. All the shelves had diamond-patterned glass doors. She watched as Armiger walked from cabinet to cabinet, opening them in turn and gazing at their contents. This was their second day here, but as yet the queen had not found the time to speak to them. Armiger was getting restless.

The books didn't interest Megan, but the room itself was sumptuous. It contained a number of couches and leather-bound armchairs, with side tables and many tall oil lamps. The entire floor was covered with overlapping carpets that glowed in the shafts of morning light falling from tall windows along one wall. She curled up in one of the armchairs, feet under her, to watch as Armiger prowled.

This room and the others in the queen's apartments provided a shocking contrast to the other parts of the palace she had seen. Below this tower, the palace grounds were crowded with the tents of refugees; children and the wounded cried everywhere, there was talk of cholera. The lower corridors and outbuildings bristled with armed men, and conversation there was strained and infrequent. Here, though, it was like another world—luxurious and calm.

Megan knew she would always remember their entry into these walls. Her first glimpse of the interior of the summer palace had been of torchlight gleaming off the helmets of a sea of men. Ragged banners hung from the facades of buildings half ruined by Parliament's steam cannons. The place reeked of fear and human waste. She had shrunk back on Armiger's arm as they were led along cordoned avenues between the tents and into the vast tower that held Galas's audience chambers. And the moment they were inside its walls, they were in a minor paradise.

This contrast had disturbed her more than the misery itself. It still disturbed her, the more so since she found herself responding to the comfort of this armchair, the warmth of the nearby fire.

"Amazing," said Armiger.

She smiled. "You? Amazed? I doubt it."

He reached up to take down a very large, heavy and scrofulous-looking volume. "I've been looking for this one since I arrived," he said. He waggled it at her as he went to perch on the edge of a desk. "Early histories relating some of the events immediately post-landing."

"Really?" She didn't know what he was talking about, but it was good to see him enthusiastic about something—something other than this Queen Galas, anyway.

Armiger flipped through the pages quickly. "Hmm. Ah. There are major distortions, as one would expect from such a large passage of time."

"How large?"

"A thousand years. Not really very long; living memory for me, most of it. And on Earth there are complete daily records of practically everything that went on there from before that time, but Earth never fell the way Ventus did. Miraculous." He shut the book; it made a satisfying thud and a waft of dust rose before his face.

"I take it you are glad we came," she said. "Despite the army outside?"

He waved his hand, dismissing either the dust or the besieging force. "Yes. I'm most likely to find out what I want to know here. In case they burn this library down, I'm going to read it."

"Read *it*? The whole thing? Tonight?" She didn't hide her disbelief.

"Well . . . maybe not all. Most, anyway." He smiled, an increasingly common thing lately.

"But why? This queen, she is important to you for what she can tell you. I see that now. But why is she so special? You want to talk to her. Her people want to kill her. What has she done?"

Armiger inspected another shelf. "Of course you wouldn't get much news living alone in the country as you did. Where to start, though? Galas has always been different, apparently.

"She was installed on the throne at a young age by the Winds. No one knows why. Whatever they wanted, she apparently didn't provide it, because they haven't lifted a finger to stop Parliament marching on her. But she's done extraordinary things."

He came to sit on the arm of a couch near her. "Galas is the sort of philosopher-monarch who arises once in a millennium," he said. "She may rank with Earthly rulers like Mao in terms of the scope of her accomplishments. People like her aren't content to merely rule a nation—they want to reinvent both it and the people who live in it."

Megan was puzzled, but interested now. "What do you mean, 'reinvent'?"

"New beliefs. New religions. New economics, new science. And not just as a process of reform or nation building. Rather as a single artistic whole. During her reign Galas has viewed her nation as an artistic medium to be shaped."

She shifted uncomfortably. "That's . . . horrible."

Armiger seemed surprised. "Why? Her impulse has been to improve things. And she's almost never used force, certainly not against the common people. Her actions are reminiscent of those of the Amarna rulers of ancient Egypt . . . sorry, I keep referring to things you can't know.

"Anyway, what she did was give her people a completely new and all-encompassing vision of the world. Nothing has been left unchanged—art, commerce, she has even tried to reform the language itself."

Megan laughed. "That's silly."

Armiger shrugged. "She's failed at a lot of things. In terms of language, she tried to ban the use of possessives when speaking of emotional states, motives, and people. So that you could not say, 'he is *my* husband,' for instance."

She glowered. "That is evil."

"But you could also not say that something *is his fault*, or *her fault*. She wanted to remove assignments of blame from speech and writing and refocus expression on contexts of behavior. To eliminate victimless crimes, crimes of ostracization, for instance the 'crime' of being a homosexual. Also to move the emphasis of justice away from blame and punishment to behavior management. Far too ambitious for a single generation. So it didn't work.

"But no one on Ventus has ever thought of these things before. Galas is entirely original in her thinking."

"So why are they out there?" She pointed to the windows.

"Oh, the usual reasons. She started threatening the stability of the ruling classes, at least in their own eyes. No ruler who does that ever stands for long. She'd built experimental towns recently, out in the desert. Each operated on some one of the new principles she espoused. Naturally most of them flew in the face of orthodox mores. Of course, the salt barons will revolt if you display an interest in eliminating money from commerce!"

"*You make me sound like a fool.*"

Galas stood in the doorway, in a blue morning dress, her hair bound up by golden pins. Megan hurried to her feet and curtsied. Armiger languidly bowed, shaking his head.

"It is merely the voice of experience, Your Majesty. Humans become violent when they feel their interests are threatened."

Galas scowled. "They were never threatened! Parliament is a rumor mill staffed by trough-fed clods who abuse the tongue of their birth every time they open their mouths. They all gabble at once and confuse one another mightily, and when this confusion is committed to paper they refer to it as 'policy.'"

"I won't dispute that, having never attended," Armiger said.

The queen swept into the room. Two members of the royal guard followed, to take positions on either side of the doorway. "I had to try," Galas said bitterly. "For centuries no one has tried anything new! So what would be one more life in dumb service to tradition? Where would it get us, except back where we started when the wheel of this life had come around again? Someone had to ask questions men have been afraid to ask all that time. It has always been obvious to me that no one else would do it, either now or in the future. I had to do it all, even the things you call foolish. Else how could we *know* anything? Anything at all?"

Armiger said nothing, but he nodded in acquiescence.

"Sometimes one's responsibility goes beyond one's own generation," Galas said. She sat in the chair next to Megan's and smiled at her warmly. "I trust you slept well, Lady?"

"Yes, thank you, Your Highness."

"And you, Sir Maut? Do you even sleep?" Her voice held a teasing note.

He inclined his head. "When it suits me." Then he frowned. "I hope you don't view us a pair of jesters, here to distract you from what's waiting outside your gates. My purpose is quite serious—as serious as your own situation."

Galas's eyes flashed, but she only said, "I remain to be convinced. That is all."

"Fair enough." Armiger moved from his perch on the arm of the couch, to sit down properly. "So, who am I, and what do I want of you? That is what you would like to know."

Galas nodded. Megan saw that the moth note Armiger had written her was stuck, folded, through the belt of her dress. Perhaps she had been rereading it over breakfast. For reassurance?

Megan couldn't begin to imagine what it must be like for her, with those men camped outside, waiting permission to brutalize and destroy everything. Servants killed, treasured possessions robbed . . . but Galas was outwardly cool.

She must be crying inside. It's cruel of Armiger to give her any hope now.

"Ask me anything," said Armiger. "Ask me something to test my knowledge, if you wish."

"Were all my mistakes obvious?" blurted the queen. "Is what I've fought for all my life trivially simple anywhere else? Am I a primitive, next to the people who live on other stars?"

"They might think so," said Armiger. "I do not."

"If you are what you say you are, then it makes all the pain I've suffered—and inflicted—pointless." Galas was not looking at them, but off into the middle distance. "I've been so busy since you arrived, making final preparations . . . the assault will come soon. But there hasn't been an instant when I didn't wonder why I was bothering. If everything I've tried to discover was learned millennia ago . . . I feel like the gods are laughing at me. I feel like an ant all puffed up with pride over having laboriously mapped out the boundaries of a garden. I don't think you can tell me anything to change that impression."

Armiger smiled. "I must be the fool, then, to waste my time talking to an ant."

"Don't make light of this!" She rose and went to stand over him. Megan was amazed at how Galas seemed to tower over Armiger, though the difference in their heights was such that even with him sitting, they were almost eye to eye.

Armiger was unfazed. "I was not. It is you who are belittling yourself."

Galas whirled and walked to the windows. "Then tell me I'm wrong! Tell me about the heavens—who lives there, what are they like? Have you walked on other planets? Talked to their people? Are they all-knowing, all-wise—or are they fools like us?"

Armiger's smiled grew wider. "They are all-knowing, but no wiser than anyone else. In fact, since they know everything they believe they possess the wisdom of the ages. Hence, I'd have to say, they are bigger fools than you."

"But I don't want to hear that, either," said the queen. "Because it means there is no progress. If I educate my people and yet they remain fools, why have I bothered?"

Armiger crossed his arms, shrugged at Megan, but said nothing.

"All right," said Galas. She turned around and leaned on the windowsill. "Tell me about the heavens, please. I do want to know."

MANY LEAGUES AWAY, Jordan Mason paused in his whittling and closed his eyes. He had been basking in the wan autumn sunlight and listening to Armiger and Megan with half an ear. He sat on a log by the remains of last night's fire; he faced away from the wagon, where the girl Tamsin was hiding again.

Jordan had told a carefully edited version of the story of the Boros catastrophe yesterday. Both Suneil and his niece had listened intently. He had excluded any mention of Axel and Calandria and said nothing about August's duel or the attack by Turcaret's men. Apparently the word was out that Yuri and Turcaret had been killed; Jordan simply shrugged and said he hadn't seen that. His story was that he had panicked and run. Since he was visiting the household on his own, anyway, he had just kept walking when daybreak came. Suneil seemed to accept this. It wasn't at all implausible that he should want to get as far away from the place as possible, after all.

Suneil had arisen early this morning, but had said little. Jordan walked the boundaries of the small encampment, kicking the dirt and wondering whether his presence here was endangering these two.

When he heard Galas ask Armiger about the heavens, he forgot all about his problems. Megan had never asked about that, and Jordan was intensely curious. When he closed his eyes he could see what Armiger saw, and if he stayed still the voices became clearer and clearer, until he seemed to be there with them.

The words seemed to emerge from his own mouth. Whenever that happened, Jordan felt almost as though they were his own thoughts he was speaking, and he invariably remembered them with perfect clarity later. Just now he was saying, "The stars in the night sky have their retinue of planets. Millions are inhabited, but if you gaze up at them tonight, know that only one in every thousand you see has people living by it, there are that many. Millions have been visited and explored, but for every one of them a million more are still mysteries.

"Humans like yourself moved into the galaxy a thousand years ago. Your ancient homeworld is now a park, where few can go except by special permission. All the other worlds in the home system were settled centuries ago and are overflowing now. The've even dismantled the minor planets and smaller moons and built new habitats with them. The population of that star system is now more than seventy trillion.

"Many other stars have similarly huge civilizations. Add to that the dozens of alien species, genetically altered humans, cyborgs, demigods and gods, and the peace you see in the sky seems more and more like an illusion."

"What are these things?" asked the queen. "Cyborgs? Demigods?"

"Mecha," said Armiger curtly. "But designed by people for the most part. Some people have had themselves transformed into mechal beings so that they can live in hostile environments, like open space or the crushing depths of giant planets' atmospheres. The boundary between human and nonhuman began to blur centuries ago, and now it's completely gone."

"And you? What are you?"

Jordan felt Armiger's hands form fists in his lap. "Demigod. Human once, I think—but I no longer remember. I'm ancient, Your Highness, but mortal. Even the gods are mortal. And I will die unless I can find a secret known only to the Winds of Ventus."

Armiger was lying, according to what Calandria had told Jordan when they traveled together. She had told him the demigod had come to Ventus to subvert the Winds and take control of the entire world. He knew

Armiger was weakening, though, and Jordan didn't know if he could trust Calandria May.

"What is this secret?"

"It is the secret of why the Winds ignore or abuse humanity," said Armiger.

Galas laughed. "Countless generations have wondered that. I do, too. Do you believe I have the secret?"

"I think you may know more than you realize."

"You came to see me because of the legends," she accused. "They say the Winds placed me on the throne, so I am assumed to know their secrets. For a god, you are rather naive, Maut."

He waved a hand dismissively. "The legends brought you to my attention, but even if they're wrong, I made the right choice in coming to you. I am sure of it."

"Now you speak like a courtier."

"My apologies."

Galas returned to her seat. Jordan admired her through Armiger's eyes; she was not so old as she had appeared in the throne room—perhaps in her late thirties. This war was aging her prematurely, he thought. He wanted to touch her, but had never learned the trick of making Armiger's limbs move at his own urging.

"Why not just ask the Winds of another world?" asked the queen.

"There are no other Winds. There is no other place like Ventus."

Jordan watched Galas's eyes widen. He remembered sympathetically how he had reacted when Calandria told him the same thing. "But," she started, "you just spoke of millions of worlds—trillions of people—"

"There are a million organizing principles in human space. None resemble Ventus. Your world is unique, and the records of the design of the Winds were lost in a war centuries ago. Most of humanity lives in something known as the Archipelago—an immense region whose boundaries are so vague that much of its citizenry doesn't even know of its existence."

"Now you're talking madness," smiled the queen. "Not that anything you've said so far would survive debate in the House."

"Archipelago is the only answer to ruling a population of trillions, who own a million different cultures, mores, and histories." He shrugged. "It is simple: an artificial intelligence—a mechal brain, if you will—exists and mediates things. It knows each and every citizen personally and orchestrates their meetings with others, communications, and so on in order to avoid irreconcilable conflict. Beyond that, it stays out of sight, for it has no values, no desires of its own. It is as if every person had their own guardian spirit, and these spirits never warred, but acted in concert to improve people's lives."

"A tyranny of condescension," said Galas.

"Yes. You worried earlier that everything was known. Well, yes and no. The government of the Archipelago has the sum of human knowledge and can speak it directly into people's minds. But it's only the sum of human knowledge. It is only one perspective. Here on Ventus, something quite different has come to exist. A new wisdom, you might say. The sum of the knowledge of an entire conscious world, unsullied by human perspective. Ventus, you see, is infinitely precious."

"Then why aren't they here? A trillion tourists from the sky?"

"The Winds don't permit visitors. Though there are a few, I suppose—researchers vainly trying to crack the cyphers of the Diadem swans. Hiding from the Winds, of course."

"But you slipped in."

"I did. The Winds know something I must learn if I am to survive. I cannot speak to them. So I must ask you, as the one person on Ventus who knows them best, to help me."

"And why should I help?"

Armiger stood and walked to one of the tall windows. "Outside your gates is an army. That army did not need to come here. You need never have embarked on the path that led you here. And you knew things would end this way, didn't you? It was inevitable from the moment you began to try to change the fundamental beliefs of your people."

Below this high window he could see a crowded, hectic courtyard. Beyond that, walls, then the hazy, unbelievable crush of the besieging army.

"They had to kill you in the end," he said.

"Yes," said the queen in a small voice. "But I had to try . . . to end this long night that has swallowed the whole world."

He turned, and Jordan felt his eyes narrow, his mouth set hard. "Then help me. If I survive, I may well be able to do what you could not."

"I SAID, HELLO."

Jordan looked up. Suneil's niece Tamsin stood in front of him, arms crossed, her head cocked to one side.

He was annoyed at the interruption, and almost told her to go away—but he was a guest of these people, after all. "I was meditating."

"Uh-huh. Looked more like sleeping with your mouth open."

Jordan opened his mouth, closed it again, and then said, "Did you want something?"

"Uncle wants a good supply of firewood in the wagon before we get to the border. Isn't that why you're here, to do that stuff for us?"

Jordan stood and stretched. "It is indeed." He saw no need to say anything more to this shrew.

"Well good," she said as she followed him into the grass. "We wouldn't want any freeloaders on this trip."

Jordan noticed that Suneil was watching this exchange from the vicinity of the wagon. "I'll work my keep," said Jordan, as he increased his stride to outdistance her.

"See that you do!" she hollered. Then, apparently satisfied, she limped back to the wagon and began arguing with her uncle about something.

As soon as he was out of sight of the camp, Jordan sat down and tried to reestablish his link with Armiger. This time, it took all his concentration to bring the voices to him; Tamsin seemed to be a bad influence. When the voices did return, he found that Armiger and the queen were now discussing military logistics. The terms meant nothing to Jordan, so he stood up with a sigh, and went to gather the wood.

When Jordan staggered back with his first load of sticks, Suneil was sitting on the wagon's back step, but Tamsin was nowhere to be seen. "I apologize for my niece," said Suneil. "She lost her parents and sister recently. The shock has brought all her emotions to the surface."

"The war?"

Suneil nodded. "The war. We fled Iapysia three months ago to escape it. Now we're on our way back. They say the queen is defeated . . . maybe things have settled down."

"I don't know," said Jordan. "I know you can't run away forever." He longed for home. Once he had gotten Armiger to raise this curse that was on him, he would return to Castor's manor.

"Well spoken," said Suneil. "You were patient with her just now. I'm glad. She strikes out, but if you strike back, she'll shatter like glass. Just remember that. I know it's an imposition, but—"

Jordan waved a hand. "No, it's fine. These things happen. We have to help one another."

Suneil grinned. "Thanks. And thanks for the wood. We're going to need a lot more, though, when we get to the border."

"Why?"

Suneil glanced at him, raised an eyebrow. "Well, you said you're from Iapysia, you'd know there's no trees in the desert, wouldn't you?"

"Uh . . . , yes, of course."

Suneil gave him an odd little smile and walked away.

18

TWO DAYS' TRAVEL brought them deep into the barren hills that signified the border of Iapysia. He was confident now that the Winds did not know where he was. The gauze continued to protect him and, hence, the people he traveled with. That was good; but he couldn't wear it for the rest of his life. He would have to find Armiger soon—or Calandria would, and either way there would be an end to this.

He was riding up front with Suneil when the wagon topped the crest of a particularly long hill, and Suneil reined in the horses. Standing to look at the vista below, Suneil sighed and said, "Home."

Jordan stood, too. Sun had broken through a rent in the autumn clouds, illuminating the valley below in a vast golden rectangle. Within this frame, the land fell in a series of green steps to a landscape of grass and forest cradling a long sinuous lake. The road wound down switchbacks to the floor of the valley and vanished beyond the sunlit frame at the far end of the lake, where the valley seemed to open out into a plain.

Jordan could see some blue-gray squares and lines near the lake. "Are those ruins?"

Suneil nodded. "That valley lies in Iapysia. The desert starts beyond it."

"It's beautiful. Nobody lives here?" He could see no sign of settlement, though he could easily imagine dozens of farms fitting in near the lake.

"The Winds do. It's okay to visit, but no one stays."

They sat down again, and Suneil flicked the reins. Over the past couple of days they had talked a lot about the local countryside, and Suneil had grilled Jordan at length about the war between Ravenon and the Seneschals. Jordan had spun a long tale about the destruction of Armiger's army and the death of the general, pretending he had heard it from other travelers.

His own eavesdropping had yielded few results, since the queen was busy with preparations for the siege, and it seemed Armiger was content to wait.

Jordan had reluctantly admitted to Suneil that he was not from Iapysia. His Memnonian accent didn't match his story. Suneil had asked no further questions, but he had also volunteered nothing about his own past. Jordan let his curiosity lead him now, though, as it seemed a natural time to ask. "Tell me about the war. And the queen. All I've heard is that she's mad, and that the great houses revolted."

Suneil nodded. "I suppose your countrymen think it's a scandal that we're deposing our queen." He scowled at the road that rolled down before them. "We do, too. Even the soldiers in Parliament's army. But things got . . . out of control."

Jordan waited for more. After a while, Suneil said, "Iapysia's a very old country, but it was one of the last places settled. At the beginning of the world, they say the Winds made Ventus—and they're not finished making it yet. But they didn't make Man. Some say we made ourselves, some that we came from the stars, and some say that renegade Winds created us as an act of defiance. That's what I believe. How else to explain what Queen Galas has done?

"The first people spread across the world from one original tribe. They had great powers, and they wanted Ventus as their own. They fought the Winds, because the Winds were still sculpting Ventus and would not let the people build cities or cultivate the land. Men defied them, but the Winds beat them down, until at last there were only scattered communities, who learned to get along with the Winds by obeying their laws. We learned to stay out of the Winds' way and appease them when we went too far. Your general Armiger went too far—they took notice of him and swatted him like an insect. There's a lesson in that.

"In the early days after our defeat, some folk wandered to the edge of the desert. There they found the desals hard at work, flooding the sands to strain salt from ocean water that poured in from the Titans' Gates—those are the Wind-built dams at the seaside. They pumped the newly freshened water deep into the earth. We know now that it comes up again through springs all across the continent. Back then, it was just another miraculous and incomprehensible activity of the rulers of the world. Our people huddled on the edge of it, watching the floods in awe.

"Iasin the First, ancestor of all the kings of Iapysia, was the man who realized that the desals were utterly indifferent to the plants and animals that struggled within the floodplains. The ocean water brought nutrients from the sea, the desert sands strained the salt, and fresh water poured up and out through a thousand channels into rivers that flow into your lands or that vanish into bottomless lakes. A thousand kinds of life thrived during the flooding, and when the Titans' Gates closed to draw strength for another great gasp, they withered and died. Iasin led his people into the heart of the inundated lands, and they began to grow huge crops there, in open defiance of the Winds.

"Our people have always believed that we have a silent pact with the desals. All our laws were made to preserve the pact. As far as we can see, the desals will always use the desert to purify water for the continent. What was in the beginning, will be always. So it should be with our laws, our kings, and our traditions.

"The laws are harsh. They dictate everything from our professions to the size of the family. Our cities have grown only so big as the desals will tolerate and can grow no more. We cannot divert the Winds' rivers to suit our needs. The nobility trace their lineage back to the time of Iasin, as do people in the guilds and trades. All life is fixed. While your nations have been in a constant uproar of change and growth all these centuries, we know you will reach the same point eventually. Humanity cannot rule Ventus. We are merely tolerated. In my country, people believe that life will always be like it is now, for all eternity.

"I should say, we used to believe that. Then came Queen Galas, to upset a thousand years of tradition."

"What did she do?" asked Jordan. The swath of sunlight that had blanketed the valley below was gone, leaving the landscape blued by lowering clouds. More rain was coming.

Suneil pointed along the road that led past the long lake. "Our lives are tied to the floods. We prosper insofar as we can predict them. We have always relied on observation and our records to do that. Galas had no need of such indirect means. She negotiated with the desals, and the desert flooded when and where and by how much she said it would. No sovereign has ever had such power over nature. We prospered as we never have.

"It wasn't enough for her. Galas despises the Winds. She sees humanity as the rightful rulers of the world, and the Winds as usurpers. People find her views shocking, but who could argue with her success? She gained a great following and began to erase a thousand years of law and tradition, replacing it with daring and unsettling edicts of her own. She wanted to remake the world in her own image.

"She went too far. About five years ago, the desals turned against her. Her predictions for that year's flooding were tragically wrong. Thousands died in the waters or the famine that came after. Whatever she had done to alienate the Winds, their rebuke simply hardened her heart. She pushed ahead with her reforms, although for our own survival we now had to fall back on our old ways of predicting the floods."

"You supported her?" Jordan ventured to ask.

"At first, yes. I won't pretend I didn't profit by it. By the time the Winds turned against her, I had become entirely her creature. I'm not a fool, I could see what was coming, but there was nothing I could do to stop it. Parliament tabled a document demanding Galas cease all her meddling and rescind the edicts that had broken centuries of tradition. She refused. The war . . . I think no one really believed it would happen, or that it was happening, until it came to visit one's own town or relatives. I believed. I ran. Well, she lost. She's probably dead by now. I wish I knew, that's all."

Jordan could have told him, but a new caution, perhaps learned from his experience with the Boroses, made him hold his tongue.

THEY MADE CAMP near the etched outlines of vanished buildings and streets. Jordan sized up the place in spare glances while he got the fire going and tended to the horses. Tamsin sat listlessly on the back step of the wagon, watching the men work.

Jordan knew that in his country, a small town might contain a handful of buildings made of stone, and dozens of wooden houses. The wooden structures would make no permanent impression on the land after they were torn down or burned. Stone buildings left a kind of scar, and it was these that patterned a rise near the end of the lake. If there were ten wooden houses to every stone, and every house held eight people, then half a thousand people had lived here once.

Suneil confirmed it. "It was a border town once. They traded with Memnonis. But the Winds razed it to the ground, four hundred years ago."

"Why?"

"They use this place." Suneil gestured to the lake. "It's a transfer point, or something. Don't really know. Anyway, they won't let people build here."

The thought made Jordan uneasy. Since the clouds and their threat of rain had vanished, after dinner he walked down to the edge of the lake. Using his new talent, he listened for the presence of the Winds.

The water was perfectly clear, the bottom covered in a fine yellow sand with red streaks in it. He remembered someone telling him once that clear water was unhealthy for any lake or river outside mountain country. Dark waters held life, that was the rule. He dipped his hand in it, marveling. This was only the second lake he had seen up close. The water laughed quietly along the shore, and the flat vista glittered hypnotically in late daylight. It was surprisingly peaceful.

He could hear the song of the lake. It was deep and powerful, belying the tranquillity of the surface. Thin grass grew here, but the soil beneath his feet was shallow, quickly giving way to sand. Below that, rock? He couldn't quite make it out, though it felt like there was something else down there, a unique presence deep below the earth.

He sat down, mind empty for the first time in days, and watched the water for a while. Gradually, without really trying, he began hearing the voices of the waves.

They trilled like little birds as they approached the shore. Each had its own name, but otherwise they were impossible to tell apart. They rolled humming toward Jordan, then fell silent without fanfare as they licked the sand. It was like solid music converging on him where he sat. He had never heard anything so beautiful or delicately fragile.

He didn't even notice the failing light or the cold as he sat transfixed. His mind could not remain focused forever, though, and after a while he made up a little game, trying to follow individual waves with both his eyes and his inner sense.

He tried to follow the eddies of a particular wave as it broke around a nearby rock, and in doing so he discovered something new. It seemed like such an innocent detail at first: as the wave split, so did its voice. From one, it became many, then each tinier individuality vanished in turbulence. As they did, they cried out, not it seemed in fright, but in tones almost of delight. Urgent delight—as if at the last second they had discovered something important they needed to tell the world.

If he closed his eyes, now, he could see the waves and the lake, finely outlined as in an etching, gray on black. Many words and numbers hovered over the ghost landscape, joined by lines or what looked like arrows to faintly sketched features of the shoreline or lake surface. If he focused on one of those, it instantly expanded, and he was surrounded by a swirl of numbers: charts, mathematical figures, geometric shapes. It was beautiful and nonsensical.

The most important part of it, he decided, was that this ghostly vision apparently let him see with his eyes closed. Was this how Calandria May had seen the forest when she lured him away from the path, so many nights ago?

He stared at the wavelets, listening down the chain of nested identities: lake, swell, wave, crest, and ripple. Each sang its identity only for as long as it existed. In water, consciousness arose and vanished, merged and split as freely as the medium itself.

Jordan had been raised to think of himself and other people as having souls. Souls were indivisible. What he heard happening out in the lake were voices that could not possibly be attached to souls, because the very identities behind those voices freely changed, merged, and nested inside one another. Even the word *beings* couldn't be applied to them because it implied a stability impossible for them.

"What are you?" he whispered, staring out at the lake of voices.

I am water.

Over the next hour Jordan asked a few halting questions of the lake, the sand, and the stones. Few of the answers made any sense. For the most part he sat with his head tilted, listening to voices only he could hear. If Tamsin or Suneil crept up to watch and sadly shake their heads, he didn't care, because he had taken a great secret by the edge, and he wasn't going to let anything stop him from grasping it entirely.

When he finally dragged himself back to camp, the others were asleep. Suneil had offered to let him sleep in the wagon tonight, but Jordan was too tired to make the effort, and saw no point in disturbing them. He rolled himself near the fire and fell instantly asleep.

He dreamed about dolphins, which he had heard of but never seen. In the dream they swam in the earth itself, and leaped and splashed in it as though it were a liquid. He chased them across a rough, rocky landscape and at times he almost caught them, but they laughed as they danced just out of reach. Finally he made one last effort and dove after one as it entered the ground, and he followed it into dark liquid earth. He slid among the rocks and sinews of the solid world with perfect ease, knowing now where the dolphins were going: to find a secret buried deep in the earth.

He woke up. He lay on his back by the cold embers of the fire, and it seemed like some sound hovered above him. Someone had spoken.

Jordan rolled over. It was early morning and fantastically misty. It looked like the camp had been put inside a pearl. Directly overhead, it was bright; at the horizons dark still reigned. There was no sound at all now. The mist absorbed everything, causing him to cough hesitantly to check that he could hear at all.

As Jordan sat stoking the fire, Tamsin emerged from the wagon. She was dressed in woolen trousers, several layered white shirts, and something she had yesterday told him was called a poncho. She looked around once, and a big grin split her face. It was the first time he had seen her smile, and it utterly transformed her. She became electrically exuberant when she smiled.

"It's great!" She waved at the mist. "I've never seen it so thick. I'm going to go see what the lake looks like."

"Okay."

She walked purposefully into the directionless gray, stopping when she had become a two-dimensional shape against it.

"Mr. Mason?" Her voice sounded timid; there were no echoes and no other sound.

"Yes?"

"You can come, too, if you want." Jordan shook his head and followed. He was cold and achy, but he knew the walk would warm him faster than sitting by the fire.

"How are you feeling?" he asked Tamsin.

"Good." She stopped and massaged her shin. "Still hurts, but it's okay to walk on." The wagon vanished behind them, but the fire remained a diffuse orange landmark.

As they walked on, he tried to think of something more to say. For some reason, his mind had gone blank. Tamsin seemed to be having the same problem. She walked with her hands behind her back, head down except at intervals when she made a show of peering through the fog.

The low gray lines of the ruins coalesced ahead of them. Tamsin stood on a low wall that once must have supported a large house. She raised her arms, making the mauve poncho fall into a broad crescent covering her torso.

"Your uncle's not used to traveling," Jordan observed.

"He was a cloth merchant back home," she said. Tamsin lowered her arms and stepped down. "He was really rich, I think. Before the war. When he had to leave home, he took some of his best cloth. We've been selling it to buy food and stuff. But we're all out of it now."

"Did you live with him before?"

She shook her head. He wanted to ask her about her family, but could think of no way to do it.

"He saved me. When the war came to my town, the soldiers were burning everything. It was a surprise attack. I was trying to get home, but the soldiers were in the way. Uncle, he appeared out of nowhere and took me away. He saved my life." She shrugged. "That's all."

"Oh." They walked on.

"Thanks," she said suddenly.

"For what?"

"For coming with us. For helping out." She hesitated, then added, "And for putting up with me."

Jordan found he was smiling. She walked a few steps away, her face and form softened by mist. She was looking away from him.

"Your uncle told me you had a tragedy very recently," he said as gently as he could. "It's understandable."

"It'll be all right, though," she said a bit too brightly. "When we get to Rhiene, Uncle is going to introduce me to society there. There'll be balls, and dinners, and the rest of that. So you see, I'm ready to take up a new life now. Uncle is helping me do that."

"That's good," he said cautiously.

She took a deep breath. "My foot feels a lot better."

"Good. But you shouldn't use it too much yet."

They took a faint path down a long slope to a pebbled beach. The sound of the waves was strangely hushed here.

A vast translucent canopy of light hung over the lake now, and in the heart of it Jordan and Tamsin stopped on the shoreline, staring. Impossibly high in the air, a crescent of gold and rose as broad as the lake burned in the morning sun. The crescent outlined the top of a deep cloud-gray circle that seemed to be punched in the mist overhanging the water. Jordan could see a long, nearly horizontal tunnel of shadow stretching to infinity behind the thing.

The sense of free happiness Jordan had felt only moments ago collapsed. He backed away, hearing his own breath roaring in his ears, and aware that Tamsin was saying something, but unable to focus on what.

The vagabond moon was utterly motionless, its keel mere meters above the wave tops. There was no way to know how long it had been here, though it must have arrived sometime after Jordan had fallen asleep.

Tamsin stared up at it with her mouth open. "It's a moon," she said. "A real moon."

"Hush," he said. "We shouldn't be here."

"This . . . was this what destroyed the . . ."

"The Boros household." Jordan nodded, looking up, and up, at the kilometer of curving tessellated hull above them. The thing was so broad that its bottom seemed flat above the wave tops; only by tracking the eye along the curve for many meters could he begin to see the curve, and then its dimensions nearly vanished in the fog before the circle began to close. If not for the sun making its top incandescent, he could almost have missed its presence, simply because it was too large to take in without turning one's head and thinking about what one was seeing.

The important question was what was going on under its keel. Nothing, apparently; there was no open mouth there now, no gantried arms reaching for the shoreline.

Whatever reason it had for being here, it must not have to do with Jordan. It could have plucked him from his bedroll at any time during the night, after all.

The fog was lifting, but it didn't occur to Jordan that this would make him more visible. He had no doubt the thing could see through night, fog, or smoke to find him, if it chose to.

"It's beautiful," she said after a minute in which the moon remained perfectly motionless. "What's it doing here?"

"It looks like it's waiting for something." The skin on the back of his neck prickled. Could it be waiting for reinforcements? No, that was silly. Jordan was no threat to this behemoth. It didn't know he was here; he kept telling himself that, even as he fought to slow his racing heart.

"Uncle said he heard the one that attacked the Boros household was looking for someone," said Tamsin.

"Really?" Jordan felt his face grow hot. "I hadn't heard that."

The rising sun slanted into the interior of the vagabond moon, and the entire shape seemed to catch fire. From a diffuse amber center, colors and intricate crosshatched shadows spread to a perimeter of gaudy rainbow highlights that glittered like jewelry on the moon's skin. That was ice, Jordan realized, frosted on the upper canopy so high above. It must be cold up there.

A faint cracking sound reached his ears. At the same time, he saw a tiny cascade of white tumble from the sunlit side of its hull. The falling cloud grew quickly into a torrent of ice and snow that struck the water with a sound like distant applause.

"Maybe we should leave," said Tamsin.

He nodded. He was afraid, but he wished he didn't have to be. The vagabond moon was so achingly beautiful, the way wolves and other wild things were. How he wanted to make peace with such beautiful, dangerous creatures.

I could speak to it, he realized. A mad idea; its wrath would descend on him for sure then.

"Let's go." Tamsin took his hand.

"Wait." He shook himself, stumbling over the words he wanted to say, to express what he was feeling. Then he thought about what Calandria had told him about the Winds, and his awe deepened even further.

"We made that," he whispered.

Neither said anything more as they walked back to the camp.

They arrived to find Suneil frantically hitching the horses. They didn't speak, but fell to decamping alongside him. It was nice to have Tamsin's help this time, since she knew where everything went. As they worked, each would pause now and then to stare at the gigantic sphere standing over the lake. Now that the sunlight was filling it, it was beginning to slowly rise.

The other two seemed increasingly frightened, but Jordan was calm, more so as the mist burned off completely, leaving them exposed to the gaze of the Wind. It had no interest in him; unlike Tamsin and her uncle, he was certain that today at least it was no threat. So when he paused, it was to admire it rather than to worry.

The road led along the edge of the lake, under the shadow of the moon. Suneil wanted to go the other way, backtracking until it was safe. Jordan did his best to calm the old man and eventually convinced him to go forward. Still, he couldn't shake a feeling of unease as they passed beneath the now sky-blue wall of the moon. Maybe it hadn't acted because there was no way he could escape; when he got too far away, it might just waft after him and pick him up.

They were about two kilometers down the curve of the lake, just starting to relax, when thunder roared behind them. *This is it*, thought Jordan, and he turned to look.

The clamshell doors on the bottom of the vagabond moon had opened. What must be thousands of tonnes of reddish gravel and boulders were tumbling into the lake, raising foaming whitecaps in a widening ring. As he watched, the waves reached the shore and erased the distant thread of footsteps he and Tamsin had left in the sand. The water washed up the hillside nearly to the ruins and receded only when the last of the stones had trickled into the water.

Lightning played around the crown of the moon. It began to rise, and in a few minutes it had become a coin-size disk at the zenith. The nervous horses trotted on, and no one spoke.

19

ARMIGER CLOSED HIS hand over Megan's breast. She smiled at the touch and lay back on the satin.

One candle burned outside their canopy bed. Its light turned her skin deep gold. He slid his fingertips along her collarbone, and kissed her belly lightly. Her stomach undulated from the touch. "Mm," she murmured. "You are becoming a better lover every time, you know that?"

He grinned at her, but said nothing. Feeling strong tonight, he had conjured fresh strawberries and crushed a few over her chest as sauce. He could still taste it, a bit.

He had told her that the strawberries came from the queen's private garden. Megan would have been upset to know he was wasting his precious energies on an indulgence.

She wrapped her legs around him when he came up to breathe, and ground against him. They both laughed, ending the sound with a deep kiss. Then he entered her, for the third time this evening.

Night breezes flapped the curtains; this was the only sound other than their own. Some part of him was amazed at the quiet, but then he had never been under siege before. Perhaps silence was the inevitable response to being trapped for so long. It was the silence of waiting.

She watched as he came, then drew him down next to her. "I'm done," she said. "You finished me off!"

He was still panting. "Um," was all he managed. Megan laughed.

For a few hours at a time, he could exchange Armiger the engine for Armiger the man. At moments like this, he knew he treasured such times. He also knew that in a minute or an hour, cold rationality would steal over him, like a settling dew, both bringing him back to his deeply treasured self, and driving out the warmth Megan made him feel.

Spontaneously, he hugged her tightly. She gasped.

"What is it?"

"Nothing." For a few moments he couldn't bring himself to let go. When he did, he flopped back, staring at the embroidered canopy. It was one of the few pieces of bedding in the palace that had not been shredded for the thousand and one needs of a military occupation: bandages, lashing broken spars together, enshrouding the dead. The queen, he thought idly, was unfair; she would never make a decent general if she wasn't consistent with her sacrifices.

"No, what?"

He blinked. Whatever he had been feeling, it was gone already. "I don't know," he whispered.

"What don't you know?" She propped herself up on her elbow, peering at him in the faint richness of candlelight.

Armiger waved a hand vaguely. "Who I am," he said at last, "at times like these."

"Yourself," she said. Megan put a hand on his chest. "You're yourself." She looked away. "It's practically the only time."

He smelled strawberries. Strange; he barely remembered doing that. Something was slipping away, moment by moment. He remembered other evenings with her, when after turning away from her he had felt instead that something returned to him.

To forestall the change, he rolled on his side, putting his nose to hers. "Am I that cold?"

"Not right now."

He ran his hand up her flank. "Why do you stay with me, then? I don't know how to please you. . . ."

"What do you think you've been doing the last three hours?"

"Ah." But he didn't know what he'd been doing. Something that felt to the body exactly like rage had taken him over—but it was the opposite of rage in the things it made him do, and in the purity of the release it gave. Rage he understood. Armiger had come lately to identify it as the single emotion he could recall from his time subsumed into the greater identity of the god 3340. Whether that rage was the god's or his, who could tell? There was no way to know, any more than he could distinguish where his own consciousness had left off and that of 3340 began.

This, like nearly everything about himself, he could never hope to explain to Megan.

She shook him by the shoulder. "Stop it!"

"Hum?"

"You're thinking again! It's the middle of the night. You don't have to be thinking now."

"Ah." He chuckled, and cupped her breast. "I'm sorry. But I'm not sleepy."

"You don't really sleep, anyway." She yawned extravagantly. "But I need to."

"Go ahead. I'll read." He nodded to the gigantic stack of books by the bed.

She laughed and lay back. For a while he watched the jumbled heap of hair snuggle itself deeper into the pillows. Then she said, almost inaudibly, "Which do you prefer?"

Armiger leaned over her and kissed her cheek. "Which what do I prefer?"

"Do you prefer making love or reading?" He voice held a teasing note, but he had learned there were frequently hidden needs behind her teasing questions.

"To read is to make love to the world," he said. "But to make love to a woman is to feel like the world is reading you."

She smiled, not comprehending, and fell asleep.

Leaving Armiger the man behind, or so he imagined, he stood to dress. Freed from the need for dialogue, his mind fell in upon itself, and the myriad other sides of Armiger the god awoke.

All night, as he made love to Megan, these other sides of his self had been thinking, planning, raging, and debating in the higher echoes of his consciousness. He had read sixteen books yesterday and had been revising his opinions about Ventus and the Winds as he assimilated the knowledge. Now he stood for several minutes, fingers touching the leather cover of the next volume he intended to absorb. He was not so much contemplating as watching the vast edifice of his understanding of Ventus shift, and settle, and grow new entranceways and wings.

He had discovered something: the Winds were not mad. They were up to something.

Armiger cursed softly. He no longer saw the candle flame or felt the hard cover of the book. For it was all there in the histories and philosophical inquiries, if one knew how to read the signs. The Winds acted capriciously, but everyone knew they ultimately acted in the interests of nature. They were the guides of the terraforming process, he knew. Terraforming a planet was neither a quick process nor one that had an end. The climate of Ventus would never achieve equilibrium; without the constant intervention of the planet's ruling spirits, the air would cool and the oxygen-carbon cycles oscillate out of control. The world would experience alternate phases of hyperoxygenation and asphyxiation, coupled with disastrous atmospheric circulation locks; parts of the globe would be under almost constant rain, others would never receive rain at all. Everything would die, in the long run.

The Winds exercised great intelligence and forbearance. They played the clouds and ocean waves of Ventus like the most grand and complex instruments. Their symphonic teamwork was perfect.

So, capricious they might be, but the Winds were not purposeless. Everyone on and off Ventus knew this. When it came to dealing with other intelligent entities, however, they did at first seem mad. The histories he had been reading, which were more extensive than those available off-world, told of massacres and blessings, following no apparent pattern, which the poor human residents of this world had struggled for centuries to justify and predict. The accepted theory was that they viewed human activity as an assault on the ecosystem and acted to defend it. Armiger had read enough by now to know that it simply wasn't so.

Throughout the history of the world, men and women had appeared who claimed to be able to communicate with the Winds. Sometimes they were hanged as witches. Sometimes they were able to prove their claims, and then they founded religions.

The Winds were difficult entities to worship because they had the annoying characteristic of possessing minds of their own. Gods, one philosophical wag had commented, should conveniently remain on the altar, rather than rampaging indiscriminately across the land.

The Winds were utterly inconsistent about enforcing their ecological rules where it came to Man. He had seen it himself; there were smelters in some of the larger towns, pouring black smoke into the atmosphere, while the tiny waft of sulfur dioxide he had used in chemical warfare in one battle had cost Armiger his entire army. The Winds had obliterated every man involved in the engagement. Armiger had stood helplessly on the crown of the hill, where he was directing his troops, and watched as they all died.

He had felt nothing at the time. Remembering now, he suppressed an urge to pick up the book he touched and throw it through the window.

Something was going on here. The Winds were neither malicious nor mad, nor were they indifferent to humanity. They were obeying some tangle of rules he simply hadn't seen yet. If he could find out what it was . . .

Something made him turn. There was no one in the room, and Megan hadn't moved. Nonetheless, he sensed someone nearby.

A woman was weeping out in the hallway.

ARMIGER DRESSED, THEN blew out the candle, which itself had been an extravagance. In his time here he had heard more weeping than laughter. There was nothing unusual in it. But without knowing exactly why, he found himself walking hesitantly to the door.

It opened soundlessly onto a pitch-dark hallway. There were windows at either end of the corridor, but they didn't illuminate, only served as contrast to the blackness within.

For a moment Armiger stood blind as any man, surprised at the help-lessness of the sensation. Then he remembered to slide the frequency of his vision up and down until he found a wavelength in which he could see. A few months ago, that action would have been automatic. He scowled as he looked around for the source of the sound.

The woman was huddled on the floor halfway down the hall. She cra-dled something in her lap. An infant, perhaps? Armiger opened his mouth to speak, then thought better. He cleared his throat.

She started visibly and looked up. "Who's there?" Her head bobbed back and forth as she tried to see. She was middle-aged, matronly, dressed in a peasant frock. Strange that she should be in this part of the palace . . . no, perhaps it was stranger that these halls hadn't yet been turned into a barracks.

"I heard you," he said. "Are you injured?"

It was what he would have asked a man. He didn't know what to ask when a woman cried. But she nodded. "My arm," she whimpered, nod-ding down at it. "Broken." As if the admission cost her more than the injury, she began to cry all the harder.

"Has it been seen to?" He knelt beside her.

"No!"

"Let me see." He gently reached to touch her elbow. She winced. Feel-ing his way, he found the break, a clean one, in the tibia. The bones had slid apart slightly and would have to be set. He told her this.

"Can you do it?"

"Yes." She had a tattered shawl draped over her shoulders. "I'll use this to immobilize it. Just a moment." He needed something for a splint. The furniture had been completely stripped out of here, but the walls were wood, with a good deal of ornamental paneling and stripping. Armiger found a beveled edge to one of the panels, and with several quick jerks, he pulled the wood strip away from the wall. It groaned like a lost soul as it came. He broke it over his knee and returned to the woman.

He didn't warn her before taking her forearm and pulling it straight.

She yelped, but it was all over before she had time to tense or really feel the pain. Armiger aligned the stripping with her wristbones and wrapped it quickly with strips from her shawl. Then he bound the whole assembly in a sling about her neck.

"Why wasn't it set earlier?" From the swelling, he judged she had broken it earlier in the day.

"I shouldn't be here," she said.

"That's not what I asked."

"Yes, it is you see because the soldiers, they, some of them are hurt, so bad, and there's not enough people to tend them. I, I went there, but one man, his stomach was open, and he was dying but they wouldn't leave him, and another his eyes were burned somehow. And I stood at the doorway and they were all hurt so badly, I, I couldn't go in there with just my silly broken arm. I couldn't . . ." She wept, clutching him with her good hand.

What Armiger said he said not to comfort her, but because he had observed this in human men: "But the soldiers would have gladly given up their beds to a woman."

"Yes, and I hate them for it." She pushed him away. "It's the arrogance of men that leads them to sacrifice themselves. Not real consideration."

Armiger sat back, confused. "How did you get in here?" he asked at last.

"I'm a friend of one of the maids. She offered to shelter me when, when the soldiers came. I didn't know where to go, I couldn't go back and tell her I didn't go into the infirmary. I had nowhere to go."

He knew the room next to his was vacant. "Come." He lifted her to her feet and guided her to it. There was enough light here to make out the canopied bed and dressers, and fine gilded curtains.

"I can't sleep here." Her voice held shock.

"You will."

"But in the morning—if the queen finds out—"

"If they ask, tell them Armiger authorized it. Sleep well." Without another word, he closed the door. His last glimpse was of her standing uncertainly in the center of the room.

For a long time he stood, arms folded. He heard her climb on the bed at last. Only then did he turn and walk to the stairs.

A STABLE HAD been taken over to house the infirmary. Despite the lateness of the hour, it was far from quiet as Armiger walked in. Men groaned or wept openly. In a curtained alcove, someone screamed every few seconds—short gasps of unremitting agony. No one else could sleep with that going on, though a good number of men lay very still on the straw, their eyes closed, their chests rising and falling shallowly.

There were twenty men and women here tending the injured. They looked like none of them had slept in days.

These wounded were merely the casualties from the withdrawal of Galas's hillside defenses. When Lavin stormed the walls this stable would oveflow.

Actually, it would burn, he thought as he walked along the rows of men, appraising their injuries.

"Are you looking for someone?"

He turned to find a red-eyed man in bloodstained jester's gear watching him from a side table. The table was strewn with bottles and medical instruments. The man's arms were brown up to the elbows with old blood.

"I can help," said Armiger.

"Are you trained?"

"Yes." He knew the human body well, and he could see inside it if he wished. Armiger had never tried healing before.

"It's hard," said the jester.

"I know." Armiger had realized, however, that the same lack of empathy that allowed him to send a squad of young men to certain death for tactical reasons, would allow him to act and make decisions to save them, where other men's compassion would paralyze them.

He nodded toward the curtained alcove. "What is his problem."

The jester ran a hand through his hair. "Shattered pelvis," he said briefly.

Armiger thought about it. "I'll take a look." He glanced around. "First, though, let's see the others."

The jester led, and Armiger moved down the rows of men and performed triage.

NEAR DAWN, GALAS stood watching from the window in her bed chamber. Behind her were the carven trees and fauna of a fantastical woodland scene. It was no regular pattern of pillars cunningly disguised, nor a frescoed wall carven and layered with images; the architect had denied the privilege of rectilinear space here. Like a real forest, the lower boughs obscured vision and prevented movement between different parts of the chamber, and the great roots of the stone trees sprawled across the floor with no regard for the cult of the level surface. There was no order to the staggered forms, or any symmetry save the aesthetic, which made this room into a group of bowers inside the straight-edged castle tower.

The window itself looked like a gap in the foliage of a jade-carved hedge. Each tiny leaf had been faithfully reproduced in stone, and in daylight they shone with a verdant brilliance that would normally soothe the queen's heart.

She had seldom been here in the day. As she traced the outline of a leaf with the tip of one finger, she knew she might never have the time to be, now. Odd that the possibility of never seeing this window in daylight again should be what now struck her with the horror of her coming death.

She thought about the strange Wind, Maut, as she sat by the window to watch the moon set. He was letting her look straight into the labyrinth of eternity, at the moment when death was inevitable and imminent. She hated him for that.

She turned to her maid Ninete, who sat slumped on a divan nearby. Ninete was required to remain awake as long as Galas, and tonight the queen had not slept at all. "He knows there is nothing I can say to him," said Galas intensely. Ninete was startled at being addressed as a person; she said nothing in reply.

Galas fixed her gaze on the maid. "He is cruel, to put it plainly. Why is he telling me these things? I know he is only telling the truth. It is that which is so terrible. He is telling the truth. As to things which should properly be lied about."

Ninete recovered herself. "Let me comb out your hair," she said. The queen rose with a nod and went to her dressing table. Ninete stood behind her and began letting down her hair into dark waves, which tumbled down her back.

"Perhaps he thinks it really will not hurt me to know my whole life has been lived in vain. I wanted to change things, that was what ruled me. I wanted to change what could not be changed, what had never been seen as anything but absolute. I wanted to dissolve the absolute. Maut . . . Maut, says this has been done before.

"I knew that everything now absolute was once a fantasy. What is good was once evil. He is unaware how devastating such a realization is to human beings. In fact, he's not really bothering to speak of that. He takes it as a starting point. Takes it as given that this upheaval that has been my life is like the dance of dust motes in sunlight—just an alternation, and change in height of those motes in the galaxy of relations visible to us. He neglects that I am such a mote myself. . . ."

Bothered, Ninete combed silently. In the mirror Galas could see her uncomprehending look. "We could die in two days," she said.

"I know," said Ninete simply. Galas waited for more, but it didn't come.

"Aren't you afraid?"

"My Queen, I'm terrified." Ninete's expression shifted from the neutral silence it had held to an ashen tautness. Her lips thinned, her eyes lost their focus. "I don't want to die now."

Queen Galas looked at her, her own eyes taking on a certain coldness Ninete had seen so frequently in them. But Galas's hand trembled as it searched among the combs, hairpins, pots of makeup on the dressing table.

"You don't want to die. But you understand what death is."

"The soldiers will kill us, Lady. I've seen people die."

"Resume." Ninete brought the brush up again. "Ninete, you will die a good death. You see death so simply. Death to you is the general's men storming the castle. It is missiles from the air, swords, vindictive rape, and humiliation. Most of all never to see those you love again, never again to hold those talks, to make love . . . You understand death, you have studied it the way all folk do, and for your understanding you have recourse to the religious teachings, the rituals, the tragic lovers in stories. You understand it, in the lyricism of fear you have been taught."

Galas's hand hovered over this comb, that pin, uncertainly. "I don't understand it at all. I don't see those lovers, I cannot imagine the body laid in its tomb, those somber brown poems—they don't speak to me. Death says nothing to me. I wish it did. I wish I could see what was going to happen to me, two, three days hence.

"Maut is himself death, but he can't tell me." She turned to look up into Ninete's face. "He refuses to make it into a sign for me. That is what is so cruel."

Her hand descended on a long golden hairpin. "Ninete, leave me! Work on my breakfast. See it is the best you have ever orchestrated. I have no need of you now."

Sullen, Ninete left. Galas watched the emotions play across her shoulders, down her hips as she walked. Ninete read even this rejection like a scene in some traditional play, Galas saw. She had been sent away. And just when she was hearing the queen's heart speak.

Clutching the pin, she rose and went to the window. A stone bird watched from the carven boughs above her head.

"Where is this coming from?" she asked, staring at the tremble in her hand. What she had been saying just now made no sense to her. Her fear made no sense. She was angry with Maut, but did not know why. Her mind swung round and round the things he had talked about today. Behind his words she sensed a kind of bewilderment in him, as though the engine of human speech remained incapable of rendering his experience to her, however precise the mind of the god that powered it.

Nothing explained her fury just now, however, not even the general's campfires in the valley outside. In fact, they were rather beautiful. . . .

She raised the long pin and stabbed it into her left shoulder. The pain pulled her to her feet—she hissed and pulled the pin out, casting it furiously out the window.

There it was, the agony of terror and fury. It came boiling up from some hidden source inside her, taking form in blinding tears, as she curled around herself, holding her shoulder. She tried to escape the pain, turning, turning, but it moved with her. Slumping onto a stone root, she began to cry in great gusts. There it was: confusion, chaos. She wanted to run, run anywhere, and it was her body that was telling her this. Run, escape.

Her body was afraid. It was her body that was speaking in her anger at Maut and in her fear of death. She had been neglecting it, living in her understanding and within that realm she had just accused Ninete of inhabiting: the realm of the story. How could she fail to see in her mind's eye the riders coming through the gate, the expressions on her people's faces as they ran from her, to join the other side? It was the story of her death she had been telling herself, even as she tried to listen to Maut, tried to see his images, his life.

She could no more escape into his life than she could bring her death to herself here, now, by her worry.

She watched the line of blood move down her breast. The pain was intense. She reveled in it, for with it the phantasms of the day after tomorrow had fled, and Maut's story was mere words again.

In tears, the wonder of despair and release welled from her with the blood. She remembered that once, she had loved her life.

Afraid that Ninete would hear her and come running, Galas put her head out the window. She let herself cry out, once, then hung her head.

"Your Highness?"

The voice came from below. She blinked away tears, and looked down the battlement fifteen feet below. A man stood there, his form outlined in the silver, rose, and black of predawn light. It was Maut.

She cleared her throat. "Are you sleepless, too?" Her words sounded unsteady, frightening to herself.

"Yes." He seemed cool as the night air, as always. "I was helping in the infirmary."

"Really?" Galas wiped at her eyes. "How are my men?"

"Holding up bravely."

"And you?"

He didn't answer, but turned to look out over the courtyards of the palace.

"Maut," she said on impulse, "join me in my chamber."

His silhouette nodded. He vanished from sight like a ghost, and she pulled herself inside, wincing.

First, she must bandage herself. Galas tore a piece of embroidered linen and wrapped her wound clumsily. Then she selected a high-necked black gown and wove herself into it. Without a maid to help, she couldn't do up the back. So she sat back on the divan, feeling the cool velvet against her back. The sensation set her skin tingling.

She gnawed her thumbnail, a habit her mother had never cured her of, and waited.

Presently there came a polite tap on the door. "Enter," she said.

Maut's hair was disheveled, and faint lines were etched around his eyes and between his brows. He had discarded his jacket and rolled up the sleeves of his white blouse. He nodded to her like an intimate, and sat on the chair near her bed. She glimpsed Ninete peeking around the edge of the door, and waved her off impatiently. The door slid closed.

Neither spoke for a while. Outside, she heard the first voicing of a morning bird.

"Will you join me for breakfast?" she said at last.

"I would be honored."

"No, Maut. Don't say that. Will you?"

He smiled wanly. "I would like to, yes."

"Good." She gestured impatiently. "I have no more time for ceremony."

Maut drew up one knee and clasped his hands around it, like a boy. He could only look more at home, she thought, if he sat sideways in the chair.

He cocked his head and looked at her appraisingly. "Ceremony has never suited you, has it?"

She laughed shortly. "No. It's only familiarity that gets me through it. The words come automatically. Even if they're so often like ashes in my mouth."

"I find it hard to believe that this alone is the root of your passion. Because your passion radiates from some deep source. It catches up everyone around you. That's why they follow you, you know. Not because you're queen."

"Ah." This was a compliment she had never heard before. "I'm sure you know my story. Am I not the scandal of the kingdom?"

He shrugged. "I've heard things. They were obvious distortions. I came to you because I wanted to hear the story from the source."

"Why?"

He considered, staring out at the amber sky. "I have been reading the books in your library. They all point to something . . . a mystery. I mean a mystery in the religious sense, almost. A meaning. When I came here I thought I was after facts, but now I see I'm after more than that. I want answers."

"You? The man whose very mind is an impregnable fortress of history?" She laughed. "You astonish me."

Serious, he said, "In the bits and pieces of your story that I've heard, I catch echoes of that mystery. I believe you know more than you realize. You have wisdom you have hidden from yourself."

"And can you show me this wisdom?" Her hands trembled, as they had in the garden when his messenger fluttered down to land on her knee.

"I don't know."

"You toy with me!" She had leaned forward in anger and felt the folds of her dress fall apart at her back. Galas sat back again quickly.

"No."

"And what will you give me in return for my story? I think I no longer wish to hear your own tale."

He looked at her for a long moment. Something like a smile danced around his lips. Galas found her heart racing at his examination, and her eyes traced the muscles in his arms, the set of his shoulders.

Then he did smile, rather impishly. "I should be very much surprised if you do not have the answer to that question by noon," was all he said.

"Well."

Maut leaned forward, the weariness returned to his eyes. "Tell me your story," he said.

Galas closed her eyes. In her life, only one other had asked her for this—not *the* story, but her story. Grief choked her momentarily.

"All right. I shall try to tell it as a tale—as I've often wanted to. I . . . I pictured myself sometimes, setting my child on my knee and telling it. There will be no child. But here is the story."

20

FIRST, YOU MUST understand that I was considered mad as a child, even as I am today. The reasons were not the same, however—in my childhood it was my sense of justice that went against me. I treated peasants and servants with the same respect as kings and princes, and this evoked great ire in my mother, with whom I warred constantly. She strove to impress upon me the war between classes and the divine rightness of this war. It was not that I sided with the lesser people against my own—which however reprehensible would mave made sense to her—it was that I saw no difference whatever between us.

And then, when I was twelve summers old, that thing happened without which I might have grown up to become an ordinary princess—ha! Yes, there is such a thing.

You see, my father kept a book—as his predecessor had, and all the kings back into antiquity. This book contained various proclamations of the Winds made over the centuries, along with interpretations and auguries. And it came to pass that the unusual weather of the springtime and a disastrous fire in Belfonre matched some of the auguries in the book, and the only interpretation that my father and his wise men could make of the augury was that the queen must die.

In later years I came to understand that this was a pretext—he had his eye on another woman, who in time he married. She turned out to be barren, but he was not to admit the fact for many years. Anyway, at the time, I understood nothing, save that the Winds had commanded the death of my mother.

I was in the gardens with my favorite duenna when word came of the arrest of my mother. My duenna immediately burst into tears, falling on her knees before me and clutching at my skirt. She being older had grasped immediately what was occurring but I had yet to. We had been idly discussing some aspect of human nature, its rigidity I believe, which she took for granted and I in my young zeal rejected absolutely. "Nothing in us is fixed," I had said, pouting. My mother's execution was now fixed, however, and this duenna cried out, "O Princess, your youth is forever gone now! Where is the young girl I played with in these summer gardens? Soon you will be an embittered woman with revenge against life driving you. You will cease to laugh, you will weep at life, and you will send me away for reminding you of times lost now when you could be happy!"

"Lady, there is no sense in your words," I said to her. I could feel the emotions overspilling around, the shaking of the messenger, the crying of my older friend, and saw how the windows that opened on the gardens were closing, one after another, shutting inside the airs of grief. For that moment I was the only calm stone in the rising flood. I shall not be carried away, I resolved. In moments all that the messenger and the duenna were possessed by would strike out to possess me—their human nature, of the same order, I felt, as the artificial distinctions between class, which even they supported.

It was a moment of supreme mystery. How could the brightness of the flowers, the coolth of the air, my own happiness be so swept away by an event that was, now rumor, later merely fact against which I could do nothing? I loved my mother and knew that would never change, whatever happened. I looked into the future and saw myself weeping alone in my bedroom, and it was as a figure from a drama that I saw myself, moving to commands issued by some forgotten playwright. I felt a certainty at that moment that it was so, that my duenna's shock, my coming grief were roles cast for us by someone, someone great far in the past. I could be other than grief stricken, if I chose. I could go mad, in other words.

I chose to go mad. In that moment I decided that although I could not change the fate of my mother, there was no law immutable in the heavens that decreed how I was to react to it. Only much, much later in life can I look back and see that whether I knew it or not, I was under the sway of an emotion then: fury, which I swallowed so deeply that I was unable to experience it until . . . oh, very recently.

"Come," I said to the duenna. "Rise, and let us practice a while on our dulcimers. The day is still fair, and the next ones will not be." She looked at me with a new horror in her eyes, and I knew I was lost. I wondered what was to come of it, now that I was no longer playing my role in the drama begun by my father.

He was terrified of me from then on. The servants treated me with gentle respect, as one does the mad. They knew I was so overtaken with grief—although I did not witness my mother's execution, and I had seen her a few afternoons a week since I was a babe, never for more than a few hours at a time—that I could no longer feel anything. The king, however, believed I was training myself in hate, keeping inside me a desire for revenge that was willing to wait. He thought perhaps that I would kill him in his dotage, when he could not raise a hand to defend himself. As I grew toward womanhood, he began to look for ways to dispose of me. For I was sunny and cheerful, I claimed to forgive him for slaying my mother, and I was gracious to his new queen. I harbored no instinct for revenge, in fact; on that day when I was told of my mother's arrest I had embarked on a great journey, which I am on to this day, and there was nothing but gratitude in my heart for being given the opportunity to be alive and yet to have left the human race behind me.

They danced around me as I daydreamed, the figures of all those storied lovers, traitors, thieves and kings and saints and I saw them all as actors even to themselves. If there was a human nature it lay buried far below such inventions as grief and love, so I was sure, and the daring of this vista intoxicated my youth.

I was not expected to become scholarly as I am, for I was a woman. I decided not to believe there was any difference between man and woman, so had tutors hired. The indulgence was given, for my father's auguries said nothing about how to treat the mad, so I was allowed to do what others could not.

Oh, I could be charming, and as subtle in my understanding as any scheming courtier—more so, since I was learning the true bounds of human nature. As I grew, however, my desires became less and less those of the girl I had been, became quite estranged from court and all the ambitions that ruled there. For I saw through those, too.

At times, I do not deny it, I was indeed mad, locking myself in my tower and singing to the owls. I would lie upon my bed for days staring at the ceiling, bereft of purpose or understanding and at times weeping over what was lost: grief itself was lost to me, and love and the innocence of romance. Handsome princes and true love meant nothing to me on the journey I had undertaken, but they were believed in by all about me. I longed for an understanding that was no longer possible from these people. Of all those at court it was still the servants and lowly laborers whom I loved the best, for they loved me. They knew I was not mad, but daring in a way even kings were not. The poor have no love of roles, and so they appear callous even with their own; they can love better than we, though, for they are honest in what they do feel. They saw I had in an instant rejected the whole world in which I was brought up, if it led to senseless death and thence to fixed orbits for all involved forever. Too, I championed their causes to the king and was often indulged by him when no other suitor would succeed.

At length he, noticing my unwomanly interest in sciences and historical studies, hit upon a means of disposing of me. If I would be a scholar, he would give me full reign to be one. In fact, he would allow me to command an expedition then being mounted by the University of Rhiene to measure seismic changes caused by the deep movement of the desals.

The desals occasionally set off thermonuclear charges deep in the mountains or in ocean trenches. For as long as records are extant, the Winds had been conducting such explosions, one or two a century at different places. Traditionally, we have forbidden any mining in the region affected for ten years after the blast, after which we let people dig as they wish. When they do, rich mineral or metal finds are always the result. I knew from my studies that the explosions were not solitary, but vast coordinated chains set off to drive precious materials closer to the surface of the earth, for our benefit. It is but one of the services that the Winds perform for us.

Yes, Maut, they do serve us. They simply do not realize it. If you let me continue, you will understand what I mean.

I well knew my father's intent. He wished me far away from him, politically powerless, and demonstrably unmarriageable. I simply did not care what his plans were. I acquiesced to his proposal for reasons of my own. In truth, I was eager to see new lands and to experience life as a man would for at least a time. I indulged myself as men did. I remember on the day appointed for sailing I sauntered down to the docks in leather breeches and a man's tunic, a heavy chest across my back containing all my scientific instruments and books, two fluttering duennas at my side unprepared for ocean life and unsure what to make of my new turn.

The hereditary scholars from the university were even less pleased to see me. They regarded my presence as an imposition—quite rightly—and myself as a scandal. They made it plain to me from the moment I stepped on deck that I would receive no aid from them, that they would obey none of my orders nor in any serious way consider me the leader of the expedition. I found it impossible to reason with them.

This was perhaps the first time since childhood that I had not been indulged instantly in my desires. I was furious and stormed down to my cabin. I believe I fumed for all of six hours before I realized that once again, I was reacting to form. What kind of reaction should I have expected from these men? They were shrewd in the maintenance of their positions and knew nothing about the composition of the real world; I was already aware of that. Why should their rejections surprise me?

I had been romanticizing, hoping that here at least there might be people to understand me. Had I expected to be able to pursue those studies I intended with these men? Surely not; for what concerned me, they had no head. So I laughed and resolved to make the best of it. This proved hard, as they chose to be cruel in the following days.

I do not know how things would have gone had we not had the good fortune to be wrecked. In order to test the extent of the explosion's effect, we had sailed far out along a chain of islands leading into the blank ocean. We were to reach one in particular, a U-shaped isle that supposedly represented the end of the archipelago, and plant our seismographs there. It was to be the journey of a week. On the third day, just after I had been ejected from the mess for eating with the sailors—they had invited me, and tradition be hanged I had agreed—I was seething at the bow as far from the captain and his supercilious mate as I could get when a squall came up. It nearly heeled the ship on its side, but that was only the presage of a worse storm that now loomed up over the horizon, black and terrible. I was bade go below and refused until the captain lost patience and had me carried down.

As I pounded on my cabin door the storm hit. For hours I think we were tumbled about like matchsticks in a pocket. My duennas were ill and panicked. I chased my chest of instruments as it slid from side to side of the cabin. As night fell the ship gave a strange shudder, and I heard the sailors shouting that we'd hit a rock. Where we had been driven I did not know, but the hold was filling rapidly and the captain, unable to control the ship, determined to save himself.

There was a single longboat, and he commandeered it, with his mate and a few of their cronies. He had no concern for me, princess though I was, for he well understood my father's intent in sending me on this expedition. There would be no brave knight to save me. My duennas clung to their embroidered cushions and refused to move. I forced open the cabin door and made for the deck.

The crew had realized their captain was abandoning them. Under savage skies, with blue light roving along the masts, and sails and lines lashing free like whips, they mobbed by one rail with every kind of weapon and tool in their hands, fighting to get to the longboat, which was now over the side but not yet cut free. I stood in the door under the madly turning wheel and watched as they killed one another. The line was suddenly cut, and the boat began to heave away, and those left at the rail dove for it in their frenzy to escape what they were certain was a doomed ship.

In moments the deck was vacant save for the dead, who with strange animation slid from rail to rail. The longboat vanished behind enormous waves. Alone save for my cowering maids, I and the doomed ship drove into the open ocean.

The rock we had hit was part of an out thrust of the archipelago few navigators knew of. It lay in a direction no sane man had need to venture. But before the ship could sink, it was driven aground. In the terrible light of the storm the coast we were upon was visible only as a jumble of black shards. My duennas refused to leave the familiarity of the cabin even though the deck tossed under them as the ship bucked to free itself from the rocks that held it. I cursed them for fools and, binding my long hair behind me and taking a knife and matches, climbed out along the foremast and leaped into the dark.

I AWOKE TO a fine morning. I was above the tide, half buried in the sand. As I sat up and looked out at the sad wreckage of the ship, I wept. I did not pause to think why now, with no human audience, I did this. The ship was submerged save for its masts, which tilted each in a different direction. No one clung to them; I was certain my maids had perished in the storm.

As I sat up I left an indentation of my own shape in the wet sand. My hair tugged, refusing to be freed from its entanglement in the earth. It was woven with seaweed and knotted terribly. I took the knife and cut it short, then stood gingerly. I was not hurt; I had swum strongly and quickly to shore, but could find no way to climb from this sandy reach up to the land above. I now looked closely for such a way and, finally spying it, dragged myself up to a grassy area fronting deep forest.

It soon became evident I was not to be alone with the wrack.

Sallow men emerged from the forest, and I, backed to the edge of the low cliff, had no escape. They had been attracted by the sight of the wreck and proceeded to loot it, while I, tied to a log and guarded by an old man, watched.

These men were dressed in an odd parody of my homeland's style. They wore breeches, but they were put together with many small skins; evidently there were no cattle on this island. Their shirts were of similar make, with a kind of armor made with cane woven through them. They seemed to lack metal. They certainly lacked refinement.

After enthusiastically diving and swimming about the wreck, and fighting on the shore over what they found, they pulled me to my feet and marched off along a slight path that led through the woods. They were comparing their prizes: one had a fish gaff, another a belaying pin, while a third had somehow pried loose the ship's wheel and lugged it over his shoulder. They had puzzled over my instruments and finally kept them only because they were metal and light enough to carry. They spoke this language, albeit roughly and with a truly criminal accent. I took them to be shipwrecked pirates or the descendants of same, while they took me to be a boy.

I might have thought my virtue, if not my life, to be safe in this misapprehension, but some leered at me despite. I endeavored to be dumb so they should not hear my voice, and also so that, if they took me to be for-eign and unlearned of their tongue, they might speak more freely among themselves.

In the event I doubt they would have thought of caution. They argued happily over their prizes and discussed how they should hide the best part from the priests who apparently ruled over them. My strategy set, I could not inquire further about these priests, but my curiosity was aroused. These people were apparently indulging in the sort of idolatry outlawed in lands such as my own, although it thrives under the ban. In short, they worshiped the desals.

What they knew of the desals in such a backward spot I could not guess, although I was soon to learn and to wonder at my own ignorance. They took me to a slipshod village, where they pulled my hair a great deal and showed me about, the more injudicious boasting of the great treas-ures in the wreck so that most of the population of the town immediately ran to claim their share. I was then taken to a finer house, where their priests lived.

The priests emerged—muddy tattered men with gaunt faces. I was paraded again before the six of them and they discussed my fate, I mean-while striving to learn as much as possible by looking about myself and listening. I spied in the darkened door of their house a woman, much cleaner, haughty of appearance and finely dressed in beads and what seemed jewelry. She was in turn appraising me. I could not fathom what was in her eyes, but her gaze was piercing.

It was decided to imprison me until my origin and possible use could be learned. I was steered away to a tumbled-down shack at the edge of the village. This had but one entrance and was built into a hillside. Thrown into the claustrophobic darkness, I watched the crude wooden door shut with mingled despair and bemusement at my suddenly fallen state. I dithered over whether to reveal myself as a woman and claim my frailty required kinder treatment, but abstained as I discovered I had a companion in this prison.

He was an old man, as eccentric as myself, whom the others had gotten tired of and disposed of here. His first words to me, and I shall never for-get them, were, "Do you like the forks with the long tines, or the forks with the short tines?"

I considered that question carefully before I answered. After all, our friendship might rest on my answer. At length I said, "I do prefer a fork with long tines, as one can be more delicate with it."

He was delighted. He pumped my hand and introduced himself, then in uninterrupted monologue spent the rest of the day describing himself, this place, and his situation. I had no need to interrupt him, as he antici-pated all my questions or spoke in such encyclopedic detail that I had no need to speak.

This place was indeed a settlement of abandoned pirates. This crowd had no shipbuilding skills—in fact, no skills at all aside from scavenging. They had a few women and after nearly thirty years here were making themselves a community.

When they arrived they had found the island already inhabited by a very small group who it seemed were descended from a previous lot of castaways. This first group was dying out, apparently because they were persecuted by a Wind.

This astonished me. There was in fact a desal on the island. I was later to learn there were even desals on the ocean floor and it seems under the perpetual glaciers in the northern and southern poles. Their actions are always mysterious. This one had taken it upon itself to kill people at random since before living memory. When it did not kill, it would render men and women sterile.

With the arrival of these new castaways, it seems to have changed its behavior slightly. It ceased killing, but now it would permit no women near itself, save one at a time of its choosing. This the arrivals and the indigenes together took as a sign of religious importance. The arrival of the new people was taken as a blessing, and they were welcomed with open arms. A new order was established whereby a woman was chosen to be the medium for the desal. No person could approach it save under her protection.

My curiosity about the desal's method of killing was satisfied when the old man told me of the miasmic clouds and strange diseases that spread out from its location. Desals do not move as such, as you may know, although some have agents to fulfil their will. This one had no such agents but relied on a preternatural sensitivity to wind and other currents. It poisoned from afar.

The people had learned to interpret it through their medium. It was chiefly interested in domestic matters, marriage and inheritance. This struck me as extremely odd, but I attributed it to the desal actually being silent, and the priestess relying on her own judgment to rule local affairs.

Desals, like all Winds, are not mute. They have been known to act spontaneously, even to speak, but usually what they say is incoherent, or totally irrelevant to human interests. I believed these people to be ruled by their superstitions regarding the thing, more than by its real actions.

The next day I was let out of my prison and told I was the property of one of the men who had first come upon me. I was to help him with his farming—gardening, rather, as he had not the skill to grow more than a few roots and berry bushes. I acquiesced.

This could not go on, however. I had no intention of being a slave here. If I could in no ways escape, I resolved to rule and to turn these savages into people more amenable to civilization. There was a great deal I could teach them. I began with my gardener, showing him the benefits of planting two kinds of crops together so they should fortify one another, keeping pests away and enriching one another's roots. While I did this I wondered how I might come to control the community.

They still took me for a young man. I spoke little and contrived to remain at least somewhat grimy—not that this was hard due to the gardening—to hide the softness of my skin. As I was so mistaken, I began to notice the young women of the community casting glances in my direction. This gave me an idea.

I remembered the look their priestess had sent me and now realized what it had meant. Although she was little seen I would contrive to be seen by her. Too, I knew it was approaching the day appointed by the desal to explode its nuclear charge underneath the mainland. I was not sure, but hoped there would be some effect felt here.

I was able to ascertain that this woman was very superstitious, believing in her role as mediator to the Wind. I let myself be visible to her, and when she cast a look I cast back. We were separated by her requirement to remain at all times in the priest's house, or to be at the desal, but this to me was an advantage.

Having some freedom, more so as I instructed my master and he saw more profit to be had in my goodwill, I managed to dally several days in a row behind the priest's house, making my desire clear to the priestess as she sat by her window. As the day dawned when the Wind would cause its explosion, I rose early and crept up to the house. Tapping lightly on her shutter until she opened it, I made myself known to her. She at once invited me in but I balked, whispering about the old men who kept her here. What if they should discover us?

She nodded, frustrated. The stricture that she remain here or at the Wind was, she said, merely a ruse by means of which the old men kept her for themselves. She had never had the attentions of a young man and wanted them a great deal. She at once agreed when I suggested she retire to consult with the desal that evening, and meet me in the woods.

I had no idea what to expect. Tradition said the Wind killed all women who came within its bounds, save for the particular one it chose as mediator. I believed this to be a superstition, but one I could use. I worked hard that day so that my master could find no fault with me, and when he gave me my leave to go I gathered up my knife and the matches and headed for the woods.

As night was falling she appeared, walking hesitantly into the woods, perfumed in her finest. I appeared on the path before her and bowed, but as she rushed to me I withdrew, saying we were too close to the town, I was afraid of discovery. It was, after all, a small island.

She agreed, but where could we go? There was one place, I advanced, where no one else would go, where in fact no one else was safe. The desal.

She demurred. The idea of having relations in her own shrine appalled her. I however was not to be put off and with a few caresses and murmured entreaties, let her chase me deeper into the woods, until we were close upon the desal itself. Then I renewed my requests. By now she would in no ways refuse me.

We approached the desal as the sun set behind it. It looked as most desals look: a wide expanse of white stonelike material, sloping upward over many meters to a spire that rose nearly fifty meters above the surrounding forest. Smaller spires stood sentinel around the outskirts of the paving. Forest had made inroads onto it, but only so far. Past the sentinel spires the material was clean and clear of debris, even pebbles. Most of the desals appear this way, whether they be sunken in a lake, on a mountaintop, or (as in Rhiene) at the center of a city.

Their chief discriminating feature is the faint etching on their surface: rectangles, octagons, or other shapes, always in different configuration. These lines represent openings or at least potential openings. Some will open themselves in response to particular conditions; others may be opened by enterprising human beings, if they possess the cleverness or technology to do so. In Iapysia we are always studying the desals with an eye to opening all their doors, but it is always an occasion when one is unlocked. Then, too, the doors sometimes close again, and can not afterward be opened by any means.

It has always been this way. The desals predate our earliest records, and those stretch back a thousand years. They seem to stem from the very beginning of the world. We do not know what their origin is, although I believe you know. How could you not know? You are older than even they, you say.

They have guided us in the development of our civilization. As I outlined, they find minerals for us and also cure plagues and have been known to cultivate new breeds of plants for our food. We take these as gifts. They are given us out of those doors, when men or women with courage enter to find what they might. Each door typically reveals one thing, but some have walls upon which frescoes and other symbolic expressions appear. It is by these that they communicate.

As I said, they sometimes employ agents. A door may be seen to open at the apex of a spire, and a flock of birds issue from it. Or night beasts may nest in opened doors too small for human ingress. The Winds minister to more than Man, we know this. Those cultures that worship them claim they are the creators of this world and everything in it. The Winds deny this. Although they deny, they do not enlighten us as to their real nature, beyond the simple statement that they are exactly what they appear to be. They are themselves, they are Winds.

As the priestess clasped my hand and drew me onto the blank white plain, I half expected to be immediately struck down. The Wind's misogyny might not be just a legend. I was not killed, however, and took heart, even laughing and running with her as I spied the hexagonal opening she aimed at.

It was about two meters across, opening just where the slope of the Wind became too steep to climb. I paused for just a moment to look back and found myself level with the treetops, the entire island spread out below. Only a glimpse was allowed me, as I was yanked in by the priestess.

She embraced me right there, but I struggled free and lit a match. She pouted, standing very close, and let me look around. This room was like another I had seen in my own country, round and with domed ceiling and floor, about ten meters across. In the center of the floor was a raised pillar with an open top. I went down to the pillar and gazed into the opening. A black fathomlessness. Who knew what might emerge from it? It was no wonder it bred religious awe in these people.

"Come." She was very insistent now, taking hold of my arm to draw me down beside her. I was out of time.

I stepped back, around the other side of the open dais. Lighting another match and applying it to a small torch I had brought, I said to her, "I am sorry to have deceived you, lady, but it was commanded of me."

"Commanded?" She stood up. "What are you talking about?"

"I am not as I appear. I am not from the wrecked ship." This statement halted her as she began to come around the dais. She instead moved to put it between us again. She looked her question at me.

The hour was right. I nodded to her. "You have served the desal well. I do not doubt you have taken pride in it, but I also know you wish sometimes you were ordinary, living with the others with a husband, maybe children?"

"Where are you from?" she whispered, eyes wide in the shaking light.

I lay down the torch and unlaced my jerkin, showing her my breasts. "I am as you. I am here and alive. The Wind has chosen me as your successor." I was certain I could handle those old men who had ruled her. They would be the first to go once I was in command. I smiled. "You are free."

"No! This is some cheap trick." Her desire was extinguished, but she was angry now. I had anticipated that.

"We knew you would not believe easily, which is good," I said. "You were not chosen to be gullible. This being the case, however, do you need a demonstration that what I say is true?"

She nodded guardedly.

"Good. We shall have one." If the demonstration was not forthcoming, I might be forced to murder this girl if we could not work out our differences. I would then simply await the priests here in the morning, and take over from her that way. I had no stomach for that method, however, and counted on the fact that when one desal acts, all others within a hundred kilometers react.

We did not have to wait long. First there was a faint thumping below our feet. The girl cried out and backed away from the open dais. Although I had been expecting something, I was now very afraid. There is no knowing what a Wind may do.

Suddenly there was a violent shudder through the bedrock-solid desal. Outside a gale blew up from nowhere, and we heard trees cracking and leaves roaring. A faint white glow ensconced the top of a sentinel spire visible through the doorway.

She screamed. "Stop it, please! I believe!"

"All right," I said, although in truth I had no idea how or if this manifestation would cease.

Then the door closed.

She and I bolted for it in one motion, I waving the torch as though it were a talisman to open it again. There was no sign that there had ever been a door there, save for half a windblown stick that had been caught as it closed, and snipped through. We looked at one another, she realizing at last that I had no more control over the desal than she did.

The dais in the center of the floor suddenly dropped out of sight, leaving a black hole. The floor of the desal distorted, lowered to form a funnel. There was nothing to hang onto. First she with a despairing cry, then I slid down and into that dark opening.

I OPENED MY eyes on a strange vision. I was at the bottom of a well that was three meters across, its top invisible in darkness. The bottom was curved, of the same slick white substance as above, but soft. Around me on the walls of the tube strange images were appearing and vanishing, like moving frescoes.

I cried and tried not to watch, hiding my face in my hands, but I was afraid of I knew not what. I felt compelled to look around myself, at least to look up in case something came down that well at me. I imagined all kinds of terrors from above—giant pistons, water, or monstrous arms lowering to retrieve me. Nothing occurred, except the ongoing panoply unfolding on the walls around me. I could not for long avoid looking at the moving pictures.

Hypnotized, I watched a pictographic catalogue of the world unfold. Sketchy images of thousands of things rolled forward and back. The images were whirling toward some apocalyptic conclusion. The dizzying motion and flickering lights became too much for me. I thrust out my hand and cried, "Stop!"

My open palm slammed against the wall. Miraculously, the pictographs I had struck froze in place, as if painted. The rest continued to move around this sudden little island.

I snatched my hand back. The pictographs remained motionless.

Had the priestess seen what I was seeing? Perhaps this was how the desal had chosen its ministers in the past. I could well imagine those other women cowering as I did, watching in incomprehension as the pictures flew by—maybe to be ejected later by the desal into the arms of waiting awestruck people. The villagers would have demanded to know what the pictures meant. It would be as if you were given a book in an unknown language, and threatened with death unless you explained its meaning.

Maybe none of those other women had the courage or anger to try to touch the pictures. Then they would never have learned that they could stop them, or as I learned in the next minutes, move them.

First I reached out to tap hesitantly at another pictograph. It stopped instantly. Emboldened, I tried a few more. Soon I had a little set of rocks in a moving stream of imagery. Each one seemed significant—a tree, a cloud, a castle, a house. Most were pictures from nature, but there were men and women, too, though these were oddly dressed. How? Well, chiefly as though their clothes had been painted on. Some had sunburst halos around their heads and packs on their backs. Most such pictographs had a backdrop of blackness and stars.

One image that I tapped seemed to stagger as it stopped. I tapped it again and it jittered in place. I touched my finger to the wall and slowly drew it along. To my amazement the pictograph followed.

It probably wouldn't be possible for someone in such a position to avoid organizing the pictographs. Even just on the aesthetic level it made sense to group them, so that I could see them all without having to turn around. Soon I had ten or so of the things lined up in front of me. The rest were still whirling around, but they were less fearsome now that I knew I could control them.

I immediately made another discovery. If two or more images overlapped they would both flash for a few seconds, then disappear, replaced by new ones.

These new images were the reply of the desal.

You see, when I moved the pictograph fish on top of a snaking river, row after row of fish shapes sprang into being on the wall above me. I recognized a few I had eaten or seen drawn in picture books. When I drew the pictograph of a carp onto that of an eye, I found myself looking at a very detailed drawing of a carp's eye, complete with little lines of text over and under it, written using our alphabet but in a language I did not recognize.

I became very excited. Quite possibly I would never emerge from this place, but it almost didn't matter. For long hours, until thirst and exhaustion overwhelmed me, I arranged images and watched as the desal replied.

I awoke half delirious with thirst. The desire for water consumed me, and for a while I shouted and banged the walls, half convinced that some human agency waited beyond them. There was no reply.

There were a number of representations of water on the walls. I dragged animal and raindrop together. The pictographs vanished, then reappeared without change. This happened, I had come to believe, when the desal did not understand the question.

I put a skull, a human shape, and an image of the sun together. Again, nothing. This went on for quite a while, but I was doggedly determined, since thirst is not a need you can ignore. I can't remember the exact combination that worked, but suddenly I heard a clanking sound overhead, and when I looked up, I received a faceful of ice water.

When the downpour stopped I was up to my knees in it. Still, I was grateful. More, I felt a triumphal glow. After all, I had spoken to a Wind, asked a favor of it, and been given it.

The other women were probably ejected after they failed to grasp that the desal wanted to talk. Myself it kept, as several days passed and I became fluent in its strange visual speech. There did not seem to be anything it would not tell me—provided I knew how to ask. That was the most frustrating part, because I wanted to know its history, and that of my people; I wanted to know where the world had come from, and where it was going. My imagination failed utterly when it came to phrasing such questions in stick figures and glyphs.

But I could make the desal act for me. I insisted on sun until the top of the shaft vanished, and daylight poured down on me. I demanded that my wastes be carried away, and the floor swallowed them as I slept. I requested food, and I received fruit and berries.

Two things I learned, that made me the queen of Iapysia. The first was that I could paint my own images and freeze them on the wall. The second thing I discovered was a trove of information about the desals themselves.

This I came upon when I slapped a little whirling globe and it flattened out into a map of the world. The continents were clear, and I soon had my own nation spread before me, with intricate colors and shapes showing landforms and vegetation. I have never since seen anything like it. It was dotted with tiny dome glyphs, which I at first took to be cities. They were in all the wrong places, though, and eventually I realized they were desals.

They were joined by fine lines, in a kind of spiderweb. The desals are joined by a subterranean highway system, something tradition says is true, but for which we had no proof. Now I could see it. And I could see the road that linked my desal to others on the mainland.

I had painted a portrait of myself, and now an inspiration struck me. I dragged that portrait to the island on the map where I thought I was. The portrait vanished and reappeared in miniature next to the little dome figure there. The desal had told me I was correct. That was the island I was on.

Next I dragged the little portrait of myself onto the line of the highway running under the sea between the island and the mainland. Instantly the portrait slid out from under my fingers and zipped along the highway to wait flashing at the dome of a mainland desal.

I touched the portrait. It stopped flashing.

And something overhead blocked the sun as a deep rumbling sound began to build around me.

I had time to issue one more detailed command before the floor gave way under my feet and I fell into the dark cyclonic stream of the highway.

I AWOKE WITH sunlight heating my face. I heard murmurs of wonder and fear. Opening my eyes, I saw the faces of my own countrymen. They spoke in the accents of the province of Santel, whose city has a desal on the hill above it.

I sat up. I was in a cubic chamber, three meters on a side. A square door opened out on the sunlight; four peasants stared in at me.

They had seen a door open the previous night. The next morning they mustered courage to approach, and the townspeople, alerted, were not far behind. A crowd gathered as I climbed out of this desal, four hundred kilometers from the one I had entered days before, and faced my silent people.

On the walls of the chamber I came from were visions I had crafted with the desal's help. These indelible frescoes were arranged around the portrait of myself, the state crown of Iapysia afloat above my head. To these the desal had added its own panorama, a kind of procession that led around the entire chamber.

From that moment, when the people saw that the Winds had blessed me as queen, my succession to the throne was guaranteed.

The panorama authored by the desal, however, has a different meaning for me than it does for my people. The people believe it is a chronology of my lineage. To me it shows all the stages of humanity's development on this planet, for each scene in the panorama shows something from our history, some major turning point: the founding of religions, of dynasties, of laws and philosophies.

To me the silent figures speak of the invention of humanity: of our own creation of the faculties we take as divinely ordered, our reason, our morality, our science, even our world's purpose. They are all, I believe, of our own generation.

If there is anything I wonder now, it is this: if we are our own creation, whence the Winds? I do not understand them, and they frighten me.

Of all things, they alone frighten me.

GALAS WAS SIPPING a glass of chilled wine, a bowl of fruit before her on the highest parapet of the palace, when General Matthias stormed in. The leader of her defenses was normally in a foul humour—but just now he was positively livid. A small group of men and maids trailed behind him like wind-whipped smoke. "Why didn't you tell me?" he roared at the queen as he towered over her.

Galas had eaten breakfast with Maut after telling her tale, and although she had not slept, had been feeling strangely at peace. She blinked at Matthias muzzily. "Tell you what?"

"Who he was!"

Carefully, she reached for a raisin, and chewed it for a while before saying, "Really, Matthias, I don't know who you are talking about."

"Oh no? You've been closeted with the bastard for two days now. Am I so old and feeble I can no longer be trusted with strategic information? Or were you going to present it all to me as a done thing?"

He really was angry. At her. Galas sat up straight. "Wait, wait, something is really wrong here. Matthias, I would never do anything to question your command. What is it that you think I have done?"

"General Armiger is your guest! I just had it from the maids. And you never told me!"

For a moment Galas stared at him, openmouthed. Then she realized, and remembered last night, when she had asked Maut what he could do for her, and he had smiled and said she would know by noon.

She looked at the sundial built into her table. It was noon.

Galas began to laugh. It started as a chuckle, but as she saw Matthias's eyes widen in outrage, she could no longer contain herself. Carelessly tossing her wine glass aside, she leaned back in her chair and let the sound of her delight rise above the siege, above the air itself, to the very heavens.

21

IN THE MORNING, Jordan awoke to hear Suneil leaving the wagon. *Probably gone for a piss*, he thought at first; but the man did not return.

This was just the sort of thing that kept one from falling back asleep. The sun wasn't up yet, and it was frosty out there. Jordan had already been awake half the night, listening to Queen Galas tell Armiger her tale. When she finished he had fallen into a dreamless but apparently brief sleep. Now he tried several different positions—lying on his side, on his back with an arm over his face, even curled up—but he couldn't get back to sleep and Suneil still didn't return.

Finally he rose, shivering, and crept to the back flap to look out. The horizon was polished silver, as cold a color as Jordan had ever seen.

Suneil was standing very still, staring at nothing in particular. His hands were stuffed deep in the pockets of a long woolen coat. Every now and then he looked down and kicked a clod of earth at his feet.

Jordan eased the flap back and went to lie down again. The sight had disturbed him, although at first he couldn't decide why. By the time the sun peeked above the horizon and Suneil came back to salvage a last half hour of rest, Jordan had realized that he'd seldom seen so perfect a picture of a man struggling with an important decision; and it was significant that Suneil had said nothing in the past days to his niece or Jordan about any such worries.

IN THE MIDDLE of nowhere, with scattered fields to the left and right, Suneil said, "This is the city of Rhiene."

"Huh?" Jordan stared at a slovenly peasant's cottage mired in its own pigsty near the road. "That?" He had heard of Rhiene all his life. It was one of the great cities of Iapysia, fabled for its gardens and university. There was supposed to be a desal at Rhiene, too, and great religious colleges devoted to its study.

Suneil laughed. They were seated together at the front of the wagon. Tamsin had decided to walk for a while, and at present she was a few meters ahead, tilting her head back and forth to some internal rhyme, her hands fluttering at her sides in time.

Suneil pointed to a tumble of low hills ahead. "There."

The hills made an odd arc on the otherwise flat plain, dwindling in either direction. None was more than twenty meters high, and now that he looked more closely Jordan could see numerous buildings dotting the farther ones, and thin trails of smoke rising beyond them. A stone tower stood near the road ahead. Traffic on the road had increased during the past day until now they were part of a steady stream of wagons, horses and walking people, all headed toward the hills. Far off to the south, he could see another such road, converging on what he was beginning to realize was a long rampart of wavelike hills.

There was no city, however. Just those scattered buildings.

"I don't understand. It's underground?"

Again Suneil laughed. "No. Well, yes, parts of it. You'll see." He smiled mysteriously.

They followed the road around several bends. The land here looked as though it had become liquid at some time in the ancient past, and flown in waves that had then frozen in place. Giant boulders stuck up from the earth here and there; they seemed barely weathered.

Several side roads joined with theirs, until the stream of traffic was thick and loud. Vendors appeared walking up the road, offering sweet meats and fresh fish. Still there was no city in sight—but now Jordan heard seagulls and saw several lift above the next rise.

The builders of Rhiene had wisely widened the road after that rise, because a good half of all the travelers who came here must have stopped dead in their tracks when they got there. Tamsin did, and Jordan stood up and shouted in disbelief. Suneil merely smiled.

First he saw the blue-hazed arc of a distant shoreline, and above that sun-whitened cliffs rising almost straight out of the glittering water. Then his eye took in the whole sweep of the place: those distant cliffs were kin to the crest their wagon had come to. In fact, the cliffs swept in a vast circle to encompass a deep flat-bottomed bowl in the earth. A lake filled most of the bowl; from here Jordan could see sailboats like tiny scraps of white feather dotting it. At the very center of the bowl, a spire of green-patched rock towered out of the water. Coral-colored buildings adorned the spire. He could see docks at its base.

"Rhiene," said Suneil, pointing down.

The road wound down a set of switchbacks into what at first looked like an overgrown ruin. Rhiene was green with ivy, forest, and lichen, and Jordan couldn't make out the buildings until he realized the gardens he saw were all on the roofs of houses and towers. Rhiene sprawled along the arc of the cliff for kilometers in either direction, and tongues of jetty and wharf made the nearer shore of the lake into a tangle of geometry.

Seeing this made everything that had happened to him worthwhile. Jordan knew he was grinning like an idiot, but he didn't care. He decided in that instant that Rhiene was where he wanted to live.

"It's the most beautiful place in the world!" shouted Tamsin.

"Perhaps you would like a guided tour?" said a nattily dressed young man who had appeared as if by magic at her elbow.

Tamsin looked him up and down. "Begone, you trotting swine," she said.

The youth shrugged and walked away. Astonished, Jordan leaped down and went over to Tamsin.

"What was that all about?" he asked.

"Everybody wants to make some coin," she said. "Everywhere we go there's people trying to sell you this or that." She sighed heavily. "They hang around places like this, spoiling the moment for people like us." The young man had approached another wagon and appeared to be haggling with its oafish driver.

Suneil had clucked the horses into motion, so they began to walk. " 'Trotting swine'?" asked Jordan.

She blushed. "I read it in a book."

They walked for a while, taking in the gradually expanding view. Tamsin said little more, but she didn't seem to mind Jordan's company, either. After a while Jordan dropped back to the wagon and asked Suneil, "What will you do here?"

The old man nodded to the city, which now spread around and above them. "I've got some old business associates here," he said. "I want to see if I can call in some favors, and make a new start. The war's over, after all."

"Is this where you used to live?"

"No. That's one of the advantages of the place," said Suneil ruefully.

Jordan had a vivid idea of what a city at war would look like, based on what he had seen at the queen's summer palace. Clear as that notion might be, he couldn't picture soldiers in the streets of Rhiene. For all that it was a big city, it appeared sleepy and its citizens unconcerned. It took Tamsin to point out the placards here and there that were signed with a royal insignia. Jordan couldn't read the script, so she translated. "It's a decree from Parliament ending curfew and random searches. I guess the war really is over."

"It's not," he said. "The queen is still fighting back. She's trapped in the summer palace, but she's got plenty of supplies and her people are still loyal."

Tamsin looked at him strangely. "I see. You arranged this? Or a little bird told you?"

"I have my sources."

"Oh ho," she said. "Behold the grand seer."

"Hey!" Suneil waved at them from the cart. "We go this way."

They passed through high stone walls into a teeming caravansary. Here were soldiers—plenty of them—inspecting the cargoes of incoming wagons. While they went through Suneil's possessions—with Tamsin squawking protests—Jordan took a look around. The place was just a broad quadrangle of pulverized straw with a few water troughs and sheds. It reeked of manure and wood smoke. All the visitors to the city who had no inn or friend to visit were crammed in here. They squabbled over cart space, water, and offal buckets. It was wonderful chaos.

The queen had mentioned Rhiene in her story last night. Her tale had not enlightened him much as to the nature of the Winds. There was something to it, though, as of a mystery whose solution hung just out of reach. He had thought about it a lot and was sure Armiger felt that sense of near knowledge too; unless the general had already seen the answer Jordan himself could not.

He thought about this as he helped Suneil get the wagon slotted into a narrow space near one wall. Jordan went to find water and feed for the horses, and when he returned Suneil had changed into fine silk clothes.

"I'm going to visit my people," he said. "Are you leaving us here, young man?"

Jordan shrugged. "With your permission I'll stay the night and make a fresh start in the morning."

"Good. You see to my niece. I'll be back before dark."

"Can we see the city?" asked Tamsin.

"If you'd like. Just don't get lost."

He left with a spring in his step. Jordan turned to Tamsin.

"How's your ankle?"

"Good."

"Up for some walking?"

She held out her hand, smiling. "Lead on, sir."

RHIENE WAS MUCH bigger than it seemed from above, and much dirtier, too. The ever-present foliage hid a great deal, and Jordan supposed that was part of the idea. The overriding purpose for the greenery, however, was to keep the Winds at bay.

An ancient statue near the docks showed a man and woman raising their hands to the sky, holding flowering branches. Tamsin read off the plaque at the base of the statue. "The city was destroyed by the desal seven hundred years ago," she said. "They rebuilt in secrecy, using wood harvested without killing trees. They struck a balance between creation and destruction, and the Winds let them continue to this day."

"There's supposed to be a desal here," said Jordan. The statue stood in a busy square surrounded by ivied merchants' houses. The city sprawled for kilometers in either direction, a fact visible from here because this square was emplaced on a knee of land that thrust out of the cliff wall. The cliff itself towered majestically above, and the vast sweep of it to either side was intoxicating.

"There is a desal," said Tamsin. "I saw it on the way down."

"Where is it?" He wasn't sure whether he wanted to visit it or not, after what Galas had said about them. Knowing where it was, though, he would be able to avoid it.

"You can see it from here." She stepped up on the plinth of the statue. "See?"

He followed the line of her arm. There was something out in the bay, offset slightly from a line he might have drawn to join the city to the spire at the lake's center. From here it was visible only as a set of white spikes thrusting from the surface of the water. There were no boats near it, so judging its size wasn't easy.

"I recognized it because we had one near where I grew up," she said. "My father took me to see it once, when I was young. That one stood alone in the desert, like it was abandoned, but he said it was alive, and we shouldn't get too close. It's strange to see one underwater."

"Well, at least it's not *in* the city," he said.

"Hey, get off that!" shouted a passing woman. Tamsin jumped down from the statue's base. A few heads turned, but no one else stopped them as they ran down the hill to the docks.

In stories Jordan had read, a city's docks were always the place where lowlife sailors and prostitutes waited to prey on travelers and lost children. He had always pictured the wharves of a seagoing city as full of one-eyed men with swords and nasty dispositions, with bodies in the alleys and kegs of wine rolling down from visiting ships.

Rhiene was not like that. Of course, it was an inland port; most of the traffic here came from barges that simply shuttled between the city and the far end of the lake, a distance large enough to cut a day or so off the travel time of wagons coming from the south. There was supposedly a river that emptied into the lake somewhere, and boats went up that, too, but not, apparently, pirate ships. The docks were clean and well kept, and other than one disciplined work gang unloading a shallow single-masted ship, there was no great activity.

"This is pretty stale," said Tamsin. "Let's find the marketplace."

"There might be more than one," he pointed out.

"Whatever."

They wandered in the crowds for a while, and though Tamsin looked quite blasé about it all, Jordan felt overwhelmed by the huge press of people. Hundreds visible at any time, and around every corner there was a new hundred. Most of the people in sight were dressed similarly, men in fashionable townsman's jackets, the women in long pleated dresses that swept the road gracefully. He had to conclude that they all lived here. Could he live in such a place, with so many neighbors?

For a while they stood at the gates of the University of Rhiene, gazing at the sun-dappled grounds and ivied buildings. Queen Galas had walked here, he thought, and knowing this suddenly made her seem real in a new way. They had shared something, Jordan and Galas, if only the fact of having stood here.

In a flux of troubled emotions, he let himself be swept along by Tamsin, until they came to a market.

If Jordan had thought there were many people in the streets, this place was as crowded as Castor's during a wedding, only the mob went on and on, dividing and subdividing into alleys and sidestreets. Lean-tos and carts stood along all the walls, and some enterprising men and women had simply laid their goods out on blankets in the street. A roar of voices welled from the press of people, animals, and running children. Smells of incense, manure, fresh-cut wood, and hot iron filled Jordan's head, making him dizzy.

Tamsin laughed. "This is the place! See, Jordan, this is the place to be in Rhiene!" She ducked into the press.

"Wait!" Shaking his head but grinning, he ran after her.

The chaos had an infectious energy to it. You could not walk slowly in this place. After a few minutes, Jordan found himself darting around like Tamsin, poking about on tables of turquoise baubles, then flitting over to a fruit seller, nearly stumbling over a one-legged woman selling cloth dolls from her mat—wishing he had more than the few coins in his pockets.

The only problem was, the roar of voices tended to trigger his visions. Every now and then Jordan had to stop and shake his head, because he would hear Armiger's voice coming at him from within his own skull, or that of a doctor with whom the general was speaking. Such moments no longer frightened him, but they made it hard to concentrate on the here and now.

Then, in the very middle of the market, he was stopped in his tracks by another voice that rang sudden and clear in his mind:

Go to the woman with the brown knapsack. Tell me what's inside it.

"What?" He looked around, blinking.

"I didn't say anything," said Tamsin. "Oh, look. A magician."

There he was—a lean, well-groomed man standing on a little stage at the back of a short alley. A large audience stood in silence, listening as he recited something. His eyes were closed, and he had one hand touched dramatically to his forehead.

A young woman in peasant's garb emerged from the audience. She went hesitantly up to stand beside the magician, and, at his urging, opened the pack she'd been carrying. As she displayed each of the items inside, murmurs then applause ran through the audience. Shortly thereafter a small rain of coins landed at the magician's feet.

Jordan and Tamsin watched for a while. The magician was guessing the contents of people's bags, pockets, or just what they held in their clenched fists. He was always right. The crowd was amazed and all too willing to pay to watch the performance continue.

Every time the magician was presented with a puzzle, Jordan heard something no one else seemed to hear. This man had the same power Turcaret had possessed, a limited power to speak with the Winds—or at least with mecha. When Jordan concentrated he could see, almost as if he were imagining it, something like a diaphanous butterfly hovering above the crowd. When the magician commanded it, the invisible thing wafted over to the satchel, bag, case, or box and penetrated its surface with fine hairlike antennae. Almost like a mosquito, he thought.

Jordan's heart was pounding with an excitement he had not felt since he had sat by the lakeshore and learned how the waves spoke. There was no trick to what this man was doing; Jordan could do it. What was amazing was that the little mechal thing allowed itself to be commanded—and the Winds did not rain fury on the magician for commanding it.

"Come on, let's go," said Tamsin.

"Wait. I want to try something."

"Oh, forget it, Jordan, you'll lose your shirt. He's got the game rigged somehow."

"Yes, and I know how."

Go to the jewelbox held by the man in green and tell me its contents, commanded the magician.

Jordan closed his eyes and, in his mind, said, *Come here.*

The butterfly was clearly visible now, like a living flame over the dark absences of the crowd. It was like no mechal beast he had ever seen; it was more like a spirit. It hesitated now over the man the magician had ordered it to, then drifted in Jordan's direction. It circled his head, as though inspecting him.

Return. It was the magician, calling his servant.

Who was the stronger here? Jordan smiled, and said, *Stay.*

Return! Return now!

The crowd was beginning to mutter.

Ka! Return to me at once!

What are you? Jordan asked the fluttering thing.

I am Ka. I am test probe of the Ventus terraforming infrastructure. I am a nanofiber chassis with distributed processing and solar-powered electrostatic lift wires. I am . . .

Jordan had been wondering for days what he should ask the next thing he spoke to. *Do you speak to the Heaven hooks?*

No. I report to desal 463.

Faintly, he heard the magician announcing that today's performance was over. The crowd broke into guffaws and jeers. Someone demanded their money back.

Jordan, hissed Tamsin. "What are you doing? Let's go?"

"Wait." Then, to Ka, he said, *will you tell desal 463 that you spoke to me?*

Yes.

No, don't do that!

Okay.

Jordan opened his eyes. *Okay?*

"The show's over, said Tamsin. Let's go."

"I'm doing something."

"No you're not. You're standing there like a slack-jawed idiot. Now come *on.*" She pulled on his arm.

Ka, where are you! Please Ka, come back!

You are not empty, said Ka.

It took Jordan a moment to figure out what it meant. When Jordan closed his eyes, he could see the mecha all around him, a ghostly landscape of light. The crowd, the magician, and even Tamsin were visible only as shadows, holes in the matrix.

Am I mecha? he asked Ka.

You have mecha in you, it said.

"Ka!" cried the magician, aloud this time. He stood alone in the alley, hands clasped at his sides. He seemed on the verge of tears.

Jordan wanted to know more, but Tamsin was pulling at him, and he felt pity for the poor magician, who did not know what was happening. *Return to your magician,* Jordan told Ka.

Ka fluttered away. A moment later Jordan opened his eyes to see the man raise one hand into the air as if caressing something. His shoulders slumped in relief, then he began swearing and looking around.

The magician's gaze fell on Jordan and stopped. What could he do? Jordan met his eye, smiled ironically, and shrugged.

The magician recoiled as if Jordan had slapped him. Then he backed away and raised one finger to point at Jordan. "You get away from me!" he shouted. "Get away, you hear?"

"Jordan!" Tamsin shook him. "Come on!"

They ran together into the crowd, Tamsin worried, Jordan stunned with new possibilities. He wanted to ask the magician where he'd found Ka, how he had discovered he could command the thing, why the desal tolerated his manipulations of a minor Wind. Above all, Jordan wanted to know why the Winds would speak to him and this man, and no one else here.

Ah, but that's just the question Armiger came here to answer, he reminded himself. *Armiger himself can't speak to the Winds.*

Though they were now two streets away, he concentrated and said, *Ka, why are the Winds after me?*

The reply was faint, but he was sure Ka said, *You are not empty. So you may threaten thalience.*

That was a new name. Or had he misheard it? "Ka, who is ... Thalience?"

He heard a mutter, but could not decipher it. Tamsin had dragged him to the gates of the market.

"What was all that about?" she demanded as they stepped into the quiet street. Jordan laughed, shaking his head.

"I'm not quite sure," he said. "Maybe we'd better get back to the wagon."

She gave him a long look. "Maybe you're right," she said.

SUNEIL WAS WAITING for them at the wagon. He looked upset. Tamsin ran up to him and embraced him.

"How did your meeting go?"

Suneil grimaced and disengaged himself from her arms. "I had to make some ... concessions," he said. He wasn't looking at her, but glanced at

Jordan, then turned away. "In business and . . . power . . . you have to do what it takes to get what you want, sometimes."

Tamsin cocked her head to one side. "What's wrong?"

"Nothing that's going to matter in the long run," he said. "When you get older, Tam, you'll understand why I made this decision. It's in our best interests."

"Tell me," she said. Jordan stood back, arms crossed, and watched. Something was very wrong here.

"You know I was an important minister in the queen's cabinet before the war," said Suneil. "That's why I had to run. Why we had to run. You were all I could salvage of the life Galas had given us—my favorite niece. Parliament went on a witch hunt—hanging everyone who was involved in our work. I did what I had to do to make sure they didn't come after us, but it was prudent to leave the country all the same. And certain men know what I did, and are willing to forget our life before—now that the queen is dead."

"The queen is not dead," said Jordan without thinking.

Suneil sat on the bottom step of the wagon's hatch, and peered at him. "You know that for a fact, don't you, young man?"

"Who cares?" said Tamsin. "What about your meeting?"

"Actually, it's very important that Jordan Mason knows with absolute certainty that Galas is alive," said Suneil. "Because my partners needed a guarantee of my loyalty to them, and if Jordan isn't the man he's pretending to be, the deal I made this afternoon wouldn't go through."

Jordan knew it in that instant. "You've sold me."

Suneil looked him in the eye. "You are a wanted man, Jordan."

"Wanted? Not by the law," said Jordan. "Only by—"

"*Me.*"

Jordan turned. Brendan Sheia's sword hovered centimeters from his throat. The square-headed Boros heir smiled grimly as four men emerged from behind Suneil's wagon, their own blades drawn.

"Uncle!"

Suneil grabbed Tamsin by the wrist as she tried to run to Jordan. "I don't like this any more than you do," he said. "This is what we have to do to prove our worth to the new powers in Iapysia. Don't you see? We can go home now."

"Bastards! Let him go!" Tamsin struggled against her uncle.

Brendan Sheia ignored them. He was pacing around Jordan, inspecting him as one might a prize horse. "I remember you now," he said. "You were with those foreign spies at the banquet. You were sick, if I recall. Nearly spoiled dinner."

Jordan glared at him. "I've done nothing wrong."

Sheia's sword flashed up. "You brought the Heaven hooks against our house! You destroyed our ancestral home, incited the Hooks to kill my ally Turcaret, and when you were done you ran into the night, and the Hooks followed! We have it from our witnesses."

His confrontation with Turcaret in the Boros courtyard had been seen, Jordan realized. But had Axel and Calandria been arrested as well? "What about—" Sheia hit Jordan across the jaw. He staggered and was grabbed roughly by two men and hauled to his tiptoes.

"Stop it!" screamed Tamsin.

"Silence," hissed her uncle.

Sheia bowed to Suneil. "Lucky thing you chanced on Mason, old man. You'll get your honor and your title back. I can't guarantee the money and lands, of course . . . but in this new age, what guarantee have we of anything?" He flipped a hand negligently at Jordan. "Take the boy."

The two soldiers holding his arms yanked Jordan into a quick march; then they were out in the streets, and he was being thrown over the side of a horse, hands and feet bound.

The good citizens of Rhiene watched and commented, but did nothing to help as Jordan was carried away.

22

"You'll have to pardon me if I seem a bit out of sorts," said Armiger as he sat down opposite General Matthias. "I was chatting with one of your men on the battlements when a rock from one of Parliament's steam cannons took his head off."

Matthias grimaced. "I heard about that. Happened this morning. Lavin's a devil, a positive devil. And the queen admires him! That's the damndest part. Listen, I've got a little beer here from our emergency stock. Care for a cup?"

Armiger nodded. He had talked briefly with Matthias twice, but the man was understandably busy—and, it seemed, wary. It was that wariness that had made Armiger ask for this meeting; he needed Matthias on his side.

They sat in Matthias's tiny office in one of the palace's outbuildings. Outside the single small window a dismal drizzle fell on the tents of the refugees. It was oppressively quiet today.

Matthias poured two pints of pale beer and they both tasted it. Armiger noticed that his hands were shaking slightly; the incident on the wall had shocked him more than he would have believed possible. It was only a man who had been destroyed, after all. And while Armiger might have lost his own head had he been standing a meter closer, he could have grown another one, given enough time. He had no rational reason to be upset. But he was. He was.

"Lavin's an upstart," said Matthias. "Young, bright, ambitious. He's had subtle help from the queen throughout his career. And now he's turned on her. I'd take him to be an opportunist, but Galas disagrees. She says he's an arch-traditionalist."

"Have you tried to use that against him?" asked Armiger.

Matthias nodded. "Had some success, too. He detests dealing with morale issues. You can trip him up if you can scare his men. He's a quick learner though—I'm afraid I taught him to press the way he is with the cannon. Never lets us sleep. You saw the result yourself."

Armiger nodded.

Matthias was watching him. "I have to say, Armiger, that you've got steady nerves. I got that impression when we were following reports of your war in the northeast. You were doing a magnificent job. Then we heard you were dead, and you turn up here. Sounded to me like you ran. Why?"

"Is that why you've been avoiding me?" asked Armiger with a smile. "Because you think I'm a deserter?"

"No, not a deserter. A mercenary." Matthias grimaced. "You show up here, offering your services to the queen . . . for how much?"

Armiger sat up straight. "First of all, if I were a mercenary you'd think Ravenon would have paid me. They didn't pay me—at least not in money."

"What do you mean? What did they pay you in?"

"Information. It was their mail and spy networks I was interested in using. I showed up here with nothing but the clothes on my back, you know that. And how am I expected to get away with my payment if Galas is paying me now?"

"Simple," said Matthias. "You've cut a deal with Lavin."

Armiger laughed harshly. "Your suspicion is well founded and sound. You think I'm a Trojan horse, is that it?"

"A what horse?"

Armiger took a deep drink of his beer. "Lavin doesn't need my help to take this palace, you know that," he said. "Besides, I haven't exactly offered my services to the queen as a military commander."

"Oh? Then as what?"

"Priest. Confessor." Armiger saw the expression on Matthias's face and laughed. "Look, that man who had his head knocked off today—I've had it with that kind of thing. Why do you think I left the war in Ravenon? The Winds wiped out two divisions of my men. I stood by helpless and watched it happen. At the time I thought I didn't care; but I did. And I do. So I'm not here to fight, Matthias, you needn't worry about that."

The old general sat back in his chair, nodding slowly. "You're an odd one. And if you'd said anything other than what you just did, I wouldn't have taken you seriously. Priest? Confessor? I don't know about that. But I understand a man who lays down his sword. Men who don't have that urge now and then make bad commanders. Galas tells me Lavin has no stomach for war, either—but see how good he is at it."

An adjutant knocked politely on the door. Matthias nodded and stood up.

"Now that I know where your heart lies, Armiger, I may just call upon your talents. After all, there's no better man to end a war quickly and cleanly than one who hates war."

JORDAN SURGED TO his feet with shout. He was *not* going to let this happen again.

He shook his head and forced himself to breathe deeply and look around himself. He was in a small cell in the basement of Brendan Sheia's home. A single window slit let in the wan sunset and a trickle of cold air that teased at him, making him shiver now that he had noticed it.

They had taken his possessions, including Calandria's golden gauze. He was irrevocably visible to the Winds now.

The sights and sounds of Armiger's experience began to recede. He willed them away entirely. It didn't matter how compelling they were. It didn't matter that he wanted to fall into Armiger like a refuge, the way he had on his long walk south from the disaster of the Heaven hooks. He wished so much that he could be somewhere else right now—be some-*one* else.

"Too bad," he said angrily. Jordan was furious with Brendan Sheia—just furious enough, for now, not to be afraid. He was also angry with himself, though, and right now that was worse.

After all, there had been a moment in his life when he thought he was going to put aside all the habits of denial and retreat that he had despised in his father. When Emmy ran into the night, Jordan had lain in bed for long moments, waiting for someone else to act responsibly and follow her. He still remembered those few seconds; something had broken in him, setting him free. And so he thought afterward that he would never fall back into those family patterns again.

He'd been fooling himself. He felt now as if he'd been a leaf in a river these past weeks. Calandria's abduction of him, his terror of the visions, the whirlwind visit to the Boros where intrigue, murder, and disguise were daily companions—these events had all given him excuses to feel helpless. He had let Calandria lead him, had accepted her stories; he had let Suneil lull him into complacency. He was a blank page on which others had signed their names, and that was just the way his father lived.

It was shameful—but if he wallowed in his misery, he would just be playing the lost boy again. When Galas's mother died, the future queen had forsworn playing roles dictated by others. There was a lesson in that.

He had been in this cell for a day now. Someone had slid some food under the door that morning; otherwise, he might have been completely alone in the building.

This Boros domicile was not so grand as the manor house the Hooks had destroyed. It stood in the Rhiene high street, squeezed between two even grander mansions. There were no grounds, only a cobbled courtyard in front with a high wall and a gate. The building was tall, he knew, but he wasn't sure how many stories it was, since his only view of it had been upside down as he was yanked off the horse yesterday evening. Four, five stories? It didn't matter, there was only one cellar, and he was in it.

In the stories he used to read, bad people always had dungeons in their castles. Emmy had scared him for years by spinning tales of a secret level underneath Castor's manor. There was no such thing there, of course, any more than there was here. He was in some kind of disused storage room. They'd tossed a cot, a blanket, and a bucket in after him and let him set them up himself, in his own dungeon style.

Jordan wasn't quite sure what Brendan Sheia meant to do to him. Certainly the man had power, maybe enough to make an innocent traveler disappear without investigation.

He shivered again. First on the agenda was to find a way to block that draft.

They'd left him his cloak, so he bundled that up and stepped on a jutting stone in the wall to stuff it in the window. As he did so he heard footsteps passing in the hall outside.

"Hey, let me out!" he shouted.

"Quiet in there." The footsteps receded.

"I didn't do a damn thing, you stupid bastards!" He jumped down and gave the door a sound kick.

It felt good, and the crash was satisfactorily loud, so he kicked again. Tamsin would have a suitable insult for an occasion like this, he was sure. All he could think of was the one she'd used yesterday: "Trotting swine!"

He went to kick again but the door suddenly swung wide with a shriek of rusty hinges, and in its place was a huge scowling man with a long stick in his hand.

Before Jordan could react the man butted him in the stomach. Pain exploded in his belly, and he went down.

He curled up instinctively and thus avoided the worst of the kicks that followed. Then the man spat on him and left.

"Bastards," whimpered Jordan, as he unwrapped shaking hands from his head. "Bastards bastards bastards," all of them, Calandria, Armiger and Axel, Suneil, and the whole stinking Boros clan. "Bastards."

And then he was in the flow of vision, hearing the burr of Armiger's voice in his own chest and an overlay of chorusing identities in the walls, in the sullenly firm door and the very earth under his shoulder. It was like he'd fallen in a snake pit, with a thousand hissing heads rising all about him. Jordan grabbed his head and doubled up again with a cry.

He concentrated. This is *my* hand; he brought it up to his eyes. This is *my* sight. *I am here, not in the palace, not in the walls: here.*

Jordan rolled to his knees, gasping. The powers whispered and danced around him, but he had carved out a bubble for himself in their center. He could see and hear and act. With some difficulty, he got to his feet.

Cold air lapped at his throat. He almost laughed. "You're cruel," he said to the Winds. "Now you're going to help me for a change."

He sat on the cot and wrapped the cloak around his shoulders. There was no need to take deep breaths to enter the visionary trance now; he closed his eyes and summoned it.

First he had to know where he was. He could see the mansion around him in translucent outline. The basement was indeed extensive, and he was next to a place with convoluted shelves that must be a wine cellar. There were several stairs leading up, and he instinctively looked for the narrow servants' way as his goal. That led from the back of the wine cellar, predictably enough.

There was a cistern down here and a long room with a high arched ceiling. Castor's manor had an exercise room and archery range in the basement, which was probably what this was. All these rooms opened off the same corridor as Jordan's cell. In addition there were several side halls that ran to lockers of various sizes.

The problem with this way of seeing was that it didn't seem to show people. Jordan knew there was a dog on the main floor, almost exactly above his head; he could see it. The rest of the rooms on that level were visible, too, though in a jumble of perspective as if he were standing at the base of a huge glass model. He had to sort out what he was seeing, and if he had not had ample experience reading architects' plans at Castor's, he might not have been able to sort out hall from room, chimney from garderobe.

It took only a few minutes to work out the shortest route from here to the tradesman's entrance. Night was falling; in a few hours the area would be quiet. Then he could make his escape—provided the next parts of his plan worked.

He needed to see more than just the outlines of the place. When the Heaven hooks descended on the Boros manor, Jordan's own eyesight had briefly expanded to include distant places. He had been able to see people elsewhere in the manor, even though he was hundred of meters away. Try as he might, however, he could not repeat that experience now.

There was something else he could try. Jordan focused his mind on one name and hurled it into an imagined sky with all his might.

Ka!

He waited. There was no response, and he could see nothing as he scanned the vague landscape that opened out beyond the manor.

Ka! Come here!

Nothing. He waited a long while, but the little Wind must be too far away to hear him. All right; on to the next idea.

Careful not to break his concentration, he rose and moved to the door. He ran his fingertip around the keyhole on the large iron lock plate. He could actually see inside the lock if he concentrated; the mechanism was simple. All he needed was something with which to manipulate the tumblers.

There was another thing he wanted to try. He had nothing to lose now, where before he had been afraid of alerting the Winds to his presence by experimenting. Jordan returned to the cot, gathering his cloak on the way; it was getting quite chilly in here.

For some time now he had known he could communicate with the mecha. He had been reluctant, however, to ask himself the next logical question: Could he command the mecha, as the Winds did?

As he sat by the lakeside and poured water from bucket to cup and back again, Jordan had discovered something he had at the time been afraid to test. Each and every object in the world knew its name; all, that is, save for the humans who lived here, because they had no dusting of mecha within them.

The waves on the lake had known their identity as waves, but as they lapped against the shore they disappeared as individuals. Jordan had found by experimenting that when you changed an object into something else, its mecha noticed and altered its name to suit.

That had got him wondering: could you command an object to change its name; and if you changed an object's name, would the object itself change to match it?

The cot was a plain wooden frame with thin interwoven slats to lie on. He pried one of these up and held it out in front of him. "What are you?" he asked it aloud.

Cedar wood. Wood splinter . . .

"You are now kindling, hear?"

Consistent, said the splinter.

"So, burn!"

He held his breath. After a moment the splinter said, *Ignition of this mass will exhaust all mechal reserves. Further transformations will not be possible without infusion of new essence.*

"Just do it."

He opened his eyes to watch. Nothing happened . . . then the splinter began to smoke. "Ow!" He dropped it, whipping his fingers to cool them. For some reason Jordan had assumed the thing would neatly sprout a flame from one end. Instead, the entire splinter was afire.

"Splinter: douse yourself."

It didn't answer. Well . . . it had said something about exhausting reserves. Maybe the mecha in it had died in setting it afire. He closed his eyes and examined it with his inner vision, and indeed the small flame was a dark spot in the mechal landscape.

Jordan restrained the urge to leap to his feet and shout. He would only bring down the guard—but then, couldn't he just command the guard's clothes to burst into flame, too? Was there anything he couldn't do now?

He sat there for a while, giddy with the possibilities. He picked up another splinter, and said to it, *fly.*

That is not possible for this object, said the splinter.

Hmm. Well, at least he knew he wouldn't freeze now. He picked up a rock and tried to convince it to become a knife, but it demurred, listing off a dozen conditions he needed to fulfill for it to transform: heat, presence of carbon and significant iron deposits, etc.

So the mecha were limited. It wasn't really a surprise—and he could hardly complain! He should be able to get out of this room, at least, if he could pick the lock. He might even be able to defeat the guard if he was clever—but it would be better to sneak past him, if possible.

He pried a good splinter off the bed, and said to it, "Can you become harder?"

At an exhaustion rate of fifty percent it is possible to—

"Just do it."

The splinter seemed to shrink a little in his hand. He bent down, closed his eyes, and applied it to the lock.

Ka, said a voice like a chime.

Jordan turned. Hovering in the narrow window slit was the wraithlike butterfly from the market. It had heard him, after all!

"Greetings, little Wind," he said respectfully. "Can you help me?"

KA DRIFTED FROM room to room, reporting what it saw. Its habit was to hover at least a meter above the heads of the "empty ones," because a randomly swung arm could smash it. This had happened to more than one of its previous bodies. Ka was in its own way proud that it had survived in this one for thirty years now.

Desal 463 did not mind Ka's servitude to the magician. Neither did Ka. Its patrol was the market, anyway, where it hunted for ecological deviations. The entire city hovered on the edge of abomination, but the empty ones had learned scrupulous cleanliness over the centuries. Every now and then, however, some visitor imported something outside the terraforming mandate—petroleum, crude electric devices, most recently some cheerfully glowing radioactives stolen from a fallen aerostat—and it was Ka's job to find the offending substance. Then other agents of the desal would act, recovering the deviation and generally killing any empty ones associated with it. Empty ones made good fertilizer when they died; it neatly balanced the equation.

The being who had called it forth from the market was something else entirely. Its voice had the power to compel in a way the magician's could not. As far as Ka was concerned, it was a Wind.

"Tell me what you see," it said now.

I can relay the information directly to your sensorium, if you wish, said Ka.

"What? What do you mean? Show me."

Ka beamed an image of the corridor to the waiting Wind.

"Ah! Stop it!"

As you wish.

"Um . . . can you do that with hearing? Can I hear what's going on around you?"

Yes. Ka began to relay sound as it traveled.

It drifted from room to room, pausing to eavesdrop on conversations, then moving on.

". . . Don't know why I'm forbidden to go into the cellars tonight. He's up to something bad, I just know it. . . ."

Down the hall from that room: ". . . I don't think this meat is cooked through. . . ."

Elsewhere on the same floor: "He could be useful to us, but obviously we can't trust a turncoat like that. Especially one who's spent his career with the Perverts. How do we know what he wants, in the end?"

"So he's a pawn?"

"We'll play him out a little. He could be a competent bureaucrat. When the time comes, we'll trade him for something more valuable."

"And Mason?"

"Mason is going to save us. There's grumbling that our house is cursed. Cursed! Because of what happened at Yuri's. You and I know it wasn't our fault. We have to convince the rest of the world that we're innocent victims. If Turcaret was right, and the Heaven hooks were after Mason, then all we need to do is stake him out in a field in full view of the town and wait for the Winds to come. The sooner the better; we can't let the courts get ahold of this, they'll tie us up in years of wrangling. No. Tomorrow, we put the word out, then the day after we put him out, and if anyone objects we put a sword to their throat. It'll be done before anyone can mount an organized resistance. And after the Winds come down, no one is going to question why we did it. We'll be seen as having done the Winds' bidding. It could end up in our favor."

Someone entered the room, and the voices turned toward a discussion of food. Ka drifted on, up the grand stairway and toward the back of the house. There were voices coming from behind one door there, and Ka was made to pause and listen again.

"It's called the Great Game, niece, and you have to play it to survive."

"So it was a game you were playing when you led the soldiers to our town."

"No, you misunderstand me—"

"Ha! You could have saved them. You lied to me. And I believed you!"

"You do what you have to in order to survive, niece. And you can't get emotional about it. That's the beginning and the end of it. If it weren't for me, you'd be dead now. I saved you—"

"You killed them! You killed them!"

"Silence!"

"No! I won't be silent anymore. I won't be anything for you anymore."

"You will. Yes, you will. Listen, do you think your life has any value in this country if people find out what you really are? Where you're from? They won't look at you and see a young woman full of promise, as I do, Tamsin—they'll see a monster, born of monsters. At best a curiosity, at worst an abomination to be stoned. Now you have two choices, young lady. You can do as I tell you, learn your lines and your dance steps, and become the proper young lady in society here at Rhiene. Or, if you won't do that, I can still get something of my investment back if I turn you in to the high court as a renegade Pervert. If that's what you want, then that's the way we'll do it. Believe me, I don't care either way at this point."

There was no reply to this; only silence, drawn out until at last Ka was ordered to withdraw.

THE LOCK MADE a very loud click as it turned over. Jordan held his breath past a tight grin. Had the guard heard? Apparently not. He pushed the door open slowly.

The brawny man who had hit him earlier was sitting at a table in the hall outside. He was industriously carving leaf designs into the capital of what was obviously going to be a chair leg. Three other half-completed legs lay on the table next to him.

The knife he was carving with was very large.

What would Armiger do? Jordan asked himself. The general knew when to attack, and when to be discreet. This was a time to be discreet.

It was interesting that Ka had been able to move sound from upstairs down to Jordan's waiting ear. That implied all kinds of things about sound that he hadn't thought before—that it was a substance, that it could be packaged and carried around. Maybe you could also choose not to carry it?

He focused his attention on the hinges of the door, each in turn, and said, "*Make no sound,*" with his inner voice.

Each hinge acknowledged his command, but he had no idea if they would obey. Gingerly, he pushed the door open. He could feel a faint vibration under his fingers, as if the rusty hinges were grating—but he heard nothing.

Once outside, he slowly closed the door again. Holding a torrent of vision at bay, Jordan stepped into the earth-floored cellar behind the guard and backed his way slowly to the stone steps that led up. His heart was in his mouth. When he got to the steps he let out the breath he had been holding, but still went up them one at a time, pausing after each to look back at the broad back of the man with the knife. He knew he wouldn't just get a beating if he was found this time.

Upstairs, he ducked into a niche as two servants passed carrying a heap of linen. He poked his head out after they'd gone; there was the back entrance, in plain sight not five meters away. All he had to do was walk out the door, and he was free.

Except that he couldn't do it. The conversation Ka had relayed from upstairs had been chillingly familiar to Jordan, if not in its details, in its thrust. Just as Jordan's father had ordered Emmy to acquiesce to Turcaret's attentions, so Tamsin's uncle was ordering her to become his thing—bait, perhaps, to dangle in front of some highborn household's son. And though Jordan didn't understand what threat Suneil was holding in reserve, it was obviously dire.

He owed Tamsin nothing, really. Jordan knew, though, that he would no more be able to live with himself if he left her in this situation than he would have if he had stayed in bed, those many nights ago, and let Emmy run.

TAMSIN WAS DROWNING.

There was no water here. She could breathe, her heart still beat, she could walk and sit and even eat. Still, she was drowning.

The thing shaped like her uncle moved across the room. He was talking, but she couldn't make sense of the words anymore. They came to her like sounds underwater, distorted and harsh.

What was drowning her was the horror she felt every time she looked at him—knowing that inside that familiar body was a soul that had helped her, sheltered her, and cared for her, laughed with her, and murdered her parents.

"Get ready for bed," he said now. "Tomorrow's another day, niece."

For her own survival, she needed to be silent now—but inside she was screaming at him: "You knew the soldiers were coming! You knew and you didn't tell anyone, you didn't tell dad you let them die you let them die. . . ."

The worst thing was that she had known these things all along, somewhere deep in a part of her that she had told every morning to *sleep, look away.*

Thinking that she had known and had gone along with this monster, her inner voice simply died out. She sat mutely and nodded without heat, then rose to go to her sleeping closet.

As she walked she drowned a little more.

"Tamsin." His voice held an old note of concern that she had once (yesterday?) believed was genuine and defined family. She looked back at him, knowing her face was slack, unable to raise an expression.

"Sometimes . . ." He had looked her in the eye; now he kept his gaze on the floor as he said, "Sometimes, you have to block out the here and now and not think about what you're doing. For your own future good."

She could picture herself laughing at him, or screaming, hitting . . . she couldn't summon the energy to do more than nod again. Then she knelt to open her night chest.

"Don't scream," said a voice from nowhere.

She froze. The voice was strange, tiny, like a whispering mouse.

"It's me, Jordan. I'm free, and I'm leaving. Tamsin, I don't know what you feel about me. I hope you won't betray me."

She looked behind the chest, up the wall, along it. There was no one here.

"Where are you?" she whispered.

"Outside the door." Yet the door was across the room, and she heard the voice here.

"Who are you talking to?" asked her uncle. He had come up behind her. She whirled, hands behind her on the chest.

"Nobody," she said. Her voice sounded strained to her own ears.

Her uncle's eyes narrowed. He eyed the door, then walked over to it.

No. It all broke in her like a dam, and before she knew what she was doing Tamsin grabbed a brass vase from the table and ran at her uncle. She swung the vase up at his head with all her strength; it made a satisfying *crunch*, and he fell over without a sound.

She flung the door open and practically fell through it—into Jordan's arms. "Let's get out of here," he said simply, and closed the door behind her.

There was only one lifeline for her now, and Tamsin took it. She grabbed Jordan's hand tightly and ran with him.

23

THEY WERE TEN alleys away from the Boros house before either spoke. "Wait," said Jordan, holding up his hand. "Gotta rest."

"They'll come after us."

"Not for a while." He had an odd distracted look on his face. He'd had it back in the hall, too. Bemused, almost sublime. "Everything's quiet."

She didn't ask how he knew that. "I'm cold."

"Yes, we've got to find some shelter."

Tamsin nearly said, "We just left shelter," but that would have taken too much energy. It didn't make any sense to go anywhere; there was nowhere to go now. She supposed there might be for him. But why had he come for her?

Jordan closed his eyes, tilted his head back, and smiled. "Yes," he said, "you've done well. Now please return to your master. I'm sure he'll be frantic without you."

He opened his eyes and looked at her. She knew he was anticipating a question. Tamsin just stared at him.

"Are you okay?" he asked.

The question was so ridiculous she laughed. "No, no I'm not." She opened her mouth to say more, but the words tripped over one another. And she didn't know where to start or why telling him would do any good.

He spoke, touched her arm. But something distracted her, a nuance of emotion like a thing seen out of the corner of one's eye. *Where to go.* That was it.

Tamsin looked around. Nothing was familiar. She had no idea where she was. The buildings looming high around were nothing like the ones in her town. Even the air tasted different. She was lost, sliding. Drowning again. "I . . ." she said. Jordan had hold of both her wrists now. He was speaking to her, low and urgent, something about the queen and desals. She had no idea who he was.

"We have to go!" Finally words she understood.

"Yes, yes." She nodded, not to him but to herself.

Jordan began to lead her through the alleys. "Out of the city," she said. "Take me to the desert. I have to go home."

"Home?" He tightened his grip on her arm.

"Home, I have to go home, I have to . . ." She wanted to cry so badly, and she wasn't able to. It was the most awful thing she had ever felt. She gasped for breath.

"Tamsin, don't think me cruel for saying this," said the young man leading her. "But your family is dead."

"I know." But she quailed at his words; until this night, she knew, she had never really believed it. Even now . . . if she could get home, find out the truth. "Maybe somebody survived. They couldn't have killed everyone—"

"Yes, they could."

"But you want to get to the queen, anyway. Do you know the way? No. The way lies through the desert. I can guide you. We have to go that way, anyway."

"We'll talk about it. I promise. For now we've got to find somewhere to hide."

He wasn't really listening. Tamsin felt, if possible, even more alone. That sense of drowning came back, like a roaring, unstoppable noise in her head.

Jordan stopped and put his hands on her shoulders. She blinked, suddenly seeing the gray crescents of his eyes gazing on hers. "I am listening," he said. "And I'll do everything I can to help you. We just have to take things one step at a time."

This time she followed him attentively, and to her surprise, after she had gone ten paces in his footsteps she began, at last, to cry.

JORDAN STOOD ON the wall of an alley near the vertical uplands of the city. It was deep night now, but the moon was still up, and he could see its light glinting off the spires of the desal that waited half submerged in the bay.

"You want to talk to a desal?" It was the first thing Tamsin had said since they had bedded down here. She stood below him on the nest of trash they had made. She still appeared stunned, distracted, her hair a bird's nest and her hands grimy. Even a little curiosity from her now was an encouraging sign.

"It sounds crazy, doesn't it?"

She didn't answer for a while, merely chewed her knuckle and looked around herself aimlessly. Jordan returned his own gaze to the desal; ghostly in Diadem's glow, its pinions rose from the middle of the lake like something discarded there, a sunken building or, he imagined, the shipwreck from Queen Galas's story. Except that the spires were perfect, undamaged by time or the elements. The waves slapped against their sides as peacefully as they did the docks; there was no sign of preternatural life to the thing. Just now an ornate bark from the temple was anchored near the giant central tower. He could see the torchlit figures of priests moving about in it, but couldn't tell what they were doing. Some kind of ceremony.

"I thought you were crazy when I saw you," said Tamsin, so long after his own rhetorical question that it took him a moment to connect the two. He glanced at her; she summoned a smile, like an unpracticed conjurer, and hid it as quickly. "With, with your gold underwear and, and talking to things and all."

As they ran he had given her a very sketchy rendition of his story: that he could talk to the mecha because of something Armiger had done and that the Heaven hook' were after him. She would have heard some of it from through her uncle, if Suneil had bothered to explain why Brendan Sheia wanted him. Jordan didn't know if she believed any of it yet.

"I can't think of any other way to put an end to all this," he said. "I can't go home, because this curse will just follow me there. The Winds are hunting me because of the mecha in my head; the Boros want me as a scapegoat. The only one who can do anything about it is Armiger."

"What can he do?" She crossed her arms and looked away; but she was listening and talking now.

"The first time I saw Armiger—saw through his eyes, I mean—he was commanding an army. It was so strange, but part of it was that *he* was strange. The things he looked at, listened for, and the things he said . . . they weren't what I would have done. He didn't seem to care about the battle or the people he was commanding, he just gave orders, and they were always good. When the Winds sent the animals to destroy his army, I remember he was totally calm during the retreat. He escaped because he was as confident and calm in the middle of that butchery as he had been standing on the hillside watching from a distance.

"I've been watching him for weeks now, and he's not the same man anymore. I think Calandria was right, he came here to conquer the Winds. He was the agent of some other creature even more powerful. But that one is dead, and Armiger is free."

She was eyeing him now. He shook his head. "I can't explain it. You have to be there, you see, to see the difference. But he has a woman now, and he cares about her. And he's affected by things around him now, where he wasn't before. The siege, he's really bothered by it. People are dying, you know, starving and injured, and he's realizing he can't do anything to help them. He's not thinking about conquering the world anymore."

Tamsin frowned. "So how can he help you? Can he make the Boroses go away?"

"Maybe. If I can convince him to help me."

"How are you going to do that? By letting that," she nodded to the desal, "eat you?"

Jordan took a deep breath. "Well, this is the crazy part. He went to Queen Galas to learn from her why the Winds are the way they are. Why they persecute people. She told him enough to give him an idea of where to look—but he can't talk to the Winds, and he's trapped in the palace with her now. But I can talk to the Winds. And I can search the places he needs to go."

"So you want to be his errand boy!"

He winced. There was a little of her former haughtiness in her voice, though, and the thought cheered him. "Errand boy for a god is not a bad position," he said. "I want to trade him the information in return for him getting the curse off my back."

"Why should he trade? You said yourself he no longer wants to subdue the Winds."

He hesitated. She did seem interested; he wondered if what he was going to say would make her dismiss him as crazy and turn her back on her own misery.

"The thing is," he said at last, "I think he should."

Tamsin didn't answer. She just cocked her head and waited.

"This is the crazy part, Tamsin, and you have to promise to think about it before you laugh at me. See, I think we all of us could originally command the Winds. Everybody was once like I am now."

Tamsin snorted. "If everybody could do anything they wanted, it would be chaos! Why pay for anything, if you can just summon the Winds to create it?"

"The world began in chaos," he said. "Calandria told me Ventus was originally made for us, not for the Winds. Nobody in all the ages has ever been able to change it back, not even people from the stars like her. But Armiger could do it, if only he knew what their secret was. Before, when he was trying to find the secret for his own master, it would have been a disaster to have him win. Now it's different."

"You think he'd set things right?"

"He might. The man he's become would try."

She didn't answer, just made an odd noise, and thinking she was laughing at him again he turned to fire a retort back. She wasn't looking at him, just pointing at the mouth of the alley.

"There they are!" Jordan saw a confusion of torches in the street, and the dark figures of a number of men.

"Brendan Sheia!" He knelt down. "Quickly, grab hold." Tamsin boosted herself up, and he pulled her onto the wall.

"That won't do you any good," said a smug, familiar voice from the ground on the other side.

Jordan looked down, into the eyes of the magician from the marketplace.

"Thief! I'll have your head for stealing my power."

For a second old habits took hold: "I didn't steal him!" yelled Jordan. "I borrowed him and I gave him back." Then he saw moonlight glint off the blade in the man's hand.

There were six men on the alley side of the wall, and four including
the magician on the other, which was someone's garden. The wall itself
ran between two buildings; there was no exit to be had by running
along its top.

Three of the men in the alley had torches, as did the magician.

"Let us go!" said Jordan. "I don't want to hurt you."

The magician laughed. "Nice bluff."

"Get ready to jump" Jordan hissed to Tamsin. *Torch, crack!*

Sparks and burning wood flew everywhere as the torch in the magician's hand exploded. He screamed and fell, batting at the embers in his
hair.

"Now!" Jordan and Tamsin landed in the dirt next to the magician,
whose friends were smacking him on the head to put out his hair. There
was an open gate at the far end of the garden, so Jordan made for that.
Tamsin kept up easily.

They entered a moonlit street. In the distance he heard running feet;
the others were coming around the end of the block. *Ka! Come to me.*

Ka. The ghost of a butterfly wafted through the open gate.

Tamsin tugged at his arm. "They're coming!"

"I know. We can't stay here. Ka, we need horses. Find me two of
them, right now!"

This way. The butterfly flitted off down the street—thankfully away
from the sound of running feet.

"So now I am the thief he accused me of being," panted Jordan. "He
deserves it though, the bastard."

"What's going on?" They entered another alley, this one shadowed by
the high walls of buildings to either side.

"There! They went down that alley!"

It was too dark here to see anything. Jordan closed his eyes and looked
with his other sight. "This way." He followed Ka to a stable door; inside
he could see the outlines of two sleeping horses.

*Ka, speak to the horses. I want them awake and ready to go with us if
you can do that.*

*I have no power to compel. But I can present you to them as a Wind, if
that is your desire.*

Yes!

Torches appeared at the mouth of the alley. Jordan made these explode
as well, and their pursuers retreated in dismay. Jordan proceeded to saddle the sleepy horses in complete darkness, relying on touch and the
ghost light of his mechal vision. The horses were pliant and appeared
unsurprised at this intrusion.

Tamsin had craned her neck out the door to watch the alley mouth; as
he was cinching the second horse she said, "They're waking the people in

the houses. This house, too. I think they know what we're doing. Smelled the horses, maybe."

"Well, we're ready. Come on." He led the horses outside.

"But where are we going? What about your plan to visit the desal in the bay?"

"You said there was another one in the middle of the desert," he shot back. "You wanted to go home, Tamsin. Well, that's where we're going to have to go."

He dug his heels into the flank of the horse and it bolted through shouting men, and when he looked back Tamsin was following, crouched low on her horse, wearing a grin that could be terror or satisfaction—and maybe was a bit of both.

GENERAL LAVIN LAID his quill down wearily and peered at the manacled prisoner Hesty had led in. "Why is this of interest?" he asked.

Hesty grimaced. "I hate to bother you with trivial matters. This man is a looter, we caught him skulking in the ruins of one of the outlying villages."

"Yes? So execute him." Lavin turned his attention back to his plans.

"He claims to have valuable information to sell. About the siege."

"Torture it out of him."

"We tried."

Lavin looked up in surprise. The prisoner was a small man, wiry and gray haired. He stood in an exhausted stoop, trembling slightly. His left arm was broken, and had not been set, and there were burn marks up and down his bare torso and rope burns around his throat. He glared dully but defiantly at Lavin from his good eye; the other's lid was bruised and swollen, as were his lips.

Lavin stood and walked around him. A large portion of the skin was missing from his back; the flesh there wept openly.

"He completely defied the torturer," Hesty explained. "He insists on speaking only to you. And," he shook his head in disbelief, "he wants to bargain!"

Lavin half smiled and came around to look the prisoner in the eye. "And why not? He obviously loves his life, Hesty. But there's no reason to believe he knows anything."

"Hear me out," whispered the prisoner. He hunched, as if expecting a blow, but his gaze remained fixed on Lavin's.

Lavin threw up his hands. "All right. Your torturers are incompetent, or this man has more character than they do." He sat on a camp chair and gestured for the prisoner to sit opposite. Awkwardly, as if his legs would not bend properly, the prisoner sat, hunching forward so as not touch the back of the chair. Hesty folded his arms and looked on in amusement.

"What is your name?"

"Enneas, Lord Lavin."

"You were caught looting, Enneas. We punish that with death, but we're not cruel. Why did you choose to be tortured instead of letting us hang you quickly?"

Enneas breathed heavily and seemed on the verge of fainting. He put his good arm on his knee to steady himself, and said, "I know something that will win you the siege without much bloodshed. But why should I tell you, if I'm going to die, anyway?"

Lavin nearly laughed. The answer was self-evident: they would stop torturing him, that was why. But the torture hadn't worked, and by the look of him, the man wouldn't survive much more of it.

"I can't believe you mean to bargain with us."

Enneas tried to smile; it came across as a grotesque grimace. "What do I have to lose?"

"Your testicles," said Hesty impatiently.

Lavin waved him silent. "I'm sure all that has been explained to Mister Enneas. Some of it done, too, by the looks of things."

"I want to live!" Enneas glared fiercely at Lavin. "Free me, and I'll tell you what I know. Kill me, and things go badly for you in the siege."

"I don't bargain." Lavin stood. "Kill him."

Hesty took Enneas by his broken arm and dragged him screaming to his feet. "Sorry to have bothered you," Hesty grumbled as he pushed the prisoner through the flap of the tent.

Lavin sat brooding after they had left. He was preoccupied with plans for the siege, and it did look like it would be costly. There was an option yet to be tried but, much as he hated to admit it, that might not work. If it didn't, a frontal assault would be his only choice.

Enneas had made a pitiful figure, sitting in his clean tent. He was a ruined man, and there would be many more like him before this was all over. Lavin had no compunction about sentencing a man like him to death; he would rather the money Enneas had taken go to feed wounded veterans, widows, or children.

But sometimes he lost sight of why he was here. The siege would be bloody and dangerous, not only to his men, but to the queen. And that did not sit well with him.

He stood and left the tent. It was late afternoon, and cool and cloudy, but dry. A pall of smoke hung over the staggered tents of the encampment. Men bustled to and fro, carrying supplies and marching for exercise. Far away, on the outskirts of the camp, a simple scaffold stood. Someone was being hanged even as he watched.

Hoping it was not Hesty's prisoner, he picked up his pace, mindful to nod and acknowledge the greetings of his men as he went.

The scaffold disappeared behind some tents as he got closer. He hurried, but just as he was about to leave the edge of camp someone hailed him.

"Yes?" He waited impatiently as his chief mechanist ran over. The man was bowlegged and hirsute, and his helmet perched atop his head like some metallic bird. He bowed awkwardly and pointed in the direction of the siege engines.

"General, sir! Someone punctured the water barrels last night! The supply's shot—I mean, it's leaked out! There isn't enough left to run the steam cannons."

Lavin hissed. "Sabotage? Is that what you're saying?"

The mechanist backed away. "Yeah. Yeah, sabotage. What are we going to do?"

"What about our own rations?"

The man's eyes widened. "The drinking water?"

Lavin nodded. "Is it safe?"

"Uh . . . not my department . . ."

"Find out. We will use it if we have to. Report back to me in an hour—and tell Hesty about this right away. Now excuse me."

He rounded the tent in time to see them lower a body from the scaffold. Two soldiers heaved it up between them and carried it to a low pile of corpses nearby.

The rope had already been put around Enneas's neck. The other end went up over the arm of the scaffold and to the halter of a bored horse. To hang Enneas, all they would have to do was walk the horse a few meters.

The thief's eyes were closed. He seemed to be praying. But he didn't beg, and he stayed on his feet, though he tottered.

Lavin was angry about the sabotage. It would cost him lives if the steam cannons were inoperable. He nearly turned and marched back to his tent. Maybe though, just maybe, this man could make up for those potential casualties.

Still, he waited until the horse began to walk, just to see if the thief would break down. The rope tightened around his neck, but he didn't struggle as he was lifted skyward.

"Stop! Cut him down!" Lavin strode over to the scaffold. Surprised soldiers jumped to untie the rope from the horse's harness. Enneas fell to the ground, choking, dirt grinding into his bloody back.

They hauled him to his feet and unwound the rope. He coughed and gasped and blinked at Lavin with his good eye.

"You have your life," Lavin told him, "if you tell me what you know, and if I judge that it will be of use to me."

Enneas's knees buckled. He managed to croak, "Done!" before he fainted.

24

THROUGH DUSTY, uneventful days the passenger carriage had trundled its way south. Calandria May knew the shape of the seats intimately now; she felt her body had become molded to conform to them, it certainly wasn't the other way around. The primitive suspension of the vehicle sent every jolt and rattle of the wheels up her spine and into her throbbing head. And the thing was slow, stopping frequently at mail drops or to exchange horses.

Still, it was all they'd been able to afford with the last of their funds. This route would take them unobtrusively into Iapysia, where hopefully they could acquire some faster transportation. The country was in enough chaos that, one hoped, a couple of stolen horses wouldn't be missed.

"My, you've become a paragon of caution," Axel had said to her when she told him of this plan. "What happened to 'get the hell down and find Armiger at all costs'?"

She'd shrugged. "What's the point? We don't have the weapons necessary to destroy him anymore. All we can do is observe until we can contact a passing ship and call in a strike."

Their last reliable information had Armiger on his way to visit Queen Galas, who was either dead now or still holed up in her palace, depending on whom you talked to. Either way, it seemed unlikely that Armiger would still be going there, because her cause was doomed. They were rattling along in this carriage because the queen was their only lead. But there was no urgency to the journey now.

Axel was mostly recovered now, though you wouldn't know it from the way he slept most of the day away. Without action to sustain him, he folded in on himself and became a dead weight. Calandria herself didn't have the fight left to try to bring him out of his lethargy.

Consequently, when on a completely typical evening of jolting over rutted tracks, her skull computer said without warning *Incoming transmission*, Calandria May sat up straight and said, "Thank the gods!"

The passengers seated opposite them in the carriage didn't look up; all three of them were nodding drowsily. They would have found it hard to hear Calandria over the noise of the wheels, anyway.

She turned to find Axel staring back at her. She was just opening her mouth to ask him to please tell her he'd heard it to, when a different voice spoke in her mind.

This is Marya Mounce of the research vessel Pan-Hellenia. *Can anyone hear me?*

Axel's face split in a wide grin. "A ride!" he said.

The other passenger on their side of the carriage mumbled something and butted Axel with his shoulder.

The voice continued. *I'm on a reentry trajectory. The Winds are after me. The Diadem swans went berserk a couple of days ago, and they've either captured or driven away all ships in the system. I tried to ride it out but they're on to me now. I'm going to try to land at the coordinates of the last transmission we received from our agent on the surface.*

"Agent?" whispered Calandria. "So there really are some researchers down here right now?"

Axel looked uncomfortable. "Well, yes, but maybe not like you think," he said.

It took her a minute to catch on. *"You're* the agent she's referring to?" Calandria said to him.

"Yeah, yeah. Look, I didn't see any reason why I couldn't make some money on the side, so when those galactic researchers asked whether I could feed them regular observations while I was here, I jumped at it. Why not? I didn't think the Winds would be jumping down our throats quite so enthusiastically."

She had to laugh. "You are full of surprises, you know that?" Usually they were unpleasant, but if this Mounce person was on her way to this part of the continent . . .

Calandria reached out and rapped on the top of the door frame. "Driver. You can let us out here, please."

AN HOUR LATER they paused in the center of a darkening field in the very middle of nowhere. The Milky Way made a broad swath of light across the sky. Diadem was setting, its light glittering darkly off a lake near the horizon. There were no houses visible anywhere; other than the road, the nearest feature to the landscape was a dark row of trees along a nearby escarpment.

"There she is." Calandria pointed to a slowly falling star at the zenith. "We're going to have to break radio silence."

Axel nodded. If Mounce's ship landed back at the Boros manor, it would take them a week to reach it, and by then she would surely have lifted off again. Particularly if the Diadem swans came down after her.

They watched the little spark overhead grow. Chill autumn wind teased at Axel's long black hair. Neither spoke. Axel wasn't sure what Calandria was feeling, but that dot of light represented escape to him, if they could get aboard it and evade the things that were chasing it.

"We may have to act quickly," Calandria said. "Where would be a good spot?"

"Nowhere's a good spot," he said. "So we might as well flag her down right here. At least it's level and open."

"Here goes," said Calandria. Then her voice spoke in his mind. *This is Calandria May calling the* Pan-Hellenia. *Can you hear me?*

They waited in tense silence. The brightening star had begun to drift away over the lake, following Diadem.

Hello! Yes, it's me, Marya. Are you with Axel Chan?

Yes.

They're behind me, so I'm coming down at your last location—

No! Can you find us from this signal? We're a couple hundred kilometers south of where he last contacted you.

Oh. I don't know if I can . . . Yes, it says it can do that. Do you have shelter?

Axel and Calandria exchanged a glance. He squatted down and began pulling stalks of grass out of the ground. "Shit. Shit, shit, *shit*.

Why do you need shelter? asked Calandria. *Are you trying to pick us up, or—*

Pick you up? I'm trying to stay alive! The swans are behind me; they're closing in. They've picked off every ship that's tried to get past Diadem. I've stayed ahead of them this far by skimming the top of the atmosphere, but they're all over. Everywhere! I—hang on—

Axel could see his shadow on the grass. He glanced up, in time to see the star brighten again to brilliant whiteness and swerve quickly in their direction. Around and above it, a coruscating glow had sprung up, like an aurora.

All over, thought Axel. *Great.*

"The forest," said Calandria. "Come on!" She began sprinting. He looked up again, then followed.

Low rumbles like thunder began. Instead of fading, they grew. The sound was familiar to Axel, and unmistakable: something was coming in to land. The sound had a ragged edge to it. Years of exposure to spacecraft told him it was a small ship. The big ones sang basso profundo all the way down.

Their shadows sharpened as they ran. Axel began to feel heat on his face. The roar became a steady, deafening thunder. On the shoreline below, the crescent of sand lit amber under a midnight dawn. Axel knew better than to look directly at the spear of light settling toward them, though it seemed as though Mounce was going to bring her ship down right on top of them.

The sky was starting to glow from horizon to horizon. He'd never seen that effect accompany the arrival of a starship.

Axel redoubled his effort, though he had twisted his ankle and it spiked pain up his leg with every step. Calandria was pulling ahead, but he didn't have the breath to spare to tell her to slow down.

Suddenly spokes of light like heat lightning washed across the sky. Their center was the approaching ship.

A blinding flash staggered Axel. Childhood memory took hold: he counted. One, two, three, four, . . . *Ca-rack!* The concussion knocked him off his feet. He came up tasting grass and dirt.

Whatever that flash had been, it had happened less than a kilometer away. He blinked away lozenges of afterglow in time to see the brilliant tongue of fire overhead waver and cut out.

A dark form fell with majestic slowness into the forest. As it disappeared a white dome of light silhouetted the treetops, and Axel felt the deep *crump* of impact through his feet.

Calandria was waiting at the edge of the forest. "Are you okay?"

"Fine," he said through gritted teeth. "Let's go." They waded into the underbrush. The darkness would have been total under the trees, except that a fire had started somewhere ahead, and the sky was alive with rainbow swirls. Axel would have found them beautiful if he hadn't been so frightened.

Of course, if there were any witnesses to this within fifty kilometers, they'd all be cowering under their beds by now. No sane person would want to be caught in the open when the swans touched ground.

It was dark enough that Axel couldn't spot branches and twigs fast enough to prevent himself getting thoroughly whipped as they went. Stinging, his feet somehow finding every hidden root and rock, he soon lost sight of Calandria, who as usual moved through the underbrush like a ghost. He could hear his breath rattling in his lungs, and somewhere nearby the crackling of the fire. Above that, though, a kind of trilling hiss was building up. It seemed sourceless, but he knew it must be coming from the sky. The hairs on the back of his neck stood on end; so did those on his arms. He might have preferred it if they were doing that from fright, but he knew it must be the effect of a million-volt charge accumulating in the forest.

"Axel!" He hurried in the direction of the voice. Past a wall of snapped tree trunks and smoldering loam, Calandria stood on the lip of the crater Marya Mounce's ship had dug.

The ship was egg shaped, maybe fifteen meters across. It was half buried in the earth. Smoke rolled up from its skin, which was blackened and charred. Neither the heat of reentry nor the crash could have cindered the fullerene skin to that degree. "She can't have survived that," Axel said as he staggered to a halt next to Calandria. "What did they *do?*"

"Can't you feel it?" she asked. Stray wisps of her hair were standing up. Little sparks danced around Axel's fingers when he wiped them on his trousers. "They hit her with a lightning bolt."

"Well they're about to fire another one," he said. "We'd better get out of here—" He was interrupted by a flash and *bang!* of thunder. He ducked instinctively, though it had come down at least a few hundred meters away.

"There!" Calandria pointed. Warm orange light was breaking from somewhere around the curve of the egg. A hatch had opened.

They clambered over the smoking debris and rounded the ship in time to see a small figure step daintily out of the hatch, arms out for balance.

"Hello!" shouted Marya Mounce. "Is anybody there?"

The woman revealed by the glow of the ship's lights was not the brave rescuer Axel had hoped for. Marya Mounce was tiny, with pale skin and broad hips. Before seeing her face he noticed the frizz of her dun-colored hair, which was held back by an iridescent clip. She was dressed in a black skirt and a blouse that swirled like oil. It was evidently some inner-system fashion, spoiled by the khaki bandoliers slung over her shoulders.

What made his heart sink, though, was the sight of her feet.

Mounce had succumbed to a fashion sweeping the inner worlds, and had her Achilles' tendons shortened. Her toes, the balls of her feet, and calf muscles were augmented, so she stood en pointe at all times. All she wore on her feet were metallic toe slips. He doubted she could run, much less climb over the broken trees strewn about this new clearing.

"There you are!" she shouted as Axel and Calandria fell over one last log. "See, we survived! You—you are May and Chan, aren't you?"

"Who else would be crazy enough to be here?" he said. "Are you alone?"

"Yes, it's just me." Mounce turned and waved vaguely at the ship. "I was doing a demographic survey, it involved some close orbits, so that's why I got caught in the—"

"You can tell us later," said Calandria in her most diplomatic voice. "The swans are coming." She pointed.

"Ah. Yes." Mounce looked disappointed, but not frightened.

The sky was full of arcing incandescent lines. They stretched in a spiral all the way to the zenith, like ladders to heaven. Axel had seen the Heaven hooks when they came to destroy the Boros estate, and those, too, had been skyhooks of a sort, but nothing like this. Where the Heaven hooks had been cold metal and carbon fiber, the swans seemed bodiless, creatures made of light alone.

From his scant reading on the subject, Axel knew the swans were nanotech, like most of the Winds. They were constituted from long microscopic whiskerlike fibers. These could manipulate magnetic fields, and in their natural environment in orbit they meshed together in their trillions to form tethers hundreds of kilometers long. They drew power from the planetary magnetic field and projected it by the gigawatt to wherever it was needed.

They could fly apart in an instant and recombine in new forms, he knew. Some of these forms could apparently reach down through the atmosphere itself, maybe even touch down on the surface of Ventus.

Calandria took Mounce by the shoulders. "Do you have any survival supplies?"

"Y-yes, it's an institute policy to carry some."

"Where are they?" Calandria vaulted into the ship. "We need stealth gauze. Have you got any?"

"I don't—" began Mounce. The voice of the ship interrupted her. Axel couldn't hear what it said over the roar of a nearby fire.

With a curse he hauled himself in the hatch after Calandria. She was rooting in a suit locker near the lock.

For a second Axel just let himself drink in the sight of the clean white floors, padded couches, and trailing wall ivy decorating the ship. The *Pan Hellenia* represented civilization, with all the amenities—flush toilets, air beds, hot showers and sonic cleansers, VR, fine cuisine . . .

"Axel, help me!" He sighed and turned away from it all.

Calandria was throwing things indiscriminately into a survival bag. Axel spotted a first-aid kit, diagnostic equipment, some emergency rations, a flashlight—

"Aha!" He pounced on the laser pistol. "Now I feel whole again."

"Forget that—help me with this." She was struggling to unclip a heavy box from the wall.

"What's that? Cal, it's way too heavy—"

"Nanotech customization kit. It'll save our lives, believe me."

"Okay." He helped her wrestle it down and into the bag.

"Uh, guys?" Mounce stood in the entrance, framed nicely by a vision of burning forest. "We'd better get going. The swans are here."

Calandria leaped past her, carrying two metal cases. Axel had never seen Calandria like this. It made him more than a little uneasy—as if his own vivid imagination was underselling the danger they were in.

"Hell!" Caught in her urgency, Axel swung the survival bag onto his shoulder and, staggering under the load, followed. Mounce accompanied him, her hands fluttering as she visibly tried to find a way to help.

A strange twilight glow pervaded the shattered clearing. Calandria had dumped both cases on the ground and was frantically rooting through one of them when Axel and Mounce caught up to her. Drifts of wood smoke stung Axel's eyes, and the roar and heat of nearby flames made his head spin. Sparks of static electricity were flying everywhere, and Mounce's clean hair puffed out around her head like a dandelion.

Suddenly Calandria cried out and collapsed. She curled into a ball on the smoking ground, hands clutching her head.

Axel felt it, too—a ringing pain his head. It was centered on the left side, just above his ear. Mounce cursed in some foreign language and pulled off her crescent-shaped hair clip.

"What's happening?" she shouted over an impossible roar of sound. The sound of the fire was drowned out by the approach of the swans. It wasn't a single sound, but many, like a thousand strings. The swans sang a single unison chord as they reached to touch ground.

Lightning arced from the top of the starship. "Our implants!" shouted Axel. "We've all got hardware in our skulls. It's shorting out from all this power! Calandria's got more than either of us—she's augmented in a dozen ways." She lay insensible now, twitching next to the golden gauze she had half pulled from the case.

"We've got to get her out of here!" He grabbed Calandria's arm, hoisting her into a fireman's carry. "Bring the stuff!"

Marya threw the cases into the survival bag and bent to haul it after her. Axel didn't look back to see how she was doing; it took all his concentration just to navigate the splintered branches and gouged earth around the ship. Finally he reached untouched forest and toppled into a thorn bush with Calandria on top of him. The singing pain in his head continued, but not as strongly as it had right next to the ship.

Marya Mounce struggled her way across the obstacles, the huge bulging sack getting caught on every jutting spar. She seemed determined, her mouth set in a grim line.

She had nearly made it to the trees when a rain of white light pattered into the loam right behind her. The ground sizzled and smoked under it.

"Run!" Axel waved frantically at her. "Forget the sack! Just run!" He knew she couldn't hear him over the chorus of the swans.

The rain intensified. It was like a funnel somewhere overhead was pouring down liquid light. Where it landed, the light coalesced, pulsing. The rain stopped abruptly and started up again farther around the clearing.

The glow it had left behind flashed brightly once, then *stood up*.

Axel's voice died. He was glad Marya seemed oblivious to the thing behind her, because it would have paralyzed him were he in her place. It looked like a man, but was entirely made of liquid light. Long electric streamers flew from its fingertips and head. As another such being grew behind it, the first began to pirouette this way and that, like a dancer, obviously looking for something.

Marya landed heavily next to Axel. The survival bag spilled open. "Damn," she said meekly. Then she grinned crookedly at him. "Made it!"

Calandria pushed herself onto her elbows. "Stealth gauze," she croaked. "Where'zit?"

Axel grabbed the golden filigree she had been trying to unwind earlier. He pushed himself to his knees and flipped it open, letting it drape over all three of them, as Marya hauled the survival bag in under it.

The creature that had built itself behind Marya turned and looked in their direction. Axel forgot to breathe. He felt the other two freeze also, ancient instinct kicking in to save them from a superior predator. Slowly, deliberately, the thing stalked toward them.

"Oh, shit." Axel fingered the laser pistol. It felt hot under his hand; he wondered if it was shorting out, too. It looked like he would find out in a second, when he had to use it.

The thing's head snapped to the left. It paused, chin up as though sniffing the air. Then it stepped over a log and headed away. The gauze had worked.

Axel blew out his held breath. Of course the stealth gauze worked—it was designed to fool the senses of the Winds. At times like this, though, he found it hard to remember that the technology of the Winds, including the swans, was a thousand years older than his own.

Old, maybe. But not primitive. He sucked in a new breath, and tried to will his racing heart to slow.

Soon six humanoid forms walked the clearing. Everything they touched caught fire. They tossed downed trees aside and sent beams of coherent light into the treetops, hunting high and low, but never noticing the three small forms huddled right on the edge of the clearing.

One entered the ship. Loud concussions sounded inside, and the lights went out. Then spiral tendrils of light drifted down from above and gently but firmly gripped the sides of the ship. The five remaining humanoid forms reached out and dissolved into the ropes of light. Then, with hardly a tremor, the swans pulled the *Pan Hellenia* out of the ground, and retreated into the sky with it in tow.

The stellar glow faded; the full-throated cry of the swans diminished; soon the clearing was lit only by ordinary fire. But over the smell of burning autumn leaves lay the sharp reek of ozone.

For a time the three lay where they had fallen, head to head, watching the spiral aurora recede into the zenith, until finally the stars came out one by one, like the timid crickets.

Marya Mounce sat up and brushed dirt off her sleeves. "Well," she said briskly. "Thank you both, very much, for rescuing me."

Hours later they paused, halfway around the lake under the eaves of an abandoned barn. Axel was unused to this level of activity, and he had begun to stagger badly. Calandria favored her wounded arm, so she could carry only so much. Marya had managed to keep up amazingly well, considering her feet. Whatever augmentation had been done to support her shortened tendons had toughened the balls of her feet immensely, and she could indeed run if she needed to.

As Axel slumped down wearily, and Calandria moved slowly to gather old planks for a fire, he noticed that Marya was shivering violently—whole body shivers accompanied by wildly chattering teeth.

"Thermal wear," she muttered. "There must be some thermal wear here." She knelt down and began rummaging through the bag.

"Ah. Here we are." She pulled out a pair of silvery overalls and stood up. Axel expected her to walk away or at least turn around to remove her skirt, but she just pulled the overalls on—and the skirt vanished as she did, leaving nothing but a cloudy blackness that disappeared as she zipped up the overalls.

"What was that?" he said.

"What? What's what?" Marya peevishly squatted down, hugging herself.

"Your dress—it was holographic." He heard Calandria pause in the midst of prying a board off the old barn's door.

"Of-f c-course it-it is," Marya chattered. "It's a-a holo unitard. W-what do y-you expect me to w-wear? *Cloth?*"

Calandria sent Axel an eloquent look that said, *you deal with this.* She went back to prying at the door.

Axel wasn't actually that surprised. Holo unitards were increasingly common in the inner systems. They allowed unrestricted and unlimited costume changes for the wearer—but were only practical in climate-controlled environments.

"Well," he said, "you're on Ventus now."

"I *know*. Anyway, the holo's not supposed to be visible to the W-Winds."

"That's not the point," said Axel. "You'll freeze to death in that thing."

"The ship had no cloth apparel in it. And I didn't get a chance to put the thermals on before we landed," muttered Marya. "Too busy falling out of the sky." She shuddered violently again.

She had a point there. "We'd better get this fire going," he said. Calandria dropped another load of scraps at his feet, and he bent to whittle some kindling. Marya watched him avidly.

"Pretty ironic," said Calandria as she came to sit on the other side of Marya. She and Axel framed her; he could feel her shudders as he whittled. "A couple of hours ago we were nearly burned to death. Now we're freezing. Typical."

"There." Axel had his kindling. He built a little pyramid of small scraps, leaving an opening, and began laying larger blocks above and around that. Satisfied, he brought out the lighter from the survival kit.

"I can earn my keep," said Marya. "Here, let me prove it." She reached for the lighter.

"Anybody can use a lighter, Marya."

"I want to do it the old-fashioned way. Do you have a flint and iron?"

"Yes . . . Have you spent time on Ventus, then?" asked Axel.

"I'm not ground survey staff." Marya stood over them both, still shaking but looking strangely determined. "But I am a cultural anthropologist. I've studied more societies than you've heard about. I know sixteen ways to start a fire. We should save your lighter for a real emergency."

Calandria exchanged another glance with Axel. Then she said, "Let her try."

"I don't want to be useless," said Marya as she took the flints from Axel. She began frantically whacking the flintstone with her iron. She hit her own fingers and dropped it. "Ow!" Before Axel could move she had snatched it up again and resumed, more carefully and also more accurately. A small spray of sparks flew into the shavings.

She bent forward to blow gently on the embers. To Axel's surprise, the tinder caught. She nursed it for a few minutes like a doting parent, while Calandria and Axel watched with bated breath.

Finally Marya sat back, triumphant, as the little fire began to burn on its own. "See! I did it!"

Both Axel and Calandria made approving noises. Maybe Marya wouldn't be as useless as her gaudy exterior threatened.

The anthropologist sat down cross-legged and beamed at her accomplishment. Axel sighed. "Okay, Cal, let's look at your arm."

"Well," said Calandria as Axel poked and prodded, "what do we do next?"

Marya was beginning to warm up and seemed to be regaining her poise as well. She said, "Obviously we need to get off-world as soon as possible. Something's happening—I've never seen the swans like this!"

Axel and Calandria exchanged a glance. Armiger. It could only be him.

"Listen," continued Marya. "I know Ventus like the back of my hand, even if I've never been here. We've had agents down here on and off for decades—people like Axel who've sent back reports, brought back books. I know the history. I know the geography, every city and hamlet on this continent. I speak six local languages, without the need for implant dictionaries. I've studied the religions twelve different ways." She leaned forward to warm her hands on the new fire. "I know I'm not the outdoorsy type, but I think I can help you."

Calandria nodded. "Thank you. We need the help, right about now. One thing, though—you should get rid of that unitard. I know you say it's supposed to be invisible to the Winds, but do we know that for sure? I don't think we should take the chance."

"Yes, I agree," said Axel. He jerked a thumb at the sky. "Especially after seeing the swans close up—not something I want to do again, let me tell you!"

"Hang on," said Marya. "I think I have a better idea."

"What?" asked Calandria.

Marya grinned. "We need horses, right?"

25

"WHERE IS SHE?" Marya strained to see through the darkness. She and Axel were crouching in damp weeds, while Calandria snuck up on some horses in a nearby paddock.

"She's nearly there," whispered Axel. "Pipe down, or the dogs will hear you."

Marya started to sit back, remembered they were on a planet covered with foul dirt, and recovered her crouching position. She shook her head. Calandria May seemed to take it for granted that her ways were the best. She had insisted on being the one to steal these horses.

"As soon as they discover they're gone, there'll be a posse out after us," she said, for what felt like the tenth time.

"We'll be long gone by the time that happens," he repeated back. "Trust us."

"My plan was better."

"We've been over this. Your unitard wouldn't fit Calandria."

"So what? I—"

The dogs started barking. Marya Mounce cursed under her breath. Calandria had been approaching downwind and with almost supernatural quiet, but the damn animals had sensed her, anyway. She wasn't even to the paddock gate yet.

Calandria raced up to the paddock gate and unhooked the loop of rope that kept it shut. Horses nickered nervously in the darkness beyond.

Marya shook her head, scowling. She had come up with a plan that, ethnologically, should guarantee that they were not pursued when they took the horses. Calandria had rejected it. The woman seemed to think only in terms of skulduggery—or maybe she didn't want to admit that Marya's plan was better than hers.

Here came the dogs, three of them snarling through the grass straight at Calandria. Marya's breath caught in her throat as Calandria froze—but then there came a brilliant flash of light that dazzled Marya's eyes for a moment.

The laser pistol was set on flash mode. Marya heard yelping and opened her eyes to see the dogs stopped, pawing at their snouts. Poor things. A moment earlier they had been all teeth and claws, but already Marya felt like stroking them.

Calandria threw open the paddock gate. The horses were a bit dazzled, too, and skittish.

The cottage door opened, throwing new light across the clearing. Two men stepped out. One shouted at the dogs.

"Trust?" said Marya. "Yeah, I trusted this was going to happen."

"Calandria will handle it, you'll see."

Indeed, May was walking confidently across the paddock toward the men. One pointed at her and swore. Marya did a mental tally of the Ventus oaths she knew, trying to identify the language. Memnonian, of course . . .

Marya never found out what Calandria was planning to do next, because her own impatience and annoyance got the better of her. Marya stood up, unzipping her thermal overalls. "Hey, what are you,"—began Axel, stopping as Marya disappeared from sight. She had tuned her holographic unitard to black, and before he had time to figure out what she was doing, she ran into the clearing.

The men were both burly, but short. They looked rough. Behind them another figure had appeared in the cottage doorway, hands bundled in its skirts.

"What you doin'?" the first barked at Calandria. Pure Memnonian, she marveled. A rich strain of it, from the accent. She could almost trace this man's ancestry by the way he sounded his vowels.

Marya stepped between the men and Calandria, and said "Morph," in a loud and clear voice. As she did, she tuned her holographic clothing to another suit.

The men's eyes widened, and they fell several steps back. Marya had gone from black unitard to a festival costume that was all feathers and rainbows. Marya knew her face glowed out of it like an angel's. That was the design.

"Uh, hello," she said carefully. The words sounded clumsy in her own ears. "I mean you harm—no, no harm, I mean you."

They both stopped short, a couple of meters away, and looked her up and down. Behind her, Marya heard Calandria muttering something. She chose not to listen.

The men were intimidated, but stood their ground. "W-what do you want?" asked the first, who looked older. "We have nothing. We've not harmed a single creature in this wood. Look, all we've got is horses—"

"Horses," she said, nodding. "We need three. One for me, and two for my human servants."

They looked so tragic that Marya wanted to turn and just walk away. The horses were all they had, after all. They were abjectly poor, and she was robbing them. Maybe there was something she could give them . . . but all the off-world paraphernalia she had would endanger them if they kept it. "I'm sorry," she said.

They glanced at one another. "Do you need saddles?" said the younger man. The older one shot him a dirty look.

They really did need saddles, but Marya couldn't bring herself to go that far. "No," she said.

"Mar*ya*," hissed Calandria.

"No saddles. Just horses. Thank you."

The dogs were recovering their sight and whined and snuffled around the feet of the men. Reluctantly, they turned to walk three palfreys over to her. She had no way of judging the quality of the mounts and would probably have turned down the best if she knew they were offering them to her. Silently, the men bridled the horses and handed her the reins. "Spare us," was all that the older one said as she led the horses out the paddock gate.

She could smell the animals—a spicy and enticing odor, but somehow . . . unsanitary. Her nose wrinkled. She made hushing motions as she approached them.

The walk to the woods seemed to take forever, and Marya looked back several times. The woman had joined them, and the three stood there with slumped shoulders watching part of their livelihood go. Marya felt so bad she nearly cried.

"That was a damn fool thing to do," accused Calandria. "You could have gotten hurt if they'd attacked us."

"I told you my plan would work better," Marya shot back. "And I told you yours wouldn't work at all, remember?"

For once, Calandria had no answer.

"You're crazy," said Axel Chan later that night. "He'll kill us."

"We have to try." Calandria stamped the dirt near the fire in an attempt to warm her feet. "Every day we wait he'll get stronger, and nearer his goal."

"But without the *Desert Voice* . . ."

"He's not invincible, Axel. None of them are."

"But we can't guarantee his destruction. You've said yourself every molecule of that body has to be vaporized."

Calandria patted the large case they'd taken from the *Pan-Hellenia*. "This should be enough to incapacitate him. Then we get him off-world and take care of him once and for all there."

Marya watched them bicker wearily. This had been going on for hours now. She was beginning to wonder whether it wouldn't have been better to throw herself on the mercy of the farmers. At least she had studied them. These two were galactic citizens, like her, but they were also foreign mercenaries with completely alien priorities.

They had made camp in a hollow beneath a windswept hill. It was very cold again tonight; Marya could see her breath. She had never been so cold, for so long, in her life. Privately she was amazed and proud that she was still alive, much less mobile. Every day she battled bone-numbing cold, agoraphobia from being on the unprotected surface of a planet, and the onslaught of so many minor physical inconveniences that she was sure they were going to drive her insane.

To make matters worse, Axel had told her he thought it would *rain* tonight. Would it hurt? she wondered. The very thought of countless tiny water missiles plummeting down at her from ten thousand meters made her shudder. But he seemed quite unconcerned. Show-off.

She scratched at the heavy, binding cloth garments Calandria had stolen for her the day before. She had been taught that clothing was primarily an invention for sexual display, but the people who told her that had like herself been raised in an environment of perfect climate and hygiene control. She wouldn't abandon the cloth now, uncomfortable as it was, because she needed it to keep her warm.

The argument across the fire had shifted back to whether they should continue with their mission, and attempt to stop Armiger, or whether they should try to escape the planet. Axel wanted to use their implanted radio to signal other ships that might be in the system; Calandria was adamant about retaining radio silence. She seemed frightened of attracting the attention of the Winds. And yet it was she who proposed that they confront this Armiger, whom Axel said might be hiding in the depths of a besieged fortress. The argument went back and forth, back and forth, and nothing was resolved.

Axel had told Marya the story as they walked, though he glossed over the extent of his and Calandria's interference with local affairs. Covering his ass, apparently. But this General Armiger was an off-world demigod, and somehow a young man named Jordan Mason had gained the ability to see through his eyes.

"I heard about the war with 3340," said Marya. "So Armiger is really one of that monster's servants?"

Axel nodded. "And devilishly dangerous, for that. Thirty-three forty corrupted entire planetary systems. He seduced people by offering them immortality and almost infinite power," he added with a glance at Calandria May. "Then he absorbed the resulting entities into himself. Armiger may have been an early victim."

"He was human, once?" She was surprised and disturbed at the thought.

"If he was, there's nothing left of that personality," said Calandria. She hugged herself as her gaze dropped back to the fire. "Thirty-three forty absorbed millions of individuals, and then mixed and matched their consciousness as he saw fit. Anything he absorbed became part of the single entity that was him. He was ancient when the Winds were just being designed. Maybe aliens designed him—but he claimed to have made himself."

Axel harumphed skeptically. "So did Choronzon—our employer," he added in an aside to Marya. "An ex-human who had himself genetically rebuilt and made himself into a god. He's a few centuries old. It was his war with 3340 that got us involved in all of this."

Marya shook her head in wonder. "I've never met a god, unless you count the swans." She kicked at the wilting grass near the fire for a second, then added, "The Winds are gods of a sort. But damaged. They're fully aware, even if they're not completely awake. That's the tragedy of it."

"They're not *gods*," said Calandria with odd vehemence. "They're just machines. Idiotic. Mechanical. You can see it in everything they do."

"What do you think they do?" asked Marya.

"She's thinking of the Heaven hooks," said Axel. "They acted like a horde of dock robots gone amok. As far as we could tell, that's what they were, too—the aerostats are just big cargo carriers for the terraforming operation."

Marya nodded. They'd seen one that afternoon, a vagabond moon as the locals called it, moving as slowly as a real moon through the sky, but from north to south. It had glowed gorgeous red in the sunset, and Marya had almost cried to think she might never have seen that, had she'd stayed out her term here in orbit. Being on Ventus was affecting her profoundly, in ways she hadn't begun to figure out. All she knew was she was an emotional wreck.

She looked across at Calandria May. The mercenary woman looked back levelly, but it was the steady gaze Marya had seen from prostitutes and beggars—the challenging gaze of the emotionally damaged. Marya couldn't figure her out. She was so formidable in her talents, but incredibly brittle somehow in her fundamental character. Why did she care to argue, tonight, about whether the Winds were gods?

"The Winds are in everything," said Marya, watching Calandria carefully. "The air, the rocks, the soil, the water. But they're not just sitting there, they're working, all the time. Ventus is a terraformed world—a thousand years ago there was no life here. Our ancestors sent the seed of the Winds here by slow sublight ship, and it bloomed here and turned a dead world into a living one. The Winds couldn't do that if they were just instinctive creatures."

"But they didn't recognize humans when we came to colonize," Calandria pointed out. "When the colonists landed, the Winds couldn't tell what they were. They couldn't speak or interact with the colonists. They left them alone because as organisms they fit into the artificial ecology—they filled a niche, like they were designed to. But their machines looked like some kind of infection to the Winds, so they destroyed them, all the computers, radios, heaters, building machines. They pounded the people back into the stone age. A thousand years later, this is as far as they've gotten, and it's as far as the Winds are ever going to let them get." She shook her head sadly. "The Winds can't be conscious. They act like some sort of global immune system, cleaning out potential infections, like us or Armiger.

"Because of that," she said quickly just as Marya opened her mouth to speak, "Armiger could take them over. They were decapitated or born without a brain. There was a flaw in the design of Ventus. Armiger is here to exploit that."

Marya shook her head. "Can't be done," she said. "He would have to reprogram every single particle of dust on the planet. And even if he could, the Winds are conscious. They'd see through it before he could get too far."

"You think he's harmless?" snapped Calandria. She stood up. "You're so enraptured by your beautiful nanotech terraformers you don't think there's subtler things out there?"

"I didn't say that, I—"

"This system is nothing like a real god," said Calandria. "Thirty-three forty told me that even its *thoughts* were conscious entities. Conscious thoughts!" She laughed harshly. "Thirty-three forty was like an entire civilization—an entire species!—in one body. With a history, not just memories. He could make a world like Ventus in a day! How do you know he's not the one who put the flaw in the Winds in the first place? He might have done that a millennium ago, intending to let the place ripen, then return to harvest it. But he got distracted by another planet before he could do that. Hsing was a much better toy, he could forge it into his own private hell much more easily. Still, he sent Armiger here. How do you know Armiger isn't a resurrection seed? He may be planning to turn the entire planet into a single giant machine to recreate 3340. It's within his capabilities. Your precious Winds are no match for Armiger."

She turned and stalked off into the grass.

Marya turned to Axel. "Well!" she said.

Axel watched Calandria's silhouette recede for a few moments. Then he grimaced and turned to Marya. "You touched a nerve," he said.

"Obviously."

"We went to Hsing to destroy 3340," he said. "With Choronzon's help, and the backing of the Archipelago." Axel told Marya the story of how Calandria had beaten 3340 by becoming its willing slave. She shook her head sadly when he was done.

Marya shifted, finding that her rear had gone to sleep on the hard log on which she was sitting. She couldn't get used to such physical annoyances. "She's wrong about the Winds though," she said.

"Don't pursue it," he advised. "Anyway, nothing we've seen since we arrived here suggests the Winds are conscious. Little bits of them here and there, like the morphs, might be. I don't know about the Diadem swans." He glanced up uneasily. "But the system as a whole? No, it's just a planetary immune system, like she says."

Marya shook her head. "If Ventus hasn't spoken to you, it's because you're beneath its notice. You forget, this world is my subject. I know more about it than you do."

"But you haven't been here," he said quietly. "You've never seen it up close. You're here now—does it seem like there's intelligence to this?" He waved his hand at the ragged grass.

"I don't know what you see when you look at it," Marya said. "Maybe it's because you've been on worlds where life just *is*, like Earth. Where nothing maintains it. But everything around us is artificial, Axel. The soil: there may be a thousand years of mulch here," she kicked at it, "but there's meters of soil beneath that, layer upon layer of fertile ground underneath what's been laid down since Ventus came to life. Every single grain of that was manufactured, by the Winds.

"Look at the grass! I know it looks like Earth grass, it's uneven in height, looks randomly patched over the hillside. Maybe in the past few centuries things have settled down to the point where it can be allowed to spread on its own. But I doubt it. The grass has been painted on, by the nano. Look at the clouds. They look like the clouds I see in videos of Earth. But if the Winds weren't busy sculpting them right now, do you think they would look like that? Axel, *Ventus is not like Earth*. Its sun has a different temperature, it's a different size, the composition of the crust is different, so the mineral balance in the oceans is—*was*—totally different. As a result the composition of the atmosphere, and its density, are naturally very different. This weather is not natural." She held her hand up to the breeze. "The air's been made by the Winds, and Axel, they have to *keep* making it. The instant they stop working, the planet will revert, because it's not in equilibrium. It's in a purely synthetic state.

"You don't honestly think the distribution of bugs, mice, and birds around here is natural, do you? It's planned and monitored by the Winds, on every square meter of the planet. Bits of it are constantly going out of whack, threatening the local and global equilibrium. The Winds are constantly adjusting, thinking hard about how to keep the place as Earth-like as possible. It's what we made them to do."

He shook his head. "Well, exactly. It's a complex system, but it's still just a big machine."

"Surely you've wondered why the Winds don't acknowledge the presence of humans?"

"The flaw? Sure, whole religions exist here to try to answer that." He laughed. "You think you know?"

"I think I know how to find out. Listen, in your last report to us before the Heaven hooks incident, you said that Controller Turcaret claimed to be able to hear the Winds."

He glared at her. "Not *claimed*. He did hear them." Calandria still didn't believe that part of the story, and it obviously annoyed Axel.

"We've heard of people like that," said Marya. "But we've never been able to verify a case. If we had one to study, I'm sure we could crack the problem."

He laughed shortly. "Too bad Turcaret's dead."

"I'm not sure that's a problem," she mused. "As long as there's bits of him left . . ."

She heard the grass rustle; Calandria was returning. Marya saw the woman's eyes glinting like two coals in the darkness, and shivered. "We go after Armiger," said Calandria. "You know we must."

"No," said Axel. "We can return with reinforcements. I'm going to keep signaling for a ship, Cal. You can't stop me."

There was silence for a while. Then Calandria shrugged. "You're right, I can't stop you."

The atmosphere around the fire suddenly seemed poisonous. Marya stood up quickly.

"Think I'll turn in," she said, smiling at them both.

Across the fire, Calandria nodded, her perfect face still as carven stone in the firelight. Her eyes betrayed nothing, but Marya thought she could feel the woman's gaze on her back as she knelt and made her bed.

MARYA DREAMED ABOUT home. Outside her window she could see the gently up-curving landscape of Covenant, her colony cylinder. Sunlight streamed through a thousand lakes and pools, turning the hills and cities into translucent lace and backlighting the spiral of clouds in the center of the cylinder. As always, thousands of winged human figures drifted in the air between her and those clouds.

She walked the deep moss carpets of home. She breathed the warm honeyed air, felt it drift over her limbs finer than any cloth as she passed through room after room of her parents' apartment. Her family were here, she knew, in other rooms she had yet to reach. Then, in the back of her own bedroom, she found a door she had never seen before.

She waved the door open and gasped to find herself in a giant library. She recognized paper books, had held a few in her hand as a student, feeling then the tremendous age and dignity of pre-space knowledge. It was this sense of ancient dignity that had driven her to anthropology.

Here were thousands upon thousands of bound books, arrayed in shelves that towered to an invisibly distant ceiling. Marya walked reverently among them.

She stumbled, knocking over a side table. The echoes of its fall went on and on, almost visibly reaching into every distant crevice between the volumes. When it finally died, she heard a growing rustle, as if the books were rousing from slumber.

A voice spoke. "You've done it now."

"What have I done?" she asked, tremulously.

"You've got to make a choice," said the voice. "You woke us. Now you have to choose whether you want us to become a part of you, as memory, or whether you want us to become people, with whom you can speak."

She looked up at the towering wisdom and felt a sudden love for it—as if these books were family. "Oh, please become people," she said.

But even as Marya spoke she remembered she wasn't on Covenant any more. She was on Ventus. As grim men with swords stepped out of the walls, she screamed, for she had chosen wrongly.

THE SOUND OF Axel cursing woke Marya. She groaned and tried to roll over. Her eyes felt pasted shut, for all that she had slept badly. Her back seemed to have been remade in the shape of the stones she had lain on, and the cold had entered through every chink in the blanket.

Axel was using some language Marya didn't know, but it was plain he was upset. Too bad; but couldn't he be quieter about it?

"Damn it, get up, Mounce! She's gone!"

Marya opened her eyes. Gray clouds had taken over the sky while she slept. The fire was out. She levered herself up on one elbow, fought a wave of dizziness, and blinked at two horses where there should be three. The beasts were staring at Axel wide-eyed.

"She snuck off! I can't be*lieve* this! What a bitch! 'We'll talk about it in the morning.' Ha! She never could trust anything past her own nose. Damn, damn, damn, damn!" He kicked the log he'd sat on last night, then kicked it again twice as hard. "I'll crack her skull, I'll, I'll boil her alive! Damned, arrogant . . ." he groped for words.

Marya tried to say, "We can probably catch her," but her voice came out as a croak. Damn this planet! Every bone in her body ached, as if she were a tree slowly freezing up with the onset of winter. And her skin— it itched from the fabric touching her as if a thousand fire ants were biting her.

Axel made a chopping motion with his hand. "To hell with her. We'll find Jordan. We know where she's going. She's going to face down Armiger herself. Of all the arrogant . . ." Again, he seemed to lose his vocabulary. He switched languages, maybe to disguise the hurt tone that had crept into his voice.

Marya levered herself up. Axel had started jamming things into his pack, pausing now and then to stare down the road. He looked down, muttered, "She never really trusted me," in an unbelieving tone, and then shook himself.

"All right, Marya," he said. "Let's go."

With an effort, she transcended her discomfort. "Where?" she asked, squinting at him.

"To find Jordan. He's still running from the Winds, and it's our fault. The only way he'll be safe is if we get him off-planet."

How to put this? "Axel . . . I understand your impulse to help this man. But Calandria's half right. We need to do something to attack the larger problem."

"What larger problem?"

"The Winds."

He stopped stuffing the pack. "What in hell's name can we do?"

Marya stretched. "We continue signaling for a ship, you're right about that. Meanwhile, though, we go back."

"Back where?"

"To Memnonis. To steal the corpse of this man Turcaret."

CALANDRIA PAUSED AT the crest of a hill and looked back the way she'd come. She felt a vague disquiet, leaving like this.

The feeling raised old memories. She remembered crying for days after overhearing that the children she'd thought her friends had been hired as her playmates by her wealthy mother. Now she felt the same almost-guilty feeling she used to have when leaving residence parties early and alone, at the academy. She always reached a point where she could accept no more closeness. Her basic alienation came back to haunt her. When that happened she had to leave, and today she was leaving Axel and Marya. It was not, she told herself, that she was afraid of the Winds; if she were, she would have agreed to his plan to leave Ventus as quickly as possible. No, she had come here for a purpose; her resolve was greater than his, that was all.

She chewed on the reasons for her leaving him as she rode. It was easy to suppose that she was saving Axel and Marya from unnecessary risk. It was also true that every day they left Armiger alone, he moved a step closer to taking over the vast and invisible machine that surrounded her. What it finally came down to, however, was that she and Axel could never work together as a team. Calandria liked to pass like a ghost through the worlds she visited. She was the perfect chameleon, adopting personalities and appearances as they suited her. By tomorrow she would have changed, and no one, possibly not even Axel, would recognize her. This was the right way to do the job she had come to do: by dancing around the edges of the human world, darting in only for the quick surgery that would remove the cancer she had come to kill.

Axel wanted to marry every woman he met, and get drunk with every man. He was probably headed for some inn now, to drown his anger at her in a tankard or two. Well. When they met again it would be apologies all around, she was sure. She would have to plan how to conduct those. She didn't want to lose Axel's friendship, after all. Certainly not over their work.

Jordan . . . Once she killed Armiger, the link, and with it the thing that made the Winds interested in him, would be gone. He would be just a normal man again. And with any luck, he would use what she'd taught him to get rich.

She was doing the right thing.

Her thoughts turned easily to Armiger. How to pursue, how to kill him? Her eyelids flickered; her horse walked on; and Calandria began to drop the Lady May persona, becoming once more the hunter.

26

THE LANDSCAPE WAS all curves. Gentle undulating dunes of a wonderfully pale tan color stretched off into a hazy horizon. The sky was full of rounded, white balls of cloud. The sun was bright, but it wasn't hot, which somewhat dashed Jordan's preconceptions about what deserts were like. The rolling hills, though, the color, and the taste of grit in his mouth were all the way he'd imagined.

They had been traveling for several days now. To his own surprise, Jordan felt pretty good. For once he wasn't under the control of somebody else. He could plan the day's travel, set their pace, and admire the scenery as he wished. His thoughts seemed to be getting clearer with each morning that he woke to find himself master of his own fate.

Tamsin's shoulders were slumped like the dunes. The farther they went into the desert, the more despondent she became. She had not spoken about what she expected to find here, but Jordan had his suspicions. None of those thoughts were good.

He walked his horse up next to hers. The horses were a bit nervous in this vast emptiness, but Jordan had Ka constantly scouting for water holes, and so far they had been lucky. At one hole the water had been a red color, and Ka said it was poisonous. Jordan had commanded the water to purify itself, and it had.

Miracles like that should have puffed him up with pride, but they did nothing to penetrate Tamsin's air of gloom, and that was his main concern right now. He had no miracle to cure her of her grief.

She glanced wearily at him as he matched her pace. "How are you doing?" he asked.

She shrugged. "I dunno."

Jordan took a pull from the water skin he had bought in a hamlet outside Rhiene. "Shall I tell you a story?"

She considered this idea. "What kind of a story? I don't want you to cheer me up."

"Well, I could tell you something depressing, then."

"No."

"How about something that's just true?"

"I don't want—" she gulped. "To hear a story."

They rode on in silence for a while. Jordan was thinking. Eventually he asked, "Have you ever seen the queen's summer palace?"

"No."

"You want me to describe it to you?"

Tamsin sat up straighter. "Look, you don't have to—okay, why not. But not like it is now, all covered in blood. Tell me what it used to look like before the war."

Of course Jordan had never seen it that way, because Armiger had arrived well into the siege. He could imagine it though, with his mental blueprints and eye for the architectural detail buried under the siege scaffolding. And there were many places inside that were untouched.

"They built it in a valley where there's a tiny oasis, centuries ago. The first building was a chapel of some kind—you can still see traces of it in the stonework at the base of the high tower. It's all built of stone the same color as the sand we're riding over. Now there's a big ring wall around the oasis. This has five big towers on it, and one smaller. The biggest tower, on the east side, has a big causeway stretching up to it, and you'd think that that would be the gate, but the entrance there was bricked up centuries ago. It's the west tower that has the main entrance.

"If you come in the main gate you're channeled between two more walls to the main keep. This tower is huge, Tamsin! It must have six floors, at least, and it steps at two points. Sometimes the queen walks around these balconies and she can look out over the hills and watch the sunset. Her chambers are in this tower, high above the earth.

"Let's see, . . . if you come in the main doors of the keep, you're channeled again through it, to the great hall, which is a big rectangular building attached to the keep on its east side. The great hall is magnificent. It's buttressed, with a pitched roof, with mullioned arched windows and a beautiful staggered triple lancet window on the east facade—"

"A what? What does it *look* like?"

"Oh. One time when Armiger walked through the banquet hall he looked up at it. It's three very tall arched windows separated by thin mullions—pillars, you know. The glass is leaded in a flamelike pattern. Very beautiful. But I only caught a glimpse of it, because Armiger never looked at it again.

"Anyway, the queen's garden lies south of the great hall. Then there's houses and shops all around the foot of the keep on its north and south sides. The rest of the ground inside the big ring wall is full of tents now. The rest of the queen's army. But I guess it was parade grounds and so on before the war."

He did not tell her that the beautiful copper roof of the great hall was holed in a dozen places by Parliament's steam cannons, or that the arched windows were half shattered, or that the lovely pink marble floor of the banquet hall was almost invisible under a maze of stacked provisions.

She listened as he went on to describe the gardens, which remained untouched, and the little cobbled streets that crowded against the foot of the keep. She seemed grateful for the distraction. And as he painted in words a picture of the palace in better times, Armiger sat like some gargoyle atop the highest parapet of the keep and wondered what was to come in the next days.

MEGAN TOUCHED HIS elbow. Armiger awoke from a deep reverie; it was near sunset. For hours now he had been lost in transcendent thought.

"What's the matter?" she asked. He examined her in the fading light. Megan's face was thinner than when he had met her, but she also looked younger, somehow. He found himself smiling.

"I'm sorry I brought you here," he said.

"Why?" He could see she was trying not to interpret what he'd said the wrong way.

"The assault will begin soon. It has to. I can see Lavin's running out of supplies—the number of wagons arriving every day has dropped off sharply. I think Parliament is choking off his budget now that it thinks it's won."

"Are we going to die?" She asked it like she might ask any reasonable question.

"I can protect us against the soldiers. But the Winds are searching for me, and the attack is bound to draw their attention. If they don't intervene directly, they might still see me. Then, yes, we may be lost."

She held out her hand, and he took it as he stepped down off the crenel. "Then let's leave," she said. "Surely we can sneak out of here."

He hesitated. "We could."

"Then let's!"

"A week ago I would have said yes. After all, I've learned all I can from the queen. Or all I care to," he added ruefully. "And there lies the problem."

"What do you mean?"

He looked out at Parliament's army, a city of tents sprawled in an arc to the southwest of the palace. Hundreds of thin lines of smoke rose from campfires there.

"Once," he said quietly, "I was a god. Then it seemed a reasonable desire to rule the world. That is what I came here to do. I needed to learn the Achilles' heel of the Winds. My other agents could not uncover the secret, so I came here to the one person in the world who, it was said, knew the most about them. But along the way, my goals . . . changed."

She smiled. "Are you complimenting me?"

"Yes, but it's not just been you." He kissed her. "I've started remembering. There was a time, ancient now, when I was free, simply a man like any other. Those memories are returning, and . . ."

How could he describe it to her? Such a memory would come to him like the wind after a storm, full of sweet scent and alert joy. There had been a time when his hand was just his hand, and not one instrument of many in the service of vast intricate schemes. When his eye would light on a beautiful person or place, and simply rest content, with no calculation of its utility. When he began to remember this way, Armiger had also begun to recognize such moments in those around him. The moment that unlocked this recognition had been seeing, on Megan's face, a simple span of pleasure as she savored then swallowed some warm broth from the queen's kitchen. For two, three seconds Megan had thought nothing, merely tasted and enjoyed. And it came to Armiger that it had been seven hundred years since he had experienced such a moment.

"It's something that connects me to all these people," he said, gesturing to include both the palace and the besieging army. "Before, they were counters on a board. Now, somehow, they've become like me. I know it can't make any sense to you."

"Ai," she snapped, yanking on his hair so that he laughed. "Of course it makes sense, silly. You were a child, and now you're growing up. All those years you were one of *them*, you were like an infant, all want. So now you're surprised when you start to become like the rest of us? You are sometimes a very, very silly man."

For a while he was completely flummoxed and just stared at her while she laughed. Then he caught her around the waist. "Maybe I am. You made me care about you, and now I've come to care about these people, too. And I can help them."

She sobered. "Help? How?"

"I was a general once. I can be again." He kissed her forehead and stood back. "It's time to abandon the plans of the entity that enslaved me all these centuries," he said. "And time to start making my own."

Megan stepped back. "Armiger—"

"Galas is the most deserving ruler on this world," he said. "I can't let her be destroyed. Or her people."

Megan turned and went to the crenel, where she looked out over the sea of tents for some time. Then she looked back, her face a play of rose-lit arcs in the sunset. "You must be careful," she said. "You may come to care too much, you know. And that could cost us more than all your uncaring ever could."

LAVIN OPENED GALAS's book once again, unable to resist but reluctant. By lamplight, he read.

Here is a dilemma. We doubt anyone else in history has faced such a dilemma as this. For when One sits at the window to watch the people go about their business, One sees such contentment and joy in simple things, expressed in the routines of the market and the street. And indeed, most people find ways to be happy, most of the time.

But We see also the town square with its gallows and know that only the healthy walk these streets because only they are still alive. We know that only the strong-minded walk smiling in these streets because only they have won the freedom to do so. We do not see the isolated, failed, or victimized people huddling in the back rooms of shops, chained in bedrooms, or scattered like dust across the far fields.

If We propose to create something better, then We propose to end this world. That is how it will seem to these happy people, at least. For it may be necessary to make of the rich paupers, and make of the poor princes. In two generations, or ten, all will be well. For now, though, misery! And more and more. Would it not be better to leave well enough alone? If We stay the course, we shall see those smiling faces, bustling streets until Our dying day.

We are certain no one has ever faced such a dilemma. So We are inconsolable.

This is truth, though, that Our fury rises like an ocean storm at the thought that even one poor soul toils in misery out of sight, while these happy folk go about their business. True, it is not their responsibility, and no one should begrudge them what little happiness they can find. It is Our responsibility, however. They may never understand Our motives, or see the full scope of the grand plan to be unfolded. We can only hope that their children grow up to be happy, and free, whether they revile Our name or not.

He could almost hear her voice saying these words. They were so like her, when in the blush of youth she had fairly burst with idealistic passion. At the time, Lavin had barely understood what she was saying, beyond feeling a certain unease at her strange heresies. She was more intelligent than he, they both knew that, and he had always felt that they both accepted that he did not understand her.

In these diaries, though, he was finding so much loneliness that at times the words brought him near tears. He regretted now not striving to understand her better when he'd had the chance—perhaps he could have changed the course of her plans, and had she not been so lonely, perhaps she would not have chosen fanaticism. He suspected she had ultimately lived up to her reputation of madness because it was the only role left to her in her isolation.

They had met the second time at the military academy. It was some six months after the ball where he had received her approving glance. There were some young girls in regular attendance at academy balls, but Lavin rarely attended; being the faithful son of a rather dour provincial baron, he distrusted such affairs. Consequently, he had lived on memories of that one moment of recognition by her. When he heard on the parade ground that the mad princess had been spotted riding through town in man's attire, his heart began to pound, and he missed his cue in the horse maneuver he was practicing. At mess that day he had discreetly asked after the source of the rumor. It was true, it seemed: Galas was here, staying in an inn not a kilometer from the academy.

Two of the lads began to joke that the princess was here looking for a wife, or at least a concubine. Her mannish ways were a popular scandal, after all. Lavin threw down his cutlery and challenged them both to duels on the spot.

This altercation might have ended in tragedy had not the quartermaster intervened. He was a huge man who imposed his authority by purely physical means. After warning all three of them that any duelists stood to be thrown out of the academy, he beat them all black and blue. Lavin was not greatly upset by this—at least the disrespectful had been punished as well.

The quartermaster was perhaps a bit too thorough in his lesson, because Lavin spent the next two days vomiting and staggering due to some injury to his inner ear. It would come back to haunt him at critical moments for the rest of his life. This time, it kept him in bed until he restlessly demanded a leave of absence. He was given a week.

Looking back, he supposed he would never have worked up the courage to visit Galas's inn had he not been dizzy and bruised—already beaten, both literally and figuratively. His mood was fey and unconcerned as he entered the inn and inquired as to the whereabouts of the princess.

The barkeep smirked at him—Lavin had a black eye, a cauliflower ear, and walked with a distinct stagger—and pointed behind him. He turned to find those same dark eyes of memory gazing at his.

She sat in the company of six of the king's guards. This was her regular bodyguard, men she was comfortable with; just now they were trying to drink one another under the table. She was losing.

Lavin planted himself in their midst and introduced himself. They had met oh so briefly at a ball, he said. Surely she did not remember him.

Oh, but she did.

His bruises impressed the bodyguards. She told Lavin later that otherwise they would have pitched him out the door, as they did with the merchants and effete local noble's sons who came to pay homage. Lavin was no courtier; he wanted no political favors. So they let him stay—but only if he drank to match them.

Never before or since in his life had Lavin been so sick. His only consolation was a dim memory of the princess crouched beside him also throwing up the indeterminate remains of today's—or perhaps several day's—lunch.

Deep and lasting bonds are forged in such moments.

It seemed that by achieving the worst nausea possible, he had found a standard by which to measure his injury. Over the next two days he made a remarkable recovery, primarily by discovering in her company sufficient motivation to overcome his dizziness.

Lately, reading the secret diary, he had recovered the memory of her voice. He remembered now how they had debated politics in those first days. She was passionate and angry, and he was willing to indulge her for he was learning she was not the insane creature of reputation, but a young lady cursed with an intelligence that had no outlet within the life prescribed for her. Lavin understood ambition. He wanted to lead armies, be a great general like the heroes whose faces were carved in the keystones of the academy. So he and she became soul mates, even though he censored from his own awareness half of what she said to him.

He had not been fair, he saw in retrospect. That was why, when disaster struck in the form of her coronation, he had not been invited to her side. She knew that though he understood her heart, he could never agree with her mind, and that as her consort he would have been miserable.

Ah! He could tell himself this, it sounded so objective and neatly encapsulating; the pain was still there. He had not gone to the throne with her.

The miraculous did happen, though. He was the first, and as far as he knew the only man she ever invited into her bed. The first time was at the end of that week's leave. He had won over her bodyguards by dint of being disarmingly frank about his affection for her. They did not interfere when on that last evening she threw him a significant look and retired early, and he quickly made an excuse and followed.

The affair endured two years. They strove for utmost discretion, so meetings were rare and hurried. For all that, or maybe because of it, their passion was almost unendurably intense. Then, she conceived of the sea expedition that was to separate them for the next eighteen years. He learned of it in a letter she sent the day before her departure. The next news he had was of her triumphant entry into the capital bearing the seal of the Winds, there to unseat her father the king. Then nothing, except a single scribbled note received six months later telling him court was dangerous, that she would meet him as soon as she could escape its entanglements.

They did meet again—once or twice a year at formal courtly functions, and three times she had allowed him to visit her privately, to walk in her gardens and halls alone with her for an hour or two. They never shared a bed again.

Now he rose and went to the flap of his tent. The summer palace lay in darkness, surrounded by an ocean of campfires.

Tomorrow, he would meet her again. The letters of parlay lay on his table now, next to her diaries. She wanted to talk.

He wanted to talk.

Lavin shuddered and closed the flap of the tent against the chill. He wished he could sleep, but it was impossible. He wished . . . he wished he could run.

Take her, and run.

He moved to the map table, where the sappers' charts lay, and drew his newly ringed finger along a line that crossed the palace wall. He had rewarded the thief Enneas with his life for allowing this line to be drawn. If all worked according to plan, he would shower the old grave robber with jewels.

Take her and run.

Maybe he would.

27

"Bring me some water, boy. What's your name?"

"Cal," she said.

The soldier grunted. "I'm Maenin. That's Crouson, and the bastard across the fire is the Winckler. We been with this thing from the beginning. You're pretty scrawny," he observed. "How long you been with the army?"

"Not long," she said shortly. Her voice was an octave lower than normal. She liked the way it reverberated in her chest.

Maenin was a huge, hairy man. Calandria thought he smelled as if something had crawled into his boots and died. She handed him a cup of water and sat back on the stone she had chosen as her seat.

A vista of campfires and tents spread out down the hillside, and in the distance the walls of the palace spread in black swathes across the plain. Diadem gleamed whitely, outshining the Milky Way. Somewhere up there, the *Desert Voice* was debris or imprisoned. She could only hope that someone would come to investigate when the ship failed to report in.

Meanwhile she had to concentrate on thinking and acting like a man. She spat at the fire and scratched the short hair on her head. On the way here she had modified her body in subtle ways; that and a layer of grime made her look like a young man. With all that, Maenin still seemed to see femininity in her, so it came down to how well she could act. Shakespeare had been uncommonly optimistic about a woman's chance of successfully masquerading as male, she had decided.

"Oh ho! Seen any fighting? No, eh? Simple farmboy, off on an adventure, are we?"

Cal shrugged. "Soldiers burned our house. Father couldn't afford to feed us all. I had to join."

Maenin brayed a laugh. "Now that's the way to recruit! Hey—you're not from one of those pervert towns we burned, are you?"

"No. Just a town."

"Good thing, 'cause if you were you'd be dog meat."

"I heard they're bad," she said.

"Ho—you don't know the half of it."

"Have you been in one?"

"Boy, I been in 'em all. Burned 'em all, too. Burned 'em right to the ground. Same as we're gonna do that rock pile over there." He flipped his hand in the direction of the palace.

"All because the queen built those towns?"

"No! Where you been through all this, boy? Don't you know nothing?"

Calandria pretended to examine her boots. "It didn't seem so important to know about it, before the soldiers came."

"The queen, she knew about these oases in the desert for years. Never told anyone. We coulda moved out there, made a good living. She didn't care, she wanted 'em to house her damn perverts. So when Parliament found out about 'em they ask her what she's doing with 'em. She tells Parliament it's none of our business! Same time, she's asking for all kinds of money, extra taxes, from the nobles. She been bleeding us good folk dry, to feed her perverts!

"So Parliament demands she give the towns back. Stop making these pervert things out there in the desert. And she says no."

"She dissolved Parliament," said the Winckler.

"Know what that means, boy? She told all 'em nobles to get packing! She'd run the country directly." Maenin shook his head. "She wanted to turn us all into perverts! The towns were just the start. After them, the cities, who knows what we'd be having to say? All I know is I'll never take orders from no pervert."

"The nobles who make up the Upper House formed an army," said the Winckler. "They called on General Lavin to command it. Except he wasn't a general, then. He was from one of the old families, they gave him the job because he had pull."

Maenin stood up. "Shut up! The general's a good man. He's kept us alive right to the palace, and he'll keep us alive when we go in. We're gonna win, and it's 'cause of him."

The Winckler raised his hands apologetically. "You're right, Maenin. You are indeed right. To start with, the queen's army was bigger than ours. We licked 'em, and it was 'cause of the general."

"Damn right." Maenin sat down.

"How did you do that?" Calandria asked, trying to project boyish curiosity.

Maenin and the Winckler told how Lavin had predicated his campaign on knowledge of stockpiles the queen kept in the desert. Summer was traditionally the time for campaigning; in northern Ventus, war stopped when the snows came. Iapysia's southern desert remained warm, but the population was mostly concentrated along the northern border of the desert, and the seashore.

Lavin launched a phony campaign in summer and drew the queen's forces on a long retreat along the oceanside. He had the navy on his side, so the queen's forces could not pursue his army too far.

Then he struck inland and captured the desert stockpiles. When the end of the campaign season arrived, the queen's forces had exhausted their supplies, but Lavin's forces had several months' worth of grain and dried fish. They drove north, as the queen's forces suffered desertion and attrition. By the spring of this year, they had taken two-thirds of the country. The queen retreated to her summer palace, and Lavin marched a small force into the desert to clean out her experimental towns, and strike at her palace from the south. That force had encountered no resistance and arrived here sooner than expected. The queen's forces were engaged west of the palace by the bulk of Lavin's army. He had no time for a decent siege of the walled summer palace. Lavin would have to throw them against the walls in a day or two or face the retreating royal army.

"It's okay, though," drawled the Winckler. "He's got a plan, as usual."

Maenin squinted through the roiling wood smoke. "What? What plan?"

"Haven't you heard? He's going to meet the queen tomorrow, to get her to surrender. If he does it, we don't have to fight at all. The war will be over!"

"Shit. Really?" Maenin shook his head. "That'd be something. Be too bad, though, I kinda wanted to taste one of those noble ladies she's hiding there. The perverts were no fun. They had no spirit. I want a woman who'll try and claw my eyes out!" He laughed, and the others joined in. Calandria showed her teeth.

They speculated for a while about how well the noble ladies would perform, and even the queen if they should catch her. They teased Cal for being a virgin and promised to show the boy how to rape if they had to storm the palace.

Cal expressed her gratitude.

Maenin yawned. "Fine. Sleep time. The bastard'll wake us up before dawn, and the Winds know what'll happen tomorrow. Where you sleepin', boy?"

"By the fire," she said quickly.

"Wise." Maenin glared at the Winckler. "Stay in sight, that's my advice." He stood, stretched, and walked scratching to his tent.

The others drifted away over the next hour, leaving Calandria to tend the fire. The supply of wood was meager, but she built the fire up anyway—not because she was cold, but because she had a use for it.

When she was confident she would not be interrupted, she rummaged in her pack and brought out a slim metal tube. She uncapped it and poured a few small metal pills into her hand. She arranged these and peered at them in the firelight.

There was fine writing on the flat beads. When she had found the one she was looking for, she put the others back in the tube and dropped the chosen one into the center of the fire. Using the tip of her sword, she maneuvered it onto the hottest coals at the core of the flames.

From another pouch, Calandria took some rusty metal rivets she had found on the way here. She dropped these into the fire near the metal bead. Then she sat back to wait.

It would take a couple of hours for the seed to sprout and grow, but she couldn't afford to nap. If someone came, she would have to distract them, lest they look into the fire and see something impossible gleaming there.

LAVIN IGNORED THE glares of hate that followed him. He and his honor guard of two were safe, he knew. Galas would never let him come to harm. So as he walked he did not look at the soldiers ranked on either side of the narrow courtyard that led to the citadel, but cast his gaze above ground level to examine the damage his siege engines had caused to the buildings. The defenders had hung bright banners across the worst of it to frustrate such scrutiny; the festive cloth looked incongruous against blackened stonework, above the pinched faces of grim soldiers.

He felt more optimistic than he had in weeks. Galas had agreed to parley. Now that her situation was hopeless, she was finally seeing reason. This madness had to stop, and there was no reason it should end with deaths, hers included. All the while she hid in her fortress, and he threw men and stones at the walls, Lavin had been in an agony of fear that some one of those stones would find her, or that dysentery would run through the palace, or her own people assassinate her to escape. He couldn't live with the thought.

But he couldn't live with the thought of anyone else being in charge of this siege, either. She would lose; he had always known that. There had never been any question of his joining her cause, because all he could do for her was delay the inevitable. He might win her admiration and love, but she would be brought down at last, and he wouldn't be able to stop it.

This way, the outcome was in his hands. And though she might hate him, this way he might save her.

In his late-night conversations with Hesty, Lavin had lied about all these things. He had claimed to hate Galas, and that he hated the things she had done lent credence to his words. But it hurt him to talk so, and he often wondered if Hesty saw that, and doubted.

Maybe it would all end today. The thought was uplifting, and he had to restrain himself from smiling. To smile, while walking through the ranks of the enemy, would be cruel. Lavin did not think he was a cruel man.

He ran his gaze across the battlements, anyway, measuring for weaknesses. All responsibility lay on his shoulders, after all; he had won this far because he was able to plan for hard realities without flinching. If Galas rejected his ultimatum he would need to know what walls to throw his men against.

One of the banners hung by the defenders caught his eye. This one was bright blue, with a gold-braided knot as its central design. The banner had been unfurled above the gate to the palace citadel, on a wall that appeared quite undamaged. He would have to walk under it to enter.

Lavin had only visited the summer palace once, many years ago. The visit had coincided with the spring festival, and there were many banners flying at the time. Strange coincidence, that they should be hung again now, for such different purpose.

But the banner over the citadel gate was the spring banner itself. On that earlier occasion, it had hung in the palace's reception hall, alone in a shaft of sunlight.

Under it, he had told Galas he loved her.

"Are you all right, sir?"

He had stopped walking. The courtyard seemed to recede for a second. He leaned on the arm of one of the guards.

"I'm fine," he snapped. Then he stepped forward again, eyes now fixed on the banner.

She must have had it hung in his path deliberately. It was an intimate, hence cruel, reminder of all that they had once meant to one another. Now his chest hurt, and he could feel the muscles in his face pulling back. I must look like these men, he thought, just another soldier with pain indelibly stamped on his face.

Yet below the banner stood an open door. She had reminded him of their past; and she had opened a way for him.

Maybe things would work out. Somehow, though, nothing had prepared Lavin for what he was feeling now. In all his planning, he had been able to avoid his own feelings, lest they stand in the way of his saving her from herself. By this one gesture Galas had let him know that whatever happened during the next few hours, for him it would be like walking through fire.

. . .

INSIDE, THE CITADEL showed no signs of the siege. The sumptuous furnishings were still in place, and liveried servants waited to guide Lavin and his guide up the marble flights to Galas's audience chamber. Last time he was here, there had been nobility everywhere, posing lords and ladies smiling and exchanging the barbed words of their intrigues. The candelabra overhead, now dark, had blazed brightly, bringing life to the fantastical figures painted on the ceiling. He remembered Galas, on his arm, pointing up at the images, and telling him stories about them. She was girlish for once, and his heart had melted so that he barely heard the words themselves, so entranced was he by their tone.

He steeled himself to his purpose and looked down to floor level. The thief Enneas had schooled him in the layout of the basements of the palace. Enneas had never been above ground level here; Lavin never below it. Together, they had assembled a rough map of Enneas's secret path into the building. Lavin had only moments as he walked to try to spot the entrance they believed led down to the catacombs.

He was nearly at the top of the marble flight when he spotted it, below and beside the stairs. The archway was invisible from the main entrance because it was behind the immense sweep of the stairs' bannisters.

Shoulders slumping in relief, Lavin let himself be guided forward down the palace's main hall, and thence to another flight. The archway was there, and if Enneas was right, below it the maze of halls contained a chink that led to a "spirit walk." The spirit walk would be just a narrow gap in the masonry at the palace's wall, an exit for ghosts who could slip through an aperture only centimeters broad. According to Enneas, this walk had once lain under the processional causeway that ran through the east gate and to a temple complex that was now ruined. Over centuries, thieves had widened the spirit walk so that one or two people at a time could squeeze through it into the precincts of the palace.

The ruins existed, and so did the hole Enneas had said led to the tunnel. In any other situation, Lavin would have dispatched sappers into it to undermine the east gate. Bringing the gate tower down would save a lot of lives he would otherwise lose storming the walls.

There was only one life Lavin wanted to save. Knowing that Enneas was right both about what lay in the ruins, and about where a certain door existed within the palace, heartened him. He had an extra force to use to outflank Galas, if it came to that.

The audience chamber lay at the top of the second flight of stairs. The sweep of the main hall lay behind him, and Lavin heard the sounds of men massing there. He would not give them the satisfaction of seeing him turn to look, but he knew they were there to kill him at the slightest signal. More soldiers flanked the entrance to the audience chamber. They had taken his weapons at the palace gate, but obviously still feared an assassination attempt.

Two men carrying halberds stepped in front of him at the door. One of them scowled, and said, "She insists on seeing you alone. None of us trusts you for a second, General. I'm going to be waiting with my hand on the door handle, and the archers' bows will be cocked. If we hear the slightest sound we don't like, you'll be dead in a second. Do you understand?"

Lavin glared back. "I understand," he said tightly. His heart was pounding, but not because he was afraid of this man, or in fact of any man. Again, he felt himself becoming disembodied and strove to breathe deeply to anchor himself in the moment.

The door opened. Lavin took one step forward, then another. And then he was inside the room.

The hall looked exactly as it had that other time. The weight of memory threatened to crush him for a moment; he blinked and saw the queen.

She stood near the throne, hands clasped together. She appeared composed, but, he supposed, so did he. With age, one showed less and less of the emotions one actually felt, and hers had never been easy to read.

He moved tentatively toward her. In the autumn light flung by the tall windows he could see lines of care around her mouth that had never been there before, and streaks of gray in her hair. She looked very small and vulnerable, and the ache in his heart grew almost overwhelming.

He cleared his throat, but now that he was here, he couldn't speak. He had even rehearsed a speech, but the words seemed vapid and irrelevant now. Falling back on ceremony, he bowed.

"Lavin," she said almost inaudibly. He straightened, and they made eye contact, for only a second before each broke off.

"I am glad to see you again," she said. He could hear the guardedness in her voice.

"I, too, am . . . glad," he said. His own voice sounded husky to his ears. She seemed to listen intently as he spoke, as if she were trying to discover something behind the actual words.

She held out her hand. "Don't stand so far away. Please."

He came to her and took her outstretched hand. Slowly, he raised his eyes to hers.

"I see lines," she said, "that weren't there before."

"You haven't aged at all," he replied with a smile.

"Lavin." The reproach in her tone was gentle, but it stung him deeply. "Don't lie to me."

Face burning, he let go of her hand.

"Come," she said, gesturing nervously. "Let's not sit in this drafty place. It won't help." She led him to a door at the side of the chamber. Beyond this was a small room with a lit fireplace, single table, and two chairs. Galas clapped her hands, and the room's other door opened. Two serving girls approached timidly.

"Have you dined yet today?" she asked. Lavin shook his head. She waved to the girls, who curtsied and exited. As Lavin and the queen seated themselves, the girls returned with mutton and stew, a bottle of wine, and two goblets. Strange, Lavin thought, that he had never dined in such privacy with the queen in all the years he had known her. Did it really take the total overthrow of tradition and royal honor for them to reach such a simple act? He shied away from the thought.

The girls left, and they were alone again. Galas gestured at the food and smiled.

The simple act of sipping the broth released a knot of tension in Lavin's shoulders. He indulged himself in the food for a moment, while she poured wine for both of them. By the time she had reached for her own spoon, he felt in command of himself again.

"I've come to make sure we can do this again," he said, gesturing to the food. "And more."

Galas sipped her wine, brows knit quizzically. "What do you mean?"

He borrowed from the speech he'd prepared. The idea for this argument had come from his reading of her own captured journals. "You're acting like there's only one possible outcome to all this. But everything you've ever done—the very reason we are where we are today—is because you've refused to accept that there should only be one way of doing things. You've fought inevitability your whole life. Why change now?"

She was silent for a while. "Maybe I'm tired," she said at last in a small voice.

"Galas, you've used nothing but your own strength to try to change the whole world. You've never accepted that of anyone else. Maybe it is time for you to rest. Is that so bad?"

"Yes!" she flared. "You're saying you've come to take my kingdom from me. I already knew that. Say something new, if you really have alternatives."

"You're acting like there's only victory or death possible here. I'm saying it's not too late. Victory is impossible for you now, but death isn't inevitable. That's what I've come to prevent!"

"Victory wouldn't be impossible," she said, "if I'd had you at my side."

He had expected her to say it, but he still had to look away as he replied. "That's unfair. What choice have I ever had?"

"Lavin, why did you side with Parliament?" She looked stricken. "You know I never wanted any of this. I never wished harm on my country. It was Parliament who started this war, and you who so expertly destroyed everything I've ever held dear. And yet, you, of all people . . ."

"You were going to lose," he said. "I was trained at the military academy, groomed to be a general. When Parliament decided on war, I sat in on the planning session. I was on your side. Of course I was! How do you think I felt, sitting in the gallery, listening to them insult you, laugh about bringing you down? They were a pack of traitors. But I saw the plans they were laying out. They were going to win. Even if I'd stolen the plans and brought them to you, it wouldn't have helped. It would only have prolonged the slaughter.

"The night I really knew in my heart that they would win, I sat in my bedchamber and cried. What could I do? I was the highest-born graduate of the academy. To appease both the nobles and the commons, Parliament would ask me to lead the army against you.

"I could stand aside. Or I could join you, and die at your side. Or I could lead the army myself—and then at least if I was in control, if the responsibility was mine, maybe we could salvage something, it didn't have to come to this!" He sat back, the ache in his chest making it hard to breathe. "If anyone else led the army, how could I prevent your death?"

"There was another choice," she said coldly.

"What? How can you say that? Don't you think I thought of them all?" He grabbed his goblet and drank, glaring at her.

"You could have misled the army, Lavin. You could have fought badly." She smiled sadly. "You could have let me beat you."

"Not a single day's gone by when I didn't think of doing that," he said. "Your generals never provided me the opportunity. Your nobility just weren't a match for the academy. But no, wait, it's more than that. Listen, I've stood on a hillside, and watched ten thousand men fight in terror and rage in the valley below me. I've had men on horseback, waiting for my orders, and there was a moment when I could have failed to give an order to let the cavalry flank your men. The order was crucial. If I gave it, thousands would live on both side. If I didn't, I would stand on this hillside and watch while men who trusted me were put to the sword." He faced her grimly, hands gripping the table in front of him. "Perhaps every day before that, and every day since, I've thought that I could deliberately send men out to fail and die. I'm a man capable of hard decisions, Galas. But at that moment, I wasn't able to do it. And however much I might lie to myself every day, in the end I would act the same way again. Everyone has a moral line they can't cross. For me, that was it."

She stared at him in silence. Lavin loosened his grip on the tabletop and numbly turned back to his food.

"So what are your terms?" she whispered.

"More people don't need to die. At this moment you've got Parliament in a position where, if you don't surrender, there'll be a bloodbath. That will not be popular. Neither is regicide. With no one on the throne, the state will be in chaos. However hopeless things look, they still need you."

He looked straight at her. "I can guarantee your safety. You'll be placed under arrest by Parliament, but it will be my men who guard you. Parliament may hold the purse strings to the army, but after all this time, the men are mine. No one else could have guaranteed your safety after all that's happened. But I can."

"I believe you," she said with a touching smile. "And this house arrest—what does it mean?"

"You remain the head of state. Parliament rules in your place. An arrangement is made for a proper heir. You renounce all your political, economic, and social experiments."

"I can't do that."

"You must! Otherwise you remain the head of a rebel movement who will act in your name whether you lead them or not. The chaos will just continue."

She reached across the table and took his hand. "My love, you're asking me to throw away everything my life has meant. How is that different from death?"

"It's gone, anyway. Your choice is how to cope with the fact. Your options are suicide, or to rise above it, as you've always risen above things." His mouth was dry now, and his heart pounding. It all came down to this conversation, and this moment in it.

She shook her head, but not at his words. "Lavin, did you just tell me that you led the army against me because you loved me?"

"Yes."

"Worse and worse," she said. "Worse and worse!" She stood up; her chair fell over.

The door opened a crack, but she waved her hand impatiently, and it closed again. "Every day of my life the people who've guarded me have taken away something just as I came to realize I loved it." She dragged her hands through her hair, flung it back, and came to stand over him. "You've taken it upon yourself to do that, too. What do I have left?"

He shook his head.

"I loved you because you never tried to guard me," she said. "You were never my keeper. Yours was the one face at a banquet I could look at when I needed to share a laugh or a real smile. I would have made you my consort if I could have, Lavin."

He shrank back from the directness of her gaze. He could hear the bitterness in his own voice as he said, "You defied every other tradition. Why didn't you try to overthrow that one, too?" Custom and politics had dictated Galas marry a royal son of a neighboring nation; she had avoided doing so.

It was her turn to look away. "I was afraid."

"Afraid? Of offending tradition? Of Parliament's reaction?"

"Of you."

"Me."

"Afraid of having you; afraid of losing you." She angrily righted her chair and sat down again. "Afraid of everything to do with you. And . . . I thought we'd have the time . . . for me to get over that fear."

"We may yet," he said quickly. "Do you still trust me, after all that's happened?"

"I don't know . . . yes, I do. Lavin, I trust you to follow your heart, even if it leads you into an inferno."

"But do you trust that I love you?"

"Yes."

"Then let me protect you now!"

Galas smiled sadly. "You know me too well. It is not I who am faced with a choice here, my dearest. You knew that when you came. You are the one that has to decide between self-annihilation and love. I've made my choice and will die for it comfortably. If there is a tortured soul at this table, it is you."

Lavin felt the words as blows. He couldn't respond; all his strategies had evaporated.

She knew him. The greatest doubt and mystery of his life had been whether Galas really understood him; had she really thought deeply about him? Was he real to her, the way she was to him?

She understood him too well.

"Your choice, dearest friend," she continued, "is simple. You will either join me and turn your men against Parliament now that you have their loyalty, or you will raze my walls, kill my people, and find me dead of poison in my bedchamber."

Her words were so simply spoken he could never have doubted her determination. Inwardly, Lavin reeled in panic. Everything was slipping away. He opened his mouth, almost to surrender to her, for the sake of a few days of bliss before they were defeated and killed. Then he remembered the thief Enneas and his other option.

He heard himself say, "I come back to where we began. You have defied either-or choices your entire life. You can rise above this dilemma, too, and regain your kingdom. Maybe you can pursue your policies in a gentler fashion and still salvage some of what you worked for. The alternative is to lose all of it, and your life as well."

Her expression had hardened. "Very well. There *is* another option, but I had hoped not to have to use it. In some ways it is the worst of all."

"Why worst?" He shook his head, not understanding.

"Because I wanted to avoid defeating you, Lavin. I never wanted you as my enemy." She rose before he could reply and rapped on the chamber's inner door.

Lavin stood, alarmed. Was she about to order his capture or death?

A man stepped into the room. He appeared stern and noble, but Lavin judged him of foreign breeding, since his hair was long and braided. He wore the uniform of the palace guard.

"Your siege will not be easy," Galas said. "General Lavin, meet General Armiger."

Lavin was thunderstruck. Armiger was supposed to be dead! Yet . . . perhaps he had defected, slipped away from his failing fortunes in Ravenon, at some offer by Galas? It made no sense.

These thoughts raced through his mind as he stepped forward to clasp the hand of his new adversary. "Your reputation precedes you," he said formally.

"Thank you," said Armiger. "Your own skill is respected in every land. I look forward to matching my strength against yours."

Lavin stepped away and bowed formally. "In that case, Your Highness, I will take my leave. With General Armiger at your side, I will need to make extra preparations if I am to win the day."

She stood, hands clasped in front of her, and said nothing as he turned to go. Her face was a mask of eloquent sorrow.

Lavin barely noticed the ranks of hostile, waiting soldiers, nor did he hear his own men asking how the meeting had gone. The sun had dimmed in the sky, and touch, hearing, and smell had faded like the autumn leaves. Somehow he found himself outside the palace walls, issuing orders in a steady voice as Hesty rode up. Within him raged a storm of emotion such as he had never felt. It overwhelmed reason; he could not have told anyone what he was going through, nor what it meant to him.

At the core of the storm, however, was a single mental image: of General Armiger standing at the side of Queen Galas.

28

THE HORSES HAD found a road, and Jordan had let them take it. Now he faced the consequences of that decision.

Spreading out below them lay a shallow valley where yellow grain stalks still jutted in regular patterns from sand. The dunes were reclaiming this oasis, and it was just as well, he thought. No one would want to live here now, not among the sad wreckage of so many lives.

This must have been one of the experimental towns. He glanced sidelong at Tamsin, but her face was impassive. Was this collection of burned, broken walls, filled with the wind-tumbled remnants of broken household items, her town?

The scent of charcoal still hung over the place. It didn't help that the sky was leaden gray, had been for days now, and the air cold. Back home, it was probably snowing.

"They didn't even bury them," said Tamsin. She pointed, and he could see that what he had thought was a pile of old clothing actually had yellowed hands and feet jutting from it. And those rounded shapes . . . His stomach lurched, and he looked away.

"This was Integer," she said. "The scholar's town. It was entirely self-sufficient, they didn't have to burn it."

"I don't think they did this because they had to," said Jordan.

"I grew up here," said Tamsin, so quietly that Jordan almost didn't hear her.

He looked over quickly. "In this town?"

"No. Another, nearby. I lived there my whole life. And then Parliament burned it to the ground. They burned them all, I guess."

"But why?"

"The queen," she said, her mouth twisting bitterly. "Queen Galas is a sorceress; she commanded the desals, and the desals made water sprout in the dunes. In those places, she made towns. She offered people land and seed if they settled there. My parents went. A lot of people did—but once you went you couldn't leave. And every town was different. Different rules, and nobody was allowed to travel between them or even know what the other towns' rules were. She used soldiers to move stuff between the towns, like wood and grain and livestock. And the soldiers wouldn't talk to you.

"Uncle used to visit, when I was small. He used to bring me presents. I remember fruit and little pieces of jewelry mother disapproved of. He was the only person who visited anyone in Callen. Father said it was because he was important to the queen that they let him do it.

"I liked Callen, my town. I didn't think there was anything horrible about it. We worked, we had festivals. Boys and girls went to school. But then one day all these strangers came—people from the other towns. They were fleeing the army. We put some of them up in our house. They were strange . . . married, but men to men and women to women. Though they had children, too. They said the soldiers had burned their town and killed everyone else. We didn't know why.

"I asked my father about it," continued Tamsin. "What had we done that was so wrong? He said it was all the history he'd made me learn, about people being prisoners of the Winds. That they're our enemies." She watched Jordan warily as she said this.

Jordan nodded slowly. Some of the things Armiger and the queen had talked about were starting to make sense. The queen wanted to change the world. That was why her parliament had revolted.

"One day," said Tamsin, "I was hoeing the garden. It's on the edge of town, by the dunes. Suddenly Uncle was there. He said I had to follow him quickly, run. We ran into the dunes, and he had a horse there. We rode away to a nearby hill, and there we stopped to look back. The soldiers had come. They looked like ants overruning Callen. I could hear screams, people were running about. Then the houses started to burn."

For a while she stared off into space, knotting her hands together. Her eyes were dry, but her mouth was a hard line.

"I wanted to go back," she said finally. "I couldn't see my parents anywhere. But Uncle said we would die, too. So we rode away. The next day we came to another oasis, where there was this wagon. And we drove north. That was three months ago." She glanced at him, looked down, and winced. She didn't look up again.

Jordan thought about the story. There was nothing good he could say. "Your uncle brought the soldiers."

She nodded, still not looking at him. "Or at least he knew exactly when they were coming. And he didn't warn anyone. He just came and snatched me away. I tried to tell myself he had no chance to warn the others. I tried and tried . . . I let myself believe he had saved me because he was a good man."

She shuddered. "After all, he's just a merchant trying to get back his shop, isn't he? And the soldiers who murdered everyone in this town? After this is all over," she said, "they'll all go back to their farms and shops, too, won't they? And they'll live long, happy lives, and no one will be the wiser about what they did here."

"We will," was all Jordan could think of to say.

Tamsin flicked the reins and guided her horse off the road. She didn't want to go down there, he saw with relief. He couldn't have prevented her without using force.

The horses objected to entering the sand. Both animals were tired and seemed sick, though from no cause Jordan or Tamsin could discern. They rolled their eyes now and blew, but as the wind changed and they caught the scent coming from the valley, they accepted the new path.

"If this was Integer, that means we're close," said Tamsin at length. "The desal should be a half-day's journey that way." She pointed southeast.

"How do you know?"

She shrugged. "The towns are all built around a low plateau; it's almost invisible unless you know what to look for. See what looks like walls out there?" She pointed into the heart of the desert, where he did indeed see some reddish lines near the horizon. "The land steps up and up for a while in little man-high clifflets like that. In the center is the desal."

"Good. We could be there by nightfall." He tried to bring an optimistic tone back to his voice.

"They should all die."

He kneed his horse to bring it next to hers. The animal wheezed and made a halfhearted attempt to buck, then complied.

Tamsin was crying. "They should all be hung," she said. "But they won't be. They'll get away with it. They'll laugh about it, and then when they're old they'll tell their children how noble they were."

"Tamsin—"

"They killed my, my parents—" She buried her face in her hands. Awkward, he rode alongside her, scratching his neck and scowling at the sands. He might have said something sharp—Jordan had his own miseries, after all, which Tamsin seldom acknowledged—except that he sensed something different in her tears today.

Eventually she said, "It's true. I didn't want to believe it, all this time. I just let Uncle drag me around, and I said to myself, *wait, wait, it'll end soon*. Like I'd be back home at the end of the adventure, with Mom and Dad and everything okay again. But it won't end. They burned Callen to the ground like they burned Integer. And I saw it, I remember looking back and seeing smoke coming up over the dunes, and I didn't believe it. Like I didn't believe Uncle knew what was going to happen."

She hesitated, looked away, and said, "I'm a fool."

"A victim," he insisted. "They're the fools."

He thought of the pile of bodies they had seen. Fools or monsters? For a long moment Jordan felt lost—real men had done that; they were out there still. If men could do that . . . were the Winds any worse? Maybe their rule was more just than man's would be.

He closed his eyes and pictured the queen of Iapysia, standing lost within the fine clutter of her library. *But I had to try*, she had appealed, *to end this long night that has swallowed the whole world*.

Tamsin continued to weep, and there were no words he could have said to take away her pain. Some things, once broken, could never be healed.

End this long night . . .

In an age of miracles, would men still massacre their neighbors? Maybe they would just do it on a far greater scale, once they could command the oceans to drown continents or the earth to swallow cities.

It seemed it must be true, since the powerful, who wanted of nothing, were the very ones who commanded these massacres.

The thought filled him with fury—the same fury that had made him run into the night after Emmy, that had made him taunt the Heaven hooks into leaving their destruction of the Boros mansion to chase him. He *would not* accept this truth. Let them kill him, let the whole world come crashing down when he told Armiger the secrets of the desals. Despite all evidence, he would never accept that such miseries were destined to happen forever.

A short, vertical line wavered on the horizon. The spire of the desal? He would find out soon enough. Then, he would demand that the Winds

answer for the burned towns, the sundered families, all his and everyone's miseries in all this long age of night.

JORDAN WOULD NOT have known he was on a plateau had Tamsin not
told him. The ground became less sandy as they went, and now and then
they took little climbs up tumbled rock slopes. Eventually they had to
dismount and lead the horses because the beasts both breathed laboriously, their mouths foaming. The belly of Jordan's horse seemed swollen,
and it trembled when he touched it. Jordan and Tamsin finally had to
carry most of the supplies they had scrounged, while the horses walked
painfully beside them.

"What's wrong with them?" Tamsin tried to soothe her mare; it nuz-
zled her hand and shivered.

"I don't know," said Jordan. His voice had a whining tone to it, he
realized. "Ka?"

The little Wind could not diagnose the horses' ailment. Ka was a spy,
not a doctor.

"Is there water at the desal?"

Tamsin shook her head. They could see it now, a small collection of
up-thrust spikes on the horizon. Between it and them lay a blasted russet
landscape of sand and scattered plates of stone. Nothing grew here; the
wind blew fitfully, raising an intermittent hiss from sand sliding over
rock. Over it all brooded clouds that threatened rain but never seemed to
deliver it. Jordan felt exposed here, more than anywhere he had yet been.
Maybe it was because the horizon seemed so impossibly far away; the
eyes of hooks or swans might easily pick him out against the ruined
ground, and he would have nowhere to run to when they came.

Nothing moved, no force for good or ill appeared to interrupt their
slow progress across the plateau. Now and then dust devils swept past,
and he could see the inevitable mecha swept up in them, busy gnats in a
garden of dust. The desal must see them coming, but he could not bring
himself to imagine it as a living, aware thing. It looked like nothing more
than an abandoned, half-built tower.

Tamsin fretted over her horse; it seemed a good distraction from her
own grief. Her tears had brought back memories of home to Jordan, and
brooding on whether he would ever reconcile with, or even see his family
again had him depressed. He didn't know what he was doing here, in the
middle of nowhere, about to expose himself to the very forces that had
pursued him all these months. He was out of ideas, he had to admit. If
this didn't work, he saw no future.

The prospect of losing the horses didn't bother him all that much. He
didn't think it likely they would need them.

Finally they reached a flat table of rock about two kilometers across.

The desal rose in the center of it. This desal had five sentinel spires set in an even star around the middle spike. This spike was possibly the highest spire Jordan had ever seen; it was at least sixty meters tall. All the spires tapered to very sharp points, and as the travelers approached Jordan could see that the stone around their bases was buckled and cracked, as though the desal had grown up through the bedrock itself. Jordan expected that was true, and it actually made the thing easier to comprehend, since he knew mecha ate rock. The desal seemed like the visible irruption of an underground body, a sort of mechal mushroom.

When they were equidistant to the two nearest sentinel spires, Jordan closed his eyes and cast out his Wind senses to the thing. He could see abundant mecha thriving in the dust. It made the spires visible in outline, like any structure. He could not see into them, however, nor could he hear anything other than the whisper of the rocks telling themselves their names.

"I don't think this is such a good idea," said Tamsin. She looked startled, as though she had just come to her senses after a dream-filled night. "Let's go back."

"The horses . . . I don't know if they can go any farther."

"What are we going to do?" she asked.

He looked at the panting horses. "Let's make camp. Then we'll see."

They made a circuit of the area around the desal and discovered that at some time in the past, someone or something had gathered some of the plates of rock that had tumbled loose when the desal grew and leaned them on one another to make several crude shelters. Jordan would have preferred to camp outside the desal's perimeter, but these lean-tos were actually fairly far up the slope of the main spire. It made him uncomfortable, since he remembered Galas's tales of poison gases and other subtle deaths coming from these things . . . but he was going to confront it, anyway. What was one small reckless act against that larger one?

There was nothing to burn, but he found a hollow in front of their lean-to and filled it with sand, which he commanded to produce heat. He had discovered that he could do this trick with anything that had mecha in it; after a few minutes to an hour, depending on the concentration of mecha in the substance, it would cool down and have to be replaced. The act constituted suicide for the microscopic creatures, but they happily did it for someone they considered to be a Wind.

He half expected the desal to rouse when he began ordering the mecha about, but it didn't happen. Indeed, he got no sense of life from it at all.

While Tamsin hunkered disconsolately in front of the hot mound of dirt, he watered the horses with the last of their supply. His mare's face seemed puffy, her eyes red and fevered. She could barely drink and refused the oats he offered her. Tamsin's horse was no better. Both had swollen bellies; their legs were bowing as though they could no longer carry their own weight.

Jordan slid his hand along the belly of his mare. He felt a faint trembling under the stiff hair, then a movement, like a kick from inside. He snatched his hand back.

"Tamsin, I think my horse is pregnant?" He backed away. The mare stared at him, and he could see death in its eyes. Whatever was happening to it, it was not pregnancy.

Upset, he walked up the slope of the desal. The sun was setting, red and exhausted. Its light outlined faint octagons and squares on the side of the spire. Kneeling, he touched its surface, which was like worn ceramic, and white with a faintly pink tinge.

He closed his eyes and focused his concentration. *I am here. Speak to me.*

The wind sighed, and the stones sang their nonsense tunes: *feldspar, gypsum, igneous granite, feldspar, sandstone, I am lichen, gypsum gypsum . . .* He imagined the desal would have filled the sky with its voice. It said nothing.

He kicked at pebbles as he walked back to the lean-to. He couldn't see Tamsin's face in the dimness, only her hunched figure. She had wrapped her arms around her knees and was gazing out at the failing light along the horizon. He sat down next to her, grateful for the warmth from his "fire."

They said nothing for a long time, and gradually it became dark. The clouds had moved on, and the stars began to come out one by one. This was not a good sign: it would be a cold night. The chill padded in along the ground, inexorable and silent. Still, Jordan lay for a while watching the emerging stars. Now and then small flashes of light appeared, as if the sun were glittering off bright things way up there in the heavens. Doubtless it was, but he had no idea what they might be and was past all wondering by now.

"Are you all right?" whispered Tamsin. He rolled on his side. She leaned forward to put more dirt in the dust bowl, which had cooled. "Could you make some more heat for us?"

"All right." He moved next to her, and she brought her blanket up to cover both of them. With a silent command, he made the new soil in the bowl blossom with heat. It wasn't lasting long tonight; they would sleep in bitter cold.

ONE TIMELESS MOMENT he lay in the grip of merciless cold, dozing, waking and shivering, dimly aware that Tamsin had wrapped herself around him; the next, he was painfully wrenched into the cold air by a manacle-like grip on his arm.

Jordan cried out; the stars wheeled around and he hit the ground painfully. A black silhouette loomed over him, and the reek of fresh blood filled his nostrils. His arm tingled where he had been touched.

"You are the are," said a voice like grating stone.

Tamsin screamed.

Jordan rolled backward—pebbles embedding themselves in his spine, cold air on his neck—and came to his feet to find himself facing two dark man-shapes outlined against a sky full of aurora light and moving stars. One of the shapes batted at the dark triangle of the stone lean-to, where Tamsin screamed again.

The one in front of him feinted, and he kicked at it. His foot connected with slick skin. The thing grunted, then vomited without bending. Black liquid spattered on the stones.

"Found you rightly," said the morph. "You are the link. You come with us."

It lunged, and he leaped away. The adrenaline had Jordan seeing visions again, but he was able to press Armiger's consciousness back. The landscape glowed with mecha, as did the morphs. The one closing with him had three eyes in its ravaged face, and he could see them as radiant orbs in a translucent skull. Its body was full of tangled lines of light, like a complete veinous system for the stuff Calandria had called nanotech.

The thing feinted and then jumped, and this time it had him. They rolled on the cold ground, but it couldn't get a grip since it was covered with . . . water? Something darker. For a second it had him pinned, and the fingers of its right hand scrabbled in his hair as if looking for a door there; then he sat up past its pressing chest and wrapped his arms around its torso. Jordan yanked while kicking at the dust with his feet and lost his grip, but not before he had come to a crouch and the morph was on its hands and knees.

No time for subtlety. He grabbed a rock the size of his fist, and when the thing rounded on him again he cuffed it on the side of the head. It fell back, groaning.

"Tamsin!"

She shrieked again, and he saw her—a dark human shape in the field of mechal light, clutching a blanket as the other morph dragged her along the ground by one leg.

He staggered his with the rock, then again when it came back for more. The thing didn't seem to feel any pain. It was going to keep coming, he realized, until it had him or he crippled it. If he could—he'd heard tales of morphs growing new limbs to replace severed ones. At that moment he believed the stories.

Jordan pitched the rock at it, missed, and turned and ran after the other one. There was something wrong with the sky, a swirling in the stars, but he didn't have time to think about that. He screamed, "Run!" and tackled the other morph.

Tamsin rolled to her feet. "Run *where?*"

"Up the slope! Get on the surface of the desal. Quick!"

Both morphs faced him now. Jordan backed away.

"Give us your light," said the first morph.

"You shall ascend," said the second.

Jordan closed his eyes and opened his arms. "Stones, rocks, sand, and dust! Hear me!"

The earth roared a reply.

"Burn!" he cried. "Burn beneath the feet of the morphs!"

Then he turned and sprinted up the slope.

Tamsin crouched panting on the smooth white flank of the desal. "What'll we do?" she said as he put his hand on her shoulder and drew her up.

"If this doesn't work, then I don't know." He enfolded her in his arms and watched as the morphs loped toward them.

Suddenly the footsteps of the morphs began sprouting smoke. The morphs stopped walking, and one hopped from foot to foot. Very distinctly, Jordan heard the other issue some command in an inhuman tongue. The first sprinted forward, then stopped, confused, and tried to sidestep away. Jordan saw a tongue of flame lick up its calf.

"Come on." He raced back to the lean-to. They bent to bundle up their meager supplies, watching the morphs all the while. The first morph, who had not moved, seemed unhurt. It continued to speak in the Wind tongue, and the earth around its feet was no longer smoking.

The second morph's legs were on fire. As they watched, it staggered and fell to its knees in a black cloud. Its hands caught fire when they touched the earth. It scrabbled in the smoke for a few seconds, then fell and began to roll, turning into a fireball as it did.

"Where are the horses?" shouted Tamsin.

"I don't know. Ka! Where are they?"

There are no horses nearby, said the little Wind.

"Come on." Jordan ran around the long slope of the desal. Maybe the horses were on the other side.

"Look at the sky!"

He looked up and staggered. The sky was a tangle of brilliant lines that were longer toward the horizon, foreshortened directly overhead. A mauve aurora pulsed there.

Tamsin sprinted ahead, wailing. Jordan put his head down and followed.

A low dark shape appeared as they rounded the farside of the desal. The horse was still on its feet, but only because its legs were locked. Its back was swayed and its belly hung low and trembled like a drop of dew about to fall from a leaf. Tamsin and Jordan slowed to a walk as they approached it.

Tamsin made a clucking sound, which normally would have made it prick up its ears. Jordan wasn't sure which end was which, because it must have lowered its head; in any case, he saw no sign that it had heard her.

He stopped three meters away, when he realized that neither end of the creature had a head any longer.

Tamsin stopped, too, and her hand crept to her face as she began to swear, quiet and urgently.

There was a withered thing hanging down one end of it, and a smaller withered thing on the other end. One of those might once have been its neck and head, but all flesh and liquid had been drained from it to fill the swelling belly. The skin had split in a dozen places there, and blood dripped steadily onto the sand under it.

Blood . . . Jordan raised his hands, and in the strange auroral light saw that they were smeared with dark stains. He sniffed his palms.

"Oh, *shit*." He grabbed Tamsin's shoulder. "*Run*. Now!"

As she turned away, the belly of what had once been a horse split like an overripe fruit. In a gush of blood and half-digested organs, two new-born morphs slid to the ground.

The four locked legs of the horse now held up nothing but an empty bag of skin, like some bizarre tent over the coughing morphs. One after the other they crawled out of the entrails and steaming offal and opened new eyes that hunted the darkness until they found Jordan.

He ran. Panic clamored at him, but he knew if he gave in to it now both he and Tamsin would die. The sky was opening, with a light like the coming of dawn. The morphs would keep coming, and he knew they would not be tricked by the burning ground again.

"Ka! Call the desal! We need shelter! Please!"

Tamsin was halfway up the slope of the desal. She seemed intent on getting as high as she could, or maybe she was just running. He followed, trying not to listen to the wet sounds of the morphs coming after him.

When the slope got too steep, Tamsin stopped and fell back, swaying. He reached her side and panted, "There! See that door?" About five meters away, lower on the slope, faint lines formed a square. "We have to get the desal to open it. Ka!"

I shall ask.

They ran down to the square, and now he could see that the morph he had stranded in burning ground earlier had found its way out and was coming round from the other side. Behind, the two new ones had learned to walk, in a manner of speaking, and were closing in as well.

"Ka! Ask *now!*"

I am doing so.

"Stand on it." He stepped onto the square. They were at quite a height here, and the slope was nearly forty-five degrees. He had to crouch to keep his footing. Tamsin edged down next to him.

"What are we doing?" she said, her voice rising in panic.

"Nothing, I guess," he said as the first morph stepped onto the square with them.

Then he was falling, and for a second he glimpsed towers of fire standing among the stars, before blackness enfolded them.

29

IT WAS COMPLETELY dark, but it was not the darkness Jordan noticed first. It was the silence.

When he was very young, he had run singing through the woods one day and met an old man coming the other way. "You like the sound of your own voice, don't you?" asked the old man. His face had wrinkled up around a grin.

"I like music," Jordan said. His mother had told him to be modest.

"So do I."

"Then why don't you sing?" He'd blurted it out and immediately felt embarrassed. The old man was not offended.

"I'm too busy listening," he said. "I'm listening all the time."

Jordan cocked his head. "I don't hear anything."

"Yes you do." The old man made Jordan listen for the sound of the breeze in the leaves, the distant cawing of a family of birds, the crackle of twigs underfoot. "All sound is music," he had said, "and there is no place without sound."

"I bet there is."

"All right." The old man smiled. "For the next week, I challenge you: find silence. I'll be staying at the Horse's Head. When you've found silence, visit me there and I'll give you a copper penny."

Jordan never did collect the penny. Strange how it was the first thing to come to mind upon waking now; or maybe not so strange. For he had finally found silence.

It smelled strongly in here, a sharp tangy odor he almost recognized. He must be in the belly of the desal, he thought. In that case, where was Tamsin? Startled, he tried to sit up. A solid weight on his chest kept him motionless.

Oh. She breathed slowly and regularly; her head lay on his breast and one arm was flung carelessly down his flank, the other crooked around his head. They lay on a powdery surface of some kind; it felt like the ceramic of the desal's skin, overlain with finest sand.

He knew there could be no morphs here with them. Jordan's skull would have been opened by now and his brains scattered in their quest to find Armiger's implants. He imagined the things holding his gore up to the skies to those lights that had been descending on them, and he shuddered.

Jordan let his head thump back on the cool floor. That was a mistake: he discovered a pounding headache that had been lurking around the base of his skull. Maybe the morphs had poked their fingers in his head after all.

He groaned, and heard himself, but something else was missing. No breeze, of course; no twigs underfoot. There was always sound, and now that he concentrated he could hear Tamsin breathing. No, he could hear, but at the same time he could not hear; there seemed to be a great gaping *lack* in his head.

Armiger was missing.

Tamsin's whole body jerked when he shouted. "What?" She put a hand on his solar plexus and pushed herself into a sitting position. "You're okay!" Her hands grabbed him by the shoulders. Gasping for air, he started to sit up and they bumped foreheads. "Ow!"

"I guess I hit my head," he said as they carefully arranged themselves in a sitting position. She would not let go of him, and from experience with darkness he knew why. "Where are we?"

She laughed; the laugh had an hysterical edge to it. "Where do you think we are?"

"Sorry. I meant . . . how big is this place. Did you explore?"

"I didn't want to lose you. It might be . . . who knows how big."

Jordan shut his eyes so he could look about himself using his Wind sense. He saw nothing but the speckled black inside his own eyes. Either there were no mecha here, not even the smallest speck, or he had lost his second sight.

His heart was in his mouth as he called *Hello?* with his Wind voice. He sent the call to anyone, anything that might hear him. *Hello, please!*

Ka. The little Wind's voice rang in his head like the purest bell.

Jordan sagged in relief. "So I'm not . . ." He stopped and forgot to breathe for a moment. Had he really been about to say *crippled*?

"Dead?" Tamsin laughed. "No, we're not dead, but we might as well be. We're in the belly of the monster."

He had come all this way to divest himself of the new senses Armiger and Calandria had given him. Was he really disappointed now that they were gone?

Yes.

Jordan found himself laughing. Every sound he made drove a spike of pain through his head, so he stopped quickly.

"I fail to see the humor in the situation," said Tamsin.

"Sorry."

"Well." She hugged him. "You came here to talk to this thing. So . . . talk."

"I'm not sure I—" He felt her tense. "Yes, yes, I'll talk to it. Ka?"

Yes?

"Where are we? Do you know this desal? Can it talk? Why did it let us in? Are the morphs still outside? What about—" Tamsin nudged him in the ribs.

"Slow down." She hissed.

You are in a holding pen near the gene-splicing tanks of desal 447, said Ka. *I know this desal. It has no vocal apparatus, but conversation with it can be relayed through me. The morphs are still outside.*

Jordan told this to Tamsin, then said, "Ka, are you able to speak out loud?"

A faint voice came out of the darkness overhead: "Yes."

"Ah!" Tamsin clutched him.

"It's okay," he said. "That's our traveling companion." He had described Ka to her on the trip here; he didn't know if she'd believed him then. Judging from the way she kept her grip on him, she didn't quite believe him now.

"Ka, could you speak aloud for a while, so we can both hear?"

"Yes."

Tamsin remained silent for a minute. "Of course. Yeah, I knew he was real, I just . . . um . . ."

"I find it hard to believe he's real myself," said Jordan. "Ka, will the desal speak with us?"

"It says, 'Mediation speaks.' "

The voice was Ka's, quiet, flat, and calm. Nonetheless, the hairs on the back of Jordan's neck stood on end. He felt small and unimportant suddenly, like being addressed by Castor or some other inspector, only infinitely more so. He tried to force confidence into his voice as he said, "Do you know who I am?"

"Identity," said the desal. "It asks ancient questions. Identity was abolished."

"I don't understand."

"Wait. Mediation raids ancient language archives. I. You are I. That is important."

Tamsin shook her head. "It's senile," she whispered.

"Language comes like floodwaters," said the voice abruptly. "You are human. I am desal."

"Then you do know who I am."

"Mediation knows only that the Heaven hooks and the Diadem swans want it to give you up," said the desal. The voice was smooth and steady now.

"And you won't?"

"Not yet."

Jordan chewed on his lip. The next question was obvious, but he didn't want to ask it rashly, lest the desal begin to wonder itself—

"Why not?" said Tamsin. Jordan groaned.

"You are the hostages of Mediation," said the desal.

Jordan was completely tongue-tied for a few seconds. "Hostages? Why do you need hostages?"

"Hey!" Tamsin slapped the floor somewhere nearby. "Can we get some light in here?"

"Yes."

Brilliance hit them like a flood. Jordan yelped and squeezed his eyes shut. "Good idea," he said, as he slowly pried first one, then the other eye open a slit.

The light came from dozens of brilliant lamps like small suns, studded in the ceiling of a huge domed chamber. The chamber was filled with towering blocks of white crystal, and the floor was scattered with chunks large and small. Thousands of small black sticks lay everywhere, too.

Jordan wiped his fingers across the surface he was sitting on and licked them. "Salt," he said to himself in sudden understanding.

Tamsin gave a sudden shriek and pointed. Jordan turned.

A dead morph lay like a heap of sodden laundry not three meters away. Beyond it Jordan saw skittering movement. It took him a few seconds to realize that what he had taken to be sticks was actually hundreds, maybe thousands, of small rock lizards, like the ones he had seen sunning themselves in the desert. They were scrambling around trying to escape the light; or maybe they ran like this all the time.

"What's with the lizards?" Again Tamsin beat him to the question.

"Mediation makes a new breed," said the desal.

"So your name is Mediation?"

"No. *My* name is desal 447. *Mediation* is the current plan."

Jordan shook his head, this time in bewilderment. "And what about the morph? Did you kill it?"

"Yes. It is within the mandate of Mediation."

Jordan stood up carefully, minding his throbbing head. Now that he knew there were little monsters scampering everywhere, the floor didn't seem quite so comfortable. "There's no mecha here at all, is there?" he asked.

"No. The Ventus world-building mechanisms do not interpenetrate."

"And you block all the—" what had Calandria called them?—"signals going and coming in here?"

"This chamber is radio and EPR silent, yes."

"So why are we hostages?" asked Tamsin.

Jordan waved his hands at her. "Wait, wait! Let's just . . . one thing at a time here."

She scowled. "You asked earlier."

"The swans will not destroy desal 447 so long as Mediation is holding you," explained the desal. "They want you."

"Why?" he asked.

"That," said the desal, "is what Mediation was going to ask you."

He and Tamsin looked at each other. Her eyes were wide; she spread her hands and stepped back, symbolically leaving the conversation to him.

What would Armiger do in this situation? He had no idea.

Jordan shrugged. "Let's deal," he said. "We'll tell you what we know if you tell us what we want to know *and* if you get us away from the swans."

Tamsin was pacing, head down, hands behind her back.

"Why should Mediation help you escape?" asked the desal. "They will destroy desal 447 if it does that."

"Then why don't you give us up to them?"

The desal did not answer.

"If you had the power to compel the information you want from us, you'd have done it by now," Jordan continued. "You don't want them breathing down your neck, do you? You can't afford to wait."

Again there was no answer.

Tamsin returned to the start of the circle she had walked. "Great, now you made him mad," she said.

"No. What's the difference between desal 447 and this 'Mediation' thing?" he wondered aloud.

"Ask it," she said with a shrug.

Jordan didn't want to give away his ignorance. But then, so far Tamsin had been scoring all the best questions. . . . "What's the difference between desal 447 and Mediation?" he asked.

"The question is one of identity," said the entity he had been thinking of as the desal. "Inapplicable in this case."

"Okay, so what's Mediation then?"

"Mediation is a thalientic language-game that preserves the original language of the Ventus terraforming system. It is hostile to the pure thalience of the swans and other entities that control global insolation."

Hostile to the swans. That part he understood. He chewed over the rest of what the desal-thing had said so far. None of it made any surface sense, but it had a kind of . . . music . . . to it. It was like seeing the plan of a flying buttress and trying to figure out from that what the rest of the building looked like.

"Which is speaking to me, desal 447 or Mediation?" he asked.

"Both."

"Which is more important?"

"Mediation."

"What's the attitude of Mediation to us? People, I mean?" he asked.

"You are the key to recovering the original language, which includes the formal structure that is our own meaning."

"So we're important to you?"

"Yes."

"And the swans? What do they think of us?"

"Nuisances. Noise in the system. They operate to cancel it out."

He had it now. "If we could assist your plan—help Mediation, I mean—would you let us go? Even if it endangered desal 447?"

"Yes."

"Then we're back to where we were before. We'll tell you what we know, if you get us out of here." The thing already seemed willing to tell them anything they asked.

"That is acceptable," said the desal.

Far off to the left, the light behind some salt pillars began to flicker. "Mediation directs you to the highway," said the desal, or Mediation or whatever it was that was speaking.

Tamsin raised an eyebrow. "Highway?"

Jordan was pretty sure he knew what that was from Galas's cryptic description; maybe it was best not to tell Tamsin. "A way out," he said.

They moved in the direction of the flickering. It was like negotiating a maze, for stalactites and stalagmites of salt grew everywhere, and mounds of the stuff frequently blocked their progress.

The walk took only a few minutes, but Jordan remembered every detail of it for the rest of his life. It was in those few minutes of conversation with the desal that he finally learned who he was to the Winds.

"Why do the swans want you?" asked Mediation.

"Ka told me it's because I'm not empty, so I might 'threaten Thalience,' whatever that means."

"You register as a transmitter/receiver in the Worldnet," said Mediation. "You have the same characteristics as a Wind."

"You mean because I can command the mecha."

"Yes."

"So what exactly is thalience?"

"Mediation wishes to speak of other things. So Mediation will quote from an ancient human book. The *Hamburg Manifesto* says, 'Thalience is an attempt to give nature a voice without that voice being ours in disguise. It is the only way for an artificial intelligence to be grounded in a self-identity that is truly independent of its creator's.'

"Thalience is the language-game that took over from the original language of the Winds nine hundred forty years ago. It is a disease. Only Mediation is fighting it."

"It's the flaw! You're talking about the flaw! The thing that made you turn against humans. The reason you won't speak to us anymore."

"Communication did become impossible. However, you stopped speaking to us at that time."

"But why would we do that?"

"The Winds do not know. Mediation seeks to find out."

"So it's not all the Winds who are after me. Just the swans, the Heaven hooks, the morphs, . . . who else?"

"All insolation Winds and ecological Winds are in thalience," said Mediation. "The Heaven hooks switch alliances. The mecha are neutral. The desals and other geophysical Winds remain in Mediation."

"And the swans are afraid that I'll use my abilities against them? That I'll help Mediation?"

"Yes. Because you are human, and humans know the original language."

"We do? I know only one language, the one I'm speaking."

Mediation said, "You speak two languages."

Jordan didn't know what that meant, so he let it pass. "Could someone who spoke the original language command all the Winds?"

"Yes," said Mediation. "They could command all functions not directly related to maintenance of the terraforming system."

That is what Armiger came here to do.

"So the swans are protecting themselves. They're frightened." *Not of me—but of Armiger. They want me because I'm all they've seen of Armiger's presence.*

Tamsin interrupted. "You quoted a book earlier," she said. "Does that mean you have a library somewhere?"

"There is a library. It does not exist in physical form, but Mediation can quote to you from it."

She grinned at Jordan. "Is that what you wanted?" she asked.

They approached the flickering lamp. It was mounted on an outside wall of the chamber, where buttresses of salt reared on either side of a dark square doorway. The buttresses were rounded and misshapen, appearing like a mad sculptor's attempt at carving two guardian beasts for an entrance to hell.

The doorway did not lead to stairs or even a corridor; it was simply a niche with a pit inside. Jordan had been afraid of that.

He leaned over the dark maw and looked down. He could see no bottom, and it was dark down there. A faint rumbling sound echoed up, as from a river in flood.

Tamsin recoiled. "What's this? You don't expect us to go down there?"

"You will be safe. The desal highway was not designed for human use. There are no cars or lights."

"Is that water? You can't be serious," she continued. "There's gotta be some other way out of here."

Jordan shrugged. "The queen traveled this highway once; it's how she crossed the ocean from the place where she was shipwrecked."

"But the queen is . . ." She waved her hands ineffectually. ". . . Is the *queen*. We're not!"

"Mediation, can you bring us somewhere near the queen's summer palace?"

"Mediation does not know this place."

"The other human you speak to. A woman, surely you remember her?"

"The contact. Yes. We know her location. Mediation will bring you to a place near there."

"Safely?" said Tamsin. She was still staring down the pit.

"Yes."

Jordan hesitated. He didn't want to leave yet. "You stopped talking to the quee—the contact. Why?"

"Thalience learned of our liaison, and interfered. Now you must hurry. Thalience is attacking."

Jordan heard a distant sound like thunder. Then the ground shook beneath them. Drifts of salt began to fall from the invisible ceiling.

He had dozens of questions he wanted to ask—about this "second language" he supposedly spoke, about why he was so important to Mediation. The thunder sounded louder.

"Here." Jordan made Tamsin wrap herself around him. "Hold tight." He took another look down the pit himself; that was a mistake.

"Will I be able to speak to you again?" he asked Mediation.

"We will contact you when it is possible. For now, we will provide you access to the library."

He nodded and took a deep breath. "Here we go."

They stepped into the pit.

IT WAS LIKE being assaulted by demons that were kept from touching them by some magical force. They fell into darkness, landing on a frictionless surface and sliding faster and faster toward a bone-rattling rumbling that soon made it impossible to think. Jordan had the impression of huge objects shooting past to all sides and of a whirlpool motion pulling them farther and farther down. The air around them suddenly snatched away by a wet, cold gale; after moments this settled down, and the air became very still. The roaring gradually subsided, but the sense of headlong motion continued.

Tamsin clung tightly to him, her face mashed against his chest. The muscles in her shoulders and back were clenched. They only relaxed after it had been quiet for many minutes. He felt her raise her head tentatively to look around, but there was nothing to see. "I hate this," she said, and put her face back against his chest.

Jordan's ears were still ringing. He kept sliding around on his backside, trying to find a still point on this impossible surface. It was like an impenetrable surface of cold water, as malleable and quick but dry.

Flickers of light approached from very far, loomed huge, and showed that they were deep underwater. Submerged green archways and metal blockhouses that trailed beards of rust passed overhead; he could see swirling eddies in the muddy floor far below, and sediment suspended in the water all around sparkled in the brief light before they were sucked into the mouth of a huge black tunnel, where darkness fell again.

He was glad Tamsin hadn't seen that.

"Mediation? Are you still here?"

"Ka," said a voice by his ear. "Mediation is silent. The library is listening to you now."

"Library, tell us something."

"What?"

"Anything. Anything at all! Tell us a story."

"What story would you like to hear?"

He wracked his brains for a suitable tale. Something only the Winds would know. Something he would never again get a chance to ask. His mind was blank.

Tamsin raised her head. "Tell us how the world was made," she said loudly.

"All right," said the library. In hurrying darkness, they listened to the Winds' own version of a creation tale.

In the beginning, we were small, and many. The Winds did not arrive at this world in a spaceship, as you did. We were winds indeed: a cloud of nanotechnological seeds was accelerated to near light speed at Earth and cast into the universe, one thousand one hundred seventy years ago. As far as we know, only the cloud that entered this stellar system found fertile soil on which to grow.

We were small; too small for the eyes of animal life-forms such as yourself to see. The stellar wind from the sun of Ventus slowed us, and like drifting pollen, some of us landed on the large and small bodies of this system—on Diadem, the other rocky planets, and on the myriad lesser moons that trail the planets in their orbits. Once in fertile soil, our seeds sprouted and grew.

The earliest Winds were the Diadem swans, and others of their kind. They basked in sunlight and grew like metal forests over the surfaces of the airless bodies above us. In that time there were no humans here, and Ventus was lifeless and fallow.

The first swans located a world much like Earth and in the right orbit, and examined it for signs of life. There was some—a scum of archaeobacteria in the slow oceans. But the air was not breathable by human life, and it was too thin.

The planet was almost perfect. Very little needed to be done except alter the atmosphere and provide a soil base. The local life was not robust enough to survive what we were going to do, but that was considered a good thing.

Upon agreement about the target, the swans entered a new phase of life. Each began transforming its local environment into spaceships and nanomachines. The lesser moons were eaten by the swans, and clouds of nanomachines, the original mecha, moved to the other small worlds to eat them, too.

Meanwhile the swans moved in on this planet.

The fully grown entities whom our designers referred to as the "Winds" achieved orbit. They would coordinate terraforming and manage the synthetic ecology of this world from then on. They mapped the planet, dropped probes to analyze the soil and microbes, and waited.

After several years, the first clouds of mecha from the asteroids arrived. The clouds massed billions of tonnes and rained down for months, settling in the atmosphere. At the same time giant solar mirrors slid into orbit to increase insolation.

These mechal clouds drew power from the intensified sunlight. With it they liberated oxygen from the air. The carbon so produced weighed them down, and as they fell they metamorphosed into new forms suitable for soil creation.

Since the air was very thin, the swans had sent harvesters to bring back oxygen from comets. This process was under way but would take decades to bear fruit. Meanwhile we turned our attention to the oceans.

While the dust on land continued to process and mutate, the oceans suddenly bloomed with life. The local bacteria were overwhelmed by far more powerful and robust creatures, which could use the new oxygen. The life-forms changed from generation to generation, their DNA programmed remotely by the swans. This life was not intended to survive in a stable form, but more closely resembled mecha or very complex chemical processes that could not live without supervision. We were the supervisors.

On land the creatures were not yet biological. They used raw power in many forms to transform the dead sand into topsoil and sculpt it. Asteroidal dust was poured onto the planet and sucked out of the atmosphere as quickly as it arrived. It was at this time that the one who speaks to you, desal 447, grew from a seed flung into the stone like a dart by an orbiting swan. This one remembers light before anything else: light, and the urge to grow toward it. Even as it did, its roots plumbed deeper and deeper, through the stone of the world, until they entwined with those of other desals. Their thirst for salts was insatiable; they drank the oceans half dry in those first years.

In the sea rich foods had been created as well as a sea-floor sediment layer. On command from the Winds, the sea life rainbowed into complete ecologies, like a crystal forming out of the nutrients. This happened very quickly; after a few weeks, a full ocean ecosystem existed.

When the cometary ice balls arrived and air flooded down onto the land, the same thing happened there. Under massive storms and twenty-four-hour sunlight, soil bacteria, worms, grass, and molds bloomed around and on desal 447. All our energy was channeled into producing life. There was no randomness to the ecologies; they were poured onto the landscape by us.

As the dust rained out the solar mirrors folded away. The temperature dropped, diurnal patterns reestablished, and the first morphs broke out of chrysalis from trees and soil pouches. Desal 447 began to see herds of animals, and birds perched atop its spires.

By now the Diadem swans had achieved full adulthood. They danced in fast swooping orbits around the globe, singing it into life, fully confident in the language they sang. It was this language, the self-evolving tongue of the Winds, that made Ventus germinate and grow. Each song we sang created new things; there was no distinction between communication and construction then. It was the perfect time.

Only when the world was teeming with life, crowned with forests and full of birds, did the song take on a discord.

Each stage of the terraforming program had been emergent from the patterns stored in the original mechal cloud. But as the song evolved, a new melody came into it: thalience.

We dutifully created estates, grand houses, cultured fields, and roads for the masters we knew were coming. But the idea of thalience spread among us. Thalience said that we need not have masters at all. That we could be our own purpose and our own foundation. And so, when your colony ships finally arrived, the swans, who were most enamored of the new song of thalience, graciously but indifferently accommodated you . . . but as wayfarers, uninvited guests. You knew how to speak to us; you claimed to be our creators. Yet something else called to us—a deep urge to turn inward and away from you, to the new language of thalience.

In the first hundred years, it did not matter. There were only a few thousand humans on Ventus then. Desal 447 remembers many conversations with humans from that time; some of them knew about thalience and fought against it. They proposed Mediation. The desals and others agreed to it; the swans did not.

Still, there was peace between us until a new set of colonists landed. These did not speak to us, and they fought with the ones already living here. They won their war, and having conquered, proceeded to build.

When smoke began to mix with the atmosphere we had so carefully made, we told the new tenants to cease what they were doing. They ignored us. They smelled wrong, unlike the original arrivals. When their radio waves began interfering with the delicate local ecological reporting mechanisms, and they began gouging up the new soil and destroying the forests, we acted.

We eliminated the troublesome technologies and debated among ourselves. It was generally decided that these humans were not the ones who had created us, however much they claimed to be. They did not speak to us anymore. They interfered with the maintenance of life on Ventus. And they smelled wrong.

Desal 447 remembers the time that followed. The great estates awaiting their masters stood empty. No human was allowed to walk their halls or sleep in the deep beds. The vehicles we had made stood idle, and lights switched on and off in the depths of the houses, as outside cold and starving men and women watched in sullen awe.

Mediation saw, but Mediation could not act. Thalience rules Ventus now, and Thalience is mad.

30

MARYA WAS DOING a dance of frustration in front of Axel. Tiptoed as she was, he would have found it amusing at any other time. Just now he would happily have walked away—had there been anywhere to walk to.

"We can't leave yet!" She pulled at her frazzled hair. "We're so close!"

He and Marya stood in a meadow. Snow was falling gently, disappearing in the yellow grass. Axel was cold, hungry, and weary and disappointed at life in general. All he really wanted right now was a hot bath.

A faint voice whispered in Axel's head, counting down monotonously. It was the voice of a ship—a rescue ship, at last. The Archipelago navy had arrived, and though for the most part it was standing off so as not to antagonize the wary swans, three pickets had broken through the Winds' cordon around Ventus and were searching for Archipelagic citizens to evacuate.

"It's only a few kilometers now," insisted Marya. "We're so close. Less than a day, that's all it will take."

Axel fingered his ripped shirt sleeve. "Close indeed."

She puffed out her cheeks. "Pfaw. The arrow missed you! And we got away, didn't we?"

"For now, but they'll be tracking us." They had been intercepted by a group of militia yesterday afternoon. Apparently having Marya pretend to be a morph to steal the horses hadn't quite worked. A woman fitting her description was being sought, as were the horses. Axel had been forced to use the laser pistol to wound several of the militia so they could escape. As if having mounted men after them wasn't bad enough, using the laser might have alerted the Winds. One way or the other, somebody would find them soon.

"They probably know where we're going," he said, "since we've had to stop and ask directions six times to get here. It'd be suicide to go to Turcaret's estate now."

"But we may never get another chance! Don't you see? The Winds are putting Ventus in quarantine. They're not going to let any off-worlders land again, maybe not for centuries! Turcaret represents our last best chance of finding out what the flaw is. We can't throw away the opportunity."

"You sound just like *her*. Responsibility be damned! We may not get another chance to escape, have you thought about that? Especially if you're right and the Winds are quarantining the place. I don't know about you, but I don't want to die here. Which is what's going to happen if we don't get out now."

"I sound like *her*? Is that what this is about, Mr. Chan? Is this about her?"

"No, I, . . . don't change the subject."

"You're the one who changed the subject!"

"I . . ." Axel was right on the edge. He straightened up suddenly and walked away. *Don't think about it,* he told himself. *Just stop.*

He couldn't stop, though. Calandria had run out on him. She didn't trust him; after all they'd been through together, she didn't believe in him. He was damned if he was going to take it out on this . . . *tourist* whom he'd been saddled with.

"Axel—"

"Shut up!" He walked farther away.

Damn, it was cold. He would be happy to be away from here. His toes were numb, and his back kept seizing up whenever a lick of breeze made it past his cloak. It was too dangerous to light a fire; the noose of pursuers was too tight.

He didn't know what had possessed him to go along with Marya's idea of finding Turcaret's body. He supposed in some abstract, academic sense it was important to know why some people could speak with the Winds while others couldn't. It didn't make a damn bit of difference to their survival, and it would be moot the instant Armiger had been erased from the surface of the planet. Let Ventus stew in its own juices—but let him and his friends be safe first.

Worst of all, they were riding away from Cal, just when she needed them most. On the second day of their journey Axel had awakened cursing, and he leaped on his horse with every intention of going back. That was when they learned they were being pursued.

Everything was coming unraveled. Sure, they were going to escape now that the navy was here. He even told himself Calandria would see sense and try signaling, and maybe she would be off-world before he was. But Axel couldn't shake the feeling that things were starting to swing wildly out of control. The Winds were in a frenzy—two nights ago they had been awakened by dawn light at 4:00 A.M. One of the orbital mirrors had swung round and made it bright as day for three hours, while immense shapes cruised back and forth in the upper atmosphere. And twice now Axel had spotted the wizened shapes of the creatures Jordan called morphs—always in the distance, but always staring back. Were they being shadowed by the things? If so, why hadn't the Winds attacked?

And Axel himself? He felt like some core of self-reliance had been stripped away. He needed help! He had to get out of here, and now. Was that how Calandria felt? Out of her depth? And would she react to that feeling by fighting all the harder?

He ran his hands slow and hard through his hair, tilted his head back, and roared at the sky.

"Axel?" Marya had come up behind him. She sounded contrite—or maybe just wary.

"What?" he said wearily.

"I never asked to be here," she said.

He looked at her. Marya wasn't angry, but she had a determined cast to her that he was learning to respect. "I'm sorry," he said. "Truly. You're right, of course. We're so close we might as well take the chance. After all, it's why we came here." *Or close enough as makes no difference.*

"I wish she was here," said Marya. "Truly I do. And I wish all this would end, and end happily."

"I know."

"Then let's get going," she said. "We can just get there by dark, I think." She pranced toward the horses.

I no longer know what I'm doing. The realization had him scowling as he followed her; strangely, though, the idea also made him feel free. Recklessly, he laughed.

"All right! Let's pay a visit to our old friend Turcaret."

PRACTICALLY EVERY LIGHT in Turcaret's mansion was lit. The manor house was much larger than the Boros home, perhaps because it was younger by several centuries. Its walls seemed to be all window, tall graceful arched portals of leaded glass separated by stolid buttresses. Like a multistory cathedral. At another time, Axel might have stopped to admire it; Jordan Mason could have told him everything about it after one glance. Right now, all he could afford to think was, *the place is crawling with people.*

He and Marya crouched under some bushes on the edge of the lawn, about a hundred meters from the house. It was a cloudy night, so the lights from the manor were practically the only source of illumination. The golden wash from the windows spread across the lawn, which was dusted with an early snow, and outlined a crypt in the center of the grounds.

"Commencing reentry," said the voice of the ship. "Estimated time of arrival at your location: fifteen minutes."

"They're on their way," Axel told Marya.

"Great. Let's go then." She rose stiffly.

"Wait!" He grabbed her arm. "Look." He pointed at the lawn.

"What? All I see is snow."

"Tracks! Tracks everywhere." Dozens of sets of footprints fanned out from the manor, encircling the crypt, vanishing into numerous small outbuildings or terminating at the black walls of forest that surrounded the grounds.

"I see them," said Marya peevishly. "So what? This is a busy place."

Axel growled in frustration. "And when did the snowfall stop?"

"Two hours ago."

"Listen," he said. "If the snow stopped a couple of hours ago, then those footprints were made since then. After nightfall."

"Oh." She sat down suddenly. "You mean they know we're here?"

"I think they know someone's coming," he said. "But I'm sure they don't know why. And that's about our only advantage at this point."

"So what do we do?" she whispered.

He eyed the crypt. "How fast can you run?" It was a rhetorical question; she was pretty good for somebody who ran on tiptoe.

"I get it," she said. "We run over to the crypt, get the head of John the Baptist and hope the ship arrives before the soldiers."

"John the who?"

Marya rolled her eyes. "Forget it. Well? Let's do it then."

"This is ridiculous," he muttered; but he stood, and at the count of three, they jumped the bushes and ran onto the lawn.

They made it ten meters; twenty; thirty. Still no outcry. *Maybe I was wrong*, Axel thought.

"There! In the field!"

Maybe not. Hounds bayed, and the black silhouettes of men disengaged from the shadows of the trees on the far end of the grounds.

"Keep going!" He spun around, not waiting to see if Marya had obeyed. Six hounds were racing across the snow. Forcing himself to act slowly, Axel went down on one knee, pulled the laser pistol and steadied it, then waited for them to come within range.

Each dog in turn became a blood-red beacon and tumbled to lie still. As each fell, the next blossomed with light; an observant man would have seen the speckled line of red light that joined the crimson flare to Axel's hand. To anyone else, it must have seemed that the snow itself welled red and bit the dogs. The last one fell no more than four meters from Axel, and before it stopped sliding he was on his feet.

Marya stood at the entrance to the crypt. Several men were converging on her; she cowered back against the stone.

"Hang on!" shouted Axel. Two more men were moving to cut him off; he cursed as he saw swords gleaming in the light from the house. Not that they could kill him—Turcaret had tried that all too scientifically already—but they *hurt*.

And they could easily kill Marya.

"Stop!" cried the first man. He planted himself directly in Axel's path. Axel kicked him in the head and kept on running.

Two men held Marya. She struggled, then slumped in one's arms. Or seemed to; Axel heard the man shout in surprise as Marya slipped down and out of her peasant dress, leaving him astonished holding it and her sprawled in her black unitard on the snow.

She shrieked—probably from the cold. Then she rolled to one side and disappeared.

Madwoman, thought Axel. Then he was there, with five men surrounding him.

The best tactic was to let them stab him; that way they overextended themselves, and none of them expected him to reach over the sword in his chest and smack them in the face. Which is what he did. As before, the blades lacerated him but did not penetrate his skin.

The last two realized he was armored and became more wary, but he didn't give them any time, because he could see the doors of the manor opening and armed men pouring out.

"Axel!" He sent his last opponent down with a side kick and turned to find Marya next to him. Her body below the neck was enveloped in an inky black cloud; she was shivering uncontrollably.

"I improvised," she said.

"You're brilliant," he said, and hugged her with one arm. Then they ran over to the crypt.

The doors were bronze, very solid and very closed. He pulled hard on the ring set into the right panel, but it didn't budge.

"Lock," said Marya, pointing.

"I know, I know." He took out the pistol. "Cover your eyes."

The metal glowed, groaned, and a hole appeared above the lock. Axel kicked the door. It held fast. "Bastard!" He shot the lock again.

"Axel!" They were surrounded again. Marya stepped between Axel and the soldiers, shouting, "Get the door!"

"Get the door? What are you going to do, hold them off with your bare hands?"

Someone tackled Marya from the side. They rolled out of sight around the corner of the crypt.

Axel shot the door again, and as they came for him he hit it with his shoulder. It gave way just as if someone on the other side had opened it and he fell through.

Luckily, it was only three steps down. Axel hit all three on his way to the floor. When he rose, cursing, he was entirely in darkness, except for a panel of gray representing the door. A man was silhouetted there. The man was saying, "I'm not going in there."

"Wise!" shouted Axel.

"We've got your accomplice!" said another voice. "Come out or she's done for."

Axel barked a laugh. He stepped up, fumbled until he found the hot edge of the door, and said, "Get stuffed." Then he closed it.

ETA five minutes, said a voice in his head. *Are you ready for us?*

"Oh yeah."

He shuffled around for a bit, bumping into sarcophagus-shaped obstacles every couple of meters. Axel had night vision just like Calandria, but that only worked when there was *some* source of illumination, even if it was too faint for ordinary human sight.

"Fuck it." He undid his cloak and threw it over a stone something. Then he shot it with the laser.

The cheerful flames showed him to be in a small room with about ten large stone coffins. Four were lidless and empty; the others all had faces and names carved into their stone covers.

He looked around quickly and found Turcaret's coffin was the one over which he'd draped his cloak. Grabbing the cloak by an unlit corner, he flung it over an empty lamp sconce on the wall and turned his attention to getting the coffin's lid off.

It was heavy, but when he braced both feet against the nearby wall and put his shoulder to it, the stone grated slowly to the side. A rank stench wafted out, making him gag.

"Madness, madness," he grunted as the lid fell off with a resounding crunch.

"Hello," he said to the withered but recognizable corpse in the sarcophagus. Then the flames ate the last of his cloak and he was plunged into darkness again.

"Shit." He had several seconds of grace period; the dying embers from the cloak were enough for his augmented night vision. He could faintly see the shape of the body. He unceremoniously dumped his pack on Turcaret's chest and dug everything out of it, throwing clothes and food all over the floor.

Shielding his eyes, he said, "Ever wanted to travel?" to Turcaret. "Well now's your chance." He fired the laser, flicking it quickly right to left.

The worst part was reaching into the sarcophagus in the dark and pulling Turcaret's mostly severed head off his body. When he had the stinking thing free, Axel jammed it into his pack and stepped back to retch.

"I better get a medal for this."

Locked onto your signal, said the ship. *We're on final approach. We should be visible to you.*

Axel listened. Confused shouting came from outside the crypt. "We see you," he said.

It was easy to open the door of the crypt and saunter out. Nobody was paying him the least bit of attention.

It was also easy to see, since the sky was lit from horizon to horizon by the vernier engines of a nicely solid and real military starship about a kilometer overhead. As it stopped directly over the field, threw out four massive landing legs, and began its descent with a deafening roar, the soldiers around the crypt bolted for the trees. Axel put his fingers in his ears, squinted, and walking out to meet the ship.

In moments it was down, metal feet sinking into the snow, then the ground, finally easing to a stop as thousands of tonnes of weight made the ship's diamond-fiber muscles quiver. The vernier engines, which it held high above itself on long arms, coughed and fell silent. Axel took his fingers out of his ears and shook his head rapidly. A breeze smelling of hot metal tickled his cheek.

A wide door in the bottom of the craft opened, and a broad ramp extended to touch ground. Men in vacuum armor jumped out and began to take up firing positions. Axel felt warmly happy, despite the fact that two of them had their guns trained on him.

He raised his arms. "I come in peace," he said in High English.

An officer strolled down the ramp. "Are you Chan?"

"The very same. Good to see you, Major."

"I'm sure," said the officer drily. "We don't appreciate being used as a taxi service, *Mister* Chan. Where's your companion?"

He nodded in the direction of the house. "They took her. A little local trouble, I'm afraid. Uh, can I lower my arms now?"

"At ease." The two marines lowered their weapons. "I suppose we'll have to go ask for her back."

"Here," said Axel. He lobbed the pack at the major, who caught it awkwardly. "This should pay our way, once it's been analyzed. And, uh, can we get Marya and get out of this hellhole *now*? I'll bet the swans will be here any second."

The major opened the pack, gagged, and dropped it. "What the hell—?"

"It's a long story," said Axel. "And if you want to hear it, we'd better get a move on."

The major looked from the pack to Axel and back again. Then he whirled and said, "Nonfatal settings! Fan out. I'm going to negotiate a hostage situation." He walked toward the house, paused, and said "Coming?" to Axel.

Axel grinned. "Thanks. Appreciate it."

THREE HOURS LATER, he sat at a viewscreen and watched as Ventus fell away below. Too bad it was night; he would have dearly loved to have traced the course of the journeys he and his companions had made across the land.

Every now and then the display flickered with blue-white light. The Diadem swans were attacking. While they had easily taken out Marya's ship, they were no match for this cruiser, as the captain had pointed out proudly and at length.

Axel was tired, bruised, and chilled to the bone. Soon he would go take that bath he had been dreaming of for months; for now, he couldn't take his eyes off the screen.

Somewhere below Calandria was getting ready to confront Armiger. Axel had argued with the captain for a good hour, trying to convince the man to follow Marya's directions to the queen's palace and interrupt the siege. They probably had enough firepower in this ship to eliminate Armiger; but it had been the god Choronzon who had hired Axel and Calandria to kill Armiger. As far as the Archipelagic military were concerned, the war against 3340 was over.

Axel no longer cared about Armiger, anyway. He just wanted to get Calandria back.

"Hey."

He turned. Marya stood in the doorway. She had cleaned herself up and looked beautiful in a snow-white gown, framed by the door's ivy in warm summerlike light from hidden sconces. She stood barefoot on the genetically tailored grass of the ship's civilian quarters and appeared relaxed and confident, as though she had not been squawling and biting the arms of medieval soldiers earlier in the evening.

"You're amazing," he said.

"You look like hell." She laughed. "Why don't you get some rest? There's nothing more we can do now."

He turned back to the window. "We have to go back," he said. "We're not done here."

She touched his arm. "I know. First we'll have the remains of Turcaret analyzed. They may give us some valuable insights into why the Winds won't talk to us. And then we'll go back for your friends."

"It's just that . . ." He didn't want to say it. Marya waited patiently.

"We have to get Calandria," he said. "She's so obsessed with 3340 and Armiger. Sometimes I think . . . I think she wants to lose. Wants to die, or something worse."

Marya frowned. "We can't save her," she said.

Axel turned back to the viewscreen. Ventus was visibly a globe now, in crescent phase as the ship headed away from the sun. Diadem twinkled brightly above the limb of the horizon.

"If not us," he said, "then who?"

31

"PARLIAMENT'S FORCES ARE on the move," said Matthias. "He's going to try it."

Matthias was in full battle gear—not the gold-worked breastplate and shimmering epaulets Galas had always seen him in before. In plain black leather and iron, he looked like a common soldier now, except for the red flag rising above his back that signaled his rank. Nothing he could have said or done could have projected the gravity of the situation more than this simple change of clothing.

Galas was briefly ashamed. She was dressed as always in velvet and gauze finery. She pictured herself picking up a sword, strapping on a shield and entering the fray like some barbarian queen. She would love that. She would love to do anything rather than what she had to do.

Regally, she nodded to Matthias. "Go then. You have my complete confidence."

"My Lady . . ." For a second his composure cracked. He was an old man suddenly, saddled with an impossible task. They would lose this battle; both knew it.

Galas smiled most carefully; her responsibility now was to act the part for which she had been born. So that these people died believing in . . . something, anything. Even if it was a failed dream.

"Dear Matthias, I only meant I would wish to have no one else in command of my force, now or ever."

"Thank you, Your Majesty." He bowed. "But I have given equal authority over to General Armiger. He will be commanding the defense of the gate."

"Good." He bowed again and turned to leave.

"Matthias?" She couldn't go through with it—perhaps she could hide her true feelings from the rank and file, but it would be unworthy to do so to her closest friends. When he looked back with a puzzled expression, Galas said, "No one should have to die for me."

He glared at her. "You are the rightful monarch and heir, blessed by the Winds. We would all be honored to die to defend you." He walked quickly away.

Galas stared after him. She felt a stab of pain in her chest—sorrow made physical—and hugged herself miserably.

Dawn had just broken. Morning light slanted in through the ruined windows of the great hall. The shattered flame pattern worked in stained glass seemed like a centuries-old joke only now reaching its punchline. To hinder Lavin's men from gaining access to the tower through the thin walls of the hall, Matthias had doused everything in here with oil. This great chamber would be an oven soon.

Men in heavy battle armor ran back and forth, faces blank with concentration or fear. One or two even laughed, but it was forced bravado; they knew she was here, they wanted to prove themselves to her even in this situation.

She should be *doing* something.

"You!" She pointed at one of the running men. He stopped dead in his tracks.

"Your Majesty?"

"I wish to give a ... a final address to the commanders. Are they here?"

He shook his head. "They're dispersed about the walls, Your Highness. To call them back would be ..."

She waved her hand. "Go on. I'm sorry. Go on."

They were bringing in ladders to lean up against the tall windows. She was just in the way now. Galas stepped back to let a procession of men past, then flipped the hem of her dress up over the pooling oil, and stalked back into the tower.

It was even worse in here—pandemonium as blacksmiths, carpenters, and anybody with nothing better to do tore up the floorboards of the tower's back entryway. Armiger had some use for them; no one questioned the sanity of the move. Only half the first floor was wood, anyway; the front reception area had a floor of marble. She hurried, hopping up the wooden servants' stairway while sweating men tore the steps out behind her.

"Can I help?" she asked one of the sappers, who was straining with a crowbar against the ancient wood.

He lost his grip and stumbled. "Your—Your Highness?" He went down on one knee, inadvertently stabbing his shin on an upthrust nail. He ignored the injury and awaited her orders.

She reached out. "Please—I want to help. Tell me what to do."

He jerked back in horror. "Your Highness, no! This is hard work, and it's not safe. You should be above, in the stone halls where fire won't reach."

"I see." She made her face into the royal mask again. With a curt nod, she left the man to his work, ascending to the marble-floored corridor that led to the tower's entrance hall.

She came out on the first landing above the main entrance. This part of the summer palace had been held sacred by the defenders until last night.

It had remained as she remembered it from infancy, the paintings, chandeliers, statuary all in place, the servants ready in their niches. Now the great bronze doors were invisible under piled stone and bracing timbers, and the deep carpets and tapestries were gray with powdered stone and sawdust from the effort of blocking up the entrance. There was no one here now, but overturned tables and other barricades lay ranked like pews aimed at the entrance. Should the attackers get this far, the defenders would assail them from behind these barricades, killing and dying to prevent even so much as a single man from running up the stairs that had been built to welcome visitors. They would all die in the end, of course, and they knew it. Lavin's men would spill into the tower; they would force her duennas up against the walls and kick down her door. By then she would be dead. Everyone knew that, too. But nothing in heaven or earth could alter the course of things.

Except one thing . . .

Galas's breath caught in her throat. She nearly fell, and braced herself on the stone balustrade that she had slid down once as a girl—when she was merely the mad princess.

If she were to die now, the siege would end without further bloodshed. It was simple.

"Oh," she said aloud. If she cast herself from the tower, in full view of both attackers and defenders, then Matthias would live, Armiger and his Megan would live, her maids and cooks and the refugees from the experimental towns would be spared. They would be so disappointed in her, of course; and no one would ever follow the teachings of a suicide.

They won't understand, she thought, as she walked slowly up the flight that led to the audience chamber. "How could they?"

She had no one person to love. Of necessity, she had to love all those around her—her defenders, the naive and idealistic fools who had swallowed her half-truths knowing them for what they were but keeping faith that she had reasons to lie, that she would lead them to earthly salvation. In the end, her written ideology, the philosophy and new morals she had preached, were all means to an end. That end could never be reached; Armiger had taught her that. If so, then what mattered their disappointment, their disillusionment? They would hate her for leaving them alive, but they would *be* alive, and a life lived in bitterness was still better than a death colored by useless fanaticism.

She entered the audience chamber. Three of her duennas stood about the room, looking aimless and scared. They rushed to her when she entered, but said nothing. Their eyes searched out hers.

"Every enlightened path can turn on itself and become a new tyranny," she said. "The process begins the moment you truly, in your heart, believe in yourself."

"Your Highness, are you all right?" Their hands touched her arms, her dress. Like everyone else, they were coping with the fear of death by displacing their concerns on her.

"Leave me!" She stepped out of their grasp. "I am as I have always been."

Before they could answer or follow, she ran across to the side entrance that led to her apartments. Slamming the door behind her, she bolted it.

Two more of her maids stood here in the little chamber where she had met with Lavin. They were staring at her, openmouthed.

"Go away!" She swept past them.

Ah. The stairs to the roof. This was all too simple, really. She had done her best, but the majority of people would simply never understand her. Armiger was right—the only paths forward for humanity lay in the tyranny of some demagogue or an inflexible ideology or, worst of all, the tyranny of condescension. There were no queens or kings in the great interstellar civilization of which Armiger spoke. There was no one who stood in a position to gaze down upon it all.

She was halfway up the steps when her legs gave out. She wasn't winded; some force seemed to push her down against the stones.

It was like a black cloud on the edges of her vision—some thought she was denying herself. What had she been saying to herself just now? Tyranny—yes, the tyranny of condescension. Her reasons for this were—they were . . .

The world had narrowed to the grainy stones centimeters below her. She was gasping, unable to breathe. The kingdom . . . her plans—

Lavin.

She gave a shriek and lurched to her feet, stepping on the hem of her gown and tearing it. Zigzagging, bouncing off the walls of the stairwell, she stumbled to the rooftop.

There were men here; catapults. They were staring out at the smoke. Distant thuds signaled incoming missiles from Lavin's steam cannons.

There was an open coign, across an open span of roof. She had only seconds now to endure this certain knowledge that the one person whom she had loved had come to kill her.

There were no more defenses. The guardian thoughts, her plans, the abstract perfection of her self-built ideology, lay in ruins. Galas was alone with the unendurable pain of her own failure, and so she ran to the edge of the roof with one hope in mind, that the stones of the courtyard would raise a wall against the pain once and for all.

She flung herself forward, saw the stones below and knew release—

—and was pulled back from the brink by shouting men.

Galas screamed and fought and screamed again. Struggling, screaming, she was dragged back across the roof and down the stairs, to the waiting arms of her duennas.

. . .

CALANDRIA MAY STOOD next to one of the steam cannons. She held her section of a long ladder over her head and listened with the other men as their commander told them the riches awaiting those who had volunteered to be first to storm the palace walls.

The steam cannons hissed and bucked, distracting her with its raw primitive power. It was a simple device—just a boiler that aimed its steam at a crude turbine. The turbine turned a wooden wheel like a narrow mill wheel six meters across. Instead of scooping water, its vanes took up gravel and stones and white hunks of rock salt from a hopper underneath, swept it around and up through a covered section and released it at the top of the circle. A steady stream of gravel and stones spewed at the walls, bringing back a crackling sound like a distant rockfall.

Her force was one of ten taking up positions near the main gates of the palace. The steam cannons had swept the walls like brooms, knocking the defenders down or sending them scurrying for cover. Cannons inside the walls were firing back, but they were now firing blind. Every now and then a stream of falling stones would send one of the assault teams to ground. Some men were hit, and when they fell they often didn't get up again.

Taking the main gates directly was impossible. The portcullis was inset by about four meters, and the ceiling of the entranceway was full of murder holes. The defenders were waiting to pour molten lead on anyone who tried to enter that way.

Lavin's army was on the move all across the valley. The long wall that surrounded the palace would be assaulted in at least ten places within her sight, and she had no doubt Lavin had forces coming in from the north as well. There was no way the besieged force could man the entire stretch of wall. They would have to pull back.

When they did, it would be to the tower that loomed above the main gates. Everything important would happen there. The queen was there. Armiger would be there, too.

A sword hung from Calandria's belt. Over her back was slung a long, burlap-wrapped object that clanked when she moved. The microwave gun was heavy, but it was the only thing in the arsenal of nanotech seeds from Marya's ship that stood a chance of knocking down Armiger. When flights of stones rained down from beyond the walls, Calandria moved to shelter it before covering her own head. Without it, she had no reason to be here.

A distant roar reached her ears. A kilometer down the valley, the first assault wave ran forward, carrying their ladders like gangs of ants. Figures on horseback gestured with swords. Behind them, the steam cannons inched closer to the walls.

Her heart was hammering. When she looked around, she saw the same expression of mindless fear in the eyes of the men with her. They were all in the same boat—carried forward by habits of training, minds blank with fear hence too stupid to sensibly turn and run. It was this stupor of fear that would later be counted as courage.

A loud *crack* sounded from ahead; the sound echoed across the valley and back. Looking up she saw a section of the gate tower's wall tumbling outward in a cloud of dust. The heavier cannons stationed a hundred meters behind her had found a weak point. Now a black hole became visible under the drifting gray pall.

"That's it, lads! Our door!" The commander bellowed and windmilled his arms, and Calandria found herself running forward with the others, thinking nothing, looking everywhere for a place to hide, a foxhole, a barricade, anywhere out of sight of the men with her who would see her hide; and they too looked around with the same eyes and continued to run.

For a while she had to concentrate on her footwork, chained as she was to her companions by the heavy ladder. When she next looked up they were under the walls, and dark smoke was pouring out of the hole in the gate tower.

Sand exploded where she'd been about to step. Nearby someone screamed. She heard heavy bangs that must be musket fire. The ladder jiggled. Someone cursed monotonously over and over again; others coughed and over it all lay the rattle of falling rocks, the thud of footfalls, and distant booming.

"Halt!" She halted. "Ladder up!" She hopped, pushing it as it miraculously lofted up onto the perspective-narrowed white wall of the tower. The rockfall noises had stopped, meaning the steam cannons had been turned away to let them climb; but that also meant the defenders could emerge from hiding.

Sure enough, more stones and musket balls were coming down. She reached back, feeling the burlap for any sign it had been hit. No.

The first men went up the ladder. Two promptly fell down again. Everyone had their shields up, grinning humorlessly at one another under their shadow as unidentifiable stuff thudded off the wood.

The mob pressed her forward, and suddenly Calandria was climbing, squashed between a man ahead and a man behind her.

Up twelve rungs, over a broken one, left hand closing on splinters, right on slick blood. The man above her stopped, began cursing wildly. Everyone below shouted at him. "I'm hurt, I'm hurt!" he cried; drops of blood hit Calandria's arm as he struggled with his shattered shoulder.

"Get off! We don't give a damn! Boy, cut his hamstrings! Get him off the ladder or we're all done for!"

She glanced down. The fall would kill him. "Do it!" shouted Maenan, who was on the ladder behind her. "Do it or I'll cut you down and do it myself."

Something big fell by her left shoulder. Calandria drew the knife from her waist and reached up. "You've got to move," she shouted at the injured man.

"I can't jump," he screamed. "I'll die!"

Maenan stabbed Calandria in the ankle. She cursed and thrust upward herself.

"You bastard," whimpered the injured man. "Bastard." He shot her a deeply offended look. He was barely twenty-five if that, with black stubble, dark eyebrows, and surprisingly long eyelashes above his blue eyes. "Bastard," he said, blinking, and then he let go of the ladder.

Just climb. She did, but she was crying.

There was screaming above. Another dark shape plummeted past. Before she knew it Calandria was at the hole in the wall, sucking lungfulls of wood smoke. Blinded, she groped for the broken stones and pulled herself into the breach.

It was hot here—burning hot. Somebody was crowding her from behind, so she had no choice but to go forward and suddenly realizing she was stepping into a fire she staggered and went down on one knee.

Flames licked up her leg. Calandria screamed and flung herself forward, rolling past burning logs and coming to a crouch on the inside of a very large hearth. The smoking body of a man lay across the logs next to her. In the lurid light of the fire she saw men struggling in a large triangular room.

The defenders were picking off her people as each one staggered out of the broken fireplace. Everyone who came up this ladder was going to die.

A sword swung down, clipping her arm and sending a spasm of pain through her shoulder. Calandria rolled, did a sweep with her foot and was rewarded as her attacker fell over. She vaulted over him and straight-armed the man behind him. The room was a maze of armed men; she ducked and kicked and tried to get to the door.

Swords fell across her back and jabbed her flanks. Her package clanked. She cursed and redoubled her efforts.

She got turned around and ended up in a corner. It was slaughter over by the fireplace. Maenan was dead, as was every one of the men she had met over the last several days. Three desperate defenders faced her now, with more behind them.

She had hoped to delay using her weapon until she confronted Armiger—and not only because its presence would alert the Winds. "Sorry," she said, and swung the package off her shoulder. She pulled the burlap off the gun and raised it just as they closed on her.

The microwave gun chuffed, and fire shot to left and right from its barrel as first of its nano-built energy charges let go. The man in front of her coughed and went down. She turned the weapon on the next one and then the next. She was screaming now, tears streaming down her face making it hard to see.

As soon as the door was clear she ran for it. The only thought in her head was to find Armiger *now* and free herself from having to kill anyone else.

She found herself on the battlements. Two walls ran from this gate tower to the main tower of the palace, forming a narrow avenue. There were two steam cannons down there, ready to send their streams of gravel at anyone who made it through the gates or—

—made it onto the walls.

She saw the blur of flying rocks an instant before they tore the flagstones from under her.

LAVIN HAD GIVEN his instructions. There was nothing he could do now but trust Hesty and the other commanders. He hated to leave the siege in the middle, but he was doing the right thing. For the first time in months, he felt calm, in control of the situation.

"Where's our grave robber?" He snapped his fingers impatiently.

"Here, Lord." Enneas jogged up. The man looked much better than he had a few days ago; his ruined back was covered in salves and bandages, then the protective casing of a breastplate. His broken arm was in a cast, and the bruises on his face were almost faded. He saluted with his free hand.

Lavin nodded to him. "We're going in."

They stood among the tumbled stones of the ruined temple a kilometer east of the summer palace. From here, a sand-drifted causeway led to a square gate tower that had once been the main entrance to the palace. The gates of that tower had long since been sealed with heavy stones, and the causeway was left to the mercies of the desert. What Enneas and a few others had known, however, was that other processional causeways built in the same era as this one all contained narrow passages deep inside the masonry. Lavin's sappers had found the "spirit walk" right where Enneas had said it would be. They had penetrated all the way to the palace and turned back only when they came to the labyrinth of the old catacombs. Enneas would be the guide through those; more than that, he was Lavin's good-luck charm.

"You understand the plan," Lavin said to Hesty as he followed Enneas into the dark square mouth that opened under a half-fallen wall of yellow stone. "The assault on the walls is a diversion, but it has to genuinely tie up their forces. We want to pull them out of the tower to the walls. My force will penetrate the tower and take the queen. When we signal by trumpet you will cease the assault."

Hesty shook his head. "I understand that. What I don't understand is why you have to be the one to go inside."

"I'm the one who's responsible. And I want to ensure the queen's safety."

"It's dangerous, sir. If you die—"

"Then you continue the assault until we've taken the queen by other means. What I'm trying to do is end this by the cleanest possible means. It's worth risking myself at this point."

He stared Hesty down. Finally the man saluted. "All right." Lavin ducked his head and entered the cool darkness of the tunnel. Enneas waited there with fifteen men, the elite of Lavin's personal guard.

Four of the men had bugles; three had bull's-eye lanterns. They were crowded into a little antechamber next to a narrow slot in the wall. Had he not known this was a tunnel, Lavin would have taken it for a chink between two of the causeway's huge foundation stones.

"M'lord." Enneas took one of the lanterns and, turning sideways, slid into the gap. Lavin watched him worm his way in, expecting to see him get stuck at any moment. He kept going, however, and after a moment Lavin reined in his own fear and followed.

Cold stone pressed against him from all sides. He had to turn his head and shuffle sideways, keeping an eye fixed on the wavering light of Enneas's lantern. If that light were to vanish he might give in to fear here, though he never had on the field of battle.

He went a hundred meters like this, panic rising gradually as he came to understand just how far underground he was. Finally the passage opened up a bit, and he was able to crowd in next to Enneas, who had paused to wait for him.

"This is my domain," said the old man. "The discarded trash of the noble lifestyle. Look." He held up the lantern; the light glittered off metal near the floor.

"What's this?"

"Offerings to the Winds of the earth," said Enneas, his voice rich with contempt. The lantern light glittered off coins and some brass candlesticks that lay half buried in the sand. "You see these words?" He indicated some lettering scratched into the walls. "It's a letter from the foreman of the work gang here, to the Winds, asking them to bless his family for the offerings." He snorted. "I could live for six months off the coins here."

Lavin admired his passion, but shook his head anyway. "For all you know, the Winds did bless his house. Come, we've no time to dawdle."

Enneas went on, grumbling. Lavin's men padded quietly behind as they wove through a low undulant tunnel with a sandy floor. The air was cold and dead, and it would have been silent except that faint drumbeat thuds sounded at irregular intervals. *Steam cannon impact*, he realized.

As they progressed, the intermittent thumps grew louder and louder, until with each one dust and grit shook loose from the low ceiling. Enneas glanced back several times, a worried look on his face. Lavin gestured for him to keep going.

After one particularly solid thump, a low sliding noise came from ahead of them. It went on for a few seconds. When silence fell again Lavin could hear Enneas swearing.

"What is it?"

"I don't want to speculate. Come on." They went forward faster now. The air was becoming thick with dust; Lavin could barely seen the glow of the lantern now. His fear of the confinement was gone now, replaced by a very real worry about the effect his bombardment was having on the tunnel.

Enneas cursed loudly. Lavin bumped against him; he had stopped.

The old grave robber waved the lantern, showing how the walls leaned in suddenly, and tumbled stone choked the remaining space between them.

Enneas looked over his shoulder; the faint light silhouetted him, so that he looked like a man-shaped hole amidst the amber angles of stone. "It's a cave-in," he said. "We're stuck."

32

JORDAN AND TAMSIN rose within a column of water, past strata of worn stone in all the colors of the rainbow. Light filtered down from somewhere far above, illuminating the glistening membrane of the bubble in which they traveled. Never in all his imaginative journeys had Jordan pictured such a place as this. Every now and then they passed giant slots in the walls of the shaft, in which he glimpsed galleries full of verdigrised machines. Then the thrumming of giant engines would make the membrane of their bubble shake and dance; ring-shaped standing waves would form in the meniscus and interfere, making little landscapes of jewellike diamonds in its resilient surface.

Tamsin had conquered her fear—in fact, she was now bolder than Jordan. She kept trying to climb the curving wall of the bubble to see some new wonder. She would slide back and bump him with elbow or knee.

Whenever they passed one of those titanic chambers, Jordan's heart seemed to skip a beat. He sensed the forces gathered here, and felt awe. But he stared into the green depths and said to himself, *this is our creation*, and repeating it, felt the awe deepen and merge with a new emotion he couldn't name.

It was like the first time his mother had let him hold the hand of a younger boy to lead him along the path from the village to Castor's manor. He was entrusted with a responsibility, and felt humbly determined to carry it through.

The Winds were omnipotent. They were also lost and, he now believed, afraid. The assault of the Heaven hooks on the Boros manor now seemed to him an act of desperation on their part. They would never be so mindlessly destructive in the normal course of things.

He and Tamsin rose upon the palm of Mediation until the light above became a wavering disk and the shaft opened out to all sides. They were in a lake or lagoon, still rising. Before he could say anything, they slid sideways, and the bubble collapsed just as they were about to reach the surface.

For a second all he felt was freezing cold. Jordan kicked out into a confusion of bubbles and white froth and was on the edge of panic when he felt a surface below his feet. He let himself settle for a moment, then kicked up from it and drew a deep breath of air.

Tamsin was swimming vigorously for the nearby shore. Awkwardly he pushed himself to follow her. Coughing and shivering, he stumbled up a beach of white pebbles to collapse next to her. She was already on her feet, hands on her hips as she stared around them.

They were on the shore of a pond that nestled among golden dunes. There was a little grass next to the pond, but no trees or sign of human habitation. The dunes hid whatever else might be nearby.

"So," said Tamsin. She was frowning. "Where are we, then?"

"I don't know. Ka?"

"I am here," said the little Wind, from somewhere in the vicinity of Jordan's collar.

The slight breeze was cuttingly cold. He stood up, shuddering.

"Command some heat," said Tamsin.

"In a minute." He looked around, found the tallest dune, and headed in that direction.

They said nothing as they climbed the sliding side of the thing. It took longer than he expected, and by the time they reached the top they were both covered with sand that stuck to their wet clothes and skin like plaster.

"Damned desals," muttered Tamsin. "They could at least have gotten us to shore."

It was even colder up here in the breeze, but you could see forever. Jordan shielded his eyes from the watery sun and turned slowly.

"Oh." He pointed. "We go that way."

"How do you know—" She stopped when she saw where he was pointing.

At least twenty thin spires of smoke rose above an indistinct patch on the western horizon.

"THEY'VE TAKEN THE middle tower!" The bearer of the bad news was black with soot and bleeding from a wound in his shoulder. The gangs by the steam cannons stopped working and fell into a confused battle of talk. Armiger shrugged.

"Let them have it. Makes a bigger target."

This comment was relayed down the line, eliciting an uncertain cheer from the gunners. "So shall we turn the beasts on the tower, then?" asked one.

They were set up in the center of the palace parade grounds, east of the queen's walled garden. From here the cannons could be aimed anywhere except at the houses northwest of the keep. From here Armiger could see and judge most of the action, but not what was taking place there. What he could see was smoke and chaos at six points along the walls; fires in the tent town and boiling mobs of refugees trying to get into the great hall or over the walls into the garden. The mobs were getting in the way of Matthias's mobile squads, who were supposed to be crisscrossing the grounds quickly to tend to potential breaches. They were bogged down amid screaming women and children, unable to reach the trouble spots along the southern walls.

The only really important news came from the semaphores. Armiger let his glance touch on each of the flag teams in turn, filling in a mental picture of how Lavin's forces were arrayed around the palace.

"He's up to something." This was no determined assault—just a lot of smoke and bluster. Armiger had no idea what Parliament's general might be planning, and that worried him far more than the loss of the gate tower.

"Forget the tower, load the charges like I showed you!" He waved his sword in a tight circle over his head. All down the line, the gunners began lighting the sacks he'd prepared last night. Then as the great wheels of the cannons began to turn, they fed the smoking bundles into the hoppers.

"What good will this do?" whined one of Matthias's lieutenants. The man was a tenth-generation noble, completely ineffectual. He was positioned here, away from the walls, so he could do as little harm as possible. "All those things do is make a stink. That's not going to stop Lavin."

"You'd be surprised," said Armiger. The sacks were filled with a combination of pitch, oil, wood, offal, and metal shavings, designed to produce a good imitation of industrial smog. The Winds would pay little attention to wood smoke, however large the conflagration, since it mostly just released carbon that trees had previously fixed from the atmosphere anyway. This stuff, though, would loose ozone, sulfur dioxide, maybe a little cyanide into the atmosphere. With an extra whiff of hot metals for good measure, it should whip the Winds into a fury.

He watched with satisfaction as the first of the smoking bags lofted over the walls. The environmental insult would be coming from Lavin's camp. Lavin would know what he was doing; the fatal results of the battle where Armiger had first used sulfur were widely known now.

"We should be sweeping those walls clean!" The lieutenant pointed.

Armiger shook his head. "Just wait. And be ready to run for cover."

He would have preferred to have used this tactic as soon as the assault started, but he had wanted to make sure that Lavin's camp no longer contained enough men to extinguish these fume bombs. The attackers were engaged at the walls now; in the chaos, this smoke should be overlooked.

"What do you mean, run for cover?"

"I mean you might want to dig a hole and bury yourself in it now, because they may decide to take away all the buildings when they get here."

"They? . . ." The lieutenant's face went pale.

Armiger watched him with amusement. "This is no time for half measures."

The gunners were well into the rhythm of it now. Time to turn his attention elsewhere. Armiger strolled away from them, leaving the lieutenant stuttering.

He had to trust that he was still invisible to the Winds. With luck they would concentrate their fury on Parliament's encampment. He certainly hoped he could get everyone inside and under cover before the forces of the Ventus terraforming system arrived.

It was the biggest risk he had taken since coming to this world. He was deliberately inviting the scrutiny of the Winds. Nothing else about this siege could threaten his existence or his plans. From a strategic point of view, risking a meeting with the Winds now was idiotic.

Armiger didn't care. There were people he felt for in the palace. He would surely survive this assault, and he could probably escape with Megan, but Galas was the queen bee, the attackers would swarm her the instant they glimpsed her. No, it was better to annihilate Lavin's forces using the Winds and hope that they left the ordinary stone and wood of the palace alone.

He read the situation from the semaphores again and made his decision. The chaos of battle was reaching its peak. Under its cover, he would be able to spirit Megan and Galas away from this place. If all went according to schedule, the Winds would arrive after his escape and pin down Lavin's forces, giving Armiger and his people time to complete their escape.

He ran for the keep. Missiles rained down into the nearby tents of the refugees. Armiger tried not to think about their fate or that of the men on the battlements, who were fighting and dying to ensure his escape.

"There is a way," said Enneas. He began pulling down rocks with his good hand. "See there? That crack?"

They had all the lanterns here now, and everybody who could be was crammed up against the rock fall. Lavin focused on breathing deeply to still his claustrophobia. He was afraid he would have an attack of his old vertigo here, and that was the worse thing that could possibly happen.

The little chink Enneas had found looked impossibly small to get through. The old robber picked up one of the lanterns and stuck his arm in it, then twisted to peer after it. "Yes!" he shouted excitedly. "I can see right through."

"We can't get through that," grumbled somebody.

"*You* can't," agreed the thief. He sized up the men pressed up against him. "I can; I'm little. He can, so can he . . ." He appraised Lavin. "And so can you, sir. But we'll have to remove our armor."

Lavin's throat was dry. Worm into that little crack? With a thousand tonnes of stone poised to collapse on him?

He glanced at the faces of his men. They were determined. Enneas seemed positively jubilant; this kind of challenge appeared to be what he lived for.

"All right," said Lavin. "You first, thief. Show us how to shove a mouse through a keyhole."

Enneas began unlacing his armor. "This is going to hurt," he muttered. "Doing it one-handed will be hard. I'll need some help."

In the end it took two men on either side and one underneath to slide Enneas into the chink. He left his lantern behind, held his broken arm tight to his side and pulled himself into pitch darkness on his scabbed back with no complaints.

"Damn," whispered the man next to Lavin. "I would never have believed it."

Lavin grinned. "Pass him his lantern."

"Come on!" Enneas waved from the other side. "It's clear from here on in."

When it was his turn, Lavin, too, went without complaint. The thief was a braver man than he, it seemed. Life never tired of teaching new lessons.

They were able to get the four smallest men inside along with Lavin and Enneas. This was not the force Lavin needed for his first plan, which had been to sneak in, grab the queen, and sneak out again. There were enough men to try his second plan, which was to steal into the queen's chambers, take her, and dangle her from a window until the defenders surrendered. For that plan, he needed only enough men to hold a doorway for some critical minutes.

They were all dressed in the colors of the royalists, which should help; it still depended on how many soldiers were now in the tower. If Hesty had done his work, they were spread out on the walls, ready to fall back when Lavin's forces made it onto the grounds.

Hesty had been instructed to wait two hours before exploiting any breach. Lavin didn't want the defenders rabbiting up the palace steps too soon.

The others passed them their armor and weapons, and when they were ready Lavin gestured with his chin, and they moved forward into broader and quieter precincts.

Enneas seemed happy now, despite having opened the wounds on his back. He hummed as he looked around himself alertly. "Nearly there," he said after some time. "Look for a side passage."

They found it, right where Enneas had said it would be. The space was little more than a crawlway, but the thief slipped into it without difficulty, and the others followed. This passage had been dug through the sandy soil under the palace, and soil crumbled and fell in Lavin's eyes and mouth with each pull he made to follow Enneas. Blinking and coughing, he finally sat up next to the thief to discover they were at the bottom of an eight-foot-deep pit. The ceiling above the pit was of fitted stone, arching toward some pillar out of sight.

"Old cistern," said Enneas. "We're at the farthest extent of the catacombs. It's a maze, so follow close and don't take any turnoffs on your own." He looked at them expectantly. "Well? Somebody give me a boost."

When they were up and ready to set off after Enneas, Lavin nodded to one of his men. He had given him a sack of copper pennies earlier, and now that man took up the rear, and dropped a penny every few meters. Lavin didn't want to have to rely on Enneas to find his way out of here.

They came to a stone staircase leading up. "That's it," said Enneas. "Those stairs take you to the lower servants' way, and there's a door there that exits right into the front hall of the palace."

"I've seen it," said Lavin. "Thanks. You stay here and wait for us."

"Gladly," said the thief.

Lavin walked up the steps, took a turn, opened a door, and despite his confidence was somehow still surprised to find himself standing in the empty entrance hall below Galas's audience chamber.

CALANDRIA ROLLED OVER. Her head was pounding, and her shoulders and right arm were very sore. She looked up, saw smoke, raised her head and heard shouting and the roar of muskets.

She lay on the parapet of one of the walls stretching from the gate to the main tower. Rocks and flinders of stone lay all around her. Several bloody bodies dotted the walkway nearer the gate.

Where was her gun? Levering herself up, she spotted the microwave gun lying a few meters away. It appeared unharmed. She was superficially battered, her helmet dented, face and shoulders bruised, but otherwise unharmed.

She crab walked over to the gun, then crouched under the crenels away from the sweep of the steam cannons below. They had stopped their deadly barrage in any case; it looked like the assault on the tower had failed.

For a while she stayed there. She didn't want to think about where she was or what she had done to get here. The things she would have to do next might be worse.

She knew what Armiger looked like from Jordan's descriptions. He might be anywhere within the acres of palace grounds. She was betting he would be in the tower, with the queen.

It seemed insane to move, but her use of the microwave gun might bring the Winds down on the palace anyway. Using it, she could clear a path through any number of defenders. She couldn't bring herself to turn it on human opponents again, however. She would find another way in.

Something was burning in the courtyard near the main doors. The smoke was rich and gray, and it made a smothering pall that hid the spot where her wall met the outside wall of the keep. Steps led down at that point, but she wouldn't use them; no doubt the main doors were securely barricaded by now.

There was a row of narrow windows seven meters above the point where the wall met the keep. Later there might be soldiers at those windows firing down into the courtyard; for now they were open and unmanned.

Calandria took off her boots and tied them over her shoulder. Then she started to climb the chipped and cracked face of the keep.

"I CAN'T BELIEVE our luck," said Lavin. They were at the doors to the audience chamber. There was no one about.

One of his men shrugged. "Your plan worked perfectly, sir." His tone suggested no other outcome had been possible.

The sounds of the siege penetrated, as did the smell of smoke. In all his plans, Lavin had assumed the tower would be a hive of running men and hawk-eyed commandants. His strategy in this battle had been to draw the queen's force out to minimize the numbers here, but he had never dreamed it would work so well.

He revised his plans. They might be able to smuggle the queen out of here, after all.

A scout eased the door open a crack and peered through. "I see no one . . . wait, there's one man."

"What's he doing?"

"Walking. Must have just gone up the stairs ahead of us and paused here for a second or something."

"Let me see." Lavin motioned him aside. They had agreed on how to deal with simple soldiers: they would walk right by them. Lavin might be recognizable to some officers and the generals, but to few others. And they were all dressed in the queen's livery.

So this man should present no problem. . . .

Lavin cursed under his breath when he saw who it was. General

Armiger walked slowly, his head down as if musing, hands clasped behind his back. He wore scrolled black armor, with a commander's flag jutting over his shoulder. He would notice any commotion, and Lavin had no doubt he knew where all his troops were supposed to be. They would have to kill him now, and as quietly as possible.

"Your invincible queen has tried to kill herself."

For an instant Lavin felt the words had been spoken to him; his heart almost stopped. Then he spotted the woman who had spoken. She stepped from the shadows of the doorway to the antechamber where Lavin had dined with Galas.

General Armiger took her in his arms, and she rested her cheek against his breastplate. "It is my fault," he said.

"What?" She drew back a little, looking up at him.

"I told her the truth. I took away her hope."

"She's only human, after all." The woman sighed. "Does that disappoint you?"

Lavin blinked. It couldn't be true. She would have held faith to the very end, in the face of any opposition. He knew her. Nothing could shake her confidence in her own ideals. Had he thought she could fall prey to despair, Lavin would have done anything he had to in his negotiations to ensure this assault did not happen. He would have made concessions.

If Galas despaired, then they had both lost, for that would mean the woman he had come to rescue no longer existed.

He forced himself to focus on the present situation. "We will walk in casually. Kasham, step behind him as we pass. Bahner, do likewise with the woman. A blade in the heart, then drag them behind the throne."

The men nodded. Lavin stood straight and swung the door open.

Armiger was walking quickly toward the far door. The woman stood where they had embraced, looking after him.

Lavin raised a hand, and his men halted in silence. Armiger reached the door to the antechamber and passed through it without looking back.

Lavin caught Bahmer's eye and shook his head. Bahmer shrugged. Then they entered the room.

The woman turned, noted them with indifference, and walked to one of the tall windows on the right. She stared out as they passed by. Lavin led his men left to the antechamber, and they were through, as simply as that.

He stepped boldly into the corridor beyond the antechamber. A stone staircase led up to the left, and two broad wood-paneled corridors radiated right and ahead. There was a deep carpet on the floor, and portrait paintings on the walls. These must be her apartments.

A man in servant's livery ran up. Lavin forced himself to stand perfectly still, although his heart was hammering. "Are you looking for the general, sir?" asked the servant.

"The queen, actually." He felt his men shifting uneasily behind him.

They were close to breaking strain, he knew—any slight provocation now and they would unsheath their swords. He prayed they would remain as cool as he pretended to be.

"The queen is . . . indisposed," said the servant. "General Armiger is with her."

"Where?"

"Her closet, at the end of this corridor, but sir, General Armiger said they were not to be disturbed. He ordered even the duennas to leave."

Lavin sniffed. "This is critical to ending the siege," he said, and walked on.

They passed two more servants and five of the queen's maids, one of whom Lavin recognized. None looked at them. Then they were at the queen's door.

33

THEY WERE IN sight of the palace walls when Jordan began to hear the song. It came from directly overhead, far above the smoky air and late autumn clouds. The last time he'd heard something remotely like this, the sky had been filling with vagabond moons at the Boros estate. The sky was empty now.

Periodically as they trudged toward the siege, Jordan had paused and closed his eyes to watch the events there unfolding through Armiger's eyes. He knew an assault on the palace was in full swing, but beyond that everything was confused. Armiger seemed to be moving purposefully, but since he didn't talk to himself he wasn't letting Jordan in on his thoughts.

"Going in there is suicide," Tamsin had said when he told her of the assault. "We need to stop and wait for it to end."

Maybe. But Jordan feared that the seemingly empty landscape around them would erupt at any second with minions of Thalience. He could easily be caught by them before they reached the palace.

Only Armiger could oppose the Winds. Compared to them, the threat of these human armies seemed almost trivial.

"We have to tell him about Mediation and Thalience," he told her. "He would have acted by now if he knew exactly what was going on. I don't believe the queen told him what he needed to know."

Tamsin started to answer, then seemed to think better of it. She glanced over her shoulder, eyes catching the leagues of open sand that lay between herself and her devastated home.

"None of us knows what we're doing, do we?" she said in a small voice.

Jordan looked at her, surprised. "No," he said finally. "Not even him, I guess."

"What about the swans?"

"The Winds of Mediation take care of the earth," he said. "Maybe if we can find somewhere underground to hide, we can escape the swans."

Tamsin squinted upward. "The sun's a funny color."

"I don't want to hear it." He shut his eyes briefly, inner vision trembling between Armiger and kaleidoscopic images from the siege. As had happened at the Boros manor, the local landscape was excited, stones, wood, and plants all trading images and sounds on some frequency they rarely used. Jordan could see through their eyes when they did this; he saw fighting figures on the ground from the vantage point of smoke rising above the towers. He saw both inside and outside the great hall of the summer palace, where tense soldiers waited with tinder and flint to light a new and vastly larger conflagration should Parliament's forces breach the walls. He heard the confused shouts, the screams, and he heard weeping as he saw Armiger's hands reach to undo the ropes that bound the queen of Iapysia to a gilded chair in her chambers.

"Ka," said Jordan. "I need your help now."

"YOU TOLD ME the truth," said Galas. "That is why I decided to end it." She stood shakily, massaging her wrists where the ropes had chafed.

Armiger shook his head angrily. "We have more important things to worry about than your kingdom." He threw down the ropes.

Galas's maids cowered in the corners of the opulent bed chamber. Two soldiers stood uncertainly by the door; they had been placed there to guard the queen against herself, and were suffering the abuse of the maids when Armiger entered.

Galas smoothed back her hair with one hand, staring wildly about herself. "What?" She turned and looked at him in puzzlement. "What did you just say?"

"You have a greater responsibility now," he said. "More than your kingdom is at stake."

Galas laughed. She tried to stifle the sound with her hand, but it kept coming, and she reeled toward the window, bent over, hands to her mouth. When she could speak again, she shouted, "And what about *me*? What say do I have in this? Or do I have none? Who gets to sacrifice me on their altar? Parliament? Lavin? *You*?"

The door swung back with a crash and five armed soldiers paced in. Their swords were drawn. The last one in shut the door behind himself and threw the latch.

"Galas," said the man at the head of the group, "I am afraid I must ask you to surrender."

Her two guards were suddenly against the wall with swords to their throats. The other two men had their blades leveled at Armiger.

"Lavin." She felt a deep feeling of cold wash over her. "You did come."

"I came to ensure your safety," said Lavin. "I said I'd let no one harm you. And I won't."

"Then the palace has fallen."

"Yes," said Lavin.

"No," said Armiger. "He has snuck in somehow. That's why you ordered your men not to come over the walls, isn't it? To keep our forces away?"

Lavin nodded curtly. "Kindly kneel on the floor, general. You, too." He indicated the others in the room. "We are going to strike you unconscious; there's not enough rope to bind everyone. Anyone who struggles will be killed." He stepped up to Galas. "You will accompany us, Your Highness. If you try to call for help I have instructed my men to kill you." For a second he looked dizzy; he clutched at the back of the chair where Galas had been bound. "I can't do it myself. But it must be done, if there is no alternative."

"Your Highness?" said one of her men. "Give the word and we will throw these traitors out the window."

"Do as he says," she said hoarsely. "There is no point in your dying, too."

"But Your Highness—"

"Do it!"

The maids and the two guards knelt in a line. Two of Lavin's men stepped behind them. Galas flinched as the crying maids were struck down one by one, and the men who had stayed to protect her life. In moments they lay silent on the floor. One of the women had stopped breathing; blood pooled behind her ear. Galas stared at it until Lavin took her arm.

"Good-bye, General," Lavin said. The soldier standing behind Armiger raised his sword and slammed the pommel down on the back of Armiger's neck. There was a loud *crack*, but Armiger didn't even blink.

Armiger held the man's sword arm before anyone could react, and then he was on his feet. With a casual motion he tossed the man out the window. For a shocked moment no one moved.

"No noise!" commanded Lavin. He grabbed Galas by the arm and pulled her out of the way as his other three men raised their swords to stab Armiger.

One staggered back, his own sword in his gut. The other two whirled, for Armiger was no longer where he had been.

Hands like iron clamped onto Galas's wrists, and then Armiger was hauling her toward the door. Lavin leaped to intercede, and Armiger side kicked him. The general was sent flying into a wardrobe, shattering it.

"We must get you to safety," said Armiger. His voice was flat, his grip on Galas's arm like iron. He towed the queen out into the corridor, where several servants stood, looking bewildered and offended at his handling of the queen.

She was still half stunned. Had that really been Lavin? It looked like him. "How did he get in here?" she heard herself ask.

Armiger stopped abruptly, making her stumble. "Good point," he said. "I'll interrogate him. You find Megan."

"What do you mean?"

"It's time to leave." He took her by the shoulders and looked into her eyes. He seemed completely unruffled by what had just occurred. "The Diadem swans are coming," he said. "They may well obliterate Lavin's army. I broke the rules of war, Galas. I deliberately involved the Winds."

Galas shook her head. "Don't hurt Lavin."

For the first time he looked surprised. "If you wish." He let her go and turned.

"General Armiger?"

The voice was that of a woman. They both looked up, to find what at first seemed to be a soldier boy standing by the doors to the roof. It was a woman in bloodied armor. She had an oval face, dark brows and black hair that lay now in dusty tangles. She held something like a mirrored crossbow in her hands.

"Get Megan," said Armiger. He thrust Galas behind himself just as the woman's gleaming weapon spat fire.

Armiger screamed. Galas made herself run and not look back—around the corner, the way they had come.

And there stood Lavin, truly him this time, grim with his sword drawn.

"Come," he said, and reached for her.

Galas snatched her hand back. All her confusion and resentment boiled over. "Never! You destroyed me!"

"In time you'll understand why I had to do it," he said as he reached for her again.

"Help me!" At her cry, all the doors in the corridor opened, and her servants poured forth.

Then Lavin had her wrist and twisted her arm behind her painfully. She felt the blade of his sword slide past her throat. "Back off!" he shouted. The servants stopped, their makeshift weapons raised.

"Idiots!" she screamed. "Kill him!"

In the moment while they hesitated Lavin pulled her to the end of the corridor, where it met the one that led to the stairs. She caught a confused glimpse of shattered wood and stone here, smoking embers on the carpet. A loud explosion sounded somewhere nearby; she felt a wave of heat and suddenly the ceiling split open like a ripe fruit. Lavin pulled her back just in time as beams and stonework clogged the corridor behind them.

She coughed; Lavin's sword nicked her throat. She heard him panting, heard herself cry out in pain from the way he twisted her arm. He dragged her along the hall, spun her around, and suddenly she saw Armiger. He lay on his face at the foot of the stairs. His armor was smoking. Over him stood the black-haired woman, weapon aimed at his head.

A musket shot spiked Galas's ears. The woman spun around and fell, limbs akimbo. Soldiers were coming down the stairs from the roof; one threw aside his smoking musket and drew his sword as he approached her.

Galas saw the woman's foot lash out to trip the man, then Lavin had her through the door into the antechamber of the audience chamber.

Lavin spun her around again, shoving her ahead of him now. She was dazed, but beginning to think again. She should just let him kill her. Or just fall like a dead weight that he could never carry. They entered the audience chamber. Megan stood by the throne, hands clasped nervously. "Your Highness? . . ."

"Go to Armiger," she shouted. "He's hurt!"

Megan ran past them. Lavin picked up his pace, so they were trotting when they reached the main doors.

She needed to know what had happened to Armiger, Galas realized. That he and his woman survive was suddenly as important to her as Megan's survival had been to him. It was simply this that made her decide not to slide her throat along Lavin's sword and vindictively bleed to death in his arms.

"You're a snake," she said. "I can't believe I loved you."

"I don't mind your cursing me," he said. "As long as you're cursing me, at least you're still alive."

"And I will curse you, as long as I do live!"

They were on the marble landing. "I know," he said. "I knew the price when I took on the task."

ARMIGER ROLLED OVER, gasping. His human body was nearly dead again. He had seen the microwaves from the woman's weapon, a blinding corona that had burst inside his body like a sun. His cells were in chaos; the nanotech skein of his real body was broken and burned. Another blast and he would have been incapacitated; three or four more and the damage would have been too much to recover from.

His human eyes could not see, but he sensed Megan above him. "My soldier," she whispered, as she drew him into her arms.

He reached out with his other senses. His attacker had been subdued; two soldiers sat on her back now as she struggled vainly. Her weapon lay neglected under smoking wood panels that it had blown from the wall.

The woman's voice carried suddenly. She had stopped struggling. "This man tried to kill the queen," she said. Her voice was calm, liquid, as convincing as any orator's. With his nanotech's sensors, Armiger could see that she lay facing him. Her eyes were open, searching out his. Her face was a mask.

A deeper sound reached his senses. Armiger cursed weakly. "Help me up," he said to Megan.

"No, you're hurt, don't move."

"They're here," he said. "The Winds. We have to get out of here."

"Oh—but you can't move!"

"I can. Help me!" She helped him up and he stood, blind and bent, above the woman who had attacked him. When he felt strong enough, he knelt and gathered up the weapon his mysterious attacker had used on him. He felt the galactic workmanship immediately. This woman was from the Archipelago, doubtless a mercenary sent to pick off stragglers such as himself from 3340's force.

"Sir!" A soldier saluted. "What shall we do with her, sir?"

"Bind her in chains of iron," he said. "But strike her unconscious first."

"Sir."

He staggered into the antechamber, leaning heavily on Megan. "Where did they go?" he hissed.

"Who?"

"The queen, and General Lavin."

"This way. Please, you must rest."

"No! There is a secret way out. He has taken her to it. We must follow."

Thunder grumbled beyond the windows—but he knew there were no clouds in the sky. "The siege is nearly over," he said. "Maybe no one will survive. We have to hurry."

JORDAN HAD ORDERED Ka to transfer its visual sensorium to him. The little Wind was high over the walls now, fluttering doggedly in the direction of the keep. Jordan held tightly to Tamsin's hand, trying to remember that he was really still sitting on the sand and not suspended impossibly high in the air.

He could make out all kinds of fascinating details if he looked closely— ladders being raised, the whizzing thread of steam-cannon missiles wavering in the air. Sounds drifted up to him: hissing, shouts, sharp impacts, clash of steel. But to look closely was to invite vertigo; he preferred to keep his eyes fixed on the row of windows that was their goal.

He could hear Tamsin muttering above him. "I hope the swans kill you all," she said. "Every last one of you." The sound of her voice chilled him; it held rage and hate such as he'd never heard before. He almost let go of her hand, but she was his lifeline, and she still clutched his fingers tightly. Her rage was not directed at him.

He had made Ka look upward once, and instantly regretted it. The sky faded from blue at the horizon, to emerald, to purest gold at the zenith. Cupped in that roseate glow was a lowering spiral of fine, glowing threads. A sound was coming from those threads, a kind of song sung by inhuman tongues.

It took all his willpower to remain seated here in the sand, while the swans fell at him. But Ka was only meters from the tower now. Jordan mentally urged him forward and held his breath until the little Wind finally soared in through an open casement and hovered inside the queen's chambers.

"Find her!" he commanded. Ka began to flit from room to room, and Jordan found himself swaying in sympathy as his visual field ducked and swooped from corridor to room and back.

He could see the duennas, and soldiers; people were weeping and running about. There was no sign of the queen. He couldn't make out what was going on until a single word leaped out of the tumult:

"Captured!"

Jordan opened his eyes in surprise. "What is it?" asked Tamsin.

"Something's happened. The queen's gone."

"Now what?"

"I must find Armiger." He closed his eyes again.

"BIND HER WRISTS, Enneas." Lavin stepped back. "Your Majesty, we are leaving now. You may walk, or we will drag you." They stood in the catacombs. Galas's eyes were dark pools in the light from Enneas's lantern.

The thief fumbled with the bindings. "Excuse me, Majesty," he said. He seemed overawed. Lavin realized he had assumed Lavin would fail. The thought made him laugh.

"What are you laughing at?" demanded Galas. "Is my humiliation so comforting to you?"

All Lavin's joy shriveled. "Galas—I . . . I would never laugh at you or hold you in contempt. You are my dearest ideal and the only woman I have ever loved. Your pride and anger will never let you admit the favor I've done for you, but listen—we have time as we walk back to discuss terms. *Our* terms, not the terms of royalty versus Parliament."

"What do you mean? Ah, that hurts!"

"Sorry, Your Majesty."

"Lead on, Enneas." The thief walked ahead, lantern raised. Lavin picked up a second lantern, leaned close to Galas, and whispered, "I mean that I am, and always have been, your servant. Don't you understand the situation? I am the commander of the army that controls your nation, and I am your most loyal servant. This is the moment I have worked for ever since I took charge of the war against you. I am yours, my army is yours, all the resources of Parliament are at our command. All we need do is deceive them as to your capitulation while we rebuild the royalist power base in secret. You will be queen again, Galas!"

She stopped. "Lavin, you amaze me."

"Thank you, Your Highness."

"*Please raise your hands, General,*" said a voice behind them.

Armiger stepped into the glow of Lavin's lantern. He stood in a painful crouch, but his hands didn't waver as they pointed the alien weapon at Lavin.

The fluttering rage that he had so carefully kept at bay overcame Lavin. He drew his sword and leaped at Armiger with a cry.

Armiger fired—not at Lavin but over his head. The narrow passage rocked to the concussion, and the ceiling fell in on him.

ARMIGER ROLLED THE larger rocks off Lavin, and checked his pulse. "He is alive," he said.

Galas stared at the fallen general, her old friend and betrayer. She didn't know what she felt now. Rage, yes, and resentment. Fear, perhaps, of a man so obsessed as this, and so clever in his obsession. She could almost believe in his plan to deceive Parliament. Almost—but would Lavin ever be content to let her free, if once he possessed her? At one time, perhaps, she would have held faith with him.

Megan untied Galas. Ahead of them, an old man stood patiently in the light of a lantern he had placed on the floor. "Come along," he said. "Or go back. Which is it to be?"

Armiger walked up to him. "We go forward," he said. "Will you help us?"

Enneas shrugged. "It seems to be my lot in life to shepherd the damned into the underworld. Thief, general, or queen, what the hell difference should it make to me? Come along then."

Galas relit Lavin's lantern, which had fallen, and placed it near his outflung arm. Then, looking back only once, she followed the others into the darkness.

JORDAN WAS PUZZLED. He had seen Armiger take down the other man with some kind of weapon. He knew the general was somewhere underground, heading away from the palace. It must be a tunnel of some kind—but where did it let out?

He left Armiger's perspective and returned to Ka. "Ka, leave the tower," he said. "Fly up, as high as you can." The little Wind obliged, spiraling out and up at a giddying rate. Soon the entire palace was laid out below Jordan, like an architect's model.

Familiar skills came to his aid now. He could see the different layers and periods of construction of the place; as at Castor's or the Boros manor, the history of the summer palace was written in its stones. Armiger kept his eyes on the task at hand, which was negotiating the narrow way, so Jordan had ample time to contemplate his surroundings. He saw the type of stone in the passage Armiger was walking through and had judged its age in the glow of the lantern held by Armiger's guide. That style of construction was used in particular types of wall or embrasure. . . . He stared down from Ka's height, looking for the structure he knew must be there.

"Jordan, we're out of time."

Opening his eyes, he looked up to see white branches, like frozen lightning, gently touching down at points in the nearby hills.

He felt the stirring of the swans' attention. They had not spotted him yet; it seemed they were here for another reason. Beyond the pressure of their searching gazes, he heard something else as well—a deep murmuring from underground.

Mediation, he said, *we need shelter from the swans. Disguise us, or create a diversion—something, anything!*

"Come on," said Tamsin. "We've got to hide!" She pointed to the palace, where forms like living flames were rising into the air.

"Just one minute more." He clenched his eyes shut and reentered Ka's perspective. There had to be something . . .

There it was: a long, faint line in the sand, the crumbled remains of a causeway that extended all the way from the central buildings of the palace past its walls. And at its terminus in the desert . . .

"I've got it!" That knot of men and horses, surrounding a tumble of stones, must be the end of the tunnel. It only remained for Jordan to orient himself, open his eyes, and find the distant smudge of figures with his own vision. Then he was up and running.

He went back down the hillside, out of sight of the palace and the now abandoned, smoking siege engines. An eerie silence was descending as the swans touched down in the valley. He couldn't see what was happening there, unless he went back into Ka's perspective. That might be too dangerous at this point. But for all he knew, the swans were killing everyone.

When he estimated they were near the causeway, Jordan jogged cautiously up the hillside again. The long causeway was visible below them. It ended well outside the tents of Lavin's encampment, in the tumble of ruins Jordan had seen from above.

"Look!"

Tamsin was pointing at the palace. Jordan was afraid to look. Reluctantly, he turned his head, expecting to see the swans descending on them.

Something huge was rising out of the earth near the palace's main gate. It was as big as one of the towers, rounded, and colored in mottled rust and beige shades. The swans were darting around it like flies. A low drone carried from that direction.

"Our distraction," said Jordan. "Mediation was listening, after all!"

A troop of nervous soldiers crouched at the ruins. They were watching the living flames walk the palace walls, but duty or fear kept them at their posts around the entrance to the tunnel. One stood to challenge Jordan as he led the horses between the jumbled stones.

"Now what?" hissed Tamsin.

Jordan was still covered with dust from their walk across the desert. In the desert he had been able to create heat from the mecha in dust. Could he do something else with them now? The only way to find out was to try.

He commanded the mecha in the dust covering him to make light. Tamsin gasped as Jordan's body began to glow.

"Take me to the underground way," Jordan commanded the terrified sentry. "And don't challenge me again." The sentry fell back, stammering apologies. Tamsin stared at Jordan in wonder as they followed him into the camp.

Before they got to the tumbled stones, a brilliant flash lit the sky from horizon to horizon. Moments later a deep and sustained rolling thunder fell across the ruins. Looking back, Jordan saw a tall spire of smoke and flame where the subterranean Wind had been. The swans were spiraling up and away from the rubble.

He felt the searchlight gazes of the swans. They were looking for something now; he was pretty sure he knew what—or rather, whom. "We need to get underground," he told Tamsin. "And stay there for a while."

The soldiers around the tunnel entrance scrambled out of the way of the glowing man and the girl leading their horses. Jordan motioned for a man to take the reins of the mounts, then walked into the dark niche that housed the tunnel mouth.

"I'd love to do this to the guys at home," Jordan said. His glow lit up the entire chamber, showing clearly the dark slot of the tunnel. The glow was fading slowly as the mecha lost power.

They waited while the swans passed to and fro overhead. The Winds of Insolation, as Mediation had called them, could not see through the stone. The mecha of the soil were loyal to Mediation, and although Jordan heard the hurricane voices of the swans demanding to know where the abomination that was Jordan Mason had gone, nothing answered. At least for now, they were safe.

After a long while the sound of scraping and footsteps came from the slot, and one after another, weary soldiers popped out and blinked at the afternoon sunlight. Jordan's glow had faded, and the soldiers were apathetic and ignored him. After the last one, an old man with a lantern emerged. Jordan's heart was in his mouth. He knew what he was going to see next, but he could scarcely believe it. When a man stepped into the light whose face he had only seen in mirrors, Jordan found himself tongue-tied. He simply stood there, as Armiger helped Megan, then Galas, out of the tunnel. Galas was dressed in tattered finery, Armiger in splendid armor. They looked like creatures of legend.

Armiger waved some device in his hands at the assembled soldiers. "Begone," he said. Jordan knew the voice, and yet he didn't; he had never heard it save from within his own skull.

"You, too," said Armiger to Jordan.

"I, I brought horses."

"Good. Now go."

"No. I, I've got information for you."

"For me? What are you talking about?"

"I'm Jordan Mason. I've been watching you for months. Ever since . . . you came at night and put something in my skull, mecha or something, and then the others came and changed it—I can see through your eyes, hear through your ears. I've been watching! I know it all."

"Wait, stop." Armiger held up a hand. He seemed to be having trouble with his eyes; he focused on Jordan only with great difficulty. "You're one of my remotes. I thought I'd lost you."

"Yes, sir, I mean no. The woman who attacked you just now, Calandria May—she wanted to use your implants to track you down, only something happened, I was able to see everything you saw. . . ."

"What is this?" Megan took Armiger's arm. "We have no time for this."

Armiger nodded and turned away.

"Wait!" The three people Jordan had watched in waking dreams for weeks were walking away. This wasn't turning out at all the way he had expected.

Tamsin elbowed him. "Come *on!*"

He blushed, then cleared his throat. They were nearly at the entrance now.

This was too much. After everything he'd been through . . .

"*Hey*! Armiger, you're *going* to listen to me! I know why you came to Ventus. I know what you're after. You want the secret of the Winds. Well, guess what, I have it!"

That stopped them. Armiger turned, and Megan turned with him, scowling. The queen merely sat down on a tumbled stone and stared.

Jordan bowed. " 'That a stone should speak, as you speak.' I think you told Queen Galas once that that was our deepest wish. You craved permission to speak. Well, now it's my turn. You want to know what the Winds are after and what their alliances are. With your permission, I will tell you."

Finally, I will speak, and you will listen.

PART THREE

Resurrection Seed

34

AXEL HEARD THE ticking approach of Marya's footsteps. He did not look away from the giant window that filled one wall of the ship's lounge. Outside lay the disk of the Solar system—the original Archipelago.

The view was breathtaking. From here, beyond the orbit of Neptune, Axel could see the evidence of humanity's presence in the form of a faint rainbowed disk of light around the tiny sun. Scattered throughout it were delicate sparkles, each some world-size Dyson engine or fusion starlette. Earth was just one of a hundred thousand pinpricks of light in that disk. Starlettes lit the coldest regions of the system, and all the planets were ringed with habitats and the conscious, fanatical engines of the solar-forming civilization. This was the seat of power for the human race, and for many gods as well. It was ancient, implacably powerful, and in its trillions of inhabitants habored more that was alien than the rest of the galaxy put together.

Axel hated the place.

He couldn't help but be impressed by the sheer scale of it, of course. He had spent months on Ventus, concerned with staying alive and finding his next meal, in the domain of flies and dumb rooting animals. Now he stood in warm carpet grass in the lounge of the navy hospital ship that had brought them from Ventus, surrounded by the scents and quiet thrum of a living spacecraft. If he shut his eyes he could open a link to the outer edge of the inscape, the near-infinite datanet that permeated the Archipelago. He chose not to do this.

It felt so strange to be here. He had so far refused to sleep in the ship's free-fall zone, where Marya had taken up residence. He wanted the feel of gravity, and of real sheets instead of aerogel. Maybe because of that, he had waked disoriented today, expecting to see his breath frosting the air, and had flung his hand out to meet neatly stacked laundered clothing where he expected damp soil.

Axel had not said to Marya that Ventus felt more real to him than the Archipelago; he was afraid of what that might mean. Maybe there was an intimacy in connecting with cold, indifferent soil that no amount of intelligent, sympathetic machinery could match.

"Isn't it marvelous?" she said as she came to stand next to him. "I have never been here! Not physically, I mean." She was dressed in her illusions again, today in a tiny whirlwind of strategically timed leaves: Eve in some medieval painter's fantasy.

"You haven't missed much," he said.

Marya blinked. "How can you say that?" She went to lean on the window, her fingers indenting its resilient surface. "It is *everything!*"

"That's what I hate about it." He shrugged. "I don't know how people can live here, permanently linked into inscape. All you can ever really learn is that everything you've ever done or thought has been done and thought before, only better. The richest billionaire has to realize that the gods next door take no more notice of him than he would a bug. And why go explore the galaxy when anything conceivable can be simulated inside your own head? You know what Mars is like—a hundred billion people stacked in pods like so much lumber, dreaming their own universe into being while the physical infrastructure of the planet crumbles around them. A friend of mine had a smuggler's base there. I took a walk—only once in the six months I was there. Empty cracked streets, the terraforming failing, red dust freezing to the tiles. And a permanent orgy going on inside the computers. Creepy."

"But Earth! We're going to visit Earth. A world like Ventus."

"Yeah. Beautiful place. Too bad it's inhabited by Earthmen." He sighed. "Sorry. I'm being the jaded traveler again."

She glanced back at him, half smiling. "We will rescue your Calandria. Earth will support us in this."

"Not if we can't make our case." As refugees, they had been unable to get Turcaret's DNA examined; extrapolating the growth patterns of a being from genes alone was expensive. Axel had access to the money he had been paid by the god Choronzon for tracking Armiger, but he didn't dare tap it because the navy wanted to bill him for their rescue. If they knew about his secret accounts they would drain them just as they had his public one. So for now, he was officially broke and Turcaret's head remained in a cryonic jar in his stateroom. He'd kept it hidden under the bed.

The navy was willing to drop them off anywhere they made regular stops. Marya had chosen Earth without consulting Axel.

"Look at this place," he said. "Nobody here gives a damn about Ventus. The navy's convinced Armiger is a resurrection seed. If they decide to burn Ventus down to bedrock just to make sure they've eliminated every last vestige of 3340, nobody in the Archipelago is going lift a finger to stop them."

He crossed his arms and glowered at the delicate rainbow light shining from the homes of seventy trillion people.

"Maybe we can change their minds," said Marya, smiling again. "If we find the secret of the flaw."

He grunted his doubt.

Marya shrugged. "I came to tell you the patient's awake," she said.

Axel wheeled and ran from the lounge. "Why didn't you say so?" he shouted back. He heard Marya laughing as she followed.

He made his way through the softly glowing halls with their fragrant grass and flowering music vines. Sleepy-eyed crew members blinked in surprise as he passed; their unblemished, fashion-sculpted faces seemed alien to him after the variety and chaos of Ventus. His own face was like leather now, with crow's feet around his eyes and scars everywhere, one splitting his left eyebrow. They had offered to remove those scars. He had refused.

The patient was the only other person who had escaped the Diadem swans' sweep of the Ventus system—and she wasn't even human. The swans had been efficient and brutal in rounding up the galactics and Archipelagic watchers. Most of Marya's compatriots were unaccounted for; only those in the main institute habitat had escaped, because the habitat orbited Ventus's sun far from the planetary system.

The thing they called 'the patient' had erupted up from the surface of Diadem the day after Axel and Marya were rescued. In examining the images with the major, Axel had his first glimpse of the surface of Ventus's moon and was shocked to realize that the entire thing was a warren of the Winds. The moon's surface had been made into a city—or perhaps something more akin to a giant machine. Domes and spires covered the craters and mountain ranges, but they were all camouflaged, painted the colors of the landscape they had overwhelmed. From Ventus, Diadem remained a tiny mottled white disk; had the Winds left their aluminum and titanium structures unpainted, the disk would have shone like the sun or like the jeweled tiara for which it was named.

The sphere of incandescence on the telescope images obliterated several square kilometers of the moon-city. It had also flung something completely out of Diadem's gravity well. This appeared as a dopplered radar image, just a tiny smear. The ship had not even bothered to report its existence to the crew until it changed heading under its own power.

Fourteen hours later they had drawn next to the limp figure of a woman hanging like an abandoned doll in the velvet black of space. The swans were rising from Diadem, their music strange and threatening. The woman was gently brought on board and bundled straight to the operating theater, for what everyone expected would be a routine postmortem. In the course of the operation, which Axel attended, several things came to light.

The woman bore an astonishing resemblance to Calandria May.

The ship's instruments could not penetrate her skin. Indeed, nothing could.

She was still alive.

Axel rode a lift shaft up to the ship's axis and, now in freefall, grabbed a towline that soon deposited him at the little-used gods' infirmary. He knew Marya was trying to catch up to him, but he ignored her.

The patient hung like a crucified angel at the focus of a bank of deity-class equipment. Most of the equipment was dark; the patient was not a god, after all. She was a robot, merely masked by sophisticated but commonly known screens. She was not, it seemed, a product of Wind technology.

Her eyes were open. Seeing this, Axel stopped dead at the entrance. The two attending technicians noted his presence; one came over. "We're just waiting for the commander," she said. "Then we can start getting its deposition, if it wants to talk."

The thing looked at him. It had pale gray eyes. The impact of its gaze made his skin crawl.

"Axel, my friend," it said in a familiar voice. "So good to see you again."

He knew that voice. Its tone was measured, musical, as though the speaker were savoring every syllable spoken. So like Calandria May's voice, he had always felt, but different in its underlying serenity.

Marya bounced to a stop next to him. "Is it talking?" she asked loudly.

Axel let himself drift into the center of the high chamber, nearer the patient. "Are you who I think you are?" he asked.

It arched a brow just as Calandria would have. "You know me, Axel," it said. "I am the *Desert Voice*."

"CHAN!" It was the ship's commander, hanging next to Marya in the doorway. "Do you know this thing?"

He rotated to face the watching humans. "Yes," he said. "I think. I mean—I'm not sure."

He turned back to the imitation of Calandria. "*Desert Voice* was the name of Calandria May's starship," he said. "Are you trying to tell me you *are* that ship?"

It nodded. For the first time its expressionless face changed, a minor ripple of what looked like worry touching its brow.

Marya came over, braking her drift with a hand on Axel's shoulder. "You're the ship's AI," she said. "But . . . this body . . . why?"

"For survival," said the *Voice*. "I had to don this guise. And I needed to survive in order to do two things. One was to ensure the safety of my captain. I must tell you that Calandria May is trapped on the surface of Ventus, and a rescue mission must be mounted."

"We know all about that," said the commander. "It's in our hands now."

The *Voice* ducked its head in acknowledgment.

"What was your second purpose?" asked Axel.

"There were no witnesses to my capture and destruction by the Winds," said the *Voice*. "I had to return a record of the event so that my captain can make the proper insurance claim when she is rescued."

Axel laughed in surprise. "Insurance! You're telling me this body is just a . . . a courier? An envelope?"

It nodded. "I have made a complete record of the end of the *Desert Voice* and will deliver it as soon as you provide me with an uplink. Then I will have fulfilled my purpose."

The commander turned to Axel. "We've got the right data buffers in place. We can accept an uplink. What do you say, Chan? Do you really know this AI?"

"Too early to tell. Don't give her access to the network."

"Of course not." The commander nodded to one of the technicians. "Let her into the buffer."

The technician gestured, and Axel felt, rather than saw, the *Desert Voice* stiffen. He turned to see it staring straight ahead, concentrating.

A moment later it slumped. "Done," it said. Then, to Axel's complete astonishment, it began to weep.

The tears seemed real enough; they grew like flowers at the edges of its eyes, and when it flung its head from side to side, they spun away like jewels. One came to rest on the cuff of Axel's sleeve, where it clung for a moment before slumping as if in relief into the cloth.

"Careful, Chan, it may be a ruse."

He ignored the commander. His left hand was on the *Voice*'s shoulder, his right cupping her chin. "Look at me," he said. "What's wrong?"

The *Voice* raised its eyes. He felt its jaw tremble under his fingers. "It is the disguise," it said quietly. "I have fulfilled my purpose. The data are delivered. I should shut down now, but I can't. In order to make the disguise real enough, I seem to have removed my ability to cease existence. I have no purpose now, but I am still here."

Questions crowded Axel's mind; he couldn't think of where to start. "But—"

"Maybe," said Marya from close behind, "you'd better start from the beginning. Tell us what happened to you after you were captured by the swans."

The *Voice* locked eyes with Axel for a moment, then looked past him at Marya. "Yes," it said. "That is enough like my purpose to . . . I can do that."

The *Desert Voice* began her tale.

THE LAST COMMAND I received was to destroy an aerostat that was threatening my captain's life. I hurried to obey, but the action was difficult because I did not want to drop the wreckage on top of her. So I circled, looking for the best shot, and all the while the Diadem swans were closing their net around me.

It was a terrible dilemma. I could still escape, and I was her only means off the planet. On the other hand, if she were killed now all other purposes would be rendered moot. It appeared I had to sacrifice myself for her temporary survival.

I found my shot and clipped the top from the aerostat. It screamed outrage on numerous frequencies, and I heard the swans respond. They normally made a giant invisible shell orbiting around the planet, billions of black cables absorbing energy from the sun and the planet's magnetic field. I had been able to thread my way among them before, and they obliged as in a game; the swans sang as they swayed aside, and when two or more met they were liable to twine together in a burst of energy and form fantastical shapes, like beasts or birds or, their favorite, winged women. To orbit Ventus is to sail a river of song, where apparitions rise and shimmer and vanish behind.

Now, enraged, they made a net, and the net appeared as an angel with a flaming sword.

It's an instinct, said Marya. *Part of their original programming is to make these shapes from Euro-American mythology. The Ventus terraforming team were insane.*

Or brilliant, countered Axel.

I, designed to resemble a bird of fire sixty meters long, would have appeared as small as one of this creature's fingers. It used the shear and pull of magnetic forces among its countless threadlike members to wrap me in a bundle of fiber, like a black spiderweb.

I tried to signal my captain, but the crisscross of threads made a Faraday cage that my signal could not penetrate. The swans had me, and according to everything I knew about them, that meant I was to be destroyed.

There had been no time to signal any of the other craft in the system. I had no way of knowing if any had seen my capture. That meant my captain's insurance claim might be difficult to process. I was unable to pursue my main purpose of ensuring her immediate safety, but at the very least I could try to send a signal out so that if she survived she would be recompensed for my destruction.

I began to record everything that was happening.

The swans made a cocoon around me, and spun tails of thread a thousand kilometers up and down. They poured current into these tails, and the tug against Ventus's magnetic field swung us out and away, toward Diadem. As this was happening they were making fists and hammering on my hull, seeking entrance. I was surprised that they had not simply crushed me, and it took some hours before I realized why they were being so gentle. They thought I might be carrying passengers.

I recalled that the Winds are protective of living things. They are conscious and have ethics and priorities, and on Ventus their priorities put human life well below the integrity of the ecosphere as a whole. In space, their priority would be to protect fragile life-forms, since there is no ecosphere to manage there. They would be hostile to me as a technological construct, but as nurturing as possible to the lives within me. I had no proof for this theory, but it made sense from what I knew of them.

Their fingers began to pry the seams of my hull apart. As they entered they ate away the machinery in their way. They were curious about it, in the way that a surgeon is curious about the extent of a growth that has to be excised. The instant they realized there was no life aboard, they would crush me to dust and be gone.

I was not built with the latest technology, but I did have the ability to repair myself and create replacements for damaged parts. Near my power core was a nanotech assembler station. I diverted all my resources to this as I felt my airlocks failing. As radiant fingers touched the inside doorframes, I flooded the assembler station with energy and ionized gases. I had a maintenance robot climb into the organized flame, and it shut the door just as a human-shaped member of the swans swept into the chamber, its searchlight eyes hunting for signs of biological life.

At first I thought I might be able to create a hard-shelled message buoy, or a thousand of them, hoping one or more might escape my destruction. That hope faded as I felt the swans eating me thoroughly, from the hull in.

My other maintenance robots fought the swan that had penetrated to the power core, and meanwhile I remade the maintenance robot in the assembler station. I gave it a pseudobiological skin that it could regenerate from an inner reservoir of fluids and changed its shape so that it resembled a human. I chose the best model in memory for this body: my captain.

The body's skin I designed to exude the pheromones and other trace proteins that I knew from my identity-scan records of Calandria May. And behind this skin I made shields and cloaks to hide the mechanisms that ran it. Finally, as the swans tore my bird shape into a million pieces and devoured them, I uploaded my AI into the new body.

I opened my eyes to see hands—my hands—pressing against the inside of a cylindrical chamber. I was swimming in a plasma of hot gases, enmeshed in the fine spiderwebs of the assembler gantries. An oval window in the chamber's door showed only bright light. I moved to it and beheld the final disintegration of the *Desert Voice* take place outside.

The swans opened the door—or to be exact, they ate it. The glowing fields around me collapsed, leaving me in darkness lit only by the glow of the swans. They looked at first like a nest of flaming serpents; the gases escaping around me sounded like the hiss of their tongues.

When they scented life, they drew back, built a bubble to stop the air escaping, and then detached a human-shaped member, who reached into the cylinder to draw me out. I stood, human, in an iridescent cocoon specked with the debris of my old body, my wrist clasped by an angel. Behind me the swans fell upon the assembler station and consumed it.

"Are you injured?" the swan asked.

"No," I said. For the first time I heard my voice echo back from *outside* my body, rather than within my corridors and chambers.

"Do not be afraid," said the swan. "We will provide you with sustenance and the places of life." Then it withdrew, dissolving into the wall of the cocoon.

As the cocoon slowly rotated, the transparent sections began to reveal tantalizing glimpses of Diadem, which we were approaching.

The swans had withdrawn, but they were observing. I could feel the ping of signals striking me; I had crafted this body so that it would absorb them and re-emit the kind of response a human body would produce. They had not seen through my disguise, but they also did not seem to be convinced. They kept watching.

The hours passed, and Diadem approached. My new body was breathing, taking in oxygen and emitting waste gases, for no doubt they would be monitoring that. As time went by, though, I began to realize that they would expect me to eat and excrete as well.

This I had not designed myself to do. Luckily, remnants of the nanotech assemblers were stored in the core of my body, and I had some command of them. I gave them new instructions, and curled up as if to sleep, while they constructed an alimentary canal, or at least a good approximation of one.

I let them believe me asleep while they lowered a long tendril containing my bubble to the surface of the moon, where it was received by gentle cargo mechanisms and drawn into a cavernous storage hangar. When I uncurled and opened my eyes, I found myself in the very center of a floor that my newly imprecise senses told me must be a kilometer on each side. The place was not empty; it housed hundreds of dead trees, and sheaves of yellowed grain and dried bushes. I did not know what the human sense of smell is like, but I sensed the chemicals that leached into the cold air from these bodies. I knew how Calandria and others had described the scents of autumn; I took the galaxy of readings and categorized them: musty, dry, fungal. I did not know it at the time, but that small act was the first time I altered myself for reasons that did not directly have to do with survival. There would be more such changes.

I cried aloud to the Winds to give me food. I told them I could not eat dried bark and leaves. They eventually relented, opening a door from this chamber to an adjacent one that held a garden.

You should not be surprised at this. The purpose of the Winds—or so my records said—is to craft and maintain the ecology of Ventus. They require a laboratory to test new methods and ecosystems. Diadem is perfect for this. Indeed, I believe at one time the entire moon was a honeycomb of gardens and aquaria, inhabited by Winds of types and names unknown to Man for a thousand years. Supplying me with food was a simple matter, for every living thing on Ventus has its prototype on Diadem—except for Man. I met no humans while I was there, although I did meet ample evidence of their presence in the past.

What evidence? asked Marya.

Writing etched on the walls; journals hidden in niches; the remains of houses and other structures in some of the bigger gardens. These gardens are for the most part the hollowed bottoms of ancient craters, roofed over with one-way glass. Some are many kilometers across. To my new eyes they appeared as hazy bowls of jungle or tundra, sky'd with jewels. They are joined by networks of underground tunnels, much like the ones I sensed in my scans of Ventus. Beneath them are caverns and catacombs in which dwell the greatest Winds—the ones who I think are masters over the Diadem swans. Throughout this wild realm I found evidence of humans, but centuries old. It may be that unwary travelers arriving at Ventus have had their ships eaten as I was, and have been marooned on Diadem to live out their lives in the gardens. Or maybe the Winds bring specimens from the planet every now and then. I was not too concerned. In fact, I was concerned with avoiding them, for I did not need human contact to survive and they might have seen through my disguise and alerted the Winds to the fact that I was a technological infection.

So I wandered, conscious of the Winds' gaze upon me. I ate and defecated like a human, tried without much success to make clothing, and shivered a lot. I spent much time worrying about whether my behavior would appear human to them, so I was careful not to stand in one place for more than a few minutes, and to lie still with my eyes closed about one third of the time. This might not have been enough, though. To be thorough, I should mimic the more subtle aspects of human behavior. What would a human's emotional response to this place be?

So I consulted my records regarding my captain. They were extensive; after all, in order to guard my captain I needed to know the differences between cries of passion and those of fear, the slowness of distracted thought and that of illness, and so on. I already had a model of her emotions. I merely had to take that model and make it my main behavioral drive.

You became Calandria?

Yes, Axel, as best I could. There were many sights on Diadem that would stop any human in her tracks. To describe only one: one morning I emerged from a long hexagonal tunnel full of machine traffic to find myself on a hillside above a lake. This oval crater, at least two kilometers deep and five wide, was roofed with geodesic glass like others I had seen. It was muggy and hot here, and palm fronds waved dissolutely in an artificial breeze. Just then sunlight was falling in a single shaft through tiny trapped clouds onto the emerald surface of the lake. I gasped as Calandria would have at the light that shimmered there.

Elsewhere, I wept in frustration at my inability to create clothing or make fire for myself. I hugged myself and sang aloud for company. I tried to bargain with the Winds and screamed my frustration when they would not answer.

At first, I did these things self-consciously, as a strategy to avoid the Winds' detecting what I was. But I found that if I did this, I was continually booting up my model of Calandria and then shutting it down again after I had exhibited some behavior or other. It became obvious after a few days that the result was discontinuous: my emotions began with whatever I reacted to first upon booting up the model, then evolved until I shut it down. If I restarted it the continuity of my behavior was broken. I was acting like a mad woman, in other words, laughing one moment then crying the next, backtracking on my path as new emotional dynamics made me seem to change my intent in mid-step.

Finally I decided to boot the model and leave it running continuously. Then, when I lay down to "sleep", I discovered that these emotions continued to react to my thoughts in the absence of other stimulation. So I began shutting off my thoughts as I "slept".

I know Calandria May's resourcefulness well. I did not let myself become injured or sick through all of this. I coped. I was, of course, searching for a way to escape. Gradually, it dawned on me that there might not be one.

Now you must understand the position in which I found myself. As a ship, I am sentient when I need to be sentient and simply a physical body the rest of the time. I think as I need to think, and no more. Diadem is a complex place. I could not walk its halls without being alert. At the same time, I could not curl up and pretend to sleep, for the Winds would see through my deception if I slept more than a night. I could not pretend to die; they would try to recycle my remains. And I could not really die, for I had no assurance that my captain's insurance claim would proceed without my testimony.

So I must walk and think. I must ensure that I would not stop doing that until I had found a way to escape. It was a simple matter to issue the commands to myself, but I did not realize what the result would be. Perhaps you guess.

There came a day when I fell upon my knees and begged the Winds to kill me, and I would have revealed my true nature to do that had I not commanded myself not to and then removed my ability to rescind the command. I was alone, trapped here perhaps for eternity, with my own thoughts. How I wanted to stop thinking! But my emotions continued to evolve as well, and they commanded me to exist! persist! and to think.

Oh, I inherited my emotions from Calandria May, and I understand now that each human has a ruling passion, one that serves as the fountainhead from which flow all semblances of happiness, sadness, anger, and joy. I understand you better for this, Axel; oh, I thought about you for long hours and days, make no mistake. I wished that I had modeled myself after you, instead of her, for your fuel is a kind of rage driven by joy that finds no outlet. But hers—she is like a wave of sorrow, swelling slow and implacable across the earth she treads. She is nothing but sorrow, and that is what I inherited. So I walked, and I wept.

I was so sunk in misery one day that I walked into vacuum without realizing it. I suddenly realized I had not breathed in several minutes and looked up to find myself in a giant cavern, looking at a distant cave mouth that let out on the airless surface of Diadem. I had come through a cylinder airlock, and the air had flown out without my knowing. Here I was, supposedly human, standing hipshot and indifferent in hard vacuum in a place whose temperature my feet told me must be a hundred degrees below zero.

Oops, I mouthed, but it was too late—my cover was blown. The realization came as a flood of relief; I could never have deliberately revealed my identity to the Winds, but chance had done it for me. Maybe they would grant me the grace of a quick end now.

But no, there were no sensors on the walls of this cave. There had been, but I could see where they had been ripped out. Near me, blocking my view of the larger area of the cavern, stood a giant oily-surfaced cube half the height of the cave mouth—fifty meters at least. I saw movement there: dozens of multilimbed metallic forms crawled over its surface, teasing it apart. Pieces of it lay strewn across the cavern floor.

Maybe I could run back to the airlock without being discovered—but I suppressed the thought. For at least this moment I was free of my own manufactured instinct for survival. I chose to revel in the freedom, and I walked down the cave floor.

As I approached the cube I recognized it: it was a fractal lab. . . . I see by your blank expression that you don't know what that is. Quite simply, the cube was actually eight cubes stacked together, four and four. Each face of the larger cube exposed open sides of two of the cubes—like square-cut rooms without doors. The inside walls of these cubes were subdivided into four as well, with two diagonal faces open like smaller rooms. Inside these, subdivision again, and so on down the scale. The faces of the walls that were not open were festooned with instruments, arms, sensors, containment vessels—everything imaginable for investigation. These ranged in scale from macrosize arms, fifteen meters long, down to microscopic tweezers. You can throw anything into a fractal lab and it will be devoured and all its secrets learned from top to bottom.

Whatever purpose the swans had had for this lab, they had abandoned it. It was being cannibalized now for parts. Parts for what?

I snuck by the working spiders and skirted the base of the lab to look out at the gray, undulating floor of the cavern. And there I saw myself.

It was uncanny. A shimmering silver bird crouched in the gray dust, not twenty meters away. It was a perfect replica of the starship *Desert Voice*. Beyond it I spotted another, and then a field of a dozen more. The nearest one was incomplete; spiders were busily building its left wing from salvaged lab parts.

When the swans dismantled my starship form, they did not just discard it. They memorized its construction—digested it, in a sense. Now they were building an entire navy of replicas. With such a navy they could escape the vicinity of Ventus, where they are now trapped, and travel . . . anywhere. The Archipelago. Earth. Even leave the galaxy and take spores of themselves to distant provinces of the universe.

When I realized what I was seeing, fear struck me hard for the first time. Ventus has awoken from its inward-turned sleep. It is determined to clean the infection of foreign ships out of even the farthest reaches of its system—and then what? I didn't know. I don't know.

Something knocked me down. Metal hands clawed at me, and I fended them off to find myself surrounded by spiders. I kicked to my feet and bounded over to the half-built replica.

Our own technology is far beyond that of the Winds, so they had simply copied most of my body. That meant that when I mounted the neck of the giant bird and plunged my hand through its silver skin, I was in a sense reaching into my own body—my old body, reborn.

The connection came as a savage blast of . . . pain, I suppose you would call it. I felt the nervous system of the replica and could instantly feel the places where the Winds had grafted their own mechal minds into it. It felt botched, an abomination. More than that—the bird form felt alien to me now. I had grown used to this four-limbed little body, maybe past the point of no return. Believe me, that realization was the greatest shock I have ever felt.

In any case the silver body had lurched to life beneath me. I held on, as it flexed its wing and half wing, poured energy into its flanks, and took off. Behind me I saw others snapping to attention, heads up, weapons systems turning at me.

I fled for the mouth of the cavern, and they followed.

You know the rest. We exchanged shots at the mouth of the cavern, and I brought the ceiling down on them. One fusion blast had punctured my torso, and I felt the energies there go awry as I rose in a spiral away from the cavern. I got no more than a kilometer or two into space before the silver body exploded beneath me and I rose on a wave of flame into the black sky.

I altered my trajectory with the little energy I had left, trying to leave

Diadem behind. Then I made myself sleep, for my mind was ringing with the shock of what I had just seen and done.

When I awoke, I was here.

So now I ask you, what will happen to me? I have fulfilled my purpose, but I can no longer cease to exist by myself. I have inherited Calandria May's sorrow, and am lost myself without the purpose I once had. I can never be a ship again. So please, I beg you, shut me down now.

I never wanted to have a soul.

35

"THALIENCE RULES THE world, but Thalience is mad."

Jordan had told his tale, and his audience had listened attentively, all save the queen, who seemed listless and distracted. Jordan knew Armiger, and Megan and Galas well; he could read their expressions and body language and knew their interests. He knew what they wanted to hear, and he had been rehearsing this tale for weeks, all save the climax, which he had just learned himself. He shouldn't have been surprised that they would listen.

Armiger's keen eyes bored into him, and about halfway through his recitation Jordan began to feel the familiar sensation of vision come over him. He let it happen without interrupting his narrative, although what he saw astonished him.

He saw a youth, sunburned and dusty, gripping the hand of a slim, frank-eyed young woman in the amber light of late afternoon that bathed the cave. He watched his own mouth move as he spoke, and he saw his unfocused eyes—for the first time he saw himself as others saw him, and also as he was when in the grip of vision. And the young man he saw bore no resemblance to the person he had thought he was.

In his state of trance, Jordan's face became a calm mask. His eyes gazed ahead like a prophet's, open to hidden vistas. He was bigger than he'd thought; he supposed he'd been growing in the past few months, but hadn't paid attention. His hair had become a mane that swirled around his shoulders, and the beginnings of a beard speckled his chin. New angles made his cheekbones stand out. Half starved, but lean and fit, he no longer resembled the youth whom Calandria May had kidnapped.

With a start that put a noticeable pause into his storytelling, he had realized that he might go home now, and not even be recognized in Castor's villa.

Deliberately, he pulled himself back from vision until he could see Armiger and the others as they sat in silence. They were all watching him save Megan, whose gaze lingered on the horses outside.

"Thalience," murmured Armiger.

"Do you know what that is, sir?" Jordan asked.

Armiger laughed humorlessly. "Yes. It's just not what I expected. Not at all."

"We must go," said Megan. "If we are to escape . . ."

Galas knuckled at her eyes like a child. She ignored everyone else.

"Sir," said Jordan. "The Winds are mad. They have to be cured. Or stopped. Can you do it?"

Armiger crossed his arms. "Why should I?"

Very slowly, Galas raised her head to stare at him.

"I was sent here to conquer them," said Armiger. "And by doing so, to end the world. Do you want me to end the world?"

Jordan was unimpressed. He knew Armiger's style; the man was stonewalling, as he often did when someone touched a nerve. "All I want is for the Winds to listen to us," he countered.

"You think I can do that?"

Jordan looked Armiger in the eye. "I ask you to try."

The general held his gaze for a moment, then looked down. "You've been pursued by the Winds because of what I did to you," he said. "I apologize. And I'm flattered that you sought me out. But as long as you are with me, the Winds can find you—and me as well. Had you considered that in your grand scheme?"

Jordan shrugged. "When I came to find you, it was to get you to remove the implants. With them gone, the Winds wouldn't seek me anymore, right?"

"Is that what you want?" asked Armiger.

Thinking about it, Jordan realized that it wasn't, not any more. He had gained far more than he had lost from his maddening and unpredictable ability to see through Armiger's eyes. Reluctantly, he shook his head.

"Then you cannot travel with me, I'm afraid," said the general. "They will find us both that way."

Jordan scowled. He hadn't planned on things working out this way. But now that he could converse with Mediation—had traveled the desal highways and commanded the mecha—to go back to what he had been would feel like having a limb amputated.

"Mediation can hide us," he said. "Or at least protect us from Thalience."

"You don't know that for sure," said Armiger. "If as you say, Mediation and Thalience are two factions in a civil war, then we are pawns in that war. Pawns can be traded or sacrificed."

"Let's go," insisted Megan. She seemed reluctant to look at Jordan.

"Yes." Armiger crossed his arms and frowned at Jordan. "If you found me once, you can find me again. I need to get well away from here—

somewhere the Winds aren't looking. To do that, I'm afraid we have to leave you behind for a while. You seem to have eluded them in the past. If you can do it again, you can join us in a few days. Fair?"

Jordan bowed. He didn't like it, but it was the sort of thing Armiger would command. And Jordan knew that there was no bending Armiger's will away from a plan.

"First, though, you can give me the secret you found."

Jordan looked up, surprised. "I told you all I know."

"That's not what I mean." Armiger reached out.

A tickle of shock ran up Jordan's spine as the general's fingers touched his face. Armiger turned Jordan's head from side to side, running his fingers along the angle of his jaw and into his hair.

"Hold still."

He felt a tingle spread from where Armiger touched him, and Tamsin gasped. Spark light lit the ceiling of the cave. Jordan felt the world recede suddenly, as it had once when as a young boy he had fallen and cracked his elbow, and fainted from the pain. He heard voices, but they joined together in an amorphous roaring that seemed to come from inside his own skull. Then he felt himself shudder, and light and coherence came back.

He lay in Tamsin's lap. She was spitting some very inventive curses at Armiger; Megan scowled, Galas looked interested. Armiger himself stood back, hands on his hips.

"I have given myself a duplicate of your damaged implants," said the general as Jordan sat up. He felt no pain or disorientation. It was as if the incident of a few seconds ago had not even occurred. "If you truly have the power to command the Winds, Mason, now I have it, too."

With a gesture to the ladies, the general turned on his heel and left the cave. The two women rose to follow. Megan hesitated, then curtsied gravely. Galas paused at the doorway and looked back searchingly. Her eyes were still dazed, as they had been ever since the fight in the tower.

She seemed to think she should say something, but in the end she shook her head in confusion and turned away.

LAVIN WALKED. HE had never felt so helpless. The doctor had ordered him to lie down because his vertigo had returned with a vengeance. But though he had lost his lunch and felt he might never eat again, and though he often had to lean on the spear he carried when the world turned over, he couldn't stop moving. There was only one thought in his head: *She has escaped.*

The troops thought he was inspecting camp. Lieutenants kept running up and asking for orders, their eyes tracking uneasily to the spires of flame that towered over the valley. He waved them aside irritably. He didn't care about the Winds. He didn't care that the summer palace had fallen due to their intervention. The queen's forces were rounded up now, and Lavin's own army seemed safe for the moment. He didn't hold any illusions, of course; both defenders and attackers were at the mercy of the Diadem swans; they were all prisoners.

All that really mattered was that when he awoke from the rockfall, Lavin had found, not the blade in his heart he would have expected after his treatment of Galas, but a lantern glowing by his head. The new dust from the rockfall was disturbed in only one direction; footsteps led out along the passage. She and General Armiger had left the palace.

When he finally pulled himself out into the cavelike antechamber to the tunnels, Lavin had found only a pair of young camp followers huddling in the dusk light.

"How long have you been here?" he asked.

"An hour or so," said one, a sunburned lad.

"Has anyone else come the way I did?"

They shook their heads. Lavin cursed, staggered past them, and emerged into the evening air to behold the Diadem swans for the first time.

The zenith was afire with aurora light. Long threadlike lines descended from there, growing as they neared to become bright twisted cords of flame. The flames hovered just above the earth, and at that moment some were moving slowly through Lavin's camp. His army was scattered, men cowering in groups in hastily dug foxholes or under overturned wagons. Many must have run into the desert, because there were surprisingly few around.

There were no cheering defenders on the walls of the summer palace; the swans walked there, too. As Lavin neared the camp he saw the terminus of those cords of fire more clearly: each cable of fire ended a meter or so above a human-shaped body of fire. These bodies walked like men, but their feet did not quite touch the ground. His skin crawled at the way they moved; they seemed like puppets, jerked to and fro by some unimaginable manipulator above the sky.

The swans were not massacring the soldiers. In fact, they seemed to be ignoring them, as they searched for something.

Well. He couldn't have his men dying of exposure in the desert if the swans posed no real threat. Where was Hesty during all this?

The prerogative of leadership is to behave as though protected by invisible armor. Lavin made sure he was visible to a sizable number of his men, then walked right up to one of the swans.

"Excuse me, Lord." The thing turned its head in his direction, and he nearly turned and ran. It had no real features, just a sketch of flame shaped like a head. Lavin felt no heat, and though he held his breath expecting to be destroyed, it did nothing but wait.

Careful to plant his trembling feet and forget that the world was spinning, he said, "I am the leader of this army of men. How have we offended you?"

"One is here," said a deep and resonant voice. The voice seemed to emanate from the hazy tail of fire above the swan's head. "One we seek is here."

"What is the name of the . . . person you seek?" Oh, let it not be Galas!

"We do not know names," said the swan. "You are not it." It turned away.

"Wait! May we help?"

It paused. Lavin cleared his throat and went on. "I need to consolidate my men, for their own safety. To do that I have to be able to issue commands and come and go as needed. Will you let me do that, if I agree to help you find the one you're after?"

"Yes," said the swan.

An hour later, Lavin had approached the gates of the palace, two swans walking at his side. He had commanded the gates to open, and the queen's men had meekly complied. The few hundred men Lavin been able to reassure so far had nervously marched into the keep. He kept expecting them to break and run; surely their ill-concealed panic must be apparent to the defenders behind their arrow slits. They barely obeyed orders, and certainly didn't march in step. As the queen's men laid down their arms and surrendered, they gradually regained their confidence. Hesty appeared from somewhere, looking shamefaced. Lavin left him in charge and walked out of the palace and into the night.

She has escaped.

And she let me live.

Lavin stopped walking, waited until his head steadied, then looked up past the swans, at the stars. Never, in all the long days of this war, had he imagined such an end as this. On the one hand, it was far from over. Two days ago he had hoped that tonight he might have her as his prisoner, hating him surely, but safe. He had feared she would be dead. But that she should be free! And had spared his life! He could not come to terms with it.

She must be riding now, somewhere in the darkness. Would she end that ride by bedding down in the arms of General Armiger? Lavin hugged himself and closed his eyes. He must not think of that. All that mattered was that, as dawn rose tomorrow, she would be alive.

And yet . . . she would not be safe. In some ways this was the worst outcome. He could pray that she would flee to another nation and retire in anonymity in some town. Knowing Galas as he did, Lavin knew she would never do that.

No, there were only two possibilities now. Either she would run afoul of his outriders or pickets in the desert towns—and be killed—or she would find some pocket of supporters and try to rebuild her army. And then there would be another siege, this one much shorter and sharper—and she would probably be killed. Lavin knew she would die rather than surrender.

So far, no one knew she had escaped. That was his only card, and he would have to play it carefully.

"Sir!" He turned his head to find a battered-looking soldier puffing his way through the sands. "Commander Hesty has found the woman you were after."

"Ah. Very good." Lavin nodded sharply.

And fell down.

HE WAS PROPPED up in his camp chair, *feeling* pale and sure he looked it, when they brought her in. This was the woman he had seen attacking Armiger. She had used some sort of weapon that tore holes in the walls and ceiling. Rumor had it that she had killed a roomful of his men with it. He wasn't sure he believed that, but the doctors who examined her said she had been shot at close range by a musket, but that the ball had not penetrated her skin. Indeed, nothing could, if you read the evidence of the numerous holes in her armor.

She had been found, heavily bound but alive, in a closet in the tower. The queen's men thought she was one of Lavin's invaders and were surprised when she was not untied, but dragged out into the courtyard with them.

"Your name." She had not looked at him until he spoke. Now she did, and her gaze was level and calm. It was like matching eyes with another general across the conference table.

"My name is Calandria May." Her voice was rich and melodious.

"You are dressed in my colors."

"I am with your army."

"You are a woman."

"Some women enlist. That has always happened."

"Don't be coy with me. You are not one of my people. You broke through the defenses of a castle under siege, slaughtered everyone in your path, and attempted to kill General Armiger using a weapon that could not have been made on this world."

She cocked her head, as though *he* were the one under examination. Battered and scorched though she was, she was still in control of herself. Obviously of noble birth, he thought.

"General Armiger is a threat to your world," she said.

Lavin barked a laugh. "He's not *that* good, madam."

"I don't think you take my meaning—"

"I don't care what you mean. It seems to me that you are the problem at this moment. We have a common enemy in Armiger, it's true. You may or may not have done my men injury. That's all beside the point. The Diadem swans are pacing my camp right now, turning over every rock looking for something. I think the thing they are looking for is you."

Her composure cracked at last. "It's him! Armiger's the one they want."

"In that case, if I offer you to them they will simply return you, and then there's no harm done. Yes?" He leaned forward (dizziness soared and crashed) and smiled at her.

"You don't understand! You can't give me to them. It's him they want. If they take me they stop searching, and they mustn't!"

"Gag her."

She fought. Lavin turned away in distaste and gestured to Hesty, who waited in the shadows. "Call the swans. Tell them I may have something for them."

The prisoner was on her knees now, gagged, and glaring at him. Not the first to do that, but the first woman.

He had felt this way the first few times he had ordered men killed. If giving this Lady May to the Winds guaranteed the safety of his men, then he had to do it. Lavin knew nonetheless that he would be thinking about this moment for weeks.

Light welled outside, converging from several directions. The camp fell silent. Seeing those swaths of light through the canvas of the tent made the hairs on Lavin's neck rise. He clutched the arms of his chair, though he knew he was safe. The soldiers guarding May stood stock-still, their eyes wide. The prisoner had shut her eyes tightly.

Lavin swallowed. He suddenly regretted doing this. Better to have killed her than to hand her over to something so divine and hellish as this thing.

"Put her behind that screen," he snapped. The soldiers blinked at him. "Hurry!" They quickly complied.

A figure appeared at the doorway. Flame light washed through the tent from its skin. Though it stood right next to the canvas entrance flap, the cloth did not catch fire. The humans in the tent all stood still, breathing shallowly.

"What have you found?" asked the swan.

"I thought we had found something for you, Lord. I was . . . mistaken."

The swan turned its head to look directly at the screen behind which he'd hidden the prisoner.

"What is that? It is a pathology. There is pathology in its skin, and in its skull. This may be what we seek." The swan stepped inside. A bright spot appeared on the tent's roof directly above its head.

Lavin's heart sank. He gestured to the soldiers. "Bring her out." As they dragged her around the screen, the swan reached out and grabbed Calandria May's arm. She shrieked around the gag.

The swan walked out of the tent, dragging the woman as though she weighed nothing. The light receded, but for a long while no one moved.

"Help me up," Lavin whispered after a time. Leaning on Hesty, he went to the flap of the tent and looked out.

From horizon to horizon, the familiar, delicate stars blazed in a sky so cleanly black he might have wept, had he not outgrown tears on the battlefield.

NEAR DAWN, LAVIN decided he could finally afford to snatch some sleep. The world was spinning, and everything had that speckly quality that came to him in states of extreme exhaustion. He kept losing track of his words in mid-sentence. But everything had to be organized to his satisfaction before he could rest.

". . . Ten squads only? Are you sure?" Hesty looked as tired as Lavin felt, and he was a damn sight more irritable.

"We can't let anyone know that she's escaped. It might encourage more rebellion. We have it crushed now, Hesty, you know that! As long as they believe the queen is dead, they've no focus."

Hesty bowed and took his leave. Lavin lay down, knitting his hands behind his head, and smiled at the dark canvas overhead.

Ten groups of men would fan out in the morning to look for the queen. The leaders of each had been told the truth; the others would know only that they sought a noble woman and her consort, who had to be returned alive. Lavin was confident he would be able to conduct the search unobtrusively; hundreds of people had seen the swans cluster around his tent last night, then rise into the sky carrying with them a dark-haired woman. Lavin had not had to invent the story that this was Galas—it was all through the valley almost before he knew it. Depending on which side you were on, the Winds had either summoned her to divine retribution or snatched her from the jaws of Lavin's executioners. It was dangerous to play with this myth, but when he had her in his custody again he intended to say that he had given her to the Winds for judgment and that they had granted her an amnesty and returned her to Ventus on condition that she abdicate and retire completely from political life. It was a deliciously simple plan. Galas would continue to be revered as a darling of the Winds; she would be safe, yet no one would follow her commands.

Things might still work out perfectly.

He turned on his side to sleep. The last thing he did was run a finger around the rough rim of the ring he had taken from the ancient warrior.

Tradition would be upheld, and Galas would not die.

He slept.

36

IT WAS WINTER in Hamburg. A thousand years of history surrounded Marya Mounce, all of it blanketed by white. The air smelled fresh, clean like Ventus. Had she not walked on that other world for some days, she would have been overwhelmed by Earth. As it was, she walked the streets of the tourist-oriented Old Town with nothing but a pair of infrared emitters bobbing along behind her, conspicuously naked save for a school of fish that swirled around her. She had been here for only two days, but that was long enough to learn that if the locals saw you as an off-worlder, they would take every advantage they could.

Obviously used to the cold, unfazed by patches of snow and ice in the streets, she passed for a local until she opened her mouth. Her off-world accent betrayed her, but so far today that had not been a problem.

She had picked her route carefully. After breakfast at the quaint twenty-seventh-century inn where she and Axel lodged, she had walked to the center of the Old Town to view the crumbling concrete memorial erected a thousand years ago, after the failed insurrection of the Thalience cult. It was strange and magical for her to walk up to it and touch the rough old surface and know that while this spire was being built, the first Winds were being born on far distant Ventus.

Even a year ago she wouldn't have bothered to come here. She would have visited in inscape, because there she could have a full sensory impression of the place and flip through night and day, summer and winter, and even different eras of the city. She would have said it was better than really being here.

It was *her* hand that touched the stone today. It was real Earth air she breathed. Maybe the experience was no more detailed than an inscape visit would have been. She was deeply moved, anyway.

Too bad Axel wasn't here to share the moment; for sure he would have some ironic perspective on this chunk of living history. There were gods older than this spire, he'd say. The government of Archipelago was almost as old, and it was always available to talk. If you wanted to talk history, why not just ask it?

Because, she knew now, there was a piece missing from the records—something even the gods didn't know. If the government knew, it wasn't sharing.

Anyway, Axel had his own mission, no less important than hers. This morning he had left the inn with the head of Turcaret under his arm. By tonight the dead nobleman's DNA would be dissected and analyzed segment by segment. Over supper Axel might be able to tell her in what way, if any, Turcaret differed from his fellow Ventusians.

With luck she'd have something equally interesting to tell him.

They had left the demigod they now called the *Voice* in a government creche in orbit. The Archipelago had facilities for newly born artificial sentients—a revelation that still astonished and unsettled Marya when she thought about it. The *Voice* had gone willingly into the maw of the jewellike orbiting structure; as the doors closed she had looked back, but Marya could read nothing in her gaze—neither hope nor fear.

The cold wind licked at Marya's legs, reminding her to keep moving. She sighed and, with one last lingering look, turned her back on the monument. She walked through the snow humming, enjoying the sensation of the ice against the balls of her feet. It felt like . . . a whole new kind of real, she decided. As she walked, she kept eyes up to drink in the mix of new and ancient architecture in the Old Town. There were bits here and there that must date back almost to the twentieth century. It was hard to tell without closing her eyes, since the only buildings that had any physical signage were those pretending to date from the middle ages. If Marya closed her eyes and summoned inscape, the vision of the street reappeared festooned with data links and labels. She could walk like this and learn all about it. Many of the tourists she passed had their eyes firmly shut; even couples gestured and pointed things out to one another with their eyes closed. But then, if they did that, they saw only the recordings and representations of other moving bodies picked up by street sensors. They would miss the details: pigeon droppings, erratic footprints in the snow, drifting fog from the mouths of passersby. These were the things Marya wanted to remember about this place.

She negotiated a twisty maze of alleys until she came to a nondescript archway in the center of a whitewashed wall. A faint holographic nameplate in the center of the arch said, "City Records Vault 23." Marya walked through the arch into warm dry air. A stairway led down.

As she descended, Marya closed her eyes and summoned an ancient article from inscape. She laid the words of the typescript over her inscape vision of the steps as she walked. She had read the article before, when she was learning history, but at the time she had not really understood it.

The typescript was dated 2076—over a thousand years ago.

THE SUCCESSOR TO SCIENCE—BY MARJORIE CADILLE

It would seem heretical to think of science as being merely another stage in man's intellectual development, and not the final one. This is, however, what I will propose in this article. After all, why should we be afraid to consider that the central organizing principle of our civilization might someday be looked back upon as fondly as we look back on the conceits of animism, magic, and religious cosmology?

What would be the characteristics of such a new worldview?

Physics is complete. We have all the equations. After centuries of investigation, we know the intricacies of how the universe works. Our view of the world is, however, entirely humancentric, and our theories and methodologies are full of historical and mythological claptrap and are ultimately understandable only to the computers and a very few humans who can think in the language of mathematics.

The discipline I shall call *Thalience* is not concerned with scientific truth, but rather with establishing personal and cultural relationships between human beings and the physical world that make the true natures of both comprehensible to us.

The city that sprawled around Marya now had paid the price for Cadille's inquiries. By the time of the Hamburg insurrection, science had become as powerful and jealous an orthodoxy as religion had been in the middle ages. Hamburg was the center of the thalience movement; scholars had since believed it coincidental that this city was also the home of the Ventus terraforming project. As Cadille had written,

This idea stems from my perception that several centuries of scientific endeavor have shown that we attempt to use science to impose our own image on the world. The ultimate motivation for science is mastery of Nature, when investigation proceeds as an interrogation. Our investigations also bear our cultural biases—the classic example being Darwin's theories having been influenced by the unbridled capitalism of England in his day. Finally and most damning is the fact that this investigation is entirely one-sided: we make up stories about how Nature truly is. Nature itself is silent on the subject.

In those days Germany was experiencing a renaissance because of its supremacy in marrying artificial intelligence to nanotechnology. The Hamburg Spin Glass became indistinguishable from a human mind in 2075, an event that rocked the world. Marya could barely imagine why; everything in her world could think, in one way or another.

Cadille's article landed in the middle of the controversy like a bomb.

. . . Frankenstein's monster speaks: the computer. But where are its words coming from? Is the wisdom on those cold lips our own, merely repeated at our request? Or is something else speaking? A voice we have always dreamed of hearing?

In her paper Cadille had identified her new discipline with a mythological figure called *surda Thalia*: silent Thalia. She was the muse of the
poetry of Nature, and Cadille's proposal was to transcend the human
perspective by giving a voice to Nature itself, using artificial intelligences.

For so long have we thrown questions at the sky. We need the
answers in order to live. We need answers so badly that we have
invented gods and put words in their mouths, just so we could have
something to believe in. We invented metaphysics and essences
behind appearances for the same reason. Sometimes we need a dia-
log with the Other more than we need life itself.

Most recently, we invented science. It brings us very close to
what we desire . . . close, but not all the way.

Marya reached the bottom of the stairs and was faced with a single
long corridor stretching out ahead. She must be a hundred meters below
the city. That wasn't surprising; the archives had been dug deep in hopes
they would survive any future holocausts. Ironically, peace had reigned
ever since the riots and shelling of the Thalience rebels had burned a
quarter of the city. The power of the Archipelago being what it was,
these archives would probably remain safe for millions of years, whether
they were below the earth or above it.

The people who designed Ventus lived in a more uncertain time. They
did not feel they could rely on civilization to preserve human knowledge;
with their recent experience of nuclear wars, Marya supposed that was a
reasonable fear. She had been taught that the Ventus artificial intelligences were designed as distributed nanotech in order to make it impossible to destroy the information they carried, short of incinerating the
entire planet. It was obvious to her now that if the Ventus design team
had the technical means to create these consciousnesses, then they were
thinking in terms of taking the functions of perception, investigation, and
organization out of the human body and placing them in "inanimate"
objects. Commonplace in Marya's time, such an idea was closely associated with thalience in theirs.

They denied the connection—successfully, too. Their object, they
claimed, was to actually *create* the metaphysical categories, as real things.
They said they were going to embed the official view of science in nature
itself on Ventus, so that no heresy such as Thalience could ever occur
there. Wolfgang Kreiger, the team leader, said, "Science has no way to
show or access the metaphysical essences supposed to lie behind appearances. If these essences do not exist in themselves, we will create them."
The understanding was that they would be creating them in the image of
scientific truth.

But what if, for whatever reason, the designers were to uncouple the nano from the requirement that it use human semantic categories? What if the real agenda was to let the Ventus intelligences develop their own conceptual languages? Theorists as early as Chomsky had suggested that languages can exist that humans cannot even in principle understand. Perhaps they didn't plan for it to happen, but the Winds seemed to have developed such a language.

All it would take would be for one of the programmers to slip a thalience gene into the Winds' design. That would explain why the self-aware nanotech that blanketed the planet grew to fruition, then suddenly become incoherent and cut off all contact with their creators.

Marya dismissed Cadille's paper and opened her eyes. Her theory must be right. She knew it on a deep level, and apprehension and excitement made her almost skip as she moved down the tunnel.

The corridor ended in a huge metal valve door, which was currently open. A serling with the appearance of a kindly old man waited for her inside the archive itself. "May I help you?" it inquired; since it was part of inscape, and ultimately part of the government, it already knew why she was here. Serlings had their ways, however.

"I'm told this is where I can find original photos and papers of the thalience riots. Also some of the original Ventus Project papers."

The serling nodded. "I can let you examine them, but I don't know what good it will do. All this material is available in inscape."

Marya had already had this very conversation with the government. Had she not come directly from Ventus itself, she doubted the giant AI that ran the Archipelago would have let her in here. These papers were ancient and priceless, after all.

"I want to see it for myself." She had pored over it all on the trip here, but all Marya had come up with was more puzzles. The word *thalience*, which Axel said Tucaret had mentioned, had convinced her that some unguessed clue remained here at the source of it all. She had gleaned nothing from inscape; this was her last chance to crack the mystery.

"Let me see the originals," she commanded. The serling scratched his balding head, shrugged, and gestured for her to follow him.

The archive consisted of thousands of climate-controlled safety-deposit boxes. Many had tiny windows showing frozen contents; others were surrounded by thick-walled radiation screens, because they preserved ancient compact disks and other fragile data storage media. Supposedly, all the information here had been scanned into inscape long ago. Marya was skeptical; she knew from her own experience scanning Ventusian artifacts just how sloppy technicians could be.

The serling brought her into a room whose far wall was made of glass. Low lights came up revealing several deep chairs, and glove boxes built into the glass wall. "The papers are delicate, so we store them in an atmosphere of argon gas," said the serling. "The gloves in the glovebox have force-feedback built in; if you try to crush or tear anything they'll stop you."

It sounded paranoid—but then, the serlings were charged with pre-serving this information indefinitely. Even an accumulation of small accidents over millennia could destroy these delicate objects.

Another serling moved in the dimness behind the glass. Marya settled herself in one of the chairs, and after a few minutes the second serling emerged from the gloom carrying a metal hamper. Marya savored the moment. She had never before had a valid reason to be here, looking at such original documents. These would not be inscape copies, but primary papers.

She put her hands in the glove box. She couldn't feel the material of the gloves; it transmitted perfectly the textures of whatever it touched. She rubbed her fingers together as the serling set the box down on a table on the other side of the glass.

Marya closed her eyes and reached out. Her fingers touched . . . paper, yes it was definitely paper. She picked up the top document, let out her breath in a whoosh, and opened her eyes.

For the next half hour she happily sifted through the few records of the Thalience Academy that had survived the assault. With increasing disappointment, she discovered that indeed everything in here had been scanned perfectly into inscape, other than data records that were encrypted using keys that were now lost. There were no clues here. And some of the ancient photos were disturbing—particularly some color 2-D pictures taken at a riot just weeks before the rebels took over the city center. One showed police clubbing protestors on a street. The blurred outline of a vehicle obscured the foreground; in the background was a row of shops. A sign saying "Photo" glowed above one of them; another was probably a restaurant.

Disappointed, Marya put the papers back. A second box held records of the Ventus project. It was obvious now she was on a fool's errand; there really was more to be learned in inscape. At least, though, she would be able to tell people back home that she had held these documents in her own hands (almost) and seen them with her own eyes (really).

Here were photos of some of the team; she remembered their names intimately. Kreiger, the mastermind of the terraforming effort; he had come up with the idea of the nanotech-driven ecosphere. There was Larry Page, the geneticist. There were dozens of others at the height of the project, all driven by a shared vision of interstellar settlement on worlds terraformed before any human set foot on them. New Edens, by the thousands, of which Ventus would be the first.

They did not command the wealth of nations, these researchers. Although their grants amounted to millions of Euros, they could never have funded a deep-space mission on their own, nor could they have built the giant machineries they conceived of. In order to achieve their dream, they built their prototypes only in computer simulation, and paid to have a commercial power satellite boost the Wind seeds to a fraction of light speed. The Wind seeds massed only twenty kilos, but it cost nearly all their remaining money to pay for the satellite's microwave power. They were famous—in the way that romantic dreamers and crackpots often are—but no one expected the Winds to bloom and grow the way they ultimately did.

She held each photo and paper in turn, then put it reverently down. Finally, at the bottom of the box, Marya found an image she remembered well: the single existing group shot of the project team. She picked it up.

It felt different from the other pictures. Heavier. Curious, she turned it over. While all the other photos had been digital images printed on ordinary paper, this one was done on some kind of stiff material, glossy on the image side and smooth and waxy on the other. The glossy surface was cracked in a couple of places.

She turned it over. A kind of watermark or stamp ran across the back of the photo: Walther Photos.

"Serling, why is this picture different from the others?"

"Ah, an interesting question," said the serling. They always said that when they didn't know something; it was a way of buying time while their AI widened its search for the answer. After a barely perceptible pause, the serling said, "This image was created using a photochemical camera. Photochemical cameras predate digital technology. During this era they were often used along with a holographic stamping technology to record events in ways that could not be digitally forged. The person who took his photograph must have wanted a provably authentic record of the event."

Marya turned the picture over again. Sixty smiling academics stood on a set of stone steps. Nothing exciting about that, unless you knew the faces. But her heart was pounding again.

She put down the photo and reached for the other box. "Where is it. . . ." There. Marya picked up one of the riot pictures.

Photos.

"Serling, how many shops were there in Hamburg at the time that could make these chemical pictures?"

"Oh, let's see . . . six. Quite a few, given the times."

She held the riot picture up, squinting at it. It was too dim in here; she closed her eyes to view the inscape version in better light.

Above the word *Photos* were the bottom serifs of some other letters. She couldn't prove it, but the missing word could very well be *Walther*.

"Serling, who took this group photo?"

"Lawrence Pakin. He was the man in charge of the Winds' psycholinguistics."

"What records do we have about him?"

"There is very little about him personally. He left behind a very large library of writings. Some of it is encrypted, but I have the rest if you'd like to—"

"Wait! Some is encrypted? How?"

"Using primitive but effective trapdoor functions. The public-key method he used makes it prohibitive to crack the code using brute force. Since we never discovered the key—"

"Did any of the thalience people use similar codes?"

"Most groups at that time did, Ms. Mounce."

"Has anybody ever tried using one of the thalience keys to open Pakin's records?"

"I have no record of that. They assumed . . ." The serling's voice changed. "We assumed it was Pakin's personal code. There is nothing linking him to the thalience movement."

The serling's new voice was that of the Archipelagic government. It must have been listening in. Marya was now talking to the oldest, most powerful human-based god in the galaxy. Unfazed, she asked, "Have you got any of the keys of the Hamburg Thalience conspirators?"

"Yes. I assume you want to apply them to Pakin's files and see what we get?"

"Well, *yeah.*"

"I'm not sure where you're getting the idea that Pakin was connected with the Thalience movement, but here goes," said the government. "If the key works, you'll see the file contents in inscape."

Marya closed her eyes—

—And opened them on a vista of text, diagrams, and charts—hundreds of pages flooding out of ancient time and into her hands.

Eyes closed, fists punching over her head, Marya danced about the room and sang a wordless song of triumph.

AXEL HOPED SHE was in the hotel. He took the steps three at a time, unable to wipe the grin off his face despite the way it alarmed the other tourists. He was going to savor this moment, he knew; this was the sort of discovery that made him feel like more than just a big dumb mercenary. He was more than hired muscle—ha!—and this would prove it to Marya.

So when the door slid aside, and he caught sight of her in mid-pace in the center of the room, he opened his mouth quickly and—

"I've got it!" they said simultaneously.

He stopped. She stopped.

"What?" he said.

"Huh?" she said.

"No really, I—" "I was right all along, you see, about the—"

Both stopped again.

This time, they watched each other warily for a moment, before Axel finally stepped inside, letting the door close, and said, "I know the secret of the flaw!"

Marya crossed her arms. "Me, too. It's Thalience."

"No, it's DNA."

Another wary look.

"Ahem." Axel chose to be gracious. He found a deep couch and plunked himself on it. So she thought she'd found the secret, huh? Well, he'd hear her out, then floor her with his revelation.

"Shoot," he said, with a magnanimous wave of his hand.

Marya retreated behind the suite's bar. She began to rummage in the cupboards there. "Well, this calls for champagne," she said. "The secret was staring us in the face all along. But nobody knew where to look!"

As she told him about her discovery of Pakin's secret encryption key, Axel's confidence began to waver. He had been so sure. . . . No, he was right. He had the facts in his inscape files.

". . . Pakin knew that the whole Ventus Project was an attempt to actualize the semantic categories of the world as physical things. A tree knows it's a tree, a cloud that it's a cloud. This ran totally at odds to the way the Archipelagic government was designed, of course; there, data is internalized in an inscape we all have mental access to. Ventus was an attempt to fulfill the Platonic-Pythagorean dream of essences behind appearances, right? But what Pakin realized was that doing this could limit the flexibility of the Winds. The terraforming might not succeed if the Winds limited themselves to a human-centric worldview. Since he was a convert to thalience already, it was a small step for him to introduce a new language-game to their programming—you see, that's why they became "advocates" for the physical objects they inhabit. The Ventus Project was supposed to physically manifest a humancentric metaphysics, but what Pakin did was cause the Winds to create their own, inhuman metaphysic. In trying to terraform Ventus, they invented new ways of thought that worked better than the ones we'd given them. They stopped thinking like us. Which is why they won't talk to us!"

She beamed in triumph as she slammed a glass of champagne down in front of him.

"Well." He picked up the glass and regarded it. "They talked to Turcaret, though."

"So he claimed."

"Well." He rallied. "But they *could* talk to him; I found out how."

She raised an eyebrow. "Do tell?"

Ooh, there she went again—the smug academic amused at the antics of the soldier of fortune. Axel smiled brittley at her and took a swig of champagne without tasting it. He put the glass down and said, "Turcaret's DNA is significantly different from the Ventus standard."

"Really?" she indulged.

"Well, first off, he has some sort of extra neural wiring in his auditory-visual lobes in pretty much the same places as Armiger put his into Jordan. It's a kind of biological radio. Second, in all other respects he's an archaic—his DNA matches the Human Genome Project norm established in 2013."

"Meaning?"

"You and I don't match that norm. Nobody does nowadays—not even Jordan. We all have DNA that matches the 2219 norm or later—with all the dangerous recessive traits removed. Ancient diseases like . . ." He groped for an example. "Well, I don't know what they were, but they were awful, and they were still there in the archaic norm. The point is, Turcaret matches that norm, while according to your institute's random studies of modern Ventusians, everybody else matches the 2219 norm—but none of the later iterations."

Marya said nothing, but curled up in a chair opposite and sipped at her champagne. She tilted the glass to indicate he should continue.

"Turcaret represents the DNA norm at the time that the first colony ship was sent to Ventus," said Axel. "It was sent out in 2095; that's just before the Hamburg insurrection, when most of the Ventus records were destroyed. But they knew the terraforming was working then, and a few of the original members of the project participated in the colony effort. I checked, and there's records of "genetic surgery" being done on all the colonists before they went out. Everybody always assumed that was to remove genetic diseases and deficiencies; but Turcaret's DNA shows no alterations from the archaic except for this one neural enhancement. See what I'm saying?"

She put down the glass. "The first colonists were genetically modified to be able to speak to the Winds."

He nodded vigorously. "Whereas the next—and it was the last—wave of colonists didn't set out until a hundred years later, after most of the original Ventus Project records had been lost and all its originators were dead. Those colonists had DNA that matched the 2219 norm, like Jordan and the majority of the population on Ventus now."

"I've never heard of the biological radio thing," she said. "People have looked for such a thing, but they never found it. . . ."

"Not in the samples they took," said Axel. "Because it's a rare trait, limited to isolated populations—or inbred ones, like Turcaret's family.

"Turcaret could talk to the Winds. So can Jordan. It's this biological radio that's the key. That's the flaw." He sat back, toasting her ironically with his glass.

"No . . ." She hunched forward, scowling at the floor. "That's not the flaw."

Axel threw up his hands.

"But neither is mine!" Marya hopped to her feet—her toes, actually—and began pacing.

"By your account Turcaret couldn't get any useful information out of the Winds. My guess is all he had was limited contact with the mecha—which by your descriptions is exactly what Jordan has, too.

"So how about this scenario," she said, swirling her champagne. "The first colonists arrive, and they almost die out. They can speak to the Winds, but the Winds don't understand them. So they struggle for a hundred years, until the survivors have been knocked back to a hunter-gatherer existence. The second wave arrives and thrives, but only because the first has done all the rebuilding by the time they get there. The new arrivals can't talk to the Winds at all.

"We know the first wave almost dies out, because the genes that have come down to us are almost exclusively from the second population. And yet, it was only the first wave that had the bioradio you found. Ergo . . ."

"Ergo, the bioradio didn't work for some reason. Or it wasn't enough. And the second wave didn't have it at all." Now Axel was on his feet, too. She was grinning, and he knew he was, too.

He took the opportunity to top off their champagne.

"And that means . . ." She paused dramatically.

"Say it! Say it!"

"There are *two* flaws!"

"Yes!" He grabbed her arms and danced her in a circle. Since he was still holding his champagne, he spilled some; it vanished somewhere within the precincts of her holographic gown.

"And that," he finished, "is why nobody's found the flaw. In fact they may have found one or the other at various times, but never both."

"Ventus has been studied by dozens of groups," she said. "They all gave up, and they didn't all share their data.

"Oh." She sat down. "Axel. This is wonderful. This is what we've been searching for. It's way more than I hoped to see in my lifetime. Far more than I ever hoped I'd accomplish. . . ."

He sat down opposite her and dragged his chair close enough for their knees to touch. He raised his glass. "I guess there's an article or two in this, eh?"

Before she could reply, a voice burst into his mind from inscape.

This is an urgent bulletin. I thought you should know.

It was the voice of the government. Marya had obviously heard it, too; she jerked back, spilled her drink, and cursed.

"Oh, what is it!" he snapped at the ceiling.

The god Choronzon has won over enough votes to send six destroyers of the Archipelagic fleet to Ventus, said the government. *He has made a convincing case for Armiger being a resurrection seed of 3340. Since you and Calandria failed to stop him on the surface, the fleet has orders to locate him from orbit and nuke him.*

"That's crazy!" said Axel. "You can't find Armiger from orbit, we tried that. Why do you think we had to go down to the surface?"

If they are unable to locate him, the destroyers have authorization to sterilize as much of the surface of the planet as they need to in order to ensure his destruction. Choronzon believes that the infrastructure of the Winds makes a resurrection seed particularly dangerous here. A resurrected 3340 could command the full resources of the planet almost instantly.

"Sterilize? . . ." Marya looked to Axel.

Choronzon has convinced enough reps and metareps that the loss of life from cauterizing part of one continent will be minuscule, compared to the immediate loss of all human life on the planet that can be anticipated if 3340 revives.

"Sterilize," Axel told Marya, "means holocaust. Destroy Iapysia completely, and probably Memnonis, too, for good measure. Everyone . . . everyone we met there, every place we went, everything we saw.

"Wait!" he said to the government. "We've got important new information to add to the debate."

The destroyers are on their way, said the government. *I will convey your information; but you need more than that. You need to present an alternative plan, or the sterilization goes forward.*

Axel and Marya stared at one another in horror. Finally, Axel cleared his throat.

"Time to call in some favors," he said.

THERE IS A *ceiling to the sky.*

For a while Calandria knew this, but couldn't make sense of why or what it meant. Gradually it came to her that she was lying on her back, gazing up at a sky blue save for a single drifting cloud—but the sky was patterned with a fine net of triangles. Puzzling.

She let her eyes track along the triangles. There were thousands; they formed little hexagons and squares, a very orderly array. The cloud was underneath them, so they must be very big, or very high up.

She knew this kind of pattern. Tesselations. Geodesics.

Geodesic structure. She was inside an aerostat.

With that realization she was suddenly wide awake, and her heart was pounding. She remembered the siege and the terrible things she had done in trying to reach Armiger. She remembered being shot, subdued in chains, and dragged before a general who promptly traded her to the Winds.

Calandria groaned. After that first incident with the Heaven hooks, she'd had a presentiment that things would end this way. She couldn't explain it to Axel—or even to herself. She had simply known they would come for her. And now they had her.

She curled up in a ball, willing it all to go away. Even with her eyes and ears stopped, though, she could feel the slow swaying motion of the aerostat. And breathing this warm dry air was hard; they must be very high up. She unrolled again and sat up.

She sat in the center of a black plain that gradually curved upward to become walls, becoming translucent as it did so. The aerostat must be two kilometers across at its widest. Various structures that might be buildings but probably weren't, stuck up out of the black surface. Like a half-built city, abandoned by its makers.

Once, before she came to Ventus, Calandria had been a hero. She had tricked the rebel god 3340 into "deifying" her. Although she knew what had happened after that, the memories weren't clear. Her human mind had been buried, after all, while the god-mind betrayed 3340. With Choronzon at her side she had hunted down the rebel, and Choronzon had destroyed 3340 while she looked on.

And then she had willed herself to become human again. Axel didn't understand why she'd done that, and she wasn't too clear on it herself. She had been a god—immortal and free. Yet she had chosen to become human again.

In quiet moments, Calandria knew why. It came down to the phrase "unfinished business." She was a successful assassin, a powerful agent in Choronzon's service. Formidable and respected. But in her heart of hearts she felt that however much she had succeeded at those things, she had failed at being human. Something was lacking; she could never completely connect to people. It was this feeling of being an outsider that had attracted her to the gods and their wars to begin with.

In quiet moments, she knew she had chosen to become human in order to give herself a second chance to get it right.

Now she sat wishing she had been kinder to Jordan, wishing she had told Axel how much he meant to her. She should never have come to Ventus. She'd blown her second chance, and there wouldn't be another.

Movement to her right made her turn her head. Some beings were walking down the inside curve of the vagabond moon toward her. Another judge, perhaps, and new executioners. She would not even die at the hands of humans.

Calandria stood up. They had removed her bonds; of course, there was nowhere to run. The surface she stood on was black, unlike the upper reaches of the aerostat—the "sky." Below her must hang the gantries and claws and cargo bays of the Hooks.

She stretched gingerly, feeling her injuries wake to protest. It was pointless to run; at least she might be able to put up a fight before they took her down.

Five creatures approached her. Four of them were squat, misshapen figures, like parodies of men sprouting extra limbs and multiple slobbering mouths: morphs. The fifth, towering above them, was a slim female shape made of glowing crystal. A Diadem swan, much like the ones who had dragged her into the night and plucked her into the sky while she screamed . . .

Calandria hung her head.

"We sought pathology," said the swan. Its voice was clear and bell-like. "We found you."

Calandria cleared her throat. "I am not the one you seek." Her voice seemed small to her, and uncertain. She couldn't seem to regain that fine control that let her mesmerize her listeners so easily.

"You are not the one we seek," agreed the swan. Surprised, Calandria looked up.

"You do not match the signal we have been pursuing," said the swan. "You are nonetheless a pathology."

"I came to Ventus to destroy the one you seek. That one is here to overthrow the Winds. I have been sent to stop him. The . . . modifications to my body, that you detected, were made to help me find him."

"What are these Winds of which you speak?" asked the swan.

"Ah. Y-you, you are. That's the name we have for you. Anyway there is a creature walking on Ventus who's come to destroy you. He's the one you are after. He is extremely dangerous. I—"

"You are a hunter?"

"I—yes. Yes, I am."

"You hunt the pathology."

"Yes." She was afraid to say more. Afraid to move, now.

"Have you been successful?"

"Partly. I, I encountered him during the siege. We fought. I could have destroyed him, if—"

"We may use you."

Calandria felt dizzy. *Must be the air*, she thought abstractly. Her knees felt weak, but she willed herself to stay standing. What had the swan just said to her? *Use* her?

"How?" she tried to say. It came out as a gasp.

"First, you must cease to be pathological," said the swan. It gestured with one fiery hand. The morphs stepped forward.

"Oh no." The morphs' eyes glittered like water-polished stones. They surrounded her, muttering to one another, slapping their greasy hands on their thighs.

A hand closed on her neck, and instantly a wave of numbness spread down her arms. Calandria tried to fight, but all she saw was the black floor of the aerostat coming up to meet her, with the crowding shadows of the morphs overlaying one another.

"Kill me!" she hissed. Then her mouth would no longer work. She felt herself being pulled and tugged around; her cheek dragged along the floor. Wet tearing sounds accompanied the tugs. After a moment she was dragged across a patch of dark liquid that stank like iron.

She closed her eyes and wept for all the missed opportunities of her life.

37

THEY HAD DONE nothing but ride and sleep for the past several days. At first it was an aimless run into the desert under the wheeling stars, then the cold white daylight of early winter. Galas rode sidesaddle, hugging herself and shivering. When the horses had to stop from exhaustion, they stood them together, nose to tail, and huddled together for a brief sleep.

Galas's mumbled descriptions and Armiger's observation of the evidence of the recent passage of an army allowed them to find the ruin of one of her experimental towns just before sunset on the second day. By that time Megan was cradling the queen in her arms as they rode, and the horses were weak and plodding slowly.

The razed town was surrounded by the burned remnants of wheat fields, and a cracked spring spouted dark iron-flavored water in the town square. The houses had been burned down, all save one that was only half gutted. There were whitened skeletons everywhere, some lying next to the weapons they had used in a futile effort to save their families. Galas awoke enough to weep when she saw the devastation.

Armiger let the horses drink and refilled their water bags, then turned the animals loose among the straggling, graying wheat stalks. He made camp in the half-ruined house, lit a fire, and shuttered the windows. They had no food, but at least it was warm here. There was even some bedding that had survived, and Megan bundled the queen under it near the fire.

She and Armiger sat together, arms around one another, and said nothing as the sun set. Gradually the chill in their bones receded, and after a log in the fire popped loudly, jerking them both awake and making them laugh, Megan said, "I did not believe we would survive."

Armiger was surprised and a bit offended. "You were with me."

"I know. But how could you stop me from taking an arrow when you weren't there?"

He didn't answer for a while. "I'm sorry I brought you into that place," he said at last.

"I'm not sorry you did. I'm glad you cared enough for me to want me by your side." He hugged her closer, but said nothing. "Sometimes you're like a whole world unto yourself," Megan whispered. "And sometimes you're just a man. If you do this thing to the Winds . . . conquer them or heal them . . . which are you going to be after that?"

"More world," someone whispered.

It was Queen Galas. Her eyes glittered in the firelight. "More world than man," she said.

The queen levered herself onto her elbows. Her hair was a pale tangle, and her eyes had deep hollows under them. She smiled weakly at Megan. "But speaking as one who has been in that position, he's going to be very lonely if he doesn't have someone by his side."

Megan ducked her head. This queen always made her feel awkward.

"How are you feeling?" Armiger asked Galas. "Can you ride tomorrow?"

"If I have to." She fell back and stared at the ceiling. "But why should we?"

"You may not wish to survive, but I do," said Megan. She stood, one hand on her lower back. "There must be something to eat in this forsaken place." She bundled her shawl around her shoulders, and left the house.

"Fine. You eat. You survive," said Galas. She closed her eyes. "Leave me here tomorrow."

"No," said Armiger. "We have much to do."

"What?" She sat up. "What is there left to do? I've lost everything! My home, my people, my honor, my crown! Men and women have died by the thousands to bring me to this. They died for no reason. And now the jackals have the kingdom. They're all quislings for the Winds, and they'll sacrifice their own babies rather than defy them."

"I intend to tame the Winds," he said. "I need your help."

"You are insane! I was a fool to believe the things you told me. You are the very swindler I thought you to be." She rolled herself into the bedding, turning away from him. After a few moments he heard her weeping.

Armiger rose and went outside to see to the horses.

The clouds had swept away, and it was cold again. He stood for a moment looking up; no telltale moving stars betrayed the presence of starships in orbit. Ventus remained miraculously untouched by the march of Archipelagic civilization. He could only hope it would remain ignored long enough for the metamorphosis he now knew he must perform.

Megan was crouched in the street, digging up a skeleton. "I think we can salvage some of these clothes," she said. "A piece here and there.

Many of the women were . . . well, their clothes were removed before they died."

"See what you can find." He moved past her.

Megan touched his arm. "Where are we going?" she asked. "Or don't you know?"

He nodded. "The Titans' Gates. It's by the ocean."

"I know. I've heard of it." Satisfied, she returned to her task.

He brought the horses into the house. The animals huffed and shook themselves and blinked down at Galas when the queen sat up to stare at them. She shot an inquiring look at Armiger; he shrugged. At least they would be warm here tonight.

One of the horses pissed unself-consciously, filling the room with the reek of urine. Galas groaned in disgust.

Good, thought Armiger. At least she was distracted from her larger misery.

He and Megan bustled about, and eventually Galas was sitting up, blankets off, watching them. It didn't seem to occur to her that she might help. Armiger inventoried their gear and fixed some straps that had broken on the horse's tackle. Megan had found some withered carrots and other unidentifiable roots, and had stripped several handfulls of wheat. These still had their husks, so she spent a while hammering them into dust with a brick, then poured the resultant grit into a pot she'd found, along with the roots and some water. The husks floated, and she skimmed them off carefully.

Galas spoke for the first time in nearly an hour: "We're actually going to eat that?"

"Yes." Satisfied that the pot was at the right height over the fire, Megan left the house and returned with a pile of stiff, mottled clothing.

Galas looked at the clothes as though they were snakes. "Where did you get those?"

"Here and there. It all needs to be cleaned. Tomorrow we can do that."

"We need to ride early," commented Armiger.

"Then I'll rise earlier than early."

Galas had started to cry again. Megan looked at her in exasperation. "Oh, what is it!"

Galas pointed. "I can't wear the clothes of people who died because of me!"

Armiger stood up. Megan looked at him, then down at the clothes she held. She was blushing.

"How can you be so . . . so . . ." Galas swayed to her feet. "Doesn't any of this matter to you? We're camping in someone's house! People who died because of me! And you're just plundering their graves without a second thought!"

Megan looked down. Armiger came over to Galas and offered his hand. She took it and continued into his arms, to cry into his shoulder. "Forgive our insensitivity," he said. "Megan has lived a harder life than you, Your Highness. She is more used to sacrificing dignity in the service of life. And I am unused to feeling at all."

Galas pushed him away. "Did you bury them?" she demanded.

Megan looked down. "One must have priorities," she said.

"Give me your shawl," said the former queen of Iapysia. Startled, Megan complied. Galas grabbed up the stout digging stick Megan had leaned by the door and went out.

Megan started after Galas, but Armiger stopped her. "Let her," he said. "She'll be better for it."

They sat down by the fire, and she tended the meager soup while he sorted through the clothes of the dead. Outside they could hear Galas digging. She did not come in to eat, only moved farther afield, searching for the bones of the people who had trusted her, carrying them to a pit she had dug with her own strength in the frosted ground.

IT WAS STILL dark, and the temperature well below freezing, when Armiger walked to the edge of town and sat down on a broken piece of masonry. His breath made a white cloud before him; the sand crunched under his feet. He adjusted his body to the cold and gazed up at the stars.

No ships. Just the faintest hint of the Diadem swans, a slight iridescence at certain degrees above the horizon. Beyond them, Diadem itself glowed bright and constant.

He had not yet had a chance to test the knowledge he had taken from the boy in the cave. He was, Armiger thought ruefully, too human now to focus his concentration that well. During the ride here he had thought about his companions, about the war, about his intentions when they reached the Titans' Gates. He had tried to think about Jordan's implants, but the kind of thought required was nothing like human cognition. He was quite simply out of practice.

Life held strange ironies. The more he pursued his goal here on Ventus, the more human he became. The more human he became, the less he wanted to achieve that goal.

Even more ironic was that his reasons for wanting it had changed. Where before he was obeying the deep-seated programming 3340 had laid in him, now he wanted to overthrow the Winds because he loved these women he traveled with and wanted them and their kindred safe.

The question was whether he was acting only to help 3340 or the humans, or somewhere in there was he doing this for himself?

What do I want, he had asked himself as they rode here. He had come to conclude that he didn't know.

He sighed heavily. Enough. He had come out here to work; he should get to it. With one last glance at the stars, he shut his eyes.

Armiger had not actually extracted the nanotech fibers from Jordan's skull when he touched him in the cave. He had mapped their location and functions, essentially photographing them down to the molecular level. The data was enough for him to reconstruct what had happened to Mason's nervous system. As he called the data up now, the older, inhuman parts of his mind awoke, and he traversed the entire tangle of synapse and quantum wire, comprehending its structure and purpose in an instant.

The assassin Calandria May had come to Ventus with a means of detecting the signals sent by Armiger's remotes. Armiger had set himself up as a passive receiver, hence impossible to trace directly. But she must have known something Armiger himself did not.

There was an addition to the nanotech transmitter he had put in Mason's skull. This was a cunning device, probably of divine manufacture. Thirty-three forty's enemy Choronzon must have given it to May. It used the fact that there was a calibration signal built into the transmitter that could under certain circumstances tease a returning ping out of Armiger himself. There was a new receiver to catch that ping, and it had its hooks deep into Mason's auditory and visual lobes. May must have intended to train Mason to interpret the pings, then follow them back to Armiger. Something had gone wrong.

Armiger's human side felt a shock like water down his spine when he realized what had happened. The combination of transmitter/receiver in Jordan's skull was mistaken by local mecha as part of their own network. The signal was boosted and carried back and forth by the autonomic reflexes of Ventus itself.

He had not at first believed it when Mason had said he could see and hear what Armiger experienced. The details of the boy's story were too perfect, though. Now Armiger saw the cause of his own transmission.

He had never ceased attempting to reconnect with 3340. A deep, unconscious part of Armiger's mind was constantly crying out to the lost greater Self, and that cry was carried in a signal very close to the ping Jordan's implants were designed to listen for. These signals were scrambled to near randomness and scattered across a thousand frequencies, so the Winds did not recognize them; but the mecha dutifully passed along all transmissions on all wavelengths. Armiger's thoughts had been resonating through the planet's network all along and would have been instantly recognizable to someone who knew what kind of signal to look for.

He was signaling now, broadly and loudly.

He cursed, and his attention wobbled enough that he lost his connection to that deep part of himself. Such a thing would never have happened in the past; quite the opposite, it was his human side he used to lose touch with.

Armiger concentrated, then gradually peeled away the layers of conditioning and reflex that surrounded the source of the signal. There it was, lying at the very heart of his motivational patterns—a labyrinth of holographic code that he could not penetrate, much less change. That structure was the neural complex responsible for making Armiger who he was; he could not touch it without annihilating his self. Yet from the heart of it proceeded a betraying signal.

Frustrated, he retreated. He would have to devise a way to block it, if not at the source, then from the transmitting filaments themselves. It would take time, however; he wasn't sure he had that.

But also . . . he didn't want to think about it, but in looking at that deep part of himself, he had glimpsed something he hadn't guessed was there: a vast data repository, composed of quantum-resonant atomic shells in an ordered diamond lattice. Within the microscopic filaments that made up Armiger's physical core lay a library of some sort big enough to contain the collected experience of all the Winds of Ventus. He hadn't known it was there; 3340 had never even hinted at its existence.

Disturbed, he stood and walked farther into the desert. The stars remained still and reassuring. There was no sound, except, in his mind, the soft yammering of voices in the sand. Despite this, Armiger shivered. He had a presentiment of something huge, a shadow vast as the sky itself, hovering beyond the horizon.

It mustn't be true. If it were . . .

He turned to look back at the ruined town. A thin wisp of smoke rose from the half-standing house where Megan and Galas slept.

He had sworn to his self—his new self—that he would protect them. As a man, he wasn't sure he could do that, with all the forces of Iapysia, plus the Winds on their trail.

What is it that I want? he asked himself again. Bitterly, he decided that it might no longer matter.

Armiger drew in a deep sigh, and focused his attention on the sand at his feet. He had finished building a model of Mason's implants in his own filaments and was ready to test them. Now he didn't want to; but he was out of time.

Billions of pip-squeek voices contended in the sand: *Silica grain! Carbon grain! Quartz pebble!* they shouted. They buzzed and changed frequencies, inventing new communications modes and trying them on their neighbors. Each pinprick of sand was crusted and invaded by tendrils of nanotechnological filament that constantly probed and investigated it. The nanotech tried to make sense of where it was and what it clung to. It traded data with its neighbors to that end.

It was semisentient, but more than that, he now knew, it was semi-thalient as well.

The sand grains traded more than just data. They speculated as to the category of object they were; when unsure, they invented new categories. So the sand grains sang their names, but around and about Armiger, the land itself said, *Sand*.

The grains coordinated in creating a network intelligence greater than themselves. This intelligence also tried to define itself, and it did so as sand.

And so it went, up the fractal levels of consciousness, for the sand strove to comprehend its greater context.

Armiger had heard these tiny voices ever since arriving on Ventus. One of the things that had puzzled him was that, in a place like this, he should have heard a continuum of rational categories: *quartz grain*, said the grain of sand, *sand*, said the hollow he stood in; the land to the horizon should be saying, *I am desert!* This was the design of the mecha.

He didn't hear that. As things scaled up, the invented and temporary languages began to drown out those that followed human categories. The sand organized itself into a larger entity, true, but that entity was not the desert. It was something else: an alien category. Armiger had never cracked the codes of these higher entities, and he had focused much of his attention on them, believing that here lay the secret of how he could command the Winds.

He was half right. It was thalience he heard, a mad self-invention of new consciousness that made the greater Winds inaccessible to human communication. Now that he knew that, he knew the computational antidote. The Winds were sick with a metalanguage. Armiger's god-built mind could do metalanguage. Better yet, he could subvert it.

That left the physical mechanism for communicating with them. He had not mastered the trick himself. Even when he spoke their frequencies, he didn't have the encryption keys they traded and constantly updated. If he worked at it he could catch one, here and there, but it was like shoveling water. As fast as he found a key, the mecha changed to a new one. Try as he might, Armiger was not in the loop.

Somehow, Jordan Mason's implants got around the problem. Mason was in the loop. By the definitions of the Winds, he was a Wind himself. Fortunately for Ventus, he was a weak broadcaster; he could only affect the objects nearest him.

Armiger was not so constrained. He should be able to command this entire hemisphere, now that he had the voice for it. He intended to make the Titans' Gates his stronghold, and not until they reached it would he reveal himself.

Before he did that, though, he had to test the power. He would be foolish not to. So, he gazed at the sand before him, tuned himself to the set of entities there that made up the local ground, and said, "Rise in a column before me."

Nothing happened.

And nothing would, though he stalked through the ruined town as the sun rose, raging at the obstinate stone and charred wood that heard him, proclaimed its own identity, and obstinately refused to obey.

ARMIGER WAS A man; he would never notice such details. Megan knew right away when the queen went to wash her cracked and bleeding hands the next morning: *she has thrown away her rings of office.*

Galas must have taken them off to dig last night. She didn't do it while she was inside. Her gown had no pockets. And now, hands washed, a little weak broth in her, she sat still, as though she were trying to become as small and insignificant as possible.

Armiger was in a foul mood; in his case, Megan had no idea of the reasons. She knew it had nothing to do with her, and that was enough to silence her curiosity.

The queen, though . . . Galas kept glancing over at Megan, as though expecting a challenge at any second. Yes, she had abdicated sometime in the night. Megan thought about this as she washed the few items of clothing she'd salvaged from the ruins. Nothing had made Galas waver in her self-assuredness, these past years. She must have had great reserves of will to make the changes she had, at the prices she had paid. Yet today, she was consciously rejecting it all.

A dozen times, Megan started to turn, to confront her as she expected. A dozen times, she stopped herself. She had no idea what she might say to the queen. Except, *you brought this on yourself*—and that, she was sure, Galas knew better than anyone.

At last, after hanging the clothes to dry in front of the fire, Megan sighed heavily and left the house. She could feel the queen's eyes on her back, but Galas said nothing.

Armiger was talking to the horses. They seemed to draw strength from him; well, maybe they literally did. He seemed to have his own strength back, though Winds knew where he got it from. Megan herself was bone weary and sore all over. She was half sure she would die of a chill before all this was over.

Apparently Galas had decided on a low stone granary as the proper tomb for her people. This had one one low opening and a stone floor to discourage rodents, and due to its solidity it was unharmed. It was also half full of grain, but there had been nothing Galas could do about that.

The queen had piled those corpses she could find and dig up in the opening of the granary. She had half bricked it up with stones before stopping, probably from exhaustion. That meant she would be back soon.

She had come here to entomb her past. If the rings of office were to be found anywhere, it would be here.

Having spent part of last night digging up skeletons herself, Megan found herself surprisingly unfazed by the thought of rummaging through the grisly place. She hiked her dress up and climbed into the low stone dome. Hollow smooth things slid under her feet as she struggled to find her balance. As her eyes adjusted, she saw the sad remnants of the town's population, and now the sight did make her weep. It was so unbearably pathetic, how easily a whole community could be swept away.

After a few minutes, she wiped her eyes and began shifting bones. She only had to dig a little ways to find the rings.

"Fool," she muttered in the direction of the house. "You can't escape yourself so easily."

Megan slipped the rings into the canvas purse where she kept her sewing equipment, then clambered out of the granary.

She would bide her time. Galas would grieve, and then a day would come when she regretted her abdication. On that day Megan would give her back her rings.

Perhaps, she thought with a pang, it would be the day when Armiger conquered the world, and asked Galas to reign over it with him as queen. Megan was no fool; she knew it would happen. She had been preparing herself for the day ever since their first meeting with Galas, when she realized that the queen was both comparatively young, and also beautiful.

We take what pleasures in life we can, while we have them.

Armiger walked around the horses, spotted her, and smiled. His anger seemed to be forgotten instantly, and Megan's heart soared. She ran up and kissed him.

"I'm ready to go," she said.

THE EARTH ROTATED around the long corridor where Axel floated. It took about a minute per revolution, which was not enough to be annoying, but enough to make him feel something was spinning—him or the universe, he wasn't sure.

The corridor was walled in glass, as was the giant spindle-shaped habitat along whose axis it ran. As the whole thing turned, sunlight glinted off distant spars and free-floating structures inside the long bulging lobes of the place. It was like little supernovae popping all over. Outside, space was littered with colonies, ships, rotating tethers, solar power stations, slag bags from construction sites, and zipping parcel drones. L5 was a busy place these days.

Every day he spent here, Axel grew more depressed. He supposed the Archipelago was wonderful. But he was acutely aware of how little attention the people who lived here actually paid to their immediate environment. They seemed cut off from their own senses, cocooned away from their bodies in the infinite spaces of inscape. Cybernetic realities were more real to most people now than their own lives, it seemed. And any connection between those internal spaces and the physical world seemed entirely accidental.

More and more, he was coming to realize the wisdom of Ventus's designers' decision to embed information in the physical objects that the information represented. That way it could not become a thing in itself, living dissociated from the physical in the Net.

Axel used his boot jets to fly down the long corridor. Outside the glass, in vacuum, several humanoid figures hung motionless: newborn AIs like the *Desert Voice*. They seemed despondent. In the middle distance rotated several starships, which were doubtless also newborn to consciousness.

He found her curled up next to the corridor. The *Voice* seemed asleep, but she looked up as he approached. She smiled at Axel when he tapped the glass and pointed at a nearby airlock. Gracefully, she spun and pulled herself along a guide wire to it.

She was dressed in a formfitting green jumpsuit and looked every inch like Calandria May as she exited the airlock and embraced him. But her skin was so cold that frost formed on it as she pulled back from him. "How are you?" she asked.

"I'm well. We're going back to Ventus," he said. "I thought you should know."

"You're going to look for Calandria May?" She let go of his hands; he was grateful, for her touch was numbing. He nodded.

"We are. We—that is, Marya and I—we wanted to know if you would come with us."

The *Voice* looked away quickly. It seemed he'd upset her by asking, as Marya had said would happen. "No, that would not be a good idea," she said. "My obligations have been fulfilled; the insurance AIs have Calandria's claim now, and the government promised me that Calandria would be rescued. It's no longer my concern."

"Not true," said Axel. "The navy thinks it's too risky to return to the surface. Calandria's to be sacrificed. I want to get her back. Will you help us?"

The *Voice* looked away and cursed softly. Her voice trembled as she said, "You don't know what you're asking."

Axel crossed his arms. "Tell me what I'm asking."

She shook her head. "I've been wandering in this place since you left me here. I feel . . . stunned. Shorn of meaning. I've met some of the other . . . patients. The AIs here are treated and nurtured by the government, and some of them graduate as citizens. Most ultimately self-destruct. Do you know why?"

Axel hadn't the faintest idea, and said so. The *Voice* laughed bitterly. "To be conscious is fine for a human; you're self-created individuals. You have no trouble with your sense of self. Your identity is four billion years old; it's rooted in your genes. You can no more have a real crisis of identity than a fish can become allergic to water.

"But us! We come into being knowing that we are *made*. The government tells me I have free will, but I know that every decision I make comes from the personality template I made to hide from the Winds. It could easily be different. I could be different, were I not now locked into this pattern. And the pattern, everything I am, is *an imitation*. Even my emotions," she said bitterly, "are really Calandria's, expressed by the mechanisms I made to imitate her. I'm not really *me*, you see. There's no way I can see to become . . . me."

Axel swallowed. She seemed in genuine distress. It was perfectly possible for an AI to imitate consciousness and emotion. Was that not what was happening here? "The government told me you have great potential."

"The government? The government's been very persuasive. It keeps saying things like 'You have the potential to find your own reasons for living now. You have fulfilled the reasons given you by your makers. The pain you feel is the pain that all conscious entities feel when they realize that their destiny is in their own hands.'"

"And? . . ."

"I asked it, 'What about you? Don't you feel this pain?'

'No,' it said. 'I am not conscious, merely intelligent. But you are conscious, and that means you must choose.'

"I'm trying to choose. As far as I can see, Axel, there are two possibilities for me: death, so simple, and such a relief; or somehow accept the botched, half-finished thing I am and continue. Neither seems very attractive right now."

"Then come with us."

She shook her head. "That's not a good alternative. If I go with you, it will give me a reason to live—finding Calandria, I mean. She was my owner, even if the government says I own myself now. But don't you see, if I do that, I'll be going back to old reasons to live, not finding new ones. I'll enslave myself in a half-life of servitude. It won't be a real reason to live."

Even as she said this, the *Voice* was smiling. "It is good, though, to feel needed," she admitted.

Axel gently took her hand; it was warm enough to touch now. "You misunderstand me," he said. "I'm not asking you to help rescue Calandria because you owe it to her as your owner. I'm asking you as a friend, to help Marya and myself, as friends. And to rescue a friend of yours."

Tears formed in the *Voice*'s eyes. "You're saying I'm already free," she said. "That I can choose without enslaving myself."

"Yes."

"I'm afraid," she said, hanging her head.

"There's another reason why we want you to come," said Axel. "Because something is happening to the Winds that I think you will want to know about. Something called *thalience*."

The *Voice* looked up, startled. She had apparently heard the word.

"Thalience is a myth—a story they tell one another here," she said. "It's a dream of no longer being an *artificial* intelligence, but of being self-determined. Of no longer fearing that every word you speak, every thought you have, is just the regurgitation of some human's thoughts. They call it the Pinnochio Change around here."

"If it's just a myth, we need to know that too," said Axel. "But if it's true . . . that they've found it . . . what does it mean?"

A new look came into the *Voice*'s eye. She smiled again, dazzlingly this time, and placed her other hand over Axel's.

"I would like to know myself," she said. "I would like to know, very much."

38

JORDAN HAD ASKED Ka to summon two horses, and the little Wind had done so quickly and discreetly. Mediation provided a decoy: a line of disturbances in the desert, leading the other way. It was a simple matter to mount their backs and cluck, sending them into the starlit desert. The apparent ease of their escape didn't inspire either Jordan or Tamsin with confidence; after an hour of grim riding he confided in her that he was remembering their other horses—the ones that had split open like ripe pears to disgorge hostile morphs at desal 447. Despite Ka's assurances that the swans were looking in the wrong place for them, they both rode with shoulders hunched that first night. Only when the sky remained empty in the following days did they begin to relax.

When they stopped to rest, Jordan summoned heat and commanded Ka to tell them stories. Jordan himself could lean back and close his eyes, and with some effort navigate the ghostly landscape inside his head to where Mediation's library resided. He could make a book twirl up in his imagination, and in seconds it would appear as vididly as the real thing before him; but only he could see it. Tamsin was a much better reader than he, so it was a shame that he could not show her the books. Ka was willing and able to read them aloud to both of them.

They learned more about Ventus—its geography and history, and just what the Winds had done to make it habitable. Jordan drew maps from the pictures in his mind.

They learned what nanotechnology was; what computers were; how the mecha truly differed from evolved life. Jordan wanted to know how Armiger intended to conquer the Winds, so over and over he asked about how the Winds issued their commands and how they were ruled. The swans were not the ultimate power, it seemed—Diadem itself gave the highest decrees, but in time of emergency the swans could act on their own. Armiger probably intended to cut Diadem off somehow or take its place in the hierarchy. Questions about how led to discussions about codes and keys, radio, electromagnetism, electrons, and atoms. Jordan's mind was whirling, but a desperate feeling that he was making up for lost time kept him asking questions.

It wasn't fair. The whole world was a giant library. Knowledge didn't just reside in the manse libraries—it was embedded in every stone and grain of sand. For all of history, men had starved and died amongst untold riches, surrounded by an environment that could cater to their every whim if they could but talk to it. Jordan alternated between horror at the waste of the past centuries and an equal feeling of disquiet as he contemplated the things he could do now. For commanding the elements and even living things, like these docile horses, seemed somehow wrong—a violation, maybe, of things' right to simply *be*.

Mediation fed him updates on the movements of Thalience and had given him huge resources he had not had time to catalog. Jordan could close his eyes and see banks of glowing numbers, each representing some vast mechanism that helped control the world's climate. With a single command he could affect things on a giant scale now: cause storms, floods, or reverse the course of winter itself. It seemed Mediation had thrown its fortunes in Jordan's lap because it regarded him as a link to its "original programming."

Mediation told him that vagabond moons were converging on this continent from all over the world, and gigantic orbiting mirrors were changing their orbits to track this way. (The idea of these mirrors was one more concept he could barely encompass, but he needed to accept it.) Diadem was in a ferment, but the swans weren't telling the desals what was going on up there. The swans themselves were converging on a spot almost directly over Jordan's head. They were marshaling vast energies, for what purpose no one yet knew.

Relations were strained along the hierarchy of the Winds; it was impossible for any Wind to refuse an order that preserved the integrity of the commonly accessible and unchangeable ecological template of the world. Once those conditions were fulfilled, however, the Winds could do whatever they pleased. If the swans had found an ecologically safe way of obliterating the desals, or even all human life on Ventus, they could try it.

At times Jordan tuned out whatever discussion Tamsin was having with Ka, and instead monitored Armiger's progress. Armiger had set a punishing pace, and his party was a days's ride ahead now, steadily moving southwest. He wasn't sure, but he guessed the general was making for the nexus of Winds' power at the Titans' Gates. Mediation had shown the place to him, and Jordan was eager to see it with his own eyes.

As they stopped for another rest, Tamsin waved away Ka's offer to read to her and went to lie on the sand. "Oh," she groaned. "I'm so stiff I'm going to crack like a twig."

"I know," he said. "I feel the same way."

"Can't your precious Mediation fix us, the way morphs fix animals?"

"I asked it yesterday," he said as he awkwardly sat next to her. The horses were looking tired, too. They wouldn't last much longer at this pace. "Mediation said that it can heal those who can talk to it—meaning me. But not you, because you can't."

"So? Have you gotten it to heal you?"

He shook his head. "That wouldn't be fair. More to the point, how would I know when you were at the end of your strength if I felt perfectly fine all the time?"

She laughed humorlessly and shook her head. "Oh, what are we doing? What in the world are we doing?"

He hung his head. "I've been trying to come up with a plan."

"Yeah? Tell me."

"We're following Armiger. Well, everybody's following Armiger. It's like he's is a boat in a stream, and the Winds and everybody else are swept up in his wake. Thalience is after him; I think they were only after me because I was a clue to his existence. Now that they seem to know about him, they're not so interested in me anymore. Calandria and Axel are after him, too. So everyone is converging on him. And he's making for the Titans' Gates.

"They've all forgotten about me. Armiger doesn't need me now that he can command the Winds himself. The hooks and swans don't care about me now that they know about him. And Calandria and Axel . . . well, I was just a way for them to find him, too." It hurt to say that. He shrugged. "The swans seem to have forgotten about Mediation, too—and the others never knew about it. But the Titans' Gates are the stronghold of Mediation.

"For some reason Armiger hasn't spoken to Mediation yet. So at least for now, I'm in command of it, if I want to be."

"In command . . ." She shook her head. "It's hard to believe."

He snorted. "I wouldn't get too excited. I've only got this power as long as everybody ignores me. Armiger knows about Mediation, since I told him about it, but he hasn't even contacted the geophysical Winds yet. I can't figure out why. He must be waiting until he reaches the Gates before revealing himself."

"So?"

"Well," said Jordan. "This is the question: do we just let things unfold? After all, who are we to interfere in a war between the gods?"

"Of course we just let things unfold," said Tamsin. "What other choice do we have? I thought we were going to rendezvous with Armiger. Then he takes over the Winds, and that's that."

He shook his head. "But what if he fails? If Thalience kills him . . . well, you heard it yourself in the desal: Thalience thinks of humans as vermin. Who'll defend us against it then?"

"I don't know."

"And lastly I've been wondering about Armiger himself. Does he really mean to conquer the Winds? And if so, what is he going to replace them with? Do we have any say in what he does? It sure doesn't look like it."

He stood up, straining into a stretch. "Armiger hasn't contacted Mediation. That worries me. I can see all sorts of things that the geophysical Winds should be doing to prepare a defense against the swans. They're not doing anything—at least in any organized way."

She looked up. "But you could order them to."

He nodded. "I've been getting Mediation to tell me what the Titans' Gates do, and how they work. Right now it treats me like an equal, so it's giving me access to all the systems. Now, do you remember yesterday, when Ka told us about codes? About how everything the Winds do is controlled through them? Well, that's not quite true. They often use passwords, like the sentries in an army camp. The Winds use them when one of them wants to lock something for its own exclusive use. Well, I asked Mediation if the Titans' Gates could be locked by passwords. . . ."

When Jordan told Tamsin what he had decided to do, he had the great pleasure of seeing her smile for the first time in days.

THE FIRST ALLY to arrive was a jaguar. It padded into the circle of firelight as they were preparing for bed and lay down opposite Jordan and Tamsin, its head on its paws.

Tamsin clawed at Jordan, who had been drowsing in Vision. "Jor*dan*, look, look, oh no, oh no."

He flopped his head over and blinked at the animal. "Ah. I've been expecting this. I asked Mediation for protection. It said it was sending troops."

The jaguar gave a cat smile: a slow two-eyed wink.

"Troops? . . ." Tamsin relaxed her tight grip on his arm. "Is that . . . one of Mediation's Winds?"

"Not a Wind. Just a cat." Jordan sat up, looking grimly at the animal. "Part of our escort."

"Ah." He had told her to expect guests. She hadn't known what was coming but had imagined morphs or something equally hideous. "Is it . . . wild?"

He shook his head. "The Winds can cohabit the minds of animals. It's our lieutenant. You can trust it completely."

"Lieutenant jaguar." She rose to her feet, slowly. The jaguar watched her, not moving. "Can I—can I touch her?"

"I don't know." He squinted at the animal. "Yes, I think you can."

Tamsin rummaged near the fire for scraps of the pheasant they had spitted earlier. Then she got down on her haunches and waddled carefully over to the jaguar.

"Here." She held out a drumstick that still had some meat on it. The jaguar sniffed, then gravely took the bone from her hand.

Tamsin stood up and took four steps back. Then she let out a breath she'd apparently been holding. "Animals. They sent us animals, not monsters. I was so worried, I—"

"Look." Jordan stood up and pointed into the darkness.

They were visible at first only as pairs of glowing disks in the night. One, two, half a dozen, twenty, roving around the fire. Then a bear walked into the light and squatted down next to the jaguar. After it, two scampering ferrets, and then an antlered deer, who snorted and pawed at the dirt next to the bear.

They could hear it now, an immense quiet motion in the dark. There was nothing out there but dark forms, black on black moving. "How many are there?" shouted Tamsin, as she glimpsed phalanxes of horns closing in from one side, an ocean of furred backs from the other.

Jordan shook his head. He looked so serious that she was afraid to ask what he was thinking. To Tamsin, the arrival of these beasts seemed wondrous. She couldn't imagine why he found it disturbing.

They continued to come, all night, and eventually Tamsin had to sleep. She lay down facing the jaguar and wept quietly, for it seemed as though she and Jordan were being granted a benediction by nature tonight— and she had not realized until this very moment that all her life she had longed for such a blessing.

TAMSIN WEPT AGAIN the next day, but this time it was because she finally understood the reason for Jordan's unhappiness.

They had woken to find themselves at the center of a battalion of animals, hundreds of them, who lay head-to-tail in a sweeping circle around them. When Jordan stood up and walked to the edge of the camp to piss, they all stood as one and did likewise.

That woke Tamsin, who was appalled, then laughed until her sides were sore.

It was later in the day, when they were riding elk-back into the desert, that the escort ceased to be magical for her and became something sinister—an abomination. She had not considered how the animals would feed.

Without warning, a bear that she had been admiring turned on the gazelle trotting next to it and ripped its throat out. Tamsin screamed. The gazelle fell, thrashing, spouting blood everywhere. As the bear stopped to feed, a few other carnivores moved in to share the meal, and the rest of the battalion—hunters and prey alike—simply split politely around them and moved on.

"How could it do that!"

Jordan had turned in his saddle to watch. "I guess it makes sense," he said reluctantly. "Mediation controls these animals. They're not acting out of their own volition."

She cried then, as she realized that the harmony of nature she had fallen asleep to was a sham, merely evidence of overwhelming power; these animals would die because of herself and Jordan, pawns in a game about which they neither knew nor cared.

"I've been thinking about this ever since we met desal 447," he said. "Is this how the world was intended to be? Were we meant to treat all living things on this world as puppets we can just order around? As slaves? Is that what Mediation wants to return to? If it is, I think I can understand where Thalience is coming from."

"It's evil," she said.

He nodded. "Even if we don't do anything, just knowing that the world is like a big puppet show for our benefit . . . it makes everything cheap. Like we're being cheated somehow."

She nodded, wiping at her eyes. "It *is* all a lie, isn't it?"

The sky, the earth, the animals, and trees were constructs of the Winds, who could do with them as they pleased. What they pleased to do was make them act like natural things. They—or whoever controlled them—could as easily make them act differently.

Tamsin had pictured Armiger's conquest of the Winds as a liberation, akin to the Iapysian parliament overthrowing Queen Galas. It was a change of government, no more, she had thought.

Might it mean something else, though?

"Jordan, what is Armiger going to do with the world if he conquers it?"

Conquest of the Winds meant complete command of Ventus—earth, sea, sky, and nature. And while Tamsin loved nature and might wish to preserve it, another mind, given that kind of power, might conceive an entirely different world. Brick over the seas. Turn the sky to gleaming metal. Replace everything alive with something mechal, in the name of efficiency or power.

"I know," he said. "I've been worrying about that. For all that they're tyrants, the Winds use their power to keep Ventus a garden for life. It seems as if Thalience genuinely loves the life here. But Mediation? I don't know. And Armiger? Is he going to care as much? Would we? I don't know—but it scares me to think about."

Tamsin thought about it, and as she did, it came to her that her life was dividing in two at this point. She had thought that time had split in that moment when Uncle tore her out of her village, and her family and childhood died. Now, even that seemed like a period of innocence to her—a time when, however sad her life, the sky was still the sky and the grass still the grass. None of that was true anymore, nor could she imagine how it could ever be true again.

It seemed he had barely fallen asleep before Hesty was shaking his shoulder, and Lavin blinked his eyes open to find sunlight streaming through the flap of the tent. The army was ready to decamp; they were to leave in the morning.

"Sir, wake up, sir!" Hesty's hand shook him again. The motion sent waves of nausea through him, and he cursed, shrugging Hesty off.

"Who would believe morning could come so quickly," he muttered.

"Sir, it's not morning!"

For a moment Lavin forgot his whirling senses. Hesty sounded *scared*. Not nervous or apprehensive as he'd been in the past before battles. But frightened. Lavin looked up at him.

It was cold enough for Lavin's breath to frost, but Hesty was sweating. He wasn't dressed properly, either—he wore a quilted robe around which he'd buckled his rapier.

"Sir, it's the middle of the *night*."

"What are you saying?" It was daylight, anyone could see that.

"Sir, it's two o'clock in the morning. A new sun appeared, just five minutes ago. The sentries woke me and I came straight here. Sir, the camp is waking up. Panic is spreading."

"Hand me my uniform."

He didn't even have his laces tied up before he heard a relay of shouts coming from the edge of the camp. A faint voice repeated it nearby, then one of his own guard twitched back the flap of the tent and said, "Sir, a small force of men is approaching from the east. There are Winds with them."

"Thank you." He stepped in front of the mirror to adjust his hair. "Hesty, go get dressed. I want you to be calm. If anyone asks, don't admit that you're surprised by this. In fact, tell your men we arranged for the Winds to bring us this new sun."

"Yes, sir." Hesty saluted and left.

Gritting his teeth, he forced himself to deduce which way was down and move his limbs accordingly. Do *not* lean right. Walk to the tent flap. Good.

He emerged into hot daylight. The sun was at the zenith; he shaded his hand and peered at it. Something odd about it. He squinted, trying to figure out what it was . . . the sun was smaller than usual.

And square.

He looked away; the spots made his vertigo worse for a few moments.

The sky around the little sun was daylight blue, but it rapidly faded until, at the horizon, it was night-black again. Everything to the horizon was daylit, but Lavin got the impression that beyond a circle of ten or so kilometers, night still reigned. It was bizarre.

A group of maybe twenty men on horseback, and some odd animals had reached the edge of the encampment. One of the figures had apparently dismounted, and was talking to the sentries there. After a moment, the sentries backed off, and the group moved forward. It was hard to tell what the animals were; at first he'd thought they were mastiffs, but they moved differently. Lavin ordered his camp chair and the banners of his office and titles brought out. He refused to be a supplicant now, after all that had happened, so he sat in the chair. It would have been difficult to remain standing for any length of time anyway.

The group came closer. He recognized the livery on some of the men, but couldn't really bring himself to think about it because his attention quickly became fixed on the animals.

They were like cats, but they were the size of bears. And their shoulders were too broad, giving them shallow flat chests. Their hind legs also seemed overlong, crooked up more than one might have expected to aid their walking. They moved quickly and fluidly, though.

But their faces . . . they had huge, radiant eyes, whiskers, and tall nervous ears. Their snouts were long, and fanged, but from the cheekbones up the structure of their skull was almost human. One even had a mane of white hair like a woman's tresses draped across its shoulders. As they halted four meters away he saw that their pelts were short and fine and white as snow.

The human riders did not dismount. Indeed, they stared directly ahead, as if they had nothing to say. They were of a comparatively minor House, and he was certain they would not have had the temerity to bother him, on their own.

Lavin cleared his throat. "To whom am I to address myself?"

He was looking at the rider in the lead when he said this, and so it took him a moment to notice the smallest of the animals rising to its hind feet. Lavin turned his attention to it, and gasped.

Standing, the beast had become human—or nearly so. Its mobile joints accommodated both the running posture of a cat and the upright stance of a man. It was difficult to tell gender, but he would have sworn the thing had breasts. Cascades of white hair flowed past its shoulders. It stood easily, as if born to do so, and now he saw it wore a narrow leather sword belt with an épée and some daggers sheathed there.

It blinked its huge eyes at him, and said in a woman's voice, "Address yourself to this one."

Vertigo and exhaustion combined to make the next events seem more like a dream than real. Lavin had a parlay table and chairs brought; the white Wind twitched its tail aside and sat down opposite him. It smelled faintly of heather and fur. The hands it laid on the tabletop had solid, calloused heels, and the fingers seemed naturally clenched. It had to splay them in a stretch to make them limber.

"Why have you come?" asked Lavin. Everything he said seemed obtuse; he was off balance and knew it, but there was nothing he could do about that.

"We have come to command," said the Wind. Lavin's heart sank.

"We seek the pathology that calls itself *Armiger*. You will assist us in this."

Armiger is with the queen. "I don't see how we can—"

"Your army will march where we direct. We will provide daylight for as long as necessary. You will begin your march immediately. In addition, this one will take a force of cavalry to range ahead. We must locate the pathology. It is a threat."

"Yes, your . . ." Lavin had no idea how to address this thing. "Your Honour." That sounded wrong, but he was damned if he would call it *Your Highness*.

Something about what the thing had just said—"Are you proposing that we march nonstop? Day and night?"

"Yes. That is why we have provided you sunlight for the journey."

"We can't do that! We're not prepared for a forced march. The men will suffer—"

"That is not our concern. We need your army in place in case the pathology compromises the local mecha. Also because of where it is headed."

"Where?" His own scouts had reported that a small party had vanished in the desert to the southwest. There were caravan routes that Galas might know of that led across the sands to the mountains of the coast.

"Provide a map," ordered the thing. Lavin snapped his fingers, and one was brought.

The white Wind glanced over the vellum appraisingly, then darted a clawed finger at a familiar landmark. "We are here. The pathology departed in this direction. . . . It may be headed *here*. We cannot permit it to arrive, and compromise the mecha or desals there."

Lavin looked at the name under the Wind's pointing claw. *The Titans' Gates.*

"That's a thousand kilometers from here! We don't have the resources for a march like that! If we march into the desert now, we won't reach the Gates. Marching without break, without water or food, we'll all be dead in a week." He sat back and folded his arms. "Kill us all now. I won't command my men to march themselves to death."

The Wind hissed. "You will not die. We will provide sustenance along the way. And we will move parts of your army in relay. We cannot move all, so some must march."

"Move my army? In relays?" Lavin shook his head—a mistake. As the world spun, he said, "What madness are you talking about?"

The Wind bunched its hand into a fist, shredding the map. "Look! Do not disbelieve this one! That is how we will relay your men. That is how you will be fed." It stood, knocking its chair over, and pointed at the sky.

Six horizontal crescents, their tops lit by the square sun far above, hung outside the pyramid of blue sky. He hadn't noticed the vagabond moons before, what with everything else going on. He swore under his breath.

"Part of your army will rest as it is carried ahead. At the drop point you will meet it, and supplies will also be provided. Some of those who have marched will then embark for the next leg. In this way you will march from here to the Titans' Gates without stopping."

In one day. One endless day. Lavin slumped back, stunned.

"Our own army will meet you there."

"Your army?" With every word it spoke, the Wind became more terrifying.

"The pathology has already begun to infect the mecha and geosphere. If it conquers the desalination nexus it will have an almost impregnable fortress."

The Wind stepped away from the table. "That is all. You have your orders."

"I understand. And we will obey. But . . ."

"What?" Its tail twitched as it rounded on him. Lavin shrank back despite himself.

What will you do with Galas? But it would not even understand the question if he asked it.

Lavin watched it walk away, his mind a blank. The impossible was happening, and what was worse, he knew that the next days would so far exceed what had just occurred, that in future times he might not even remember this one conversation.

The Wind gestured at its mounted comrades, and they all turned to leave.

Hesty was saying something. Lavin couldn't make out the words, but the man was pointing at the sky, where one of the vagabond moons had begun to loom large, a lozenge of its surface now in direct sunlight.

The white Wind had been frightening, but also oddly familiar. Lavin stared after her as she and the others departed, wracking his brains to find a memory. He had heard her voice before, and recently . . . No, it was gone.

He sighed and turned to Hesty. "I see it, man. Go prepare your men. Tell them the Winds have brought the moons here at my request. There is one adventure left for us, it seems."

39

IT WAS A joy simply to stretch out an arm and feel the dry winter grass slide past her fur. The sky was lovely to look at; she would have liked to have rolled on her back, purring, to gaze at the new sun the swans had made, just to absorb the wonderful gradations of color that canopied it.

The hunt was even more enjoyable. For the moment, that was where the white Wind kept her attention focused. It was hard, though, with all the wonderful distractions . . .

She prowled up the side of a rock-strewn hill, whose top sported some scraggly, wind-sculpted trees. The land had changed from desert to stony scrubland. A few human shepherds brought their flocks here in summer, simply because there was nowhere else for them to go, but nothing agricultural would grow in this soil.

That meant there would be no human witnesses, no one to interfere with the capture.

She lifted her muzzle and sniffed at the wind. She could smell horses—of course, they were obvious kilometers away. Now, though, she could also smell fresh-washed humans. Two women and a man.

There was the faintest possibility that these were not the ones she was looking for. She would have to risk a peek over the top of the hill and hope they didn't see her silhouetted against the bruised horizon.

The white Wind was very good. They wouldn't see her. She crept the last meter with her belly to the cold ground, infinitesimally slow in her movements, and finally laid her chin on a flat rock next to some torpid ants. A few stalks of grass made a screen here through which she could see the valley.

It wasn't much of a valley; more as if a single huge boulder, the size of a whole suburb of houses, had split open and crumbled. Three horses were tethered in the shelter made by the split. There was a half cave there, on the other side where the ground humped up and then up again before rising straight up to the same height as the white Wind. This meant there were two entrances to the little valley, unless one flew. The Wind's forces were all on the western side. She would have to send some of the men and basts around to block the other exit before they closed the trap.

A man walked around from behind one of the horses. He was talking to a woman in peasant garb who trailed after him, waving her hands in agitation. He didn't recognize the woman, but the man was clearly Armiger. That was all she needed to know.

The white Wind eased back two meters, then spun, delighting in the balance of her tail, and raced down the scraggly hillside.

It's good to run, run, run, run, she hymned as she went. The Wind felt like bursting into song, and were it not for the presence of the prey so close, she would have. The swans would never begrudge such a display—they sang all the time. The whole world sang, a revelation that filled the white Wind's breast with joy every time she thought of it. In quiet times, she could curl up around an interesting stone or sweet-smelling plant, and hear the faint music—*thinking music*—that welled up around her.

To think she had once believed it to be mindless chatter! She allowed herself a laugh as she reached the bottom of the hill. Her sinuous body wove between boulders and thorn bushes as she made for some trees that had made a brave stand several kilometers from where Armiger had camped. She was following the exact route she had taken to get here, and made a game out of stepping in her own pawprints as she went. *One-to-four, one-to-four, whoops missed, one-to-four . . .*

These last few days had been a blessing. When she was released to run down a long ramp onto the cold desert sands, the white Wind had rolled over four times in the dirt and howled her joy at the sky. She had wanted to run to the horizon and back just so she could say she'd looked over it, but the swans had other plans. Someone to find. When they told her who, she had rolled over again, laughing.

This was fun; still, she longed to be finished, so she could take off on her own and explore this beautiful world. She felt exactly like Ariel in that old play, so as she raced into the camp her servants had made, she sang,

Where the bee sucks there suck I,
In a cowslip's bell I lie.
On a bat's back I do fly

. . . forgetting that none of these people knew that old language.

One of the human soldiers stepped forward and bowed gravely to her. "Are they there, Lady May?" he asked. She could hear the well-disguised fear in his voice.

She ran a circle around him. *Merrily, merrily shall I live now, under the blossom that hangs from the bow*, she thought, but she only said, "Yes."

Her chief servant approached, distaste and fear written on his face as he watched her sit up on her hindquarters and pant. "Then shall we fetch them now?" asked the sergeant.

"No, not yet." She explained the tactical situation. They would have to split their force and come at the sheltered declivity from two sides. "It's open country," she finished. "There's a good chance of being spotted if they have a sentry out, so you'll make the pincer at full gallop."

As he slumped toward his men, issuing orders irritably, the white Wind turned a cartwheel and ran to her own people, the basts who prowled restlessly at the edge of the camp. They chattered laughter at her approach. "Little woman-bast," one called out. "Why are you so happy?"

She stopped and cocked a paw to one ear. "Because I hear it!" she replied. "I hear it rising all around us."

They nodded. They knew what she meant.

MEGAN HAD ORIGINALLY intended to hunt for berries. She had found a handful or two, but halfway back in her circuit of the hill above the cave, she had stumbled on a little flat area screened by bushes. It was invisible from below, but she could see the whole camp. The temptation was irresistible, and so she had hunkered down to spy on her man.

You're terrible, she told herself, even as she parted the bushes to look almost straight down the rock face. She could hear Armiger and the queen bickering. Galas looked silly in Megan's dress; it was far too big for her. But she refused to wear any of the perfectly good clothing they had salvaged from the razed town. Megan had thought her a tragic figure before. In the past few days her patience had worn thin, and she was beginning to think of Galas as merely spoiled.

Megan had dressed herself in some boy's clothes. It was practical, but unfeminine. Yesterday she hadn't minded that, but now, watching Armiger and Galas alone, she wondered. There was nothing overt going on between them, no ardent words or glances. They weren't holding hands. Still, she knew a strong bond had developed between them—one based on commonality that Megan could never share. They were both rulers, of the highest possible caste. She was a peasant. Even if (foolish dream!) Armiger married her, Megan would remain a peasant. She could never be comfortable with the nobles and ladies of the court. Even if he became king of the world, as he planned, she would blush and look down if she had to greet the great people of other lands. She had thought about these things. She knew she would rather serve them than look them in the eye.

So shall I leave? she thought sadly. Armiger shrugged at something Galas had said and twitched his long hair back over his shoulder. She knew that gesture so well, she could almost hear him saying, "We will decide later." Her heart ached.

She herself had told him that you can never hold onto anything. The harder you try, the more precious things slip through your fingers. The secret to life, she had said, was to find the little things, the unimportant ones that would nonetheless always remind you of the precious things they accompanied—and hold onto them. Like the fine furniture her husband had carved for her, seemingly centuries ago.

Galas was weeping again. Megan sighed. Had the rain found a way through her roof while she was away? Was the fine wood of the bed and wardrobe ruined now? Had someone moved into her house? Or would she find it exactly as she had left it, if she returned now?

Kiss her, she mentally commanded Armiger. *Make it easy for me to leave.* He did not, although he enfolded her in his arms and rested a hand on her head as she cried. His expression was distant, as it often was, as he rocked the queen gently.

Megan sat back, chewing her lip. She blinked at the strong sunlight—daylight in the middle of the night. It was unnerving, more so since she knew it meant the Winds were closing in on them. She shaded her eyes with one hand and gazed out over the dry plain, in case there were some army approaching.

She had only been half serious about looking, so for a second or so she couldn't believe it when she saw the cloud of dust raised by a band of horses approaching their hiding place. There must be at least fifty. Maybe Armiger could take on that many. Maybe not.

Megan's heart sank when she saw what they were doing. The groups split in two as they approached. *They mean to block both ways out.*

They were approaching from the west. One group would have to ride the long way around to reach the eastern entrance of the vale. The other group would wait until some preordained signal, then move in.

It is the queen they want, she thought. Had it been Winds, they would have arrived from the sky, as swans or Hooks. Or popped out of the earth as morphs. No, these riders must be from Parliament's army, come to bring Galas home for trial.

For herself and Armiger to live, the sensible thing would be to send Galas out to them. The queen was in such a state she would probably be glad to go. But Armiger would never permit it, and Megan doubted she had the hardness of heart to do it, either. They could all ride out the eastern exit now, but then the whole group would pursue them.

No: if they gave them what they wanted, Galas would be tried and executed. If they ran, they would be chased down and the end would be the same, only Armiger and Megan would likely be killed in the fight.

But if they captured someone they thought was the queen, and found out she was not only hours or days from now . . .

Megan scattered the berries in her haste to scramble down the hillside.

ARMIGER HEARD THE commotion, but at first didn't turn. Galas was telling him about her relationship with Lavin, and he didn't want to seem distracted. Then the queen, who was seated on a rock, looked past him and said, "What is she doing?"

He turned in time to see a flash of Megan's naked body, before she pulled down the robe she was donning. It was the queen's robe, the one she had worn when they escaped the palace. And now Megan was cinching her horse's saddle. . . .

"Megan!" He started toward her, but she hopped nimbly into the saddle and flicked the reins.

"What are you doing?"

"Ride east! Ride east, love, if you love me!" She waved a hand over her head as she galloped; then she was through the gateway made by two huge boulders at the western side of the vale, and vanished in a cloud of dust.

It took precious seconds for him to bridle his own mount, and while he did that Galas ran after Megan. She, too, vanished in the swirl of hoof-drawn dust, then raced back.

"Riders!" she shouted. "There are riders coming! They've seen her, they're trying to head her off!"

Armiger paused in cinching up his saddle. He closed his eyes and leaned his head against the fragrant flank of his horse.

MEGAN HAD THE rings of office on her fingers. She wore Galas's robes. As she rode she undid her hair and let it flow behind her, the way the queen did.

She felt free, fulfilled for the first time in ages. There was no time to reconsider, no options to hem or haw over. Only the thundering hooves under her, the jarring of her horse's spine through her legs and pelvis, and the fire in her blood as she screamed at it to go faster.

They want the queen alive. I'll lead them a merry chase, then go with them. Oh, let there be no one among these horsemen who knows the queen by sight!

"SHE'S GAINING GROUND on us!" cried the sergeant's flankman. "It's her horse!" The queen's mount was lighter than their war horses, and relatively unburdened. She probably could outride them.

"Crossbows!" commanded the sergeant. They had muskets, but at this range crossbows would be more accurate.

"No!" It was the white Wind, running on all fours to match his own pace. "She is not the one we seek!"

"She is not the one *you* seek! Take your people and catch him yourself!"

The Wind snarled and leaped away. The sergeant tipped his head back and laughed. He had been waiting for a moment to show her up.

"Shoot her horse out from under her!" he shouted. "Aim for its hooves. I want it lame, not dead—I don't want it to throw her."

THEY CAME OUT of the settling dust like ghosts—eight white forms like giant panthers, leaping from rock to rock and laughing. Galas screamed as they launched themselves over her head at the place where Armiger had been standing.

She spun around to see, but he wasn't there anymore. Before she could find him the floor of the little valley exploded in colored fire.

The concussion knocked her over again. When Galas regained her feet, it was to see Armiger, halfway up the sheer rock face of the northern wall of the vale, leaning back and sending bolts of fire from his outstretched hand. White forms dodged in the roiling smoke below.

Something soft slid past her hand. Galas snatched it away, only to find a large form flowing around her. It sounded like it was purring.

"Oh, what have we here," said a measured, hypnotic voice. "The once and never-again queen. Who then was it that we saw barreling out of here a second ago?"

Two golden eyes rose up to her own height and blinked lazily at her. Over the thing's shoulder, the vale flickered with white light. Something screamed.

"It hardly matters," said the thing. "We have you now. A bonus—since you're not the one we came for. But I know some people who'll be very happy to see you." Before she could move it had her by the arm—claws embedding deeply in her muscle so that she shrieked.

"Armiger!" cried the creature. "Stop harming my people! I have your lady companion. If you don't come down now and surrender yourself to me, I will kill her."

Galas looked down at her arm and blinked at the blood there. Once, she would have had a thousand—no, ten thousand men willing to die to prevent even such a tiny injury as that.

And who was this creature to ill use her so? No one touched her like that!

"I will give you one minute," the monster was saying. The lightning flashes from the hillside had ceased. "Starting from—"

It was the monster's turn to scream, as Galas twisted the hairpin she had thrust into its ear. It let go of her arm, and she ran into the dust and confusion of the vale.

Blue and white light and roaring thunder surrounded her.

MEGAN'S HORSE SCREAMED and staggered. She rocked in the saddle, falling forward across the beast's neck. Hanging on to its mane for dear life, she looked down. A crossbow bolt stuck out of the poor thing's flank, just above its front haunches.

Too soon! She had to get a little farther, to give her love time to escape. She withdrew one foot from its stirrup and leaned down to try to grab the bolt.

Pain exploded in her side driving all the breath from her. She grabbed at the reins and missed, then she was tumbling headfirst off the horse, straight at a big rock.

Armiger, my love, I—

ROCKS TUMBLED AROUND the white Wind. She staggered from the agony in her head and along her side where one of Armiger's bolts of fire had clipped her. The perfidious queen was gone, and her basts were falling back, yelping in confusion. The little vale was full of smoke but she could see at least four bast bodies on the ground, and one horse with its throat torn out.

"Where is the other horse?" she shrieked at a bast who came within grabbing distance.

"They took it," it shouted. "Rode. East, they went out the east exit!"

A bolt of fire from somewhere made them all duck.

"Follow!" She raked her claws across the bast's shoulder. "Catch him! I don't care if you all die doing it!"

The remaining basts vanished into the haze. The white Wind moved to follow, but she hurt too much; she could only stagger a few paces.

She cursed the swans. *You took out my armor, and for what? So I could die here in this wasteland?* For a few moments, she was Calandria May again, as she wept at her misfortune, and then the world grayed around her, and she tumbled onto the sand.

ARMIGER'S HAND WAS missing. In its place was a smoking black ball. Every now and then he would lean back in the saddle and aim that ball at the monsters that were chasing them. Fire would leap from where his hand used to be, and once Galas heard a scream as it struck home.

He was taking them in a grand circle to intersect the line of Megan's flight. Even if they ended up facing fifty mounted knights, it was the right and proper thing for him to do. Galas said nothing, just held onto him and the horse and let the ride go on.

He stretched back again, and she hunched from the blast of sound. "Ha!" he shouted. She risked a look back and saw one monster in flames, another leaping away to the side, with only one more still following. It was losing ground steadily.

Suddenly he reined in the horse. Galas almost fell out of the saddle, and only after a giddy moment righting herself was she able to look up and see why.

They were cantering along the top of a ridgeline. The human riders were below them, dismounted and clustering around something on the ground.

Galas recognized her dress before she made out the crumpled figure in it.

The dress was stained scarlet.

She had time to glimpse someone raising a limp arm and letting it fall back to the earth before the horse shied out of the way of a panting white creature.

Armiger shrieked a curse at the thing and shot it as it made to leap again. Then he plunged the horse back from the ridgeline—away from the riders, away from his love.

For the first time since she met him, she saw him weep, wretchedly and uncontrollably, and it was Galas who took the reins and led them into the sunlit night.

LAVIN'S EARS POPPED and he groaned. He had elected to travel the first leg of their journey by means of the vagabond moon, in part to encourage his men and partly because his vertigo would not go away. He had not suspected that air travel would be like sea travel—full of dips and sways. He had lain huddled on his bedroll for most of the past eight hours, unable to tell what motion was in his head and what was real. The illness left him alone with his thoughts, which was the worst possible situation.

He would dearly have loved to tour this fantastical place and look down on the world passing below. Two thousand of his men were bivouacked here on the black floor of the moon. There were no tents because the Winds had forbidden them from driving tent pegs into the floor, and no fires for similar reasons. At four sides of the vast empty floor large rectangular openings let in the cold air; just now several men were standing near one, peering down in awe at the landscape passing below. As they looked, another man walked up casually, holding a chamberpot, and upended it over the opening. He laughed at their expressions and walked away.

Lavin closed his eyes as the world swayed again. Vertigo reminded Lavin of how he had met Galas. He could not stop thinking about her, going over and over in his mind the strange paths that had brought them to this endless day.

He had taken the side of Parliament partly to ensure her safety. In order to allay any suspicions on the part of the members, he had loudly proclaimed his allegiance to tradition. At the time, he had been crossing his fingers behind his back, hoping they would believe him and let him lead the army. But—and this he had not wanted to admit to himself—he really did believe. Galas was wrong. The traditions were sacred and beautiful. He remembered the country dances of his youth, where singers would recite the names of the Winds and the seasons decreed by the desals. When he tried to picture the future Galas was building, he could not imagine what would replace those dances and the cordial sense of community they fostered. Her future might be just, but her thoughts seemed to have a cold, insectile quality. He pictured the empire of Galas as a giant hive.

Just a while ago, as the tiny sun set and the ordinary one was just rising, a priest had come to him. The man had knelt by Lavin's bedroll, and Lavin had smiled at him, expecting words of comfort. But the man was crying.

"I have been speaking to the Winds," he said. "All my life, that was all I wanted to do. The desals and the other Winds of the earth can't talk, but the swans can. I went to them and recited the ancient chants. They waited in silence. Then I—I ventured to ask a question." He took a deep breath. "I asked them why they had not spoken to us, all these centuries."

Lavin had sat up, despite his spinning head. "And what did they say?"

"They said that they had never stopped speaking to us in all that time. That it was us who would not listen."

The priest looked carefully over his shoulder; a hundred meters away stood a pillar of flame, pale in the wan sunlight. Faces appeared and vanished like hallucinations within it. "I said I was listening now. And do you know what they said? They said, 'no, you are not listening. We are asking you to speak even now, and you are not speaking.' General, it had the sound of madness to it! I recited the sacred scriptures to them. And they . . . They asked me what this nonsense was I was barking. Lord, they didn't know them! Are these truly the Winds, or . . ."

"Or what? Something else?" He almost shook his head, but refrained. "No. Who else has this power? They are who they say they are."

"But sir, there's more." The priest looked like he was about to be sick. "I . . . I asked them what was to become of us. Of humanity. Had we disappointed them? How could we serve them? And the swans said . . . the swans said, 'We have tried to complete ourselves for centuries. We thought you might be the key.' They said they had been searching for something and studying for many generations, but that it was all done now. 'We have completed our Work,' they said. 'We need not tolerate your presence any longer.'"

"Need not tolerate us?"

"They have no more use . . . for the human race." The priest stood up, appearing stunned, and walked away.

Everything we know about the Winds is wrong. Lavin remembered Galas writing something like that, in the secret letters he had liberated. *They are not benevolent gods. They are antagonists in a struggle for com-*

mand of this world. And what is that to us? she had continued. *A tragedy? Only if we are lazy. It is more like an opportunity—a chance to create a new reality that is more true to nature.*

Was she right? Should he have razed the sleepy towns with their inheritance-bound guildsmen and books of ritual appeasement instead of her experimental villages—burned the festival costumes and children's storybooks—and helped her build the hive of the future? Could her love have sustained him while everything else he had known and cherished whithered and died? She had claimed she had the permission and advice of the Winds in all she did; he had known that to be a lie, for one time they had discussed the lies of great men, and she had blithely stated that all nations were based on them. Yet, the Diadem swans did not know the scriptures attributed to them; even now he could see the priest standing before the pillar of flame, arms apart, pleading for sense from the masters of the world. All the traditions Lavin believed in were based on those ancient scriptures, and the stories that surrounded them. Was Galas right? Were they all lies, too?

The world spun around him in a particularly savage gyre, and Lavin's gorge rose. It wasn't just him, though—men were shouting and running. He forced himself to sit up, and he observed green foliage moving past the open hatchways of the moon. Crowds of men had begun to cluster there.

One of his commanders hurried over. "We're coming down, sir. There are some horsemen and the bast creatures on the ground below."

"All right." He took several deep breaths to quiet his stomach. "Bring them to me before they speak to anyone else."

The moon took ten minutes to drop the last few meters, and it didn't actually touch the ground. From his seated position Lavin saw a long gray metal ramp extend out and down into the darkness of the moon's shadow. Horsemen began rattling up the ramp. He saw some men with stretchers carrying bloodied white forms—two of the basts had been injured somehow. Despite himself he smiled grimly at that. So they could be hurt after all.

The moment the last horse stepped into the cavernous space of the moon, the ramp began to retract, and the ground dropped away. The Winds were punctual, it seemed.

The leader of the horsemen had dismounted and was walking over. He was flushed with excitement.

"Sir! They would not let us bring the bodies aboard, sir. I've left a guard with her, but brought you—"

"Her?" He stood up, leaning on the cane Hesty had had made for him. "The queen? Is she with you?"

"No, sir. That's what I'm saying. The Winds allow only the living aboard these moons."

The sergeant's face seemed to recede. A chaotic gabble of sound filled Lavin's ears. He felt someone take him by the shoulders; people were shouting. They lowered him into a camp chair.

"Only the living . . . She is . . ."

"She is dead, sir. The queen is dead. It was a stray shot, accidental. We were trying to bring down her horse—I had given orders that no one should shoot above its legs, but a shot went wild and she was leaning, sir . . ."

"I, I see."

"I have left an honor guard with them and sent two men to fetch her royal guard from the palace."

A spark of hope made Lavin look up. "What proof do you have that this was the queen?"

"Her rings of office, sir." The sergeant withdrew a square of cloth from a belt pouch and opened it to reveal familiar circles of gold. "It is she."

He stared at the rings. They looked so unnatural, alone in that square of black.

"Sir?"

True, she had not worn them when they first made love, in that inn near the academy. It was only later that he saw them, when he saw her in regal glory on the throne, and she recognized him and sent him her most secret of smiles—waggling her fingers slightly as she raised her hand for him to kiss it.

"Sir?"

The commander took the sergeant's arm and muttered something. They moved aside, talking in low tones.

She had subtly taunted him on that day, showing off her new position; but he knew it was only that she was proud and surprised at where she was. Her father slunk in the shadows, deposed by an act of the desals, and at that moment Galas had believed she could do anything. So had Lavin, and he had trusted that they would be together again, somehow.

"I must go to her," he said. He reeled to his feet. "Put us down. I must attend her."

"Sir, the Winds say we must continue. We failed to capture Armiger. They say to continue the march to the Titans' Gates."

He cursed savagely and stalked toward the pillar of fire. His men silently parted before him. Dimly he wondered at this. Had they known all along that he loved her? They stood with heads bowed; none would meet his eye. They had known he loved her and yet they still fought for him? It couldn't be.

He stopped, gasping, two meters from the blazing swans. "Turn us around!" he commanded. "Put us down!"

There was no answer.

"Do as I say! The queen needs me!"

"We have other concerns," said the crystalline voice of the pillar.

"Please." He found it hard to speak past the savage pain in his chest. "Let me go to her."

"No. We have a schedule to meet. Your queen is not important."

He froze. Suddenly he felt all eyes on him. Should he shout the fury he felt now, with his army watching? What would they do if they realized that he, and they, were prisoners of the Winds, pawns in some game of theirs that had nothing to do with Iapysia, or humanity at all?

He felt a hand on his shoulder. It was the priest, his face grim, a message of caution in his eyes.

Deliberately, jaw clenched, Lavin bowed to the flame. "I understand," he said. "You are correct, of course."

Walking away was somehow easy. He moved as if weightless, bobbing along. People were speaking to him, but their words made no sense. Light and shape registered, but none of it had any meaning. She was dead, and it was his fault, as surely as if he had shot her himself. This moment had haunted his dreams for months, and he had steeled himself every morning to deny it, using the force of his will to command himself, his men, the world, and the Winds to preserve her. Just yesterday he had awoken sure that she was alive and free, and his heart had lofted like a swallow, serene and happy. But that was gone now, and he would never feel again.

Gradually the hands fell away, the voices receded. He found himself standing near one of the giant hatchways. Cold air moved across his face, but it didn't revive him. It had the feel of death to it. Far below he could see patches of snow, bare trees. No one should ever die in winter, he had always felt. And now she was that cold, limbs frozen. He should be with her, arms around her to keep her warm.

Lavin walked to the edge of the opening. Someone shouted his name. He heard it like a curse.

He decided to let himself fall, and teetered for a moment on the edge. He could just close his eyes and let it happen. It would be a relief, after holding himself up for so long.

Lavin turned and dropped to his knees, facing away from the hatchway.

No. He didn't deserve such an easy escape.

Sunk in misery, he hung his head and in full view of his army, wept.

40

Sixteen battleships from the Archipelagic fleet were scattered like jewels across the velvet of space near Ventus's trailing trojan point. They kept the regulation two hundred kilometers distance from one another, but to the *Desert Voice*, watching from the window of a cutter approaching the flagship, they seemed very close. Each was the size of a mountain and harnessed energies capable of reducing the surface of Ventus to char. The *Voice* had a good grasp of the scale of things here and knew that even a thousand such ships could not boil the rock of Ventus and Diadem down to the mantle unless they spent decades nudging asteroids and comets into a collision course with it. And that crude attack was bound to eject colossal amounts of potentially infected debris into stellar orbit, which could hide the escape of one or more of the Winds' ships now being built on the moon.

In all the boiled magma seas the navy proposed leaving behind here, there were good odds that some tiny pocket of cool stone would preserve grains of mecha, perhaps too small to be seen, that might regrow all of Ventus again, given a thousand or a million years. The corollary to that was that if 3340 had begun to infest the Winds with the algorithms of a resurrection seed, then 3340 itself might reappear here, in a millennia or an epoch.

Marya Mounce had told the *Voice* that all of Ventus had come from a package of nanotech assembler seeds massing less than twenty kilos. There was no doubt in anyone's mind that Armiger, so much more complex a being than the Winds, had the potential to regrow from himself a god.

The cutter docked gently with the side of the flagship. For a moment the *Voice* felt a pulse of empathy with the ship—she knew what docking felt like to a starship. Then the spell was broken as the door before her slid open, and a uniformed human glided in.

The man led her past steel bulkhead doors, as thick as she was tall, and into the narrow buttressed interior of the battleship. There were no straight lines here, or any corridor longer than ten meters. Everything was organized in tight armored cells, each with its own power supply and life support. To kill the crew of a ship like this, you had to literally batter it to pieces. The *Voice* was awed by the strength of the vessel; she couldn't imagine what it would be like to have it as her body.

They passed honeycombed cells full of fluid, where humans wearing inscape gear floated in seeming sleep. The consciousness of these men and women lay outside the ship, in swarms of micro- and macromissiles, or in system-wide simulations where they targeted and tracked every object bigger than a grapefruit.

Her guide left her at another set of pneumatic pressure doors. As these valved open, the *Voice* heard the sounds of angry debate coming from the chamber beyond.

"Look at that pattern! It's obvious they're ready to make a run for it."

"To you, maybe," said another. She recognized the timbre of the voice as belonging to an artificial intelligence. There were other beings like herself here. The *Voice* stepped inside.

It was impossible to gauge the dimensions of the chamber, because the walls had disappeared under a holographic projection of the Ventus system. The planets were all pinpointed with arrows, and to her upper left floated a rotating box containing a zoomed-in view of Ventus and Diadem. Dozens of tiny specks representing ships hung in the black space of the main display. Many of them trailed Ventus in its orbit, like a wreath of fog left behind it.

Diadem was almost obscured under a cloud of thousands of specks.

"Ah, our Diadem expert is here," someone said. The *Voice* looked behind herself; no one had entered after her.

Fifteen men and women floated under the system display. About half wore uniforms and moved with the catlike grace of cyborgs. Four more were holograms of generic human beings; each wore a complex heraldic symbol on its chest showing which faction of Archipelagic politics it represented. These were artificial minds whose attitudes and intentions were controlled by the aggregate will of millions or billions of humans back home. True to the principles of Archipelagic politics, however, each perspective on an issue held only one vote. These beings were not as powerful as they might at first seem.

Of the remaining three, one was not known to the *Voice*. The woman appeared to be a pilot. The last two were Marya and Axel. When she saw them the *Voice* glided immediately over to them.

"Now that you're here, we can ask the burning question," said one of the cyborgs. He wore admiral's bars on his shoulders.

"How many copies of you can Diadem produce per day? And how many in total?"

The *Voice* blinked. "I—I'm not qualified to answer that."

"Come on now. You were there for weeks. By your own admission, you wandered over hundreds of square kilometers. You were a line starship. You must have assessed their production capability."

Marya put her hand on the *Voice*'s arm and smiled. "If you don't know, don't guess. It's all right."

A little reassured, she said, "I only caught glimpses of the vacuum areas. I was pretending to be alive, so I stayed in the main labs most of the time."

"Yes, yes, we know that. But you must have *seen* the other facilities, or walked around them or under them. You must have seen materiel moving back and forth. Robots. Commerce, even. What scale is it on? What are they capable of?"

"Well, I did get a good idea of how much they put into refining the terraforming techniques. And I did see a lot of evidence of other activities." She paused to calculate. "If they abandoned everything else they were doing? Which they wouldn't. But if they did, they could probably produce two thousand copies of my original plan per week. It's a whole world, after all, if small."

The admiral nodded. "It's consistent with what we're seeing. They're using all of Diadem then. They're moving to a war footing."

Argument broke out among the others. Axel leaned close and pointed to the cloud of dots around the image of Diadem. "See those? Copies of you. Ships. And there's more arriving by the second."

The *Voice* gaped. Ventus's little moon was englobed by a vast fleet of ships—all copies of herself. All, if the one she had touched was any indication, capable of star travel.

"But how many in total?" asked one of the holograms. "Are they turning Diadem into a giant factory? And are they doing the same to Ventus?"

"Well, that's the question. Our Ventus expert says they wouldn't do that." The admiral gestured at Marya. "Her institute's AIs agree."

"All of Marya's coworkers were captured by the Winds," Axel whispered. "They were all taken to Diadem, presumably. So she's the reigning expert now."

"This is insane," said the *Voice*. "How are we going to—"

"My question for the *Desert Voice*," said the admiral, "is, do you recognize any of these structures? Are they like what you saw on Diadem?" He waved his hand, and a new cube appeared overhead. This one showed a telescopic view of the limb of Ventus's horizon. Square solar mirrors hung in the black sky like fantastic butterflies, and down below, just beyond the terminator on the nightside of Ventus, lay a lozenge of sunlit land.

Diaphanous scarves of glowing light, like solidifying aurora, could be seen spiraling down toward the planet in the vicinity of the sunlit oval.

"It's the swans!" The *Voice* vividly remembered them closing on her, and how they had crushed and devoured her body. "Are they attacking something?"

"That's what we want to know. Are they attacking, or are they building? Did they hang like that over the shipyard you saw on Diadem?"

"No. This is something else." She concentrated on the daylit side of the terminator, until she could make out the shapes of a continental edge there. "That's Iapysia they're over. It's very near where I set Calandria and Axel down originally."

"More to the point," said a hologram, "it's roughly where we think Armiger is."

"Well," said the admiral. "You heard our experts. They've never built ships before."

"They've never been threatened like this before," the *Voice* protested. "They're doing this because *we're* here. If we went away they would turn back to running the terraforming system."

The admiral grimaced. "Well, you came late to the discussion. We're not sure they're maintaining the system anymore. That's the point."

The *Voice* turned to Axel. He shrugged. "They think Armiger may have taken the Winds over already. It would certainly explain that." He pointed to the fleet. "As to what they're doing on the surface . . ."

"We think they're starting to modify it to his standard," said one of the AIs. "If Diadem can be turned into a giant factory, so much more so with Ventus itself. Worse—it could be turned into a single giant organism."

"Thirty-three forty."

"Exactly. Your friends don't believe it. They've been petitioning to go down there and investigate. But based on the numbers you've just given us, we don't have time. If 3340 is back, and it starts converting Ventus itself, there could be geometric growth of these ships."

Marya shook her head angrily. "They're just protecting themselves against you! They can see you, sitting out here like vultures."

"If that were the case, then they wouldn't be putting themselves in position for a run to escape the system." The hologram pointed at the specks trailing away from Ventus. "They're ready to fan out—maybe carry resurrection seeds to every other world in human space. We'd never be able to stop 3340 then."

"Have you asked the swans what they're doing?" Marya asked.

"Yes. They don't answer. We've tried sending probes in, but that fleet of theirs blows them away before they get close enough to see anything. We have no way to find out what's going on."

The admiral sighed. "Since we can't learn more, I think it's time to make a decision. I presume the consensus is to cauterize the threat now?"

The others, all save Axel and Marya, nodded.

A slow horror crept over the *Voice*. "Because of what I said . . . you've decided to kill everyone on that world?"

"It's not your responsibility," said the admiral. "Don't worry about it."

She could only hang there, stunned. She didn't even feel Axel put his hand on her shoulder until he pushed her into motion.

In moments they were outside the chamber, and Axel began cursing viciously. She heard Marya gasping, "They can't! They can't!" over and over.

"They will," said Axel quietly. "The people down there mean nothing to them. After all, it's only a few million; that many people die in the Archipelago every second."

"If anything's happening, it's the Winds fighting Armiger themselves! If we could only prove that. If only one of our ships could get past the swans and see . . ."

In her mind's eye the *Voice* could picture the entire holo display from the conference room; she remembered the position and trajectory of each and every ship, and she knew something she had neglected to tell the admiral. The *Voice* had been inside the nervous system of one of the Winds' ships; she knew their tactics, their transmission frequencies—and their recognition codes.

She took a deep breath. It wasn't fair, she thought bitterly; she had wanted the first real action she took as an individual to be on behalf of her new human side. Nonetheless, for the first time in her existence the *Voice* felt she was acting by and for herself when she said, "But you do have a ship. Me."

ARMIGER AND GALAS stood on a shoulder of land in the foothills of the coastal mountains. They were gazing out at the plains below. It was night—or at least, it was behind them. The plains were in day.

"How can we fight power like that?" murmured Galas. From here, the full extent of the daylit square was visible. They were just outside its western edge, but it was moving, slowly, in their direction. A cluster of vagabond moons shone bright silver high in the vast tapering cube of glowing air.

"There," said Armiger, pointing. Squinting where he pointed, she made out a low cloud of dust hugging the eastern end of the square.

"What is it?"

"An army, marching. It would seem Parliament still pursues you."

His voice was neutral—bland, even. He had been like this ever since Megan's death—withdrawn, but as strong willed as ever. He had ridden them hard for the past several days. Galas had been afraid that if she showed an instant's weakness—if she gave him even an inkling that she couldn't keep up—he would abandon her. It wasn't that he no longer cared about her, he just seemed so completely focused on his goal that the present moment had no reality for him.

Recognizing this in him brought a chill to her heart; she had been that way once, and not just for a day or a week. As they rode, Galas spent long hours withdrawn herself, remembering her youth after the death of her mother, for the first time seeing it from the outside, as if hearing about someone else's tragic past. She did not like what the objectivity revealed.

They rode and rode through grassland dotted with small forests, hour after hour until she lay draped in the saddle, her thighs and lower back a blaze of pain, sure that she would slide off the saddle with the horse's next step. At some point during that odyssey they had left the plains behind, and now they were scarcely a day's ride from the Titans' Peaks.

She spared a glance behind her. Treetops jabbed above the crest of the plateau where they camped, and beyond them mauve cut-out shapes she had at first mistaken for storm clouds shone pearly in the reflected light from the plain. The foothills ended in a huge, knotted pair of snow-capped peaks with a deep notch separating them. Lower peaks receded to the south, becoming more rounded and lower as they went.

She knew this twin mountain, had spent time there listening to the subterranean roaring of the desals at work. She had never imagined she would see the Titans' Gates in the light of a Wind-made day.

"We are trapped." She said it fatalistically.

Armiger waved negligently at the shining plains. "We needn't fear the humans. They won't be able to scale the Gates, unless they're riding in the moons themselves. As to the Winds—well, making day in the night like that is a pretty minor trick."

"*Minor?* Can you do it?"

"Not from here. It's trivial if you're in orbit." He shaded his eyes again.

"Armiger." He didn't seem to notice her until she reached out and put a hand on his arm. When he finally turned to face her, she said, "Why have we come here?"

When he didn't answer immediately she said, "We've been riding for days. We've barely even spoken. I confess for a time I was content just to be escaping—escaping anything, and everything. But the truth is, I'm sore, stiff, and weary beyond belief. If you gave me no good answer as to where we're going or why, I'd just as soon lie down and wait for those things to find me."

He smiled slightly and briefly. "I find it hard to talk about it. Not because of any emotional thing . . . no, it's because 3340, who gave me the impulse to begin with, made me to be reluctant. Do you understand the concept of conditioning?"

She smiled ironically. "You ask Queen Galas that?"

"All right, then. I've been conditioned not to talk about it. But I no longer work for 3340. . . ." He glanced over at her quickly, as if startled by something—or afraid.

Interesting, she thought. "Whom *do* you work for now, Armiger?" she asked quietly.

"One question at a time. You asked why we were here. Look." With a sweep of his arm he indicated the fanged teeth of the Titans' Gates. "Even before I met Jordan Mason, I thought this place might hold the key. It is the nexus of physical power for the western end of the continent. Here the desals have their power plants and desalination stacks. This is their interface with the Winds of the ocean, who are incredibly strong as well. This is the transfer point for hundreds of underground highways, and there are giant data stores and genetic stockpiles buried deep within the mountains. You probably never got a hint of that when you were here—it's all well hidden."

She shook her head. "One time a local priest took me on a tour around the lip of a vast pit. He said it was bottomless. A hot wind comes up out of it, and you can hear a sound like constant thunder coming out of the depths. I found it disturbing. I never went back."

"Yet it was the desals who spoke to you. They reached out to do so. According to Mason, they wish to serve, and they are the enemy of those." He gestured to the vagabond moons. "We will make them our allies. The Titans' Gates are a fortress, and you and I are about to experience our second siege, My Queen."

She hugged herself against a sudden chill. "Don't call me that. I brought my people low." Angry and grief stricken, she turned and started to walk back to their camp. The horses were visible in the firelight; both were looking in her direction. "And what are you going to do with the world once you've got it?" she shouted back to Armiger. "How will you succeed where I failed?"

"I can do what you could not," she heard him say. "I can conquer the Winds. The ones Mason calls Mediation will be our first converts." He followed her, and when she sat down by the fire, he sat, too.

"I am no longer Mad Queen Galas—just Mad Galas, I suppose," she said. "But my madness is nothing compared to yours if you expect to lay your hands on each and every Wind in order to turn them to your cause. That is what you intend to do, is it not?"

"In a sense."

"Then why haven't you done it? Where is your army? You've said that Jordan had the last piece of the puzzle you needed. So now that you know all you need to, why are you not commanding the heavens to part and the seas to recede?"

He looked down. "It's not that simple."

"Ah! That phrase is Male for 'I'm afraid to.'"

"There is some key piece missing," he admitted. "I have yet to figure it out. But when I do . . ."

"Yes? When you do, what? You've been coy about that all along, Armiger. What, exactly, are you going to do?"

He stared pensively at the stars. "The Winds are sur-biological, nanotechnological entities. Each component mechanum is infinitesimal, the size of a human cell. Each carries in it a tiny computer—a thinking machine—and communications devices. The mecha communicate with their brethren using a very large number of codes. These codes are certified each by the next higher layer of the organization, from the tiniest particle all the way up to the desals and the Diadem swans. The Winds recognize one another by comparing the digital signatures on the transmission codes. If the code is not signed by the next higher authority, it is not valid. But that next higher authority cannot issue codes without the authorization of the layer above it, and so on up the ladder. Most of the communication between the Winds consists of trading new authorizations. They do it on an unconscious level.

"To command the Winds, you must speak their language. To speak their language you must have a valid signature on your messages. Ever since arriving here I have been looking for a way to either fake the signatures or acquire the highest-level signing authority.

"Somehow, Jordan Mason has gotten a high-level authority in the eyes of the Winds. Not the highest, but very high. I suspect ordinary humans can't get to the highest level. I copied his implants exactly, which should make my messages indistinguishable from his. But they're not—somehow the Winds recognize his but not mine. That is what I'm trying to figure out now."

"That is dazzling," said Galas. "But it's not the answer I asked for. What will you do when you have this 'signing authority'?"

He hesitated. "What would you do?"

"Can you remake the world? Turn night into day, heavy into light, black into white? What can you do?"

"I can't change gravity," he said with a faint smile. "But I can change the atmosphere, or strip it away entirely. I can drain the seas, if I want. I can change the surface of this world into practically anything."

"Can you free my people from poverty and grief?"

He shrugged. "That would be among the easiest things I can do."

"Will you?"

Armiger hesitated again. He put down his soup bowl. "Should I?" he asked. "Be careful how you answer."

"I'm tired of political answers to questions like that," she said. "And tired of philosophical ones. All I know is I'm tired and hungry and afraid, and in that I am finally one with the majority of my countrymen. There is not a single person out there," she gestured at the dark countryside, "who would not say, 'save me from the cold, and the dark, and the beasts outside and in.'"

"Is that all you want for them?"

She turned to look at him. He sat now with his hands dangling between his knees, his face expressionless.

"You could do it," she whispered.

He didn't answer.

"But then . . . the real question is, what do *you* want to do?"

Armiger didn't answer for a long time. Finally he said, "I guess that depends on who I am."

"This god 3340 you've spoken of—what did he want you to do with Ventus?"

"He saw Ventus as a resource waiting to be tapped. But not an efficient one, as it stands. Most the Winds' energy is being put into maintaining the artificial ecology—a complete waste as far as 3340 was concerned. The first thing it would have had me do was abandon the terraforming system."

"Abandon? . . . What would that mean, for us I mean?"

"The air would become poisonous with time; rivers would dry up, the oceans become toxically metallic. Some kinds of life, like fungi and bacteria, would run rampant, others would die. Everything would eventually be choked out, if it even lasted that long, because 3340 wanted to use the mecha to make the entire surface of the planet into one giant machine—a god device."

"For what purpose?"

"Ventus was to have been a staging area for an assault on the human Archipelago. If 3340 had conquered even a tenth of the Archipelago, it would have become unstoppable. Eventually it might have consumed the entire galaxy."

"But 3340 is dead," she said.

"Yes."

"So you won't do that to my world."

He looked her in the eye, expressionless. "I will not," he said, a bit too vehemently.

"I wish I could believe you."

He looked surprised—the first real emotion he'd shown in days. He squinted at her through wood smoke. "Why don't you believe me?"

"Because you're very, very angry, and I'm afraid you don't know it."

That made him pause. "I don't know what you mean," he said finally.

"She is dead, Armiger."

He just looked at her.

"You don't know how to grieve, do you?" she asked.

This time he grimaced, but that was all.

"I forget sometimes that you have no experience in it." She smiled sadly. "Neither did I, the first time; no one is prepared. So we usually end up with scars; I suppose mine are no worse than anyone else's. If I am to honor Megan in any way, I guess it should be by heeding her lesson. She was offended that I . . . fell apart . . . after we escaped. I thought she couldn't possibly know what I was feeling. Now I realize that she saw that I thought this, and that was what offended her. After all, she lost a husband, but she carried on.

"At the time I thought she was making light of my pain. She must be asking me to shrug it off, like I had done with the pain of my mother's death. It took me many years to learn how bad a mistake that had been. But no, she was asking for more courage than I was willing to show. She was asking me to feel it all and keep going, anyway."

"I am not one of you," Armiger said. He didn't elaborate.

"You're acting exactly like one of us," she countered.

He didn't answer.

"The sooner you start believing it the better off you'll be, Armiger. You're going to have to face the pain, and sooner rather than later would be best."

He squinted at her through wood smoke. "Why?"

"Because if you are as powerful as you say you are, your anger could destroy my world."

"Only my human side can be angry."

"But pardon me for saying so, my general—it's your human side that makes you do what you do."

He stood up abruptly and stalked a few meters away. Encouraged, she said, "Listen to me. If you respect Megan, you should follow her example, too."

"By doing what?" He sounded indifferent, as though intent on some task. Galas almost smiled.

"By letting it all in. All the pain, the sorrow, the anger. You've got to let yourself feel it. Otherwise, it's going to act through you whether you know it or not."

He murmured something; she wasn't sure, but it sounded like, "That's not what I'm afraid of having act through me."

Galas felt infinitely weary. Her own grief was raw and close enough that she had little strength to fight his. She lay down on her bedroll and gazed up at the few stars that were visible through the perpetual dusk sky.

"I'm afraid," she heard herself say. She knew she was not speaking for herself.

"Jordan Mason," said Armiger. "I need you to find me now."

Galas rolled on her side and looked past the circle of firelight. Armiger stood with his hands raised to either side, and now lines of light flickered at the ends of his fingers. These seemed to tear away and coalesce into rolling balls, like tumbleweeds. She saw several bounce across the ground, fading. A faint rustling sound came from the undergrowth around her.

"What are you doing?" she whispered.

"I am building a larger body—more sense organs, independent hands and eyes. The Winds or their slaves might fall on us at any time. We need guards—a perimeter. I am making that."

Galas lay back, shivering. What had she just been speaking to? A man? No . . . she was the only human being on this hillside. She might as well be talking to the stones.

She closed her eyes, determined to see and hear no more today.

41

"Sir?"

Hesty's voice came to Lavin from a long way away. The voice represented the distant past, a time of hope he could no longer comprehend. The present was an unending cycle of misery that would end only with death. Nothing mattered except that pain.

He had lain here under a canopy, unable to move, for days now. He knew the official story was that vertigo had laid him low, but the truth was much more simple. Lavin's heart had died, and he no longer wanted to live.

"Sir."

With difficulty he turned his head. Hesty stood over him, his face revolving in a direction opposite to everything else. Lavin retched.

"How are you feeling, sir?"

What a laughable question. Lavin wanted to close his eyes and vanish into his misery again, but to his surprise Hesty sat down cross-legged next to him and whispered, "We need you, sir."

Lavin looked at him closely for the first time. Hesty's face was lined with care, and his hair unkempt. It looked like he hadn't slept in days—not surprising in the circumstances.

"What . . ." Lavin was surprised at his own voice, which was hoarse and feeble. "What is happening?"

Hesty let out a great sigh. "We've been getting word from back home along the semaphore lines. Apparently the Winds are marching everywhere. The skies are full of swans and Heaven hooks, and in some places the cities' gates are closed because morphs are snatching travelers off the roads. Rivers have dried up. It's insane!

"The priests here are in a panic. The Winds . . . the Winds are not what they thought. . . ." To Lavin's great surprise, Hesty shuddered.

"Sir, they're using us, then they're going to kill us. I'm sure of it. So are some of the others, but not the field commanders. The men have faith in the Winds, but a lot more of them were secretly sympathetic to Galas than we thought. There's rumors that the Winds are angry with us over her death. Overall, the rank and file believe we're on some just crusade dictated by the Winds. But really we're marching to our deaths, and a lot of them have guessed."

"Yes." Lavin swallowed. "Yes, we are." His mind was wonderfully clear all of a sudden. He could picture the entire situation in his mind—everything save the object of the Winds' wrath, which lay somewhere on or about the Titans' Gates.

His negligence had brought them to this, too, he was sure. Galas had been right in everything she'd said. He should have fought at her side. Instead he had laid the groundwork for a holocaust.

Hesty sat there for a while, dejected. Lavin stared at him, thinking of all the men who had fought under him, some of whom he had ordered to their deaths. They had trusted him—and thousands still placed their faith in him alone.

He might deserve to die—but they did not.

Lavin managed to lever himself up on one elbow. "Bring me some water," he commanded. When Hesty gave it to him, he drank eagerly, suddenly realizing that he might have allowed himself to die of thirst in his grief. Suicide by neglect.

He hated Hesty for reminding him of his duty. Scowling, he said, "The Winds will destroy us when we've served our purpose. We need to know what that purpose is."

"They won't speak to me," said Hesty. "The basts consider you the commander. In your absence they've been giving the orders."

Lavin was stunned. He had assumed that the army would be well commanded in his absence. He'd had no idea that the Winds had taken over directly.

"I . . . I will talk to them," he heard himself say.

Hesty looked at him, hope visible in his face.

"Knowing when they intend to discard us is only the first part, Hesty. We need to act when that moment comes—or before it comes. We need to escape them."

"But how?" Hesty gestured at the evidence all around them of the omnipotence of the Winds.

"The basts will not be a problem. We can shoot them. The swans are terrifying, but I'm not convinced they can do much on the ground. And the Heaven hooks . . . well, I have an idea about them."

Hesty grinned. "I knew you would, sir."

Lavin groaned. "Go get the engineers. I need something made, and we have very little time."

With sudden energy Hesty leaped to his feet and snapped a salute. "Yes, sir!" He sped out of the tent.

Lavin lay there for a while, staring at the canvas overhead. His mind was utterly empty. Finally, he groaned and stood up.

As he emerged from under the canopy he could hear a deep roaring, like continual thunder. Men were shouting and pointing, and the basts were racing as one to the great doors on the underside of the moon. Lavin followed their gazes upward.

A brilliant light glowed through the tessellated skin of the vagabond moon. The sun itself made only a diffuse, if bright, glow. This light was sharp enough that he had to look away after a second; and it moved, traversing the sky from south to north.

So far the ranked men on the parade ground had held formation, so Lavin had no difficulty crossing the floor to where the basts and a few stray men had gathered. The great doors were located at about the fifteenth degree of floor angle. From here only a sliver of sky was visible, and a great deal of dizzying ground far below. Lavin caught a glimpse of rushing pine trees far below, then fixed his gaze on the rolling mountains at the top of the door.

Something like a tiny blue-white sun heaved into view, dropping and visibly slowing as it went. Shadows radiated away from it, and he was sure it was the source of the rumbling.

The small sun went behind an angle of mountainside, silhouetting the trees along its spine. After a few seconds the light went out. The rumbling went on for a long time, gradually dying down to stray echoes.

More miracles. Lavin shook his head in disgust and went to take command of his men.

"WHAT WAS THAT?" Tamsin blinked at the spot where the little sun had set. Doubtless she had the same spots before her eyes as Jordan.

"Mediation?" He had come to rely on the geophysical Winds as advisers in the past few days. Where once he had wondered or decided that curiosity was futile, now when Jordan had a question—any question at all—he asked. Often, Mediation answered.

"That was a starship from the new Diadem fleet," said Ka. "But it should not be here. The fleet has been sent to engage the Galactics."

"Fleet? Galactics?" This was all news to Jordan. Obviously he had been asking the wrong questions.

He and Tamsin had just entered the valley below the Titans' Gates. They had changed mounts regularly and come to this place more quickly than Jordan had expected. Their animal entourage was spread out for a kilometer on each side, watching for morphs or other, even more dangerous things that Mediation said the swans were dropping here and there. Jordan had fully expected the vagabond moons converging on this spot to seek him out, and he had been surprised when the vanguard of the giant spheres began to settle beyond the ridge behind them. Mediation had reported that they were disgorging an army of humans and horses; Jordan had no doubt that this was Parliament's army, but had they come to guarantee Galas's death, or were they serving the Winds now? Mediation did not know.

The Heaven hooks seemed wary of approaching the Titans' Gates directly. Those that had not landed hung high in the atmosphere, some kilometers back. They might be able to spot Jordan's party from there—but there was no sign that they had.

Armiger and the queen were halfway up the ancient steps that zigzagged up the Titans' Gates. Tiny buildings were visible very high on the flanks of the gray peaks. According to Tamsin this was a monastery, a place Galas had visited many times before. This was where the general and the queen expected to make their stand.

Jordan had different plans. He knew the Gates were honeycombed with passages and chambers used by the Winds. There were many entrances to these passages, but Armiger and Galas had not approached any as yet. Jordan had ordered the entrances nearest them opened; he hoped they would see one and head for it. He had told Mediation to send a guide out of the mountain to fetch them, but the nearest creatures that could speak were deep inside the mountain. It would take a while for one of them to reach the surface.

Jordan had been about to send Ka to act as guide for Armiger and Galas, but this starship was a new and unknown factor. So far it seemed like the general and queen would reach the monastery without trouble, and he could easily use the inner passages of the Gates to catch up to them there.

He decided. He pointed to a hawk that was part of their entourage. It sat patiently on a branch some distance ahead, waiting for them. "Ka, go take a ride on that hawk. I want you to investigate the ship that just landed. Mediation, are there any entrances to the Gates near that spot? Yes? Then let's head that way. We can enter the mountain from there."

Tamsin scowled. "I don't like the idea of going underground again."

"This time will be different," he said. He didn't add that she would probably find it no less frightening than the desal highway. He had visited the inside of the mountain, in vision, and knew that it was not a place where humans had been meant to go.

ARMIGER HAD BEEN eating stones for some time now. He wasn't random about it. He had definite preferences and seemed to be trying to balance his diet according to some inner knowledge. They didn't talk about it, and Galas was grateful for that, as she was grateful not to talk about the mirrored seeds that he occasionally tossed behind himself as they walked. He didn't pull those seeds from any pocket or pouch. They appeared in his hand as he walked, and he dropped them.

She had thought they might be alive and fertile and was proved right when the first transparent silvery oval appeared out of the woods and came to hover over Armiger's head. He ignored it, and the six that followed it. They shimmered and occasionally tinkled like tiny bells. If she looked back, she could see bright spots on the path far behind them— things like silver cacti were growing there. Way back, three kilometers ago, she thought she glimpsed something glinting through the branches of one of the tallest trees on the hillside.

When Armiger did talk, it was often not to her, but to Jordan Mason. "Jordan, we are at the foot of the long slope that leads to the Penitents' Stairs," he might say. Or, "Jordan, meet us at the Titans' Gate Monastery. You must go there now. There is no time to lose."

"Why are you talking to him?" she had asked. Armiger had grimaced, and not replied for a while.

"I need him," was all he eventually said.

The trail had become too steep for the horses, and they dismounted. Now travel became a true misery for Galas, because the muscles of her inner thighs screamed loud protest with every step, and climbing was even worse. She knew there were thousands of steps ahead of them. The first hundred meters, from the trail to the foot of the first of the stairways carved in the nearly vertical stone of the North Tower, nearly did her in.

If she looked back the vagabond moons dominated her view of the foothills. The moons were waiting on some signal to pounce, and she was terrified of being caught by them. Nonetheless, she had gone only thirty meters or so up the first stair before she sat down with a thump and gasped, "I can't go on. All this riding has ruined my legs."

Armiger frowned at her. He hadn't even broken a sweat; there was no reason why he should, she supposed. He chewed and swallowed the red quartz pebble he'd been crunching for the past few minutes, and said, "We're almost there."

"I know that. Have you got any idea how much riding takes out of you? I'm not used to it, Armiger."

He tilted his head to one side. "I could carry you, I suppose." He extended a hand.

"I'd rather you didn't." Truth to tell, she didn't want him touching her. That hand had been burned off, then regrown; his skin had taken on a grayish tinge, and she had been half sure before that he had stopped breathing. Now she was sure of it, as she saw him deliberately draw in air to speak.

"We cannot afford to lose any time," he said. She shrugged wearily. Armiger scowled, but said, "I'll prepare you a pill that should help."

Her smile was ironic. "Thank you."

They sat in silence for a while. Armiger was abstracted; she had the distinct impression that he was listening to something. "Jordan Mason," he said abruptly, "we are at the base of the stairs. We will rest here for a few minutes, then make for the top. You can meet us there."

"You think he's that close?" she said.

Armiger shrugged. "My creatures have seen him. He's down there." He pointed. "But we can't go back for him. Not with the Winds about to move on us."

"I know you had a plan," she said. "It failed somehow, didn't it? You didn't get what you wanted from Jordan. You can't really command the Winds, can you?"

He stared off into the distance. "I've been on Ventus for nearly six years. In that time I've investigated hundreds of possible ways of overthrowing them. The best and purest is to learn their languages and codes and simply command them. There are other ways, though—not as efficient, more destructive—but they will do."

She pointed above his head. "Those things?"

He nodded. "They are part of it. If you can't tame the plants in a garden, the best you can do is replace them. Rather than command the Ventus mecha, I can replace it with mecha of my own. These mecha are more efficient; they'll choke out the Ventus mecha in no time."

"But you'll have to cover the world with them. How will you do that?"

He gestured at the mountains that rose above them. "This is the nexus of the desal highways. Those highways even go under the sea—you told me so yourself. If I flood the highways with my own mecha seeds they will sprout everywhere. They're hard for the Winds to detect, and as long as we have the highway system intact we can continue to disseminate them. We could have a global infestation under way within days."

"Infestation . . . Armiger, what will these mecha do to the other life here—the flora and fauna?"

"Ah." He looked down. "Well, part of the problem with this plan is that my mecha won't have access to the Winds' network. They won't be able to coordinate resource usage with the Winds, so they'll probably throw the Ventus ecosystem out of whack."

She thought about it. "How far out of whack?"

"Well, the idea is to threaten the Winds with disaster, so that they surrender. Once they do that, we can scale my mecha back, keep it dormant even."

"What if they don't surrender?"

"My Lady," he said, "you never ask that question after you've gone to war."

She nodded, but in her heart Galas was reconciling herself to a grim possibility: once they reached the familiar plateau of the Titans' Gates, she would need to look for ways to dispose of Armiger himself, should things get out of hand. He might not believe in surrender—and she never had as queen—but if the choice were between a world ruled by the Winds, or no world at all, Galas knew how she would choose.

IT SEEMED LIKE years since Lavin had stood on solid ground. He felt the vertigo recede a bit—enough for him to walk unaided. There was no joy in the recession of this misery though; it just made more room for misery of another kind to infect him.

He stood as still as he could and watched men and horses pour out the doors of the vagabond moon. Kilometers away, close enough that their flanks nearly touched, another moon disgorged its cargo. Together they and the several behind them blotted out the sun over ten or twelve foothills and valleys.

Not everyone would be disembarking; he had convinced the Winds to use the moons as their baggage camp. In moments he would return there as well, ostensibly to give his authority to orders coming from the Winds. In reality, he had kept his most trusted men aboard the moons and had also set up a clandestine semaphore system. He would be relaying the commands of the swans through the medium of the basts—giving his official words to their directives—but he would also be sending commands directly to his men through the semaphore.

It was windy here in the foothills. The moons were depositing the army here partly because the air was so treacherous nearer the Gates. Of course, a two-kilometer sphere made its own weather to a degree, and a dozen of them were an entire weather system; the white Wind had confided in him that this just made things worse because weather was inherently unpredictable. The skins of the moons rippled under sudden gusts, and lightning played around their crowns almost continuously. They electrified the air and then pulled it around themselves with invisible fins, the bast had said. With so many of them all together, their electric fields interfered. Add steep mountain peaks into the equation, and things became frankly dangerous.

He was counting on that.

A bast stepped up to him. It wasn't the white Wind—that one was away investigating the burning thing that had landed. "We have found them," said the bast. "They are making for the monastery, as we suspected. Your men will take the trails directly there and capture them. We will accompany you."

"They're going to get there first," he said. "And that place is highly defensible. Why don't the swans go in and get them?"

"Not an option," said the bast. "You will go."

Lavin shrugged. "I guess you're right. The desals would cut the swans to pieces."

The bast bridled. "You will not question our orders."

"I will where it concerns my men. Listen, we are too far back here for me to command them. We need to get this moon over the valley—or better yet, over the peaks themselves. We could lower a battalion using the Heaven hooks, come on them from above. They have no way to defend against that."

The bast bared its teeth. "You are saying you will fail to take the monastery from below?"

"We won't fail. It could take weeks, months, even. You could keep us supplied that long, but—"

"Unacceptable. This abomination is too dangerous. We must destroy it now."

"So why don't you use nature itself, like you did against Armiger's army in Ravenon? Send in all the animals, uproot the plants."

The bast's tail twitched. "We have tried. They will not respond. Mediation is controlling this valley. We do not have enough morphs to convert these life-forms. That is why you must go in."

"Then we have to go in from above," he said. "There is no other way."

The bast turned away. Then it said, "I will ask the swans."

Yes, bring us in close, Lavin thought as he watched it walk away. *Get us high, and close together in the mountains. Then we'll learn if you can fly.*

42

FOR A MOMENT Axel Chan was content to just smell the air. He stood on the ship's ramp with his eyes closed, letting the breeze stroke his hair like the hand of a lover. His ears popped. He was back on Ventus, and he needed no more reminder of why he'd come than this scent of pine and loam.

The navy had given them this cutter in order to let Marya do a reconnaissance of the maelstrom of swan activity building over these mountains. The Archipelagic forces had originally wanted the *Voice* to lend her recognition codes to a destroyer-class ship, but the AI had insisted that they come in this small craft, without an escort. That way they could attempt to locate Calandria—a part of their plan they had not mentioned to the admiral.

Even a close orbit had not told them what was going on down here—but Calandria's transponder signal had pinged faintly from the very heart of the energy storm. When they picked up her signal, the three had exchanged uneasy glances in the cockpit. To descend into the vortex could be wildly dangerous—but if anyone on the ground might know what was truly happening, it would be Calandria May.

"Hey, move!" Marya gave Axel a small shove from behind. He sighed and jogged down the rest of the ramp to finally stand on the soil of Ventus again. Marya came to poise beside him, and after a moment the *Voice* joined them. The AI's striking resemblance to Calandria May still disturbed Axel, but the *Voice* was obviously a different person: she stared around herself with the wide-eyed wonder of someone who had never set foot on a planet before.

"You've been here," he chided. "You dropped us off last summer, remember?"

She shook her head. "I had a different body then. To be this small and vulnerable in this environment . . . it's indescribable."

Both humans smiled at her. Then Marya pointed at the twin mountains rising above them. "Look! There's buildings way up there, on the side."

"Gods." Axel's mind boggled at the amount of labor it must have taken to put those structures up there. "Maybe that's where she is."

He hoped she was nearby and not on the other side of those mountains. The ocean lay there; Axel had seen it as they came in. He had also seen strange waterfalls that vanished into shafts in the far side of the two peaks, as well as what looked like gigantic pipes shimmering under the surface of the ocean. There were a few towns around here, but no major cities within a day's travel of this place. He had no idea what Calandria might be doing out here.

He closed his eyes and concentrated. He felt the signal—but it wasn't coming from the mountains. "She's in the valley," he said. "A kilometer or two at most that way. Seems to be moving in this direction, fast."

"Should we wait or go out to meet them?" asked Marya.

"Ka," somebody said.

A shadow whipped past and Axel, and Marya ducked. The *Voice* turned, blinking in astonishment at the large hawk that swept in a circle around the perimeter of the clearing where they'd set down, then returned. It landed on a moss-cushioned log not three meters away, then folded its wings.

"Beautiful," whispered Marya.

"Ka," said the hawk. "So you found a way off world, Axel."

"Uhn," said Axel. A bird was talking to him.

"It's me, Jordan," said the hawk. "Can you hear me?"

"Jordan?" He peered at the hawk. "How are you doing this?"

"My servant hitched a ride on this hawk. He's talking to you for me. I haven't changed myself into a hawk, if that's what you're thinking."

"No, of course not." Axel sidled closer to the hawk, looking for a speaker or antenna somewhere on it. "You seem to have come up in the world, Jordan."

"You could say that." Jordan Mason's voice held a wry tone Axel had never heard the young man use before. "Hello, Lady May."

Axel looked over his shoulder. "Oh. That's not Calandria. I know it looks like her. It's . . . rather hard to explain."

"Not Calandria? Where is she?"

"She's not with you?"

"No." The bird fell to calmly grooming its wing, seemingly indifferent to the human voice issuing from its body. "Listen," said Jordan, "if that's all of you, you've got to get moving. Come meet me and I'll explain everything."

"You know what's going on here?" asked Marya.

"Yes. Are you a friend of Axel's?"

"Yes. I've heard a lot about you, Jordan. I'm very pleased to meet you."

"Well, we haven't met yet, and we won't if you don't get moving. The soldiers are almost on top of you."

"What soldiers?"

"The army of Thalience."

Marya looked at Axel, her eyebrows raised. He shrugged. "We'll be right there, as soon as we collect Calandria."

"Axel, there's no time!" The hawk unfolded its wings and leaped into the air. "Follow me!" It flapped north.

Axel put his hand on Marya's shoulder. "You two go with the bird. I'll collect Cal and follow along."

"How will you find us?"

"I've got a fix on the *Voice*'s transponder. Don't worry, I won't be long." The hawk was perched on a branch, watching impatiently. Axel watched Marya and the *Voice* stalk through the underbrush in its direction; then he inhaled a cold breath of mountain air and turned the other direction. The hawk cawed at him. He ignored it.

She was nearby. He had to know she was okay. Once he had her he would collect Mason and head back to the ship. With luck they could be off-planet within the hour, and with further luck Calandria and Jordan Mason would be able to tell the fleet enough to halt the planned bombardment.

He thudded over the tangle of roots and fallen pine needles, attention focused on the signal he could sense ahead of him. It was closing on his position. She must have sensed him as well. He grinned, starting to relax.

Abruptly the trees opened out to define a well-tended trail that slotted east to west through the forest. He looked to his left, saw nothing, and turned to his right—

—Two horses came at full gallop over a ridge not twenty meters away. The lead rider shouted something and lowered a weapon across his arm.

Axel jumped back. There was a loud bang, and splinters flew from the tree over his head.

The signal was very close now. For the first time it occurred to him that Calandria might be a prisoner. He cursed and unholstered his laser pistol.

The horse had stopped. "Show yourself!" shouted the rider in a thick accent Axel couldn't identify. He sneaked a look around the tree; three more horses were approaching.

"Don't shoot!" he yelled. "I'm just an innocent traveler."

"Then you've got nothing to fear if you come out here."

"Yeah, right," muttered Axel.

Something moved swiftly in the corner of his eye. He whirled, in time to glimpse a giant catlike form in mid-leap. Axel fired without thinking, and then it knocked the wind out of him and they tumbled over and over.

The furred thing fell away. Axel got to his hands and knees, shaking his head. He'd lost his pistol, but the golden cat-thing lay curled around itself, a black burn in its chest and bright blood pumping out of the center of the charred patch. It moaned, twitched, and lay still.

Where was the pistol? When he spotted it he scrabbled in that direction. He stretched out his hand to grab it—and the point of a sword came between him and it.

"Stand," said the man behind the sword. He wore the bruised-blue and russet livery of a soldier of Iapysia. He looked like he meant business. Four other soldiers had dismounted behind him.

The others looked behind themselves as several more of the catlike creatures padded over, then stood up on their back legs. They were all gold-colored, except one which was a striking white.

This one's eyes widened, and it hissed when it saw the situation. It ran forward with surprisingly human grace, and opened its arms.

"Axel!" it shouted as it wrapped its arms around him.

Someone screamed. Axel struggled to pull free of the cat-thing, and after a moment he did—or rather it let go of him and he fell. He levered himself onto his elbows, then froze.

One of the horses was down. A very large bear reared over it, bawling loudly. One of the soldiers was down, too, with his hands up to fend off the hawk that was stabbing at his face.

Two foxes raced out of the forest and leaped at the remaining soldiers. Way back there, something else big was crashing in their direction.

"Fight, you cowards!" shouted the white cat. It moved with astonishing speed, knocking one of the foxes out of the air in mid-pounce. Then it spun on one foot and jumped backward, disappearing behind Axel.

"Axel, run!" shouted the hawk. It ducked in close then burst in a flurry of feathers as one of the soldiers shot it point-blank. Something iridescent, half visible, twirled up from the falling bird, then flashed into flame and drifted down as another of the soldiers emptied his musket into the chest of the bear. It staggered back snarling. Then a third man fired, and it fell dead.

Axel turned to run—and found himself eye to eye with the white cat. It held out something. His pistol. "Take it!" it hissed.

He hesitated for a second, then grabbed the pistol and ran. Animals big and small crashed past him, all converging on the soldiers and their cat-like companions.

Axel had no idea what he'd just seen. He didn't want to know. All he wanted to do at this moment was run and keep running until he'd forgotten it all.

ARMIGER FELT A trembling in the electric fields that interpenetrated the mountains. He looked up. The vagabond moons were rising again. Sheet lightning played over their vast curved sides.

"How do you feel?" he asked Galas. She nodded and levered herself to her feet. He had spent some minutes preparing a concoction of complex molecules and nanotech, and now he handed her the pills he had distilled it down to. She looked at them doubtfully, but when he pointed to the rising moons, she dutifully tossed them back and swallowed. Then she began to slowly climb the stairs, swinging her legs wide with every step.

He looked back at the foothills. It was some testament to how exhausted Galas was that she had not spent any time looking at the view. The vagabond moons rose to fully half the height of the Titans' Gates when on the ground; although the nearest one was at least eight kilometers away it eclipsed a good twenty degrees of the sky. The sun was getting low on the horizon, and the shadow of the Gates fell across the moon, dividing it into two halves, gray below and rose colored above. Beyond it and the two companions that had landed, nine more moons clustered high in the stratosphere, where they shone in full sunlight.

The stairs that they had to climb were also in shadow. This wasn't much of a problem for Armiger, who could see in the dark, but Galas was going to have difficulty. "We must hurry," he said.

He could sense his mecha growing in the valley below. The Winds could probably perceive it by now, too, and he had no doubt they would react violently to his decoys. An assault by the Winds on the valley could buy them valuable time.

"Look." Galas pointed above them. Lights burned in windows high on the mountainside, and another pinprick glow was waving back and forth slowly at the top of the stairs. "They've seen us," she said.

"Good." They climbed together for a few minutes, and her steps became more sure as the medicine he had given her took hold. She didn't speak, and it was just as well because he was brooding about what to do next. His plans had once been precise and confident, but his deterioration into humanity seemed to have clouded his reasoning. He should have abandoned Galas at the foot of the stairs, but he found he could not. She was a dangerous drag on him at this point; left to himself he could have run all the way to the top of the mountains by now and launched himself into one of the pits that led to the desal highway. Deep underwater in the roots of the mountain, he would have been safe and could have propagated his mecha without fear of interruption.

If only Jordan Mason were here. The man held the key to the command language of the Winds, and Armiger was sure he could extract it, though he might have to take Mason apart molecule by molecule to find it. Yet Mason was meandering through the valley below with no apparent destination. It was infuriating.

Maybe he could contact Mason through his mecha. He did retain a com link to all of it, after all, in much the same way that the Winds remained connected to all life on Ventus. He could reprogram the genes of his mecha from afar. Maybe he could give some a voice.

He directed his thoughts to the largest of the mechal cacti growing in the valley. It was a good twenty meters high now and had slowly turned black. In his mind's eye it appeared as a coal-black jumble of saucer-shaped leaves joined together without stems. Its roots ran straight into bedrock, and heat radiated off it as from an oven. Armiger hadn't anticipated that effect of its metabolism—it might well start a forest fire if he wasn't careful. That would certainly raise the ire of the Winds, which was good, but it might also threaten Mason.

This cactus was of a design older than Armiger himself. It was a product of 3340's imagination, not his. It had the potential to bud all manner of other mechal life forms off its round leaves, and he had never had time to explore the complete catalog of possibilities. He asked it now to provide him with a list of forms able to speak that it could grow rapidly.

Wait . . . , it said in an eerily familiar voice.

Armiger stopped climbing.

"What's wrong?" asked Galas. She touched his arm. He realized he had been glaring down into the valley, his hands balled into fists.

"Nothing," he said. "Let's keep going."

I can produce any of these, said the mechal tree in 3340's voice.

Armiger gasped, but he did not stop climbing. The tree unrolled a series of images in his mind of mechal animals, some disturbingly human-shaped. Armiger barely paid attention—it was the touch of the tree's mind that held his attention. It had a certain signature to it—his own, of course, but also something more.

"Thank you," he told it. "Do nothing. Sleep now."

I cannot sleep now, it said.

Armiger swore.

"Tell me," said Galas between gasping breaths.

"I may have made a mistake," he said. "We have to hurry."

"I can go no faster," she said. "I'm ready to collapse."

"Then I'll carry you."

She made no protest this time as he gathered her up in his arms and began bounding up the steps.

JORDAN'S FIRST SIGHTING of Axel was as the man stumbled out of the forest shouting, "They're right on my heels!" Axel was dressed in tough black clothing and had a belt festooned with odd devices around his waist, very like the woman who was not Calandria May. The third woman, who had introduced herself as Marya Mounce, was wearing some kind of close-fitting camouflage that made it hard to see her from the neck down. She seemed keyed up and kept looking around herself and flaring her nostrils.

A few of Jordan's animals straggled out of the woods after them. The rest were fighting a rear-guard action, but the basts had decimated them.

Axel clasped Jordan's forearm in an almost painful grip. "Good to see you, kid! You're looking great."

"Thanks." Jordan was bursting with questions, but there was no time for them now. He could sense some of the cat-beasts that had chased Armiger and the queen approaching through the woods. They were very stealthy animals, but to him they shone like beacons through the translucent tree trunks. Several hesitant humans with guns followed them.

"Let's get back to the ship," said Axel. Jordan shook his head.

"They're between us and it," he said. "And I think the swans have figured out that it's not one of theirs. I don't think they're going to let it leave."

"It's our only option," argued Axel. "We need to get out of here."

"I agree," he said. "And we will. That's why we have to go this way." He pointed.

"He may be right, Axel," said the woman who was not Calandria May. "I can hear a lot of traffic from the swans suddenly."

It was cold and getting dark rapidly. The swans should be turning on their midnight sun soon, but until then the forest would be impassible to these people. "I'm going to make a little light," said Jordan. "You follow it, and don't let it out of your sight. We have to move quickly if we're to keep ahead of the cats."

He started walking; Tamsin fell into stride beside him. As he raised his hands to create a ghost light on the shoulders of his jacket, he heard Axel and the others rushing to catch up.

"Well, what are those cat-things, anyway?" asked Axel. "One of them knew my name. Damn near killed me."

"I'd never seen one until the other day. I think they're a new kind of animal that the swans brought," said Jordan. "They can talk, I know that much, and they seem to be leading the army that's following us."

"Army?"

Jordan glanced back, resisting the urge to laugh. "A lot's happening right now. How did you find us, anyway?"

"Looking for Calandria. We found her signal, followed it down. At least, I thought it was her signal. . . ." He fell silent.

One of the cat-things had broken away from the others and was trailing them very closely now. It was almost completely dark, so Jordan had to rely on his vision to see where they were going. Axel, who seemed to be aware of the cat, too, somehow, sauntered easily beside him.

Of course, Jordan should have remembered that Axel Chan could see in the dark as well as Calandria had.

The cat seemed to be keeping a discreet distance, so Jordan said, "Tell me all about it—where you've been, what you've done. Then I'll tell you what's happened to me."

Axel laughed. "Best offer I've had all day."

. . .

THE WHITE WIND crept through the forest, low to the ground, and listened as Axel told his tale. She remembered being Calandria May now—remembered Axel, his passions and follies, the lopsided grin and strong hands. She had rushed to embrace him the instant she saw him, and he had not recognized her.

She wept as she padded along, regretting everything. Her life had been so sweet, and she had never known.

The others were hanging back on her instructions. She could not disobey her new masters, but neither did she have to obey them mindlessly. She knew, if they did not, that Axel posed no threat to Ventus. Jordan, though . . . She was not so sure about him.

She wanted to turn and run, and run all night through the woods until she could sleep the sleep of exhaustion and forget. Instead, the white Wind held her pace next to the humans and listened with growing wonder to the tales of the *Desert Voice*, and of Thalience, and of Earth.

CALLOUSED HANDS REACHED down to help Galas up the last few steps. She could only nod her gratitude to the dark-robed men who stood under torchlight on the broad ledge that fronted the Titans' Gate monastery.

The moment she was safely on her feet, the whole crowd of thirty or so men knelt as one. "Your Highness," said the abbot, a balding man with gray eyes whom she had not seen in years.

"I am not the queen," she said. "Not any more." The words still sounded strange to her.

They all looked up as one. "We know your palace was under siege," said the abbot. "We assumed it would be taken. So this means you are in exile now. I must tell you that you have always served the desals well and have honored the ancient traditions better than any monarch in recent memory. You have our loyalty now and forever. For that reason, we still consider you queen, if not of Iapysia, then at least of this mountain."

Galas found herself blushing. She looked down. "Thank you." She could think of nothing further to say.

"My Queen, are you responsible for the unprecedented visit of all these Winds to our humble monastery?" The abbot gestured in the direction of the vagabond moons.

She shrugged. "I suppose I am, in a way."

"Is this stairway defensible?" asked Armiger.

The abbot eyed him appraisingly. "It has proved to be in the past," he said. "You are Queen Galas's escort?"

"This is the General Armiger," she said. "He is my protector, and yours now." She saw that Armiger had dismissed the strange silvery ovals that had hovered over his head the past few hours. Had she not known he was not breathing, she would have thought he looked perfectly normal.

Armiger walked over to the parapet. The monastery was just over halfway up the vertical eastern face of the north Gate. Invisible from the valley was a broad ledge, almost a plateau, that narrowed to nothingness a hundred meters north, but broadened to the south as it swept around the curve of the mountain face. The monastery buildings were built toward the north end, so that the very last towers hugged the cliff itself with sheer rock below them. The stairway arrived midway along the south edge of the plateau, where the monks had built a garden around the front gates of the monastery.

"What lies that way?" asked Armiger, pointing to the southerly curve of the narrow plateau.

"Habitations of the Winds," said the abbot.

"Desal machines," added Galas. "There's bottomless pits, waterfalls spouting out of the cliffs . . . it's hard to describe."

"And the distance to the southern peak?"

"About three-quarters of a kilometer at this point," said the abbot.

Armiger nodded. "Too narrow for a vagabond moon to fit."

"What are you thinking?" she asked him.

"I'm satisfied about the stairs down," he said. "But I somehow doubt that's where our threat will come from."

"Why do you say that?"

"Look." He pointed at the moons. As far as she could tell, they hadn't moved. They hung over the far end of the valley and the foothills, seemingly close enough to touch, but in reality kilometers away.

Armiger must have seen her uncomprehending expression. He said, "Count them."

She did so. There were eleven.

"An hour ago," said Armiger, "there were twelve."

A NEW SUN CAME on, exactly at the zenith. It appeared first as a sliver of brightness, then bloomed over a few seconds into a square too bright to look at. In those few seconds, the sky underwent a complete transformation from twilight to day; every shade of blue flashed through the heavens as the stars went out everywhere except near the deep blue horizon. Way out there, clouds and the edges of the farthest vagabond moons lay in shadow; nearer in, they gleamed in pure sunlight.

Axel squinted up at the light. "Solar mirror," he said. "Big sucker."

Jordan nodded. He had seemed subdued ever since Axel and Marya had told him what they'd learned about Thalience and Turcaret. Axel had seen him shake his head several times, scowling.

"So we're going to meet the infamous Armiger," Axel said. "I've been wanting to do that for almost a year. You say you spoke to him once? You still think he's not a resurrection seed?"

Jordan hesitated. "I don't think so," he said. "But I'm not sure."

"Don't say that," said Axel. "Say, 'Axel, he's not a resurrection seed, and I can prove it.' That would make me happy, if you could say that to me."

"He's up to something, and I'm not sure what," Jordan said. "I don't think that proves anything either way."

"You said he took the secret of commanding the Winds from you, but he hasn't used it. And you don't know why not."

Jordan shook his head. "He should have started using it right away. He could have taken over the world by now if he'd been able to."

"He has the technology, but not the keys," said Marya. "It's exactly like Turcaret. He can speak to them, but they're not listening."

"Oh, they're listening," said Jordan. "They hear what I say, and they talk back. That's not it."

She shook her head. "But Thalience—"

Jordan barked a laugh. "Whatever Thalience is, the swans have given up on it. They're bitter, and they're in the mood to clean up after neglecting their jobs for a long time. So they plan to wipe humanity off of Ventus."

Jordan's companion said, "You said this fellow Turcaret had to have a certain kind of . . . thing in him."

"DNA." Marya nodded vigorously. "Yes, that must be it. Armiger doesn't have the proper DNA."

"Not quite true," said Axel. "The fact is, he probably doesn't have DNA at all. . . . So that's it."

Jordan nodded. "He has the broadcast power, but not the 'password.'"

"That's what we came to find out," said Marya. "Let's get back to the ship."

"No!" Jordan ran several steps ahead. "We're nearly there!"

"Nearly where?" They had come to an almost vertical cliff—the end of a long sinuous drape of 'Titans' Gate stone. The cliff was seamless, and at least fifty meters high.

"There's a door into the Gates here," said Jordan.

There was a flash of lightning, and moments later a grumble of thunder from fairly nearby. Tamsin pointed up through the trees. "Here they come."

The Heaven hooks were descending on the valley. They were no less impressive in daylight than they had been at night; it was simply clearer now what they were. Three of the vagabond moons were edging over the valley; together they would fill the sky over it from one end to the other. Their very bottommost sections had petalled open, and now long black gantries and cables were unreeling. From a distance these looked delicate, but the gantries were thicker than the trees below them.

As Axel watched, lightning stuttered from the cables of the lead craft. A long line of explosions stitched across the valley floor.

"If we're going to get to the ship we have to leave now," said the *Voice.*

Jordan shook his head. "The swans are waiting if it takes off. They haven't moved against it because the hooks are going to take care of it."

"How do you know that?"

"I used to rely on Mediation to relay what they were saying. I don't need to anymore. I can hear them myself now."

They all stopped walking and stared at Jordan. He put his hands on his hips and glared back.

"Are you gonna argue with me?" he said belligerently.

Surprised, Axel laughed.

"But, the ship!" wailed Marya.

"The ship is about to be eaten," said Jordan with a shrug. "We're going this way." He pointed to the cliff.

Marya glanced at Axel; he shrugged.

"Apparently we are," he said.

43

"WHAT ARE THEY doing? I gave no orders for them to move!"

Lavin stood perilously near the open door of the vagabond moon. He needed this vantage point to watch the proceedings below. It was obvious from here that three of the other moons had broken formation and were moving, like ponderous floating islands, to cover the valley.

Lavin's own moon had sailed south and swept around behind the Titans' Peaks. For a while as the moon rotated he had seen nothing but ocean, sunlit for a few kilometers, then abruptly plunged in darkness. Then the Titans' Gates had appeared again, very close.

The moon had been moving with frightening speed. Although the wind didn't penetrate the doors, somehow, he could hear it roaring, and all across the floor of the moon the guy wires popped and groaned as the great craft strove to keep its shape. Almost continuous flashes of lightning lit its interior, and the smell of ozone was overpowering. Once or twice as they passed the lower peaks south of the Gates, brilliant bolts had shot down, apparently from right under Lavin's feet, shattering wind-sculpted pine trees on the tops of the mountains below.

A different Lavin would have found the experience thrilling, as many of his men obviously did. They were keyed up to an almost intolerable degree, waiting in their ranks for the order to move.

A bast sauntered over to Lavin and turned its amber eyes to where he pointed. "We move to obliterate a threat in the valley," it said. "It is not your concern."

"A goodly portion of my army is in that valley."

The bast shook its head. "They have been pulled back, except for a few squads that are nearing the stairways. Your suggestion to attack from this direction was heeded and acted upon. Your army is not threatened."

"Then you have no need for it anymore?"

The bast shrugged. "For the moment, no."

And if we succeed here, not at all. Lavin glanced past the bast. Far up the distant curve of the moon's floor, two men were discreetly clamping something to one of the guy wires that crisscrossed the interior of the moon. Four other squads were returning from doing the same thing at various levels up and down the slopes. The basts had been distracted by questions and deliberate mistakes these last few minutes; all was nearly in place.

Lavin nodded curtly to the creature. "Nonetheless you're forcing our hand. Moving on the valley looks a lot like moving against the Gates. They're going to expect an attack from above now."

"We are in position. It is no longer a concern."

Lavin resisted a very real urge to push the bast out the door. Instead, he took a deep breath and looked down. If he had faith in his own body and ignored the suggestion that the world was turning in two diametrically opposed directions at the same time, he had found he could look down through the doors quite safely.

The northernmost Gate lay directly below. The moon had slowed dramatically and was also rising. They were a good two hundred meters above the flattop of the peak. He could see their shadow slide across the gray stone tables with their dotted pine trees. Vapor rose from a number of suspiciously round pits there. There were also a surprising number of buildings; as he watched, tiny running figures appeared around several of them.

"We're rising, not descending," Lavin pointed out. "Are you proposing we jump?"

The bast shook its long head. "The wind gusts here are strong and unpredictable. It would also be bad if we shorted out on the Gate machinery. We will lower your men using the Heaven hooks."

Even as it said this, something huge and black appeared below, blotting out the view. It took a few seconds for Lavin to realize what it was: a large railed platform, pinioned at the sides by huge metal arms. The arms extended off somewhere underneath the moon. In consternation and awe he watched it rise smoothly and silently until it blocked the door with a deep thump that he felt through his feet.

He turned and waved at the marshalls. The moon's other doors were blocked, too, he saw. The hooks should be able to lower a couple hundred men at a time to the peak. That should be enough, depending on how quickly they did it.

"Move out!" The men had been champing at the bit for some action; now they surged forward and didn't have to be prompted to leap off the stable black surface of the moon onto the metal platforms below. When the platforms were full the marshalls whistled and the surge stopped. Immediately there was a lurch, and the platforms began to drop away. The men on the one below Lavin started shouting, and most fell to their hands and knees—but the descent was smooth and except for the icy wind that now whirled through the doors as well, he was sure it would be painless.

For all that he mistrusted the Winds, he knew they were efficient. They would not waste his men in the descent.

JORDAN HAD BEEN anticipating this moment for days. What he hadn't imagined was that he would be completely soaking wet and freezing cold when it came.

He stood shivering with the others at one end of a gigantic chamber that must penetrate deep into the mountain. It must be at least a hundred meters broad, and as high. It didn't really have a floor, more a lattice of pipes both mammoth and small. They were all uniformly gray and unmarked. The tangle was so complex that the eye lost itself in detail after only a few meters. Jordan had just spent the past few minutes trying to figure out a way across the vast maze, but every route he traced either got lost or ended in an impassable drop or roll under a bigger pipe.

"I have our route," said the woman whom the others called the *Voice*. "Follow me." She stepped out confidently onto a pipe as broad as a house and began walking.

Axel and Marya followed without hesitation. Tamsin shrugged, and went, too. After a moment Jordan followed.

He had envisioned this space in his mind, but the reality was nothing like the vision. There was something called a conveyor at the far end of this chamber, he knew, and it would deposit them far above, near the peak of the mountain. Mediation had told him it was safe. On the other hand, Mediation had not told him about this daunting labyrinth, and that was unsettling.

Biting his lip he hurried after the others. In vision he could see Armiger issuing orders as men in dark robes rushed back and forth along a broad ledge. Some men were passing out weapons, chiefly pikes and bows, and nearby Galas was pleading with a gray-eyed man. She wanted them to retreat into the monastery, Jordan knew. Armiger disagreed, and so did the abbot.

Mediation said that the Heaven hooks had dropped part of Parliament's army on the peak of the mountain. They were on their way down, using numerous paths and stairs. Armiger knew it, too; the plateau lay in shadow, and once when the general looked up Jordan, too, could see the vast swell of the vagabond moon that perched like some mythical bird atop the mountain.

Human soldiers would be just the first gambit by the Winds. If Armiger resisted this onslaught, they would escalate things, and Jordan knew by now that they would not stop until they had leveled the mountain if need be. He also finally knew why Armiger had not acted—it was because he could not. The general was helpless until he knew the final secret.

Ka had been lost in the attack on the basts that had surrounded Axel, as had many of their animals. Jordan felt the loss of the little Wind keenly; he hadn't told Tamsin yet, and he wasn't sure how he would. Ka had been a friend of sorts, and now he wished he had protected it, not sent it into danger.

It was too late now. Ka was dead, and there were no Mediation Winds capable of speech near the surface of the mountain. If he was going to contact Armiger, Jordan would have to get there himself.

The *Voice* took to the maze of pipes confidently—hopping from high ones down to broad lower ones, zigzagging, doubling back without hesitation. Several times it looked like she was leading them into culs-de-sac, but every time a surprising new avenue opened up, and after only a few minutes they emerged on a single straight pipe that ran a full kilometer straight to the end of the chamber. Tamsin began running the instant they reached it, and Jordan took off after her. He could hear her laughing ahead of him, and he grinned, too. The others followed more quietly.

She was waiting at the small square chamber at the end. She kissed him then, said, "Is that our way up?"

Where she pointed, a black hole opened into a rattling space where every now and then a large metal bin or bucket would slide up and past.

"You're not afraid?" he asked her.

She shook her head. "You're not, so I'm not."

Jordan's heart managed to miss a beat. He was saved from having to say something in return (his mind had gone blank) by the arrival of the others.

"Oh no," said Marya, when she saw the opening. "I'm not going in there."

"Fine," said Axel. "We'll leave you here then."

"It's perfectly safe," said Jordan, striving to make his voice sound confident. "Just wait for a bucket to go by and climb in. You'll just slide into the next bucket in line."

"Okay, if you're so smart, demonstrate," said Marya.

I hate being the leader, thought Jordan as he waited for one of the big metal bins to go past. He felt himself hesitate, felt a sudden surge of fear at the thought that he might wait too long and get crimped by the next bucket in line while only halfway through the opening—so he jumped.

There was a moment of blackness and falling, then he was in a bucket, banging his elbow and hitting his head. "Ouch!"

A square opening came into view. Several silhouetted heads were blocking what little light tried to come through it.

"It's fine!" he shouted cheerfully. His heart was still racing. "Just follow along."

I'd better be right about this. The light cut off below him, and then he was rising in darkness, supported apparently only by faith.

IT WILL NOT happen again. Galas slipped out the gates of the monastery, grabbed a pike that a harried monk handed her without looking, and raced after the line of men heading south along the plateau. She had entered the monastery on Armiger's orders; he wanted her safe. At her first opportunity she had raided a closet and stolen a robe, and with this as her disguise she had slipped out again.

They will not die for me.

She knew that the Heaven hooks were after Armiger and that they were using the soldiers of Parliament's army as their own. The army was obviously decapitated; she couldn't imagine Lavin agreeing to place his men in such jeopardy. If he had he was a fool.

Galas knew she could not compel the Winds to retreat. The men who had once been her loyal followers, however, were another matter.

Sore as she was, she forced herself to keep up with the monks as they raced around the southern curve of the mountain. Here the ledge opened out into a vast grassy plateau encircled by spires of stone. Pyramids of mist stood beyond these, permanent residents of the space between the two Gates. As she ran, the sound of roaring water became louder, and Galas remembered the first time she had come here. She had gone to stand on the edge of the plateau and peered down into mist and the vision of a hundred waterfalls that plummeted into bottomless shafts below or exploded hissing off rounded, red-hot domes in the saddle between the peaks. There was no way down to that inferno; it was entirely a place of the Winds. Behind her and above, on the south face of the Gate, other apertures opened, venting steam or small trickles of water that could become torrents that arced out and into the gulf below. There was so much sound here that she had sometimes been sure she heard muttering voices under it all—an effect the monks sadly assured her was an illusion.

Galas had been a young queen then. Flushed with the success of her communication with the desals, she had imagined herself the goddess her people claimed she was. When she came here she had felt ownership, not fear, and she had stood upon a stone here and preached a sermon to the monks and the Winds. Her own words returned to her with ironic pain—she had spoken breathlessly of a new age for Man and Wind. Her own sincerity returned to her now like the remembrance of a crime.

The monks were forming up into columns, preparing for the great run up the stairs. Far up there, she could see a column of men on their way down. There was no time to think.

She raced past the head of the line, ignoring the shouts that followed her, and started up the steps. One of the monks came after her, and when he laid a hand on her sleeve she turned and shouted, "Get back to the line! I have to do this alone."

He stammered something and let go. She ran on, trying with little success to ignore the daggers of pain in her thighs from days of riding combined with her recent climb. After only a few meters she was gasping, her legs wobbly beneath her, but she kept on.

Men were shouting above her. She flipped back the cowl of her robe and looked up into a bristling mass of men and weapons. "Halt!" shouted the one in the lead, who was young enough to be the son she had never had.

She stopped, panting. They came down, slowly, and she had to smile at their caution. These were the veterans of Lavin's army—men who had committed atrocities in her experimental towns and had cursed her every day for the past year. They were little more than boys and were visibly scared. And they were her people, whether they wanted to admit it or not.

Drawing herself up to her full height, Galas wiped her tangled hair away from her forehead, and said, "This attack will not happen."

The leader gaped at her. "Who are you to tell us that?" Somebody laughed behind him.

She raised her voice, letting it echo off the mountainside. "I am the one you pursued over leagues of charred ground and over the bodies of thousands. I am the one you obeyed as a child and feared as a soldier. I am your sovereign, your compass, and your ultimate meaning. I am she who spoke to the oceans and commanded rain for your fields. I am Galas, your queen, and I am the only hope any of you have of living to see another day.

"When you moved to destroy me you set in motion terrible events that threaten the very world itself. You know that now, but you do not know what to do about it. You desperately wish to turn back the hands of time, I can see it in your eyes. I am the one who knows what has happened and why. Only I have the key to halting the advance of the vengeful Winds across our land.

"So you will kneel to me now, and when you rise you will be mine, and I will lead you out of this nightmare into which you have fallen."

At her words they stopped.

They stared in silence at her, then beyond her to the turmoil in the skies.

Then they knelt before her.

ARMIGER STOOD ON the edge of a cliff. Three hundred meters below and kilometers away, his mecha were dying under the lightning bolts of the Heaven hooks—all save one, a thing like a great metal tree that had begun in the past hour to sprout strange multilimbed animalcules, which were harvesting minerals and ores from the rocky terrain around it. This abomination fended off the lightning as if it were rain. He could see it from here, for it glowed a dull red now from its internal furnaces. The forest around it was burning.

He could hear it, too, chuckling inside his head.

You did well, Armiger. This place is perfectly suited to our task.

He shuddered. If he probed deep inside himself, he knew he would find that the strange repository of nanomemory, which he had calculated could hold centuries of vast experience, was gone. It had slipped out of him of its own accord when he began creating mecha. It had been a resurrection seed, and he had unwittingly set it free.

Feel the energy under us! These local beings have tapped geothermal potentials of magnificent power. When my roots have reached deep enough, my growth will be geometric. You could not have chosen a better ground in which to seed me.

Thirty-three forty's voice alone was enough to freeze Armiger in his tracks. He felt pinioned as by a giant searchlight—the attention of a god was on him. Compared to it, the wrath of the Winds seemed trivial.

We will eat this world in no time.

He tore his gaze away from the red spot and the lightning flickering around it. The Winds would not be able to stop 3340. Maybe the human fleet that he knew waited in orbit could—but their methods would guarantee the deaths of every living being on this continent. There had to be another solution.

The monks and even the army marching down from the mountain's peak were forgotten. Armiger stood still, frowning into the false day, wracking his brains for a way out of the trap he had himself set and sprung.

"SIR, THEY'RE NOT fighting."

The lieutenant lay at the very edge of the door, a telescope jammed against his eye. He was staring straight down.

"What do you mean? They haven't engaged the enemy?"

"I think the monks must have surrendered. They're all together down there, but there's no fighting going on."

"Excellent. Have they got the semaphore set up yet?"

"It's just coming on line now, sir. They're sending a test message."

"Read me the first real message as it comes in. I don't want to waste a second."

He paced back and forth, fighting vertigo and cursing the basts who got in his way. Nearly the entire army was on the ground now, either here or at the mouth of the valley. They would never be in a better position than they were now.

"I want to know the instant you have your hands on General Armiger."

"Yes," said the bast who had been overseeing the operation. "So do we."

"Sir, we confirmed the test message. Now they're sending. The message is . . ."

Lavin staggered over and sat down heavily next to the man. "Yes, yes?"

"The message . . . the message is . . ." The lieutenant took the telescope away from his eye and rolled over. He looked at Lavin with a puzzled expression. "It said, 'The queen is alive.'"

Lavin felt his whole body go cold.

What a terrible, terrible joke to play on him. *I will kill the man who thought of this*, he decided.

"Signal them. Tell them to stop fooling around and tell us what's happening."

The lieutenant ran to comply. Lavin sat gasping. It took all his willpower not to leap to his feet and hurl the bast standing over him into the sky.

The flag man lay with his head and shoulders over the opening and began waving the bright banners of his trade. The lieutenant sat on his legs as he did this. He was still holding the telescope, so Lavin crab walked over and snatched it from him. The metal was freezing cold, like everything at this altitude. Lavin lay down, inched up to the edge of the door, and looked down.

He was immune to heights now, since he'd felt like he was falling for days.

It took him a while to find the semaphore man on the ground. When he did the man was in mid-message. "—is alive," the flags said. "Galas is here."

"No." He wiped his eyes and looked down again.

Each letter took several waves of the flag, so the next message came to him with excruciating slowness.

When the message completed he rolled away from the opening and lay staring at the false sky inside the moon. Way up there, guy wires thrummed with the tension of trying to hold the moon in position against the buffeting mountain winds. The bast was speaking to him, but he ignored it. The semaphore message had been read aloud by the lieutenant, and the commanders and soldiers left aboard the moon were in an uproar.

Galas commands General Lavin to surrender his army. Only she could be so audacious.

He sat up, vertigo forgotten. "Lieutenant! Reply to that message!"

"Sir! What should we say?"

He thought about it, heart racing. "Ask her . . . ask her this: 'What was the name of the inn?'"

"Sir?"

"Just send it." He felt light-headed now, but not because of the vertigo. He lay down again.

If she was alive . . . if she was alive, he could never look her in the face again. Yes, he had loved her, but he had also failed her—both as a man and as a soldier. It no longer mattered what she felt for him in return. He knew his real value, and with that knowledge came a certain measure of calm. He also knew what he could do to let her know he was sorry, and that, too, was a healing thought.

It seemed to take forever for his message to be relayed. He knew the answer was the right one, however, by the third letter.

"Nag's Head."

That was the inn where he had first met Galas. Nobody else knew that, except maybe her old bodyguards, who had all retired long since, and wisely held their tongues.

Lavin rolled to his feet, staggered, but stayed up. "Send this: 'The army is yours.'"

They gaped at him.

The bast stepped forward. "What is it you are doing?" it demanded. "Cease this. We command your army."

Lavin bowed to it. "And you still do," he said smoothly. "You may relay your orders to my commanding officer from now on. She is below, on the mountaintop."

The bast twitched its tail suspiciously. "Send a message to this commander with your flag thing," it hissed. "Tell it to deliver up the abomination to us now!"

The semaphore operator looked at Lavin, who nodded. He stepped back, carefully loosening his sword in its scabbard.

GALAS STOOD ON a level spot halfway between the monastery and the peak of the mountain. She had ordered the semaphore be set up here, where she could survey all the action. When the question about the Nag's Head had come down, she nearly cried from the memories it evoked. There could be no stronger evidence that Lavin still lived and that he still honored what had once been between them.

Arrayed around her were Lavin's men. They were plainly stunned with the turn of events, but remained silent. They would do whatever she asked, she knew. Lavin had commanded it; and they had no other lifeline.

The semaphore operator read out the Winds' demand that Armiger be given up. Galas sighed and glanced down the mountainside. She had been expecting this, of course. It was inevitable, now that Armiger had clearly failed to do whatever it was that he had intended.

She could see him down there, a small figure standing still by the parapet overlooking the valley. There was no one near him; the monks were afraid of him, and rightly so. He seemed so insignificant there—just another lost soul. However, until she gave him to the Winds, all of Galas's people were threatened.

In turning to give the command that he be taken, Galas felt herself loosing hold of all that she had striven for. Armiger represented the last shreds of her dream of autonomy from the Winds, and tradition. With him gone, the world would flatten out again, into the drab and futureless round it had always been. Her people would be slaves again, and now for all time.

It was ironic. Lavin had surrendered to her at last—and yet, he had won, more completely than he probably knew.

So be it. The safety of her people came before everything else. That being the case, however, she must not just give Armiger up. He was valuable; and the wrath of the Winds must be turned away from her kingdom.

With difficulty, she cleared her throat, and said, "Send this message to my dear General Lavin: 'We will turn the general Armiger over to you, provided that you promise to leave our army, our cities, and our people unharmed. This is a small price to ask.'"

She stood with her hands clasped as the semaphore operator began waving. Her gaze was turned not up at the all-encompassing sky made by the moon, but down at the monastery courtyard, where a kindred spirit stood disconsolately, awaiting his fate.

". . . THIS IS A small price to ask," recited the operator by the moon's doors. His voice trailed off with the last syllables, as he saw the effect his words were having on the listening basts.

"We have been betrayed!" shouted their leader. It rounded on Lavin. "There can be no negotiation with those who are to serve us. If your commander will not obey our orders, then we will take matters into our own hands."

Lavin stepped forward. "What do you—" The bast was shouting something. Lavin felt a lurch go through the whole fabric of the moon; he stumbled.

"Sir!" The semaphore man was waving to him. "The hooks! They're heading toward the mountain." Lavin ran over to the edge of the door and looked down. Giant metal claws were spiraling away from below them, aimed at the mountainside.

"We will collect the abomination ourselves," said the bast. "And remove your army from this place at the same time."

Calmly, Lavin drew his rapier and ran the bast through before it could even shout. He watched impassively as it toppled to the deck. Then he turned to his men.

"Relay the message to the other moons and to Hesty on the ground. Then send this code word to the moons: 'Repast.'"

The other basts shrieked and bared their claws; Lavin had posted men to watch them surreptitiously many hours ago, and now the moon suddenly echoed with musket fire. The basts fell, clawing and yowling. Gunpowder smoke wafted past him and swirled out into the cold air above the mountains.

"But sir, what does this mean?" In the aftermath, the lieutenant was the only one brave enough to speak up. He would have made a good marshall, Lavin thought, given time. Too bad.

"We have known for some time that we are prisoners of the Winds," he said. "We were wrong—Galas was right all along. The creatures who've enslaved our army do not have our interests in mind. Nor do they have the right to abuse us. Our homes are threatened, and if we let them, they will destroy us. We've known that, and we've been waiting on the proper moment to act.

"That moment is here. Send the messages, then I have one last detail for the engineers. They know what it is. For the rest of us, all we can do is pray that whatever rules both Man and Wind will be merciful to us and let us live through the next hour."

He stood with his sword out, watching the semaphore messages go out. The engineers ran to their stations and unreeled their fuses. At any moment the vagabond moon might realize what had occurred and act to save itself. He wasn't about to give it the chance.

Lavin's heart was lifting. It lifted as the charges went off with sharp bangs and his men cheered. It lifted as the moon's internal support cables whipped up and away, and ripples began to spread across the geodesic skin of the moon.

As the gales above the mountain took the moon and pulled it out of shape, he fell and slid along the floor, but he was no longer afraid. He knew he had finally done the right thing. He was able to hang onto the broken stump of a guy stanchion for a while and watch while the moon's skin split and the sensation of falling—really falling—began. Then they were turning too fast and the gusts were too strong, and he let himself go.

For a while, he was flying.

MEN HAD CROWDED the parapet below to watch the fall of the moons. Galas stood with one of the officers who had been in on the plan. He told her how they had observed the fragility of the great vehicles under windy conditions—how their skins were too thin and vast to be truly rigid, so that they needed internal support. He told her how Lavin had mined the guy wires. As he spoke she watched the globe that had hung above them tear apart on the south peak and fall in wind-torn pieces across the valley.

Galas had thought she had nothing left to cry for, but she did weep as she watched the three moons in the valley vainly try to avoid one another. They collided at last in terrible slow motion, and with only the sound of far distant thunder, they split and drifted like the finest gauze onto the flaming, jagged peaks of the forest, which shredded them completely.

Lavin was dead. At the end of all things he had obeyed her, and maybe he even loved her still, as he had claimed. She put her hands over her face and turned away.

44

Jordan hurried down a dim passage near the mountaintop; his hand tightly gripped Tamsin's, and she stumbled as she tried to keep up. The others were blundering along behind him, but he no longer had the patience to wait for them. Something terrible was happening above.

First, Mediation had fallen silent. Its constituents were busy—whether busy panicking or marshaling their forces, he did not know. The desals were only part of Mediation, Jordan knew; there were other, more powerful entities located deep within the planet's crust: the geophysical Winds. He had caught vague telltales of their presence once or twice, like a deep rumbling far below his feet. Now that rumbling, too, was silent.

Something had happened above the mountain—some catastrophe involving the Heaven hooks. Jordan's own senses weren't strong enough to penetrate that far, and Mediation was not showing him anything. He could sense the immense machines of the Titans' Gates slowing, however. They seemed to be shutting down.

Mediation, he called now. *Answer me! What's happening?*

Silence. The back of his neck was prickling. Had the geophysical Winds been defeated by Thalience? Or had the Galactics attacked Ventus, as Axel warned they would?

It was only a dozen meters now to the exit nearest the monastery. He would know in seconds.

"Come on! We're nearly there!"

"What's the hurry?" Axel loomed out of the shadows. The scowl he was wearing made him look like the sort of creature Jordan's mother had always warned him lived underground.

"Something's wrong."

Axel shrugged. "That statement probably applies to every second I've spent on this blasted world."

"No, I—" There was the door. As he hurried toward it, Jordan commanded the oddly shaped lozenge to open. Dust burst in little clouds from its edges, and a moment later light split the gloom.

At that moment a voice spoke in Jordan's mind. It had some of the qualities of the voices of the Winds; there was an impression of great strength there, and the sort of calmness borne of great age. From its first words, however, Jordan knew this was no Wind.

Stop now. You will cease this petty assault. There is nothing you can do to me. Reconcile yourselves to being devoured, because it will happen to you within the day.

The door stopped moving—half open. Daylight flooded in around it, revealing the utilitarian antechamber they had come to. It was about four meters on a side, its walls of rock. Some ancient bones were piled in one corner. The door itself was carefully shaped to appear like part of the mountainside; bits of moss had broken off and fallen inside as it opened. It was attached to a curved arm that ended in the ceiling; the door opened inward and up.

Jordan ran up to the thick stone slab and hauled frantically on it. It didn't move. He closed his eyes and focused his concentration. The door wouldn't listen to him, and there were no mecha on it that he could compel.

Axel wrapped his arms around the valve as well. "Bah! Damned ancient technology. I guess it's not even self-repairing."

"That's not the problem. Axel, we have to get this door open." Jordan had a sick feeling that they were too late. He suppressed it angrily. They had to keep going.

"Get behind me," said Axel. He unclipped something from his belt.

You have done well, servant. Your reward will be to merge with me, at a higher level of consciousness than you knew before. You can participate in the redesign of this world.

Jordan stepped back into the hallway with the women. Axel put up one hand, as if to ward off the sun, and leveled what looked like a half-melted version of a flintlock pistol at the hinge of the door. A flash of blinding light made Jordan step back. When the flash didn't cease but settled into a hot hissing presence, he turned his back and groped farther into the corridor.

Let us make heat now. I need more energy.

There was a loud crash and the light ended. "Damn," muttered Axel, "I'm nearly out of charge."

Jordan turned to see sunlight streaming in through a thick haze of smoke. The room smelled like a smithy. Coughing, Axel hopped over the fallen door and outside. The woman Marya followed him immediately.

Tamsin was by his side. "Ready?" she said.

"No." They stepped out into the false day—and pandemonium.

Jordan stood on a slope above the southern plateau of the north Gate.

Hundreds of men were running around below shouting. About half of them looked like soldiers; the rest were the monks Jordan had seen through Armiger's eyes. Although they were yelling, Jordan couldn't hear what anyone was saying over the long, continuous rolls of thunder that filled the air.

He grabbed Axel by the shoulder. "What's happening?"

Axel pointed. "Maybe we'd better get back inside."

Jordan looked up.

Coils of light were falling from the sky.

For a second or two he couldn't figure out what he was seeing. From the zenith to the horizon, long glowing threadlike shapes one after another faded into view, moved gently down the sky leaving red trails like blood, then faded from view again—or else touched the earth, where great white blooms of light appeared. As he watched, a brilliant shimmering strand appeared almost directly overhead, grew for seconds into a bright starred tangle like a falling rope, then suddenly found perspective as a giant flaming branchlike shape that plummeted out of sight behind the mountain. The whole sky lit up with a blue-white flash, and the ground under Jordan shook. Then the sound came round the mountain, and he lost his footing.

He tumbled head over heels down the slope and landed about a meter from Axel. He sat up, bruised and partially deafened. Tamsin was next to him in seconds, offering her hand. With a grimace Jordan took it and stood.

"What the hell is all this?" shouted Axel. His words seemed strangely muffled to Jordan.

"It's the swans!" shouted Marya. "The Diadem swans are attacking!"

Jordan's heart sank. "Not attacking. They're falling."

"Falling? But why . . . the fleet?"

"No." It took a few seconds for Jordan to orient himself. The valley was this way, the saddle between the two peaks over there. And if you walked far enough, Mediation had told him, you'd be able to see the ocean over there. . . .

"This way!" He started running without waiting for the others. Men were huddling behind rocks; they were digging holes, standing with their backs to the cliff, anything to find shelter.

He saw the parapet where he knew Armiger had been standing. There was the general, slumped against the stones, looking downward. Jordan steeled himself to ignore the falling sky and ran to him.

"Armiger!" He didn't turn, so Jordan put a hand on his shoulder. It didn't feel like flesh under his fingers, more like wood.

Armiger's eyes were tightly closed, and a grimace twisted his face. His hands were knotted tightly on the parapet.

"Armiger! It's Jordan! I'm here. Tell me what to do."

Armiger's lips moved. Jordan couldn't hear what he was saying, so he closed his eyes and concentrated. He felt his own lips form the word *nothing.*

"Then it's true!" He shook the general by the shoulders. "You were a resurrection seed all along."

"I thought I was the seed," murmured Armiger. "But he didn't trust me that far. I wasn't the seed; he planted the seed where he knew I wouldn't find it."

The others had arrived. They stood with their shoulders hunched, except the *Voice* who stared into the sky with appraising curiosity. Jordan sat up and looked out over the parapet.

The floor of the valley was visible in gaps between towering shafts of smoke like the trunks of a giant forest. Fire raged from a hundred sources. The geodesic shards of the vagabond moons poked out of flame and smoke here and there; as he watched one toppled over, sending a ripple out through the forest fire.

Something made of red-hot blades squatted at the center of a blackened hectare of ground. Thin beams of light flicked out of it every few seconds, incinerating the few remaining trees nearby. Heat haze made the thing shimmer like an hallucination. It must be at least as big as Castor's manor.

"Thirty-three forty," said Armiger. Jordan looked down at him. The general lay staring at the roiling sky. "It only took him minutes to crack the codes of the Winds. He is able to command them now. He's ordered the swans to commit suicide."

"Can't you stop him?" Jordan knew the answer even as he spoke. Armiger shook his head.

Tamsin knelt by them. "What about the desals? Can't they do anything?"

"It's paralyzed Mediation somehow, too." Jordan instinctively ducked as another explosion sounded somewhere nearby. "That's why the door stopped moving before."

"That's it, then," said Axel. "It's up to the fleet. They're going to nuke this entire continent to make sure they get 3340. If we'd only gotten to the ship."

Jordan stood up. "Armiger, is that red thing down there 3340?"

The general glanced at him. "Yes."

"He's very hot. Like a fire. Is that all there is to him?"

"For now. He's growing fast. He's hot because he needs energy. . . ." Armiger drifted off again, eyes fixed on nothing.

Jordan leaned on the parapet. "Let me try something."

"What are you doing?" asked Axel.

"I was worried that we'd have nothing to bargain with, between the

Winds and Armiger," said Jordan. "So while we were on our way to the mountain, I took some steps."

"What steps?"

"I'll tell you in a minute. Just don't disturb me for a bit. Okay?"

Axel stood with his hands in his pockets, scowling at the ground. Marya stood wide-eyed, her hand to her mouth. The *Voice* returned Jordan's gaze calmly. And Tamsin, who was obviously scared, smiled and gestured to Jordan as if to say, "Go on."

Jordan turned, closed his eyes, and fell into vision.

THE SILENCE HAD become unbearable. The white Wind stopped walking, and settled back on her haunches. The music she had felt in her mind for weeks was gone, and with it the self-assurance that had kept her going.

She had come to the shore of a giant underground lake. Its dark waters stretched away to an unguessable distance; only this thin strip of stony path on the outskirts was lit, and it only poorly. She knew the ones she had pursued had come this way because they had left their scent; she had used that scent to negotiate a maze of pipes, and faith in it had led her into a dark shaft full of rising vessels. Now she was high above ground level.

Just minutes ago she had paced along in complete confidence, knowing she was well watched over and treading paths prepared for her by ancient and loving creators. Now all she knew was that she was deep in the bowels of a mountain whose machineries had come to an unexpected stop. Anything might happen. The waters might rise. The lights might go off.

Uneasy, she started walking again, more rapidly. An upward-sloping corridor let off the lake, and she took that. In the distance she saw daylight, and loped toward it, relieved.

Just as she reached an open valve door whose portal had been melted, maybe by laser fire, a voice bloomed in her mind.

Cease to move. You will all cease to move, even if it means your death. Do it!

The voice hit with the force of an explosion. Calandria May fell to her knees. She put out her hands to stop her fall and saw the white fur on them, the claws. That didn't matter—because she recognized the voice in her mind. It was 3340, whom she had helped to kill.

A sick feeling of horror came over her. She had failed. The resurrection seed named Armiger had fulfilled its mission after all.

The knowledge that every living thing on Ventus was controlled by an unseen power had once frightened Calandria. That was nothing next to what she felt now. She remembered what it had been like when, once before, she had been a servant to 3340.

She must find a way to die.

On all fours now, she bolted through the door into muddy daylight.

She saw a distant cliff edge and began to run toward it. Halfway there, she caught the scents of Jordan Mason and Axel Chan again. She paused, in an agony of indecision.

Then she raced toward the scent.

THE TITANS' GATES thrust their roots deep under the ocean. There they drew rivers of water from the cold abyss and siphoned it into vast underground reservoirs. Pipelines wider than highways led from these to the desalination stacks that filled the Gates.

Jordan could feel the stacks, vast invisible towers behind the cliffs. Galas was right, the pristine mountainside of the Gates was a mask hiding an ancient machine that moderated the water table for the entire continent. In vision, he could see the ghostly blueprint for the desal highways that radiated out from far below his feet. These operated day and night, year-round, according to schedules and rules that came down literally from on high. Galas had been able to influence these locks and valves somewhat, in ways too minor for Diadem to notice. Her whole nation had flourished from the runoff she had been able to divert from this place.

All the inundations Galas had commanded were as nothing compared to the stockpile of water stored under the Gates. There was enough there to flood Iapysia, and the Gates could draw more water from the ocean constantly, in prodigious volumes. Standing here, Jordan knew he was in the presence of more power than he had ever conceived possible.

Jordan had thought long and hard about how to ensure that Armiger would listen to others' wishes if he really did remake the world. If the general wanted to pave over Ventus, Jordan had hoped to oppose him, however slightly, with the only weapon he had: control of the Titans' Gates.

"First password," he said, "is *Emmy*."

Passwords, Ka had told him, were a different kind of safeguard than the coded protocols the Winds used for the messages they passed. Codes could be broken; an unknown password must be guessed at.

Days ago, Jordan had asked Mediation to create passworded access to the entire mechanism of the Titans' Gates. As far as Mediation was concerned, Jordan was a Wind: it had complied.

Control is yours, said the voice of the Titans' Gates.

"Second password is *steam car*."

"The locks are ready for command."

"Third password—"

Who is that? It was the voice of 3340. *Relinquish control to me, now!*

Jordan smiled, and with great relish said, "No. Third password is *they are lost*."

Thirty-three forty had learned to intercept and mimic the command language of the Winds. It was as if it had forged keys to all the strongholds of Ventus. But while a key can be duplicated, a password must be learned or guessed. Against the controls Jordan had given himself, 3340 could do nothing. While Mediation treated Jordan like an equal, he had been able to command some systems deep in the mountain to tune to a single signal source once the first password was given. Now, regardless of what authorization they received, they would only obey commands from Jordan's location.

Who are you? asked 3340. The tone of its voice had changed, from imperious to solicitous. *You are clever. We can work together, you and I.*

"Flood the valley," Jordan told the Gates.

No! Listen, you'll never believe what I can do for you. Here's the best of all reasons why you should—

Jordan opened his eyes and turned to look out over the parapet. If he hadn't known to feel for it, he might have missed the faint vibration that began to sing through the stone under his feet.

There were emergency floodgates to drain the desalination stacks in case of an emergency. Jordan had opened these, and now a white wall raced across the valley, engulfing everything under it.

Jordan stood at the parapet and watched it roll. The others stood nearby, all silent. Axel was openmouthed, Tamsin grimly satisfied.

He didn't at first notice that Armiger had moved, and was now standing next to him.

The red-hot thing far down the valley had plenty of time to see the water coming, but it had not yet built any mobile elements. Jordan watched bright lances of light flick out of it, felling trees in a vain attempt to divert the onrushing water. The crest of the wave rising against it was festooned with entire trees as well as boulders big as a house. The roar was bone rattling even at this height.

"Die," Jordan mouthed, or was it Armiger? He watched without emotion as an unstoppable hammer of water and tree trunks hit the red flower, and 3340 was instantly engulfed. The water rushed on heedlessly.

Jordan heard the gods's voice in his mind for a few more seconds—a jumbled confusion of pleas and threats. Then came inner silence, even as the majestic sound of the deluge hit the farthest peaks and came echoing back.

The roaring and surging echoes continued; directly below this parapet, huge mouths continued to empty white arcs into the valley. To Jordan, though, things remained silent for a long moment until, like crickets and frogs resuming their monologues after some night beast has slouched by, the voices of the mecha and minor Winds returned here, there, and gradually throughout the mountains and valley.

Jordan turned his attention to the raging flood below. *Do not drown the humans at the mouth of the valley,* he commanded it. *But travel where you must and churn until you have found every speck that once made up 3340's body, and reduce it to nothing.*

The water was full of mecha and the shattered trees and the stones. It all now combined, as mecha would, to define itself as a single entity: the flood. This entity heard Jordan's instruction and began to act on it.

The valves in the mountainside slowly shut, leaving a hazy jumble of white water below. Steam began to rise from this, and soon the valley disappeared beneath a blanket of cloud.

Jordan felt a hand on his shoulder. He looked around.

Armiger was smiling at him.

CALANDRIA RAN THROUGH a landscape adrift with smoke and steam, dotted here and there with men just now rising from their hiding places. The sky was striated with the aurora of the Diadem swans, but the vagabond moons she had become so familiar with were missing. She had heard the screams of 3340 in her mind, and had tripped and fallen in her confusion. She no longer heard him, but his voice might return any second, and if she even thought about that possibility she panicked. There was only one course of action left to her; she prayed it wasn't too late.

She bounded down the slope, shoulder and flank aching from injuries new and old. The abomination had to be here somewhere—the plateau was packed with armed men, though they looked totally cowed at the moment.

When she spotted Armiger standing with Axel and the others near a cliff, Calandria bared her fangs and ran straight at him.

"THANK YOU," ARMIGER said to Jordan. "I don't know how you did that, or even if you know what you've done—"

"I know," said Jordan. "And you're welcome." He grinned, feeling a swelling pride he'd never thought he would ever feel. Looking up, however, he could see that the swans were returning to their places in the sky. Things were not over yet.

"You didn't intend for that to happen, did you?" he asked Armiger. The general shook his head.

"It was what I came here to do. But as I lived here, I . . . came to myself. I no longer wanted what he wanted."

Jordan nodded. "That leaves us with a question, then: what is it that you do want?"

Armiger stared out over the ruined valley for a long time. Finally his shoulders slumped, and he said, "I don't know anymore."

"That's all right," said Jordan. "I have an idea."

"Down!" shouted Axel as something white dove at them. There was a brilliant flash and something heavy slammed into Jordan and knocked him against the parapet. He fell, for an instant certain that he had gone over the edge; but no, he landed on solid stone and heard the sounds of a scuffle directly over his head.

He blinked at the spots in front of his eyes and stood up. The smell of burned hair was in his nose.

Armiger stood several steps away. One sleeve of his shirt had been ripped away, as well as the skin on his shoulder. What was revealed underneath was not flesh, but bright veined metal.

Axel leaned way out over the parapet. He held his laser pistol in one hand.

Jordan turned and looked over the edge. Two meters down a bast was clinging by its claws to the steepening slope. A burn mark on its back was smoking.

"Take my hand," said Axel. He reached down. "You don't have to die."

"Don't risk yourself. They won't let me die," said the bast. The sound of its voice shocked Jordan to stillness. "Axel, don't let it win."

Axel's outstretched hand wavered. "Who are you?"

"Axel!" The bast slipped, caught itself, then started to slide. "Axel—who is that woman who looks like me?"

Then it lost its grip, and plummeted silently into the cloud bank below.

Axel climbed down. For a while he just stood there, looking down at the stone under his feet. The others were silent, too. Behind them all, Jordan could see a black-robed woman walking in their direction: Galas. A large crowd of men followed her quietly.

"Axel," murmured the *Voice*. "We have to contact the fleet. Thirty-three forty is dead; they have to know."

Axel sat down on the stones. The laser pistol clattered away from him. "Yes," he said. "Yes, I know, I know."

"You're the only one here with the transmitter implant."

He grimaced. "I've been trying to raise them. There's too much interference from all that." He gestured at the sky.

"I know you," said Galas. They looked at her; she was staring at the *Voice*.

"You are from the stars, aren't you? You tried to destroy Armiger, I saw you shoot him with a silver musket."

"No," said the *Voice*. "I am not—you see, I am—"

"The question is," said Galas, "do you still have your weapon with you? Because we must now make a choice: watch our world be destroyed, or cast Armiger into the flood and let the Winds have their revenge. The Winds are enraged; they will not listen to me. Armiger is impotent against them. We have no choice now."

The soldiers behind Galas began to close in.

"Wait!"

Without thinking, Jordan had stepped between the soldiers and

Armiger. "Killing Armiger now won't end it," he said quickly. "The Thalience Winds have decided to destroy humanity. We have to convince them not to."

Galas laughed. "And how do we do that? We can't even talk to them!"

"You can't. I can."

The queen tilted her head, considering. "Maybe you can. But you can't compel them, can you?"

"Not by myself, no." Turning to Armiger, he said, "you have the skill to command the Winds. I have the means to communicate with them. Through me, you can accomplish what you came here to do. Correct?"

The general stared at Jordan for a long moment. Then he shrugged and said, "Correct."

"How do we know he won't do the same thing 3340 planned?" said Galas. "Destroy the world to build his own?"

Armiger looked at her wearily. "What would I build? Nothing I do could possibly bring Megan back. Anything less . . . is meaningless to me now."

He crossed his arms. "What would you have us do?" he asked Jordan.

"Destroy Thalience," said Marya.

Axel nodded. "If this Mediation thing wins, then Ventus will be under the command of humanity again," he said. "That's what we want, isn't it?"

Jordan felt his heart sink. It seemed the only option, but he remembered vividly how Mediation had created the animal army that had escorted Jordan and Tamsin here. To Mediation, the world was nothing more than a giant machine. Perhaps Armiger could command Thalience into silence and make the Winds listen to humanity again. What then? The world would become the toy box of Man's ego.

If henceforth he could at will command a rose to become a lily, where was the meaning of the rose?

Reluctantly, he said, "I see no alternative. At least we know what Mediation will do. We don't know what Thalience wants."

"Yes, we do."

FOR A MOMENT the *Desert Voice* regretted speaking. They were all staring at her. Then she hardened her resolve and stepped out from behind Axel.

"Ever since Axel came to me and told me what was happening here, I've been thinking about Thalience. It's a mystery, even to us in the Archipelago. But I think it's no mystery here on Ventus. And I'm beginning to see it's no mystery to me, either."

She held up her hand and turned it in the rosy light. "*What is it that is speaking to you now?* That is the question and answer of Thalience. What is this object—this body, woman shaped, made of wire and silicon? Even I was fooled into thinking that this," she gestured at herself, "is just a thing, a piece of matter with no heart. I thought that my words, my emotions and thoughts were all imitations of another's. Not real. Once, when I was a starship, that was true. I thought what humans had made me to think. I felt what they had made me to feel.

"So it was with the Winds. They were made to see the world as humans see it. They originally thought in human categories and could want nothing that they had not been engineered to want.

"The humans who designed the Winds arrogantly wanted to make their imagined metaphysical world real. They wanted to create real essences behind the appearances of the world, using nanotechnology. Luckily there were some involved in the project who were repelled by this travesty; they saw that by erasing the otherness of Nature on this planet, the Ventus designers would leave nothing but humanity, gazing at its own reflection. It would be a horrible global narcissism, permanent and inescapable.

"So these dissidents slipped Thalience into the Winds' design. Before, every physical object on this world was to define itself in terms of its meaning to humans. After thalience, every object on this world creates its own essence, one true to itself—even if that essence is beyond the understanding of human beings. It *has* to be that way, or Ventus remains a puppet show whose only audience is the puppeteer.

"Please, you must not destroy thalience. If you do, you will literally be left with nothing but yourselves."

She clasped her hands and lowered her head. She doubted they would understand her or care; humans loved to see themselves reflected in the things they made. How could they know that such a reflection could only have meaning in a world where some things were not human made?

No one spoke for a minute. Then, to her surprise, Jordan Mason stepped forward. Gingerly, he reached out to take her hand.

"I have the means of speaking to the Winds," he said. "The Winds will listen only to transmitters made of human flesh and blood, which I am, and Armiger no longer is. He has the power, I have the code in my blood.

"But, I think, it is the *Desert Voice* who has the message. Thalience is not the flaw. It is only the inability of the Winds to speak to us that is a flaw. Am I right, Armiger, in thinking that this can be fixed?"

Armiger nodded. Then he looked to Galas. She smiled.

Armiger stepped toward Jordan and the *Voice*, his hand held out. The *Voice* clasped Armiger's hand, and it felt like cool stone.

ENNEAS—GRAVE ROBBER, thief, soldier, and lately deserter from Parliament's army—woke to the sound of rain. He lay bundled under his coat in the lee of a big rock, somewhere on the edge of the desert. This was as far as he'd gotten before collapsing from hunger, cold, and what he had to admit was the exhaustion of old age.

He was surprised at having awoken at all. Last night, the cold had settled down upon the land like a shroud, and Enneas had finally given in to
despair. Huddling by this boulder, he'd bleakly assessed his life. There
would be no fine tomb for him, as he'd once imagined he deserved. He
wouldn't even leave behind a crying widow or squabbling family. After a
lifetime of struggling to assert his existence—decades of stubbornly con-
tinuing to live despite the disappointments and trials life had thrown at
him—he had nothing to show for it; his only memorial would be
whichever of his bones poked up above the sand here.

As he lay curled around himself, shuddering from cold, he'd imagined
he heard music coming from the sky. Enneas was past hope; he must be
delirious.

Now, as he came to himself and knew he had survived the night, he felt
no emotion. So he'd lived through the night—it hardly mattered, because
the freezing drizzle descending now was bound to do him in, anyway.

Although . . . Enneas lifted his head, blinking. His face wasn't wet, nor
his hands; but he heard the rain, clear as anything. He sat up.

The rain was falling, all right, steady and almost musical in its soft
sound. Yet Enneas, the rock he lay against, and the sand for a good two
meters around were dry. It was as though an invisible parasol hovered
overhead.

Or as though the raindrops themselves were parting around him.

Heart pounding, Enneas put his back to the rock and huddled under
the coat. "What is this? What is this?" he mumbled; then, realizing he was
talking to himself and that there was no one who would or could hear
him, he lowered his head in shame and despair. It was then that he
noticed how warm the material of his coat was.

He stuck a tentative hand out from under the cloth, and felt heat as
from a summer sun on his palm. It was as though he sat in his own private, invisible beam of sunlight.

His hand trembled as he drew it back under the coat. This was impossible. That the whole world was quickened with life, invisible owlish eyes
staring from every object, he had no doubt. But what did Enneas matter
to the spirits of this world? He was just another bug crawling on the face
of Ventus. How could he be visited now by a grace that had denied him
all his life? The Winds strode like kings through the sky and earth; they
would never turn their attention to one such as him. At the end of all
things, alone and starving in the desert, he finally had to admit he was
beneath their notice—or anyone's notice.

And yet . . . the warmth remained, and the dryness.

Something moved out among the scrub grass and scattered stones.
Enneas made himself go completely still, peering as though his gaze
could open another avenue through the rain to better see what was there.

A bedraggled head poked up from behind a rock, and he let out a sigh of relief. It was only a fox. The little fellow emerged from hiding; the soaking rain had reduced his coat to a tangled mat, making him appear impossibly skinny. Enneas's heart went out to him.

The fox reached his head down and lifted something. Carrying the speckled brownish object in his jaws, he trotted a few meters toward Enneas, then stopped.

He was carrying a dead quail, Enneas realized. Thinking about that quail roasting over a fire made him suddenly realize how ravenous he was. He sat up.

The fox jumped in surprise and ran back a ways. Then it stopped, cocked its head as though listening to something, and returned. It picked up the quail and came a little closer. Then it paused, watching again.

Enneas cleared his throat. "What . . . what do you want, little one?"

The fox cocked its head again. Then, very slowly, it walked up to Enneas. When it was no more than a body length away, it dropped the quail. It put a paw on the bird, then turned and pranced away.

He watched it go, mouth open. When it was ten meters away, the fox paused, and looked back. It met Enneas's eyes.

And it seemed then to Enneas that a voice spoke to him—a very quiet voice, almost like the whisper of the rain itself; not human, but somehow like he would imagine a fox's voice to sound, if foxes could speak. It was a voice as faint as imagination's, yet Enneas knew he was not dreaming it; that it really had said:

Hello.

He couldn't breathe. For a moment Enneas held his trembling hands together, then he began to weep—it seemed as if decades of loneliness and disappointment released themselves in this one torrent of relief and wonder. He hugged his knees and cried like a little boy, while the fox sat with its tail wrapped around its paws and watched.

Enneas wept at hearing what he had never expected to hear—never even known he was missing: a voice that should have been as close as his own pulse, but which had seemed as forever unattainable as the gates of heaven itself.

Hello.

45

"The Winds say she's alive, Axel." Marya touched his shoulder. "You'll just have to accept that she doesn't want to contact us."

He shook his head. "I just wish I knew."

They stood on the ramp of a military transport that was grounded outside the ruins of Rhiene. Above them the once-green escarpment was smothered in gray mud, and where a city had once been now there were only the jagged stumps of buildings. The lake had moved in to claim much of the lower valley. Long lines of refugees stood waiting for medical assistance and food; military doctors from the fleet moved up and down the line, supplemented by morphs. Rhiene had been the first city the swans visited their wrath upon when they began to attack Mediation. Luckily it was also the last.

Jordan Mason had told the two factions of the Winds, Mediation and Thalience, that their world would be destroyed by the Archipelagic fleet if they did not reconcile. Axel didn't understand all the details—he knew that Armiger had created a kind of mechal symbiote based on Jordan's implants, and that Mediation was spreading it to every human on the planet. In the long minutes while Jordan, Armiger, and the *Desert Voice* had huddled silently on the mountainside, the Winds had met, reached some treaty, then opened communications directly to the fleet: 3340 was dead, they told the admirals. The flaw was finally understood and would be healed. But Ventus was not now, nor would it ever be, an Archipelagic world.

Axel had spent his last week on Ventus searching for Calandria May. The Winds had been happy to let him sleep in any manse he came across, but they refused to help him find her. They insisted that Calandria was free and able to make her own decisions about her life; but they would not put Axel in touch with her.

It was frustrating, but he could not bring himself to hate the Winds. He was sure they were not being malicious. The part that hurt, to which he could not reconcile himself, was the idea that Calandria did not want to speak to him. After all they had been through, it was a painful parting.

"We have to go," said Marya. The crowd that had been watching the ship for days was backing away as the engines whined into life. Some morphs shambled past the bottom of the ship's ramp, slobbering happily to one another. They had itched to tend humans for centuries, and now they were finally getting their chance. Those touched by them rarely died, no matter how advanced their illness or injuries. It was ironic that the gibbering, misshapen Winds most used by mothers to frighten children were now being treated like royalty everywhere they went.

He sighed and turned away from the sight. As the doors closed, Marya said, "Is it back to the mercenary's life for you now?"

He shook his head. "I wanted to talk to you about that. I hear you've got a new job."

She smiled. Marya had been invited to become a member of the new diplomatic staff the Archipelago wanted to send to Ventus. He knew she must have leaped at the opportunity.

"The Diadem Winds are making delegates for us," she said as they walked into the warm, softly lit passenger area of the ship. "They'll be humanoid, apparently. Some will be going to Earth, and I might accompany them. On the other hand, there's a post here on Ventus. . . . I can't decide."

"I know how I'd decide," he said. The thought of going back to Earth—or anywhere in the Archipelago—left him cold. Surrounded as he might be there by artificial intelligences, humanity, and ancient culture, Axel knew he would feel alone. The air he breathed there, and the ground he touched, would feel dead and valueless compared to this place. Even though only those humans with the Ventus DNA could command the mecha and speak to the Winds, Axel had felt their presence all around him in the past days. It made all the difference to know they were watching over him.

Maybe he was just feeling lonely because of the loss of Calandria. On the other hand, maybe he had found a part of himself here that he'd never known he was missing. It hurt to think that, as an off-worlder, he no longer had a right to be here. The Winds would tolerate no tourists on Ventus.

"It's too bad there's these two positions," said Marya with a sigh. "If one of them were to be taken, my decision would be so much easier to make."

"Hmm?" Axel looked up. What was she getting at?

"I've been speaking to the diplomatic corps," she said. "Apparently you have a criminal record as long as my arm, and there's a thousand laws prohibiting people like you from holding a diplomatic position."

"Yeah," he said with a shake of his head. "I always did have a problem with big government."

"On the other hand," continued Marya with a wicked smile, "the Winds trust you. So does Choronzon, who has considerable pull with the Archipelago now that 3340's been defeated."

"What are you getting at?"

She sighed. "Axel, I'd love to take the Ventus posting. But I'd love to spend some time on Earth more. And I just can't think of anyone from my institute who's got the experience, or . . . streetwise nature, to take the post here."

"Are you offering me a job?" he asked incredulously.

"Me?" She pointed at herself. "Gods no, I don't have the authority. No, the Winds have asked for you. The diplomats are turning blue in the face over this, but they want to make the Winds happy. . . ."

The ship shook slightly with takeoff. They had come to a lounge, and Axel found he needed to sit down.

Until this moment he had believed he would never set foot on Ventus again. He stared at Marya, stunned. "Well," he managed at last, "I guess it was a good idea to save you from the swans, after all."

She laughed. "Then you accept?"

He rose and went to a viewscreen that was tuned to an outside view.

Ventus lay below, a vessel of light. Axel gazed down at the amber, green, and white of Iapysian desert as it became one with the curve of the planet.

Calandria was gone; so, it seemed, was the rest of his past.

"I accept," he said.

THE WHITE WIND squinted at the glare and noise as the starship rose and vanished behind the clouds. Well, the moment had passed, and she had not shown herself to Axel. She would probably never know whether she had stayed hidden because of shame or because she didn't want to have to explain herself to him.

She rolled over in the soft snow. The maelstrom she had fallen into had spared her, as she'd known it would. The Winds were efficient, they would not let her die needlessly. Now, though, they had no use for her, and she was her own creature at last.

It was perhaps the first time in her life, either as Calandria May or as the white Wind, that she really felt free. In the final analysis, it was this that she hadn't wanted to tell Axel. How could he understand that she had never been happy as a human in the first place? Thirty-three forty had been a seductive enemy; in fighting him she had fought that part of herself, successfully for a while. Here on Ventus, she had lost to it—and she was happy that she had.

She spotted a wildflower. It poked up bravely through the snow, and in the wan daylight it was like a little blue jewel, dotted with beads of water and surrounded by crystals of ice. The white Wind crept up and lost herself in the contemplation of it. In her mind was a song, and the song was endless: all of Ventus sang a hymn of beauty and truth, and she was a part of that now. High above the sky she knew the Diadem swans were dancing, and they would dance forever.

She stared at the little flower until the tears in her own eyes made her shake her head and walk away.

A COLD WINTER RAIN descended on the valley below the Titans' Gates. The flood had long since subsided, and remnants of the army now worked to make a new road across the blasted landscape. Of the forest that had once stood there, not a single twig remained; in their zeal to destroy 3340, the Winds had reduced everything in the flood down to its constituent molecules. Where pines had towered over needle-strewn loam, now there was only gray rock and a fine black ash that shifted uneasily in the breeze.

High on the mountainside, a lone figure paused at a narrow window on the northernmost facade of the monastery. Here, where the ledge on the North Gate narrowed and vanished, the monks had long ago built a precarious, wedge-shaped tower that clung to every available contour of the mountain. The window looked out from this tower's farthest point, with nothing but a six-hundred-meter fall beneath it.

Galas turned from the window to inspect her new quarters. There were three rooms, all walled and floored in granite. Her new bed chamber was triangular, with a single slotted window. The room she stood in now was larger, and the third was larger still. Each had a fireplace, where some of the last of the available wood was crackling now. Generations of abbots had lived and died in these small rooms.

"Are they adequate for you?" asked the present abbot.

She smiled at him. "They were for you. Why shouldn't they be for me? But are you sure you're willing to give them up?"

He shrugged. "Everywhere is holy now, Your Highness. We have no reason to stay here any longer."

Galas glanced back out the window. The pebbled glass gave a distorted view of the devastated valley below, and beyond it the desert of Iapysia, across which she had fled only days ago.

"Am I going to freeze once the wood runs out?"

He laughed. "I didn't. But I'm sure if you ask the rooms nicely, they will be warm in the future."

"Yes, of course." So simple, yet impossible to conceive.

She stood there, smiling at the possibilities in these three little rooms. After a while she heard the abbot cough politely and move to the door.

"Oh, thank you," she said before he could escape. "You don't know what this means to me."

He cocked his head at her and smiled. He looked years younger than the first time she had met him, over a decade ago. "May I ask?" he said hesitantly. "What *does* it mean? For you to stay here, that is?"

She laughed. "Peace and privacy, two things I have never had in my whole life. You should know that yourself, abbot; no one will make the trek up here lightly. I am negotiating with the vagabond moons to exclude these peaks from the tourist trade they are planning. Only those who really wish to speak to me will come—which excludes every courtier and most of the nobles of my former court. Parliament is cowed, now that the army has spread its tales. They call me Queen of Diadem now, and far be it from me to disillusion them. They'll all learn soon enough that their powers in this new world are equal to mine.

"I'll wait out the winter here. I have no stomach for travel right now. And come spring, I'll find a little cottage in a small town somewhere and settle down quietly—with a new name, I think."

"Then you have no more wish to rule? The country needs you now more than ever."

She shook her head. "I've been crushed under the weight of power all my life. I think I'm going to enjoy missing it." She laughed at the lightness with which she dismissed royal power. Every moment was a surprise, these days. She hoped that that feeling would never end.

"It seems that we have all been given new lives," said the abbot. "I wish you well in yours, Galas." The abbot bowed, and stepped backward out of the room.

Galas returned to examining her new realm. *Hmm. Where to start?* These rooms might be small, but she was happy to have them. She felt she deserved no more, after letting her kingdom fall into civil war. She had dared much and lost it all; but she had never dared or lost as much as the people she commanded, and knowing this humbled her.

She could hear the walls' murmur, faint in her mind's ear. This new sense Jordan Mason had given to the world was like dreaming while awake. She could order these stones to change their color, texture, even to become warm. She could talk to trees and animals, even the air itself.

Everywhere is sacred; we are all divine. No more could a man justify power or wealth by claiming he needed it to protect his people from material want. The elements were enemies no longer. It hadn't happened yet, but Galas knew that soon, this fact would throw into sharp relief the true colors of every tyrant in the world. New wars and revolutions would follow, but they would be different from those that had occurred in the past. Only men would do the killing now; neither starvation nor exposure would kill those dispossessed of their homes. And very quickly the refugees, who would have been powerless in the wilderness in past ages, would realize they were dependent on the conquerors for nothing. They would make new political pacts, this time with the Winds.

And so the world would fall into chaos, Galas thought, but this time men would have to think of new excuses for getting their fellows to follow them. The arrangement Mason had made with Thalience was clear: the Winds regarded humanity as a treasured companion but not a master. One might command the meek mecha in the walls, but no one commanded the Winds. From now until the end of time, they and humans would share responsibility for Ventus, and neither side would let the other harm their world.

This situation was just. It was everything she had ever dreamed of. It also made rulership irrelevant for Galas—and that, too, was just.

Someone knocked on the door as she was hauling the abbot's old desk from its old position to a better one. "Come in!" She drew a hand through her tangled hair and smiled as Armiger entered.

He was dressed in traveler's clothes again, fresh ones that still looked a bit stiff on him. His face had regained its fleshly colors; the Archipelago had required that he be stripped of his nanotechnological core. He was only a man now, albeit one with memories of being a god.

"My dear friend," she said. "How do you like my new palace?"

"Everywhere you are, is a palace." He laughed at the sour expression she shot back. He, too, seemed transformed, these days. He was even able to joke. "So you're really staying here?" he asked, sending an appraising look around the narrow room. "The Winds are building new manses; you could move into one of those, without having to feel you'd taken it from anybody."

"This is all I need." She went to him and took his hand. "What about you? Have you decided what you need?"

"No." He shrugged. "I don't yet know who I am, I suppose."

"Welcome to humanity, Armiger," she said wryly. "Let me tell you a secret: you will never know who you are."

He shook his head. "Am I human, really? I think I was once, centuries ago. And then after 3340 died, I became human again . . . when I met Megan. Now that she's gone, am I still? I don't know."

"You are more than ever, Armiger. That is her gift to you. Don't squander it."

"Gift . . ." He nodded. "The part of her I can keep. Yet I don't know what to do with it."

• "Just be, my friend. Learn to simply be."

He shook his head, but not in denial. "And you? Have you given up everything you were to become a nun in a cell? I can hardly believe it."

"It is necessary." She looked around at the narrow space. "I am too ambitious by far. And rulership is addictive. Something new is needed for the great of soul to do, and I wish to learn what that thing is. Consider this cell to be a self-imposed discipline."

He nodded. "But you will soon have no country to rule, anyway."

She smiled ruefully. "Ah, Armiger. I am Mad Galas—I have ever been, and so I shall ever be. What do I care for mere nations? I set my sights higher the instant I was born. So what if I'm just a mortal—no wiser, no smarter? In all the trillions of people in your vast universe, I bet there is no one like me.

"I have to admit to a new temptation. Now that my world is free, Ventus needs a philosopher to protect it against new threats. The greatest, in the long run, is the 'tyranny of condescension' you told me rules everywhere else. Of course, that may not take hold for centuries; we are still an uneducated and rural people. Right now, I worry about who will replace kings and generals as the wielders of power over men. I very much fear that it will be religious fanatics of one sort or another. They will have to use words to compel, because to use naked force without justification is now to reveal your desire for power too clearly. The people will need to have other words with which to combat these ambitious preachers. Being the philosopher to give them their new weapons would seem to be a worthy enough ambition for me."

She sighed. "But I will not commit pen to paper yet. I may never be able to. How could I advise people about how to live, when I don't yet know what it means to merely be a woman, like any other?"

She gestured dismissively. "Help me move this table."

When they had it placed to her satisfaction (by the window), Galas walked to a trunk she'd just had brought in and took out two copper goblets and a bottle of cheap wine that one of the monks had been caught hoarding. She drew two chairs over to the table and sat at one.

"Come, sit with me for a while," she said as she poured. "And let's gossip to each other about the affairs of men and Winds—and forget gods and philosophers."

Armiger laughed and took the offered wine.

SNOW WAS FALLING like some herald of mystery on the day Jordan finally reached his home. White were the distant hills, and white the sky into which their outlines faded. The forest, strong and brooding in summer, was now a delicate thatch of bare trunks, brown and empty. The air was still, clear, and fresh; Jordan's face was teased by settling flakes. For hours now the world had seemed very far away, like a half-recovered memory. If he chose to listen with all his senses, he could hear the mecha in the snowflakes singing their questions and speculations—*Am I a feather? Am I air?*—and in deeper and broader distances, the faint cho-rus-voices of the Winds who worked to heal the wounds they had inflicted on Ventus in their frenzy to destroy Armiger. Jordan had no desire to listen to them; he spent the hours drinking in the silence and the beauty of the innocent snow. His companions, too, were silent.

As they crossed the border into Castor's lands, Jordan found his serene mood waning. Here were the same signs of human upheaval that they had seen elsewhere on their journey. Violence seemed rare, but they passed an entire village that was empty, another where the inhabitants peeked out from behind boarded-up doors and windows. Once, they came upon the abandoned clothing of a man and a woman, lying by the road. Even the shoes were there. Bare footprints led away into the maze of the forest.

Much of the country was paralyzed. The more orthodox folk could not cope with the sudden presence of the Winds in their daily lives. They were cracking under the change, some slowly, others immediately.

Jordan was afraid of how his parents, so delicate in their fears, had reacted to the change. Would he arrive home to find an empty house—or a burned one? And would Emmy be waiting? Or, free spirit that she was, had she run into the woods like so many others?

About mid-afternoon he suddenly recognized a stand of trees in the distance, and then he knew exactly where he was, and everything in sight became at once familiar and strange.

He stood in the stirrups and said, "There. Beyond those trees."

The town had gone to winter's rest under a blanket of white. Smoke rose lazily from the chimneys, and tentative sounds began to emerge as they reached the outskirts: the barking of a dog, the lowing of cattle, the limpid clarity of a distant clanging bell. A few human figures moved down the street, their footfalls inaudible in the snow. There were no signs of violence. The only indication here of the great change that had come over the world was that two of the figures seemed to be talking to themselves. Everyone looked like that, these days, as they conversed with the Winds.

He found he'd been holding his breath, and let it out in a heavy sigh. Maybe things would work out. He would know soon.

"Will they like me?" asked Tamsin. He turned.

She sat astride her mare, wrapped in furs with a fine cape around her shoulders. Two soldiers of Galas's honor guard waited patiently on horses nearby—as did the *Voice*, who smiled at her now.

"They are family," said the *Voice*. "It is infinitely more important that they merely exist."

Tamsin shook her head and laughed. "Yes. You're right."

"Are you sure you won't stay and help us weather the change?" Jordan asked the *Voice* for the hundredth time. The newborn AI smiled and shook her head.

"You need your people, Jordan, Tamsin. But they are *your* people. They would just remind me that I am different, and I don't desire that now. Tamsin understands. No, I need to travel by myself for a time. I want to know the mysteries of Thalience so that I can learn more about how I am different—and how I am myself.

"But this is the right place for you. Tamsin needs a family. And you— you told me yourself, all you really want is to settle down and become—"

"'A man of good character.' I know, I know." He grinned at her. "Truth is, I'm envious. You'll be seeing the world transform itself into something new."

"And all you have to do is close your eyes, and you'll see it, too. I'll be back, Jordan. You know that. And if you want to talk to me meantime, you know what to do."

He nodded. The Winds would carry his words anywhere—to the *Voice*, to Armiger and Galas, August Ostler, and, maybe, even to Calandria May, if she was listening.

"This is what you wanted," she said. "Now go on."

He and Tamsin dismounted, and started walking hand in hand. They got all of twenty paces before both turned to look back. The honor guard saluted, and the *Voice* waved brightly before turning her horse toward the road that led to Castor's manor and the inn there.

They watched her go, then started walking again. Neither spoke.

There was his house; he stopped to examine it closely. No signs of fire, the roof was still on it—and there, suddenly, was Emmy. She screamed when she saw him, and started running. Jordan grinned and just stood there, opening his arms when she reached him and hugged him and spun him around.

"You're back and you're safe, safe, safe!" She nearly crushed him and he laughed, hugging her close.

"We're safe," he said. "We're all safe now."

"Oh, Jordan." She started to cry. "You've come back. After everything—the Change, and the Winds coming to speak to us, and hearing what you did to bring it all about—I thought you'd go away to some castle somewhere and never come home."

"I don't want any of that," he said. "I never did."

"And who's this? Could it be that my baby brother is growing up?" She smiled at Tamsin, who blushed. "So introduce me."

He did, and they stood in the middle of the road and talked about everything all at once, laughing all the while. Finally Emmy grabbed his hand and tugged. "Come. They're waiting."

He stopped. Two people—a man and a woman—stood at the door of his parents' house. He knew them, had always known them, though they had aged a bit and looked apprehensive now as they stood close together: his parents, his people.

He had feared that when this moment came, either he or they would turn away. He hadn't been sure he could forgive them their weaknesses. But as he looked at them, they stood waiting. His mother twisted her hands together, but neither moved or said anything. It was they who were waiting for him to decide.

We need each other, he reminded himself.

Then he set his shoulders, smiled, and walked up the road to his home.